U0138647

2011 不求人文化

2009 懶鬼子英日語

我識出版集團
I'm Publishing Group
www.17buy.com.tw

2006 意識文化

2005 易富文化

2004 我識地球村

2001 我識出版社

2011 不求人文化

2009 懶鬼子英日語

I'm 我識出版集團
I'm Publishing Group
www.17buy.com.tw

2006 意識文化

2005 易富文化

2004 我識地球村

2001 我識出版社

2011 不求人文化

2009 懶鬼子英日語

I'm 我識出版集團
I'm Publishing Group
www.17buy.com.tw

2006 意識文化

2005 易富文化

2004 我識地球村

2001 我識出版社

2011 不求人文化

2009 懶鬼子英日語

I'm Publishing Group
www.17buy.com.tw

2006 意識文化

2005 易富文化

2004 我識地球村

2001 我識出版社

Examination KING

考來考去
都考
這些新多益單字

（隨身版）

NEW TOEIC

使用說明
User's guide

〔全書單字來源〕

• 數十本坊間新多益考試暢銷書籍

• 98年06月～101年10月期間100篇英文新聞（如：CNN、BBC）、英文商用文章（如：TIMES、NEWSWEEK、THE CHINA POST）

• 2005年～2012年ETS TOEIC歷屆考古題

• 總計約50,000個英文單字，篩選出80%最常考、易混淆的必考單字1,800個

單字屬性及出現機率圓餅圖

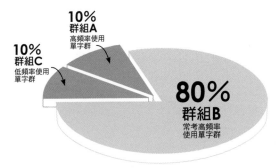

10%
群組A
高頻率使用
單字群

10%
群組C
低頻率使用
單字群

80%
群組B
常考高頻率
使用單字群

〔首創電腦統計單字出現次數〕

群組A

高頻率使用單字群：此群組單字為
10%超簡單出現頻率高達250次以
上常見英文單字，此類單字多為主
詞、冠詞、連接詞，簡單名詞及
動詞等等。如：a, the, you, is,
and, but, or...etc.

群組C

低頻率使用單字群：此類單字多為
10%不常用、不規則、超難記的專
業用詞，出現頻率低於50次以下的
單字。如：alvaron, argentine,
bracelet, bucaiemu,
colossal, dignitary...etc.

群組B

常考高頻率使用單字群：此群組單字為
80%CNN、BBC、英文報章雜誌、ETS TOEIC
考試中心常用、常考的單字。出現次數約介
於50～250次。 如：abnormal, abstract,
aggravate, bid, brag, circuit, debate...etc.

（更多單字與詳解，請見本書內文）

出現次數

| 450 |
| 400 | A |
| 350 |
| 300 |
| 250 |
| 200 |
| 150 | B |
| 100 |
| 50 |
| 20 | C |
| 0 |

300個單字   1800個單字   3900個單字

使用說明
User's guide

1. 最有效的單字學習法

匯整出新多益考試中這些80%CNN、BBC、英文報章雜誌常用的單字。每個單字均有KK音標、字母拼讀法、例句,讓讀者不但會背、會讀、會寫也懂得靈活運用。

1.
abandon [ə`bændən]【aban·don】**Ⅴ**拋棄、放棄 **Ⅵ**放縱、縱情
We finally abandoned his reformist ideas.
我們終於放棄了他的改良主義思想。
🔵 desert, discard, forsake (放棄、離開)
🔴 conserve, maintain, reserve (維持、保留)

2.
abate [ə`bet]【ab·ate】**Ⅴ**減少、緩和
We abate nothing of our just requirements: not one jot or little do we recede.
我們的正當要求絕不打任何折扣。我們一絲一毫也不退讓。
🔵 reduce, lessen, decrease (減少、緩和)
🔴 increase, augment, raise (增加、擴大)

3.

---

2. 同、反義字彙補充

學會高頻率單字再學同、反義字彙、片語補充,保證有效倍增單字力。

3. 高分錦囊,考試重點大破解

補充說明該單字「字首、字根、字尾」組合結構及相關常考片語,加深單字背讀印象。仔細研讀,保證穩坐考場常勝軍寶座。

105
on me.
● 此單字多用於否定句。
● **abide by**忠於、遵守
● 字首:**a**加強語氣
  字根:**bide**等待、停留
● **resolve v.** 解決、決定
● **pressure n.** 壓力
● **superior n.** 上司、長官

211
的、異常的
g methods
● 字首:**ab**離開
  字根:**norm**標準
  字首:**al**屬於…的
● **essential a.**必要的

4 電腦統計單字出題次數

集結坊間新多益書籍、新多益考古題、英文雜誌（TIMES、NEWS WEEK、THE CHINA POST）、英文新聞（CNN、BBC）及各類商業詞彙，利用電腦比對嚴選出最常考的1,800個字。出現次數達100次以上用深色表示，100次以下用淺色表示。數字愈大，表示ETS TOEIC考試中心愈會出。

- superior n. 上司、長官

　211

- 字首：ab離開
　字根：norm標準
　字尾：al屬於…的
- essential a.必要的
- method n.方法
- quantity n.數量
- quality n.質量
- according to ph.依據

5 聽力、口說能力強化MP3

全書單字由專業外籍教師錄音，聆聽最標準的發音並大聲朗讀，加強聽力與口說能力。

is　 MP3 01-01

高 分 錦 囊
　248

縱情
- 字首：ab離開
- finally ad. 最後地
- reformist n. 改革者a. 改良主義的

6 新多益全真模擬試題＋詳細解析

隨書附贈新多益考試擬真試題組及精闢詳細解析。高頻率單字＋模擬試題＋詳細解析＝必勝黃金組合！英語大師獨家解題技巧，完全掌握致勝關鍵。

LISTENING TEST　MP3 02-01

In the Listening Test, you will be asked to demonstrate how well you understand spoken English. The entire Listening Test will last approximately 45 minutes. There are four parts, and directions are given for each part. You must mark your answers on the separate answer sheet. Do not write your answers in the test book.

PART 1

Directions: For each question in this part, you will hear four

測驗簡介
Introduction

何謂 NEW TOEIC 測驗？

TOEIC是Test of English for International Communication （國際溝通英語測驗）的簡稱。NEW TOEIC是針對英語非母語之人士所設計的英語能力檢定測驗，測驗分數反映受測者在國際職場環境中，與他人以英語溝通的熟稔程度。測驗內容以日常使用之英語為主，因此參加本測驗毋需具備專業的辭彙。NEW TOEIC是以職場為基準點的英語能力測驗中，世界最頂級的考試。全球有超過四千家企業使用多益測驗，每年有超過200萬人應試。

NEW TOEIC 測驗會考的題型有哪些？

新多益測驗屬於紙筆測驗，時間為兩小時，總共有二百題，全部為單選題，分成兩大部分：聽力與閱讀，兩者分開計時。

〔第一大類：聽力〕

總共有一百題，由錄音帶播放考題，共有四大題。考生會聽到各種各類英語的直述句、問句、短對話以及短獨白，然後根據所聽到的內容回答問題。聽力的考試時間大約為四十五分鐘。

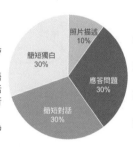

〔第一大題〕
照片描述 10題／4選1
〔第二大題〕
應答問題 30題／3選1
〔第三大題〕
簡短對話 30題／4選1
〔第四大題〕
簡短獨白 30題／4選1

〔第二大類：閱讀〕

總共有一百題，題目及選項都印在題本上。考生須閱讀多種題材的文章，然後回答相關問題。考試時間為七十五分鐘，考生可在時限內依自己能力調配閱讀及答題速度。

〔第五大題〕
單句填空 40題／4選1
〔第六大題〕
短文填空 12題／4選1
〔第七大題〕
單篇文章理解 28題／4選1
雙篇文章理解 20題／4選1

NEW TOEIC 測驗會考的內容有哪些?

NEW TOEIC的設計,以職場的需要為主。測驗題的內容,從全世界各地職場的英文資料中蒐集而來,題材多元化,包含各種地點與狀況,舉例來說:

一般商務	契約、談判、行銷、銷售、商業企劃、會議
製造業	工廠管理、生產線、品管
金融/預算	銀行業務、投資、稅務、會計、帳單
企業發展	研究、產品研發
辦公室	董事會、委員會、信件、備忘錄、電話、傳真、電子郵件、辦公室器材與傢俱、辦公室流程
人事	招考、雇用、退休、薪資、升遷、應徵與廣告
採購	比價、訂貨、送貨、發票
技術層面	電子、科技、電腦、實驗室與相關器材、技術規格
房屋/公司地產	建築、規格、購買租賃、電力瓦斯服務
旅遊	火車、飛機、計程車、巴士、船隻、渡輪、票務、時刻表、車站、機場廣播、租車、飯店、預訂、脫班與取消
外食	商務/非正式午餐、宴會、招待會、餐廳訂位
娛樂	電影、劇場、音樂、藝術、媒體
保健	醫藥保險、看醫生、牙醫、診所、醫院

(雖然取材自這麼多領域,但考生毋需具備專業的商業與技術辭彙)

NEW TOEIC 測驗的適用範圍為何?

本測驗主要為測試英語非母語人士身處國際商務環境中實際運用英語的能力,為全球跨國企業所採用,其成績可作為評估訓練成果、遴選員工赴海外受訓、招聘員工、內部升遷等之標準;亦可作為個人入學及求職時之英語能力證明。

NEW TOEIC 測驗的計分方式為何?

考生用鉛筆在電腦答案卷上作答。考試分數由答對題數決定,再將每一大類(聽力類、閱讀類)答對題數轉換成分數,範圍在5到495分之間。兩大類加起來即為總分,範圍在10到990分之間。答錯不倒扣。

近年來，根據統計新多益全球考生已經突破600多萬人，超過10,000間公司企業、學校、政府機構採用新多益測驗的成績，使新多益考試成為各大企業徵才的重要指標。與全民英檢的難度做比較，新多益的難度大約介於全民英檢中級以上，中高級以下。

該如何掌握並準備新多益測驗？是許多讀者與考生都有的共同疑惑。首先，從單字開始。想在聽力及閱讀測驗中拿高分，關鍵即為「字彙量」。字彙量不夠意味著英文基礎不夠紮實，唯有充足的字彙量，在考場上才能游刃有餘。因此，我識出版社將2010年出版且廣受好評的《考來考去都考這些新多益單字》內容加以修訂，書名改為《考來考去都考這些新多益單字（隨身版）》，縮小原書的尺寸，方便讀者攜帶，希望能獲得更多讀者的青睞。

《考來考去都考這些新多益單字（隨身版）》一書，不僅集結坊間新多益書籍、考古題、各類英文報章雜誌、新聞英文及各類商業詞彙，並用電腦嚴選出最常考、常用的1,800個單字，並搭配同、反義詞、實用商業例句及單字相關補充，讓讀者及考生能用最少的時間，掌握最多新多益考試的高頻率單字。

　　《考來考去都考這些新多益單字（隨身版）》一書，還附贈「新多益全真模擬試題及詳細解析」，除了掌握高頻率的新多益單字之外，並實地模擬練習新多益測驗考題，讓讀者及考生們能在考場上輕鬆拿高分，是考前三個月衝刺必讀的新多益祕笈考用書。

　　相信這本《考來考去都考這些新多益單字（隨身版）》一定可以幫助莘莘學子、社會新鮮人、上班族，奠定並增強英語能力，克服新多益測驗的挑戰，增加職場上及考場上的優勢及競爭力。最後，希望各位讀者及考生都能戰勝新多益。

目錄
Contents

abbr 縮寫詞
a 形容詞
ad 副詞
aux 助動詞
conj 連接詞
n 名詞
num 數字
ph 片語
prep 介系詞
v 動詞
（美）美式用語
（英）英式用語
（法）法式用語

全書單字取材於：
①10本坊間新多益考試暢銷書籍
②50篇英文新聞、商業文章
③2005~2012年ETS TOEIC歷屆考古題
→ 總計約50,000個單字，以電腦統計出題率高達80%
　的實用單字1,800個

高頻率單字

 **A 家族 abandon~axis**

 01-01

高 分 錦 囊

1.
abandon [ə`bændən] 【aban·don】 Ⅴ拋棄、放棄 n放縱、縱情 **[248]**
We finally abandoned his reformist ideas.
我們終於放棄了他的改革主義思想。
📖 **desert, discard, forsake**（放棄、離開）
📖 **conserve, maintain, reserve**（維持、保留）

• 字首 ab離開
• finally ad. 最後地
• reformist n. 改革者a. 改良主義的
• idea n. 想法、思想

2.
abate [ə`bet] 【ab·ate】 Ⅴ減少、緩和 **[156]**
We abate nothing of our just requirements: not one jot or little do we recede.
我們的正當要求絕不打任何折扣。我們一絲一毫也不退讓。
📖 **reduce, lessen, decrease**（減少、緩和）
📖 **increase, augment, raise**（增加、擴大）

• 字首：a加強語氣
  字根：bate減少、緩和
• requirement n. 需要、必需品
• jot n. 一點兒、極少
• recede v. 退後、降低

3.
abide [ə`baɪd] 【a·bide】 Ⅴ堅持、忍受 **[105]**
I resolved to abide the pressure my superiors put on me.
我決定忍受上司們向我施加的壓力。
📖 **wait, endure, tolerate**（等待、忍受）
📖 **start, depart, leave**（開始、離開）

• 此單字多用於否定句。
• abide by忠於、遵守
• 字首：a加強語氣
  字根：bide等待、停留
• resolve v. 解決、決定
• pressure n. 壓力
• superior n. 上司、長官

4.
abnormal [æb`nɔrml] 【ab·nor·mal】 a反常的、異常的 **[211]**
Where it is essential to change the sampling methods and quantity according to the quality of the goods and the abnormal circumstance in the packages.
根據到貨的品質和包裝異常情況，需適當變更抽樣方法和數量。
📖 **irregular, eccentric, odd**（不規則的、古怪的）
📖 **normal, regular, usual**（正常的、規則的）

• 字首 ab離開
  字根：norm標準
  字尾：al屬於…的
• essential a.必要的
• method n.方法
• quantity n.數量
• quality n.質量
• according to ph.依據
• circumstance n.情況、環境

5.
abolish [ə`balɪʃ] 【abol·ish】 Ⅴ廢止、革除、取消 **[184]**
Repeated rebuffs couldn't abolish his enthusiasm.
他的熱情不會因屢次的受拒而減少。
📖 **cancel, endure, put an end to**（廢除、徹底破壞）
📖 **establish**（建立、設立）

• 字首：a加強語氣
  字根：bo拋、扔
  字尾：ish使成為…
• rebuff n.斷然拒絕
• enthusiasm n.熱情、熱忱

6.
abortion [ə`bɔrʃən] 【abor·tion】 n流產、墮胎 **[85]**
The issue of abortion has been a hot potato in western countries for a long time.
很長時間以來，人工流產在西方國家一直是一件很棘手的事。

• 字首：a無、不
  字根：bor=born出生
  字尾：tion情況、狀態
• hot potato ph. 棘手的事、難題

7.

abound [ə`baʊnd] 【a·bound】 **V** 富於、充滿、大量存在

Most employees in the company abound in good abilities.

公司裡的大部分員工都很能幹。

- **flourish, teem, overflow**（豐富、充滿）
- **lack**（缺乏、不足）

- 字首：a無、不
  字根：bound邊界、範圍
- employee n.員工
- ability n.能力
- be abundant in ph.富有、富於

177

8.

abrupt [ə`brʌpt] 【a·brupt】 **a** 突然的、魯莽的、陡峭的

The abrupt business trip gave me lots of trouble.

臨時出差對我造成許多麻煩。

- **sudden, hasty, precipitous**（突然的、倉促的）
- **gradual, deliberate**（逐漸的、深思熟慮的）

- 字首：ab離開
  字根：rupt破裂
- trip n.旅行、行程
- trouble n.煩惱、困擾

134

9.

absent [`æbsnt] 【ab·sent】 **a** 缺席的、缺少的

There were many members absent, so the program had to be put off.

因為很多會員不在場，活動只好延期。

- **away, truant**（離開、逃學的）
- **present**（在場的）

- absent without leave ph.曠課（職）、不假外出
- absent of mind ph.心不在焉
- 字首：ab離開
  字根：sent感覺、出現
- member n.會員
- put off ph.推遲、拖延

215

10.

absolute [`æbsə,lut] 【ab·so·lute】 **a** 絕對的、完全的

The supervisor has an absolute mandate for these proposals.

總監完全有權提出這些建議。

- **complete, thorough, entire**（完全的、全部的）
- **relative, comparative, conditioned**（相對的）

- absolute alcohol【化】純酒精
- 字首：ab離開
  字根：solu釋放
- supervisor n.監督人
- mandate n.命令、指令
- proposal n.建議、提議

278

11.

absorb [əb`sɔrb] 【ab·sorb】 **V** 吸收、吸引、兼併

Local small businesses are absorbed by multi-national ones.

本土小公司被多國際巨頭吞併了。

- **incorporate, engross, assimilate**（合併、吸收）
- **extract, dissimilate**（拉出、不同）

- be absorbed in ph.全神貫注於
- local a.地方性的
- business n.商業、交易
- multi-national a.多國際的

199

12.

abstract [`æbstrækt] 【ab·stract】 **a** 抽象的、難懂的 **n V** 摘要

In the end, the vice-president abstracted the most important points from his long speech.

最後，副總從自己的長篇演說中提取出最重要的幾點。

- **unconcrete, difficult, hard to understand**（抽象的、難懂的）
- **concrete**（具體的、有形的）

- vice- 副的、代理的
- important a.重要的
- speech n.演講
- 字首：abs離開、離去
  字根：tract拉、拔出

121

13.

absurd [əb`sɜd] 【ab·surd】 **a** 荒謬的、不合理的、可笑的

His colleagues were shocked by his absurd behavior.

同事們對他那荒謬的行為感到震驚。

- **foolish, ridiculous, impossible**（愚蠢的、不可能的）
- **reasonable, rational, sensible**（合理的、意識到的）

- colleague n.同事、同僚
- shock v.震驚、撞擊
- behavior n.行為

78

14.
abundant [ə`bʌndənt]【abun‧dant】**a** 豐富的、大量的、充裕的

The East of China is endowed with abundant human resources that should be properly developed and utilized.

中國東部人力資源豐富，應當好好開發利用。

同 plentiful, bounteous, ample（大量的、豐富的、足夠的）
反 rare, scanty（稀有的、罕見的、不足的）

- in abundance ph.充足、豐富
- endow v.捐贈、賦予
- human resource ph.人力資源
- properly ad.恰當地、徹底地
- develop v.發展、成長
- utilize v.利用

194

15.
abuse [ə`bjuz]【ab‧use】**v n** 濫用、辱罵、虐待

In any case, we're opposed to abusing power for personal gains.

在任何情況下，我們都要反對濫權謀私。

同 injure, maltreat, severely scold（傷害、責備）
反 heal, praise（治癒、讚美）

- 字根：ab含否定的意思 字根：use使用
- oppose v.反對、反抗
- power v.權力、勢力
- gain n. 獲得、增加

144

16.
academic [͵ækə`dɛmɪk]【ac‧a‧dem‧ic】**a** 大學的、學術的、純理論的 **n** 學者、大學教師

He is leaving the academic field to take a job in industry.

他將要離開學術界到企業界去工作。

同 theoretical, intellectual, professor（理論的、智慧的、教授）
反 empirical, ignorant（經驗的、不學無術的）

- academic dissertation ph.學位論文
- academic freedom ph.學術自由
- field n.知識專業領域
- industry n.企業、工業

201

17.
accede [æk`sid]【ac‧cede】**v** 答應、同意、繼承

I whispered to my boss that she shouldn't, on any account, accede to the proposal.

我低聲對老闆說無論如何絕不能同意這個提議。

同 assent, consent, grant（同意、贊成）
反 demur, dissent, oppose（猶豫、反對）

- accede to ph.同意、就任
- 字首：ac朝向
- 字根：cede前進
- whisper v.低語、私語
- on any account ph.無論如何
- proposal n.提議、提案

194

18.
accelerate [æk`sɛlə͵ret]【ac‧cel‧er‧ate】**v** 使增速、促進、增加

The State Council warns that the inflation in the region will accelerate and reach a 10-year high in 2009.

國務院警告說這一地區的通貨膨脹將會加速，在2009年將達到近十年來的最高點。

同 hurry, hasten, speed up（加速、急趕）
反 decelerate, retard（使減速、降低…的速度）

- 字首：ac朝向、往…
- 字根：celer快速
- 字尾：ate使成為…
- council n.政務會、地方議會
- inflation n.通貨膨脹
- region n.行政區域
- reach v.達到、抵達

184

19.
accept [ək`sɛpt]【ac‧cept】**v** 接受、相信、承擔

The low salary did not dispose me to accept the position.

微薄的待遇使我不願接受這項工作。

同 adopt, approve, agree（接受、同意）
反 refuse, reject, decline（拒絕、衰退）

- acceptance n. 接受、贊同
- 字首：ac朝向 字根cept：拿取
- salary n.薪資
- dispose v.傾向於
- position n.職務、工作

212

20.
access [`æksɛs]【ac‧cess】**n** 進入、接近 **v**（電腦）取出資料

We strive to retain access to the resources that make company tick.

我們設法獲取公司賴以運轉的資源。

同 way of approach, entry（進入、接近）
反 retreat（退出）

- access to ph.能接近、進入、瞭解
- 字首：ac前進 字根：cess走動
- strive v.努力、抗爭
- retain v.保留、擋住
- resource n.資源

145

21.
accessible [æk`sɛsəbl] 【 ac·ces·si·ble 】 🅰易接近的、可到達的
These commercial secrets are not accessible to the public.
這些商業機密是大眾無法得到的。
🔵 **reachable, attainable, achievable**（可達到的、可獲得的）
🔴 **inaccessible**（達不到的、難進入的）

- 字首：ac朝向
- 字根：cess走動
- 字尾：ible與…的
- commercial a.商業的
- secret n.祕密
- the public ph.大眾
267
107

22.
accessory [æk`sɛsərɪ] 【 ac·ces·so·ry 】
🅽配件、附加物、從犯 🅰附屬的
The client asked me to buy him some accessories for a car.
顧客讓我幫他買些汽車配件。
🔵 **addition, supplement, accomplice**（額外、補充、共犯）
🔴 **abatement**（減少）

- 字首：ac朝向
- 字根：cess走動
- 字尾：ory與…有關
- client n.顧客、委託人
284

23.
accident [`æksədənt] 【 ac·ci·dent 】 🅽事故、意外事件
My father has kept a reserve fund in case of accidents.
我父親已籌備了一筆準備基金以防不測。
🔵 **casualty, mishap, catastrophe**（意外事情、災禍、大災難）

- by accident ph.偶然的、意外
- without accident ph.安全地
- reserve v.儲備、保留
- fund n.資金、存款
- in case of ph.如果發生
202

24.
acclaim [ə`klem] 【 ac·claim 】 🅽🆅歡呼、喝采
Despite the popular acclaim of the new project, the board of directors harrumphed.
儘管這個新計劃受到普遍支持，董事會仍不同意。
🔵 **applaud, praise, cheer**（向…鼓掌、歡呼、鼓勵）
🔴 **dispraise, criticize, scold**（毀謗、批評、責罵）

- 字首：ac朝向
- 字根：claim喊叫、聲音
- despite prep.儘管、任憑
- the board of directors n.董事會
- harrumph v.表示不同意、發哼聲
167

25.
accommodate [ə`kɑmə,det] 【 ac·com·mo·date 】
🆅使適應、調和、向…提供
One flat can accommodate a family of three.
一個套房可容納一個三口之家。
🔵 **supply, adapt, adjust**（提供、適應、調整）
🔴 **exhaust, derange, disturb**（耗盡、擾亂、妨礙）

- accommodation n.住處、膳宿
- accommodate-accommodated-accommodated
- flat n.套房
220

26.
accompany [ə`kʌmpənɪ] 【 ac·com·pa·ny 】 🆅陪同、伴隨
A remittance must accompany all orders.
所有訂單均須附匯款。
🔵 **convoy, escort, squire**（護衛、陪同）
🔴 **leave**（離開）

- 字首：ac朝向
- 字根：company陪伴、夥伴
- remittance n.匯款
- order n.訂購、訂貨
167

27.
accomplish [ə`kɑmplɪʃ] 【 ac·com·plish 】 🆅完成、達到、實現
We have accomplished our mission successfully.
我們成功地完成了任務。
🔵 **achieve, complete, finish**（完成、達到）
🔴 **abandon, frustrate, imcomplete**（拋棄、失敗、不完整）

- 字首：ac朝向
- 字根：compl=complete完成
- 字尾：ish使成為
- mission n.任務
- successfully ad.成功地

28.
accord [ə`kɔrd] 【 ac·cord 】 **n** **v** 一致、調和、給予　　96

Employers must accord employees the respect they are due.

雇主必須給予員工應有的尊敬。

同► **agree, conformity, harmony**（一致、調和、同意）

反► **disagreement, diaccord, differ**（不一致、爭論、相異）

- in accord with ph. 與……一致
- out of one's accord with ph. 與……不一致
- with one accord ph. 一致地
- of one's own accord ph. 自願地、主動地
- respect n. 尊敬、尊重

29.
accordance [ə`kɔrdəns] 【 ac·cor·dance 】 **n** 一致、符合、給予　　116

An agreement is concluded at the moment when an acceptance of an offer becomes effective in accordance with the provisions of this Convention.

協議是按本公約規定對發價的接受生效時訂立。

同► **concurrence, correspondence, endowment**（相同）

- in accordance with ph. 依照、根據
- conclude v. 締結條約
- offer v. 給予、提供
- effective a. 有效的
- provision n. 供應、規定

30.
account [ə`kaunt] 【 ac·count 】 **n** 帳目、帳戶、利益　**v** 解釋、導致　　210

To write off an account receivable is to reduce the balance of the client's account to zero.

核銷這項應收帳款是要將該客戶的帳戶餘額減至零。

同► **record, bill, statement**（帳目、解釋、記錄）

- on one's own account ph. 為了某人的緣故、利益
- on account ph. 賒帳
- on account of ph. 因為
- on no account ph. 不論如何也不要
- of...account ph. 有…重要性

31.
accountant [ə`kauntənt] 【 ac·coun·tant 】 **n** 會計師、會計員　　115

The accountant gave a breakdown of the wages.

會計交出一份工資明細表。

同► **bookkeeper, cashier, teller**（出納員、記帳人）

- 字根：accoun帳戶
- 字尾：ant做某事的人
- breakdown n. 分類、分析
- wage n. 薪水、報酬

32.
accrue [ə`kru] 【 ac·crue 】 **v** 產生、增加　　126

To accrue bond interest payable for five months ended August 31st.

到8月31日止的5個月的未付債券利息。

同► **aggrandize, increase, enlarge**（強化、擴大）

反► **decrease, diminish, reduce**（減少、縮減）

- bond n. 字據、債券
- interest n. 利息、趣味性
- payable a. 應支付的、到期的

33.
accumulate [ə`kjumjə‚let] 【 ac·cu·mu·late 】 **v** 累積、積聚　　174

They set to work accumulating a huge mass of money.

他們開始累積大量的金錢。

同► **collect, compile, gather**（聚集、收集）

反► **dissipate, scatter, waste**（驅散、消失）

- accumulation n. 積累、積聚
- accumulative a. 積累的、堆積的
- accumulator n. 積累者、聚財者
- mass n. 團、大量、眾多

34.
accurate [`ækjərit] 【 ac·cu·rate 】 **a** 準確的、精確的　　140

She gave an accurate account of the project.

她對該項企劃做了準確的闡述。

同► **correct, exact, precise**（正確的、準確的）

反► **inaccurate, incorrect**（不精準的、不正確的）

- 字首：ac朝向
- 字根：cur關心
- 字尾：ate有…性質的
- strive v. 努力、抗爭
- account n. 解釋、說明
- project n. 計劃、企劃

35.
accuse [əˋkjuz] 【 ac·cuse 】 **V** 指控、譴責、把…歸咎於
Employees accused their boss of having broken his word.
員工指責老闆不守信。
同► **blame, charge, denounce**（指責、譴責）
反► **absolve, defend**（寬恕、防禦）

- accuse...of ph.控告、譴責
- employee n.員工
- break v.打破、毀壞

36.
accustomed [əˋkʌstəmd] 【 ac·cus·tomed 】
a 慣常的、習慣的
I'm not accustomed to working overtime.
我不習慣加班。
同► **customary, habitual, routine**（習慣的、普遍的）
反► **unaccustomed, uncustomary**（不習慣的、不熟悉的）

- accustom v.使習慣於
- be accustomed to ph.習慣於
- overtime n.加班時間、超過時間

37.
achievement [əˋtʃivmənt] 【 achieve·ment 】
n 完成、達成、成就
He didn't want such special credit for his achievement.
他並不希望他的貢獻獲得如此特殊的榮耀。
同► **accomplishment, exploit, fullfilment**（成就、功勳）
反► **failure**（失敗）

- 字首：achieve完成、實現 字尾：ment情況、性質
- special a.特別的、特殊的
- the board of directors n.董事會
- credit n.榮譽、讚揚

38.
acknowledge [əkˋnɑlɪdʒ] 【 ac·knowl·edge 】
V 承認、就…表示謝意、告知收到
We acknowledge your quotation dated Oct 22nd with thanks and want to place you our order no.563 as enclosed.
我們已收到您於10月22號的報價，並將向你訂貨，訂單號為563。
同► **admit, concede, recognize**（承認、給予）
反► **disapprove, contradict**（不贊成、否定）

- acknowledge the corn ph.認錯
- 字首：ac朝向 字根：knowledge知道、瞭解
- quotation n.報價單、估價單
- order n.訂購、訂貨
- enclose v.把…封入

39.
acquaint [əˋkwent] 【 ac·quaint 】 **V** 使認識，介紹
It takes time to acquaint oneself with new co-workers.
熟悉新同事是需要花點時間。
同► **apprise, make familiar, notify**（通知、使熟悉）
反► **exhaust, derange, disturb**（耗盡、擾亂、妨礙）

- acquaintance n.瞭解、相識的人
- acquaint oneself with ph.知悉
- acquaint sb. with ph. 把…通知某人
- be acquainted with ph. 瞭解

40.
acquire [əˋkwaɪr] 【 ac·quire 】 **V** 獲得、得到
Gradually they acquired experience in how to do the work.
他們漸漸地獲得了如何做這工作的經驗。
同► **gain, obtain, get as one's own**（獲得、取得）
反► **forfeit, lose, miss**（遺失、喪失）

- 字首：ac朝向 字根：company陪伴、夥伴
- acquire the skills ph.掌握技能
- gradually ad.逐步地、漸漸地
- experience n.經驗

41.

177

acquisition [ˌækwə`zɪʃən] 【ac·qui·si·tion】 n.獲得、取得

More married women now work than ever before in our history, sharing their husbands' preoccupations with the acquisition of greater wealth and position.

現今婦女比歷史上任何時代的婦女投入工作還多，分擔她們丈夫的事業，以期待獲得更多的財富和更高的地位。

🔄 acquirement, obtainment, procurement（取得、獲得）

- acquisition of assets ph.資產購併
- acquisition of land ph. 土地徵用
- acquisition order 徵用令
- preoccupation n. 專心的事物
- wealth n.財富、財產

42.

61

acrophobia [ˌækrə`fobɪə] 【ac·ro·pho·bia】 n.懼高症

Suffering from acrophobia; abnormally afraid of high places.

患懼高症的症狀是反常地害怕高處。

- 字首：acro高 字尾：phobia病痛
- suffer v.遭受
- abnormally ad.反常地、不規則地

43.

290

act [ækt] 【act】 v.扮演、舉止表現 n.行動、行為

Would you please act your position!

請你做事要有一個與自己職位相稱的樣子。

🔄 behave, do, perform（行動、表演）

- act on ph.奉行、按照…行動
- act as ph.扮演
- act for ph.扮演、代理
- act against ph.違反

44.

281

activate [`æktəˌvet] 【ac·ti·vate】 v.使活動、使活潑

This would be effective if you could adequately activate everything on the screen by the touch of a finger.

當你需要執行螢幕上的內容時，只需要用手指觸碰就可以了。

🔄 actuate, animate, stimulate（激勵、使興奮）
🔄 enervate, depress, stagnate（使失去活力、腐敗）

- 字根：active活躍的、活潑的
- 字尾：ate使成為…
- effective a.有效的
- adequately ad.適當地、充分地
- screen n.螢幕

45.

117

acute [ə`kjut] 【a·cute】 a.尖銳的、激烈的、嚴重的

Whatever happens, we should avoid the acute angle with others.

無論如何我們都應避免與他人的正面衝突。

🔄 astute, exquisite, keen（敏銳的、劇烈的）
🔄 blunt, chronic, dull（不鋒利的、慣性的）

- acute accent n.尖重音
- acute angle n.銳角
- acute triangle n.銳角三角形
- happen v.發生、碰巧
- avoid v.避免、躲開

46.

210

adapt [ə`dæpt] 【ad·apt】 v.使適應、適合、改寫

A reasonable man adapts himself to the world, the unreasonable one persists in trying to adapt the world to himself.

理智的人使自己適應世界，不理智的人硬想世界適應自己。

🔄 adjust, alter, modify（調節、修改）
🔄 unfit（使不相宜）

- adapt oneself to ph. 使自己適應於
- adapt...for ph. 改編、改寫
- 字首：ad朝向 字根：apt適當
- reasonable a.通情達理的
- unreasonable a.非理智的

47.

129

add [æd] 【add】 v.添加、增加、補充說

In recent years fashion has encouraged men to add more colors to their wardrobes.

最近這幾年，時尚界激勵男人挑選多花色的服裝。

🔄 increase, put together, sum up（增加、總和、組合）
🔄 decrease, eliminate, subtract（減少、消滅）

- addition n.加法
- add insult to injury ph. 雪上加霜
- add in ph.把…包括在內
- add up ph.把…加起來
- add up to ph.總計達

48.

addict [ə`dɪkt]【ad·dict】 **V**使入迷、使成癮 **n**入迷的人

She addicted herself to the study of antiquity.

她沉迷於研究古代的事物。

回 **attract, captivate, enchant**（吸引、著迷）

- 字首：ad朝向
  字根：dict說、言
- **antiquity** n.古代的遺物

164

49.

adept [ə`dɛpt]【ad·ept】 **a**熟練的、內行的 **n**內行

She is adept in the operation of all the machines in the factory.

她精通於工廠裡所有機器的操作。

回 **apt, expert, proficient**（易於…的、精通的）

反 **inept**（不適當的、無能的）

- **adept at** ph.善於
- **adept in** ph.善於
- 字首：ab朝向
  字根：ept適當
- **operation** n.操作、運轉
- **machine** n.機器、機械

107

50.

adequate [`ædəkwɪt]【ad·e·quate】 **a**適當的、足夠的、勝任的

Our company does not have an adequate inventory to supply the demand.

我們公司存貨不足，難以滿足客戶的需求。

回 **ample, enough, sufficient**（大量的、足夠的）

反 **deficient, inadequate, slender**（不足的、不適當的）

- 字首：ad朝向
  字根：equ平等
  字尾：ate有…性質的
- **inventory** n.存貨清單
- **supply** v.供給、提供
- **demand** n.需求

129

51.

adhere [əd`hɪr]【ad·here】 **V**黏附、遵守、追隨

It is necessary to adhere to the principle of equality and mutual benefit in conducting international economic exchanges.

開展國際經濟往來，應堅持平等互利。

回 **cling, cohere, stick**（黏著）

- **adhere to** ph.黏附、堅持
- 字首：ad朝向
  字根：here黏著
- **principle** n.原則、原理
- **mutual** a.相互的、彼此的
- **benefit** n.利益、優勢
- **conduct** v.帶領、經營

174

52.

adjoin [ə`dʒɔɪn]【ad·join】 **V**貼近、毗連

It is prohibited to adjoin a postcard any merchandise.

禁止在明信片上附貼商品。

回 **be close to, border, connect**（毗鄰、連結）

反 **disjoin**（分開）

- **adjoin to** ph.鄰近、連接
- 字首：ad朝向
  字根：join連接
- **prohibit** v.禁止
- **postcard** n.明信片
- **merchandise** n.商品、貨物

166

53.

adjust [ə`dʒʌst]【ad·just】 **V**調節、校正、解決

She must learn to adjust herself to English work rhythm.

她必須學會適應英國的工作節奏。

回 **alter, arrange, make suitable**（改變、修正）

反 **derange, disturb**（擾亂、搞亂）

- **adjust to** ph.使自己適應於…
- **adjust-on-hand** n.調整現有庫存量
- **rhythm** n.節奏、律動

180

54.

adjourn [ə`dʒɜn]【ad·journ】 **V**使中止、休會、延期

The program was adjourned until next Thursday.

該專案延至下星期四討論。

回 **postpone, recess, suspend**（使中止、休會、延期）

反 **begin, convene**（開始、召集）

- **adjournment** n.休會、延期
- 字首：ad離開
  字根：journ每日、白天

144

55.
administrate [əd`mɪnəˌstret] 【 ad·min·is·trate 】 **V**管理、支配

Administrate periodical official training and inspection as superordinate as regulation required.

依上級要求管理定期培訓和檢查工作。

🔵 **control, manage, take over**（控制、管理）

- administration n.管理、行政
- periodical a.定期的
- training n.訓練
- inspection n.檢查、審視
- superordinate a.上級的 n.上級
- regulation n.規定、條例

286

56.
admire [əd`maɪr] 【 ad·mire 】 **V**欽佩、稱讚

We admire the way she is able to shrug off unfair criticism.

我們很佩服她能對不公的批評意見不予理會。

🔵 **adore, appreciate, respect**（崇敬、欣賞、尊敬）
🔴 **abhor, desprise, criticize**（厭惡、鄙視、批評）

- admiration n.欽佩、稱讚
- 字首：ad朝向 字根：mire-miracle驚奇
- shrug off ph.不理會
- unfair a.不公平的
- criticism n.批評

241

57.
admit [əd`mɪt] 【 ad·mit 】 **V**承認、允許、可容納

We have to admit that she's a highly competent career woman.

我們必須承認她是個非常能幹的職業婦女。

🔵 **allow, consent, grant**（同意、承認）
🔴 **banish, exclude, forbid**（排除、禁止、拒絕接納）

- admittance n.入場許可
- admit of ph.容許
- admit to ph.承認
- industry n.企業、工業
- 字首：ad朝向 字根：mit送
- competent a.有能力的

203

58.
adopt [ə`dɑpt] 【 ad·opt 】 **V**採取、收養

They would adopt payment by installments for their present business transactions.

這次商業交易他們將採取分期付款方式。

🔵 **accept, assume, choose**（選擇、採納）
🔴 **discard, reject**（拋棄、拒絕）

- an adopted son n.養子
- 字首：ad朝向
- 字根：opt選擇
- payment n.付款
- installment n.分期付款
- transaction n.交易

104

59.
advance [əd`væns] 【 ad·vance 】 **V**前進、進展 **N**前進、預付

The payment by the buyer was therefore an advance payment for an executory contract which the seller had not performed.

買方所付之款項是一份應於訂立後再履行而賣方尚未履行的契約而約付的預付款。

🔵 **accelerate, further, proceed**（促進、進行）
🔴 **block, obstruct, recede**（阻塞、撤回）

- in advance ph.事先、預先
- in advance of ph.在（時間或空間）之先
- advance contract n.預簽合約
- advance copy n.新書樣本
- advance payment n.預付款
- executory a.未生效的

149

60.
advantage [əd`væntɪdʒ] 【 ad·van·tage 】 **N**優點、利益 **V**有利於

As a country has huge labor resources, labor export is an advantage for its participation in international economic activities.

當一個國家擁有巨大的勞務資源，勞務輸出是該國參與國際經濟活動的優勢。

🔵 **benefit, favor, privilege**（利益、有利於）
🔴 **disadvantage, handicap**（不利條件、使不利）

- have an advantage over ph.勝過
- have the advantage of ph.由於…處於有利條件
- have an advantage of sb. ph.知道某人所不知道的事
- take advantage of ph.利用
- resource n.資源

270

61.
advent [`ædvɛnt] 【 ad·vent 】 **N**出現、到來

With the advent of modern methods of communication, the whole world has been transformed into a single mechanism.

由於近代通信方法的出現，整個世界已轉變成為一個統一的機體。

🔵 **approach, arrival, access**（到達、接近）
🔴 **departure, retreat**（離開、撤退）

- 字首：ad朝向 字根：vent來
- modern a.現代的
- method n.方法
- communication n.通信、傳達
- mechanism n.結構

181

62.
adventure [əd`vɛntʃə] 【ad·ven·ture】 **v.n.**冒險

It gives us the power to predict and to design, to understand and to adventure into the unknown.

它使我們有能力預言和設計，理解和探索未知的領域。

同► enterprise, venture, exploit（冒險精神、開拓）

- adventure novel n.冒險小說
- adventure playground n.冒險園
- 字首：ad朝向
  字根：venture來
- predict v.預言
- design v.設計

129

63.
adversary [`ædvə͵sɛrɪ] 【ad·ver·sary】 **n.**敵手、對手

It is wrong to overestimate the strategic insight of one's adversary as it is dangerous to underrate it.

過度高估對手的戰略遠見是錯誤的，低估也是危險的。

同► antagonist, enemy, opponent（敵人、對手）
反► supporter（支持者）

- 此單字常用於否定句。
- adversarial a.敵手的
- overestimate v.對…評價過高
- strategic=strategical a. 戰略的
- insight n.洞察力
- underrat v.低估、輕視

168

64.
advertisement [͵ædvə`taɪzmənt] 【ad·ver·tise·ment】 **n.**廣告、宣傳

The theme of an advertisement must be clear and distinctive.

廣告的主題是必須清晰突出的。

同► announcement, broadcast, statement（廣告、廣播、說明）

- 字首：ad朝向
  字根：vert轉
  字尾：ise使成為…；
  ment性質、狀態
- theme n.主題、題材
- clear a.清楚的
- distinctive a.有特色的

167

65.
advise [əd`vaɪz] 【ad·vise】 **v.**忠告、勸告、通知

Please advise us immediately after you have obtained the necessary import license.

貴公司得到所需進口許可證後，請立即通知我們。

同► admonish, counsel, warn（告誡、商議、勸告）

- 字首：ad朝向
  字根：vise看見的
- immediately ad.立即、馬上
- obtain v.得到、獲得
- import v.進口
- license n.許可證

213

66.
advocate [`ædvəkɪt] 【ad·vo·cate】 **v.**擁護、提倡 **n.**擁護者

We advocate a policy of gradual reform.

我們擁護逐步改革的政策。

同► defend, support, speak in favor of（提倡、主張）
反► impugn（責難、抨擊）

- 字首：ad朝向
  字根：voc喊叫、聲音
  字尾：ate行動
- policy n.政策
- gradual a.逐步的
- reform n.改革

177

67.
aerobics [͵eə`robɪks] 【aer·o·bics】 **n.**有氧運動

My muscles are sore from doing aerobics mechanics.

練有氧運動，我的肌肉一直痠痛。

同► wait, endure, tolerate（等待、忍受）
反► start, depart, leave（開始、離開）

- muscle n.肌肉
- sore a.痛的
- mechanics n.技術

62

68.
affection [ə`fɛkʃən] 【af·fec·tion】 **n.**感情、影響

Our gratitude will pour out in open expressions of affection for you and the great movement that you guide.

我們將向您和您所領導的活動表達感激之情。

同► admiration, friendly feeling, love and respect（愛慕、情義）
反► coldness, dislike, hatred（討厭、冷淡）

- gratitude n.感激之情
- pour v.倒、灌
- expression n.表達
- movement n.運動、活動
- guide v.帶領

184

69.

affiliate [ə`fɪlɪˏet]【af·fil·i·ate】**n**分會、成員**v**使緊密聯繫

Our company was founded five years ago as an affiliate of United Trading Company.

本公司創立於5年前，是聯合貿易公司的關係企業。

同► **member**（會員）

121
- affiliate with ph.與…有密切聯繫
- company n.公司
- found v.建立
- united a.聯合的
- trade n.貿易

70.

affirm [ə`fɝm]【af·firm】**v**斷言、證實

We can not affirm what should be done the next step.

我們不能肯定下一步該做什麼。

同► **assert, confirm, certify**（斷言、證實）
反► **deny, negate**（否定、取消）

239
- affirmation n.斷言、肯定
- 字首：af朝向
  字根：firm堅決、穩固
- step n.步驟

71.

affordable [ə`fɔrdəbl]【af·ford·able】**a**負擔得起的

In big cities, taxis are plentiful and affordable for the middle-class.

在大城市裡，大量而充足的計程車更加適合中產階級的消費能力。

126
- afford v.買得起
- 字首：af朝向
  字根：ford涉水而過
  字尾：able可…的
- plentiful a.豐富的
- middle-class a.中產階級的

72.

agenda [ə`dʒɛndə]【agen·da】**n**議程

A Council of 500, elected from all but the poorest class, prepared the agenda of the assembly.

公民大會的議程由500人組成的議會負責，這500人幾乎從最低階層中推選出來。

同► **programme, schedule, timetable**（程序、時間表）

274
- agendum（單數）待辦事項
- agenda setting n.議程設定
- council n.會議
- elect v.選舉
- prepare v.準備
- assembly n.集會

73.

aggravate [`ægrəˏvet]【ag·gra·vate】**v**惡化、加重、激怒

That is the way to aggravate rather than to resolve contradictions.

這個辦法只會使衝突惡化，而無法解決衝突。

同► **exasperate, infuriate, provoke**（使惱怒、加劇）
反► **mitigate**（使緩和）

133
- aggravation n.惡化
- aggravated assault n.重傷害
- 字首：ag朝前
  字根：grav重
  字尾：ate行
- resolve v.解決

74.

aggregate [`ægrɪˏget]【ag·gre·gate】**v n**聚集、總計

The aggregate number of employees in our company is five thousand this year.

今年公司雇用的人員總計5000人。

同► **accumulate, amass, total**（累積、合計）
反► **segregate**（分離、離析）

164
- in the aggregate ph.總計
- aggregate fruit n.聚合果
- 字首：ag向前
  字根：greg聚集
  字尾：ate行動
- employ v.雇用

75.

aggressive [ə`grɛsɪv]【ag·gres·sive】**a**侵略的、好鬥的

Mike was an aggressive salesman who did his job quite well.

邁克是個積極有幹勁的推銷員，他工作相當出色。

同► **belligerent, combative, offensive**（好戰的、進攻的）
反► **defensive**（防禦的）

149
- aggressiveness n.侵犯、進取
- 字首：ag朝向
  字根：gress行走
  字尾：ive有…傾向
- salesman n.銷售員
- quite ad.完全、相當

76.
agitate [ˋædʒəˏtet] **[ag·i·tate]** **V** 使激動、攪動

They sent agents to agitate the local people.

他們派情報人員煽動當地的民眾。

⊕ **disturb, inflame, instigate**（激動、擾亂）
⊗ **calm, soothe, quiet**（使鎮定、使平靜）

- agitation n.攪動、激動
- 字根：ag做、行動
  字尾：it走動
  字尾：ate進行一項行動
- agent n.間諜
- local a.當地的

181

77.
agony [ˋægənɪ] **[ag·o·ny]** **n** 極大的痛苦

He relinquished his labour of agony, and turned consoled at once.

他放棄了那痛苦的工作，馬上獲得了慰藉。

⊕ **anguish, grief, torment**（苦惱、悲痛）
⊗ **comfort, relief, solace**（安慰、慰藉）

- agony column n.人事廣告欄
- relinquish v.放棄
- labour n.勞動
- console v.安慰
- at once ph.立刻、馬上

208

78.
agreeable [əˋgriəbḷ] **[agree·able]** **a** 令人愉快的、符合的

We found him the most agreeable.

我們覺得他極容易相處。

⊕ **appropriate, graceful, palatable**（合適的、使人愉快的）
⊗ **disagreeable, odious**（不同意的、令人作嘔的）

- agree v.意見一致
- agree on / upon ph.對…取得一致意見
- agree to ph.同意
- agree with ph.和…意見一致
- agreeable food n.可口食物

234

79.
air [ɛr] **[air]** **n** 天空、空氣 **V** 使通風、發表

The program is merely a castle in the air because it is simply impracticable.

這計劃不過是空中樓閣（即不可能的實現的計劃）而已，因為它根本行不通。

⊕ **atmosphere, heaven, sky**（大氣、天空）
⊗ **sea**（海洋）

- air bag n.安全氣囊
- air ball n.籃外空心球
- air base n.空軍基地
- in the air ph.不具體
- castle n.城堡
- impracticable a.不能實行的

210

80.
airliner [ˋɛrˏlaɪnɚ] **[air·lin·er]** **n** 大型客機

The airliner from New York landed a few minutes ago.

來自紐約的客機在幾分鐘之前降落了。

- an air-liner 定期班機
- 字首：air空中
  字根：liner班機
- land v.使降落

74

81.
aisle [aɪl] **[aisle]** **n** 通道、側廊

The usher came down the aisle towards them.

接待員沿著通道向他們走去。

⊕ **artery, corridor, passageway**（通道、走廊）

- aisled a.有狹長通路的
- usher n.接待員

149

82.
alarm [əˋlɑrm] **[alarm]** **n** 警報器、鬧鐘 **V** 使恐懼、驚慌

They felt a vague alarm.

他們隱約感到一種不祥的預兆。

⊕ **frighten, jolt, startle**（使驚嚇、使慌亂）
⊗ **assure**（向…保證）

- alarm clock n.鬧鐘
- fire alarm n.火災警報器
- vague a.模糊不清的

211

83.
album [`ælbəm] 【 al·bum 】 ⋒相簿、唱片集、文集

Her latest album is a compilation of all her best singles.

她最新的一套唱片是她最佳單曲唱片集。

⟨同⟩ anthology, catalogue, scrapbook（選集、目錄冊）

- album of views n.風景畫集
- Family Album U.S.A. ph.走遍美國
- latest a.最新的
- compilation n.編輯物

【104】

84.
alcohol [`ælkə͵hɔl] 【 al·co·hol 】 ⋒酒精、含酒精飲料

Notice: it is illegal to sell alcohol to anyone under the age of 18.

注意：販賣酒給未滿18歲的公民是違法的。

⟨同⟩ booze, intoxicant, liquor（酒類、酒精）

- alcohol-in-glass thermometer n.玻璃管酒精溫度計
- alcohol abuse n.酗酒
- notice v. 注意
- illegal a. 非法的

【251】

85.
alert [ə`lɝt] 【 alert 】 ⓐ機警的、靈活的 ⋒警戒 ⓥ使警覺

My boss had been painfully alert.

我老闆一直都有強烈的警覺。

⟨同⟩ attentive, nimble, vigilant（機警的、靈敏的）
⟨反⟩ languid, sluggish, torpid（懶散的、倦怠的）

- alertness n.警覺、敏捷
- painfully ad.費力地、強烈地

【120】

86.
alien [`eliən] 【 alien 】 ⋒外國人、外星人 ⓐ外國的、性質不同的

Their behavior is alien to our ethical values.

他們的行為和我們的倫理標準格格不入。

⟨同⟩ extraneous, foreign, strange（外來的、外國的）
⟨反⟩ akin, kindred, native（本國的、同族的）

- behavior n.行為
- ethical a.道德的
- value n.價值觀

【114】

87.
alienate [`eljən͵et] 【alien·ate】 ⓥ使疏遠、使轉移

Worse still, by arrogantly dismissing these as uninformed opinions are not worthy of our rebuttals, we would forfeit good opportunities for self-improvement and alienate our audiences.

依舊很糟的是，自大地把這些意見當成無知的而不理會，不值得我們去爭辯，這樣的態度會讓我們失去改進自己的機會，也會使我們和觀眾越來越疏遠。

⟨同⟩ disunite, estrange, separate（使疏遠、分開）
⟨反⟩ conciliate（使和好）

- 字根：alien外國人 字尾：ate進行一項行動
- arrogantly ad.傲慢地
- dismiss v.讓…離開
- uninformed a.無知的
- rebuttal n.抗辯
- forfeit n.喪失
- opportunity n.機會

【149】

88.
allege [ə`lɛdʒ] 【 al·lege 】 ⓥ宣稱、斷言、提出

His reputation is blemished by a newspaper article that alleged he'd evaded his taxes.

由於報上一篇文章聲稱他曾逃稅，使他的名譽受到損害。

⟨同⟩ declare, profess, plead（斷言、宣告）
⟨反⟩ deny, suppress（否認、鎮壓）

- 字首：al加強語氣 字根：lege讀
- reputation n.名譽
- blemish v.玷汙
- evade v.躲避

【163】

89.
alleviate [ə`livɪ͵et] 【 al·le·vi·ate 】 ⓥ減輕、緩和

Not only alleviate the symptoms, but effect a permanent cure as well.

不但要治標也要治本。

⟨同⟩ allay, ease, moderate（使緩和、減輕）
⟨反⟩ astonish, pain（使痛苦、使吃驚）

- alleviation n.減輕、緩和
- 字首：al加強語氣 字根：levi輕 字尾：ate行動
- symptom n.症狀
- effect v.產生
- permanent a.永久的

【181】

90.
alliance [ə`laɪəns] 【al·li·ance】 **n**結盟、聯姻

These islands tried to forge an alliance.

這些島國試圖建立同盟。

同- league, treaty, union（結盟、聯合）
反- division（分開）

- ally v.使結盟
- island n.島
- forge n.編造

91.
189

allocate [`ælə͵ket】【al·lo·cate】 **v**分配、分派

We allocate 10% of revenue to publicity.

我們撥出10%的營業收入用於廣告宣傳。

同- allot, dispense, distribute（分配、分發）
反- withhold, monopolize（保留、獨佔）

- 字首：al朝向
  字根：loc地方
  字尾：ate行動
- revenue n.收入
- publicity n.廣告宣傳

92.
261

allowance [ə`lauəns] 【al·low·ance】 **n**津貼、零用錢、允許
v供應

Retired workers need not to come hat in hand to ask for supplementary allowance.

退休工人就不必卑躬屈膝地請求追加補助費了。

同- allotment, fee, ration（費用、配給量）

- 字根：allow允許
  字尾：ance性質
  字尾：ate性質
- retired a.需要、必需品
- come hat in hand ph.乞求施捨
- supplementary a.追加的

93.
217

alter [`ɔltɚ] 【al·ter】 **v**改變、修改

No bidder shall be permitted to alter his bid after the bid has been open.

開標以後，任何投標人都不准再修改投標。

同- change, diversify, modify（改變、多樣化）
反- preserve, fix（維持、使固定）

- alter ego n.心腹朋友
- alter-isness n.更改或改變某事物的真實性
- bidder n.投標人
- permit v.允許
- bid n.投標

94.
127

amateur [`æmə͵tʃur】【am·a·teur】 **n**業餘從事者、外行人

Although my father is only an amateur, he's a first-class golf player.

雖然我父親只是個業餘愛好者，但也是一流的高爾夫球高手。

同- apprentice, dabbler, dilettante（見習生、一知半解者）
反- expert, professional, specialist（專家、內行）

- amateur dramatics n.業餘戲劇活動
- amateur edition n.私人收藏本
- enthusiasm n.熱情、熱忱
- 字根：amat喜愛
  字尾：eur從事某種活動或職業的人

95.
164

ambiguous [æm`bɪgjuəs] 【am·big·u·ous】 **a**含糊不清的

His ambiguous directions confused us and we did not know what we should do.

他模稜兩可的指導使我們困惑。

同- dubious, equivocal, weasel-worded（有疑問的、含糊的）
反- clear, definite, explicit（清楚的、明確的）

- ambiguity n.意義不明確
- 字首：ambi二
- direction n.指導
- confuse v.使困惑

96.
241

ambition [æm`bɪʃən] 【am·bi·tion】 **n**抱負、野心 **v**追求

Her son was filled with ambition to become a great entrepreneur.

她兒子一心想成為偉大的企業家。

同- aspiration, desire, motivation（志向、積極性）

- ambitious a.野心勃勃的
- 字首：ambi二
  字尾：tion行為、性質
- be filled with ph.充滿
- entrepreneur n.企業家

97.

amend [əˋmɛnd]【a·mend】 **V** 修改、改善、改過自新

The motion to amend the club's constitution was defeated by 30 votes to 10.

修改俱樂部章程的提議以三十票對十票被否決了。

(同) **emend, improve, rectify**（改進、改正）

(反) **deprave, deteriorate, impair**（惡化、損壞）

> `169`
> • amendment n.修正
> • 字首：a 加強語氣
>   字根：mend 修補
> • motion n.提議
> • constitution n. 章程
> • defeat v. 擊敗

98.

amity [ˋæmətɪ]【am·i·ty】 **n** 友好、和睦

The two nations had lived in perfect amity for many years before the recent troubles.

兩國在產生紛爭之前和平共處了許多年。

(同) **harmony, goodwill, peace**（友好、和睦）

(反) **enmity, hostility**（敵意、不合）

> `79`
> • 字根：ami 喜愛
>   字尾：ty 狀態
> • perfect a.想的
> • recent a.最近的
> • trouble n.紛爭

99.

amount [əˋmaunt]【am·ount】 **n** 總數、數量 **V** 合計

I didn't expect the bill come to this amount.

我不希望帳單費用超出這個金額。

(同) **quanity, sum, volume**（總計、數量）

(反) **part**（部分）

> `211`
> • a great amount of ph.許多、大量的
> • amount to ph.總計為
> • amount to the same thing ph.結果相同
> • in amount ph.總計
> • expect v.期望
> • bill n.帳單

100.

ample [ˋæmpl]【am·ple】 **a** 大量的、足夠的、寬敞的

You'll have ample opportunities to ask questions after talk.

會談結束後你有大量機會提問。

(同) **abundant, plenty, sufficient**（大量的、足夠的）

(反) **deficient, insufficient, meager**（不足的、缺乏的）

> `98`
> • ampleness n.富裕、充足
> • 字根：ampl 足夠、擴大
> • opportunity n.機會
> • question n.問題

101.

amplify [ˋæmpləˏfaɪ]【am·pli·fy】 **V** 增強、擴展、詳述

I must ask them to amplify their statement.

我必須請他們對其說法作進一步的說明。

(同) **broaden, elucidate, expand**（擴大、說明）

(反) **abbreviate**（縮短）

> `124`
> • amplification n.
> • 字根：ampl 擴大
>   字尾：ify 使成為…
> • statement n.陳述、說明

102.

amuse [əˋmjuz]【a·muse】 **V** 使歡樂、給…提供娛樂

We may also amuse ourselves in the magnificent Workers Palace of Culture.

我們也可以在富麗堂皇的工藝館裡消遣娛樂。

(同) **delight, entertain, tickle**（使歡樂、娛樂）

(反) **annoy, bore, tire**（使煩惱、使厭煩）

> `180`
> • magnificent a.壯麗的
> • palace n.皇宮
> • culture n.文化

103.

analogy [əˋnɑlədʒɪ]【anal·o·gy】 **n** 相似、類比

He drew an analogy between the brain and the vast computer.

他打了個比方，將巨型電腦比作人的大腦。

(同) **comparison, resemblance, similarity**（比照、相似）

(反) **difference**（不同）

> `194`
> • 此單字常與介系詞between 連用
> • 字根：logy說話
> • draw v.逗引說話
> • brain n.腦袋
> • vast a.巨大的

104.
analyze [ˈænḷˌaɪz] 【 an·a·lyze 】 **V** 分析、解析

We should analyze the problem as a whole.

我們應該把問題作一個整體分析。

同 diagnose, dissect, examine（分析、細查）
反 synthesize（合成）

- **239**
- analysis n.分析、解析
- 又作analyse
- as a whole ph.整體來看

105.
ancestor [ˈænsɛstə] 【 an·ces·tor 】 **n** 祖先、先驅

The ancestor of the modern bicycle can only be seen in the picture.

現代自行車的先驅只能從照片上看到了。

同 antecedent, forefather, forerunner（祖先、先驅）
反 descendant（後裔）

- **141**
- ancestry n.列祖列宗
- ancestress n.女祖先
- ancient a.古代的、古老的
- modern a.現代的
- bicycle n.自行車

106.
angle [ˈæŋgḷ] 【 an·gle 】 **n** 角度、觀點 **V** 使角度移動

I realized I was looking at it from the wrong angle.

我承認我看待問題的角度錯誤。

- **201**
- triangle n.三角形
- angle for ph.謀取
- angle of attack n.攻角
- realize v.領悟

107.
animal [ˈænəmḷ] 【 an·i·mal 】 **n** 動物

Animal growth or production yield is the ultimate concern of the farmer.

農場主人最關心的是牲畜的生長或其產品的生產量問題。

同 beast, brute, creature（動物、家畜）
反 human, mineral, plant（人類、礦物、植物）

- **128**
- animal husbandry ph. 畜牧業
- animal kingdom ph.動物界
- animal magnetism ph. 吸引力的能力
- animal spirits ph.精力充沛
- 字首：anim精神、靈魂
- yield v.出產

108.
animate [ˈænəˌmet] 【 an·i·mate 】 **V** 使有生命、鼓舞 **a** 有生命的

Jakson's arrival served to animate the whole party.

傑克遜的到來使聚會的整個氣氛活躍了起來。

同 inspire, vivify, alive（鼓舞、活躍、活著的）
反 depress, enervate, inanimate（使沮喪、無生氣的）

- **164**
- animation n.活潑、激勵
- 字首：anim精神、靈魂 字尾：ate使成為…
- arrival n.到達
- serve v.提供

109.
anniversary [ˌænəˈvɝsərɪ] 【 an·ni·ver·sa·ry 】 **n** 週年紀念、結婚週年 **a** 週年的

We're very happy to be invited to your tenth anniversary celebration.

我們很高興能受邀請參加你們的十週年慶祝會。

同 annual, centenary, red-letter day（一年一次的、紀念日）
反 daily, perennial（每天的、終年的）

- **177**
- anniversary ring ph.結婚週年戒指
- 字根：anni年
- 字根：vers轉
- 字尾：ary性質
- invite v.邀請
- celebration n.慶祝活動

110.
annoy [əˈnɔɪ] 【 an·noy 】 **V** 使生氣、打擾

Jack really annoyed me in the meeting this morning.

傑克在晨間會議上惹惱了我。

同 bother, irritate, make angry（打擾、使生氣）
反 gratify, please, relieve（使高興、緩和）

- **123**
- annoyance n.惱怒、打擾
- meeting n.會議

111.

announce [əˈnaʊns] 【an·nounce】 **V**宣佈、通知、播報

She announced the winner of the competition to the excited audiences.

她向興奮的觀眾宣佈此次比賽的獲勝者。

同 broadcast, declare, proclaim（宣佈、通知）
反 conceal, hide, withhold（隱藏、保留）

- 245
- announcement n.通知、宣佈
- 字首：an朝向
- 字尾：nounce報告
- competition n.競賽
- excited a.興奮的
- audience n.觀眾

112.

annual [ˈænjʊəl] 【an·nu·al】 **a**一年一次的、全年的 **n**年刊

Companies publish annual reports to inform the public about the previous year's activities.

公司向公眾發佈了年度報告說明上一年度公司經營狀況。

同 anniversary, once a year, yearly, yearbook（每年的、年刊）
反 daily, perennial（每天的、終年的）

- 217
- annual interest ph.年息
- annual meeting ph.年會
- annual salary system ph.年薪制
- 字根：ann年
- 字尾：ual屬於…的
- publish v.發表
- previous a.先前的

113.

anonymous [əˈnɑnəməs] 【anon·y·mous】 **a**

匿名的、無特色的

The money was donated by an anonymous benefactor.

這筆錢由匿名捐助者捐贈。

同 innominate, nameless, incognito（匿名的、隱姓埋名的）
反 famous（著名的）

- 114
- anonymous remailer ph.電腦匿名轉信站
- 字首：an否定的意思
- 字根：onym字、名
- 字尾：ous充滿…的
- donate v捐贈
- benefactor n.捐助者

114.

answer [ˈænsə] 【an·swer】 **V** **n**回覆、答辯、答案

I've just called him but there was no answer.

我剛才給他打電話但是沒有應答。

同 reply, respond, retort（回覆、回嘴）
反 ask, inquiry, query（詢問、打聽）

- 208
- answer for ph.對…負責
- answer sheet ph.答案紙
- answer to ph.符合
- answer up ph.迅速回答
- ring v.打電話

115.

antibiotic [ˌæntɪbaɪˈɑtɪk] 【an·ti·bi·ot·ic】 **n**抗生素 **a**抗菌的

A new potent antibiotic will shortly be available.

一種新的高效抗生素不久將在市面銷售。

- 64
- antibiotics n.抗生素（用作複數）
- 字首：anti對抗
- 字根：bio生命
- 字尾：tic與…有關的

116.

anticipate [ænˈtɪsəˌpet] 【an·tic·i·pate】 **V**預期、預先考慮、先發制人

It's always best to anticipate a problem before it rises.

問題在發生前能預料到總是最好的。

同 await, foresee, expect（期待、預知）
反 despair（絕望）

- 184
- anticipation n.預期
- anticipator n.佔先者
- 字首：anti先
- 字根：cip拿
- 字尾：ate行動

117.

antipathy [ænˈtɪpəθɪ] 【an·tip·a·thy】 **n**反感、引起反感的事物

There was an undercurrent of antipathy between us.

我們兩人之間潛伏著一股反感的暗流。

同 hatred, strong dislike, spite（厭惡、惡意）
反 sympathy（同情）

- 53
- 字首：anti相反
- 字根：pathy感覺、痛苦
- undercurrent n.暗流

118.

anxiety [æŋˋzaɪətɪ] 【anx·i·ety】 n焦慮、渴望

Children normally feel a lot of anxiety about their first day at school.

一般來說，小孩對第一天上學都很緊張。

🔄 angst, eagerness, dread（憂慮、渴望）

🔄 ease, easiness, insouciance（安心、不在乎）

- anxious a.擔心的
- anxiety-depression neurosis ph.憂慮性精神官能症
- normally ad.通常

119.

apartment [əˋpɑrtmənt] 【apart·ment】 n房間、公寓

They have six luxurious aparments for sale.

他們有六套豪華公寓要出售。

🔄 chamber, flat, suite（房間、公寓）

- apartment block ph.【英】公寓大樓
- apartment building ph.【美】公寓大樓
- 字首：apart分開 字尾：ment性質、狀態
- luxurious a.奢侈的

120.

aperitif [ɑperiˋtif] 【aper·i·tif】 n【法】開胃酒

This wine makes an excellent aperitif and is ideal with seafood, cream soups and salads.

這種葡萄酒是種優等的開胃酒，搭配海鮮、奶油湯和沙拉一起食用較理想。

- excellent a.優等的
- ideal a.理想的、完美的
- seafood n.海鮮
- cream n.奶油
- salad n.沙拉

121.

apparatus [ˌæpəˋretəs] 【ap·pa·ra·tus】 n設備、器官、機構

We have installed wireless apparatus on board.

我們已在船上安裝了無線電設備。

🔄 equipment, gear, tackle（設備、裝置）

- install v.安裝
- wireless n.無線電
- board n.船艙

122.

appeal [əˋpil] 【ap·peal】 vn呼籲、上訴、有吸引力

They will appeal to a great variety of sources of information.

他們將求助於多種資料來源。

🔄 beg, entreat, plead（懇求、辯護）

- appeal for ph.懇求
- appeal to ph.向…呼籲、吸引
- variety n.多樣化
- source n.根源、來源

123.

appendix [əˋpɛndɪks] 【ap·pen·dix】 n附錄、附加物 v加附錄於

The seller shall undertake the design work with respect to the Contract Plant, details of which shall be as the Appendix 8.

賣方應承擔本合同項目的設計工作，詳見本合約附件八。

🔄 annexation, appendage, attachment（附加物、附著）

- 字首：ap添加 字根：pend懸掛
- undertake v.承擔
- detail n.詳述

124.

apologize [ˋpɑləˌdʒaɪz] 【a·pol·o·gize】 v道歉、辯護

This is pure slander and I'll sue him for defamation if he doesn't apologize.

這純屬污蔑，如果他不向我道歉，我就告他誹謗。

🔄 ask forgiveness, beg pardon, express regret（道歉、認錯）

- 字根：apology道歉 字尾：ize使成為
- apologize to sb. for sth. ph.為…向…道歉
- slander n.誹謗
- defamation n.誹謗

125. `148`

appetite [ˋæpəˌtaɪt] 【ap·pe·tite】 n食慾、慾望

The patient feels pretty well, but she doesn't have much of an appetite.

病患精神還不錯，不過胃口不太好。

同►craving, desire, hunger（渴望、食慾）

- patient n.病人
- pretty ad.相當

126. `81`

appetizer [ˋæpəˌtaɪzə] 【ap·pe·tiz·er】 n開胃的食物

Pickled vegetable of Sichuan flavour is a good appetizer and affords a lingering after-taste.

川味泡菜清口開胃，令您回味無窮。

同► delicacy, snack（佳餚、點心）

- appetizing a.刺激食慾的
- pickled a.醃漬的
- flavour n.味道
- lingering a.逗留不去的

127. `232`

applaud [əˋplɔd] 【ap·plaud】 v向…鼓掌、稱讚

The viewers cheered and applauded the young man's artistry.

觀眾對這位年輕人的才藝報以讚歎和掌聲。

同► approve, cheer, clap（贊成、拍手）
反► disapprove, disject, reprobate（不贊成、駁斥）

- applause n.鼓掌、喝采
- 字首：ap加重語氣
  字根：plaud鼓掌
- artistry n.藝術性

128. `131`

appliance [əˋplaɪəns] 【ap·pli·ance】 n器具、設備、救火車

AAA Group Electric Appliance Co., Ltd. is specialized in developing better coffee machine to satisfy the customer's request.

三A集團電器有限公司以專門研發和更好的咖啡機來滿足顧客的要求。

同► device, inplement, tool（設備、工具）

- application n.申請
- specialize v.專門化
- develop v.發展
- request n.需求

129. `266`

apply [əˋplaɪ] 【ap·ply】 v申請、適用、實施

We intend to apply economic sanctions.

我們打算實施經濟制裁。

同► ask, petition, request（請求、申請）
反► answer, grant（答應、同意）

- applicant n.申請人
- ask for v.請求得到
- apply to v.向…申請
- intend v.打算
- economic a.經濟上的
- sanction n.國際制裁

130. `245`

appoint [əˋpɔɪnt] 【ap·point】 v任命、指定、委任

Appoint people on their merits; do not resort to malpractice in personnel placement.

堅持任人唯賢，反對用人上的不正之風。

同► assign, elect, nominate（提名、分配）
反► innominate（無名的）

- appointment n.約會
- merit n.價值、優點
- resort v.訴諸
- malpractice n.不法行為
- placement n.佈置

131. `94`

apposite [ˋæpəzɪt] 【ap·po·site】 a適當的、貼切的

The successful copywriter is a master of apposite and evocative verbal images.

成功的廣告文字撰稿人是貼切且能引起共鳴的大師。

同► applicable, acceptable, fitting（適合的、相稱的）

- 字首：ap加強語氣
  字根：pos放置
  字尾：ite有…傾向的
- copywriter n.廣告文編寫人
- master n.大師
- evocative a.喚起…的
- verbal a.言辭上的

132.

appraisal [ə`prez!] 【ap·prais·al】 **n** 評價、估價

An appraisal firm or corporation may properly use a corporate signature with the signature of a responsible officer.

一個評估事務所或公司在有權負責的經理人員簽字的條件下使用法人印章。

⊜ **assessment, estimation, evaluation**（評估、評斷）

- appraisal fee **ph.**房屋估價費
- corporation **n.**財團法人
- properly **ad.**恰當地
- corporate **a.**公司的
- signature **n.**簽名
- responsible **a.**承擔責任的

`104`

133.

apprise [ə`praɪz] 【ap·prise】 **v** 通知、評價

The secretary came to apprise us that the erection of the monster machine had been successfully completed.

祕書來通知我們說那台巨型機器已順利安裝成功。

⊜ **acquaint, inform, prime**（通知、提供）

- 字首：ap加強語氣 字根：prise緊握、抓住
- secretary **n.**祕書
- erection **n.**建立
- complete **v.**完成

`132`

134.

approach [ə`protʃ] 【ap·proach】 **n** 接近、方法 **v** 接近、找…商量

When is the best time to approach my employer about an increase in salary?

什麼時候最適合與我的雇主討論加薪事宜？

⊜ **advance, access, entrance**（接近、靠近、入口）
⊗ **hinder, recede**（隱藏、退去）

- approach control **ph.**航空進場管制台
- employer **n.**雇主
- increase **n.**增加
- salary **n.**薪資

`204`

135.

appropriate [ə`proprɪˌet] 【ap·pro·pri·ate】 **a** 適當的

In entering into a contract, the parties shall have the appropriate capacities for civil rights and civil acts.

當事人訂立合約應當具有相應的民事權利能力和民事行為能力。

⊜ **fitting, proper, suitable**（適當的、相稱的）
⊗ **inappropriate, unfit, unsuitable**（不適當的、不適合）

- contract **n.**合約
- party **n.**當事人
- capacity **n.**能力
- civil **a.**市民的
- right **n.**權利
- act **n.**行為

`231`

136.

approximately [ə`praksəmɪtlɪ] 【ap·prox·i·mately】 **a** 大概、近乎

She was involved in HR practices and handled approximately 200 employees of the organization.

她曾參與人力資源管理實務並管理公司大約二百名員工。

⊜ **about, around, nearly**（大約、將近）

- 字首：ap朝向 字根：proxim接近 字尾：ate有…性質的 ly副詞字尾
- involve **v.**忙於
- HR=human resource 人力資源
- handle **v.**管理
- organization **n.**組織

`257`

137.

approve [ə`pruv] 【ap·prove】 **v** 贊同、同意、批准

The General Manager approved the issue of quality policy, quality objective and quality commitment.

總經理已批准發佈品質方針、品質目標和品質承諾。

⊜ **accredit, accept, ratify**（同意、批准）
⊗ **ban, object, oppose**（禁止、反對）

- approve of **ph.**贊成
- 字首：ap加強語氣 字根：prove證明
- issue **n.**問題
- quality **n.**品質
- objective **n.**目標
- commitment **n.**承諾

`211`

138.

arbitrary [`ɑrbə,trɛrɪ] 【 ar·bi·trary 】 **a** 任意的、反覆無常的、專制的

With respect to price reform, comprehensive supplementary measures will be taken to control the rise of prices and put an end to arbitrary price hikes.

在進行物價改革時，必須採取一系列綜合配套措施，以控制物價上漲。

🔘 **dictatorial, unreasonable, willful**（任意的、無理的）

- reform n.改革
- comprehensive a.廣泛的
- supplementary a.增補的
- measure n.措施
- hike v.上升

139.

argue [`ɑrgju] 【 ar·gue 】 **v** 爭吵、辯論、提出理由

The price clause is an important part of a contract, where the buyer and the seller argue the most.

價格條款是合約裡最重要條款，這是買賣雙方爭論較多的地方。

🔘 **object, debate, quarrel**（反對、辯論）
🔘 **agree, consent, reconcile**（同意、妥協）

- argue away ph.爭день論不休
- argue out ph.把…辯論清楚
- argue with ph.和…爭辯
- clause n.條款

140.

arise [ə`raɪz] 【 a·rise 】 **v** 升起、出現、喚醒

Arise in price will make people postpone expenditure.

價格的上升會使人們降低支出。

🔘 **ascend, appear, rise**（出現、產生）
🔘 **descend, fall**（下降、降落）

- arise-arose-arisen
- arise from ph.由…引起
- 字首：a加強語氣
  字根：rise升起
- postpone v.延遲
- expenditure n.消費

141.

arrange [ə`rendʒ] 【 ar·range 】 **v** 安排、佈置、商妥

It's simpler and cheaper for both of us to arrange the multimodal combined transport.

安排聯運對我們雙方都既簡單又經濟。

🔘 **classify, organize, settle**（安排、設置）
🔘 **derange, disarrange, disturb**（擾亂、使心神不寧）

- arrange for ph.為…作安排
- combine v.結合
- transport n.運輸

142.

array [ə`re] 【 ar·ray 】 **v** 整隊、打扮 **n** 列陣、衣服

A lectern and a platform were set up on the East Side, facing an array of seats arranged in a semicircle.

廳的東側設置了主席臺和講臺，面對講臺排列著呈半圓形的一排排座位。

🔘 **display, order**（排列、展示）
🔘 **conceal, hide**（隱藏）

- lectern n.講桌
- platform n.平臺
- set up ph.建立
- semicircle n.半圓形

143.

arrest [ə`rɛst] 【 ar·rest 】 **v n** 逮捕、抑制、阻止、吸引

The beautiful style of the book arrested the readers.

這本書優美的筆調吸引了讀者。

🔘 **capture, interrupt, stop**（阻止、中斷）
🔘 **acquit, release**（宣告…無罪、釋放）

- beauty n.優美
- reader n.讀者

144.
arrival [əˋraɪvl̩] 【 ar·riv·al 】 **n** 到達、新生兒

The goods you shipped us have become moldy on arrival because of heat during transit.

你們送來的貨物因途中受熱受潮運達時已經發霉。

同 advent, appearance（出現）
反 departure（離開）

- goods n.商品、貨物
- arrival lobby ph.入境大廳
- ship v.用船運
- moldy a.發霉的
- heat n.熱度
- transit n.運送

145.
artery [ˋɑrtərɪ] 【 ar·tery 】 **n** 動脈、道路幹線

The Yangtse River is one of the main arteries of traffic in China.

長江是中國的交通要道之一。

同 blood vessel, channel, pipe（血管、要道）
反 vein（靜脈）

- main a.主要的
- traffic n.交通

146.
article [ˋɑrtɪkl̩] 【 ar·ti·cle 】 **n** 物品、文章、冠詞

Every article has a price tag on it.

商品都標了價格。

同 composition, essay, item（作品、項目）

- article of faith ph.信條
- tag n.標籤

147.
articulate [ɑrˋtɪkjəˏlet] 【ar·tic·u·late】 **a** 發音清晰的、口才好的 **v** 清楚地說話

Articulate your words so that we can understand what you are saying.

說話要清楚，這樣我們才能聽明白你的話。

反 inarticulate（口齒不清的）

- understand v.瞭解

148.
artificial [ˏɑrtəˋfɪʃəl] 【 ar·ti·fi·cial 】 **a** 人造的、不自然的、人為的

Developments in artificial intelligence (AI) programs, have led chemical companies to experiment with many applications, including control.

人工智慧(AI)程式的發展，化學公司對其多方面的應用展開了試驗，其中也包括控制。

同 fake, false, sythetic（假的、人造的）
反 artless, genuine, natural（真的、自然的）

- artificial currency ph. 人造貨幣
- artificial nail ph.水晶指甲
- artificial respiration ph.人工呼吸
- intelligence n.智慧
- chemical a.化學的
- experiment n.實驗
- application n.運用

149.
ASAP **abbr** 越快越好

I would appreciate it if you can deliver your products ASAP.

如果您能儘快出貨，我會非常感激。

- 即as soon as possible的縮寫
- appreciate v.感激
- deliver v.傳送
- product n.產品

150.
ascend [əˋsɛnd] 【 as·cend 】 **v** 上升、追溯、攀登

The smoke ascended miles away, so the mountain climbers could be rescued.

煙裊裊升到幾里外，所以登山客得以獲救。

同 climb, mount, rise（攀爬、登上）
反 descend, fall（下降、落下）

- ascendance n.優勢
- ascendancy n.優越
- 字首：a加強語氣 字根：scend攀、爬
- climber n.登山者
- rescue v.援救

151. (177)

ascertain [ˌæsɚˋten]【as·cer·tain】**v** 確定、查明

She still kept her lips tightly compressed, as if determined fully to ascertain her longitude and position before she committed herself.

她依舊一言不發,彷彿打定了主意,在沒有完全弄清自己的處境以前絕不隨便發表意見。

同 **determine, clear up, find out**（決定、探查）

- 字首:as 朝向
- 字根:certain 確信的
- **tightly** ad.緊密地
- **compressed** v.壓縮的
- **longitude** n.經度
- **commit** v.把…付諸於

---

152. (192)

ascribe [əˋskraɪb]【as·cribe】**v** 把…歸因於、把…歸屬於

He ascribed his failure to bad luck.

他認為他的失敗是運氣不好引起的。

同 **arrogate, assign, attribute**（把…歸於）

- **ascription** n.歸屬
- **ascribe to** 把…歸因於
- 字首:a 在
- 字根:scribe 寫
- **failure** n.失敗

---

153. (123)

asleep [əˋslip]【a·sleep】**a** 睡著的、靜止的、麻木的

I fell asleep as soon as my head hit the pillow.

我頭一碰到枕頭就睡著了。

同 **sleeping, dormant, numb**（熟睡的、靜止的、麻木的）

反 **alert, awake**（機敏的、清醒的）

- **fall asleep** ph.睡著
- **as soon as** ph.一…就…
- **pillow** n.枕頭

---

154. (75)

asocial [eˋsoʃəl]【a·so·cial】**a** 反社會的、不好社交的、自私的

Staying in other's house makes Dabbie lack of familiy education, which shapes her solitary and asocial characters.

寄養生活使黛比缺少家庭教育,性格變得孤僻、不合群。

反 **social**（社會的、社交的）

- 字首:a 無、不
- 字根:social 社會的
- **lack** n.缺少
- **education** n.教育
- **solitary** a.孤獨的

---

155. (215)

aspect [ˋæspɛkt]【as·pect】**n** 方面、觀點、外觀

I find this aspect of my job particularly congenial.

我覺得我工作的這一方面特別適合我。

同 **look, perspective, view**（外觀、觀點）

- **aspect ratio** ph.圖像縱橫比
- 字首:a 朝向
- 字根:spect 看
- **particularly** ad.特別
- **congenial** a.協調的

---

156. (131)

aspiration [ˌæspəˋreʃən]【as·pi·ra·tion】**n** 熱望、志向、呼吸

The generalship was his aspiration.

將官職位是他夢寐以求的目標。

同 **ambition, breath, intention**（目標、呼吸、意向）

- 字首:a 加重語氣
- 字根:spir 呼吸
- 字尾:ation 性質
- **generalship** n.將官之職

---

157. (145)

assault [əˋsɔlt]【as·sault】**n** **v** 攻擊、抨擊

Trainee commandos are put through an exhausting assault course.

受訓的突擊隊員要參加令人筋疲力盡的突擊課程。

同 **attack, invasion, offense**（攻擊、襲擊）

反 **defense, protection, safeguard**（防禦、保護）

- **assault and battery** ph.人身傷害
- **assault course** ph.野戰訓練場
- **trainee** n.受訓者
- **commando** n.突襲部隊
- **exhausting** a.使人精疲力竭的

158.
assent [ə`sɛnt] 【 as·sent 】 **V n** 贊成、同意

I translated her silence as assent.

我認為她沉默不語就是同意了。

🔵 **agree, approve, consent**（同意、贊成）
🔴 **disagree, dissent, oppose**（不同意、反對）

183
- assent to ph.同意
- 字首：as朝向
  字根：sent感覺
- translate v.解釋
- silence n.沉默

159.
assemble [ə`sɛmbl] 【 as·sem·ble 】 **V** 集合、聚集、組合

Over 1000 people were assembled at the hall to honor the general manager's visit.

有一千多人聚集在大廳歡迎總經理光臨。

🔵 **collect, compile, gather**（聚集、收集）
🔴 **dismiss, disperse, dissolve**（疏散、分解）

165
- 字首：as加強語氣
  字根：semble相類似
- hall n.大廳
- honor v.尊敬

160.
assert [ə`sɝt] 【 as·sert 】 **V** 主張、斷言、顯示

The asserted that his client is not guilty.

律師們辯稱他們的訴訟委託人是無辜的。

🔵 **declare, pronounce, state**（宣稱、聲明）

168
- assert oneself ph.堅持自己的權利
- 字首：as朝向
  字根：sert參加
- attorney n.律師
- client n.委託人

161.
assess [ə`sɛs] 【 as·sess 】 **V** 估定、徵稅、評價

It is these documents that enable the importing customs to assess consignments at the correct rate of duty.

進口國海關憑藉這些證件按正確稅率對貨價估價徵稅。

🔵 **gauge, measure**（評估、測量）

129
- document n.文件
- enable v.使能夠
- custom n.海關
- consignment n.運送
- rate n.比率

162.
asset [`æsɛt] 【 as·set 】 **n** 財產、有價值的物品、有利條件

An asset is anything that is owned by a business and has value to a business (or other organization or entity).

資產是實業單位（或其它組織、實體）所擁有，或對實業單位有價值的任何東西。

🔵 **account, fund, valuable things**（估價、財源）
🔴 **liability**（不利條件）

151
- own v.擁有
- value n.重要性
- entity n.實體

163.
assign [ə`saɪn] 【 as·sign 】 **V** 分配、指定、把…歸於 **n** 受讓人

It's one of the preconditions to explore the employee's capability to assign each employee a proper post.

給員工分配合適的崗位，是發揮員工才能的前提。

🔵 **allocate, allot, distribute**（分配、指定）

194
- assignment n.任務
- precondition n.先決條件
- explore v.探測
- proper a.適合的

164.
assimilate [ə`sɪmḷet] 【 as·sim·i·late 】 **V** 吸收、同化

Northern Europeans assimilate readily in America.

北歐人在美國容易受同化。

🔵 **absorb, blot up, digest**（消化、吸收）
🔴 **dissimilate**（不同）

147
- assimilation n.同化作用
- 字首：as加強語氣
  字根：simil使類似
  字尾：ate使成為
- readily ad.很快地

165.
assist [əˋsɪst]【as·sist】 **v**幫助、支持、參加

The most common use of a computer was to assist in accounting and financial statement preparation activities.

電腦最普通的用途是參與核算和財務報表的制定工作。

同 **aid, help, support**（幫助、支持）

反 **hamper, oppose, resist**（阻礙、抵抗）

> ▸ 194
> • 字首：as加強語氣
> 字尾：sist站立
> • financial a.財政的
> • statement n.陳述
> • preparation n.準備

166.
associate [əˋsoʃɪet]【as·so·ci·ate】 **v**聯想、使聯合、交往
n夥伴、有關聯的事物

My mom always admonishes me not to associate with bad companions.

媽媽經常訓誡我不要跟壞人為伍。

同 **combine, connect, companion**（使聯合、合夥人）

反 **dissociate**（使分離、將…分開）

> ▸ 154
> • associate with與…交往
> • associate degree ph.美國大學修滿兩年課程之肄業證書
> • associate professor ph.副教授
> • 字首：as朝向
> 字根：soci社會的
> 字尾：ate行動

167.
assume [əˋsjum]【as·sume】 **v**假設、承擔、呈現

We assume that the partners agree to a profit-sharing plan providing for salaries and for interest on beginning capital balances.

我們假設合夥人同意有關支付薪資和期初資本利息的利潤分配方案。

同 **conceive, presume, suppose**（假定為、想像）

反 **abdicate, conclude, prove**（放棄、結束、證明）

> ▸ 214
> • assumption n.假定、設想
> • 字首：as朝向
> 字根：sume使用
> • capital a.重要的
> • balance n.平衡

168.
assure [əˋʃur]【as·sure】 **v**向…保證、使確信、弄清楚

Anticipate the need for borrowing and assure the availability of adequate amounts of cash for conducting business operation.

預測需要償還的借款，保證有足夠的現金滿足企業經營的需要。

同 **convince, guarantee, insure**（擔保、確保）

反 **alarm, frighten, scare**（使恐慌、驚恐）

> ▸ 221
> • assure of ph.向…保證
> • assurance n.保證、保險
> • 字首：a加強語氣
> 字根：sure確定的
> • anticipate v.預期
> • availability n.有效
> • adequate a.適當的

169.
athlete [ˋæθlit]【ath·lete】 **n**運動員、身強力壯的人

The athlete was within an inch of breaking the record.

那個運動員差點打破記錄。

同 **ballplayer, player, sportsman**（運動員）

> ▸ 89
> • athlete's foot ph.香港腳
> • 字根：athl競賽
> 字尾：ete從事某項行動的人
> • inch n.少許
> • break v.打破
> • record n.記錄

170.
attach [əˋtætʃ]【at·tach】 **v**裝上、使依附、把…歸·

Fill out the application form, attach a grade notice and explain what subject should be checked and what the question is.

填寫申請表（附成績通知單），註明申請檢查科目及疑問之處。

同 **add, affix, fasten**（裝上、附上）

反 **detach**（拆卸）

> ▸ 217
> • attachment n.連接、附件
> • attach importance to ph.重視
> • attach to ph.屬於
> • be attached to ph.附屬於
> • fill out ph.填寫
> • application n.申請

171.

attack [əˋtæk] 【at·tack】 **V** **n** 攻擊、抨擊、侵害

Oil industry supporters may attack a state coastal zone program by showing an impermissible burden on interstate commerce.

石油工業的支持者們可能會證明某個州的沿海區域規劃對各州商貿交往造成了不允許有的負擔來攻擊該規劃。

同- **ambush, assault, invade**（襲擊、攻擊）
反- **defend, protect, guard**（防禦、保護）

234
- attack ad n.攻擊性競爭廣告
- attack-fax n.攻擊或抹黑對手的傳真
- industry n.工業
- coastal a.海岸的
- burden n.重擔
- interstate a.州與州之間的
- commerce n.商業、貿易

172.

attain [əˋten] 【at·tain】 **V** 達到、獲得 **n** 成就

We are now confident that we can attain our first goal ahead of schedule, this year or the next.

現在我們可以說第一步的原定目標是可以提前在今年或明年完成。

同- **arrive, get to, reach**（到達）
反- **fall**（失敗）

175
- attain to ph.達到
- 字首：at朝向
  字根：tain握、持
- confident a.有信心的
- goal n.目標
- ahead of ph.在…之前

173.

attempt [əˋtɛmpt] 【at·tempt】 **V** **n** 企圖、嘗試

In computer security, an attempt to gain access to a system by posing as an authorized user.

在電腦安全學中，試圖以裝成一個合法使用者來獲取對某系統的使用權。

同- **endeavor, strive, try**（試圖、努力）
反- **abandon, quit**（放棄）

184
- make an attempt at doing sth. ph.試圖做…
- security n.安全
- gain v.獲得
- access n.接近
- authorized a.經認可的

174.

attend [əˋtɛnd] 【at·tend】 **V** 出席、前往、照料、伴隨

In case of absence of the meeting, the director shall entrust another person to attend and vote for him with a trust deed.

任何一名董事如不能出席會議，應以書面委託的形式指定一名代理出席會議和行使表決權。

同- **administer to, be present, go to**（照料、出席）
反- **defy, disregard, ignore**（不理會、忽略）

204
- attendance n.出席
- attend on ph.照料
- attend to ph.注意
- 字首：at朝向
- in case of ph.如果發生
- absence n.缺席

175.

attendant [əˋtɛndənt] 【at·ten·dant】 **a** 伴隨的、出席的 **n** 陪從、侍者、伴隨的事物

Being a good flight attendant means making your passengers feel relaxed.

當一個好的空服員就是要讓乘客們感到旅途輕鬆愉快。

同- **assistant, servant, steward**（助手、服務員）

129
- 字根：attend照料
  字尾：ant做某事的人
- passenger n.乘客
- relax v.放鬆

176.

attention [əˋtɛnʃən] 【at·ten·tion】 **n** 注意力、照顧

Attention, please! These tickets are available on the day of issue only.

請注意！這種車票僅在發售當天有效。

同- **concern, consideration, thoughtfulness**（照料、關照）
反- **carelessness, inattention, indifference**（不小心、冷淡）

207
- attention-getting a. 引人注意的
- pay attention to ph. 關心、注意
- available a.有效的
- issue n.發行

177.
attentive [ə`tɛntɪv] 【at·ten·tive】 a 注意的、殷勤的
The first batch of solar energy kitchen has come out after the attentive and hard work of several months.

在幾個月專心竭力的工作後第一個太陽能廚房問世了。

同► accommodating, assiduous （熱於助人的、勤勉的）
反► absent-minded （心不在焉的）

- attentiveness n.注意 `154`
- batch n.一批生產量
- solar a.太陽的
- come out ph.出現
- several a.數個

178.
attest [ə`tɛst] 【at·test】 v 證實、表明、宣誓
I encourage you to contact my references who will attest to my career commitment, academic performance and work ethic.

我希望你能與我的推薦人聯絡，他們會對我的學習成績、職業道德和敬業精神提供證明。

同► swear, testify, vouch （證明、發誓）

- attest to ph.證明 `181`
- 字首：at加強語氣
  字根：test證據
- encourage v.鼓勵
- reference n.推薦人
- academic a.學術的
- ethic n.倫理標準

179.
attitude [`ætətjud] 【at·ti·tude】 n 態度、看法、姿勢
We adopted an active attitude towards drawing on overseas fund to make up for domestic fund shortage.

我們採取積極的態度吸引海外資金以彌補國內資金短缺。

同► opinion, standpoint, viewpopint （意見、看法）

- attitude to / toward `245`
  ph.對…的態度、看法
- adopt v.採取
- draw on ph.利用
- overseas a.海外的
- domestic a.國內的

180.
attorney [ə`tɝnɪ] 【at·tor·ney】 n 律師、法定代理人
For more information on citizenship and naturalization, contact an attorney who is specialized in immigration law.

想瞭解更多關於公民身份和入籍方面的資訊可諮詢移民律師。

同► agent, counselor, lawyer （代理人、律師）

- attorney at law ph.【美】 `71`
  律師
- attorney general ph.首席檢察官
- citizenship n.公民身分
- naturalization n.外國人的歸化
- immigration n.移民

181.
attract [ə`trækt] 【at·tract】 v 吸引、引起注意
Grow from what works: Once you know what works, you can start to build more campaigns Ad Groups to attract your potential customers.

熟能生巧：一旦你知道了整個工作程式，你可以開始建立更大的廣告宣傳計劃和廣告組來吸引你的潛在客戶。

同► allure, charm, fascinate （吸引、引誘）
反► distract, repel （拒絕、使分心）

- attractive a.有吸引力的 `249`
- attraction n.吸引力
- 字首：at朝向
  字根：tract拉
- Ad n.廣告
- potential a.潛在的

182.
attribute [ə`trɪbjut] 【at·tri·bute】 v 把…歸因於、認為…是某人所有 n 屬性
Public perception can also create a legal right for an attribute of a product.

公眾的認知也能為產品的某個屬性創造法律權利。

同► ascribe, assign, give （把…歸因於）

- attribute to ph.歸因於、因為 `184`
- 字首：at加強語氣
  字根：tribute分配
- perception n.看法
- legal a.合法的

183.
audience [ˈɔdɪəns]【au·di·ence】**n**聽眾、觀眾、謁見
Grant a private audience to a foreign ambassador.
准予外國大使私人謁見。
同 spectator, turnout, reception（觀眾、接見）

- audience rating **ph.**收視率
- 字根：audi聽
  字尾：ence執行某行動的人
- grant **v.**同意
- ambassador **n.**大使

211

184.
audition [ɔˈdɪʃən]【au·di·tion】**v**聽覺 **n**試聽
She was a bundle of nerves before the audition.
面試前她極為緊張。
同 ear, hearing（聽覺）

- 字根：audi聽
  字尾：tion行為、性質
- bundle **n.**大量
- nerve **n.**憂慮

121

185.
authentic [ɔˈθɛntɪk]【au·then·tic】**a**可靠的、真正的、有效的
The century-aged shop boasts authentic technology, and its product quality is absolutely reliable.
百年老店正宗工藝，品質絕對可靠。
同 actual, legitimate, real（真實的、合法的）
反 false, fictitious, spurious（偽造的、虛構的）

- century **n.**世紀
- boast **v.**誇耀
- technology **n.**技術
- absolutely **ad.**絕對地
- reliable **a.**可靠的

105

186.
authority [əˈθɔrɪtɪ]【au·thor·i·ty】**n**權力、當權者、官方
A certificate of legal operation (transcript) issued by the competent authority of the country where the enterprise is located.
由該企業所在國的有關當局出具的開業合法證書（副本）。
同 administration, government, sovereignty（權力、官方）

- authorize **v.**授權、認可
- certificate **n.**證明書
- operation **n.**經營
- transcript **n.**副本
- enterprise **n.**企業

238

187.
automatically [ˌɔtəˈmætɪklɪ]【au·to·mat·ically】**a**自動的、無意識的
This is an automatically generated file; it will be read and overwritten.
這是一個自動生成的檔案，它可讀可寫。
同 account, fund, valuable things（估價、財源）

- automation **n.**自動操作裝置
- generate **v.**產生
- file **n.**檔案
- overwrite **v.**重覆寫在…上面

141

188.
autonomy [ɔˈtɑnəmɪ]【au·ton·o·my】**n**自治、有自主權的國家
Branch managers have full autonomy in their own areas.
分支機構的經理在其管轄範圍內有充分的自主權。
同 freedom, liberty（自由）

- autonomous **a.**自治的
- 字首：auto自動
  字尾：nomy治理
- branch **n.**分支

135

189.
avail [əˈvel]【a·vail】**v**有用、有利於 **n**效用、利益
The obligor may avail itself of any set-off against the assignee.
債務人可以向受託人主張抵銷。
同 advantage, benefit, profit（利益、效用）

- available **a.**可用的
- avail oneself of **ph.**利用
- obligor **n.**債務人
- assignee **n.**受託人

123

190.

average [ˈævərɪdʒ] 【av·er·age】 **n**平均、中等 **a**平均的、普通的 **v**使平衡

243

Gasoline now costs an average of $3.15 a gallon; seven cents shy of the record set last May, according to AAA.

據美國汽車協會的資料顯示汽油現在的平均價格是每加侖3.15美元，僅比去年五月的記錄低了七分美金。

同 common, general, moderate（普通的、中等的）
反 special（特別的）

- on the average=on average=on an average ph.平均
- gasoline n.汽油
- gallon n.加侖
- AAA=American Automobile Association abbr.美國汽車協會

191.

averse [əˈvɜs] 【av·erse】 **a**反對的、不願意的

110

Quite naturally, these managers are averse to depriving themselves of able subordinates.

很自然地，這些主管不願意失去能幹的下屬。

同 against, reluctant, unwilling（不願意、反對）
反 willing（願意）

- 字首：a否定
  字根：verse轉
- deprive of ph.使喪失
- subordinate n.部屬

192.

avert [əˈvɜt] 【av·ert】 **v**避開、防止、擋開

215

Try to avert a facedown between the two nations, a political facedown during the primaries.

盡量避免在初選中造成這兩國之間形成政治對峙。

同 avoid, prevent, prohibit（防止、避免）

- avert a strike ph.取消罷工
- 字首：a離開
  字根：vert轉
- facedown n.對手或敵人間的對抗
- primary n.初選

193.

aviation [ˌeviˈeʃən] 【avi·a·tion】 **n**飛行、航空學、飛機

81

The civil aviation department shall take effective measures to mitigate environmental noise pollution.

民航部門應當採取有效措施，以減輕環境雜訊污染。

同 flight, aeronautics（飛行、航空學）

- avaiation security ph.飛航安全
- 字首：avi鳥
  字尾：ation行為、性質
- mitigate v.減輕
- pollution n.汙染

194.

avoid [əˈvɔɪd] 【a·void】 **v**避開、避免、使無效

257

So pervasive advertisements are that no one can avoid being influenced by them.

廣告是如此盛行，每個人都難免不受它們的影響。

同 escape, elude, snub（避開、躲開）
反 approach, confront, face（靠近、面對）

- pervasive a.普遍的
- advertisement n.廣告
- influence v.影響

195.

award [əˈwɔrd] 【a·ward】 **v**授予、判給 **n**獎狀

188

An award of aggravated damages is still compensatory.

加重性損害賠償仍然是補償性的。

同 medal, reward, trophy（獎品）

- award-winning a.獲獎的
- aggravated a.嚴重化的
- compensatory a.補償的

196.
aware [əˋwɛr] 【a‧ware】 a 知道的、明智的、閱歷深的

The challenge for translators and interpreters is to be aware of these differences.

翻譯員和口譯員所面對的挑戰就是要瞭解這些差異。

囫 **conscious, cognizant, knowing**（知道的、察覺的）
囵 **ignorant, unaware**（無知的、忽略的）

- be aware of **ph.**意識到
- challenge **n.**挑戰
- translator **n.**譯者
- interpreter **n.**口譯員

197.
axis [ˋæksɪs] 【ax‧is】 n 軸、核心

67

The Allies triumphed over the Axis powers in World War II.

在第二次世界大戰中，同盟國打敗了軸心國。

- ally **n.**同盟國
- triumph **v.**獲得勝利

MEMO

MEMO

abbr 縮寫詞
a 形容詞
ad 副詞
aux 助動詞
conj 連接詞
n 名詞
num 數字
ph 片語
prep 介系詞
v 動詞
（美）美式用語
（英）英式用語
（法）法式用語

全書單字取材於：
①10本坊間新多益考試暢銷書籍
②50篇英文新聞、商業文章
③2005~2012年ETS TOEIC歷屆考古題
→ 總計約50,000個單字，以電腦統計出題率高達80%
　的實用單字1,800個

高頻率單字

B家族 backup~bywork

 MP3 01-02

高 分 錦 囊

198.
backup [`bæk‚ʌp] 【back·up】 **n** 備用 **a** 備用的 **v** 備份
When the main system fails, the backup system takes over.
當主系統不能運作時,備援系統立即投入工作代替之。

219
• backup copy ph.備份檔案
• take over ph.接管

199.
bacteria [bæk`tɪrɪə] 【bac·te·ri·a】 **n** 細菌
A microscope magnifies bacteria so that they can be seen and studied.
顯微鏡把細菌放大,使人們得以看見並研究它。

143
• bacterium (單數)細菌
• microscope n.顯微鏡
• magnify v.放大

200.
baggage [`bægɪdʒ] 【bag·gage】 **n** 行李、精神包袱
Fill in the baggage declaration for inward passengers.
請填寫入境旅客物品申報單。

同 bag, luggage, package(行李)

231
• baggage car ph.行李車
• baggage claim ph.行李提領處
• baggage room ph.行李寄放處
• 字根:bag袋子

201.
balance [`bæləns] 【bal·ance】 **v n** 平衡、協調、結算
To bring balance of payments into equilibrium and insure that the flow of trade and capital contributes to their development goals.
使收支平衡以確保貿易和資本的流動有助於他們的發展目標。

同 equalize, stabilize, steady(平衡、穩固)
反 unbalance(不平衡)

207
• balance beam ph.平衡木
• balance of payments ph.國際收支平衡
• balance of power ph.國際間的均勢
• balance of terror ph.恐怖的制衡
• equilibrium n.均衡

202.
balcony [`bælkənɪ] 【bal·co·ny】 **n** 陽臺、包廂
Each studio flat is equipped with a bathroom, a kitchenette and a balcony.
這種公寓套房配有衛浴、小廚房和陽臺。

同 porch, terrace, veranda(陽臺)

124
• studio flat ph.一室的公寓房
• equip v.配備
• kitchenette n.小廚房

203.
ballet [`bæle] 【bal·let】 **n** 芭蕾舞、芭蕾舞音樂
The best of you have not only discovered your conscience—the very best of them—are taken into the major American ballet companies.
只有其中少數佼佼者才可得到美國的主要芭蕾舞團的聘請。

113
• ballet dancer ph.芭蕾舞蹈家
• conscience n.良心
• major a.主要的

204.
bankrupt [`bæŋkrʌpt] 【bank·rupt】 **a** 破產的、失敗的
v 使破產、枯竭 **n** 破產者
The debtor also may apply to the people's court to declare itself bankrupt for debt repayment.
債務人也可以向人民法院申請宣告破產還債。

同 insolvent, busted, penniless(破產的、失敗的)

201
• 字首:bank銀行 字尾:rupt破裂
• debtor n.債務人
• court n.法院
• declare v.宣佈

B

205.
banner [`bænɚ] 【ban·ner】 ❶旗幟、標語 ❷傑出的

Be his banner unconquered, resistless his spear.

祝他旗開得勝，所向無敵。

🔄 **banderole, flag**（旗幟）

- banner ad ph.網站廣告條幅
- banner headline ph.報紙通欄大標題
- resistless a.無法抵抗的
- spear n.矛

206.
banquet [`bæŋkwɪt] 【ban·quet】 ❶盛宴、款待 ❷參加宴會、宴請

We had a court wedding first and then held a banquet in a restaurant.

我們先登記註冊結婚，然後在餐廳宴客。

🔄 **affair, feast**（宴會、盛宴）

- wedding n.結婚
- restaurant n.餐廳

207.
bargain [`bɑrgɪn] 【bar·gain】 ❶討價還價 ❷交易、特價商品

Nothing is a bargain if you don't need it.

如果你不需要的東西根本不值得去討價還價。

🔄 **agreement, contract, sale**（協議、交易）

- 用於否定句時，可解釋為「預期」
- bargain basement ph.百貨店的地下廉價商場
- bargain bin ph.廉價處理商品專區

208.
barrier [`bærɪr] 【bar·ri·er】 ❶障礙物、界線、剪票口

They could come to terms if they came truly to grips instead of scolding at each other over a barrier of misunderstanding.

如果他們能夠認真妥善處理而不是相互猜疑、指責對方，他們是可以達成協議的。

🔄 **barricade, fortification, obstruction**（障礙物、設防）

- barrier crash ph.障壁試驗
- barrier island ph.屏障島
- barrier reef ph.堡礁
- grip n.理解
- scold v.斥責
- misunderstanding n.誤解

209.
basis [`besɪs] 【ba·sis】 ❶基礎、主要部分

Since 1992, special IPR courts have been set up in major cities such as Beijing and Shanghai on the basis of their specialized collegial panels.

自1992年起根據各自專業人員組成的情況，在北京和上海等一些主要城市設立了專門的智慧財產權法庭。

🔄 **base, foundation, principle**（基礎、基本原則）

- basis point ph.基點
- on the basis of ph.根據
- IPR=intellectual property rights abbr.智慧財產權
- collegial a.學院的
- panel n.專門小組

210.
batch [bætʃ] 【batch】 ❶一批、一群

The boss owned a batch of adept technical workers of handicraft and an excellent administration team.

這老闆擁有一批工藝嫻熟的技術工人和優秀的管理團隊。

🔄 **bunch, cluster, pile**（束、群、堆）

- batch number ph.批號
- batch production ph.批量生產
- adept a.內行的
- handicraft n.手工藝品
- administration n.管理

211.
batter [`bætɚ] 【bat·ter】 ❶連續猛擊、磨損 ❷糊狀物、打擊手

The police battered down the door to rescue the hostage successfully.

警方把門打破成功地救出人質。

🔄 **beat, smash, thrash**（打、擊）

- 字根：bat拍打
  字尾：ter表示連續動作
- rescue v.營救
- hostage n.人質
- successfully ad.成功地

212.

bazaar [bə`zɑr]【ba·zaar】 n.市場、義賣

`61`

The high-grade mattress offered by this bazaar assures you of a luxurious comfort.

本商場供應高級床墊讓您享受奢侈的舒適。

🔁 **market, mart, rialto**（市場、集市）

- high-grade a.高級的
- mattress n.床墊
- offer v.提供
- assure v.擔保
- luxurious a.奢侈的

213.

beam [bim]【beam】 n.橫樑、光線、笑容 v.照耀、發送、眉開眼笑

`57`

The beam from the streetlamps showed gangsters walked back and forth in front of the bank.

路燈的光線照出一群歹徒徘徊在銀行門口。

🔁 **shine, timber, bar**（發光、橫槓）

- beam bridge ph.樑橋
- beam-ends n.船樑末端
- streetlamp n.街燈
- gangster n.歹徒
- back and forth ph.前後來回

214.

befall [bɪ`fɔl]【be·fall】 v.降臨、發生

`71`

I've prepared for the worst that can befall me.

我已準備好了應付可能發生的最壞的情形。

- 尤指不幸的降臨
- prepare v.準備

215.

beforehand [bɪ`fɔr,hænd]【be·fore·hand】 v.預先、提前地 a.預先

`52`

Nothing is as good as it seems beforehand.

世事往往不如預料中那麼好。

🔁 **afterward**（事先）

- 字首：before在…之前 字尾：hand手
- as...as 和…一樣

216.

behave [bɪ`hev]【be·have】 v.表現、行為檢點

`149`

Behave in a confident manner that attracts attention and respect.

表現出自信而受到注意和尊重。

🔁 **comport, deport, act**（舉止、行動）

- behavior n.行為
- behave in a disorderly manner ph.做出…不檢的行為

217.

behalf [bɪ`hæf]【be·half】 n.利益、代表

`151`

The legal guardian must act on behalf of the child.

法定監護人應該維護這個孩子的利益。

🔁 **benefit, gain, welfare**（利益）

- on behalf of ph.代表
- guardian n.保護者

218.

belittle [bɪ`lɪtl]【be·lit·tle】 v.輕視、貶

`81`

Do not belittle what he has achieved.

不能小看他取得的成績。

🔁 **decry, derogate, underate**（低估、輕視）

- achieve v.達到

219.

benchmark [`bɛntʃ,mɑrk]【bench·mark】 n.基準

`102`

It can be used by the organization to achieve the benchmark of its performance against that of external organizations and world-class performance.

組織透過自我評定可將其業績與外部組織和世界級的業績進行水準上的對比。

🔁 **criterion**（標準）

- benchmark country ph.基準國
- external a.外界的

220.
beneficial [ˌbɛnəˈfɪʃəl] [ben·e·fi·cial] **a** 有益的、有權益的

International trade is beneficial for all participants.

國際貿易對所有參加國都有好處。

🔄 **advantageous, favorable, profitable**（有益的）
🔄 **fruitless, harmful, vain**（無用的）

- 字首：bene好
  字根：fit製作
  字尾：ial與…有關的
- trade n.貿易
- participant n.參與者

217

221.
betray [bɪˈtre] [be·tray] **v** 背叛、洩露、把…引入歧途

In failing to return the money, he betrayed our trust.

他未能歸還那筆錢而辜負了我們的信任。

🔄 **deceive, divulge, mislead**（誤導、洩露、欺騙）
🔄 **support**（支持）

- fail v.失敗
- return v.歸還
- trust n.信任

149

222.
beverage [ˈbɛvərɪdʒ] [bev·er·age] **n** 飲料

Brisk market sales were concentrated in food, household electrical appliances, beverage and clothing.

市場暢銷產品主要集中在食品、家電、飲料和服裝類。

🔄 **drink, potable**（飲料）

- brisk a.興旺的
- concentrate v.集中
- household a.家庭的
- electrical appliance ph.電器

131

223.
beware [bɪˈwɛr] [be·ware] **v** 注意、小心

Beware lest you should fall into this mistake again.

請注意不要再犯這種錯誤。

🔄 **look out, take care, watch out**（小心、當心）

- beware of ph.小心…
- lest conj.免得
- mistake n.錯誤

121

224.
bewilder [bɪˈwɪldɚ] [be·wil·der] **v** 使迷惑、使迷路

Don't be bewildered enough to do silly things.

不要糊裡糊塗地去做傻事。

🔄 **confuse, mystify, puzzle**（使迷惑）
🔄 **guide**（指引）

- bewilderment n.迷惑、混亂
- silly a.愚蠢的

81

225.
biannual [baɪˈænjuəl] [bi·an·nu·al] **a** 每年兩次的

The airfield, less than an hour's drive west of London, is home to Britain's biannual air show.

該機場在倫敦以西不到一小時的車程舉辦英國雙年航空展。

- 字首：bia二
  字根：ann年
  字尾：al屬於…的
- airfield n.飛機場

75

226.
biennial [baɪˈɛnɪəl] [bi·en·ni·al] **a** 兩年一度的

The World Chambers Congress, also biennial, provides a global forum for chambers of commerce.

兩年一次的國際商業大會為商業提供全球論壇。

- 字首：bi二、雙
  字根：enn年
  字尾：ial屬於…的
- forum n.討論會
- chamber n.會議廳
- commerce n.商業

124

227.
bid [bɪd] [bid] **v n** 命令、出價

There is big difference between your bid and our price.

你方的出價與我方的價格差距太大了。

🔄 **direct, instruct, order**（命令、吩咐）

- bid figure ph.大數（交易員術語）
- bid price ph.買價
- difference n.差異

211

228. `145`

bilingual [baɪˋlɪŋgwəl]【bi·lin·gual】**a**雙語的 **n**通兩種語言的人

International travel has grown to the point that many hotels find it necessary to employ bilingual or even multilingual staff.

國際旅行發展迅速，許多旅館都有必要雇用能講兩種或多種語言的職員。

- 字首：bi二、雙
  字根：lingu語言
  字尾：al與…有關的
- multilingual a.使用多種語言的
- staff n.全體職員

229. `54`

billiards [ˋbɪljədz]【bil·liards】**n**撞球

Billiards isn't popular here.

這裡不流行玩撞球。

- 此單字後接單數動詞
- popular a.流行的

230. `125`

biography [baɪˋɑgrəfɪ]【bi·og·ra·phy】**n**傳記

I have read a biography of Abraham Lincoln.

我讀過一部亞伯拉罕林肯的傳記。

同 autobiography, life story, record（自傳、記錄）

- 字首：bio生命
  字根：graphy撰寫某學科

231. `81`

bland [blænd]【bland】**a**和藹的、無刺激性的、淡而無味的

In fact, most vegetables in the U.S. are rather bland in taste.

事實上，美國大部分的蔬菜味道很淡。

同 gentle, mild, smooth（和藹的、溫和的）
反 poignant（味道濃烈的）

- in fact ph.事實上
- vegetable n.蔬菜
- taste n.味道

232. `104`

blaze [blez]【blaze】**v**燃燒、閃耀、爆發 **n**火焰、記號

London was a blaze of pageantry and colour.

倫敦到處是輝煌的慶典、色彩斑瀾。

同 fire, flame, flare（火焰、閃光）

- blaze away ph.連續猛擊
- pageantry n.盛會

233. `235`

bleed [blid]【bleed】**v**流血、犧牲、悲傷、放掉

At the end of the shift or work day, close the cylinder valve and bleed the pressure off the regulator and torch equipment.

在下班或工作結束的時候，關閉鋼瓶閥門，放出調整器和吹管設備內的壓力。

同 grieve, pity, sorrow（悲傷）

- bleed-bled-bled
- cylinder n.汽缸
- pressure n.壓力
- regulator n.調節器

234. `241`

blink [blɪŋk]【blink】**v**眨眼、閃爍、視若無睹 **n**眨眼睛、一瞬間

The problem exists; one simply cannot blink it away.

這個問題是存在的，誰也回避不了。

同 blaze, flutter, twinkle（閃爍、眨眼睛）

- exist v.存在
- simply ad.完全地

235. `108`

blossom [ˋblɑsəm]【blos·som】**v**開花、興旺、發展 **n**花、成長期

At sunrise riverside flowers blossom more red than fire, in spring green river waves grow as blue as sapphire.

日出江花紅勝火，春來江水綠如藍。

同 bloom, flower, develop（開花、發展）

- in blossom ph.開花（指樹木）
- be in blossom ph.開花（強調狀態）
- come into blossom ph.開花（強調動作）
- riverside n.河邊
- sapphire a.天藍色的

236.

94

blunder [`blʌndə] 【 blun·der 】 **v** 犯大錯、跌跌撞撞地走 **n** 大錯

Without experience, we couldn't avoid blundering and shall no doubt blunder again.

沒有經驗就無法避免犯錯，無疑地會再發生。

⑩▸ mistake, error, flounder（犯錯、錯誤）

• no doubt ph.無疑地

237.

85

blunt [blʌnt] 【blunt】 **a** 鈍的、直率 **v** 遲鈍、減弱

The finest edge is made with the blunt whetstone.

寶劍鋒利是用鈍的磨刀石磨出來的。

⑩▸ dull, unsharp, candid（鈍的、坦率的）

⑫▸ acute, keen, sharp（尖銳的、敏銳的）

• bluntness n.鈍
• edge n.刀口
• whetstone n.磨刀石

238.

278

board [bord] **n** 木板、佈告牌、董事會 **v** 登上、膳宿

The board of directors has a chairman and may have one vice-chairman if necessary.

董事會設一名董事長，可以視需要設副董事長。

⑩▸ wood, lumber, committee（木板、委員會）

• board and lodging ph. 供應食宿
• board of trade ph. 同業公會
• board of director ph. 董事會
• chairman n.董事長

239.

215

bond [bɑnd] 【blood】 **n** 債券、結合力、字據 **v** 使結合

Floating rate bond: Bond on which the is established periodically and calculated with reference to short-term interest rates.

浮動利率債券：這種債券的息票是定期確定的，並參照短期資金利率來計算。

⑩▸ connection, link, attachment（聯結）

• bond indenture ph. 債券契約
• bond paper ph.證券紙
• bond-servant n.奴隸
• floating rate ph.浮動利率
• establish v.建立

240.

194

bonus [`bonəs] 【 bo·nus 】 **n** 獎金、紅利、津貼

The firm offered her a generous bonus as a sweetener.

公司提出給她一筆可觀的紅利藉以拉攏她。

⑩▸ extra, premium（額外之物、獎金）

• bonuses為其複數形
• generous a.慷慨的
• sweetener n.好處

241.

174

booklet [`buklɪt] 【 book·let 】 **n** 小冊子

A booklet describing GE integrity policies which every GE employee is required to sign and reacknowledge annually.

描述通用電器公司職業道德政策的小冊子，每個員工需在此上簽字並每年再次確認。

⑩▸ brochure, handbook, pamphlet（小冊子）

• 字根：book書本 字尾：let小事物
• integrity n.正直
• require v.需要

242.

84

boom [bum] 【 boom 】 **v** 迅速發展、發隆隆聲 **n** 隆隆聲

The English language boom stems from a variety of sources: world trade, diplomacy, pop culture, science and so on.

英語的迅速普及是有各種根源的，如：世界貿易、外交、大眾文化、科學等等。

⑩▸ flourish, swell, roar（繁榮、增長、轟鳴）

⑫▸ slump（下跌）

• boom box ph.發很大聲響 的箱子
• boom car ph.勁爆音響汽車
• boom-and-bust n.大繁榮 後緊接著發生嚴重的不景氣
• stem from ph.起源於
• diplomacy n.外交
• variety n.多樣化

243.
border [`bɔrdə] 【 bor·der 】 n 邊緣、邊界 v 圍住、毗鄰
The United States borders on Canada.
美國毗鄰於加拿大。
同 **edge, margin, termination**（邊緣、邊界）
反 **inside, interior**（裡面、內部）

> • Border Gateway Protocol=BGP ph.外在閘道通信協定

244.
bounce [bauns] 【 bounce 】 v n 跳躍、彈起、解雇
I thought once I got a job and things would bounce back.
我原以為一旦獲得工作，情況就會恢復原樣。
同 **jump, recoil, resile**（跳動、反彈）

> • bounce flash ph.跳燈
> • job n.工作

245.
bound [baund] 【 bound 】 a 受約束的、有義務的 v n 跳躍
I'm bound to say I disagree with you on this point.
我必須聲明不同意你這一點。

> • be bound to ph.對…有義務的
> • bound for ph.準備前往
> • bound from ph.束縛型
> • bound to ph.一定會做

246.
boycott [`bɔɪkɑt] 【 boy·cott 】 v n 聯合抵制
The African-American residents of the city were asked to boycott the bus company by walking and driving instead.
他們要求該市的美國黑人居民步行和自己開車來抵制公車公司。
同 **blackball, revolt, strike**（聯合抵制、反對）

> • resident n.居民
> • instead ad.作為替代

247.
buyout [`baɪaut] 【 buy·out 】 n 全部買下、買斷
They staged a management buyout to preempt a takeover bid.
他們籌劃買下資方的全部產權以便搶先得到出價的好處。

> • 來自於片語buy out
> • stage v.籌劃
> • preempt v.先佔有
> • takeover n.接收

248.
brace [bres] 【 brace 】 v 支持、使防備、鼓起勇氣 n 支柱、一對
A series of health foods prepared by our factory can surely brace you and give you lots of go.
本廠保健系列食品是您精神振奮、精力充沛的保證。
同 **support, strengthen, tighten**（支撐、加固）
反 **loose, relax**（鬆開、放鬆）

> • a series of ph.一系列
> • health n.健康
> • factory n.工廠

249.
bracket [`brækɪt] 【 brack·et 】 n 撐架、括弧、類別 v 用托架固定、圍住、排除
In Japan, 18 percent of teenagers aged 15 through 19 work, while in Germany, 30.8 percent of teenagers in that age bracket work.
日本15歲到19歲的青少年中只有18%打工；德國這一年齡層的青少年打工的占30.8%。
同 **enclose, join**（圍住、結合）

> • percent a.百分比
> • teenager n.十幾歲的青少年

B

250.
brag [bræg] [brag] **v.**吹噓、誇耀
Average sales records are nothing to brag about.
銷售成績平平沒有什麼值得吹噓的。
boast, crow, vapor（吹噓、自誇）

- brag-bragged-bragged
- average a.平均的
- record n.記錄

`84`

251.
brainstorm [`bren.stɔrm] [brain·storm] **n.**集思廣益、腦力激盪
After months of futile labor, the scientists had a brainstorm and solved all problems.
在數月努力徒勞無功後，科學家們集思廣益所有問題都迎刃而解。
hurry, hasten, speed up（加速、急趕）
decelerate, retard（使減速、降低…的速度）

- brainstorming n.集體研討
- futile a.無效的
- scientist n.科學家
- solve v.解決

`124`

252.
breach [britʃ] [breach] **v.n.**破壞、破裂
The breach of contract damages as stipulated in the contract shall be regarded as compensation for the losses resulting from breach of contract.
合約中規定的違約金可視為違反合約的損失賠償。
break, gap, quarrel（鬧翻、絕交）

- breach of promise ph. 毀約
- breach of peace ph. 妨害治安
- damage n.損害
- stipulate v.規定
- compensation n.賠償

`159`

253.
breakdown [`brek.daun] [break·down] **n.**故障、崩潰
Cars should cross the desert in convoy in case there is a breakdown.
汽車應該結伴穿越沙漠，以防拋錨。
collapse, disruption, malfunction（倒塌、故障）

- 源自於片語break down
- breakdown lane n.在公路旁供給行車緊急停止的狹道
- breakdown lorry ph.救援車輛

`201`

254.
breakthrough [`brek.θru] [break·through] **n.**突破、突破性進展
Seizing the historic opportunity of Western development to make a breakthrough in the population and family planning work in the western region.
抓住西方大開發的歷史機會，推動西部地區人口與計劃生育工作取得突破性進展。
discovery（發現）

- 源自於片語break through
- seize v.抓住
- population n.人口

`195`

255.
breathtaking [`brɛθ.tekɪŋ] [breath·tak·ing] **a.**驚人的
An airplane offers you an unusual and breathtaking view of the world.
飛機為你帶來非凡且令人驚訝不已的地球景色。
exciting, marvelous, surprising（驚奇的）
gradual, deliberate（逐漸的、深思熟慮的）

- airplane n.飛機
- offer v.提供
- unusual a.不平常的
- view n.景色

`174`

256.

`101`

breed [brid] 【 breed 】 **V**養育、繁殖、引起 **n**品種、類型

Deeply involved with this new technology is a breed of modern business people who have a growing respect for the economic value of doing business abroad.

深深迷戀這種新技術的是一種現代商人，而這些人越來越看重在國外經商的價值。

同 cultivate, produce, raise（養育、培育）

* breed-bred-bred
* technology n.科技
* grow v.成長
* respect n.方面

257.

`75`

brew [bru] 【 brew 】 **V**醸造、調製、策劃 **n**醸製飲料

Their politics were a strange brew of idealism and self-interest.

他們的政治主張是理想主義和自我利益的奇特混合。

同 plan, plot, scheme（圖謀、策劃）

* brew-up n.沏茶
* politics n.政治
* idealism n.理想主義
* self-interest n.利己主義

258.

`291`

brief [brif] 【 brief 】 **a**簡短的、草率的 **n**概要、簡報

Britain is a brief name of the United Kingdom of Great Britain and Northern Ireland.

不列顛是大不列顛及北愛爾蘭聯合王國的簡稱。

同 concise, short, terse（簡短的、簡潔的）
反 long, prolonged, verbose（延長的、冗長的）

* brevity n.簡潔、短促
* brief period of enthusiasm ph.三分鐘熱度
* in brief ad.簡言之

259.

`204`

brilliant [`brɪljənt] 【 bril·liant 】 **a**光輝的、傑出的、極為順利的

He was a brilliant debater and his gift of repartee was celebrated.

他擅長辯論，以敏於應答著稱。

同 bright, intelligent, sparkling（明亮的、出色的）
反 dull, gloomy, melancholy（陰暗的、憂鬱的）

* brilliantine n.美髮油
* debater n.辯論家
* repartee n.機敏的應答
* celebrate v.頌揚

260.

`125`

brisk [brɪsk] 【 brisk 】 **a**活潑的、興旺的、尖酸的 **V**使活潑、使興旺

Business was brisk at the beginning of the year, but now it is slack.

年初生意還興隆，沒想到現在竟蕭條了。

同 active, spry, vivacious（活潑的、快活的）
反 dull, inactive, sluggish（無聊的、呆滯的）

* briskness n.輕快、清新
* slack a.蕭條的

261.

`196`

broadcast [`brɔd͵kæst] 【 broad·cast 】 **V n**廣播、散佈

Channel 5 will broadcast the news at 10 o'clock.

第5頻道將於十點播放新聞。

同 announce, publish, distribute（散佈、宣揚）

* broadcast fax n.同時向多方發送的傳真
* channel n.頻道

262.

`144`

brochure [bro`ʃur] 【 bro·chure 】 **n**小冊子、廣告冊子

Your new catalogue and brochure will, of course, continue to have our best attention.

你們的新目錄及宣傳資料當然會持續吸引我們的關注。

* catalogue n.目錄
* continue v.繼續
* attention n.注意

B

263.
bronze [brɑnz] 【 bronze 】 **a** 青銅色的 **n** 青銅色、青銅製品

An outstanding feature of the cathedral is the impressive group of four bronze horses over the central entrance way.

這座大教堂的明顯特色是令人印象深刻的中央入口處的四匹銅馬。

同 **copper**（青銅色的）

- **67**
- Bronze Age ph.青銅器時代
- bronze medal ph.銅牌
- outstanding a.傑出的
- cathedral n.大教堂
- impressive a.令人印象深刻的

264.
brood [brud] 【 brood 】 **v n** 孵化、沉思

People do brood over bygone wrongs sometimes.

人們有時候對於過去的冤屈總是無法忘卻的。

同 **meditate, ponder**（沉思）

- **77**
- brood on / over / about ph.沉思
- brood patch ph.孵卵斑
- bygone a.過去的

265.
browse [brauz] 【 browse 】 **v n** 瀏覽、隨便翻閱、吃草

Valid username and password are required to browse this website.

瀏覽該網站要求有效的用戶名和密碼。

同 **read, scan, graze**（翻閱、吃嫩葉）

- **231**
- valid a.有效的
- username n.用戶名稱
- password n.密碼
- website n.網站

266.
bruise [bruz] 【 bruise 】 **n** 傷痕、水果等碰傷 **n** 受傷、搗碎

Don't drop the peaches, they bruise easily.

水蜜桃容易碰傷，要輕拿輕放。

同 **injure, hurt, wound**（傷害、挫傷）

- **175**
- drop v.落下
- peach n.桃子

267.
brutal [`brutl] 【 bru·tal 】 **a** 殘忍的、嚴苛的

We had another brutal winter.

我們又度過了一個嚴冬。

同 **barbarian, coarse, savage**（粗暴的、殘忍的）

- **61**

268.
buckle [`bʌkl] 【 buck·le 】 **v** 扣住、使彎曲、全力以赴 **n** 釦子、彎曲

Slip the seat belt into buckle and pull tight.

把安全帶穿進帶釦，然後抽緊。

同 **fasten, hook, bend**（扣緊、使彎曲）

- **94**
- buckle up ph.繫安全帶
- slip v.滑動
- seat belt ph.行車安全帶
- pull v.拉
- tight a.緊緊地

269.
bud [bʌd] 【 bud 】 **n** 花蕾、萌芽、少女 **v** 發芽

If a bud opens, gather it. Let your bud wait for an empty bough.

花開堪折直須折，莫待無花空折枝。

同 **flourish, sprout**（開始生長）

- **61**
- bud scale ph.芽鱗
- gather v.摘
- empty a.空的
- bough n.大樹枝

270.
budget [`bʌdʒɪt] 【 budg·et 】 **n** 預算、一批 **v** 編入預算、安排

With an auspicious beginning, our company has made a balanced budget in the first year's business, and has had a small surplus as well.

本公司開張大吉，第一年便收支平衡還略有結餘。

同 **allowance, ration, schedule**（編入預算、安排）

- **274**
- budget account ph.預算帳戶
- budget airline ph.廉價航空公司
- budget defitit ph.預算赤字
- auspicious a.吉利的
- surplus n.盈餘

271.

buffet [`bʌfɪt] 【buf·fet】 n 自助餐、毆打 v 揍、打

The delicious food court grandly brings forth local-flavor buffet lunch, NT$38 dollars per person.

美食廣場隆重推出風味自助午餐，每個人38元。

- buffet car ph.餐車
- food court ph.美食廣場
- grandly ad.盛大地
- bring forth ph.產生

272.

bulk [bʌlk] 【bulk】 n 體積、大部分 a 大量的分 v 顯得重要

Our client is all for speciality product, not the kind of thing to sell in bulk to wholesaler.

我們的客戶都是經營專業產品，而不是那些大批出售給批發商產品的。

同 lump, mass, majority（大部分）

- bulk mining ph.大量開採
- bulk scale ph.整批零售
- in bulk ph.大批
- client n.客戶
- wholesaler n.批發商

273.

bulletin [`bʊlətɪn] 【bul·le·tin】 n 公報、新聞快報、期刊 v 公告

Electronic bulletin board systems (abbreviated as BBS) provide on-line services generally on a smaller scale.

電子公告牌系統（簡稱BBS）通常在一個較小範圍內提供網路服務。

同 circular, newsletter（公告、新聞快報）

- bulletin board ph.佈告牌
- system n.系統
- abbreviate v.縮寫
- on-line a.連線作業的
- service n.服務

274.

bully [`bʊlɪ] 【bul·ly】 n 欺凌弱小者、惡霸 v 威脅、橫行霸道

A neutral nation will never seek hegemony or bully others, but will always side with the Third World.

中立國永遠不會稱霸，也不會撻伐他國且支持第三世界。

同 badger, pester, tease（欺凌）

- bully beef ph.罐頭牛肉
- bully boy ph.以武力推行其計畫的人
- bully tree ph.橡皮樹
- seek v.尋求
- hegemony n.霸權

275.

bump [bʌmp] 【bump】 v n 碰撞、猛擊

They expected to bump against serious opposition.

他們預期會遇到強烈的反對。

同 collide, hit, shake（碰、撞）

- bump into ph.無意中遇到
- expect v.預期
- serious a.嚴重的
- opposition n.反對

276.

burden [`bɝdn] 【bur·den】 n 負擔、重載 v 使負擔於、煩擾

The cost reduction achieved in this way will benefit patients and the society in burden alleviation.

集中招標採購降低的採購成本，有利於患者減輕社會負擔。

同 hard work, load, task（負荷、艱難）
反 lighten, reduce（減輕、減少）

- burden of proof ph.提供證據之責任
- reduction n.減少
- benefit v.受益
- patient n.病患
- alleviation n.減輕

277.

burglar [`bɝglɚ] 【bur·glar】 n 夜賊 v 偷盜

Darkness curtained the burglar's movements.

黑暗掩蓋了竊賊的行動。

同 housebreaker, robber, thief（夜賊、破門盜竊者）

- burglar alarm ph.防盜自動警鈴
- darkness n.黑暗
- curtain v.遮掉
- movement n.行動

B

278.
bureaucracy [bjuˋrɑkrəsɪ] 【bu·reauc·ra·cy】 n 官僚政治、繁文褥節

The citizens have the rights to oppose bureaucracy and a cumbersome apparatus.

人民有權反對官僚主義及龐大的機構。

🔄 **govenment**（政府）

- oppose v.反對
- cumbersome a.麻煩的
- apparatus n.政黨組織

`201`

279.
bust [bʌst] 【bust】 v 爆裂、破產 n 失敗、破裂、胸部

His company went bust.

他的公司破產了。

- bust a move ph.跳舞
- bust-up n.爆裂

`91`

280.
buzz [bʌz] 【buzz】 v 發出嗡嗡叫、謠言流傳 n 嗡嗡聲、流言

He buzzed off the rumor on purpose.

他故意散佈謠言。

🔄 **murmur, whizz, rumour**（嗡嗡的叫聲、謠言）

- buzz around / about ph.忙亂
- buzz crusher ph.掃別人興的人
- buzz saw ph.電動圓鋸
- on purpose ph.故意地

`145`

281.
bygone [ˋbaɪ.gɔn] 【by·gone】 a 過去的 n 過去不愉快的事

The ferry service of bygone days has been replaced by that tunnel.

往日的渡口已被那個隧道取代。

🔄 **antiquated, back**（過去的、過時的）

- ferry n.渡輪
- replace v.取代
- tunnel n.隧道

`126`

282.
bypass [ˋbaɪ.pæs] 【by·pass】 v 繞過、置…於不顧 n 旁道

There was a growing tendency for big businesses to bypass clearing banks in the lending and borrowing process.

大企業在存款或借款過程中有繞過清算銀行的趨勢。

🔄 **blink, skip**（視若無睹、略過）

- 源自於片語pass by ph.經過
- bypass surgery n.繞道手術
- tendency n.趨勢
- lend v.把…借給
- borrow v.借入

`184`

283.
byproduct [ˋbaɪ.prɑdəkt] 【by·prod·uct】 n 副產品

Refinery and petrochemical operations produce a variety of byproduct gases.

煉油廠和石油化工生產中生成各種副產氣體。

🔄 **outgrowth**（副產物）

- 字首：by次要
  字尾：product產品
- refinery n.精煉廠
- petrochemical a.石油化學的
- operation n.運作

`121`

284.
bywork [ˋbaɪ.wɜk] 【by·work】 n 副業、兼職

Proofreading for publishings is one of Chris's byworks.

替出版社作校對是克里斯的副業之一。

- proofread v.校對
- publishing n.出版社

`75`

MEMO

abbr 縮寫詞
a 形容詞
ad 副詞
aux 助動詞
conj 連接詞
n 名詞
num 數字
ph 片語
prep 介系詞
v 動詞
（美）美式用語
（英）英式用語
（法）法式用語

全書單字取材於：

① 10本坊間新多益考試暢銷書籍

② 50篇英文新聞、商業文章

③ 2005~2012年ETS TOEIC歷屆考古題

→ 總計約50,000個單字，以電腦統計出題率高達80% 的實用單字1,800個

高頻率單字

 C 家族 **cabin~cutting edge** 🎧01-03

高分錦囊

285.
cabin [`kæbɪn] 【cab·in】 **n**小屋、客艙 **v**住在小屋裡
He has a seat over the wing, so he cannot see much out of the cabin window.
他的座位在機翼上方，所以看不到窗外的許多景色。
🔁 **bungalow, cottage, compartment**（小屋、火車小客房）

- **cabin altitude ph.**座艙壓力高度
- **cabin boy ph.**船上的服務員
- **cabin crew ph.**總稱航班空服員
- **cabin cruiser ph.**有艙房的汽艇

131

286.
cable [`kebl] 【ca·ble】 **n**鋼索、電纜、越洋電報 **v**發電報
As soon as we're able to give you further information regarding our supply of compressors, we will cable you again.
關於提供壓縮機一事，一旦有進一步消息，我們立即發電報告知。
🔁 **telegraph, wire**（電纜、電報）

- **cable car ph.**纜車
- **cable modem ph.**纜線數據機
- **cable television ph.**有線電視
- **information n.**資訊
- **supply n.**提供

145

287.
cafeteria [ˌkæfə`tɪrɪə] 【caf·e·te·ri·a】 **n**自助餐廳
I have my meals in the cafeteria all along.
我都在自助餐廳吃飯。

- **meal n.**膳食
- **all along ph.**始終

94

288.
calculator [`kælkjəˌletɚ] 【cal·cu·la·tor】 **n**計算器、計算者
This pocket calculator needs two batteries.
這個袖珍計算器需用兩顆電池。

- **pocket a.**袖珍的
- **battery n.**電池

105

289.
calendar [`kæləndɚ] 【cal·en·dar】 **n**日曆、行事曆
Letters of credit, bank guarantees and tender bonds shall be valid for one calendar month beyond the validity of the tender.
信用證、銀行保函和投標保函的有效期應比標書有效期長一個月。
🔁 **agenda, schedule**（日程表）

- **calendar month ph.**曆月
- **calendar year ph.**曆年
- **guarantee n.**保證書
- **tender n.**投標
- **validity n.**有效

144

290.
call waiting **ph**電話插播
You couldn't have gotten a busy signal because I have call waiting, the call should have gotten through.
我有電話插播所以電話不可能佔線，你應該可以打得通啊！

- **signal n.**信號
- **get through ph.**接通電話

117

291.
campaign [kæm`pen] 【cam·paign】 **n**戰役、競選活動 **v**參加競選、作戰
The new managing director will act as spearhead of the campaign.
新上任的常務董事將在這場運動中掛帥。
🔁 **crusade, movement**（運動、活動）

- **director n.**董事
- **spearhead n.**先鋒

151

247

292.
cancel [`kænsḷ] 【can·cel】 **V**互相抵消、刪去、取消
The $10 dollars I owed him and the $10 dollars he owed me cancel out.
他與我各欠對方十元，正好相互抵消。
同 delete, erase, repeal（刪去、取消）

- **cancel former order ph.**改單
- **owe v.**欠

117

293.
candidate [`kændədet] 【can·di·date】 **n**候選人、應試者
Michael was the strongest candidate for the job.
麥可在求職應徵者中是具備最好的條件。
同 applicant, nominee（申請人、被提名人）

- **candidate gene ph.**候選基因
- 字根：candid白的
  字尾：ate執行某一職責的人

105

294.
capable [`kepəbḷ] 【ca·pa·ble】 **a**有能力的、能幹的
With my rich experience, I am capable and competent.
憑藉我豐富的經驗，我可以勝任自己的工作且具有競爭力。
同 theoretical, intellectual, professor（理論的、智慧的、教授）
反 empirical, ignorant（經驗的、不學無術的）

- **capable of ph.**能…的
- 字根：cap取
  字尾：able能…的
- **competent a.**有能力的

183

295.
capacity [kə`pæsəti] 【ca·pac·i·ty】 **n**容量、能力、資格
He accompanied the supervisor in an advisory capacity.
他以顧問身份做總監的隨行人員。
同 clever, intelligent, sagacious（能幹的、有天賦的）
反 incapable, unable（無能的）

- **capacity management ph.**能力管理
- **capacity requirements planning ph.**產能需求計畫
- **capacity utilization rate ph.**產能利用率
- **accompany v.**伴隨

164

296.
capital [`kæpətḷ] 【cap·i·tal】 **n**首都、資金 **a**首要的、致命的
Our corporation has enough capital to build another factory.
我們公司有足夠的資金來興建另一家工廠。
同 chief, leading, important（主要的、重要的）
反 trivial（不重要的）

- **capital account ph.**固定資產帳戶
- **capital appreciation ph.**資產增值
- **capital assets ph.**資本
- 字根：capit首要的
  字尾：al屬於…的

180

297.
caption [`kæpʃən] 【cap·tion】 **n**標題、字幕 **V**加標題於
It must be consistent from dialog to dialog, in the exact same place and caption.
各個對話方塊應該保持一致，即相同的位置和相同的標題。
同 heading, headline, title（標題）

- 字根：capti重要的
  字尾：on量
- **consistent a.**前後一致的
- **dialog n.**對話
- **exact a.**確切的

146

298.
capture [`kæptʃə] 【cap·ture】 **V n**捕獲、引起注意
The candidate captured 80% of the votes.
那位候選人獲得百分之八十的選票。
同 arrest, catch（捕獲）
反 acquit, rescue（無罪釋放、營救）

- 字根：cap取
  字尾：ture狀態、性質

C

299.
carbon [ˈkɑrbən] 【car·bon】 n 碳、複寫紙
You'll need to keep the carbon copy of the receipt of your record and give me the original.
你必須保留收據的複寫本存檔，然後把正本給我。

- 字首：carb碳
  字尾：on單位
- carbon copy ph.複寫的副本
- receipt n.收據
- original a.原始的

300.
cargo [ˈkɑrgo] 【car·go】 n 貨物
Insurance brokers will quote rates for all types of cargo and risks.
保險業務員依貨物的種類及風險來評定其費率。
同 **freight, load**（貨物）

- cargo boat ph.貨船
- cargo plane ph.貨運飛機
- quote v.報價
- risk n.風險

301.
carnival [ˈkɑrnəvl] 【car·ni·val】 n 狂歡、嘉年華會、巡迴演出
The carnival celebrations in Brazil are world famous.
巴西的嘉年華會慶祝活動是舉世聞名的。
同 **fate, festival, jamboree**（嘉年華會、宴飲狂歡）

- 字根：carni肉
  字尾：al與…有關
- celebration n.慶祝
- famous a.有名的

302.
carry out ph.完成、實行
No matter what industry we do, we must carry out our duties.
無論我們從事什麼行業，我們都應履行自己的職責。
同 **accomplish, actualoze, prosecute**（完成、執行）

- industry n.行業
- duty n.責任

303.
carry-on [ˈkærɪɑn] 【car·ry-on】 a 可隨身攜帶的
Put your carry-on baggage on the belt, please.
請把隨身攜帶的行李放在傳送帶上。

- baggage n.行李
- belt n.傳送帶

304.
cash register ph.收銀機
We stand in a queue at the cash register.
我們在收銀台前排隊。

- queue n.行列
- register n.收銀機

305.
cast [kæst] 【cast】 v 投擲、投射、丟棄
I was able to cast off such an uninteresting task.
我終於擺脫了這麼一項乏味的工作。
同 **fling, pitch, throw**（投擲、拋扔）

- cast a spell over ph.施魔法
- cast aside ph.拋棄
- cast away ph.丟掉
- cast the first stone ph.首先批評

306.
casual [ˈkæʒuəl] 【ca·su·al】 a 偶然的、漫不經心的、臨時的 n 臨時工
When I'm not at work I wear casual clothes in bright colors, just for a change.
我不上班的時候就穿鮮豔的服裝來點變化。
同 **contingent, random, unexpected**（偶然的、隨便的）
反 **planned, regular**（有計劃的、規則的）

- casual shoes ph.休閒鞋
- casual wear ph.休閒裝
- bright a.鮮明的
- change n.改變

214

307.
catalogue [ˋkætəlɔg] 【cat·a·logue】 **n.v.**目錄、登記

This order is the first from the new catalogue.

這筆訂單是新目錄的第一項。

同 **index, list, inventory**（目錄、一覽表）

• 亦可寫作catalog
• order n.訂購

308.
cater [ˋketɚ] 【ca·ter】 **v.**提供飲食、滿足需要

They aim to cater for private individuals as well as for groups.

他們服務目標有私人也有團體。

同 **coddle, indulge, provide**（滿足、提供）

105
• cater to ph.為…服務
• cater-corner a.成對角線的
• cater-cousin n.遠親
• private a.私人的
• individual n.個人

309.
caution [ˋkɔʃən] 【cau·tion】 **n.v.**謹慎、警告

The factor of mutual agency suggests the need for exercising great caution in the selection of a partner.

相互代理權的特點決定其必須慎重選擇合夥人。

同 **admonish, alert, warm**（警告、告誡）
反 **carelessness**（不小心）

168
• cautious a.謹慎的
• mutual a.互相的
• selection n.選擇
• partner n.夥伴

310.
cell phone **n.**大哥大、行動電話

The cell phone industry asserts the technology is safe.

手機業堅稱手機技術夠安全可靠。

104
• cellular a.細胞組成的
• assert v.聲稱
• safe a.安全的

311.
cellar [ˋsɛlɚ] 【cel·lar】 **n.**地下室、酒窖、最低點

My grandfather had kept a good cellar for a long time.

我祖父藏有大量好酒許多年了。

同 **basement, crypt, vault**（地下室、儲藏室）

91
• grandfather n.祖父
• keep v.保存

312.
celebrity [sɪˋlɛbrətɪ] 【ce·leb·ri·ty】 **n.**名人、名聲

Most executives reduce their need for celebrity and replace it with a desire for reputation.

大部分的管理者降低對想成名的慾望，取而代之的是對聲望的嚮往。

同 **glory, notable**（榮耀、名人）

127
• celebrity worship syndrome ph.名人崇拜症候群
• executive n.經理
• reduce v.減少
• desire n.渴望
• reputation n.聲望

313.
census [ˋsɛnsəs] 【cen·sus】 **v.**實施統計調查 **n.**人口調查、統計數

At present, all data collected through the census are under computer processing program, and the advance tabulation of major figures has been finished.

目前，人口普查全部資料正在用電腦進行資料處理，主要資料的快速匯總工作已經結束。

同 **head count, poll, statistics**（人口統計、數據）

161
• census-taking n.進行人口普查
• process v.處理
• advance a.先行的
• tabulation n.製表

314.

271

certain [ˈsɝtən] 【cer·tain】 a 確定的、某種程度的

Beyond a certain distance we are out of contact with our branch.

超過一定的距離範圍，我們與分公司的訊號就會中斷。

- definite, positive, sure（確信的）
- doubtful, uncertain（不確定的、可疑的）

- 字根：cert確定
- beyond prep.越過
- distance n.距離
- branch n.分公司

315.

167

certify [ˈsɝtəˌfaɪ] 【cer·ti·fy】 v 證明、保證

There are at least three witnesses to certify that this is your signature.

必須有三個見證人證明這的確是你的簽名。

- confirm, depose, verify（證明、確認）

- 字根：cert確定
  字尾：ify使成為…
- witness n.證人
- signature n.簽名

316.

189

certificate [səˈtɪfəkɪt] 【cer·tif·i·cate】 n 證明書、憑證

An certificate of insurance has the same effect as an insurance policy.

保險憑證與保險單具有同樣的效力。

- document, testimonial, voucher（證書、證明）

- certificate authority ph.憑證授權
- certificate master ph. 文憑教師
- certificate of deposit ph.銀行存款單
- Certificate of deposit(CD) 定存單

317.

211

challenge [ˈtʃælɪndʒ] 【chal·lenge】 n 挑戰、質疑 v 向…挑戰、懷疑

The new position challenged me to study harder during the spare time.

這個新職位激發我在業餘時間更加努力學習。

- confront, defy, dispute（挑戰、懷疑）

- position n.職位
- spare time ph.業餘時間

318.

107

champion [ˈtʃæmpɪənˌʃɪp] 【cham·pi·on】 n 冠軍、提倡者 v 擁護、支持

Rayan won the champion at the annual tennis tournament.

雷恩贏得年度網球錦標賽的冠軍。

- advocate, victor, winner（提倡者、優勝者）

- win v.贏得
- annual a.一年一次的
- tournament n.錦標賽

319.

86

chant [tʃænt] 【chant】 n 聖歌、詠 v 吟誦、歌頌

The crowds chanted their demand: "Work for all!" in front of the city hall.

群眾在市政府前齊聲呼喊著他們的要求：「給大家工作！」

- carol, hymn, psalm（聖歌、讚美詩）

- crowd n.人群
- demand n.要求
- in front of ph.在…前面
- city hall ph.市政府

320.

124

character [ˈkærɪktə] 【char·ac·ter】 n 性格、特色、人物

To sum it all up, in this area the entirety of people's characters is still high, either cultural characters or others.

總而言之，這一地區的人的整體素質還是比較高的，無論是文化素質還是其它素質。

- disposition, temperament（性格）

- character assassination ph.毀謗名譽
- character reference ph.品德信譽見證人
- sum v.總結
- entirety n.全體
- cultural a.文化的

321.

charter [ˈtʃɑrtɚ] 【char·ter】 **n**特許狀、包租 **v**發執照給、租

The travel firm specializes in charter flights.

這家旅遊公司專門經營包機業務。

同 **lease, rent, treaty**（包租、特許狀）

- charter member ph.社團或公司的創始會員
- charter party ph.備船契約
- charter school ph.特許學校
- charter flight ph.包機

322.

chase [tʃes] 【chase】 **v n**追捕、驅逐

I never ceased to chase after my dream in the vigorous youth.

在精力充沛的年輕時代，我從未停止過追求自己的夢想。

同 **follow, pursue, run after**（追求）

- chase about ph.到處跑
- chase after rainbows ph.想入非非
- chase down ph.找出
- chase the dragon ph.吸食海洛因

323.

checkout [ˈtʃɛkˌaut] 【check·out】 **n**結帳離開的時間、付款臺

Guests must finish checkout before noon, or they will be charged for the day.

旅客必須在中午前辦理手續離開否則將收取全日費用。

- 源自片語check out
- guest n.旅客
- charge v.索價

324.

chef [ʃɛf] 【chef】 **n**廚師、主廚

The chief chef asked his assistant to take care of the roasting.

大廚叫他的助手負責燒烤。

- chef-d'oeuvre 【法】傑作
- chief a.主要的
- assistant n.助手
- roast v.烤肉

325.

cherish [ˈtʃɛrɪʃ] 【cher·ish】 **v**珍愛、懷有希望

Most Americans cherish freedom and independence.

大多數美國人都鍾愛自由和獨立。

同 **adore, treasure, worship**（珍愛、愛護）

反 **disregard, hate, neglect**（漠視、討厭）

- freedom n.自由
- independence n.獨立

326.

chief [tʃif] 【chief】 **n**首領、長官 **a**等級最高的、主要的

Jim was appointed chief engineer of the project.

吉姆被委任為該項工程的總工程師。

同 **authority, head, leader**（首領、領袖）

反 **subordinate, subservient**（次要的、充當手下的）

- Chief Acquisition Office (CAO) ph.首席兼併官
- Chef Cultural Office (CCO) ph.文化總監
- Chef Executive Officer (CEO) ph.總裁
- appoint v.任命
- engineer n.工程師

327.

chip [tʃɪp] 【chip】 **n**碎片、缺口、炸洋芋 **v**削、切

To pay for their purchases, people will use smart cards, which contain a tiny chip, instead of cash.

人們在購物付款時，將使用裝有微型卡片的智慧卡而不再使用現金。

同 **bit, crumb, piece**（屑片、碎片）

- chip in ph.插話、捐助
- chip on one's shoulder ph.容易發怒
- chip-proof a.不會破碎的
- purchase v.購買
- smart card ph.電腦卡

328.

chopsticks [ˈtʃɑpˌstɪks] 【chop·stick】 **n**筷子

The Easterns use chopsticks while the Westerns use knives and forks.

東方人用筷子西方人用刀叉。

- knife n.刀
- fork n.叉

329.
chord [kɔrd]【chord】**n.**弦、和音、感情

It also struck a chord in American, where the book has sold more than 1 million copies.

這本書在美國也引起了迴響銷售一百多萬冊。

- 字根：chor唱歌
- strike v.打動
- million n.百萬
- copy n.本、冊

330.
chore [tʃor]【chore】**n.**家庭雜務、例行工作、困難的工作

He finally caught on as a chore with an outfit in New Zealand.

他終於在紐西蘭的一個牧場裡找到打雜的工作。

- outfit n.裝備

331.
choreography [ˌkɔrɪˋɑɡrəfɪ]【cho·re·og·ra·phy】**n.**編舞、舞藝

The choreography respects the subject-matter.

舞蹈設計應顧及舞蹈的主題。

- 字根：chor跳舞
  字尾：graphy學術
- matter n.主題

332.
chorus [ˋkorəs]【cho·rus】**v.**齊聲朗誦、合唱 **n.**合唱隊、異口同聲

We chorused its approval by loud cheering.

我們異口同聲大聲歡呼表示贊同。

同► **choir, unison**（合唱隊）

- 字根：chor唱歌
- approval n.同意
- cheer v.歡呼

333.
chronic [ˋkrɑnɪk]【chron·ic】**a.**慢性病的、長期的、慣性的

The dietary nutrition and physical activity are closely related to the chronic diseases.

飲食營養和體力活動與相關慢性病關係密切。

同► **constant, lasting**（長期的、慣常的）
反► **acute**（急性的）

- chronic fatigue syndrome ph.慢性疲勞症
- 字根：chron時間
  字尾：ic與…有關的
- dietary a.飲食的
- nutrition n.營養
- physical a.身體的
- disease n.疾病

334.
cinema [ˋsɪnəmə]【cin·e·ma】**n.**電影院、（總稱）電影

I haven't been to a cinema for I don't know how long.

我都記不清楚究竟有多久沒看過電影了。

同► **film, motion picture, photoplay**（電影、影片）

- cinema novo ph.新潮電影
- cinema verite ph.記錄電影

335.
circuit [ˋsɝkɪt]【cir·cuit】**v.**繞…運行 **n.**環形、一圈、電路

Integrated circuit has had a very significant impact on digital system development.

積體電路的出現與發展使數位系統的設計工作發生了巨大的變化。

同► **ambit, circle, orbit**（環道、周圍）

- circuit board ph.電路板
- circuit switching ph.迴路切換
- 字根：circu圓、環
  字尾：it走動
- significant a.重要的
- digital a.數位的

336.
circulation [ˌsɝkjəˋleʃən]【cir·cu·la·tion】**n.**循環、流通、發行量、通貨

This paper has a circulation of more than thirty thousand.

這報紙的發行量達三萬多份。

同► **rotation, spreading, coinage**（循環、流通、貨幣）

- 字根：circul圓、環
  字尾：ation狀態

337.

circumscribe [ˋsɝkəmˌskraɪb]【cir·cum·scribe】

Ⅴ環繞、限制、為…下定義

We should not circumscribe our activities by any inflexible fence of rigid rules.

我們的行為不應該被死板、不知變通的規則給限制住。

⬛ **bound, encompass, surround**（限制、環繞）

- 字首：circum圍繞
  字尾：scribe劃出
- inflexible a.不可彎曲的
- rigid a.堅硬的

338.

circumstance [ˋsɝkəmˌstæns]【cir·cum·stance】

ⁿ環境、境遇、細節

Where it is necessary to change the sampling methods and quantity according to the quality of the goods and the abnormal circumstance in the packages.

根據到貨的品質和包裝異常情況，需適當變更抽樣方法和數量。

⬛ **condition, situation, state**（情況、情勢）

- 字首：circums圍繞
  字尾：tance性質、狀況
- method n.方法
- quantity n.量
- abnormal a.不正常的

339.

circus [ˋsɝkəs]【cir·cus】 ⁿ馬戲團、馬戲表演場

The visiting circus was an excitement to every child in town.

馬戲團的到來使鎮上每個孩子都感到興奮。

⬛ **big top, carnival, rodeo**（雜技、馬戲）

- visiting a.訪問的
- excitement n.刺激

340.

cite [saɪt]【cite】 Ⅴ引用、表揚、想起

The manager cited a previous project to support his argument.

經理引用了以前的專案來佐證他的論點。

⬛ **mention, quote, refer**（引用、舉出）

- previous a.先前的
- argument n.論點

341.

claim [klem]【claim】 Ⅴⁿ要求、主張

Debenture holders have a prior claim and accept the least risk.

債券持有人有優先索賠權，風險最小。

- lay claim to ph.對…提出權利要求
- put in a claim for sth. ph.就某物的損壞提出賠償要求
- debenture n.公司債券

342.

clarify [ˋklærəˌfaɪ]【clar·i·fy】 Ⅴ澄清、闡明

An example will help to clarify what he means.

舉個例子將有助於澄清他的意思。

⬛ **explain, refine, simplify**（澄清、闡明）
⬛ **confuse**（困擾）

- 字根：clar清楚
  字尾：ify使成為…
- example n.範例
- mean v.意指

343.

clarity [ˋklærətɪ]【clar·i·ty】 ⁿ清楚、明晰

Wherever clarity and simplicity are important, these tips will guide you there.

通過瞭解這些提示後，你就會明白合約清晰、簡明是多麼地重要。

⬛ **clearness, limpidity, transparency**（清澈）

- simplicity n.簡明
- tip n.提示
- guide v.指導

344.
clash [klæʃ]【clash】**v.n.**碰撞、衝突、不協調　　●181

Our views clash on the new tax.

我們在新稅法上意見不協調。

📖 **conflict, contradict, oppose**（發生衝突、牴觸）

- clash with ph.與…衝突
- view n.觀點
- tax n.稅

345.
clasp [klæsp]【clasp】**v.**緊抱、扣住 **n.**扣子、緊握　　●121

My boss gave my hand a warm clasp.

老闆熱情地握了握我的手。

📖 **buckle, clip, hook**（緊握、扣住）

- clasp knife ph.摺刀
- clasp sb. bythe hand ph.緊握某人的手。
- warm a.溫暖的

346.
classification [ˌklæsəfəˈkeʃən]【clas·si·fi·ca·tion】　　●145
n.分類，分級

The criteria governing the classification of wastes shall be established by the Competent Authority.

垃圾分類的標準由主管部門制定。

📖 **categorization, distribution, sorting**（選別、分級）

- criteria n.標準
- establish v.建立
- competent a.合格的
- authority n.當局

347.
clearance [ˈklɪrəns]【clear·ance】**n.**清除、空隙、清倉大拍賣　　●167

This voucher entitles the bearer to 20% off any purchases over NT$200. Excludes weekly advertised specials and selected clearance lines.

凡持有贈券購物200元以上者，憑此券可享受八折優惠，但不包括每週特價商品和清倉貨品。

- voucher n.收據
- bearer n.持有人
- entitle v.給…題名
- exclude v.除外

348.
clerk [klɝk]【clerk】**n.**辦事員、店員　　●215

I got a job as a bank clerk.

我得到一份銀行職員的工作。

📖 **cashier, teller, bookkeeper**（職員、辦事員）

- clerk of works ph.現場監工員
- bank n.銀行

349.
client [ˈklaɪənt]【cli·ent】**n.**顧客、委託人　　●234

Analyze client equipment and operations to determine servicing and supply needs.

對客戶的設備及其運行情況進行分析以決定提供何種服務和物品。

📖 **customer, patron, prospect**（顧客、客戶）

- client state ph.附庸國
- analyze v.分析
- equipment n.設備
- operation n.操作
- determine v.決定

350.
climate [ˈklaɪmɪt]【cli·mate】**n.**氣候、社會趨勢　　●115

I could not stand the terrible climate in the U.K..

我忍受不了英國糟糕的氣候。

📖 **weather**（氣候）

- stand v.忍受
- terrible a.糟糕的

351.

climax [ˋklaɪmæks]【cli·max】 **n** 頂點、高潮 **v** 達到頂點或高潮

His election to the general manager was the climax of his career.

他當選為總經理是他職業生涯的頂峰。

`232`
- election n.選舉
- general manager ph.總經理
- career n.事業

352.

cling [klɪŋ]【cling】 **v** 黏著、緊握不放、依附、堅持

My superior isn't a man who clings to old routines.

我上司不是一個墨守成規的人。

⑩ adhere, hold, grasp（黏附、緊握、堅持）

`184`
- cling to ph.緊握不放
- superior n.長官
- routine n.慣例

353.

clockwise [ˋklɑkˏwaɪz]【clock·wise】 **a** 順時針方向的

Turn the lid clockwise if you want to fasten it tightly.

如果你想把蓋子旋緊就按順時針方向轉即可。

⑮ anticlockwise（反時針方向）

`97`
- 字首：clock時鐘
  字尾：wise方向
- lid n.蓋子
- fasten v.繫緊

354.

clone [klon]【clone】 **n** 翻版、複製品、植物克隆

A clone is identical with the original animal or plant.

複製動植物與母本動物或植物完全相同。

⑩ copy, reproduce（複製、再生）

`55`
- identical a.一致的
- original a.原始的

355.

closet [ˋklɑzɪt]【clos·et】 **n** 壁櫥、小房間 **a** 私下的、祕密的 **v** 密室會談

The supervisors were closeted together in the office.

總監們在辦公室裡密談。

⑩ cabinet, cubby, wardrobe（壁櫥、衣櫥）

`116`
- closet drama ph.只供閱讀而不適合上演的劇本
- closet queen ph.非公開的同性戀者

356.

clue [klu]【clue】 **n** 線索、暗示 **v** 為…提供線索

I'm not going to guess the answer if you don't give me a clue.

如果你不給我提示的話我永遠猜不到答案。

⑩ evidence, hint, sign（線索、提示）

`205`
- clue in / up ph.向…提供情況
- clued-up a.十分瞭解的
- guess v.猜

357.

cluster [ˋklʌstɚ]【clus·ter】 **n** 串、群 **v** 使成群

There was a cluster of fans around the actress, asking for autographs.

女演員周圍簇擁著一群粉絲跟她要簽名。

⑩ bunch, group, set（串、群、組）

`164`
- a cluster of ph.成群的
- cluster bomb ph.子母彈
- fan n.狂熱仰慕者
- actress n.女演員
- autograph n.親筆簽名

358.

clutch [klʌtʃ]【clutch】 **v n** 抓住、掌握、控制

Keep out of his clutches.

別陷入他的掌握中。

⑩ hold, grasp, stick（抓牢）

`124`
- clutch at ph.試圖抓住
- clutch bag ph.女用無帶提包
- clutch pedal ph.離合器踏板
- in the clutches of ph.在…的控制下

359.
coach [kotʃ]【coach】 n.教練、【美】公車、【英】長途公車

Their football team has a very experienced coach.

他們的足球隊有了一個很有經驗的教練。

同 **tutor, bus, carriage**（指導、公車、馬車）

> 124
> • coach dog ph.達爾瑪提亞短毛狗
> • coach station ph.長途汽車站
> • football n.足球

360.
coalition [ˌkoəˋlɪʃən]【co·a·li·tion】 n.結合、聯合

There is no coalition of members of the corporation.

公司的各部門之間沒有結合。

同 **conjunction, integration, union**（結合、合併）

> 162
> • coalition cabinet ph.聯合內閣
> • corporation n.公司

361.
coherent [koˋhɪrənt]【co·her·ent】 a.一致的、連貫的、有黏性的

We seem to have no coherent plan for saving the company.

我們似乎沒有個一致的挽救公司計劃。

同 **accordant, congruent, consonant**（一致的、相連接的）

> 182
> • 字首：co共同
> 字根：her黏著
> 字尾：ent有…狀態的
> • plan n.計畫

362.
coincide [ˌkoɪnˋsaɪd]【co·in·cide】 v.同時發生、重疊、巧合

Their opinions did not coincide on this case.

在這個案例裡他們的意見不一致。

同 **concur, correspond, happen together**（相符、巧合）

反 **contradict**（與…相矛盾）

> 114
> • coincidence n.巧合
> • coincide with ph.與…相一致
> • opinion n.意見

363.
collaborate [kəˋlæbəˌret]【col·lab·o·rate】 v.共同合作、勾結

We would ask you to collaborate with us in this work.

我們願意邀請你們在這項工作中和我們合作。

同 **cooperate, unite, work together**（合作、共同研究）

> 210
> • collaboration n.合作
> • 字首：col共同
> 字根：labor工作
> 字尾：ate進行一項行動

364.
colleague [ˋkɑlig]【col·league】 n.同事、生意上的熟人、加盟

His colleague, Michael, is in charge of the customer service.

他同事麥克負責客戶業務。

同 **buddy, companion, comrade**（同事、同行）

> 219
> • be in charge of ph.負責
> • consumer n.客戶

365.
collect [kəˋlɛkt]【col·lect】 v.收集、聚集 a.電話受話人付費的

As I had no money with me, I made a collect call.

因為身上沒錢，我打了一個由對方付款的電話。

同 **accumulate, assemble, gather**（收集）

反 **distribute, scatter**（分開、分散）

> 240
> • 字首：col聚集
> 字根：lect聚集

366.
collide [kəˋlaɪd]【col·lide】 v.碰撞、衝突

The interests of the two multi-national Enterprises collide.

兩大跨國公司利益發生衝突。

同 **bump, clash, conflict**（碰撞、衝突）

> 188
> • interest n.利益
> • multi- (字首)多
> • enterprise n.公司

367.
colloquial [kəˋlokwɪəl] 【col·lo·qui·al】 **a**口語的
My English is fluent but not colloquial.
我英語講得很流利但不夠口語化。
🔄 **conversational, dialectal, vernacular**（口語的）
🔄 **literary**（文言的）

- 字首：col聚
  字根：loqu說
  字尾：ial屬於…的
- fluent a.流利的

368.
collusion [kəˋlɪʒən] 【col·lu·sion】 **v**共謀、勾結
Each company acts independently; no collusion is present.
每個公司都獨立行動，沒有相互勾結。
🔄 **conspiracy, complot**（共謀）

- 字根：lus遊戲
- independently ad.獨立地
- present a.在場的

369.
combat [ˋkɑmbæt] 【com·bat】 **vn**戰鬥、反對
Drastic measures were taken to combat the property prices roared.
採取強烈措施對付房價激增。

- 字首：com共同
  字根：bat打架
- combat aircraft ph.戰鬥機
- combat troops ph.戰鬥部隊

370.
combine [kəmˋbaɪn] 【com·bine】 **v**使聯合、化合 **n**企業聯合
They are going to combine the three departments soon.
他們很快就要合併這三個部門了。
🔄 **associate, connect, join**（結合、聯合）
🔄 **separate**（分開）

- combine harvester ph.聯合收割機
- department n.部門

371.
comedy [ˋkɑmədɪ] 【com·e·dy】 **n**喜劇、喜劇成分
We didn't appreciate the comedy of the situation.
我們沒有感覺到在這個情況下有趣的一面。
🔄 **drollery, farcicality, joking**（滑稽、玩笑）
🔄 **tragedy**（悲劇）

- comedy of intrigue ph.陰謀喜劇
- comedy of manners ph.風尚喜劇
- appreciate v.察知
- situation n.情況

372.
comfort [ˋkʌmfət] 【com·fort】 **vn**安逸、慰問
If so, what comfort did we expect to derive from it?
如果這樣，我們指望從中得到什麼慰藉呢？
🔄 **console, solace, sympathize**（安慰、撫慰）
🔄 **affliction, discomfort, grief**（悲痛、苦惱）

- comfortable a.舒適的
- comfort station ph.公共廁所
- comfort women ph.慰安婦
- derive v.得到

373.
command [kəˋmænd] 【com·mand】 **vn**指揮、命令、掌握
The examiner commanded all examinees to submit the test papers immediately.
主考官命令所有應試者立刻交卷。
🔄 **direct, instruct, order**（指揮、命令）
🔄 **comply, forbid, obey**（順從、妨礙）

- at one's command ph.可自由使用
- be at sb.'s command ph.服從某人
- have a command of ph.掌握
- examiner n.主考官
- examinee n.應試者

374.
commemorate [kəˋmɛmə͵ret] 【com·mem·o·rate】 **v**慶祝、紀念
We commemorate the founding of our nation with holidays for a week.
我們放假一星期以慶祝國慶。
🔄 **celebrate, honor, observe**（慶祝、紀念）

- 字首：com聚集
  字根：memor記憶
  字尾：ate進行一項行動
- founding a.創辦的

375.
commence [kə`mɛns]【com·mence】**Ⅴ**開始、著手
The conference will commence at 2 p.m.
會議將在下午兩點開始。
同► begain, start, fire away（開始、著手）
反► conclude, end, finish（結束、完成）

- commence on ph.著手
- commence with ph. 從…開始
- conference n.會議

`157`

376.
commend [kə`mɛnd]【com·mend】**Ⅴ**稱讚、推薦
Reprove your husband privately and commend him publicly.
對丈夫要私下責備，公開讚揚。
同► approve, compliment, praise（稱讚、賞賞）

- reprove v.責備
- privately ad.私下地
- publicly ad.公開地

`168`

377.
commercial [kə`mɝʃəl]【com·mer·cial】**ⓐ**商務的、商業性的 **ⓝ**商業廣告
Pays visits to existing and potential clients in view of entering contracts with them, especially commercial clients.
拜訪現有的和有潛力的客戶尤其是商業客戶，與其保持聯繫。
同► marketing, mercantile（貿易的、商業上的）

- commercial bank ph. 商業銀行
- Commerical paper (CP) ph.商業本票
- commercial traveler ph.商品推銷員
- potential a.潛在的

`211`

378.
commitment [kə`mɪtmənt]【com·mit·ment】**ⓝ**託付、承諾、支持、犯罪
I felt I did not have to make such a commitment to you.
我覺得我沒有必要對你作出那樣的承諾。
同► commission, oath, obligation（委任、誓言）

- 字首：com一起 字根：miti送 字尾：ment性質
- have to ph.必須

`98`

379.
commission [kə`mɪʃən]【com·mis·sion】**ⓐ**傭金、委任、委員會 **Ⅴ**委託
In short, it is an important responsibility of our Commission to choose young cadres for promotion.
總之，選拔年輕幹部是我們委員會重要責任之一。
同► consign, entrust, commit（委託）

- commission plan ph.委員市政制
- 字首：com共同 字根：miss送 字尾：ion情況
- responsibility n.責任
- cadre n.幹部

`201`

380.
commodity [kə`mɑdətɪ]【com·mod·i·ty】**ⓝ**商品、日用品、有價值之物
In Japan, rice is a significant commodity for import.
米是日本的一項重要進口商品。
同► product, ware（商品）

- commodity future contract ph.期貨契約
- rice n.米
- significant a.重要的
- import n.進口

`194`

381.
community [kə`mjunətɪ]【com·mu·ni·ty】**ⓐ**社區、公眾
We did it for the good of the community.
我們為了公眾的利益而做這件事。
同► district, town, society（社區、社會）

- community center ph. 社區活動中心
- community chest ph. 社區福利基金
- community property ph.夫妻或團體共有的財產

`181`

382.

communicate [kə`mjunə,ket] 【com·mu·ni·cate】 Ⅴ傳遞、傳染、通訊

Did she communicate my messages to you?

她有沒有把我的信息轉告你？

🔄 **convey, inform, report**（傳達）

- message n.信息

383.

commuter [kə`mjutə] 【com·mut·er】 Ⅲ通勤者

During the peak hours, many commuters take mass transportation to work.

尖峰時間，許多通勤者搭乘大眾交通工具上班。

🔄 **passenger**（乘客）

- commuter belt ph.月票居民帶
- peak hour ph.尖峰時刻的
- mass a.大眾的
- transportation n.運輸工具

384.

compact [kəm`pækt] 【com·pact】 ⓐ緊密的、小巧的、簡潔的 Ⅴ使緊密、簡潔

The computer looks compact and functional.

這台電腦看起來小巧而實用。

🔄 **brief, concise, short**（緊湊的、簡潔扼要的）

- compact car ph.小型汽車
- compact disc player ph.CD放音機
- functional a.實用的

385.

comparison [kəm`pærəsn] 【com·par·i·son】 Ⅲ比較、對照

This emerged by a comparison of factory capacity and output figures.

這一點只要將其工廠的生產能力和產量數字比較一下就可以看出。

🔄 **contrast, confronting, collation**（比較、對照）

- emerge v.顯露
- capacity n.能力
- output n.產量

386.

compassion [kəm`pæʃən] 【com·pas·sion】 Ⅲ同情、憐憫

The plight of the refugees arouses their compassion.

難民的困苦引起他們的同情。

🔄 **clemency, mercy, sympathy**（憐憫）
🔄 **cruelty, harshness**（殘忍、嚴厲）

- 字首：com共同
  字根：pass感覺
  字尾：ion性質
- plight n.困境
- refugee n.難民

387.

compensation [,kɑmpən`seʃən] 【com·pen·sa·tion】 Ⅲ補償、賠償金、報酬

I had earned that money over many years at IBM, through deferred compensation as well as retirement and pension benefits.

那筆錢我是在IBM公司賺了好幾年的，其中有推遲領取的補償金還有退休和養老金。

🔄 **payment, reimbursement, remuneration**（報酬、賠償）

- earn v.賺得
- defer v.推遲
- retirement n.退休
- benefit n.利益

388.

compete [kəm`pit] 【com·pete】 Ⅴ競爭、媲美

Depreciation of our currency makes it easier for domestic companies to compete with foreign companies.

本國貨幣貶值使本國企業較易與外國企業競爭。

🔄 **contest, rival, vie with**（競爭、對抗）

- compete against ph.與…競爭
- compete with ph.與…競爭
- depreciation n.貶值
- currency n.貨幣
- domestic a.國內的

---

389. `188`

competent [ˈkɑmpətənt] 【com·pe·tent】 **a** 有能力的、足夠的、恰當的

Michel proved to be a very competent manager.

麥克證明了自己是一個很能幹的經理。

🔄 **adequate, capable, effective** (有能力的、合格的)
🔄 **incapable, incompetent, inefficient** (無能力的、無效的)

- prove v.證明
- manager n.經理

---

390. `104`

complement [ˈkɑmpləmənt] 【com·ple·ment】 **n** 補充物、全數 **v** 補充、與…相配

We've taken on our full complement of new trainees for this year.

我們今年招收的新學員已經滿額了。

- full a.滿的
- trainee n.新生

---

391. `147`

complex [ˈkɑmplɛks] 【com·plex】 **a** 複雜的、複合的 **n** 複合物、綜合體

A petrochemical complex is to be built there.

那將建造一個石油化學聯合企業。

🔄 **complicated, confused, mixed** (複雜的、難懂的)
🔄 **plain, simple** (簡單的)

- complex number ph.複數
- complex sentence ph.複合句
- 字首：com一起
  字根：plex折、疊
- petrochemical ph.石油化學的

---

392. `98`

compliance [kəmˈplaɪəns] 【com·pli·ance】 **n** 承諾、順從

The appointment and removal of managers shall be in compliance with legal procedures and shall be publicly announced.

經理的任命與免職應按照法定的程序，並向社會公告。

🔄 **conformity, concession, obedience** (順從、服從)
🔄 **command, denial** (命令、拒絕)

- appointment n.任命
- removal n.免職
- procedure n.過程、程序
- announce v.公佈

---

393. `156`

compliment [ˈkɑmpləmənt] 【com·pli·ment】 **v** **n** 讚美、恭維、問候

She presented her compliment to the entrepreneur, and hoped the enterprise would succeed.

她向企業家致敬並祝其成功。

🔄 **congratulation, flatter, praise** (讚美、恭維)
🔄 **insult** (羞辱)

- compliment on ph.讚揚
- compliment slip ph.贈禮便條
- entrepreneur n.企業家

---

394. `94`

comply [kəmˈplaɪ] 【com·ply】 **v** 順從、遵從

This was a clause we could never comply with.

這個條件是我們絕對不能順從的。

🔄 **assent, obey, yield** (應允、順從)
🔄 **deny, refuse, reject** (拒絕、否認)

- comply with ph.遵守
- 字首：com共同
  字根：ply折疊
- clause n.條款

C

395.

component [kəm`ponənt]【com·po·nent】 n 構成要素、零件 a 組成的

Increased reliance in the international trade will be a necessary component of the reform procedure.

更加依靠國際貨易是這個改革過程中必不可少的組成部分。

🔄 **constituent, element, portion**（部分、成分）

- component stereo ph. 立體聲組合音響
- 字首：com共同
- 字根：pon放置
- 字尾：ent…的狀態
- reliance n.信賴
- procedure n.程序、步驟

（214）

396.

composer [kəm`pozə]【com·pos·er】 n 作曲家、調停者、作家

The beautiful moonlight inspired the composer.

美麗的夜色使作曲家文思泉湧。

🔄 **author, creator, inventor**（作者、創造者）

- 字首：com聚集
- 字根：pos放置
- 字尾：er從事…的人
- inspire v.刺激

（104）

397.

composition [͵kɑmpə`zɪʃən]【com·po·si·tion】 n 寫作、作品、成分

Regarding English composition is concerned, more practice is the best way.

就英語作文而言，多練習是最好的方法。

🔄 **combination, composite, mixture**（組成、混合物）

- regarding prep.就…而論
- concern v.涉及
- practice n.練習

（157）

398.

composure [kəm`poʒə]【com·po·sure】 n 平靜、鎮靜

We shouldn't lose our composure in trouble!

在遇到困難時，我們應保持冷靜！

🔄 **calmness, pease, serenity**（鎮定）
🔀 **haste**（急促）

- lose v.失去
- trouble n.困難

（167）

399.

comprehensive [͵kɑmprɪ`hɛnsɪv]【com·pre·hen·sive】 a 廣泛的、有充分理解力的

The company is a comprehensive corporation that specializes in the developing, manufacturing and trading of automobile devices and parts.

此公司是從事專業汽車設備、配件的開發、生產和貿易的綜合性實業公司。

🔄 **inclusive, thorogh, widespread**（廣泛的、全面的）
🔀 **incomprehensive**（無包括性質的）

- comprehensive school ph.綜合制中學
- 字首：com共同
- 字根：prehen抓住
- 字尾：sive有…傾向的
- manufacture v.製造
- automobile n.汽車
- device n.設備

（179）

400.

compress [kəm`prɛs]【com·press】 v 壓縮、概括出資料

You'll have to compress the work of three months into one.

你必須將三個月的工作壓縮在一個月內完成。

🔄 **condense, press, squeeze**（壓緊、壓縮）

- 字首：com聚集
- 字尾：press壓縮

（175）

401.

comprise [kəm`praɪz]【com·prise】 v 包括、由…組成

Industrial unions usually comprise a number of diverse groups.

產業工會一般由各式各樣的集團所組成。

🔄 **consist of, contain, include**（包含、由…組成）

- 字首：com共同
- 字根：prise握緊
- industrial a.產業的
- diverse a.不同的

（184）

402.

compromise [ˋkɑmprəˏmaɪz]【com·pro·mise】 **n** 妥協、折衷　**v** 妥協、讓步

I hope they shall come to a compromise.

我希望他們能達成妥協。

同 concede, yield（妥協、讓步）

- 字首：com一起
- 字根：promise答應

165

403.

compulsion [kəmˋpʌlʃən]【com·pul·sion】 **n** 強迫、強制力

Compulsion will never result in convincing us.

強迫永遠不會使我們信服。

同 impulse, oppression（強迫）

反 freedom, liberty（自由）

- 字首：com共同
- 字根：puls推
- 字尾：ion性質
- result in ph.導致
- convince v.說服

145

404.

compute [kəmˋpjut]【com·pute】 **v n** 計算、估算

Besides calculations, the most frequent use for a compute is probably information retrieval.

除了計算工作以外，估計最頻繁的用途大概是資料檢索。

同 calculate, estimate, figure（計算、估算）

- 字首：com共同
- 字根：pute計算
- frequent a.頻繁的
- retrieval a.恢復

169

405.

concede [kənˋsid]【con·cede】 **v** 承認、讓步

The candidate conceded that she had lost the election.

這位候選人承認她已經在競選中失敗。

同 admit, confess, grant（承認、容許）

反 deny（拒絕給予）

- 字首：con聚
- 字根：cede屈服
- candidate n.候選人
- election n.選舉

144

406.

concert [ˋkɑnsət]【con·cert】 **n** 音樂會、和諧

The champion had her head turned by a concert of praise.

冠軍因受到異口同聲的讚頌而忘乎所以。

同 music, harmony, recital（音樂會、和諧）

- concert hall ph.音樂廳
- concert party ph.各自買了股票後再合併的一群人
- champion n.冠軍
- praise n.讚美

96

407.

concierge [ˏkɑnsɪˋɛrʒ]【con·cierge】 **n** 門房、旅館服務台職員

One copy of this form will be forwarded to Concierge Desk.

這申請單的影本將送到禮賓部櫃檯。

- form n.單子
- forward v.轉交

79

408.

conclusive [kənˋklusɪv]【con·clu·sive】 **a** 決定性的、確實的

Where a party suspends performance without conclusive evidence, it shall be liable for breach of contract.

當事人沒有確切證據中止履行的應當承擔違約責任。

同 decisive, irrefutable, ultimate（確定性、最後的）

反 inconclusive, questionable（非決定性的、有疑問的）

- 字首：con一起、共同
- 字根：cluse關閉
- 字尾：ive有…傾向的
- suspend v.暫時取消
- performance n.表演
- breach n.違反

143

409.

concur [kənˋkɝ]【con·cur】 **v** 同意、同時發生、合作

My colleagues rarely concur on any issues.

我的同事們在任何問題上都很少有一致的意見。

同 acquiesce, coincide, cooperate（意見相同、同時發生）

- concur with ph.同……一致
- 字首：con共同
- 字根：cur跑
- rarely ad.難得

121

410.
condition [kənˈdɪʃən]【con·di·tion】**n**條件、情況
Everybody wishes to ameliorate his own condition.
改善自己境況的願望人皆有之。
⑯ circumstance, situation, specification（條件、情況）

- wish v.希望
- ameliorate v.改善

(287)

C

411.
conductor [kənˈdʌktə]【con·duc·tor】**n**領導者、指揮
The conductor read Beethoven with astonishing insight.
這位指揮家以驚人的洞察力闡釋貝多芬的作品。
⑯ administrator, director, leader（領導者、管理人）

- 字首：con聚集
  字根：duct引導
  字尾：or從事…的人
- astonishing a.令人驚訝的
- insight n.洞察力

(115)

412.
confederate [kənˈfɛdərɪt]【con·fed·er·ate】**n**同盟國、共謀者 **v**使結盟
The robber was caught, but his confederate got away.
這個搶劫犯被抓住了，但他的同夥卻逃脫了。

- Confederate States ph.美國南部聯邦
- 字首：con共同
  字尾：federate結成同盟
- robber n.搶劫者

(104)

413.
confer [kənˈfɜ]【con·fer】**v**協商、給予
I'll confer with the supervisor about your suggestion.
我將把你的建議和總監磋商。
⑯ consult, discuss, talk over（商量）

- 字首：con共同
  字根：fer拿來、帶來
- supervisor n.上級
- suggestion n.建議

(194)

414.
conference [ˈkɑnfərəns]【con·fer·ence】**n**會議、討論會
An international conference will be held in Shanghai next month.
一個國際性的會議下個月將在上海舉行。
⑯ forum, convention, council（會議、討論會）

- conference call ph.電話會議
- 字首：confer協商
  字尾：ence性質、狀態
- international a.國際性的

(215)

415.
confess [kənˈfɛs]【con·fess】**v**承認、坦白
I confess that I can hardly venture, at my age, to look for such promotion.
我承認在我這年齡已幾乎不大敢冀望這樣的晉升。
⑯ admit, concede, consent（坦白、承認）
⑬ conceal（隱瞞）

- confess to ph.承認
- 字首：con共同
  字根：fess承認
- venture n.冒險
- promotion n.提升

(198)

416.
confidential [ˌkɑnfəˈdɛnʃəl]【con·fi·den·tial】**a**祕密的、表示信任的
This conference and the entire arrangement are supposed to be confidential.
這次會議以及整個的安排應該都是保密的。
⑯ private, secret, unpublishable（機密的）

- confidential communication ph.不能對第三者洩漏之祕密
- a confidential secretary ph.機要祕書
- 字根：fid信任
- entire a.整個的

(94)

417.
configuration [kənˌfɪgjəˈreʃən]【con·fig·u·ra·tion】**n**結構、配置
Differentiate between command and configuration.
要把命令和設置區分開來。
⑯ formation, silhouette, sketch（結構、輪廓）

- configuration management ph.配置管理
- configuration management board ph.配置管理委員會
- differentiate v.區別
- command n.命令

(81)

075

418.

confine [kən`faın]【con·fine】**v** 限制、禁閉 **n** 邊界

We'll confine our discussion to the main issue during conference.

會議期間我們將只討論主要問題。

同► **enclose, imprison, restrain**（限制、監禁）

- confine to ph.把…限制在
- 字首：con聚集
  字根：fine限制
- main a.主要的

〔**215**〕

419.

confirmation [ˌkɑnfə`meʃən]【con·fir·ma·tion】**n** 確認、批准

The offer rates depend on our final confirmation.

該報盤以我公司最後確認為準則。

同► **determination, institution, proof**（決定、證明）

反► **denial**（拒絕）

- 字首：con共同
  字根：firm堅定的
  字尾：ation性質
- depend on ph.視…而定

〔**164**〕

420.

conflict [`kɑnflɪkt]【con·flict】**n v** 衝突、爭執

There is an important conflict of interest in the world of product development.

在產品開發領域中存在著重大的利益衝突。

同► **clash, fight, opposition**（衝突、矛盾）

- conflict between ethnic groups ph.族群衝突
- conflict manage ph.衝突管理
- conflict with ph.與…牴觸
- 字首：con共同
  字根：flict打擊

〔**179**〕

421.

conform [kən`fɔrm]【con·form】**v** 遵照、符合、使一致

Activities are checked to determine whether they conform to planned actions.

決定那些是否按照計劃行動的工作，都要加以核查。

同► **assent, comply, obey**（遵照、符合）

- conform to ph.符合
- 字首：con共同
  字根：form形成
- determine v.決定

〔**201**〕

422.

confront [kən`frʌnt]【con·front】**v** 面臨、對抗、對照

Doctors often confront such urgent choices.

醫生經常會遇到這樣刻不容緩的抉擇。

同► **encounter, face, meet squarely**（面對、遭遇）

反► **avoid**（避免）

- confront danger ph.勇敢地面對危險
- 字首：con共同
  字根：front正面
- urgently ad.緊急地

〔**134**〕

423.

conjuncture [kən`dʒʌŋktʃə]【con·junc·ture】

n 事情同時發生、緊要關頭

At this conjuncture in our nation's affairs, we need a firm leadership.

當國家危急之時，我們需要堅強的領導。

同► **concurrence, simultaneity, context**（同時發生、事態）

- 字首：con聚集
  字根：junct連接
  字尾：ure表示行動
- firm a.堅定的

〔**88**〕

424.

conquer [`kɑŋkə]【con·quer】**v** 征服、攻取、贏得讚譽

By now, fast-food restaurants were ready to conquer the world.

目前為止，速食餐廳已快速風靡全球。

同► **overtake, overwhelm, vanquish**（戰勝、征服）

反► **submit, surrender**（屈服、投降）

- 字首：con共同
  字根：quer尋找
- fast-food restaurant ph.速食餐廳

〔**141**〕

---

425. `104`

conscience [ˋkɑnʃəns] 【con·science】 n 良心、道德、善惡觀念

You cannot in all conscience regard that as fair pay.

你在良知上總不能認為那樣的報酬算是合理的吧。

🔄 ethnics, morals（良心、道德）

- conscience clause ph. 良心條款
- conscience money ph. 悔罪金
- conscience-stricken a. 良心不安的

426. `194`

conscious [ˋkɑnʃəs] 【con·scious】 a 有知覺的、意識到的、故意的

Language learning usually necessitates conscious mimicry.

一般來說，學習語言就要進行有意識的模仿。

🔄 awake, cognizant, sensible（有知覺的、察覺到的）
🔄 involuntary, unconscious（無意識的、不小心的）

- conscious of ph. 意識到
- 字首：con共同
  字根：sci知道
  字尾：ous充滿…的
- mimicry n. 模仿

427. `98`

consecutive [kənˋsɛkjutɪv] 【con·sec·u·tive】 a 連續不斷的、連貫的

It shall have sound business performance and remain profitable for the last three consecutive years.

公司經營業績良好最近3年連續盈利。

🔄 continuous, following, serial（連續的、始終一貫的）
🔄 alternate（輪流的、交替的）

- consecutive thought ph. 連貫的思考
- 字首：con共同
  字根：secu緊跟
  字尾：tive有…傾向的
- profitable n. 有利的

428. `115`

consensus [kənˋsɛnsəs] 【con·sen·sus】 n （意見等）一致、合意

The Keynesian consensus view was that the government could be treated exogenously.

凱恩斯主義的一見見解認為政府可以被看成是外生性的。

🔄 concordance, conformity, unison（一致、合意）

- 字首：con共同
  字根：sens感覺
- exogenously ad. 外生性地

429. `54`

consignee [ˏkɑnsaɪˋni] 【con·signee】 n 受託者、收件人

A recipient entity refers to the consignee or consignor specified in the purchase contract and shipping invoice.

收貨單位是指購貨合約和貨運發票中載明的收貨人或者貨主。

- 字首：con聚集
- 字根：sign標記
- 字尾：ee動作承受者
- recipient n. 接受的

430. `215`

consist [kənˋsɪst] 【con·sist】 v 組成、構成、一致

For this very reason forward markets rarely consist entirely of hedgers.

正因為這一理由遠期市場很少全由套利交易者組成。

🔄 comprise, include, make up（組成、構成）

- consist in ph. 在於
- consist of ph. 由…構成
- 字首：con共同
  字根：sist站立
- hedger n. 模稜兩可的

431. `117`

consolidate [kənˋsɑləˏdet] 【con·sol·i·date】 v 合併、鞏固

Several small businesses are planning to consolidate to form a large powerful company.

幾家小企業正計劃合併成一家實力雄厚的大公司。

🔄 combine, integrate, merge（結合、鞏固）

- 字首：con共同
  字根：sol單獨
  字尾：id…狀態的
  字尾：ate進行一項行動
- powerful a. 強大的

150

432.
consultation [ˌkɑnsəl`teʃən] 【 con·sul·ta·tion 】

n諮詢、會議、參考

This agreement is hereby made on the basis of the existing contact and consultation of both sides.

雙方根據已有的聯繫與協商特簽下此協定。

同 consideration, deliberation, dicussion（商量、討論）

• hereby ad.藉此
• basis n.根據
• existing a.現存的

147

433.
consumer [kən`sjumə] 【 con·sum·er 】 **n**消費者、消耗者

We are running your consumer survey now.

我們正在處理你的消費者意見調查。

同 buyer, customer, purchaser（消費者、用戶）
反 producer（生產者）

• consumer confidence ph.消費信任度
• consumer credit ph.消費者信用貸款
• consumer durables ph.耐用消費用品
• consumer goods ph.消費品

254

434.
contact [kən`tækt] 【 con·tact 】 **vn**接觸、聯繫 **a**接觸的

He tried in vain to get into contact with the local branch.

他試圖與當地分部取得聯絡但沒有成功。

同 approach, connect, reach（接觸、聯繫）
反 isolation（隔離）

• contact lens ph.隱形眼鏡
  字首：con共同
  字根：tact接觸
• in vain ph.白費
• branch n.分局

104

435.
contagious [kən`tedʒəs] 【 con·ta·gious 】 **a**接觸傳染的、會蔓延的

Measles is a contagious disease.

麻疹是一種傳染性疾病。

同 epidemic, infectious, spreading（傳染的、容易感染的）

• 字首：con聚集
  字根：tag接觸
  字尾：ious充滿…的
• measles n.麻疹
• disease n.疾病

251

436.
contain [kən`ten] 【 con·tain 】 **v**包含、控制

Our observations may contain a grain of truth for you to refer to.

我們的意見也許會有千慮一得之處供你參考。

同 include, hold, restrain（包含、限制）
反 exclude, release（拒絕、釋放）

• 字首：con共同
  字根：tain握、持
• observation n.觀察
• gain v.獲得
• truth n.真實

188

437.
contemporary [kən`tɛmpəˌrɛrɪ] 【 con·tem·po·rar·y 】 **a** **n**當代的（人）、同時代的（人）

A very significant proportion of contemporary Americans are descendants of merchants, craftsmen, and professional people

當今美國人中，商人、手工業者和專職者的後裔佔很大一部分。

同 coeval, synchronal, simultaneous（同時期的）

• 字首：con共同
  字根：tempor時間
  字尾：ary有…性質的
• proportion n.部分
• descendant n.後裔

151

438.
contempt [kən`tɛmpt] 【 con·tempt 】 **v**輕視、恥辱

For outward glamour, or rank they have nothing but a cool contempt.

對於表面的榮譽、職稱、地位這類東西他們是不屑一顧的。

同 disdain, haughtiness, scorn（輕蔑、藐視）
反 esteem, honor, worship（尊敬、崇拜）

• contempt of court ph.蔑視法庭
• outward a.表面的
• glamour n.魅力
• rank n.等級

439.

contend [kən`tɛnd] 【con‧tend】 **v** 競爭、爭論、堅決主張

The firm is too small to contend against with large international companies.

這家公司太小無法與國際性的大公司抗爭。

⑮ fight, struggle, quarrel（爭奪、競爭）

- **148**
- contend with ph.對付
- 字首：con一起
- 字根：tend爭

440.

contentment [kən`tɛntmənt] 【con‧tent‧ment】

n 滿意、滿足

His mood of contentment was beginning to lapse.

他怡然自得的心情漸漸消失了。

⑮ satisfaction（滿足）
⑯ discontentment, misery（不滿足）

- **111**
- mood n.心情
- lapse n.流逝

441.

contest [`kɑntɛst] 【con‧test】 **n** 競爭、比賽

A bitter contest has been developed between the two men for that position.

那兩個人為得到這一職位展開了激烈的競爭。

⑮ game, sport, tournament（競賽、比賽）

- **217**
- bitter a.激烈的

442.

context [`kɑntɛkst] 【con‧text】 **n** 上下文、來龍去脈

By maintaining a very consistent layout, the writer will be able to keep his bearings between context shifts.

維持一致的版面編排，作者才能在不同上下文的轉換中保有相同的思維。

⑮ contextual relation, meaning（上下文）

- **269**
- 字首：con聚集
  字尾：text正文
- maintain v.維持
- consistent a.前後一致的
- layout n.佈局

443.

continue [kən`tɪnju] 【con‧tin‧ue】 **v** 繼續、仍舊

Regardless of your choice of design deliverable, your team should continue to work closely with the construction team throughout implementation.

不管最後提交的設計方案是什麼，在開發和實施的整個過程中設計團隊要繼續緊密地和實施團隊一起工作。

⑮ endure, last, persist（繼續、持續）

- **188**
- regardless of ph.不管
- deliverable a.可以傳送的
- construction n.建造
- implementation n.履行

444.

contractor [`kɑntræktɚ] 【con‧trac‧tor】 **n** 立契約者、承包商

Chase up the contractor and get a delivery date.

找到那個承包商要他定一個交貨的日期。

⑮ builder, carpenter, maker（立約人、承包人）

- **94**
- 字首：con共同
  字根：tract拉
  字尾：or從事…的人
- chase up ph.為某一目的而尋找
- delivery n.交貨

445.

contrary [`kɑntrɛrɪ] 【con‧trar‧y】 **a** 相對的 **n** 相反

I will come on Monday unless you write me to the contrary.

我星期一會來除非你寫信叫我不要來。

⑮ conflicting, different, opposite（相反的、對立的）

- **215**
- contrary to ph.與…相反
- 字首：contra相反
  字尾：y有…性質的
- unless conj.除非
- on the contrary ph.正相反

C

446.
contradict [ˌkɑntrəˋdɪkt]【con·tra·dict】**ⅴ**反駁、否認、矛盾
I am not in a position either to contradict or affirm this statement.
我既不能否定又不能肯定這一說法。
🔄 **conteract, dispute, refuse**（反駁、反對）
🔺 **avow, confirm, recognize**（承認、確定）

> 169
> • 字首：contra相反
> 字根：dict說
> • affirm v.證實
> • statement n.陳述

447.
controvert [ˋkɑntrəˌvɝt]【con·tro·vert】**ⅴ**反駁、爭論
The statement of the last witness controverts the evidence of the first two.
最後一個證人的陳述反駁了前兩人的證詞。
🔄 **altercate, impugn, wrangle**（辯駁、反駁）

> 184
> • 字首：contro相反
> 字尾：vert變
> • witness n.證人

448.
convene [kənˋvin]【con·vene】**ⅴ**集合、聚集
The Chairperson of the Commission shall convene an annual regular session of the Commission.
委員會主席應召開委員會的年度例會。
🔄 **assemble, gather, rally**（集合、召喚）
🔺 **adjourn**（中止、休會）

> 211
> • convention n.集合
> • 字首：con共同
> 字根：vene來
> • chairperson n.主席
> • commission n.委員會
> • regular a.定期的

449.
conversant [ˋkɑnvɚsn̩t]【con·ver·sant】**a**熟悉的、親近的
I'm not particularly conversant with the document.
對於這個檔案我所知甚少。
🔄 **acquainted, familiar, up-to-date**（熟悉的、精通的）

> 74
> • particularly ad.特別
> • document n.文件

450.
converse [kənˋvɝs]【con·verse】**ⅴⅰ**談話 **a**相反的
He's willing to converse with anyone about the quotations on the stock market.
他願和任何人談論股市行情。
🔄 **communicate with, discuss, talk**（交談）

> 147
> • conversation n.談話
> • 字首：con共同
> 字根：verse轉
> • quotation n.語錄
> • stock n.股票

451.
convert [kənˋvɝt]【con·vert】**ⅴ**轉變、使皈依 **n**皈依者
You are about to convert an HTML message to plain text.
您要把一條HTML的訊息轉換為純文字。
🔄 **change, transform**（轉變）

> 194
> • convertible n.敞篷車
> • 字首：con一起
> 字根：vert轉變
> • HTML=Hypertext Markup Language電腦超文字標記語言

452.
conveyance [kənˋveəns]【con·vey·ance】**n**運輸、表達、交通工具
Fares do not include conveyance between railway stations and steamer piers.
運費中不包括火車站至輪船碼頭之間的運輸費用。
🔄 **expression, transmission, transport**（表達、運輸）

> 61
> • 字首：con共同
> 字根：vey道路
> 字尾：ance行為
> • fare n.費用
> • pier n.碼頭

C

453.
convince [kən`vins] 【con·vince】 **V** 使信服

Only by reasoning can we convince people completely.

只有以理服人才能使人心悅誠服。

同 persuade, pledge（使確信、使信服）

- 字首：con共同
  字根：vince打敗
- completely ad.完全地

454.
convoke [kən`vok] 【con·voke】 **V** 召集

The king convoked parliament to cope with the impending danger.

國王召開國會以應付迫在眉睫的危險。

反 dissolve, prorogue（分解、休會）

- 字首：con聚集
  字根：voke呼叫
- parliament n.國會
- cope with ph.處理
- impending a.逼近的

455.
coordinate [ko`ɔrdn̩et] 【co·or·di·nate】 **V** 協調、調整
a 同等重要的

The Federal Reserve Board, an independent government agency, was established in 1913 to help stabilize and coordinate the nation's commercial banks.

成立於1913年的聯邦儲備局是一個獨立的政府機構，這個機構協助穩定和協調全國的銀行。

同 equal, equipotent, equivalent（同等的、協調的）

- coordinate clause ph.並列子句
- 字根：ord次序
- independent a.獨立的
- agency n.代辦處
- stabilize v.使穩定

456.
corporate [`kɔrpərɪt] 【cor·po·rate】 **a** 共同的、團體的

It is impossible to break down corporate income into interest on capital, rent on real estate, and profits of the enterprise.

無法把公司收入按資本和利息、不動產和租金和企業利潤區分開來。

同 collective, connected（共同的、連貫的）

- corporate area network ph.企業區域網路
- corporate bond ph.公司債
- corporate culture ph.企業文化
- corporate hospitality ph.商業應酬

457.
corporation [͵kɔrpə`reʃən] 【cor·po·ration】 **n** 社團法人、公司、【英】市政府

A smaller corporation can seldom raise much capital by issuing bonds.

一家小企業不可能通過發行債券累積更多的資本。

同 business, company, enterprise（法人、公司）

- corporation tax ph.企業稅
- 字首：corpor團體
  字尾：ion性質
- seldom ad.很少
- bond n.債券

458.
correct [kə`rɛkt] 【cor·rect】 **V** 改正、責備 **a** 正確的、恰當的

His appreciation of her chances of getting the promotion was correct.

他對她晉升機會所作的賞識是對的。

同 accurate, proper, true（正確的、得當的）
反 false, inaccurate, wrong（錯誤的、不正確的）

- 字首：cor聚集
  字根：rect指導
- appreciation n.鑑識

459.
correspondence [͵kɔrə`spandəns]
【cor·re·spon·dence】 **n** 通信、信件、一致

We inform you that we have this day removed to ABC City, where all correspondence should be addressed in future.

自即日起已經遷至ABC市，日後請寄該址特此奉告。

同 letter, message, missive（信件、書信）

- correspondence course ph.函授課程
- correspondence school ph.函授學校
- inform v.通知
- address v.給…寫信

460.
corrupt [kəˋrʌpt] 【cor·rupt】 **a** 腐敗的、墮落的 **v** 腐敗、墮落
The corrupt judge dismissed the case without a hearing.
腐敗的法官沒有聽審就駁回了這個案子。
同 **crooked, evil, rotten**（墮落的、邪惡的）

- 字首：cor共同
  字根：rupt破裂
- judge n.法官
- dismiss v.駁回

461.
cosmopolis [kazˋmapəlɪs] 【cos·mop·o·lis】 **n** 國際都市
On the occasion of the Shanghai World Expo, especially the outstanding theme, the commercial services should seize the rare opportunity to develop and improve, which is the responsibility in realizing the functions of the cosmopolis.
上海世博會的舉辦特別是其鮮明的主題為商業服務的發展與提升提供了難得的機會，也是商業服務在實現國際化大都市功能中應當承擔的責任及機會。

- 字首：cosmo世界
  字根：polis城市
- occasion n.機會
- theme n.主題
- commercial a.商業的

462.
cost-effective **a** 開銷適當的、有成本效益的
Assuming that this can be achieved in a cost-effective manner, it will translate into business success.
如果能夠以較為合算的成本實現上述目標，就能取得商業上的成功。
同 **econmical**（經濟的）

- assume v.假設
- manner n.方法
- translate v.轉變

463.
counteract [ˌkauntɚˋækt] 【coun·ter·act】 **v** 對抗、抵消
Our work calls for mutual support. We shouldn't counteract each other's efforts.
工作要互相支持，不要互相對抗（打消、妨礙）
同 **balance, neutralize, offset**（打消、妨礙）

- 字首：counter相反
  字尾：act行動
- mutual a.互相的
- support n.支持

464.
countermand [ˌkauntɚˋmænd] 【coun·ter·mand】
v 撤銷、收回命令
If the goods are not shipped in June, we shall be compelled to purchase elsewhere and may have to countermand our order.
若無法在六月裝船我們只能撤回訂單去別處採購。
同 **annul**（廢除、取消）

- 字首：counter相反
  字根：mand命令
- compel v.強迫
- purchase v.購買

465.
coupon [ˋkupɑn] 【cou·pon】 **n** 折價券、贈獎券
The coupon is not valid if detached.
折價券撕下無效。
同 **cheque, stub, tag**（贈券）

- valid a.有效的
- detach v.拆卸

466.
courier [ˋkurɪɚ] 【cou·ri·er】 **n** 送地急件的信差、嚮導
Send by express mail or courier such as Federal Express.
用特快專遞郵寄或者送快信的人例如聯邦快遞公司來寄件。
同 **messenger, postman, runner**（送快信者、郵差）

- courier travel ph.幫他人托帶行李的旅行
- express mail ph.快捷

C

467.
courtesy [`kɝtəsɪ] 【cour·te·sy 】 n.禮貌、殷勤、好意

I know to offer a guest tea is a Chinese traditional courtesy.

我知道給賓客敬茶是中國的一個傳統禮節。

🔄 **gentleness, good manner, politeness**（好意、禮貌）
🔄 **discourtesy**（無禮）

- courtesy bus **ph.**免費接客車
- courtesy call **ph.**禮節性拜訪
- courtesy light **ph.**門控車室照明燈
- traditional **a.**傳統的

468.
coverage [`kʌvərɪdʒ] 【cov·er·age 】 n.覆蓋範圍、新聞報導

The X-Carrier offers customers comprehensive coverage of trade corridors, with some of the fastest transit times in the industry.

X快遞公司的服務範圍廣泛，提供業內最快捷的運送服務。

- comprehensive **a.**廣泛的
- corridor **n.**通道
- transit **n.**運輸

469.
crash [kræʃ] 【crash 】 n.碰撞、墜毀、爆裂聲

He completely lost his marbles after the stock market crash.

股票市場崩盤後他完全失去理智。

🔄 **break, shatter, smash**（撞擊、砸碎）

- crash barrier **ph.**防撞護欄
- crash course **ph.**速成課
- crash diet **ph.**應急食物
- crash dive **ph.**急速下潛
- crash helmet **ph.**安全帽

470.
crash landing n./迫降著陸

The pilot was highly commended for having handled the crash landing successfully.

這名機長因成功使飛機迫降而得到高度讚賞。

- pilot **n.**機長
- commend **v.**稱讚
- handle **v.**操作

471.
crave [krev] 【crave 】 v.渴望獲得、懇求

To have a native-born Nobel Laureate is what most developing and developed countries crave for as an unparalleled honour.

多數已開發和開發中國家都渴望能夠培育出一個諾貝爾得獎人為國爭光。

🔄 **covet, lust, want**（渴望獲得、迫切需要）

- Nobel Laureate **ph.**諾貝爾獲得者
- unparalleled **a.**空前未有的
- honour **n.**榮耀

472.
credible [`krɛdəbl̩] 【cred·i·ble 】 a.可靠的、可信的

Quality of products appeared credible won the praise of users.

產品品質上等、信譽可靠，深得用戶的好評。

🔄 **believable, plausible, reliable**（可信的、可靠的）
🔄 **incredible, unbelievable**（不可信的）

- 字根：cred相信
  字尾：ible可…的
- quality **n.**品質
- praise **n.**讚揚

473.
credit [`krɛdɪt] 【cred·it 】 n.信譽、賒帳、銀行存款 v.相信

That means the credit agencies are happy to award CPDOs their highest (AAA-style) rating.

這就意味著信用機構樂意給予CPDO他們最高的評級（AAA制）。

🔄 **brief, faith, trust**（信用、信賴）
🔄 **discredit**（敗壞名聲）

- credit account **ph.**賒銷帳項
- credit card **ph.**信用卡
- credit crisis **ph.**信貸危機
- credit freeze **ph.**信貸凍結
- credit hour **ph.**學分

474.
criterion [kraɪ`tɪrɪən] 【cri·terion 】 n.標準、準則

Practice is the sole criterion of truth.

實踐是檢驗真理的唯一標準。

🔄 **benchmark, norm, prototype**（標準、準則）

- practice **n.**實踐
- sole **a.**唯一的

475.

criticize [ˋkrɪtɪ͵saɪz]【crit·i·cize】**V**批評、評論

Some people criticize the boss, but they're too mealy-mouthed to say so in her presence.

一些人批評老闆，但是他們很虛偽，當著老闆的面從不提這事。

⑰ condemn, reproach, slam（批評、譴責）

⑰ admire, eulogize, praise（讚美）

• mealy-mouthed a.說話婉轉的
• presence n.存在

(181)

476.

cross-reference **N**前後參照 **V**使前後對照

Adds a cross-reference from processes on a page to other processes on the same page of your flowchart.

將工作流程圖中的某一頁前後對照後，將其加入同一頁的其他流程裡。

• flowchart n.流程圖

(54)

477.

crossroads [ˋkrɔs͵rodz]【cross·roads】**N**十字路口、轉折點

I'll stop for you at the crossroads.

我在十字路口等你。

(144)

478.

crisis [ˋkraɪsɪs]【cri·sis】**N**危機、病情危險期

A good leader can make an appropriate decision in any crisis.

一個好的領導者可以在任何危機時作出適當的決定。

⑰ emergency（緊急關頭）

• crisis management ph.危機管理
• appropriate a.適當的
• decision n.決定

(210)

479.

cruise [kruz]【cruise】**V****N**巡航、漫遊

The liner is making a round-the-world cruise.

客輪正在做環球航行。

⑰ navigate, wander, voyage（巡航、漫遊）

• cruise car ph.【美】巡警車
• cruise liner ph.巡航挺
• cruise ship ph.遊輪
• liner n.班輪

(124)

480.

cue [kju]【cue】**N**暗示、提示

Act according to circumstances; take cue and act accordingly.

見機行事。

⑰ clue, hint, signal（提示、暗示）

• cue ball ph.撞球檯上的白色球
• cue card ph.舉示給演員的提示板
• according to prep.根據

(215)

481.

cuisine [kwɪˋzin]【cui·sine】**N**烹調、菜餚

Chinese cuisine culture has a long history and also a profundity for its variety.

中華民族的飲食文化源遠流長博大精深。

• cuisine minceur ph.【法】清淡菜
• cuisine nouvelle ph.【法】法國新潮派烹調

(61)

482.

cultivate [ˋkʌltə͵vet]【cul·ti·vate】**V**耕作、培養

A series of policies have been put forward to support and cultivate high-tech key industries at different aspects.

我們推出了一系列政策，從不同的層面對高新技術重點產業給予扶持和培育。

⑰ develop, improve, train（栽培、培養）

• put forward ph.提出
• high-tech a.高科技的
• aspect n.方面

(185)

483.

curious [`kjuəriəs] 【cu·ri·ous】 **a**好奇的、奇怪的

Our meeting was taking place in a curious atmosphere of assumed consensus.

我們的會議是在一種裝作意見一致的奇妙氣氛中進行的。

同 inquisitive, peculiar, snoopy（奇怪的、好奇的）
反 incurious, indifferent, unnchalant（不好奇的、漠不關心的）

- take place ph.發生
- atmosphere n.氣氛
- consensus n.一致

484.

curriculum [kə`rikjləm]【cur·ric·u·lum】 **n**學校的全部課

The course coordinator explained the curriculum for all new-comers at the orientation.

新生訓練時，課程協調員向新生解釋學校課程。

同 hurry, hasten, speed up（加速、急趕）
反 decelerate, retard（使減速、降低…的速度）

- curriculum vitae ph.【拉】履歷、簡歷
- coordinator n.調停者
- orientation n.對新生的情況介紹

485.

currency [`kʌrənsi]【cur·ren·cy】 **n**貨幣、流通、流行時期

She wasn't able to rake much currency together at such short notice.

她無法在接到通知後這麼短的時間內湊齊大筆現金。

同 cash, money（貨幣）

- currency risk ph.貨幣風險
- 字根：curr跑 字尾：ency性質
- rake v.迅速獲得

486.

curtain call **nph**要求演員謝幕的掌聲或歡呼聲

Do not just sit on your hand when actors make curtain call.

演員謝幕時不要坐著不鼓掌。

同 cash, money（貨幣）

- curtain n.舞台上的幕

487.

custom [`kʌstəm]【cus·tom】 **n**習俗、慣例、（大寫）海關

Our baggage has cleared the Custom.

我們的行李已通過海關檢查。

同 habit, tradition（習慣、傳統）

- custom-built a.非現成的
- custom-made a.客製的
- baggage n.行李
- clear v.獲得批准

488.

customer [`kʌstəmə]【cus·tom·er】 **n**顧客、買主

A satisfied customer is the best advertisement that we hope to have.

顧客滿意是我們所期望的，它是一種最好的廣告宣傳。

同 client, patron, vendee（顧客、主顧）

- customer relationship management ph.客戶關係管理
- customer value ph.顧客價值

489.

cutback [`kʌtˌbæk]【cut·back】 **n**減少、電影倒敘

Because of a cutback in defense orders, the Harrington Company decided to shut down its research and development department.

由於國防訂貨的削減，哈林頓公司決定關閉其研究和開發部。

同 diminution, reduction（減少）

- defense n.防禦
- shut down ph.停工
- department n.部門

490.

cutting edge **nph**最前線、最重要的位置

California is on the cutting edge of trends that spread nationwide.

加州正位於全國時尚的最前線。

同 contemporary, original, progressive（先進的、原始的）

- edge n.邊緣
- spread n.散佈
- nationwide a.全國性的

MEMO

abbr 縮寫詞
a 形容詞
ad 副詞
aux 助動詞
conj 連接詞
n 名詞
num 數字
ph 片語
prep 介系詞
v 動詞
（美）美式用語
（英）英式用語
（法）法式用語

全書單字取材於：
①10本坊間新多益考試暢銷書籍
②50篇英文新聞、商業文章
③2005~2012年ETS TOEIC歷屆考古題
→ 總計約50,000個單字，以電腦統計出題率高達80%
的實用單字1,800個

▷ D 家族 database ~ dynamic 🎧 01-04

491.
147
database [`detə,bes] 【 data·base 】 **n** 資料庫
Development of Database Construction and On-line Services in 2003-2004
2003-2004年資料庫建設發展及線上服務狀況。

- database management ph.資料庫管理
- database management system ph.數據庫管理系統

492.
88
dazzle [`dæz!] 【 dazz·le 】 **v** 使眼花、使迷惑 **n** 燦爛
Children's food whose names are of every description dazzle people.
如今名目繁多的兒童食品讓你眼花撩亂。
⊕ flash, glaze, glare（使目眩）

- description n.敘述

493.
162
deadline [`dɛd,laın] 【 dead·line 】 **n** 截止期限、截稿時間
The reporter's deadline is 8 p.m. for the morning edition.
記者上午版發稿的截止時間是前一天的下午八點。

- reporter n.記者
- edition n.版本

494.
141
dealer [`dilə] 【 deal·er 】 **n** 商人、業者
The dealer reduced the price for cash down.
這家商店對付現金的人減價優惠。
⊕ merchant, seller, vendor（商人）

- 字首：deal交易
  字尾：er從事…的人

495.
214
debate [dı`bet] 【 de·bate 】 **v n** 辯論、討論
A fierce debate on the tax cut was going on.
一場圍繞著減稅的辯論正在激烈進行中。
⊕ contend, discuss, dispute（辯論、討論）

- fierce a.激烈的
- tax n.稅收

496.
163
debit [`dɛbıt] 【 de·bit 】 **n** 借方 **v** 把…記入借方
If the currency has to be paid out abroad, it is registered as a debit.
如果需要對外付出外匯則應填入借方。
⊗ credit（貸方）

- debit balance ph.借方餘額
- debit card ph.借方卡
- debit note ph.欠款單

497.
181
debt [dɛt] 【 debt 】 **n** 債、負債、情義
Due to poor management, the factory is deeply in debt.
由於經營不善該工廠負債累累。
⊕ amount due, obligation（債、借款）

- debt collector ph.收帳人
- debt of honour ph.賭債
- Debit service 還本付息
- debt / equity ratio ph.負債股東權益比

D

498.
decade [ˋdɛked] 【 de·cade 】 **n.**十年

The operating margins are on track to top 14% — their highest level in a decade.

營業毛利也有望達到10年來的最高水準14%。

- track **n.**行蹤
- top **n.**頂點

499.
decay [dɪˋke] 【 de·cay 】 **v.n.**腐朽、衰退

They are figuring out a way to stop the decay of the ancient building.

他們在想辦法阻止這古老建築的朽壞。

反 **crumble, rot, spoil**（腐朽、衰敗）
反 **develop, flourish, prosper**（發展、茂盛）

- figure out **ph.**想出
- ancient **a.**古代的
- building **n.**建築

500.
deceive [dɪˋsiv] 【 de·ceive 】 **v.**欺騙、蒙蔽

Advertisers are now forbidden to deceive the public with false claims.

現在不允許廣告商用假話來欺騙群眾。

同 **beguile, betray, lie**（欺騙、蒙蔽）
反 **undeceive**（使醒悟）

- 字首：de在…之下
  字尾：ceive奪取
- forbid **v.**禁止
- claim **n.**要求

501.
decelerate [diˋsɛləˏret] 【 de·celer·ate 】 **v.**使減速、降低速度

Also, further government tightening could decelerate the current outflow of bank liquidity into equity markets.

同時政府進一步實施緊縮政策也會減緩目前銀行資金流入股票市場的勢頭。

同 **brake**（煞車、制動）
反 **accelerate**（加速）

- 字首：de減少
  字根：celer加速
  字尾：ate進行一項行動
- outflow **n.**流出
- liquidity **n.**流動性

502.
decent [ˋdisṇt] 【 de·cent 】 **a.**正派的、體面的、親切的

He spent three year in a manufactory before finding a decent job.

他在一家製造廠做了3年才找到一份像樣的工作。

同 **adequate, proper, suitable**（體面的、像樣的）
反 **coarse, indecent, vulgar**（粗俗的）

- manufactory **n.**製造廠

503.
deceptive [dɪˋsɛptɪv] 【 de·cept·ive 】 **a.**迷惑的、虛偽的

Her working style is deceptive; what she has to say is very profound.

她的工作態度虛偽，她說出話卻來是很有深度的。

同 **fallacious, illusive, slippery**（騙人的）

- profound **a.**深奧的

504.
decide [dɪˋsaɪd] 【 de·cide 】 **v.**決定、下定決心

After you decide to buy groceries, the particular check-out aisle you select may not be important.

在你決定購買日用品之後選擇哪個櫃檯付款不重要。

同 **clinch, determine, judge**（解決、決定）
反 **hesitate, revoke, waver**（猶豫、取消）

- decide against **ph.**決定不
- decide on **ph.**選擇
- decide upon **ph.**考慮後決定
- 字首：de向下
  字根：cide降落
- grocery **n.**食品雜貨

---

505. `75`

decimal [`dɛsɪml̩] 【de·cimal】 **a** 十進位的、小數的 **n** 小數

The first two figures after the decimal point indicate tenths and hundred respectively.

小數點後的頭兩位數分別表示十分位和百分位。

- decimal place **ph.** 小數點右邊第一個數字的位置
- decimal point **ph.** 小數點
- decimal system **ph.** 十進制
- 字首：deci十

---

506. `104`

decisive [dɪ`saɪsɪv] 【de·ci·sive】 **a** 決定性的、確定的、堅決的

Opening to the outside world is a decisive policy for the country to promote its modernization.

實行對外開放是這國家推進現代化建設的一項重大決策。

- **definitive, determining, emphatic**（決定性的）
- **indecisive**（優柔寡斷的）

- promote **v.** 提升
- modernization **n.** 現代化

---

507. `188`

declaration [ˌdɛklə`reʃən] 【dec·la·ra·tion】 **n** 宣佈、陳訴、申報

He made a declaration to the effect that he would soon resign.

他發表一項聲明，大意是他將很快辭職。

- **announcement, avouchment, proclamation**（宣佈、申訴）

- declaration of secrecy **ph.** 保密聲明
- resign **v.** 辭職

---

508. `219`

decline [dɪ`klaɪn] 【de·cline】 **v** **n** 下降、衰退、婉拒

The decline of sales embarrassed the company.

銷路下降使公司陷於財政困難。

- **sink, refuse, reject**（下降、婉拒）
- **accept, choose, thrive**（接受、選擇）

- 字首：de向下
  字根：cline傾斜
- embarrass **v.** 尷尬

---

509. `151`

decorate [`dɛkəˌret] 【de·cor·ate】 **v** 裝飾、佈置

Bright posters decorate the streets.

鮮豔的廣告點綴著街道。

- **adorn, ornament**（裝飾、修飾）

- bright **a.** 明亮的
- poster **n.** 海報

---

510. `211`

decrease [`dikris] 【de·crease】 **v** **n** 減少、減小

Rectify the credit balance of trust business, decrease the risk of various trust assets and guarantee the payment of trust liabilities.

調整信託業務存量，降低各項信託資產的風險，保障信託負債的按時支付。

- **diminish, lessen, curtail**（減少、減小）
- **add, increase, extend**（增加、擴展）

- 字首：de向下
  字根：crease上升
- rectify **v.** 改正
- asset **n.** 資產
- guarantee **n.** 保證

---

511. `85`

decree [dɪ`kri] 【de·cree】 **v** **n** 法令、判決

He is to be the new ambassador to Japan by decree of government.

他受政府之命將擔任駐日本的新大使。

- **command, dictate, pronounce**（命令、裁定）

- decree absolute **ph.** 絕對判決
- ambassador **n.** 大使

512.

deduction [dɪˋdʌkʃən] 【de·duc·tion】 **n.**扣除、扣除額、推論

He pays to the seller the full amount of the sight draft, without any deduction.

他向賣方支付即期匯票的全部金額不打折扣。

⊗ **induction**（歸納）

- 字首：de向下
- 字根：duct引導
- 字尾：ion性質
- **draft n.**匯票

513.

dedicate [ˋdɛdəˏket] 【ded·i·cate】 **v.**以…奉獻、舉行落成典禮

Our professional team dedicates their talent and expertise to insure the highest quality service money can buy.

本公司專業團隊以其優異的才能和專長來確保為客戶提供最高品質的服務。

⊗ **bless, devote, hallow**（奉獻、供獻）

- **dedicate to ph.**奉獻給
- **talent n.**天才
- **expertise n.**專門知識
- **insure v.**保證

514.

deduce [dɪˋdjus] 【de·duce】 **v.**演繹、推論、追溯

From the presence of so many people at the party, we can deduce that it is a welcomed one.

從參加聚會的人數之多，我們可以看出這次聚會是受人歡迎的。

⊕ **infer, glean, reckon**（演繹、推斷）
⊗ **induce**（歸納）

- 字首：de向下
- 字根：duce引導
- **welcomed a.**受歡迎的

515.

deduct [dɪˋdʌkt] 【de·duct】 **v.**扣除、減除

In no circumstance is it allowed to deduct or delay the payment.

不得扣除或者無故拖欠勞動者的工資。

⊕ **remove, subtract, withdraw**（扣除、減去）

- 字首：de向下
- 字根：duct引導
- **circumstance n.**情況
- **delay v.**延遲

516.

deem [dim] 【deem】 **v.**認為、持某種看法

I deem it highly important and necessary to help the needy.

我認為幫助窮人是很重要且必要的。

⊕ **consider, regard, think**（認為、視作）

- **necessary a.**必須的
- **needy a.**貧窮的

517.

deface [dɪˋfes] 【de·face】 **v.**毀壞、損壞

The wall has been defaced with slogans.

那堵牆因貼滿標語而面目全非。

⊕ **blemish, damage, mar**（損傷、磨損）

- 字首：de在…之下
- 字根：face外表
- **slogan n.**標語

518.

default [dɪˋfɔlt] 【de·fault】 **v. n.**違約、不履行責任、缺席

If on default by the contractor, the guarantor shall satisfy and discharge the damages sustained by the employer thereby.

如果承包人違約，則保證人應賠償業主因此而承受的損失。

⊕ **absence, delinquency**（缺席、懈怠）

- **default route ph.**電腦路徑表格記錄
- **default value n.**電腦內定值
- **satisfy v.**滿足
- **discharge v.**履行

519.
defeat [dɪˋfit]【de‧feat】**v.n.**擊敗、使失敗
After defeat of the new competitor, the prices can rise again.
新的競爭者被擊敗之後，價格就會重新上漲。
同 **beat, overcome, surpass**（戰敗、打敗）
反 **lose, conquest, triumph**（征服、勝利）

• competitor n.競爭者
• rise v.上升
225

520.
defect [dɪˋfɛkt]【de‧fect】**n.**缺點、不足之處 **v.**逃跑
A defect of vision prevented him from focusing accurately.
視力上的缺陷使他不能準確對焦。
同 **deficiency, flaw, weakness**（缺點、缺陷）
反 **merit**（優點）

• 字首：de在…之下
  字根：fect製作
• prevent v.防止
• accurately ad.正確地
115

521.
defend [dɪˋfɛnd]【de‧fend】**v.**保衛、防禦
We shall defend our city, whatever the cost may be.
不管代價如何，我們要捍衛我們的城市。
同 **advocate, protect, shield**（防禦、保衛）
反 **accuse, assail, attack**（指責、攻擊）

165

522.
defendant [dɪˋfɛndənt]【de‧fend‧ant】**n.**被告**a.**辯護的
If the defendant refuses to appear in court without justified reasons, the court may make a judgment by default.
被告無正當理由拒絕出庭，法院可以缺席判決。

• 字首：defend防禦
  字尾：ant做某事的人
• refuse v.拒絕
• justified a.有正當理由的
104

523.
defense [dɪˋfɛns]【de‧fense】**n.**保護、防禦、辯護
Most of our defense budget goes for conventional forces and manpower.
我們大部分的國防預算是用在常規軍事力量和人員上面。

• defense mechanism ph.防禦機制
• budget n.預算
• conventional a.普通的
• manpower n.人力資源
211

524.
defiance [dɪˋfaɪəns]【de‧fi‧ance】**n.**違抗、藐視、挑戰
His defiance of the law cost him dearly.
藐視法律使他付出沈重的代價。

• in defiance of ph.違抗
• law n.法律
94

525.
deficiency [dɪˋfɪʃənsɪ]【de‧fi‧cien‧cy】**n.**缺乏、不足、缺陷
Her entreaties were vain, and I was appointed to supply the deficiency.
她的請求是白費的，我奉命來補這個缺。
同 **famine, shortcoming, shortage**（不足）
反 **adequacy**（足夠）

• deficiency disease ph.營養缺乏病
• 字首：de在…之下
  字根：fic製作
  字尾：ency性質
• entreaty n.懇求
• appoint v.指定
131

526.
deficit [`dɛfɪsɪt] 【def·i·cit】 **n**不足額、不足

The current trade deficit indicates a serious imbalance between our import and export trade.

當前的貿易赤字表明我們的進出口貿易嚴重失調。

🔄 **shortage**（不足）
🔃 **surplus**（過剩）

115
- a foreign trade deficit **ph.**外貿逆差
- **deficit spending ph.**赤字開支
- 字首：de在…之下
  字根：fic製作
  字尾：it走動
- **indicate v.**指出

527.
define [dɪ`faɪn] 【de·fine】 **v**解釋、限定、使明確

Top management shall define quality objectives and measurements that shall be included in the business plan and used to deploy the quality policy.

最高管理者應規定賣徹品質目標和測量方法，它們應包括在經營計劃中。

🔄 **clarify, describe, explain**（解釋、使明確）

210

528.
definitive [dɪ`fɪnətɪv] 【de·fin·i·tive】 **a**決定性的、最後的、限定的 **n**限定詞

This isn't a definitive answer.

這並不是決定性的答案。

🔄 **consummate, terminative, ultimate**（最終的、具有決定性的）
🔃 **provisional, tentative**（臨時的、嘗試的）

178
- 字首：de在…之下
  字根：fin限制
  字尾：it走動
  字尾：ive有…傾向

529.
deform [dɪ`fɔrm] 【de·form】 **v**使變形、變畸形

There is no material but will deform more or less under the action of force.

在力的作用下沒有一種材料或多或少地變形。

🔄 **disfigure, deface, make ugly**（使不成形、變醜）
🔃 **beautify, embellish**（美化、裝飾）

121
- 字首：de在…之下
  字根：form形狀
- **material n.**材料
- **force n.**力

530.
defy [dɪ`faɪ] 【de·fy】 **v**公然反抗、向…挑戰

We defy the available methods to estimate them quantitatively.

我們不能採用現有的方法進行定量估算。

🔄 **disregard, ignore, resist**（公然反抗、蔑視）

94
- **available a.**可得的
- **method n.**方法
- **estimate v.**估算
- **quantitatively ad.**分量上

531.
degenerate [dɪ`dʒɛnəˌret] 【de·gen·er·ate】 **v**衰退、退化 **a**衰退的

At this point, arguments seem to degenerate into emotional displays.

在此處，爭論似乎淪為情緒發洩。

🔃 **develop, evolve**（發展、逐漸形成）

151
- 字首：de在… 之下
  字根：gen產生
  字尾：ate進行一項行動
- **argument n.**爭論
- **emotional a.**感情上的

532.
degrade [dɪ`gred] 【de·grade】 **v**使降級、使丟臉

The politician was degraded for his corruption.

這位政客因為貪汙而被降級。

🔄 **demote, lower, reduce**（降級、減少）
🔃 **exalt, promote, uplift**（提高、升起）

104
- 字首：de在…之下
  字尾：grade分數
- **politician n.**政客
- **corruption n.**貪汙

533.
delay [dɪˋle]【de·lay】**v n** 耽擱、延遲

Discrepancies might cause delay of shipment or refusal of payment.
異議會造成延遲交貨或對方拒付。

🔵 **detain, postpone**（使延期、耽擱）
🔴 **hasten, hurry**（急速、匆忙）

- 字首：de在…之下
  字尾：lay放置
- discrepancy n.差異
- refusal n.拒絕

【277】

534.
delegate [ˋdɛləgɪt]【del·e·gate】**n** 代表 **v** 委派…為代表

His ability to delegate authority not only expedited work but impelled every subordinate to perform beyond his own suspected capacity.
他的授權負責不僅促進了工作效率而且迫使每一部屬不得不竭盡所能以求速達成任務。

🔵 **agent, envoy, representative**（代表）

- 字根：leg派遣
- authority n.當局
- expedite v.促進
- subordinate a.次要的
- impel v.推動

【281】

535.
delete [dɪˋlit]【de·lete】**v** 刪除、劃掉

If you delete 50 words, we can put the whole story on one page.
如果你刪掉50個字，我們可以把整篇報導安排在一個版面上。

🔵 **censor, erase, obliterate**（減少、刪除）

【135】

536.
deliberate [dɪˋlɪbərɪt]【de·lib·er·ate】**a** 深思熟慮的、不慌不忙的 **v** 仔細考慮

She went about her work in a systematic and deliberate manner.
她工作時有條理而不慌不忙。

🔵 **consider, ponder**（仔細考慮）
🔴 **hasty**（匆促的）

- systematic a.有條理的
- manner n.方法

【121】

537.
delicate [ˋdɛləkət]【del·i·cate】**a** 脆的、嬌弱的、精美的

It contains no fibers and can therefore be used safely in areas such as hospitals or where delicate electronic instruments are manufactured or used.
本產品不含任何纖維因而可安全用於醫院製造或使用精密電子儀器等的地方。

🔵 **fragile, tender, soft**（脆的、溫和的、柔軟的）
🔴 **crude, gross**（粗糙的）

- fiber n.纖維
- hospital n.醫院
- electronic a.電子的
- instrument n.工具

【104】

538.
delimit [diˋlɪmɪt]【de·lim·it】**v** 劃定…的界限、限定

Delimit warning zone and exercise local transportation control.
劃定警戒區實行局部交通管制。

- 字首：de向下
  字根：lim限制
  字尾：it走動
- warning a.警告的
- transportation n.交通

【133】

539.
deluxe [dɪˋlʌks]【de·luxe】**a** 豪華的、高級的

Our apartments deluxe furnished with wall-to-wall carpeting and brand new furniture.
我們的公寓裝潢考究配有全新傢俱而且全部鋪設地毯。

- deluxe building ph.書本精裝
- apartment n.公寓
- furnish v.裝備
- wall-to-wall a.鋪滿整個地板的

【67】

540.

delighted [dɪˋlaɪtɪd] 【 de·light·ed 】 a高興的、快樂的

I am delighted to comply with such an order.

我非常願意遵守這命令。

🔃 **cheerful, glad, happy**（快樂的）

- comply with ph.遵守

541.

demand [dɪˋmænd] 【 de·mand 】 v n 要求、請求

If an existing partnership has exceptionally high earnings year after year, the present partners may demand a bonus as an admission of a new partner.

如果現存合夥企業每年都能獲得很高的利潤，現有合夥人可能要求新合夥人提供額外津貼。

🔃 **inquire, need, require**（查問、需要）
🔄 **furnish, provide, supply**（提供）

- demand bill ph.見票即付的支票或匯票
- demand deposit ph.活期存款
- demand loan ph.活期付款
- demand management ph.需求管理
- demand note ph.即期票據
- 字首：de向下
  字根：mand命令

542.

democracy [dɪˋmɑkrəsɪ] 【 de·moc·ra·cy 】 n 民主、民主國家

Economic growth and political democracy can develop hand in hand.

經濟增長和政治民主是可以齊頭並進的。

🔃 **commonwealth, republic**（民主政體）
🔄 **autocracy, despotism**（獨裁統治）

- 字首：demo人民
  字根：cracy政體
- growth n.成長
- hand in hand ph.連在一起地

543.

demonstrate [ˋdɛmənˌstret] 【 dem·on·strate 】 v 論證、證實、示範操作

Quality records shall be maintained to demonstrate conformance to specified requirements and the effective operation of the quality system.

品質紀錄應維持以證明產品符合規定要求與品質系統之有效運作。

🔃 **clarify, illustrate, manifest**（證明、說明）

- 字首：de向下
  字根：monstr表現
  字尾：ate進行一項行動
- maintain v.維持
- requirement n.需要

544.

demote [dɪˋmot] 【 de·mote 】 v 使降級

An employer who has lost confidence in the ability of an employee may demote him.

雇主對雇用員之能力失去信心時得予以降職。

🔃 **degrade, lower, reduce**（降級）
🔄 **promote**（提升）

- 字首：de向下
  字根：mote移動
- confidence n.信心

545.

denial [dɪˋnaɪəl] 【 de·ni·al 】 n 否認、拒絕、自制

I told the doorkeeper about the denial of all callers.

我告知傳達室不接見任何客人。

🔃 **denegation, disavowal, rejection**（否認、拒絕）
🔄 **affirmation, confirmation**（確認）

- 字首：den拒絕
  字尾：ial有…傾向
- doorkeeper n.門房
- caller n.訪問者

546.

denote [dɪˋnot] 【de‧note】 Ⅴ指示、表示

Article 3 Patent agencies stated here denote service organs that apply for patents or handle other patent-related affairs on behalf of their consignors and within their authorized powers.

第三條條例所稱專利代理機構是指接受委託人的委託，在專利許可權範圍內，辦理專利申請或者辦理其他專利事務的服務機構。

🔵 imply, indicate, signify（表示、意味）

- 字首：de向下
  字根：note標記
- patent n.專利
- affair n.事件
- on behalf of ph.代表
- consignor n.委託者

547.

denounce [dɪˋnauns] 【de‧nounce】 Ⅴ指責、告發、彈劾

Any contracting party may denounce this treaty by notification addressed to the director general.

任何締約方均可退出本條約，退約時應通知總幹事。

🔵 blame, condemn, reproach（指責、指控）

- 字首：de向下
  字尾：nounce報告
- treaty n.條約
- notification n.通知

548.

dentist [ˋdɛntɪst] 【den‧tist】 ⋂牙科醫生

He had an appointment to see the dentist but he chickened out of it at the last moment.

他已預約牙醫但時間到了卻不敢去。

- 字首：dent牙齒
  字尾：ist動作的實踐者
- appointment n.約定

549.

deny [dɪˋnaɪ] 【de‧ny】 Ⅴ否認、拒絕給予

We should not deny the importance of authority and should centralize power wherever necessary, otherwise, time will be wasted, at the least.

我們不能否定權威，該集中的要集中否則會耽誤時間。

🔵 refute, reject, renounce（否定、拒絕）
🔴 affirm, concede, confirm（確認）

- deny oneself ph.節制
- deny oneself ph.不會見
- centralize v.集中
- otherwise ad.否則
- waste v.浪費

550.

departure [dɪˋpartʃə] 【de‧part‧ure】 ⋂離開、違背、偏差

They accepted his judgment that they had better put off their departure.

他們接受了他所提出的延期的意見。

🔵 exit, leaving（離開）
🔴 arrival（抵達）

- departure lobby ph.
  出境大廳
- departure lounge ph.候機室
- departure tax stamp
  ph.離境印花稅票
- departure board ph.飛機
  起飛
- put off ph.拖延

551.

depict [dɪˋpɪkt] 【de‧pict】 Ⅴ描述、描寫

The sales budget is intended to depict what products will be sold in what quantities at what prices.

銷售預算主要用於描述企業銷售什麼產品、數量是多少和價格如何。

🔵 characterize, describe, portray（描出、敘述）

- 字首：de向下
  字根：pict畫、繪
- intend v.指出

552.

deport [dɪˋport] 【de‧port】 Ⅴ移送、驅逐

This would make it easier to track students, revoke their visas and presumably deport them if they drop out.

這樣對外國留學生的追蹤工作、拒簽工作更容易進行，而且更能把那些中途退學的留學生驅逐出境。

- deport oneself ph.持…舉
  止
- revoke v.撤回
- drop out ph.退出學校

553.
deposit [dɪ`pazɪt] [de·pos·it] **V n** 放置、沉澱、儲存
I want to deposit these checks into my savings account.
我想把這些支票存進我的儲蓄帳戶。
同 lay, place, pledge (放置、保證金)
反 draw (開支票)

- deposit account ph.儲蓄存款
- deposit ship ph.存款單
- 字首：de向下
  字根：pos放置
  字尾：it走動

211

D

554.
depreciation [dɪ͵priʃɪˋeʃən] [de·pre·ci·a·tion]
n 跌價、貶值、輕視
Depreciation of our currency makes it easier for domestic firms to compete with foreign firms.
本國貨幣幣值下跌使本國企業較易與外國企業競爭。
同 diminution (降低)

- the rate of depreciation ph.折舊率
- 字首：de在…之下
  字根：preci價值
  字尾：ation性質
- domestic a.國內的
- compete v.競爭

104

555.
depress [dɪ`prɛs] [de·press] **V** 使沮喪、壓低、使蕭條
Does mass unemployment depress wages?
大量人口失業會使工資降低嗎？
同 deject, lower, reduce (使沮喪)
反 encourage, inspire (鼓勵、刺激)

- 字首：de向下
  字尾：press壓擠
- mass a.大量的
- unemployment n.失業
- wage n.薪資

205

556.
deprive [dɪ`praɪv] [de·prive] **V** 剝奪、使喪失
To deprive of a benefit or a part of one's wages, especially as a punishment.
從工資中扣掉一部分或扣掉利益用來表示懲罰。
同 take away, take from (剝奪、從…奪走)
反 entitle, impose (給…權力)

- deprive of ph.剝奪
- benefit n.利益
- punishment n.處罰

132

557.
derive [dɪ`raɪv] [de·rive] **V** 取得、衍生出、起源
It is from their celebrities that many Americans derive their sense of nationhood.
許多美國人從他們的名人身上找到了民族自豪感。
同 acquire, obtain, secure (取得、得到)

- derive from ph.由…得來
- derived image ph.攝取影像
- derived object ph.衍生物件
- celebrity n.名人
- nationhood n.國家的獨立

128

558.
descend [dɪ`sɛnd] [de·scend] **V** 下降、下斜、來自於
To descend to particulars, just what work do you do every day?
現在談具體的，你每天到底做些什麼工作？
同 decline, fall, plunge (下來、下降)
反 ascend, rise (上升)

- descend from ph.起源於
- descend on / upon ph.突然襲擊
- descend to ph.向下延伸至

146

559.
describe [dɪ`skraɪb] [de·scribe] **V** 描述、描繪、形容
Would you be able to describe a typical day on the job?
您能描述一下這個職位的日常工作內容嗎？
同 characterize, depict, portray (描繪、敘述)

- 字首：de向下
  字根：scribe寫
- typical a.典型的

257

560.

deserve [dɪ`zɜv] 【de·serve】 ☑該得、應受

About income, I think most people deserve more than what they get.

談到收入,我想大多數人都應得到比他們現在得到的更多些。

- **You deserve it.**你罪有應得。
- 字首:de在…之下
- 字根:serve奴隸
- income n.收入

73

561.

desktop [`dɛsktɑp] 【desk·top】 ☐桌上型電腦

In some versions, you can even drag tiny window thumbnails from one desktop to another.

在一些版本中你甚至可以將這些微型視窗從一個桌面拖曳到另一個桌面。

- **desktop operating system** ph.桌面作業系統
- **desktop publishing** ph.小規模出版業
- **desktop video** ph.桌面影像系統

225

562.

design [dɪ`zaɪn] 【de·sign】 ☐計畫、圖謀 ☑設計、計劃

A new design concept which includes luxury, beauty of the new cell phone will be available in the market next month.

全新設計理念包含豪華美觀流線型的手機即將在下個月上市。

⚫ **depict, picture, sketch**(設計、構思)

- **design management** ph.設計管理
- **design management plan** ph.設計管理計畫
- 字首:de在…之下
- 字根:sign標記
- concept n.概念

94

563.

designate [`dɛzɪɡ‚net] 【de·sign·ate】 ☑指定、稱呼、委任 ☐指定的

We'd like to designate New York as the loading port, for it has larger accommodation capacity.

我們想指定紐約港作為裝船港因為它的輸送量大。

⚫ **indicate, specify, nominate**(指出、任命)

- loading n.裝貨
- port n.港口
- accommodation n.調節
- capacity n.生產力

184

564.

desire [dɪ`zaɪr] 【de·sire】 ☑☐渴望、要求

I can select anyone I desire to fill vacant positions.

我可以選我喜歡的人去填補這些空缺。

⚫ **covet, fancy, wish**(渴望)
⚫ **despair**(絕望)

- select v.選擇
- fill v.填補
- vacant a.空缺的

105

565.

desolate [`dɛslɪt] 【de·sol·ate】 ☐荒蕪的、孤寂的 ☑使孤寂

The foreigner felt desolate in the strange country.

外國人住在異國感到孤寂。

⚫ **barren, empty, vacant**(荒蕪的)
⚫ **cheerful, happy, joyful**(快樂的)

- 字首:de在…之下 字根:sol單獨 字尾:ate有…狀態的

112

566.

despise [dɪ`spaɪz] 【des·pise】 ☑鄙視、看不起

We should not despise plain features, or a laborious yet honest occupation.

我們不應該看不起相貌平常的人,也不應該看不起辛苦而正直的職業。

⚫ **disdain, loathe, scorn**(鄙視、厭惡)
⚫ **appreciate, esteem, respect**(感激、尊敬)

- plain a.樸素的
- feature n.相貌
- laborious a.費力的
- occupation n.職業

567.

dessert [dɪˋzɜt] 【des·sert】 ⓝ餐後甜點

After dinner, we had ice-cream for dessert.

吃過晚飯之後我們吃霜淇淋作為甜點。

ⓢ **hors d'oeuvre** (開胃小菜)

- 此單字易與desert (n.沙漠) 混淆
- dessert wine ph.飯後甜酒
- dessertspoon n.甜點匙

61

D

568.

despair [dɪˋspɛr] 【des·pair】 ⓥⓝ絕望

Defeat after defeat filled us with despair.

接二連三的失敗使我們感到絕望。

ⓢ **depression, grief, sadness** (沮喪、悲傷)
ⓐ **desire, hope, optimism** (希望、樂觀)

- defeat n.失敗
- fill with ph.充滿

211

569.

destination [ˌdɛstəˋneʃən] 【des·ti·na·tion】 ⓝ目的地、目標、終點

The buyer shall undertake in-land transshipment from the quay or container yard at the destination to the storage place at his own cost.

買方應自費負責將貨物從目的港碼頭或集裝箱貨場轉運到買方倉儲地。

ⓢ **ambition, goal, objective** (目標、目的地)

- destination wedding ph.旅遊結婚
- undertake v.負責
- transshipment n.轉載
- quay n.碼頭
- storage n.儲藏

243

570.

destruction [dɪˋstrʌkʃən] 【de·struc·tion】 ⓝ破壞、毀滅

Over confidence was the reason of his destruction.

自負是他垮臺的原因。

ⓢ **demolition, implosion, wreckage** (破壞)
ⓐ **construction, establishment** (建立)

- 字首：de在…之下
字根：struc建立
字尾：tion狀態
- confidence n.信心

156

571.

detach [dɪˋtætʃ] 【de·tach】 ⓥ使分離、分開、派遣

He had to detach himself from social activities for the time being in order to concentrate on his studies.

為了專心致志於學業，他只好暫時拒絕社交活動。

ⓢ **separate, unfasten, delegate** (分開、派遣)
ⓐ **attach, join** (繫上)

- 字首：de在…之下
字根：tact接觸
- concentrate v.專心

211

572.

detail [ˋditel] 【de·tail】 ⓝ詳情、細節 ⓥ詳述、選派

The order form means the form on which a buyer can fill in the detail of his intended purchase as an order to supply.

訂貨表格指訂單的貨品供應表格，買家把意欲購買的細節填寫便可。

ⓢ **elaborate, itemize, commission** (詳述、選派)

- detail-oriented person ph.吹毛求疵的人
- 字首：de相反
字根：tail切、減
- supply v.提供

204

573.

detain [dɪˋten] 【de·tain】 ⓥ留住、拘留、耽擱

The port drug administration shall adopt mandatory administrative measures to seal up and detain all the drugs.

港口藥品監督管理局應當對已進口的全部藥品採取查封、扣押的行政強制措施。

ⓢ **delay, retard** (留住、使耽擱)
ⓐ **free, liberate** (自由)

- 字首：de在…之下
字根：tain握、持
- drug n.藥物
- administration n.管理
- mandatory a.命令的

155

574.
detect [dɪˋtɛkt]【de·tect】**v** 發現、察覺
Do I detect a note of irony in your voice?
聽起來你是在說反話吧？
同 **discover, perceive, recognize**（發現、察覺）
反 **conceal, hide**（隱藏）

• note **n.** 注意
• irony **n.** 諷刺
• voice **n.** 聲音

575.
deteriorate [dɪˋtɪrɪəˏret]【de·te·ri·o·rate】**v** 惡化、墮落
The planned quality of the product does not deteriorate.
規定的產品品質沒有下降。
同 **decline, degenerate, worsen**（使惡化）
反 **ameliorate, limit**（限制）

576.
determine [dɪˋtɜmɪn]【de·ter·mine】**v** 決定、確定、影響
Since public agencies can receive subsidies, considerations of profitability do not determine the difference between floor and ceiling prices.
由於公共機構可以得到補貼所以最低價與最高價差額並不決定於賺取利潤的考慮。
同 **decide, ascertain, affect**（決定、確定、影響）
反 **hesitate**（猶豫）

• receive **v.** 接受
• subsidy **n.** 津貼
• consideration **n.** 考慮
• profitability **n.** 有利
• floor **n.** 底價
• ceiling **n.** 最大限額

577.
detest [dɪˋtɛst]【de·test】**v** 厭惡、憎惡
I detest all affectation.
我厭惡一切矯揉造作的行為。
同 **hate, loathe, scorn**（厭惡）
反 **adore, love**（喜愛）

• affectation **n.** 裝模作樣

578.
detract [dɪˋtrækt]【de·tract】**v** 降低、減損、使分心
Getting help from others won't detract from your achievement.
向他人尋求幫助不會減少你的成就。
同 **divert**（使分心）

• 字首：de 向下
  字根：tract 拉
• achievement **n.** 成就

579.
devalue [diˋvælju]【de·val·ue】**v** 降低價值、減少重要性
Be selective in distributing your cards. Otherwise you may devalue them, or hoard them.
不要亂發你的名片，不然你不是令你的名片貶值就是使它們沒有發揮應有的作用。

• 同 devaluate
• 字首：de 在之下
  字尾：value 價值
• distribute **v.** 散佈
• hoard **v.** 隱藏

580.
deviate [ˋdivɪˏet]【de·vi·ate】**v** 脫離、越軌
Our sample might be afraid slightly to deviate from specification required, please advice if acceptable.
我公司所提供的樣品恐怕與所要求的規格略有不同，能否接受請告知。
同 **deflect, divergent**（偏斜、轉向）

• 字首：de 向下
  字根：via 道路
  字尾：ate 行動
• specification **n.** 規格
• advice **n.** 通知

581.

device [dɪ`vaɪs] 【 de‧vice 】 **n** 設備、裝置、謀略

The Safety Assessor performs clinical assessment of information on reported adverse drug and device experiences including accurate data entry of the assessment into the safety database.

安全評估員負責對所報告的藥品和醫療機械不良事件相關資訊進行臨床評估包括將評估結果準確輸入到安全資料庫中。

⑩▸ implement, instrument, scheme（設備、計畫）

> **121**
> • assessor n.評估員
> • clinical a.客觀的
> • assessment n.評價
> • adverse a.不利的
> • accurate a.正確的

582.

devise [dɪ`vaɪz] 【 de‧vise 】 **v** 設計、發明、遺贈

We must devise a scheme for earning money during the vacation.

我們必須想出在假期中賺錢的計劃。

⑩▸ create, invent, plan（設計、發明、策劃）

> **132**
> • scheme n.計畫
> • vacation n.假期

583.

devote [dɪ`vot] 【 de‧vote 】 **v** 奉獻、把…專用

He withdrew from newspaper work to devote his full time to writing.

他退出新聞工作以便專心寫作。

⑩▸ assign, consecrate, dedicate（奉獻、專心於）

> **144**
> • devote oneself to ph.
> 專心於
> • withdraw v.離開

584.

devoted [dɪ`votɪd] 【 de‧vot·ed 】 **a** 獻身的、虔誠的、摯愛的

Abalard was Lord Haart's the most devoted follower.

阿芭拉是哈特領主最忠實的追隨者。

⑩▸ dedicated, faithful, loyal（熱心的、忠實的）

> **138**
> • devoted to ph.專心致力於
> 工作
> • follower n.追隨者

585.

diagnose [`daɪəgnoz] 【 di‧ag·nose 】 **v** 診斷

A system 370 based IBM licensed program used to monitor a network, manage it, and diagnose its problems.

IBM公司銷售的一種以370系統為基礎的特許程式，用它來監視網路的工作情況管理IBM的電腦網路以及診斷網路中可能出現的問題。

⑩▸ analyze, deduce, interpret（診斷、分析）

> **151**
> • licensed a.得到許可的
> • monitor v.監控
> • network n.網路

586.

diagram [`daɪə‚græm] 【 di‧a·gram 】 **n** 圖表 **v** 用圖解方式表示

We reproduced a same working schematic diagram.

我們複製了一份同樣的施工簡圖。

⑩▸ graph, figure, plot（圖表）

> **212**
> • 字首：dia穿越
> 字尾：gram圖像
> • reproduce v.複製
> • schematic a.圖式的

587.

dialogue [`daɪə‚lɔg] 【 di‧a·logue 】 **n** 對話、交談、意見交換

The dialogue deadlocked over the wage issue.

交談因工資問題而僵持住了。

⑩▸ conversation, speech, words（對話）

⑫▸ monologue（獨白）

> **117**
> • 字首：dia穿越
> 字尾：logue說話
> • deadlock v.僵持

588.
diameter [daɪˋæmətə] 【di·am·e·ter】 n 直徑、倍數
The diameter of the column has now decreased to 2,000 feet.
這時水柱的直徑已減少到2000英尺。
反 radius（半徑）

- column n.圓柱
- decrease v.減少
- foot n.英呎

589.
dictate [ˋdɪktet] 【dic·tate】 v 口述、聽寫、命令 n 命令
Assuming that both goods are competitively supplied, the relative costs of each good will dictate relative prices.
假設這兩種商品是在有競爭的情況下供給的，那麼每種商品的相對成本就能確定其相對價格。
同 direct, instruct, rule（命令、要求、指定）
反 obey, submit（遵守）

- 字根：dict說、言
  字尾：ate進行一項行動
- competitively ad.有競爭地
- relative a.相關的

590.
dictionary [ˋdɪkʃəˏɛrɪ] 【dic·tion·ar·y】 n 字典、辭典
He cooperated with his colleagues in compiling this dictionary.
他和同事們協力編纂這部辭典。
同 glossary, lexicon（辭典、專業辭典）

- 字根：dict說、言
  字尾：ion性質
  字尾：ary領域
- cooperate v.合作
- colleague n.同僚
- compile v.編輯

591.
dictum [ˋdɪktəm] 【dic·tum】 n 格言、名言
"Don't put off till tomorrow what should be done today" is the dictum of unanimous common sense.
「今日事今日畢」是一致公認的名言。
同 proverb（諺語）

- 字根：dict說、言
- put off ph.推遲
- unanimous a.一致同意的
- common sense ph.常識

592.
difficult [ˋdɪfəˏkəlt] 【dif·fi·cult】 a 困難的、難相處的
Bad managers are a dime a dozen but a good one is diffcult to find!
壞的老闆簡直多如牛毛，碰見一個好的真難！
同 arduous, hard, rough（難的、困難的）
反 easy, simple（簡單的）

- a dime a donze ph.太平常

593.
digest [daɪˋdʒɛst] 【di·gest】 v 消化、領悟、整理 n 摘要
His rudeness is hard to digest.
他的莽撞令人難以理解。
同 absorb, ingest（消化、吸收）

- 字首：di向下
  字尾：gest運送
- rudeness n.無禮貌

594.
diffuse [dɪˋfjuz] 【dif·fuse】 v 擴散、傳播 a 散開的、冗長的
The Aegean Trade Company Ltd will diffuse olive oil's culture and conduct healthy life in coming day.
此貿易公司在未來的日子裡將以傳播橄欖油文化引導全新健康生活概念為已任。

- 字首：dif分散
  字尾：fuse流、瀉
- olive n.橄欖
- cultre n.文化

595.
dignity [ˋdɪgnətɪ]【dig·ni·ty】 n.尊嚴、尊貴

A man's dignity depends not upon his wealth but upon his character.

一個人的高尚與否不取決於他的財富而是取決於他的品格。

同 **stature, majesty, nobility**（威嚴、高貴）
反 **indignity**（輕蔑）

- depend upon ph.視…而定
- wealth n.財富
- character n.性格

596.
digital [ˋdɪdʒɪtl]【dig·i·tal】 a.數字的、指狀的 n.鍵

Digital products require humans to do the heavy lifting.

數位產品需要人來完成大量工作。

- digital asset management ph.數位資產管理
- digital camera n.數位相機
- heavy a.大量的

597.
dilemma [dəˋlɛmə]【di·lem·ma】 n.困境、進退兩難

I was on the horns of a dilemma when I was offered another job.

別人又給了我一個工作我不由得進退兩難。

- horn n.觸角

598.
diligent [ˋdɪlədʒənt]【dil·i·gent】 a.勤勉的、費盡心血的

One can become the master of his trade provided he is diligent and tries hard.

只要自己努力行行出狀元。

同 **industrious, hard-working**（勤勉的、用功的）
反 **idle, lazy**（懶惰的）

- master n.大師

599.
dilute [daɪˋlut]【di·lute】 v.稀釋、削弱

In real life, all of our collective experiences dilute the impact of any single one.

在現實生活中，我們積累的全部經歷會沖淡任何單一事件對我們的影響。

同 **reduce, weaken**（稀釋、使薄弱）
反 **dense**（密集）

- collective a.收集的
- impact n.影響

600.
dim [dɪm]【dim】 a.暗淡的、模糊的 v.變模糊

However dim the prospects may be today, we intend to continue this effort.

無論今日希望如何黯淡我們都打算繼續努力。

同 **darkish, faint, vague**（模糊的、微暗的）
反 **bright, clear, light**（亮的、清楚的）

- dim sum ph.點心（中國廣東話譯音）
- dim-out n.燈火管制
- dim-wit n.傻瓜
- prospect n.前途
- effort n.努力

601.
dimension [dɪˋmɛnʃən]【di·men·sion】 n.尺寸、面積、範圍

You furnished a whole new dimension to their efforts.

你為他們的工作開創了一個全新的領域。

同 **capacity, range, size**（面積、大小）

- 字首：di分開
  字根：mens測量
  字尾：ion性質
- furnish v.供應

602.
diminish [də`mɪnɪʃ] 【di‧min‧ish】 **Ⅴ**減少、變小、削弱權勢

Paying taxes would diminish profits and increase the risk of loss by confiscation of the goods.

納稅會減少他們的利潤並增加商品被徵收的風險。

同 decrease, lessen, reduce（減少、減小）

反 increase, magnify, raise（增加、變大）

- 字首：di向下
  字根：min小
  字尾：ish使成為
- profit n.利益
- confiscation n.徵收

603.
diploma [dɪ`plomə] 【di‧plo‧ma】 **n**畢業文憑、執照、文書

Regardless of whether or not it is for the sake of a diploma or a promotion, a person's life often cannot help but face countless tests.

無論是為了升學文憑還是為了職稱，人的一生中往往不得不面對無數次的考試。

同 certificate, degree（文憑、證書）

- regardless of ph.不管
- promotion n.提升
- countless a.數不盡的

181

604.
directory [də`rɛktərɪ] 【di‧rec‧to‧ry】 **n**工商名錄、使用手冊 **a**指導的

Functionally, this dialog offers two things: it lets users name a file, and it lets them choose which directory to place it in.

從功能而言，對話方塊提供了兩種功能，即允許用戶命名檔案並且選擇存放的目錄。

同 catalogue, handbook, manual（目錄、手冊）

- directory enquiries ph.
  電話號查詢臺
- 字首：direct指導
- 字尾：ory領域
- functionally ad.功能地
- file n.文件夾

145

605.
disable [dɪs`ebl] 【dis‧a‧ble】 **Ⅴ**使失去能力、使傷殘、使無資格

If problems continue, disable or remove any newly installed hardware or software.

如果問題依然存在，禁用或者移除最近安裝的軟硬體。

同 cripple, debilitate, enfeeble（使無能、使殘廢）

反 enable（使成為可能）

- 字首：dis不、無
  字尾：able能、可以
- remove v.移除
- install v.安裝

123

606.
disaster [dɪ`zæstə] 【dis‧as‧ter】 **n**災難、不幸、徹底失敗

GM is so big and powerful that it can withstand a disaster or two.

通用公司是個大且實力雄厚的公司，遇到一、兩次災難還是頂得住。

同 casualty, misfortune, tragedy（災害、不幸）

- disaster area ph.災區
- disaster film / movie
  ph.災難片
- disaster loss ph.災害損失
- withstand v.禁得起

177

607.
disburse [dɪs`bɝs] 【dis‧burse】 **Ⅴ**支付、支出

On approval, we will disburse the fund to your designated bank account directly.

一經批核貸款將於扣除手續費後直接存入您指定的銀行帳戶。

- approval n.准許
- fund n.資金
- designated a.指定的

125

608.
discard [dɪs`kɑrd] 【dis‧card】 **Ⅴn**屏棄、拋棄

Select the refined and discard the crude.

取其精華，去其糟粕。

同 get rid of, reject, scrap（拋棄）

- refined a.精煉的
- crude a.粗糙的

81

609.
discern [dɪˋzɝn] 【 dis‧cern 】 **V**辨別、認識、領悟
We could discern from his appearance that he was upset.
我們從他的樣子可以察覺出他的不悅。
同 behold, realize, recognize（看出、察覺到、領悟）

- appearance n.外表
- upset a.心煩的

610.
discharge [dɪsˋtʃɑrdʒ] 【 dis‧charge 】 **V n**排出、解雇、釋放
232
A person insufficient to the discharge of his duties.
一個不能執行自己任務的人。
同 dismiss, release, unload（卸下、釋放）
反 charge（索價）

- insufficient a.不足的
- duty n.責任

611.
discipline [ˋdɪsəplɪn] 【 dis‧ci‧pline 】 **V n**紀律、訓練、懲罰
132
He must both assemble power and discipline its use.
他必須聚集力量，另一方面又要限制力量的使用。
同 chastise, groom, train（懲戒、訓練）

- assemble v.聚集

612.
disclose [dɪsˋkloz] 【 dis‧close 】 **V**露出、透露
125
The company and its controlling shareholders shall timely and
accurately disclose relevant information to all shareholders.
上市公司及其控股股東應及時準確地向全體股東披露有關資訊。
同 expose, reveal, uncover（使露出、顯露）
反 conceal, hide（隱藏）

- 字首：dis無、不
  字根：close關閉
- shareholder n.股東
- relevant a.有關的

613.
discount [ˋdɪskaunt] 【 dis‧count 】 **n**折扣、貼現率**V**商品打折
132
We have adjusted our price and given you a special discount
of 3 percent.
我們對價格作了調整，給你們百分之三的優惠折扣。
同 deduct, remove, subtract（打折扣、減少）
反 premium（加價）

- discount bond ph. 貼現債券
- discount rate ph.折扣率
- discount shop ph.折扣店
- discount window ph.貼現窗口
- 字首：dis分開
  字尾：count計算
- adjust v.校準

614.
discourage [dɪsˋkɝɪdʒ] 【 dis‧cour‧age 】 **V**使沮喪、勸阻、不允許
189
We discourage waste of time on items irrelevant to the object
of study.
我們避免把時間浪費在與研究物件無關的專案上。
同 deter, prevent, hinder（阻止、使沮喪）
反 encourage（鼓勵）

- 字首：dis無、不
  字尾：courage鼓勵
- waste n.浪費
- irrelevant a.不恰當的

615.
discover [dɪsˋkʌvɚ] 【 dis‧cov‧er 】 **V**發現、發覺
251
I was horrified to discover that we didn't have any dealers'
orders to build these cars.
我吃驚地發現我們生產這些車子根本就沒有收到經銷商的訂單。
同 expose, observe, reveal（發現、發覺）
反 miss（錯失）

- 字首：dis無、不
  字尾：cover蓋
- horrify v.使恐懼
- dealer n.商人

616.
discredit [dɪsˋkrɛdɪt]【dis·cred·it】**v** 使丟臉、不信任、懷疑

They no longer try to discredit the technology itself.

他們不再試圖懷疑這種技術本身。

同 **doubt, humiliate, shame**（懷疑、使丟臉）

反 **credit**（相信）

• 字首：**dis** 無、不
  字尾：**credit** 相信
• **technology** n.技術

131

617.
discrepancy [dɪˋskrɛpənsɪ]【dis·crep·ancy】**n** 不一致、差異

The price tag says $100 and you charged me for $120. How do you explain the discrepancy?

貨物標籤上寫的是100美元，你向我索價120美元這個差額該怎麼解釋？

同 **divergence, inconsistency, variance**（差異、不同）

• **tag** n.標籤
• **charge** v.索價

94

618.
discrete [dɪˋskrit]【dis·crete】**a** 分離的、不連接的

A project's objectives are usually very clear cut and often divisible into discrete component parts.

專案的目標通常十分明確並且可以分解成若干個子項目。

• **discrete data** ph.離散數據
• 字首：**dis** 向下
  字根：**crete** 分離
• **divisible** a.可分割的
• **component** a.構成的

84

619.
discriminate [dɪˋskrɪmə͵net]【dis·crim·i·nate】
v 區別、辨別、差別待遇

They may not limit, segregate, classify, discharge, or force retirement upon their employees so as to discriminate against persons in this age group.

不可以對雇員限制、區分、解聘、或強迫退休造成對此年齡段的歧視。

同 **distinguish, segregate, separate**（區別、識別）

• **discriminate against** ph.歧視
• **classify** v.將…分類
• **retirement** n.退休

121

620.
discuss [dɪˋskʌs]【dis·cuss】**v** 討論、商談

I wanted to discuss my company's outstanding account.

我想談一下我公司豐厚的利潤。

同 **consult, debate, talk over**（討論、商談）

• **discussion** n.討論
• **outstanding** a.傑出的
• **account** n.利益

251

621.
disease [dɪˋziz]【dis·ease】**n** 疾病、弊病 **v** 使生病

The epidemic disease was kept under control by the authorities' vigorous action.

當局採取有力措施控制住此種傳染病的蔓延。

同 **ailment, illness, sickness**（病、疾病）

反 **health**（健康）

• **epidemic** a.流行性的
• **vigorous** a.強有力的

211

622.
disguise [dɪsˋgaɪz]【dis·guise】**v n** 假裝、掩飾、隱瞞

Losing that job was a blessing in disguise really, and I found a much more enjoyable career.

失去那份工作真的是塞翁失馬知禍非福，我找到我更喜歡的職業。

同 **conceal, hide, mask**（掩飾、隱瞞）

反 **show**（顯示）

• **blessing** n.幸事
• **enjoyable** a.快樂的
• **career** n.事業

101

623.
disgust [dɪsˋgʌst] 【 dis·gust 】 **v** **n** 厭惡、作嘔

With a gesture of infinite understanding, disgust, noble indifference, he threw up his hands and started to walk out.

他帶著無限的瞭解、厭惡、儼然不屑的神色及無可奈何地站起身就走出去。

⊕ **nauseate, revolt, sicken**（使作嘔、使厭煩）
⊗ **delight, please**（使高興）

- gesture n.姿態
- infinite a.無限的
- noble a.高貴的
- indifference n.漠不關心

624.
disincline [ˏdɪsɪnˋklaɪn] 【 dis·in·cline 】 **v** 使不願

Her delicate constitution disinclined her from such an arduous job.

她纖弱的體質使得她不願擔任如此艱巨的工作。

⊗ **incline**（有意）

- delicate a.纖弱的
- constitution n.體質
- arduous a.艱鉅的

625.
dismay [dɪsˋme] 【 dis·may 】 **v** **n** 沮喪、驚慌

We were all looking at each other in dismay and at a loss for words.

我們都面面相覷不知說什麼才好。

⊕ **bewilder, confuse, frighten**（使驚慌、使沮喪）
⊗ **cheer**（歡呼）

- at a loss ph.困惑不解

626.
dismiss [dɪsˋmɪs] 【 dis·miss 】 **v** 解散、離開、解雇

The boss threatened to dismiss him from his job, but it's all a bluff.

老闆威脅說要解雇他但這不過是恐嚇而已。

⊕ **discharge, expel, fire**（離開、遣散、解雇）
⊗ **assemble, employ**（聚集、雇用）

- 字首：dis離開
  字根：miss送
- threaten v.威脅
- bluff n.嚇唬

627.
dispatch [dɪˋspætʃ] 【 dis·patch 】 **n** 派遣、發送、迅速處理

I'd like to reconfirm the dispatch date on those ES-37S we ordered a month ago.

我們一個月前定購的那批ES-37S我要再確認一下，什麼時候出貨。

⊕ **forward, send, transmit**（派遣、發送）

- dispatch box ph.公文箱
- dispatch list ph.派工單
- dispatch rider ph.騎機車
  或騎馬之通訊員
- reconfirm v.再確認

628.
dispel [dɪˋspɛl] 【 dis·pel 】 **v** 驅除、消除

The company is trying to dispel rumors about a take-over.

公司力圖澄清有關控制權轉移的流言。

⊕ **disperse, scatter**（驅散、消除）

- 字首：dis向下
  字根：pel驅趕
- rumor n.謠言

629.
dispense [dɪˋspɛns] 【 dis·pense 】 **v** 分配、執行、免除

Let's dispense with formalities and get down to work.

讓我們免去那些俗套並開始工作吧。

⊕ **allocate, distribute, grant**（分配、分發）

- dispense with ph.省掉
- formality n.拘泥形式
- get down to ph.開始認真
  對待

630.
disperse [dɪ`spɜs] 【dis·perse】 **V** 驅散、傳播

They talked like this for a few minutes, while the other occupants in the room began to disperse to their various tasks.

他們這麼交談了幾分鐘，屋裡的其他人紛紛離去做各自的事情了。

🔁► **distribute, scatter, spread** (傳播、散發)
🔀► **collect, withdraw** (收集、收回)

- occupant n.居住者
- various a.各種各樣的
- task n.工作

131

631.
displace [dɪs`ples] 【dis·place】 **V** 移開、取代、撤換

Televisions have displaced motion pictures as American most popular form of entertainment.

電視取代了電影的地位成了美國最為普遍的娛樂方式。

🔁► **disturb, supersede, unseat** (移開、廢棄)
🔀► **establish, place** (建立、放置)

- 字首：dis分開
  字尾：place放置
- motion picture ph.電影
- popular a.受歡迎的
- entertainment n.娛樂

173

632.
display [dɪ`sple] 【dis·play】 **N** 陳列、顯示、炫耀

The store displays its wares in the window.

商店把各種物品陳列在櫥窗內。

🔁► **flaunt, exhibit, illustrate** (展示、表現)
🔀► **conceal, hide** (隱藏)

- 字首：dis分開
  字尾：play表演
- ware n.商品

124

633.
disport [dɪ`sport] 【dis·port】 **V** **N** 娛樂

Every Sunday, they disport themselves either in the parks or in the mountains.

每週日他們或去公園或去爬山作為娛樂。

84

634.
disposal [dɪ`spoz!] 【dis·posal】 **N** 處理、配置

The sanitation department is in charge of garbage disposal.

環境衛生部門負責處理垃圾。

🔁► **elimination, release, removal** (處置、解決)

- 字首：dis分開
  字根：pos放置
- al與…有關
- sanitation n.公共衛生
- garbage n.垃圾

161

635.
disposition [ˌdɪspə`zɪʃən] 【dis·po·si·tion】 **N** 性格、傾向、配置

The fact that the seller is authorized to retain documents controlling the disposition of the goods does not affect the passage of the risk.

賣方受權保留控制貨物處置權的單據，並並不影響風險的轉移。

🔁► **character, inclination, temperament** (性情、氣質)

- 字首：dis分開
  字根：pos放置
  字尾：ition性質
- retain v.維持

157

636.
disproof [dɪs`pruf] 【dis·proof】 **N** 反證、反駁

He could not believe even with the disproof before his eyes.

連反證都擺在眼前他還不能相信。

- 字首：dis相反
  字尾：proof證據

112

637.
dispute [dɪ`spjut] 【dis·pute】 **V** **N** 爭論、質疑

We're in dispute with the management about overtime rates.

我們正與資方交涉加班費問題。

🔁► **argue, debate, quarrel** (爭論、爭執)
🔀► **agree** (同意)

- 字首：dis無、不
  字根：pute考慮
- overtime a.超時的

143

638.
disregard [ˌdɪsrɪˋgɑrd]【dis‧regard】 **v.n.**不理會、忽視、漠視

More and more entrepreneurs know that if they disregard the well-being of their fellow staff and workers, their ventures will implode.

越來越多的企業家意識到如果他們不關心員工的話，最終會對企業造成不利影響。

同 ignore, neglect, skip（不理、忽視）
反 regard（注視）

- 字首：dis無、不
- 字尾：regard注視
- entrepreneur n.企業家
- staff n.總稱全體員工
- venture n.冒險
- implode v.內暴

194

639.
disrupt [dɪsˋrʌpt]【dis‧rupt】 **v.**使分裂、使混亂 **a.**破裂的

Civil activities shall have respect for social ethics and shall not harm the public interest, undermine state economic plans or disrupt social economic order.

民事活動應當尊重社會公德，不得損害社會公共利益，破壞國家經濟計劃擾亂社會經濟秩序。

同 disorder, jumble, tangle（使混亂）

- 字首：dis分開
- 字根：rupt破
- civil a.國民的
- ethics n.倫理學
- undermine v.暗中破壞

89

640.
disseminate [dɪˋsɛməˌnet]【dis‧sem‧i‧nate】 **v.**散播、宣傳

It is an important purpose of hosting the Olympic Games to carry forward and disseminate the Olympic spirit.

宏揚和傳播奧林匹克精神是舉辦奧運會的重要宗旨。

- host v.主辦
- forward ad.向前
- spirit n.精神

94

641.
dissent [dɪˋsɛnt]【dis‧sent】 **v.n.**不同意、不信奉國教

He felt her shoulders give a wriggle of dissent.

他察覺到她的肩膀扭動表示反對。

同 demur, differ, disagree（提異議）
反 assent, consent（同意）

- dissent from ph.與⋯意見不一
- 字首：dis分開
- 字根：sent感覺
- shoulder n.肩膀
- wriggle n.扭動

110

642.
dissident【dis‧si‧dent】 **a.n.**持不同意見的(人)、不贊成的(人)

The authorities decide to damp down the dissidents' activities by imposing a curfew.

當局決定實行宵禁以抑制持不同政見者的活動。

- 字首：dis無、不
- 字根：sid坐
- 字尾：ent⋯狀態的
- damp v.抑制
- curfew n.宵禁

81

643.
dissipate [ˋdɪsəˌpet]【dis‧si‧pate】 **v.**驅散、消失、浪費

The office boy tried to dissipate the smoke by opening a window of the meeting room.

辦公室小弟打開窗子試圖使會議室內煙消散。

同 dispel, spread, waste（驅散、浪費）
反 accumulate（累積）

- office boy ph.辦公室小弟
- smoke n.煙霧
- window n.窗戶
- meeting room ph.會議室

104

644.
distill [dɪsˋtɪl]【dis‧till】 **v.**蒸餾、提煉、滲出

Economists adjust current prices for the rate of inflation in order to distill out the real gains in production.

經濟學家通過扣除通貨膨脹因素可以得出生產的實際效益。

同 dribble, gasify, squeeze（滴下、蒸餾）

- adjust v.調節
- current a.現今的
- inflation n.通貨膨脹

645.
distinct [dɪˋstɪŋkt]【dis‧tinct】**a** 清楚的、顯著的、難得的

With increasing specialization, however, the publishing became, by the 19th century, an increasingly distinct occupation on its own.

隨著專業化進展，出版業在19世紀逐漸進為一個獨立行業。

同 **clear, exact, obvious**（明顯的、確定無誤的）
反 **indistinct, vague**（不清楚的、模糊的）

- 字首：dis分開
  字根：stinct刺
- specialization n.專門化
- publishing n.出版業
- century n.世紀
- occupation n.職業

646.
distinguished [dɪˋstɪŋgwɪʃt]【dis‧tin‧guished】
a 卓越的、著名的、高貴的

The managers of the future will be clearly distinguished from their predecessors.

未來的管理者很顯然會與他們的前輩不同。

- Distinguished Service Cross ph.美國銅十字英勇勳章
- predecessor n.前輩

647.
distort [dɪsˋtɔrt]【dis‧tort】**v** 扭曲、曲解、使失真

The bias of a journalist can easily distort the news.

記者的偏見很容易扭曲新聞的報導。

同 **contort, twist**（扭、曲解）

- 字首：dis分開
  字根：tort扭
- bias n.偏見
- journalist n.記者

648.
distract [dɪˋstrækt]【dis‧tract】**v** 轉移、分心、使困擾

It was all a ploy to distract attention from his real aims.

那純粹是障眼法用以轉移人們對他真正意圖的注意力。

同 **bewilder, confuse, disturb**（迷惑、使困擾）
反 **attract, concentrate**（吸引、專心）

- distract from ph.使從…分心
- 字首：dis分開
- 字根：tract拉
- ploy n.計謀
- attention n.注意

649.
distress [dɪˋstrɛs]【dis‧tress】**n** 悲痛、貧困、危難 **v** 使苦惱

Company in distress makes the sorrow less.

患難中的同伴減少了你的悲苦。

同 **afflict, upset, torture**（使痛苦、使苦惱）
反 **comfort, relief, solace**（安慰、減輕）

- company n.同伴
- sorrow n.悲痛

650.
distribute [dɪˋstrɪbjut]【dis‧trib‧ute】**v** 分配、分開、散佈

The firm should distribute on the principle of equal pay for equal work.

公司應按照同工同酬的原則進行分配。

同 **allot, dispense, spread**（散佈、分配）
反 **assemble, collect, gather**（聚集、收集）

- 字首：dis分開
- 字根：tribute分配
- principle n.原則
- equal a.相同的

651.
distributor [dɪˋstrɪbjətɚ]【dis‧trib‧u‧tor】**n** 分配者、批發商

We'll send you a letter of appointment and can sign a full distributor contract.

我們將給你們一份聘書並簽訂一份完整的銷售合約。

- 字首：dis分開
  字根：tribut分配
  字尾：or從事…的人
- appointment n.約定

D

652.

disturbance [dɪsˋtɝbəns] 【 dis‧tur‧bance 】 **n**擾亂、打擾、不安應

When a disturbance breaks out in a place due to the leaders there didn't take a firm, clear-cut stand.

凡是擾亂的地方都是因為那裡的領導者態度不堅決。

🔄 **disarrangement, interruption, perturbation**（計畫打亂、情緒紛亂）
🔁 **arrangement**（安排）

- 字首：dis分開
  字根：turb擾動
  字尾：ance性質
- break out ph.爆發
- clear-cut a.清楚的
- stand n.立場

98

653.

dissuade [dɪˋswed] 【 dis‧suade 】 **v**勸阻

I tried to dissuade her from investing her money in stocks and shares.

我曾設法勸她不要投資股票交易。

🔄 **deter, discourage**（勸阻）
🔁 **persuade**（說服）

- 字首：dis分開
  字根：suade力勸
- invest v.投資
- share n.股份

121

654.

diverse [daɪˋvɝs] 【 di‧verse 】 **a**不同的、多變化的

The ABS market is highly diverse in terms of structures, yields, maturities and collateral.

資產支援型證券市場是一個在結構、收益、到期日以及擔保方式上都高度多樣化的市場。

🔄 **distinct, several, various**（不同的、多種的）
🔁 **same, similar**（相同的、類似的）

- 字首：di分開
  字根：verse轉變
- in terms of ph.依據
- yield n.收益
- maturity n.支票到期
- collateral n.擔保品

145

655.

divide [dəˋvaɪd] 【 di‧vide 】 **v**劃分、分發、使對立 **n**分歧

He agreed to divide the prize between Tom and Ann.

他同意把這筆獎金分給湯姆和安兩個人。

🔄 **separate, share, spilt**（使分開、劃分）
🔁 **unite**（使結合）

- agree v.同意
- prize n.獎金

151

656.

divorce [dəˋvors] 【 di‧vor‧ce 】 **v n**離婚、分離

They demanded the divorce of the subsidiary from the parent firm.

他們要求子公司與母公司分離。

🔁 **marriage, marry**（結婚）

- demand v.要求
- subsidiary n.子公司

78

657.

dizzy [ˋdɪzɪ] 【 diz‧zy 】 **a**頭暈目眩的、愚蠢的 **v**使頭暈眼花

Don't become dizzy with success.

別因為勝利而沖昏了頭。

🔄 **giddy, vertiginous**（暈眩的）

- success n.成功

64

658.

doctrine [ˋdɑktrɪn] 【 doc‧trine 】 **n**教條、學說、教誨

The vote that followed, establishing the doctrine as official company policy, was unanimous.

接下來進行的表決把這一原則正式奉為公司的方針。

🔄 **belief, creed, dogma**（信條、政策）

- vote n.投票
- official a.官方的
- unanimous a.一致同意的

105

659.
document [`dɑkjəmənt] 【 doc·u·ment 】 n 文件、證據

As a user works on a document for an extended time, she may desire a repository of deleted text.

當長時間處理一個文檔她可能期望存在一個已刪除文本的資料庫。

🔄 **archive, credentials, paper**（文件、證件）

- document management ph.文件管理
- 字根：docu指導
  字尾：ment性質
- repository n.儲藏處
- delete v.刪除

660.
domestic [də`mɛstɪk] 【 do·mes·tic 】 a 家庭的、國內的、馴養的

Depreciation of our currency makes it easier for domestic firms to compete with foreign firms.

本國貨幣幣值下跌使本國企業較易與外國企業競爭。

🔄 **family, household, internal**（家庭的、國內的）
🔄 **foreign, wild**（國外的、野外的）

- domestic science ph. 家政學
- domestic tragedy ph. 家庭倫理悲劇
- domestic violence ph. 家庭暴力
- depreciation n.貶值
- compete with ph.競爭

661.
dominate [`dɑmə‚net] 【 dom·i·nate 】 v 支配、統治、俯視

She never quite so much dominated a situation as she permitted it to dominate her.

她常常不能控制局面而是讓局面控制了她。

🔄 **control, lead, rule**（支配、統治）

- 字根：domin統治
  字尾：ate進行一項動作
- permit v.允許

662.
donate [`donet] 【 do·nate 】 v 捐贈、捐獻

The United States corporations donate to charity and other nonprofit purposes some $1,600 million annually.

美國各大公司每年為慈善事業和其它非營利事業捐款約16億美元。

🔄 **bestow, contribute, give**（捐贈、給予）

- 字首：don給予
  字尾：ate進行一項動作
- charity n.慈善
- nonprofit a.非營利的

663.
donor [`donɚ] 【 do·nor 】 n 供獻者

Southeastern United States has also acted as a donor region.

美國東南部也是主要充當供應地區。

🔄 **contributor**（貢獻者）

- donor card ph.器官捐獻卡
- 字首：don給予
  字尾：or動作實踐者

664.
doom [dum] 【 doom 】 v 註定、判決 n 厄運、判決

The tyrant encountered his doom after just one year dominion.

那暴君僅統治一年就結束了。

🔄 **condemn, convict, sentence**（判定、判決）

- doom and gloom ph.前景黯淡
- tyrant n.暴君
- dominion n.統治

665.
doubtless [`dautlɪs] 【 doubt·less 】 ad 無疑地、大概

The rapid proliferation of microcomputer will doubtless cause many social dislocations.

微型電腦的迅速推廣無疑會引起許多社會問題。

🔄 **certainly, undoubtedly, unquestionably**（無疑地）

- 字首：doubt懷疑
  字尾：less無
- rapid a.快速的
- proliferation n.激增
- dislocation n.混亂

666.
download [`daun‚lod] 【 down·load 】 v 下載

It takes several minutes to download this file.

下載這個檔案要花幾分鐘的時間。

🔄 **upload**（上傳）

- download limit ph.BBD 站所允許接收檔案的最大量
- 字首：down向下
  字尾：load運載

667.

downgrade [`daʊnˌgred] 【down·grade】 **V**降級、降低
N下坡

His job is downgraded in the reorganization of the office.

在公司改組中他的工作被降級了。

反 upgrade（升級）

- 字首：down向下
- 字尾：grade等級
- reorganization n.改組

668.

down payment **PH**分期付款的頭款

As for your payment term, are they down payment or unasked payment?

貴公司的付款條件是下訂金還是分期付款？

- term n.期限

669.

draft [dræft]【draft】 **N**草稿、匯票、徵兵

A documentary draft offers greater security to the exporter.

跟單匯票對出口商來說更為保險。

同 outline, sketch（草稿）

- draft board ph.兵役委員會
- draft card ph.兵役應徵卡
- draft dodger ph.逃避兵役者
- security n.安全
- exporter n.出口商

670.

drain [dren]【drain】 **V**流出、耗盡 **N**排水管、消耗

The country suffered from a continual brain drain because of bad economy.

那個國家因經濟不景氣人才不斷外流。

同 dry, exhaust, deprive（排掉水、耗盡）

反 flood, fill（填滿）

- drain away ph.枯竭
- drain off ph.流掉
- drain tap ph.車輛的排氣閥門
- suffer from ph.受…之苦

671.

drama [`drɑmə]【dra·ma】 **N**戲劇、劇本、戲劇性

He was not satisfied with the drama critic panning his new play.

他不滿於這位戲劇批評家對自己新劇本的苛評。

同 play（戲劇）

- drama queen ph.喜歡小題大做的人
- satisfy v.滿意
- panning n.一頓痛斥

672.

dramatic [drə`mætɪk]【dra·mat·ic】 **A**戲劇性的、充滿激情的

The Special Economic Zones are providing dramatic examples.

經濟特區提供了突出的例子。

同 operatic, theatrical（戲劇的）

- dramatic irony ph.戲劇性諷示
- dramatic monologue ph.戲劇性獨白
- 字首：drama戲劇
- 字尾：tic屬於…的

673.

drastic [`dræstɪk]【dras·tic】 **A**激烈的、嚴厲的

A drastic reformation of the present housing system has been carried out.

目前的住房制度正在徹底改革。

同 extreme, fierce, severe（激烈的、猛烈的）

- reformation n.改革
- carry out ph.完成

674.

drawback [`drɔˌbæk]【draw·back】 **N**缺點、障礙、撤銷

A drawback is made on customs duties on imported goods when they are later exported.

進口貨物日後出口時將退還其進口關稅。

同 disadvantage, fault, shortcoming（缺點）

- 字首：draw拉
- 字尾：back向後
- import v.進口
- export v.出口

675.
dread [drɛd] 【 dread 】 **v.n.**懼怕、擔心

Meeting new leader filled him with vague dread.

會見新領導者使他感到莫名的害怕。

同 fear（懼怕）

- dreadful a.令人恐怖的
- vague a.模糊不清的

61

676.
drill [drɪl] 【 drill 】 **v.**鑽孔、訓練**n.**鑽、訓練

The class is chopped into small groups for oral drill.

為進行口語訓練，班級分成若干小組。

- chop v.砍成
- oral a.口頭的

77

677.
drought [draʊt] 【 drought 】 **n.**乾旱、不足

Right now there's a drought of adequate leadership.

現在缺少能勝任的領導人。

同 aridity, dehydration（乾旱）
反 wet（溼）

- right now ph.現在
- adequate a.適合的

104

678.
drugstore [ˋdrʌɡˏstor] 【 drug‧store 】 **n.**藥房、雜貨店

His next job was that of a helper in a drugstore.

他的下一個工作是在一家雜貨店裡當幫手。

同 pharmacy（藥房）

- 字首：drug藥
  字尾：store店家
- helper n.幫手

94

679.
dual [ˋdjuəl] 【 du‧al 】 **a.**雙的、雙重的 **n.**雙數

The road opened out into a dual carriage way.

這條路已擴展成了雙向車道。

同 twofold, double, duplicate（雙重的、二倍的）

- dual citizenship ph.
  雙重國籍
- dual personality ph.
  雙重性格
- carriage n.四輪馬車

125

680.
dubious [ˋdjubɪəs] 【 du‧bi‧ous 】 **a.**半信半疑的、曖昧的

The results of this policy will remain dubious for long time.

這項政策的效果長期內難以確定。

同 doubtful, questionable, uncertain（可疑的、不明的）
反 precise, trustworthy（明確的、可信的）

- dubious about ph.懷疑
- dubious of ph.懷疑
- 字首：dub二、雙
  字尾：ious充滿…的

141

681.
due [dju] 【 due 】 **a.**應支付的、合適的、到期的

The ticket is past due.

這張票過期了。

反 undue（不適當的）

- due bill ph.借據
- due date ph.借限
- due to ph.由於

174

682.
duplex [ˋdjuplɛks] 【 du‧plex 】 **a.**雙重的、二倍的**n.**雙層樓公寓

With his large family, renting a duplex might be just what he needs.

像他這樣的大家庭租套兩層樓的公寓剛剛好。

同 twin（雙重的）

- duplex apartment ph.
  套樓公寓
- 字首：du二、雙
  字尾：plex折疊
- rent v.租借

81

683.
duplicate [`djupləkɪt] 【du·pli·cate】 n 複製品、副本
a 複製的、一對的

Type the file in duplicate.

請把這文件打成一式兩份。

- 字首：du二、雙
  字根：plic折疊
  字尾：ate有…性質的

D

684.
durable [`djurəbḷ] 【dur·able】 a 持久的、耐用的 n 耐用品

Our firm's new anti-theft safety locks are both sturdy and durable.

本廠新推出的防盜保險鎖，結構堅固經久耐用。

⮂ **enduring, permanent, perpetual**（耐久的、堅牢的）

- durable goods ph.耐用品
- 字根：dur延續
- 字尾：able能…的
- sturdy a.堅固的

86

685.
dynamic [daɪ`næmɪk] 【dy·na·mic】 a 有活力的、動力的

Until 1300 the Chinese civilization was dynamic and its learning became widespread.

華夏文明直到1300年還充滿活力，它的學術傳播四方。

⮂ **active, animated, energetic**（有生氣的）

⮂ **static**（靜態的）

- dynamic accuracy ph.
  動態經度
- dynamic analysis ph.
  動態分析
- dynamic balance ph.
  動態平衡
- 字首：dynam力
  字尾：ic與…有關的
- civilization n.文明

53

MEMO

MEMO

abbr 縮寫詞
a 形容詞
ad 副詞
aux 助動詞
conj 連接詞
n 名詞
num 數字
ph 片語
prep 介系詞
v 動詞
（美）美式用語
（英）英式用語
（法）法式用語

全書單字取材於：
①10本坊間新多益考試暢銷書籍
②50篇英文新聞、商業文章
③2005-2012年ETS TOEIC歷屆考古題
→ 總計約50,000個單字，以電腦統計出題率高達80%
　的實用單字1,800個

高頻率單字

 E 家族 earnings~extreme (MP3) 01-05

> 高 分 錦 囊

686.
earnings [ˋɝnɪŋz] 【earn·ings】 n收入、利潤
We must show our annual earnings in the tax form.
我們必須在稅單上註明我們的年收入。
➡ **fee, gross, revenue**（工資）

> • earnings per share date ph.每股盈餘宣佈日
> • earnings-related a.與收入相關的

687.
eclipse [ɪˋklɪps] 【e·clipse】 v n蝕、遮蔽
The country's economy may well eclipse others' in size in 15 years or so.
該國的經濟的規模在15年左右的時間裡可能超越其他國家。

688.
ecology [ɪˋkɑlədʒɪ] 【e·col·o·gy】 n生態學、生態環境
Make a thorough face-lift of the country's ecology system.
徹底改變該國的生態面貌。
➡ **nature**（自然）

> • 字首：eco環境
> 字尾：logy學術
> • thorogh a.徹底的
> • face-lift n.翻新

689.
economy [ɪˋkɑnəmɪ] 【e·con·o·my】 n經濟、節省 a廉價的
The employees of our firm practiced economy in doing everything.
我公司的雇員做任何事都力行節約。
➡ **saving**（節省、節約）
➡ **luxury**（奢侈的）

> • economy class ph.經濟艙位
> • economy of scale ph.規模經濟
> • firm n.公司

690.
edible [ˋɛdʒəbl] 【ed·i·ble】 n食品 a可食用的
Although there has been a general uptrend in world exports of fats and oils, the growth has been mainly limited to edible oils.
儘管世界出口油脂呈上升趨勢但這種增長卻主要限於食用油。
➡ **comestible, delicious, eatable**（可食用的）
➡ **inedible**（不可食用的）

> • 字首：ed吃
> 字尾：ible可…的
> • uptrend n.改善的趨勢
> • growth n.成長

691.
editorial [ˌɛdəˋtorɪəl] 【ed·i·to·ri·al】 a編輯的 n社論
Yesterday the first column of the front page was devoted to an important editorial.
昨天報紙的頭版頭條刊登了一篇重要社論。
➡ **column**（社論）

> • front a.前面的
> • devote v.專用於

692.
educate [ˋɛdʒəˌket] 【ed·u·cate】 v教育、培養
The magazine is designed to educate and not merely entertain.
這本雜誌不僅是為了娛樂而且是為了教育而設計的。
➡ **discipline, guide, instruct**（教育、訓練）

> • 字首：e出
> 字根：duc指導
> 字尾：ate進行一項行動
> • magazine n.雜誌
> • entertain v.娛樂

693.
effective [ɪˈfɛktɪv] 【 ef·fec·tive 】 **a** 有效的、起作用的、實際的
The contract will be effective with two signatures.
合約要雙方簽名才有效。
同 efficacious, productive（有效的）
反 ineffective（無效的）

- cost-effective **a.** 符合成本效益的
- effective number of pixels **ph.** 有效畫素
- signature **n.** 簽名

154

694.
efficiency [ɪˈfɪʃənsɪ] 【 ef·fi·cien·cy 】 **n** 效率、功效
Efficiency lies on good organization.
高效率依賴於良好的組織。

- organization **n.** 組織

112

695.
effuse [ɛˈfjuz] 【 ef·fuse 】 **v** 瀉出、散發
The country effuses warmth and hospitality.
這國家洋溢著人情味和好客精神。

- 字首：ef向外
  字根：fuse流、瀉
- hospitality **n.** 殷勤

94

696.
ego [ˈigo] 【 e·go 】 **n** 自我、自尊心
Losing the match made quite a dent in my ego.
比賽失敗對我的自尊心打擊極大。
同 oneself, self-esteem, psyche（自我、自尊）

- ego idea **ph.** 自我理想
- ego massage **ph.** 自我鼓勵
- ego trip **ph.** 自私自利
- dent **n.** 凹痕

104

697.
eject [ɪˈdʒɛkt] 【 e·ject 】 **v** 逐出、噴射
We were ejected because we had not paid the rental.
我們因未付房租而被趕了出去。
同 eliminate, expel, remove（驅逐、排除）

- 字首：e向外
  字根：ject投擲
- rental **n.** 租金

123

698.
elaborate [ɪˈlæbərɪt] 【 el·abor·ate 】 **va** 精細製作（的）、詳盡（的）、複雜（的）
He represented an elaborate research design and his boss laughed him down.
他提出一個詳盡的研究計劃被他的老闆笑著否定了。

- elaborate on / upon **ph.** 詳細說明
- represent **v.** 提出
- laugh down **ph.** 用笑聲拒絕

147

699.
elapse [ɪˈlæps] 【 e·lapse 】 **v** 時間消逝、過去
Nationalized natural resources assets elapse waits to be prevented from various aspects.
國家自然資源資產流失有待於從各個方面加以制止。
同 expire, pass, slip away（過去、經過）

- 字首：e向外
  字根：lapse掉落
- asset **n.** 資產
- various **a.** 多方面的
- aspect **n.** 方面

92

700.
elastic [ɪˈlæstɪk] 【 e·las·tic 】 **a** 有彈性的、靈活的、開朗的
This pact slowly erodes as members defect and outside demand gets more elastic.
隨著成員國的背叛以及外部的需求變得更有彈性，這個協定就慢慢地失去約束力。
同 flexible, pliable, stretchable（有彈性的）
反 inflexible, rigid, stiff（無彈性的、堅硬的）

- elastic band **ph.** 橡皮筋
- 字首：e向外
  字根：last持久
  字尾：ic能…的
- erode **v.** 侵蝕
- defect **n.** 缺點

701.
electric [ɪˈlɛktrɪk] 【 e·lec·tric 】 a 電的、令人震驚的

The amount paid to the electric company might vary from to check, but it probably stays within 5 or 10% of the last check written to them.

支付給電氣公司的每筆帳目可能有變動，變動可能在上次帳目的5~10%內。

同 **cordless, galvanizing**（電的、令人激動的）

- electronics n.電子學
- electric blanket ph.電毯
- electric chair ph.電椅
- electric eye ph.光電池
- electric guitar ph.電吉他
- electric piano ph.電子琴
- probably ad.大概

702.
elegant [ˈɛləgənt] 【 el·e·gant 】 a 高雅的、精緻的

His elegant piece of reasoning impressed me deeply.

他簡要明確的論證給我留下深刻的印象。

同 **fine, refined, tasteful**（優美的、高雅的）
反 **inelegant**（粗野的）

- impress v.印象
- deeply ad.深刻地

703.
elementary [ˌɛləˈmɛntərɪ] 【 el·e·men·ta·ry 】 a 基本的、初級的

Countries differ greatly even in such elementary matters as education and standards of living.

各國甚至在教育和生活標準等這些基本事情上也大不相同。

同 **basic, fundamental, primary**（基本的、初步的）
反 **advanced**（進階的）

- elementary particle ph. 基本粒子
- elementary school ph. 小學
- standard n.標準

704.
elevate [ˈɛləˌvet] 【 el·e·vate 】 v 舉起、提高、振奮

He was elevated to the position of a department manager.

他被提升為部門經理。

同 **boost, lift, raise**（舉起、使上升）
反 **degrade**（降低）

- elevator n.電梯
- 字首：e向外
  字根：lev舉起
  字尾：ate進行一項行動
- department n.部門

705.
elicit [ɪˈlɪsɪt] 【 e·lic·it 】 v 引出、引起的

It operates a monetary reward scheme to elicit information on textile origin fraud.

海關推行了獎金獎賞計劃，鼓勵市民提供有關紡織品產地來源欺詐活動的資料。

同 **secure, summon**（引出、引起）

- operate v.運作
- monetary a.財政的
- reward n.獎金
- textile a.紡織的
- fraud n.詭計

706.
eligible [ˈɛlɪdʒəbl] 【 el·i·gi·ble 】 a 有資格當選的、合適的 n 合格者

Anyone who has worked here for over two years is eligible for sick pay.

凡在這工作了兩年以上的人都有資格獲得病假工資。

同 **desirable, qualified, suitable**（有資格的）

707.
eliminate [ɪˈlɪməˌnet] 【 e·lim·i·nate 】 v 排除、淘汰、忽視

Alternatives must be pre-screened to eliminate those which have lower potential.

為了排除那些沒有多大前途的方案必須進行預先審查。

同 **discard, exclude, reject**（排除、去除）
反 **add, maintain**（增加、維持）

- alternative n.二擇一
- screen v.審查
- potential n.潛能

708.
elite [e`lit] [e·lite] n精華、優秀份子

The power elite inside the corporation are controlling personnel policy.

公司內部的一群握有實權的精英控制著人事政策。

- corporation n.公司
- personnel n.總稱人員
- policy n.政策

709.
eloquent [`ɛləkwənt] [el·o·quent] a雄辯的、有說服力的

The speaker made an eloquent appeal for human rights.

該發言人就人權問題發出了強有力的呼籲。

⑩ **expressive, fluent, meaningful**（善辯的、意味深長的）

- 字首：e向外
  字根：loqu說話
  字尾：ent…狀態的
- appeal for ph.懇求

710.
embark [ɪm`bark] [em·bark] v上船、從事、投資

He is about to embark on a new business venture.

他就要開始新的商業冒險活動。

⑩ **board, depart**（搭乘、起程）
⑫ **disembark**（登陸）

- embark on / upon ph. 從事
- be about to ph.即將
- venture n.冒險事業

711.
embarrass [ɪm`bærəs] [em·bar·rass] v不好意思、為難、使拮据

We are greatly embarrass by your omission to enclose the packing list with other documents.

貴方沒有把裝箱單和其他貨運單據一起寄來會使我們為難。

⑩ **abash, perplex, shame**（使困窘、使為難）

- omission n.省略
- enclose v.封入
- document n.文件

712.
embed [ɪm`bɛd] [em·bed] v栽種、把…嵌進

Our company wishes to take the way of technology authorizing to cooperate with equipment manufacturers of cable TV at home, to embed the broadband inserting function in the cable TV equipment.

我們公司可以採取技術授權的方式與國內有線電視設備廠商合作，將寬頻接入功能嵌入到有線電視設備中。

⑩ **enclose, fix, inset**（埋藏、使固定）

- 字首：im進入
- cooperate with ph.合作
- equipment n.設備
- cable TV ph.有線電視
- broadband a.多頻率的
- insert v.插入

713.
embezzle [ɪm`bɛzl] [em·bez·zle] v盜用、侵佔

She insinuated to us that her partner has embezzled fund.

她旁敲側擊地指出她的合夥人盜用了資金。

⑩ **steal, thieve, rob**（偷、竊取）

- insinuate v.暗指
- fund n.資金

714.
embody [ɪm`badɪ] [em·bod·y] v使具體化、包含

The budget is a short-term (typically one year), quantitative and detailed plan, which embodies the set of common goal established by the high level of management.

預算是短期的數量化的和詳細的計劃，它是企業高層管理者所制定的一整套組織目標的具體表現。

⑩ **comprise, embrace, include**（包括、包含）

- budget n.預算
- short-term a.短期的
- quantitative a.量的
- common a.普通的
- goal n.目標

715. `165`

embrace [ɪm`bres]【em‧brace】Ⅴ Ⅱ 擁抱、包含

Both parties must embrace the end objective.

雙方必須擁護最後的目標。

🔄 clutch, hug, grasp（擁抱、抱住）

---

716. `143`

emerge [i`mɝdʒ]【e‧merge】Ⅴ 浮現、顯露、擺脫

We could supposedly emerge as a smaller but healthier company.

我們可以作為一個規模較小但較為健康的公司而東山再起。

🔄 appear, loom（出現）
🔄 submerge（淹沒）

- supposedly ad.根據推測
- healthier a.較健康的

---

717. `211`

emergency [ɪ`mɝdʒənsɪ]【e‧mer‧gen‧cy】Ⅱ 緊急狀況、非常時刻

He was throughout his period the masterful opponent of all emergency measures.

在他的任期內，他是一切緊急措施的最有力的反對者。

🔄 crisis, exigency, pinch（緊急情況、緊急時刻）

- emergency alert ph. 預警信號
- emergency brake ph. 緊急煞車
- emergency room ph. 急診室
- opponent n.敵人

---

718. `104`

emotion [ɪ`moʃən]【e‧mo‧tion】Ⅱ 情感、激動

Emotion should never be a substitute for sound policy.

感情不能代替政策。

🔄 affection, feeling, sentiment（感情、情感）

- 字首：e向外
  字根：mot動
  字尾：ion性質
- substitute for ph.代替

---

719. `62`

empathy [`ɛmpəθɪ]【em‧pa‧thy】a 移情

Empathy is an effective tool to use when dealing with conflict in a team.

在處理團隊內的衝突中換位思考是一種有效的工具。

- 字首：em向內
  字尾：pathy感覺
- tool n.工具
- deal with ph.處理

---

720. `51`

emperor [`ɛmpərə]【em‧per‧or】Ⅱ 皇帝

The emperor ordained that all foreigners be expelled.

皇帝下令將所有外國人驅逐出境。

🔄 monarch, sovereign（皇帝）
🔄 empress（皇后）

- ordain v.規定
- foreigner n.外國人
- expel v.驅逐

---

721. `165`

emphasize [`ɛmfə͵saɪz]【em‧pha‧size】Ⅴ 強調、使顯得突出

They are enthusiastic in improving community environment and emphasizing the interests of citizens.

她們通常致力於改善社區的環境，重點關注民眾的利益。

🔄 highlight, punctuate, stress（強調、著重）

- emphasis n.強調
- enthusiastic a.熱情的
- improve v.改善
- community n.社區

722.
empirical [εm`pɪrɪkl̩] 【 em·pir·i·cal 】 **a**經驗主義的

Voluminous empirical evidence now available shows that the statement, far from being an exaggeration, probably was an understatement.

實際上大量的證據表明，這種說法非但沒有誇大甚至還可能是打了折扣的。

ⓢ **theoretical** (理論的)

ⓐ **rare, scanty** (稀有的、罕見的、不足的)

- voluminous a.大量的
- evidence n.證據
- available a.可得的
- exaggeration n.誇大
- understatement n.不充分的陳述

`79`

723.
employ [ɪm`plɔɪ] 【 em·ploy 】 **vn**雇用、使用

Firms can now produce huge quantities and employ the division of labor to much greater advantage.

現在廠商可以生產大量產品，可以更充分地利用分工。

ⓢ **hire, engage, occupy** (雇用、利用)

ⓐ **dismiss** (解散)

- employ oneself in ph.忙於、從事於
- employer n.雇主
- employee n.職員
- huge a.巨大的
- division n.分配

`145`

724.
empower [ɪm`pauɚ] 【 em·pow·er 】 **v**授權、准許

In the event that the chairman is unable to discharge his responsibilities, he shall empower a vice-chairman or another director to represent the joint venture.

董事長不能履行職責時，應授權副董事長或其他董事代表合營企業。

ⓢ **authorize, entrust, warrant** (授權於、允許)

- 字首：em向內
  字根：power權力
- unable a.不能的
- responsibility n.責任
- joint n.結合

`112`

725.
enchain [ɪn`tʃen] 【 en·chain 】 **v**束縛、吸引住

Mrs. Penniman's imagination was restless, and the evening paper failed on this occasion to enchain it.

佩尼曼太太的想像又開始不停歇，連她手中的晚報此刻也無法使它平靜。

- imagination n.想像
- evening paper ph.晚報
- fail v.失敗
- occasion n.時刻

`72`

726.
encircle [ɪn`sɝkl̩] 【 en·cir·cle 】 **v**環繞、包圍

A similar system is used to contact the communication satellites that now continually encircles the earth.

人們正把同樣的系統用來與目前繞地球飛行的通訊衛星保持聯繫。

- 字首：en向內
  字尾：circle圓圈
- satellite n.衛星
- continually ad.一再地

`135`

727.
enclosure [ɪn`kloʒɚ] 【 n·clo·sure 】 **n**圍住、圍牆、附件

A business letter with a supplemental enclosure.

一封帶有補充附件的商業信函。

ⓢ **corral, paddock, fence** (圈用地、圍牆)

- enclose v.裝入
- supplemental a.補充的

`140`

728.
encounter [ɪn`kaʊtə] 【en·coun·ter】 **V.n.**遭遇、意外地遇見

149

- encounter group **ph.**交心心理治療小組
- undertake **v.**著手做
- bound to **ph.**一定會

If you undertake the project, you are bound to encounter difficulties.

如果你承接這項工程的話，免不了會遇到許多困難。

come across, confront, meet（遇到、遭遇）

729.
encourage [ɪn`kɝɪdʒ] 【en·cour·age】 **V.**鼓勵、支持、促進

157

- 字首：en加強語氣字尾：courage勇氣
- liberalize **v.**自由化
- initiative **n.**主動

Economic policy is liberalized to encourage initiatives in production.

放寬經濟政策以鼓勵生產的積極性。

inspire, promote, urge（發起、激發）
discourage（使沮喪）

730.
endeavor [ɪn`dɛvə] 【en·deav·or】 **V.n.**努力、盡力

123

- 同endeavour
- customer **n.**顧客

We make every endeavor to satisfy our customers.

我們盡全力使顧客滿意。

strive, struggle, tackle（努力）
neglect（疏忽）

731.
endorse [ɪn`dɔrs] 【en·dorse】 **V.**簽名、批註、贊同

94

- committee **n.**委員會
- prevail **v.**戰勝
- proposal **n.**提案

The committee hoped to prevail on them to endorse the proposal.

委員會希望說服他們贊同這項提案。

assign（簽名）

732.
endow [ɪn`daʊ] 【en·dow】 **V.**捐贈、賦予

81

- endow with **ph.**給予
- tourism **n.**旅遊業
- property **n.**資產
- beneficial **a.**有利於

To develop tourism, property right deal system must be reformed and modern property right system should be established to endow the manager with right of use, beneficial right and right of management.

發展旅遊產業必須改革產權交易制度、建立現代產權制度，使經營者具有使用權、受益權和處置權。

bequeath, provide, supply（捐贈、資助）

733.
educe [ɪ`djus] 【e·duce】 **V.**引出、推斷

104

- 字首：e向外字根：duce引導
- pupil **n.**學生

The teacher was unable to educe an answer from her pupils.

老師無法從學生口中得到任何答案。

unconcrete, difficult, hard to understand（抽象的、難懂的）
concrete（具體的、有形的）

734.
endurance [ɪn`djurəns] 【en·dur·ance】 **n.**忍耐、持久力、苦難

95

- 字首：en向內字根：dur持久字尾：ance行為
- complete **v.**完成

Through hard work and endurance, we will complete this project.

透過努力工作和堅持，我們將會完成這項方案。

backbone, fortitude, stamina（忍耐、耐久力）
weakness（虛弱）

735.

energetic [ˌɛnɚˈdʒɛtɪk]【en·er·get·ic】**a** 精力旺盛的、積極的

Some of the most energetic protectionist measures are erected against agricultural products in all countries.

有一些最厲害的保護主義措施，用來反對所有國家的農產品。

active, peppy, vigorous（精力旺盛的）

- protectionist n.貿易保護主義者
- erect v.建立
- agricultural a.農業的

736.

enforce [ɪnˈfors]【en·force】**v** 實施、強迫、堅持

Do you have any statistics that would enforce your argument?

你有加強你論點的統計資料嗎？

compel, force（強迫）

- 字首：en加強
  字尾：force力量
- statistics n.統計
- argument n.論點

737.

engage [ɪnˈgedʒ]【en·gage】**v** 保證、訂婚、從事於

I will engage for his behaviour if you decide to employ him.

如果你能決定雇用他，那麼我可以擔保他的行為。

- engage in ph.從事於
- behavior n.行為

738.

engineer [ˌɛndʒəˈnɪr]【en·gi·neer】**n** 工程師、機械工

Joe is an engineer, but he does some translation as a sideline.

喬是工程師，但他也從事一些翻譯工作當副業。

- 字首：engin引擎
  字尾：er從事⋯的人
- translation n.翻譯
- sideline n.副業

739.

enhance [ɪnˈhæns]【en·hance】**v** 提高、增加

Passing the English examination should enhance your chances of getting the post.

通過了英語考試可以增加你獲得這個職位的機會。

enrich, improve, uplift（提高、改善）

- pass v.通過
- examination n.考試
- chance n.機會
- post n.職位

740.

enlighten [ɪnˈlaɪtn̩]【en·light·en】**v** 啟發、教育

In Britain, the charter of incorporation of the BBC enjoins it to enlighten as well as to entertain, while the Independent Television authority has the duty to supervise the program content of the commercial television companies.

在英國，BBC的規定使其具有教育和娛樂功能，而獨立電視臺則有責任監督商業電視公司的節目內容。

educate, illuminate, instruct（教育、啟發）

- 字首：en向內
  字根：light亮
  字尾：en使成為
- charter n.許可證
- entertain v.娛樂
- supervise v.監督

741.

enormous [ɪˈnɔrməs]【e·nor·mous】**a** 巨大的、龐大的、兇暴的

An enormous gap remains between the advanced countries and the developing countries.

在先進國家和發展中國家之間仍然存在著巨大的差距。

great, large, vast（巨大的）

little, small, tiny（小的、微小的）

- gap n.差距
- developing country ph.發展中國家

742.
enrich [ɪnˋrɪtʃ]【en·rich】Ⅴ使富裕、使肥沃

Going travelling around the world can enrich your life.

到世界旅行可以豐富你的人生。

🔄 better, enhance, improve（加強、提高）
🔄 impoverish（使貧窮）

● 字首：en向內
字尾：rich富有

132

743.
enroll [ɪnˋrol]【en·roll】Ⅴ登記、註冊、使入會

I was admitted to your university last fall, but could not enroll owing to my work engagement.

去年秋天我獲准貴校申請，但因工作期限未滿而沒能前去註冊。

🔄 enter, register, sign up（登記）

● admit v.同意
● owing to ph.由於
● engagement n.雇用期

173

744.
en route ⅢⅢ【法】在途中

Jerry stopped en route and got some flowers for his girlfriend.

傑瑞在途中停下來買花要送給女友。

● 意同於on the way

52

745.
ensure [ɪnˋʃur]【en·sure】Ⅴ接著發生、因⋯而產生

Three competing store owners rented adjoining shops in a mall. Observers waited for mayhem to ensure.

三個互相爭生意的商店老闆在一間購物中心租用了毗鄰的店鋪。旁觀者等著看好戲。

🔄 follow（接著發生）

● owner n.所有人
● adjoining a.毗鄰的
● observer n.旁觀者
● mayhem n.有意的破壞

87

746.
entail [ɪnˋtel]【en·tail】Ⅴ必須、使承擔、限定繼承

Failing to meet the time limit shall entail reapplication for inspection.

超過期限的應當重新報驗。

● re-application n.重新申請
● inspection n.檢察

94

747.
enterprise [ˋɛntɚͺpraɪz]【en·ter·prise】ⁿ事業、冒險精神、進取心

The funds in need will mainly be drawn from accumulation within the enterprise.

所需資金主要取自於企業內部的資本增值。

🔄 business, venture（事業）

● 字首：enter進入
字尾：prise緊握
● accumulation n.資本增值

101

748.
entertainment [ͺɛntɚˋtenmənt]【en·ter·tain·ment】
ⁿ娛樂、款待

The public is not satisfied with light entertainment anymore.

公眾再也不滿足於輕鬆的娛樂片了。

🔄 amusement, recreation（娛樂）

● be satisfied with ph.滿意
● light a.輕鬆愉快的

105

749.
enthusiasm [ɪnˋθjuzLͺæzəM]【en·thu·si·asm】ⁿ熱情、熱誠

Hard work and enthusiasm can lead to success.

努力工作及熱忱可以導致成功。

🔄 keenness, passion（熱情）

● enthusiastic a.熱心的

74

750. `154`

entice [ɪn`taɪs] 【en·tice】 **V**誘使、慫恿

Advertisements are designed to entice people into spending money.

廣告宣傳的目的是誘使人花錢。

同 attract, lure, seduce（引誘）

- advertisement n.廣告
- spend v.花費

751. `177`

entire [ɪn`taɪr] 【en·tire】 **a**全部的、完全的

A conscientious person, when drafting a report, also puts a handsome cover page on it and makes enough photocopies for the entire department.

一個盡責的人在起草一份報告時，還會在報告上加一個漂亮的封面並為整個部門影印足夠的份數。

同 plenary, total, whole（全部的、完全的）

反 partial（部分的）

- conscientious a.誠實的
- draft v.打草稿
- handsome a.漂亮的
- cover page ph.封面
- photocopy n.影印

752. `94`

entitle [ɪn`taɪt!] 【en·ti·tle】 **V**給…權利、題名

Their qualifications entitle them to a higher salary.

他們的資格使他們可以得到較高的薪金。

同 label, name, title（命名）

反 deprive（剝奪）

- 字首：en向內
  字尾：title標題
- qualification n.資格
- salary n.薪資

753. `54`

entity [`ɛntətɪ] 【en·ti·ty】 **n**實體、存在、本質

A corporation is separate legal entity chartered by the state.

股份有限公司是州政特許的獨立的法律主體。

- separate a.單獨的
- legal a.合法的
- charter v.發執照給

754. `51`

entrée [`ɑntre] 【en·trée】 **n**主菜

Would you like a baked potato or mashed potatoes with your entree?

您想要烤馬鈴薯還是馬鈴薯泥來搭配您的主菜呢？

- bake v.烤
- potato n.馬鈴薯
- mash v.搗成糊狀

755. `88`

entrepreneur [ˌɑntrəprə`nɝ] 【en·tre·pre·neur】 **n**企業家、承包人

Every entrepreneur expects his products to enjoy a reputation in the world market.

在國際市場上享有聲譽是每位企業家對自己產品的期望。

- 字首：entrepren企業
  字尾：eur從事某種行業的人
- expect v.期待
- reputation n.名譽

756. `97`

epidemic [ˌɛpɪ`dɛmɪk] 【ep·i·dem·ic】 **a**流行性的、極為流行的**n**流行病、流行

Buying goods on the installment plan has become epidemic in recent years.

近幾年來，用分期付款購物十分流行。

同 contagious, prevalent, widespread（傳染性的、流行的）

- installment plan ph.分期付款購物法
- recent a.最近的

757.
episode [ɛpəˌsod]【ep·i·sode】n.一個事件、插曲、一齣戲
That episode was still so vivid to her.
對她來說，當時的情景仍然歷歷在目。
🔄 **affair, event**（事件）

• vivid a.栩栩如生的

758.
epoch [ˈɛpək]【ep·och】n.時代、重要時期、新紀元
We are entering upon a new epoch in the history of civilization.
我們正進入人類文明史上的新紀元。
🔄 **age, era, period**（時代）

• epoch-making a. 意義重大的
• history n.歷史
• civilization n.文明

759.
equable [ˈɛkwəbl̩]【eq·ua·ble】a.穩定的、寧靜的
I like working with John because he's so calm and equable.
我喜歡和約翰一起工作因為他性情沈著穩重。
🔄 **stable, calm**（平穩的、恬靜的）

• 字首：equ平等的
  字尾：able能…的
• calm a.沈著的

760.
equal [ˈikwəl]【eq·ual】a.相等的、勝任的
The firm should distribute on the principle of equal pay for equal work.
公司應按照同工同酬的原則進行分配。
🔄 **equivalent, equal**（相同的）
🚫 **unequal**（不相等的）

• equal opportunity ph. 機會均等
• equal sign ph.等號
• equal to ph.能勝任
• 字首：equ相同
  字尾：al屬於…的
• distribute v.分配

761.
equity [ˈɛkwətɪ]【eq·ui·ty】n.公平、普通股
Corporations' earnings accumulated separately from its paid-in equity capital.
股份有限公司的盈利是在其繳入的業主權資本之外單獨累積的。

• 字首：equ相同
  字尾：ity狀態
• earnings n.利潤
• accumulate v.累積

762.
equipment [ɪˈkwɪpmənt]【e·quip·ment】n.裝備、設備
The equipment has all been field-tested.
這些設備都已經過實地試驗。
🔄 **apparatus, contrivances, implements**（設備）

• 字首：equip裝設備
  字尾：ment性質

763.
equivalent [ɪˈkwɪvələnt]【e·quiv·a·lent】a.相等的、等值的
的 n.相等物
Import restraints are equivalent to a sales tax and often apply to necessities.
進口限制相當於銷售稅而且往往是針對必需品。
🔄 **equal, like**（相等）
🚫 **different**（不同的）

• 字首：equiv相等
  字尾：al屬於…的
  字尾：ent…狀態的
• restraint n.限制
• apply to ph.適用於

764.
erase [ɪˈres]【e·rase】v.擦去、消除
These effects of the exchange-rate depreciation do not erase the effect of initial loss of export income.
匯價下跌的這些影響並不會消除最初的出口收入損失的影響。
🔄 **cancel, delete, obliterate**（擦掉、刪去）

• 字首：e向外
  字根：rase刮、擦
• exchange v.交換
• depreciation n.降價
• initial a.最初的
• income n.收入

765.

erect [ɪ`rɛkt] 【 e·rect 】 **V** 豎立、建立、安裝

I tried to erect a facade of imperviousness and self-confidence.

我竭力裝出一副不受外界干擾十分自信的樣子。

同 build, construct, frame（建立、建造）
反 demolish, destroy, ruin（破壞、毀壞）

- 字首：e 向外
  字根：rect 直立
- facade n.表面
- imperviousness n.不為所動
- self-confidence n.自信

766. **57**

erroneous [ɪ`ronɪəs] 【 er·ro·ne·ous 】 **a** 錯誤的、不正確的

The newspaper published a retraction of the erroneous report.

那家報紙聲明撤回那篇錯誤的報導。

同 false, incorrect, wrong（錯誤的、不真實的）

- 字根：erron 錯誤
  字尾：eous 有…性質的
- retraction n.撤回
- report n.報導

767. **114**

erupt [ɪ`rʌpt] 【 e·rupt 】 **V** 爆發、噴出、發疹

It is what drives you, and everything you do in building your brand should erupt from that passion.

這是你的動力，為你所建立品牌而所作的每件事情都應該在熱情中爆發。

同 burst forth, vomit（噴出、排出）

- 字首：e 向外
  字根：rupt 破裂
- brand n.品牌
- passion n.熱情

768. **120**

essence [`ɛsn̩s] 【 es·sence 】 **n** 本質、要素、精華

Speed is of the essence in dealing with an emergency.

在處理緊急事件時，速度是非常重要的。

同 meaning, substance, pith（實質、重要性）

- speed n.速度
- deal with ph.處理
- emergency n.緊急事件

769. **154**

esteem [ɪs`tim] 【 es·teem 】 **V n** 尊重、評價

Please accept this little gift in token of our esteem.

請接受這個小禮物以表示我們的敬意。

同 appreciate, cherish, respect（尊重）
反 despise, disesteem（不尊重、鄙視）

- self-esteem n.自尊
- accept v.接受
- gift n.禮物
- in token of ph.代表

770. **211**

estimate [`ɛstə.met] 【 es·ti·mate 】 **V n** 估計、評價

My estimate of the situation is not so optimistic.

我對形勢的估計不那麼樂觀。

同 evaluate, judge, value（估計、評價）

- situation n.情況
- optimistic a.樂觀的

771. **95**

eternal [ɪ`tɝn̩] 【 e·ter·nal 】 **a** 永恆的、永存的、不朽的

Kunming, the capital of Yunnan province, enjoys the fame as the "City of Eternal Spring".

雲南省省會昆明市素有「春城」的美譽。

同 everlasting, permanent, perpetual（永久的、不停的）
反 momentary, temporary（短暫的、暫時的）

- eternal triangle ph.三角戀愛關係
- eternal verity ph.基本道德準則
- province n.省份

772. **87**

etiquette [`ɛtɪkɛt] 【 et·i·quette 】 **n** 禮節、規矩

According to etiquette, you should stand up to meet a guest.

按照禮節你應該站起來接待客人。

同 decorum, manner, propriety（禮節、禮儀）

- according to ph.依據
- guest n.賓客

E

773.
evaluate [ɪ`vælju‚et]【e‧val‧u‧ate】**Ⅴ**評估、評價

They had no idea how to evaluate from a financial perspective about what management was doing.

這些人根本不知道如何從財務角度來評價當前的管理工作。

- 字首：e向外
  字根：valu價值
  字尾：ate進行一項行動
- financial a.財政的
- perspective n.觀點

774.
event [ɪ`vɛnt]【e‧vent】**n**事件、情況、結果

In the unlikely event of a strike, production would be badly affected.

罷工未必能發生，若一旦發生，生產勢必受到嚴重影響。

(同)▸ **incident, occurence**（事件、情況）

- event gal ph.每次都會出席舞會的女大學生
- event horizon ph.重大的轉捩點
- event movie ph.電影大片
- strike n.罷工
- affect v.影響

775.
eventual [ɪ`vɛntʃuəl]【e‧ven‧tu‧al】**a**最終的、結果的

The eventual decision came after weeks of deliberation.

經過數星期的考慮後，最終決定出來了。

(同)▸ **basic, fundamental, primary**（基本的、初步的）
(反)▸ **advanced**（進階的）

- deliberation n.深思熟慮

776.
evidence [`ɛvədəns]【ev‧i‧dence】**n**證據、跡象**v**證明

She went through the company's accounts, looking for evidence of fraud.

她仔細審核公司的帳目查找欺騙作弊的證據。

(同)▸ **clue, indication, proof**（證據）

- evidence-based education ph.事實教育
- 字首：e向外
  字根：vid看
  字尾：ence性質
- fraud n.欺騙

777.
evil [`ivl]【e‧vil】**a**邪惡（的）、討厭（的）、不幸（的）

There is, I believe, in every disposition a tendency to some particular evil.

我相信，一個人不管是怎樣的脾氣都免不了有某種邪惡。

(同)▸ **bad, sinful, wicked**（罪惡的）
(反)▸ **good, virtuous**（好的）

- evil eye ph.惡毒眼光
- evil-eyed a.眼光惡毒的
- evil-minded a.惡意的

778.
evoke [ɪ`vok]【e‧voke】**Ⅴ**喚起、引起

We will be gratified if our efforts evoke your enthusiasm.

如果我們的努力能引起您的共鳴會是我們最大的心願。

(同)▸ **induce, prompt, summon**（引起、召喚）

- 字首：e向外
  字根：voke呼喊
- gratify v.使高興

779.
evolution [‚ɛvə`luʃən]【ev‧o‧lu‧tion】**n**發展、進化

Our watchword is: "Evolution, not revolution."

我們的口號是：「要循序漸進，不要劇烈變革」。

(同)▸ **development, evolvement, progression**（發展）
(反)▸ **devolution**（轉移）

- watchword n.口號
- revolution n.革命

780.

evolve [ɪˋvɑlv] 【 ev·olve 】 **V** 逐步形成、釋放、引伸出

How did you evolve this very personal and original style?

你是怎樣逐步形成這種很有個性且具獨創性的風格的？

⊞ **advance, develop, grow** （發展、促進）
⊠ **degenerate** （衰退）

- 字首：e向外
- 字尾：volve滾轉
- personal a.個人的
- original a.有獨創性的

151

781.

example [ɪgˋzæmpl] 【 ex·am·ple 】 **N** 樣本、榜樣

When, for example, a user creates an invoice for a customer without an ID number, most applications reject the entry.

例如，當使用者創建一張沒有顧客號碼的發貨單時，多數程式會拒絕輸入。

⊞ **illustration, model, pattern** （樣品、範例）

- for example ph.例如
- invoice n.發票
- ID=identification n.識別
- reject v.拒絕
- entry n.進入

241

782.

exceed [ɪkˋsid] 【 ex·ceed 】 **V** 超過、勝過

What is the probability that today's demand will exceed our inventory?

今天銷售量超過庫存量的概率是多少？

⊞ **excel, surpass** （勝過）

- 字首：ex向外
- 字根：ceed走動
- probability n.概率
- inventory n.存貨清單

108

783.

exceptional [ɪkˋsɛpʃənl] 【 ex·cep·tion·al 】 **a** 例外的、特別優秀的

A few exceptional men might rise above circumstance.

少數特別優秀的人可能不受環境的制約。

⊞ **extraordinary, outstanding, remarkable** （特別的）
⊠ **common, ordinary** （普遍的）

- 字首：exception例外
- 字尾：al屬於…的
- rise above ph.克服
- circumstance n.環境

94

784.

excess [ɪkˋsɛs] 【 ex·cess 】 **N** 超過、過度 **a** 過量的、額外的

Last year's profits were in excess of one billion dollars.

去年的利潤超過了10億美元。

⊞ **additional, extra, surplus** （額外的、過剩的）

- excess baggage ph. 過重行李
- excess material analysis ph.呆滯材料分析
- excess postage ph.應補的欠資郵費
- 字首：ex向外

125

785.

exchange [ɪksˋtʃendʒ] 【 ex·change 】 **V N** 交換、兌換

The world saw a return to a floating exchange rate system.

世界又恢復到浮動匯率制度。

⊞ **change, interchange, switch** （交換、替代）

- exchange rate ph.外匯率
- exchange rate mechanism ph.匯率體制
- exchange student ph.交換學生
- floating a.流動的

146

786.

excise [ɛkˋsaɪz] 【 ex·cise 】 **V** 割去、向…徵收消費稅 **N** 貨物稅

The excises on alcohol and tobacco had increased last year.

自去年開始，菸酒稅已調漲。

- Customs and Excise ph.關稅與消費稅
- alcohol n.酒
- tobacco n.菸草

101

787.
exclaim [ɪksˋklem] 【 ex·claim 】 Ⅴ 呼喊、大聲叫嚷

Till now, it's still unable for us to exclaim whether his theory could withstand the trial.

到目前為止我們還不能說他的理論是否經得住考驗。

🔊 **clamor, shout**（呼喊）

- 字首：ex向外
  字根：claim喊叫
- withstand v.抵擋
- trial n.試驗

788.
exclude [ɪkˋsklud] 【 ex·clude 】 Ⅴ 拒絕接納、排除

The easiest way to capture that buying power on behalf of domestic industry is simply to exclude imports.

要想引起本國工業的購買力，最容易的方法就是簡單地剔除進口數額。

🔊 **bar, forbid, prohibit**（排斥、禁止）
🔊 **include**（包含）

- exclusive a.唯一的
- 字首：ex向外
  字根：clude關閉
- capture v.引起注意
- on behalf of ph.代表

789.
excruciating [ɪkˋskruʃLetɪŋ] 【 ex·cru·ci·at·ing 】
ɑ 極痛苦的、難忍受的、極度的

The afternoon wore on with excruciating slowness.

下午的時間慢得令人難受。

790.
excursion [ɪkˋskɝʒən] 【 ex·cur·sion 】 ⋂ 遠足、短程旅行、離題

Your comments are an excursion from the major theme.

你的話偏離了主題。

🔊 **journey, outing, trip**（旅行、出遊）

- 字首：ex向外
  字根：curs跑
  字尾：ion狀態
- theme n.主題

791.
execute [ˋɛksLkjut] 【 ex·e·cute 】 Ⅴ 實施、執行、將…處死

We would thank you to execute the order as soon as possible.

感謝您能儘快安排所訂購的貨物並早日交貨。

🔊 **carry out, perform**（執行、完成）

- as soon as possible=ASAP 盡早

792.
executive [ɪgˋzɛkjutɪv] 【 ex·ec·u·tive 】 ⋂ 執行者 ɑ 執行的、行政上的

Each staff executive had specific performance objectives and his bonus was pinned to achieve them.

每個部門主管人中都有具體的工作目標實現，這些目標達到就可以拿到獎金。

🔊 **administrative, directing, managing**（經營的、管理的）

- executive flu ph.主管流行感冒
- executive management ph.主管經理管理層
- Executive Mansion ph. 白宮
- Executive officer ph. 執行官
- executive order ph. 美國總統之行政命令

793.
exempt [ɪgˋzɛmpt] 【 ex·empt 】 Ⅴ 免除、豁免

Members of the service staff shall be exempted from dues and taxes on the wages which they receive for their services.

服務人員就其服務所得之工資免納稅。

🔊 **free, except, release**（免除、釋放）

- exempt from ph.免除
- tax n.稅

E

794.

exert [ɪg`zɝt]【ex·ert】**v.**盡力、發揮、運用

- exert oneself **ph.**努力
- catch up with **ph.**趕上

We must exert ourselves to catch up with them, or it would be too late.

我們要奮起直追，否則就太晚了。

🔁 **employ, utilize**（使用、利用）

795.

exhaust [ɪg`zɔst]【ex·haust】**v.**耗盡、筋疲力盡、詳細研究

- exhaust pipe **ph.**排氣管
- tariff **n.**關稅

The effects of a tariff on the well-being of consumers and producers do not exhaust its effects on the importing nation.

關稅對消費者和生產者的福利影響，並沒有包括它對進口國的影響。

🔁 **consume, drain, empty**（排出、消耗）
🔃 **replace, replenish, supply**（提供、補充）

796.

exhibit [ɪg`zɪbɪt]【ex·hib·it】**v.**展示、顯示**n.**展示品

- exhibition **n.**展覽會
- complete **a.**完整的
- bottling **n.**裝瓶

We're interested in importing a complete bottling machine for exhibit and sale.

我們有興趣進口一整部裝瓶機，以備展示和銷售。

🔁 **display, flaunt, show**（陳列、顯示）

797.

exhort [ɪg`zɔrt]【ex·hort】**v.**規勸、激勵

- more than **ph.**不只
- permit **v.**允許

I do more than permit, I exhort you.

我不但允許而且還鼓勵你這樣做。

🔁 **advise, coax, urge**（促使、勸戒）

798.

exist [ɪg`zɪst]【ex·ist】**v.**存在、生存

- failure **n.**失敗
- successor **n.**成功者

The word "failure" does not exist in a successor's mind.

成功者心中沒有失敗這個字。

🔁 **live, subsist**（存在、生存）

799.

exotic [ɛg`zɑtɪk]【ex·ot·ic】**v.**異國的、外來的

- exotic species **ph.**外來物種
- melting pot **ph.**文化熔爐
- brew **n.**質地
- flavor **n.**風味
- brew **n.**質地

East meets west in Hong Kong, and from this melting pot comes a brew that has given the SAR its flavor as one of the world's most exotic cities.

香港特別行政區是一個中西合併的熔爐，其多元混合的成份使之躋身於世界上最具異國風情的城市之列。

🔁 **foreign, strange**（外來的、陌生的）
🔃 **endemic, indigenous, native**（本國的、地方性的）

800.

expand [ɪk`spænd]【ex·pand】**v.**展開、膨脹、詳述

- expansion **n.**擴展
- expand on / upon **ph.**詳述
- exploit **v.**利用
- resource **n.**資源

We should exploit our rich resources to expand the economy.

我們應該利用我們豐富的資源發展經濟。

🔁 **broaden, enlarge, increase**（展開、增加）
🔃 **abridge, contract, shrink**（縮短、縮小）

188

801.
expect [ɪk`spɛkt]【ex·pect】**V**期待、盼望、(用進行式)懷孕
What do you expect for a starting salary?
你心理理想的起薪是多少？
同► **anticipate, hope, think**（預期）
反► **despaire**（絕望）

• 字首：ex向外
　字尾：pect看

91

802.
expedition [ˌɛkspɪ`dɪʃən]【ex·pe·di·tion】**n**遠征、探險隊、迅速
In June 2009, our expedition, two years in the planning, was finally underway.
在2009年6月，我們籌備了兩年的考察工作終於開始了。
同► **journey, pilgrimage, trek**（遠征、旅行）

• 字首：ex向外
　字根：ped足
　字根：it走動
　字尾：tion表示一項行動
• underway a在進行中的

145

803.
expel [ɪk`spɛl]【ex·pel】**V**驅逐、排出、開除
Two attaches at the embassy are expelled from the country.
大使館的兩名隨員已被驅逐出境。
同► **dismiss, eject, remove**（驅逐、排斥）

• 字首：ex向外
　字根：pel推動
• attach n.伴隨
• embassy n.大使館

216

804.
expend [ɪk`spɛnd]【ex·pend】**V**花費、消費、耗盡
Don't expend all your energy on such a useless job.
不要把你的精力全花在這無益的工作上。
同► **consume, spend, waste**（花費、用完）

• expense n.費用
• 字首：ex向外
• 字根：pend付款
• energy n.精力

81

805.
expert [`ɛkspɚt]【ex·pert】**n**專家 **a**熟練的、內行的
It seems impossible to find the right balance between catering to the needs of the first-timer and the needs of the expert.
看來很難找到一個合適的平衡點以同時滿足新手和專家的要求。
同► **handy, masterful, proficient**（熟練的、靈巧的）
反► **amateur, amateurish**（外行的）

• Expert Systems ph.專家系統
• balance n.平衡
• first-timer n.新手

77

806.
expertise [ˌɛkspɚ`tiz]【ex·per·tise】**n**專門知識
Actually, I was hoping to rely on some of your marketing expertise.
我還希望仰仗你的專業行銷知識來有所突破。

• rely on ph.仰賴
• marketing n.行銷學

205

807.
expire [ɪk`spaɪr]【ex·pire】**V**期滿、呼氣、斷氣
Our trade agreement with Holland will expire at the end of this year.
我國和荷蘭的貿易協定今年年底期滿。
同► **cease, end, vanish**（終止、消失）
反► **retreat**（退出）

• expiration n終結、期滿
• agreement n.協議

241

808.
expiration date **ph**有效期限
"Term" means the term of the contract from the effective date through the expiration date.
「合約期限」指本合約從合約生效日至合約期滿日之間的期間。

• term n.期限
• effective a.有效的

E

809.

explicit [ɪk`splɪsɪt] 【 ex‧plic‧it 】 **a** 詳盡的、清楚的、直率的

After this very explicit financial statement came the most important part of the report!

在這段非常簡單扼要的財政情況說明後就是這篇報告的最重要部分！

同 candid, clear, distinct（清楚的、明確的）
反 ambiguous, implicit, vague（模擬兩可的）

• **Explicit knowledge ph.** 外顯的知識
• 字首：ex向外
  字根：plic折疊
  字尾：it…的
• **financial a.** 財政的

114

810.

exploit [`ɛksplɔɪt] 【 ex‧ploit 】 **v** 開發、利用、剝削 **n** 功績

One who owns the patent right enjoys the exclusive right to exploit it.

持專利權的人享有實施這項專利的絕對權力。

• **patent n.** 專利
• **exclusive a** 獨有的

123

811.

explore [ɪk`splor] 【 ex‧plore 】 **v** 探險、探測

Some American oil companies are helping you explore China's offshore oil resources.

美國的幾家石油公司正在幫助你們勘探中國近海的石油資源。

同 investigate, hunt, search（探究、搜索）

• **exploration n.** 探測
• **offshore a.** 近岸的

181

812.

export [ɪks`port] 【 ex‧port 】 **v n** 輸出、出口

Suppose it's an export deal and we've bought ex-works and sold C.I.F.

假設這是筆出口交易，我們按工廠交貨買進以到岸價格賣出。

反 import（進口）

• **export promotion ph.** 鼓勵出口
• 字首：ex向外
  字尾：port港口
• **C.I.F.=Cost, Insurance & Freight abbr.** 包括運費、保險費在內的對岸價格

222

813.

expose [ɪks`poz] 【 ex‧pose 】 **v** 使暴露、接觸到、揭露

As far as possible, a teacher should expose the students to real life situation.

教師應該盡可能地使學生接觸實際生活。

同 disclose, display, uncover（揭露、顯示）
反 conceal, cover, hide（隱藏、覆蓋）

• **exposition n.** 闡述
• 字首：ex向外
  字根：pose放置
• **situation n.** 情況

145

814.

expound [ɪk`spaund] 【 ex‧pound 】 **v** 解釋、詳細說明

You have enough time to expound your views to everybody.

你有足夠的時間向大家闡明你的觀點。

同 demonstrate, explain, illustrate（解釋、澄清）

• 字首：ex向外
  字尾：pound放置
• **view n.** 觀點

189

815.

expropriate [ɛks`proprɪˌet] 【 ex‧pro‧pri‧ate 】 **v** 徵收、剝奪…的所有權

They may have made a big loan to an infrastructure project, which the government might seek to expropriate.

某些銀行可能向某項基建項目提供巨額貸款，而這些貸款可能被政府強行沒收。

• **loan n.** 貸款
• **infrastructure n.** 基礎建設
• **seek v.** 尋求

124

816.
exquisite [`ɛkskwɪzɪt`] 【 ex·qui·site 】 ⓐ精美的、劇烈的、靈敏的
The hostess had exquisite taste in clothes.
女主人對衣著十分講究。
⑯ delicate, enchanting, superb（精美的）

- 字首：ex向外
- 字根：quis尋找
- 字尾：ite有⋯性質的
- hostess n.女主人
- taste n.品味

`121`

817.
extend [ɪk`stɛnd`] 【 ex·tend 】 ⓥ延長、擴展、給予
We can extend to you a special first order discount of 2%.
你是第一次訂貨，我們可以特別給予2%的折扣。
⑯ lengthen, stretch, provide（延伸、給予）
⑳ contract, shrink（縮小）

- 字首：ex向外
- 字根：tend伸展
- discount n.折扣

`215`

818.
extent [ɪk`stɛnt`] 【 ex·tent 】 ⓝ廣度、範圍、程度
Business declined to such an extent that the company had to close up.
生意如此清淡，公司只好停業。
⑯ degree, expanse（程度、廣度）

- 字首：ex向外
- 字根：tent伸
- decline v.下降

`219`

819.
extension [ɪk`stɛnʃən`] 【 ex·ten·sion 】 ⓝ伸展、延期、電話分機
For further information, please contact 64320776, extension 809.
如需瞭解更詳細的資訊請撥64320776分機809。
⑯ diffusion, elongation（擴散、延伸）

- extension course n.公開講座
- extension lead ph.接線
- 字首：ex向外
- 字根：ten伸展
- 字尾：sion性質

`194`

820.
exterior [ɪk`stɪrɪə`] 【 ex·te·ri·or 】 ⓐ外部的、對外的 ⓝ外部
The interior of the house corresponded with the exterior.
房間內部的陳設跟室外很協調。
⑯ external, extrinsic, superficial（外部的、表面的）
⑳ interior（內部的）

- exterior angle ph.外角
- Exterior Gateway Protocol ph.一個通信協定
- correspond v.符合

`94`

821.
exterminate [ɪk`stɜmə͵net`] 【 ex·ter·mi·nate 】 ⓥ消滅、根絕
We've made great efforts to exterminate mosquitoes and flies.
我們作了很大努力來消滅蚊蠅。
⑯ destroy, eliminate, eradicate（消滅、毀壞）

- mosquito n.蚊子
- fly n.蒼蠅

`104`

822.
external [ɪk`stɜnəl`] 【 ex·ter·nal 】 ⓐ外面的、對外的
ⓝ外表、形式
Our external trade has expanded during the recent years.
我國的對外貿易近幾年來有所發展。
⑯ exterior, outer（外面的、表面的）
⑳ internal（內部的）

- external trade ph.外貿
- External Viewer ph.外部閱覽器
- external-combustion engine ph.外燃機

`198`

823.
extinct [ɪk`stɪŋkt`] 【 ex·tinct 】 ⓐ熄滅的、絕種的、失效的
My hope of getting some employment was extinct.
我要找到工作的希望落空了。
⑯ dead, past, obsolete（死的、滅絕的）

- extinct book ph.絕版書
- extinct volcano ph.死火山
- 字首：ex向外
- 字根：tinct刺

`126`

824.

extinguish [ɪkˋstɪŋgwɪʃ]【ex·tin·guish】 **V**熄滅、使消失

Repeated rebuffs couldn't extinguish my enthusiasm.

我的熱情不會因屢次的受拒而減少。

⊜ **crush, smother, quench**（熄滅、平息）
⊗ **ignite, kindle, light**（點亮、點燃）

• rebuff n.失敗
• enthusiasm n.熱情

127

825.

extort [ɪkˋstɔrt]【ex·tort】 **V**敲詐、侵占

It shall be strictly forbidden to extort confessions by torture and to collect evidence by threat, enticement, deceit or other unlawful means.

嚴禁刑訊逼供和以威脅、誘、騙以及其他非法的方法收集證據。

• 字首：ex向外
  字根：tort扭曲
• confession n.承認
• enticement n.引誘
• deceit n.欺騙

141

826.

extract [ɪkˋstrækt]【ex·tract】 **V n**取出、提煉、摘錄

We can extract pleasure from a party.

我們可以從聚會中得到快樂。

• 字首：ex向外
  字根：tract拉
• pleasure n.快樂

188

827.

extraordinary [ɪkˋstrɔrdn̩ˌɛrɪ]【ex·traor·di·nar·y】
a特別的、離奇的

Extraordinary profits resulted for the firms during a twenty-year period.

在二十年的時間裡，這些公司都賺到了巨額的利潤。

⊜ **exceptional, special, wonderful**（特別的、卓越的）
⊗ **common, normal, standard**（普遍的、標準的）

• extraordinary
  ambassador ph.特派大使
• 字首：extra額外的
  字尾：ordinary普通的

129

828.

extreme [ɪkˋstrim]【ex·treme】 **n a**末端(的)、極度(的)、激烈(的)

During spasms of extreme activity he relied on his assistants to screen his more impetuous commands.

在工作極端緊張的時候，他依靠他的助理去檢查他那比較倉促的指令。

⊜ **drastic, excessive, radical**（極端的）
⊗ **moderate, proper, temperate**（適度的、溫和的）

• extreme sport ph.
• 極限運動
• extreme tourism ph.
• 極限旅遊
• spasm n.痙攣
• screen v.審查
• impetuous a.魯莽的

194

E

MEMO

abbr 縮寫詞
a 形容詞
ad 副詞
aux 助動詞
conj 連接詞
n 名詞
num 數字
ph 片語
prep 介系詞
v 動詞
（美）美式用語
（英）英式用語
（法）法式用語

全書單字取材於：

①10本坊間新多益考試暢銷書籍

②50篇英文新聞、商業文章

③2005~2012年ETS TOEIC歷屆考古題

→ 總計約50,000個單字，以電腦統計出題率高達80%
的實用單字1,800個

> | F 家族 **fabricate~fusion** 01-06

高分錦囊

829.
fabricate [ˋfæbrɪ͵ket] 【fab·ri·cate】 **V**製造、偽造、杜撰
Obviously, he fabricated an excuse for his absence.
他提出的缺席理由顯然是瞎編的。
圓 creat, forge（製造、捏造）

• excuse n.藉口
• absence n.缺席

82

830.
facilitate [fəˋsɪlə͵tet] 【fa·cil·i·tate】 **V**使容易、促進、幫助
It would facilitate matters greatly if you could inform them in advance.
如果你事先能通知他們，事情會容易進行得多。
圓 assist, ease, help（幫助）

• 字根：facil容易
  字尾：it走動
  字尾：ate使成為
• facility n.便利
• inform v.通知

194

831.
factor [ˋfæktɚ] 【fac·tor】 **N**要素、代理商 **V**分解、代理
As economies grow, there are major changes in technology, factor supplies, and demands.
當經濟增長時，在技術、生產要素供應量和需求方面會有重大的變動。
圓 cause, element, ingredient（因素、起因）

• factor in ph.將…納入
• 字首：fact製作
  字尾：or事物

181

832.
fake [fek] 【fake】 **V**偽造、假裝 **N**冒牌貨、騙子 **A**假的
The salesman cheated me into buying a fake.
那個推銷員騙我買了假貨。
圓 false, mock, unreal（假的）
反 genuine, real, true（真實的）

• fake bake ph.打腫臉充胖子
• salesman n.銷售員
• cheat v.欺騙

105

833.
fancy [ˋfænsɪ] 【fan·cy】 **V N**愛好、想像 **A**花俏的
We cannot fancy a life without electricity.
我們不能設想生活中沒有電會怎樣。
圓 dream, imagine, visualize（想像）
反 plain（樸素的）

• fancy ball ph.化妝舞會
• fancy dan ph.愛賣弄的人
• fancy fair ph.義賣場
• fancy oneself ph.自以為
• fancy-free a.無拘束的
• fancy-sick a.有相思病的

114

834.
fare [fɛr] 【fare】 **N**車費、乘客、伙食
Let me go shares with you in the taxi fare.
我和你分攤計程車費吧。
圓 charge, fee, toll（票價）

• fare card ph.儲值卡
• fare-thee-well / fare-you-well n.完美

229

835.
farewell [ˋfɛr͵wɛl] 【fare·well】 **V N**告別 **int**再會
I think it's time to bid farewell for tonight.
我想今晚就到此為止。
圓 cheerio, good day, so long（再會）

• farewell party ph.歡送會
• bid v.向…表示

81

836.
far-fetched [`far`fɛtʃt] 【far·fetched 】 **a** 牽強的
- explanation n.解釋
- convince v.使確信

Your far-fetched explanation could hardly convince anybody.
你的解釋有多穿鑿附會之處，很難讓大家心服口服。

837.
fascinate [`fæsn͵et] 【fasci·nate 】 **V** 迷住、使呆住
- fascination n.著迷
- toy n.玩具

The children were fascinated by the toys in the shop window.
孩子們被商店櫥窗裡的玩具給吸引住了。
圓 attract, enthrall, intrigue （使著迷）

F

838.
fasten [`fæsn̩] 【fas·ten 】 **V** 繫緊、抓住、集中於

Don't fasten the responsibility on others.
不要把責任推到他人身上。
圓 attach, bind, tie （繫緊）
反 loosen, unfasten, untie （放鬆）

839.
fatal [`fetl̩] 【fa·tal 】 **a** 致命的、命中注定的
- tick n.滴答聲

Each tick of the clock was bringing the fatal hour nearer.
隨著時鐘的每一個滴答聲，關鍵的時刻越來越近了。
圓 dead, mortal （致命的）

840.
fatigue [fə`tig] 【fa·tigue 】 **V n** 疲勞、勞累
- persist in ph.堅持
- carry on ph.繼續
- in spite of ph.不管

He persisted in carrying on his work in spite of great fatigue.
他雖然疲倦極了，可是仍然堅持工作。
圓 exhaust, tire （疲勞）

841.
favorable [`fevərəbl̩] 【fa·vor·a·ble 】 **a** 贊同的、有利的、討人喜歡的
- 字首：favor贊成
  字尾：able易於…的
- transnational a.跨國的

A favorable aspect about a transnational corporation is that they provide jobs in foreign countries.
跨國公司在國外提供就業機會，這是它受歡迎的一面。
圓 approving, profitable, salutary （贊成的、有幫助的）
反 adverse, unfavorable （反對的）

842.
feasible [`fizəbl̩] 【fea·si·ble 】 **a** 能實行的、合理的、合適的
- minimize v.減少
- authority n.職權
- decentralize v.使分散

To minimize this cost, authority should be decentralized wherever feasible.
為了減少這方面的損失，可把職權作適當的分散。
圓 attainable, practical, workable （可實行的、可能的）

843.
feast [fist] 【feast 】 **n** 盛宴、享受、節日 **V** 盛宴款待、享受
- feast on ph.盡情欣賞
- feast-or-famine ph.不是極好就是極差
- customarily ad.習慣上
- intellectual a.智力的

Customarily, he began the day in Tokyo with an intellectual feast.
在東京，他通常以接收新知來開始自己一天的生活。
圓 banquet, feed, treat （盛宴）

844.
feature [`fitʃə`] 【 fea·ture 】 n特徵、面貌、特寫

Contrasts are a vital feature of environment design.

協調是環境設計的一個重要的特點。

同► **characteristic, mark, trait**（特徵、特色）

- feature fatigue ph.功能疲勞症
- feature film ph.故事片
- feature-length a.長篇的
- vital a.重要的

845.
feeble [`fibl`] 【 fee·ble 】 a虛弱的、微弱的、拙劣無效的

Feeble and uncertain securities were thrown upon the market.

拙劣無效的或者沒有把握的證券都向市場拋售了。

同► **frail, powerful, weak**（虛弱的、衰弱的）
反► **intense, strong, tough**（強壯的、熱情的）

- feeble-minded a.低能的
- uncertain a.不明確的
- security n.安全
- throw upon ph.拋起

846.
feminine [`fɛmənɪn`] 【 fem·i·nine 】 a女性的、嬌柔的

Feminine craft was alert to prompt it.

女性的手腕會警覺地提醒她說出適當的話語。

反► **masculine**（男性的）

- feminine rhyme ph.第二節無重音的雙音節韻
- craft n.手腕
- alert a.警覺的

847.
ferry [`fɛrɪ`] 【 fer·ry 】 n擺渡、渡輪、渡口 v運送

The right to charge tools is usually incident to a ferry.

索取通行稅的權利通常附屬於擺渡營業權。

- 字根：fer拿來
  字尾：ry一項行動
- incident a.附隨的
- proposal n.提議、提案

848.
fertile [`fɝtl`] 【 fer·tile 】 a肥沃的、多產的、豐富的

A fertile and needful trade flowed between our countries.

在我們兩國之間進行著繁榮和互惠互利的貿易。

同► **abundant, enriched, productive**（多產的、豐富的）
反► **barren, sterile**（貧瘠的）

- 字根：fer帶來
  字尾：tile與…有關的

849.
festival [`fɛstəvl`] 【 fes·ti·val 】 n節日、慶祝活動 a節日的

He asks whether we have ordered the plan for the spring festival.

他問我們是否為春節訂了計劃。

同► **holiday, jubilee**（節日）
反► **weekday, workday**（平日、工作日）

850.
fiction [`fɪkʃən`] 【 fic·tion 】 n總稱小說、虛構、謊言

The hypothesis no longer belongs to the realm of science fiction.

這種假設已不是科學幻想。

同► **fable, legend, myth**（虛構、捏造）
反► **fact, nonfiction**（事實、非小說類散文學）

- 字根：fict製作
  字尾：ion性質
- hypothesis n.假設
- belong to ph.屬於
- realm n.領域

851.
finale [fɪ`nɑlɪ`] 【 fi·nal·e 】 n終曲、結尾

By the time the pop group went into the finale of their act, the audience was at fever pitch.

流行音樂樂團演奏終曲時，觀眾的情緒沸騰了。

同► **conclusion, end, termination**（結局、終結）
反► **prelude**（前奏、序幕）

- pop group ph.流行樂樂隊
- audience n.觀眾
- fever pitch ph.極度興奮

165

852.
finance [faɪˋnæns] 【 fi‧nance 】 n財政、資金支援 a融資

Shanghai will turn into an international center of economy, finance, trade and shipping.

上海將建成國際經濟、金融、貿易、航運中心。

🔊 **aid, sponsor, subsidize**（資金支持）

- financier n.財政者
- finance company ph.貸款公司
- Finance company subsidiary ph.財務子公司
- finance house ph.信貸公司

196

853.
finish [ˋfɪnɪʃ] 【 fin‧ish 】 vn完成、結束

His sense of duty pricked him on to finish the work on time.

他的責任心驅使他按時完成工作。

🔊 **complete, end, terminate**（結束、完成）
🔊 **begin, commence, start**（開始）

- finish off ph.毀滅
- finish up with ph.以…告終
- finish with ph.完成
- 字首：fin最終 字尾：ish使成為
- prick on ph.驅使

83

854.
finite [ˋfaɪnaɪt] 【 fi‧nite 】 a有限的 n有限之物

We must accept finite disappointment, but we must never lose infinite hope.

我們必須接受有限的失望，但是千萬不可失去無限的希望。

🔊 **bounded, limited, restricted**（有限的）
🔊 **infinite**（無限的）

- 字根：fin限制 字尾：ite有…性質的
- disappointment n.失望

54

855.
fire alarm nph火警

The people poured back into the building when they heard the fire alarm.

一聽到火警警報，人們就紛紛回到大樓裡。

- alarm n.警報
- pour v.湧流

58

856.
fire extinguisher nph滅火器

Always have a fire extinguisher handy when working with a blowpipe.

工作中使用汽油吹焰管時，請將滅火器放在觸手可及之處。

- extinguisher n.滅火器
- handy a.近便的
- blowpipe n.吹管

144

857.
fiscal [ˋfɪskl̩] 【 fis‧cal 】 a財政的、會計的、國庫的

Fiscal revenue of local governments kept sustained and rapid growth.

地方財政收入持續高速增長。

🔊 **financial, monetary, pecuniary**（財政的）

- fiscal year ph.會計年度
- revenue n.收入
- rapid a.快速的

75

858.
fitness [ˋfɪtnɪs] 【 fit‧ness 】 n健康、適合

They're doing exercises to improve their fitness.

他們為增強體質而做體操。

- exercise n.運動
- improve v.改善

51

859.
flat [flæt] 【 flat 】 a平坦的、蕭條的 n套房

If they won't cooperate, our plan will fall flat.

如果他們不肯合作我們的計劃就會落空。

🔊 **horizontal, dull**（平的、蕭條的）
🔊 **bumpy, rough**（崎嶇不平的）

- flat cap ph.低頂圓帽
- flat iron ph.熨斗
- flat out ph.竭盡全力
- flat show ph.樣品公寓
- flat switching ph.平裝

143

860.
flatter [`flætɚ] [flat·ter] **v** 奉承、阿諛、使高興

We flatter ourselves that we can do without their help.

我們自以為沒有他們的幫助我們也可以辦到。

同 adulate, blandish, fawn（諂媚、奉承）

• flatter oneself **ph.** 自以為

861.
flaw [flɔ] [flaw] **n** 缺點、裂縫 **v** 使破裂師

This type of success was almost without flaw, as he saw it.

在他看來，這種成就簡直是無懈可擊。

同 blemish, defect（裂紋、瑕疵）

862.
flea market **n片** 廉價市場、攤市

The flea market offers the most practical commodities at the most favorable prices.

跳蚤市場以最實惠的價格提供最實用的商品。

• flea **n.** 跳蚤
• practical **a.** 實際的
• commodity **n.** 商品

863.
flexible [`flɛksəbl] [flex·i·ble] **a** 可彎曲的、柔順的、靈活的

Flexible exchange rates yield an intermediate outcome in the face of capital-flow shocks.

變動匯率在面臨資本流動衝擊時能產生一種緩衝的效果。

反 inflexible（不可彎曲的）

• flexible response **ph.** 機動反應戰略
• 字根：flex 折疊
  字尾：ible 易…的
• intermediate **a.** 中間的
• outcome **n.** 結果

864.
flight [flaɪt] [flight] **n** 飛行、航班、航程

Flight 123 to Sydney is now boarding at gate five.

飛往雪梨的123次航班正在五號登機門登機。

同 aviation, gliding, soaring（航行）
反 alight, fall（降落）

• flight attendant **ph.** 空中服務人員
• flight crew **ph.** 機組人員
• flight deck **ph.** 駕駛艙
• flight lieutenant **ph.** 空軍上尉
• flight sergeant **ph.** 空軍上士

865.
fling [flɪŋ] [fling] **v n** 投擲、揮動、嘗試

Why did you fling your money away on that risk?

你為什麼要浪費錢去冒那個風險？

同 cast, throw, toss（擲、拋）

• fling dirt at **ph.** 中傷
• fling mud at sb. **ph.** 中傷某人

866.
floppy [`flɑpɪ] [flop·py] **a** 鬆軟的、懶散的

High-speed information transfer between a floppy disk and data memory frequently occurs directly between these two devices, by passing the CPU.

在軟碟與資料記憶體之間的高速資訊傳輸，常常是跨過中央處理機直接在這兩個部件之間進行的。

• floppy disk **ph.** 電腦軟式磁碟片
• high-speed **a.** 高速的
• frequently **ad.** 經常地

867.
flourish [`flɝɪʃ] [flour·ish] **v** 茂盛、繁榮、炫耀

No new business can flourish in the present economic climate.

在目前的經濟氣候中，任何新生意都興旺不起來。

反 decay, decline, fall（衰落、降下）

• climate **n.** 趨勢

868.
fluctuate [ˋflʌktʃuˏet] 【fluc·tu·ate】 **V**變動、動搖

The rate of industrial injury insurance premium varies according to different trades, and it may fluctuate with the situation of the individual enterprise.

工傷保險費率隨著不同貿易和企業狀況而有所不同。

• industrial a.工業的
• premium n.保險費
• according to ph.依據

869.
flush [flʌʃ] 【flush】 **V**湧流、沖洗 **a**充足的

The firm is flush with funds.

這家公司有充足的資金。

• flush of hope ph.希望的曙光

870.
flutter [ˋflʌtɚ] 【flut·ter】 **V n**飄動、興奮

She had found it well to flutter ahead.

她發覺最好的辦法是振翼前進。

• flutter echo ph.顫動回聲
• flutter kick ph.淺打水

871.
focus [ˋfokəs] 【fo·cus】 **n**焦點、調焦 **V**聚焦、集中

Many companies have begun to focus on serving the needs of people with their products, and are spending the time and money to do upfront design.

很多公司開始重視如何使產品滿足使用者的需求並投入時間和資金來進行前期設計。

• adjust, concentrate（集中、調節）

• focus on ph.集中於
• upfront a.預付的

872.
fold [fold] 【fold】 **V**摺疊、失敗 **n**摺疊

What he ought to do, he thought, was to fold up the Marliss Corporation.

他想現在當務之急是讓馬里斯有限公司倒閉。

• bend（折）
• unfold（打開）

• fold-up a.適於摺疊的
• ought to應該

873.
fondness [ˋfɑndnɪs] 【fond·ness】 **n**喜愛、溺愛

Years after his graduation, his teachers and friends at Yale still remembered him with great fondness.

他畢業多年，耶魯的老師和朋友們提起他還是稱讚。

• 字首：fond喜愛的
  字尾：ness一項行動
• graduation n.畢業

874.
forbid [fɚˋbɪd] 【for·bid】 **V**禁止、防止

They forbid entry to unauthorized people.

他們禁止未經許可的人員入內。

• bar, prohibit, taboo（禁止）
• allow, permit（同意）

• forbid-forbade-forbidden
• entry n.進入

875.
forecast [ˋforˏkæst] 【fore·cast】 **V n**預測、預言

The sales forecast had to be done before the pricing and scheduling.

銷售預測必須在價格估計和生產安排之前進行。

• foretell, predict（預報、預測）

• 字首：fore向前
  字根：cast投擲
• schedule v.安排

876.
foremost [`for͵most`] 【 fore·most 】 **a** 最前的、最重要的

Work therefore is desirable, first and foremost, as a preventive of boredom.

因此人們願意工作，最重要的是工作可以防止無聊感。

📖 **dominant, main** （最重要的）

📖 **aftermost** （最後頭的）

- preventive a.預防的
- boredom n.無聊

877.
foresee [for`si`] 【 fore·see 】 **v** 預見、預知

No one can foresee precisely what course it will take.

沒有誰能夠正確地預料事情將如何發展。

📖 **anticipate, prophesy** （預知）

- foresee-foresaw-foreseen
- 字首：fore向前
  字尾：see看
- precisely ad.精準地

878.
foreshadow [for`ʃædo`] 【 fore·shad·ow 】 **v** 預示 **n** 預兆

Public health officials fear that because of vast underreporting, recorded statistics foreshadow much more severe conditions.

公共衛生官員害怕因為通報率嚴重偏低，實際的情況可能比記錄的統計數字更為嚴重。

- official n.官員
- vast a.大量的
- statistics n.統計資料
- severe a.嚴重的

879.
forestall [for`stɔl`] 【 fore·stall 】 **v** 搶先行動、先發制人

I have my objection all prepared, but Stephens forestall me.

我已做好準備要提出反對意見，不料斯蒂芬斯卻搶先了一步。

- objection n.反對
- prepare v.準備

880.
forfeit [`fɔr͵fɪt`] 【 for·feit 】 **v n** 喪失、罰金

Bidder shall have the right to refuse to grant such an extension of validity of bid without forfeit their bid bond.

投標人有權拒絕延長投標有效期限並不會因此而失掉其投標保證金。

📖 **lose, sacrifice** （失去）

📖 **aquire, benefical** （獲得）

- extension n.延長
- validity v.正確的

881.
forge [fɔrdʒ] 【 forge 】 **v** 鍛鍊、偽造、穩步前進

A boat sailing against the current must forge ahead or it will be driven back.

逆水行舟，不進則退。

📖 **progress** （前進）

- boat n.船
- sail v.航行
- current n.水流
- ahead ad.向前

882.
formal [`fɔrml̩`] 【 for·mal 】 **a** 正式的、拘謹的、整齊的 **n** 正式社交活動

In the civil procedure a confession is a formal admission.

在民事訴訟程式中，供認是一種正式的承認。

📖 **casual, informal** （隨便的、不正式的）

- formal dress ph.禮服
- 字首：form形式
  字尾：al屬於…的
- procedure n.過程
- confession n.承認

883.
formula [`fɔrmjələ`] 【 for·mu·la 】 **n** 客套語、公式、準則

For the gray area in between, no simple formula would suffice.

在這兩者之間的灰色地區任何簡單的方案都是不夠的。

📖 **cliché, formulary, principle** （做事之定規）

- formula car ph.方程式賽車
- formula literature ph.公式文學
- suffice v.足夠

884.
formulate [`fɔrmjə,let] 【 for·mu·late 】 **V**用公式表示、規劃、配製
He thought it is time to formulate some plan of action.
他認為這是該籌畫什麼行動計劃的時候了。
🔟▶ **define, describe, put**（闡述、說明）

885.
forthcoming [,for`kʌmɪŋ] 【 forth·com·ing 】 **a**即將來臨
的、樂意幫助的
The secretary at the reception desk was not very forthcoming.
接待處的祕書不太主動。
🔟▶ **approaching, imminent, near**（來臨的、行將到來的）

• secretary n.祕書
• reception n.接待

886.
forum [`forəm] 【 fo·rum 】 **n**討論會
Whispers around downtown predict major cutbacks soon at Forum East.
商業界人士私下預料，東城新區工程不久將大幅度縮減。
🔟▶ **plaza, square**（公會所、廣場）

• whisper v.私下告訴
• predict v.預測
• cutback n.減少

887.
forward [`fɔrwəd] 【 for·ward 】 **V**轉交、促進 **a**向前的 **ad**向前
Please clear the goods and forward them by rail to our address, carriage pay.
請將該貨物關後通過鐵路交本公司運費已付。
🔟▶ **deliver, send**（發送、遞送）

• forward market ph. 期貨市場
• forward roll ph.向前翻滾
• forward-looking a.向前看 的
• carriage n.運費

888.
foster [`fɔstə] 【 fo·ster 】 **V**養育、培養 **a**養育的
We should foster capital investment in areas needing development.
我們應鼓勵在需要發展的地區投資。
🔟▶ **feed, nourish, nurse**（養育、培育）

• foster child ph.養子女
• foster father / mother ph.養父（母）
• foster- pref.收養的
• investment n.投資

889.
fraction [`frækʃən] 【 frac·tion 】 **n**小部分、破片、分數
Naturally, only a fraction of our huge investment was ever making public.
自然地，我們巨額的投資中只有一小部分是公之於眾的。
🔟▶ **division, portion, segment**（部分、片段）
🔄▶ **integer**（完整）

• fracture n.破碎
• 字首：fract打碎
• 字尾：ion性質

890.
fragile [`frædʒəl] 【 frag·ile 】 **a**易碎的、脆弱的、精細的
We offer courier service for fragile goods, and we'll pay the full price for anything damaged.
本公司承接易碎品特快專遞業務，如有損壞，照價賠償。
🔟▶ **brittle, frail**（易碎的、脆弱的）
🔄▶ **solid, tough**（堅硬的、固體的）

• 字首：frag打碎
• 字尾：ile易…的
• courier n.送遞急件
• damage v.損壞

891.
fragrant [`fregrənt] 【 fra·grant 】 **a**香的、芳香的
Coffee is a fragrant beverage.
咖啡是一種香味濃郁的飲料。
🔟▶ **aromatic, perfumed, odorous**（芳香的）

• beverage n.飲料

892.

franchise [ˈfrænˌtʃaɪz] 【fran·chise】 **n** 選舉權、**v** 給予特權、經銷權

This is the firm that has an exclusive franchise to offer bus service in the city.

這是一家在這個城市的公共汽車服務方面擁有獨佔權利的廠商。

- franchise organization ph.特許加盟組織
- exclusive a.獨有的

893.

fraud [frɔd] 【fraud】 **n** 欺騙、騙子、假貨

She went through the company's accounts, looking for evidence of fraud.

她仔細審核公司的帳目，以查找欺騙作弊的證據。

同 cheating, swindle, trickery（欺騙）

- Fraud Squad ph.詐欺行為偵查組
- account n.帳目

894.

freight [fret]【freight】 **n** 運費、貨物、貨運

The aircraft company deals with freight only; it has no travel service.

這家航空公司只經營貨運業務不經營客運。

同 cargo, load, shipment（貨物、負荷）

- freight car ph.運貨車廂
- freight train ph.集裝箱列車

895.

frequent [ˈfrikwənt]【fre·quent】 **a** 頻繁的、慣常的 **v** 常到

It is advisable to check the instrument by frequent calibration.

最好通過經常的校準來檢查儀器。

同 common, habitual, prevalent（頻繁的、慣常的）

反 infrequent, rare（不平常的、稀少的）

- frequent filer ph.飛行常客
- frequent shopper program ph.購物積點計畫
- instrument n.儀器
- calibration n.劃刻度

896.

friction [ˈfrɪkʃən]【fric·tion】 **n** 摩擦、不和

There is a great deal of friction between the management and the work force.

勞資雙方之間存在大量矛盾。

同 clash, conflict, scraping（摩擦、衝突）

- friction cost ph.與證券買賣有關的費用
- friction tape ph.絕緣膠帶
- management n.管理
- force n.勢力

897.

fuel [ˈfjuəl]【fu·el】 **n** 燃料、刺激因素 **v** 刺激、加燃料

Many small plants in that country closed down for lack of fuel.

由於燃料不足，那個國家很多小工廠都關閉了。

同 combustible（燃料）

- fuel cell ph.燃料電池
- fuel injection ph.燃油噴射
- fuel-efficient vehicles ph.省油車
- lack n.缺少

898.

fulfill [fulˈfɪl]【ful·fill】 **v** 執行、實現、達到目的

The question is how to fulfill our production plan as soon as possible.

問題是如何儘快地完成我們的生產計劃。

同 complete, perform（執行、完成）

- production n.生產

899.

function [ˈfʌŋkʃən]【func·tion】 **n** 官能、職務、集會 **v** 起作用的

Who would like to feel left out at such a function?

在這樣的場合誰會願意受到冷落呢？

同 act, operate, work（起作用）

- function key ph.功能鍵
- function word ph.虛詞

900.
fund [fʌnd] 【fund】 **n**基金、存款

● pension n.養老金
● several a.數個

166

The pension fund owns shares in several major public companies.

該養老基金在幾家主要出售股份給公眾的公司中均有股份。

同 **assets, stock, supply**（資產、財產）

901.
fundamental [ˌfʌndəˈmɛntl̩] 【fun·da·men·tal】 **a**基礎的、原始的 **n**基本原理

● historically ad.歷史上地
● reform n.改革

94

Historically, there have been few fundamental reforms in corporate power.

從歷史上看來，大公司的權力從未發生過根本的改革。

同 **basic, elementary, essential**（基礎的、根本的）

902.
furnish [ˈfɝnɪʃ] 【fur·nish】 **v**配置、提供

● clause n.條款
● sufficient a.足夠的

87

First you must find out the clause of the quality problems and furnish sufficient evidence.

首先你得查查有關品質問題的條款並提供足夠的證據。

同 **equip, provide, supply**（供應、提供）

903.
furnishing [ˈfɝnɪʃɪŋ] 【fur·nish·ing】 **n**裝備、（常用複數）傢俱、服飾

● impart v.給予
● elegance n.優雅

58

The furnishings of the room imparted an air of elegance.

這個房間的傢俱給這房間一種優雅的氣氛。

904.
furniture [ˈfɝnɪtʃə] 【fur·ni·ture】 **n**傢俱、設備

● suitable a.適合的
● humidity n.濕度
● preseration n.保存

61

A suitable relative humidity is important for the preservation of furniture.

適當的相對溫度對保護傢俱是十分重要的。

同 **chattels, equipment**（傢俱、設備品）

905.
furthermore [ˌfɝðəˈmor] 【fur·ther·more】 **ad**此外、而且

● inflation n.通貨膨脹
● erode v.腐蝕

211

Furthermore, inflation erodes other kinds of government revenue.

此外，通貨膨脹損害了政府的其他各種收入。

906.
fusion [ˈfjuʒən] 【fu·sion】 **n**熔解、融合

● fusion bomb ph.氫彈
● fusion cuisine ph.混合菜式
● 字首：fus流、寫
　字尾：ion性質
● association n.聯盟

165

The association of Inter-Americana fusion covers North, Central, and South America, establishes a central office in Montevidei.

美洲國家廣播協會包括北美、中美和南美國家，總部在蒙特維。

同 **liquefaction, melting, refining**（融解）

MEMO

abbr 縮寫詞
a 形容詞
ad 副詞
aux 助動詞
conj 連接詞
n 名詞
num 數字
ph 片語
prep 介系詞
v 動詞
（美）美式用語
（英）英式用語
（法）法式用語

全書單字取材於：
①10本坊間新多益考試暢銷書籍
②50篇英文新聞、商業文章
③2005~2012年ETS TOEIC歷屆考古題
→ 總計約50,000個單字，以電腦統計出題率高達80%
　的實用單字1,800個

高頻率單字

➤ | G 家族 gadget~gym

高 分 錦 囊

907.
gadget [`gædʒɪt] 【gadg·et】 **n.**小機件、小玩意兒
She has a gadget that lets her send e-mails, play games, and take notes.
她有一個可以讓她發郵件玩遊戲和記筆記的小設備。
➤ appliance, device, instrument（器械）

- e-mail n.電子郵件
- note n.筆記

`57`

908.
gamble [`gæmbḷ] 【gam·ble】 **v.n.**賭博、冒險
Setting up this business was a bit of a gamble.
創辦這樣的公司有點冒險。
➤ bet, risk, wager（賭博、冒險）

- gamble in / on ph.投機
- set up ph.創辦

`88`

909.
garage [gə`rɑʒ] 【ga·rage】 **n.**車庫、汽車修理廠
The truck that had a breakdown was towed to the garage.
那輛故障的貨車被拖到修車廠。
➤ auto repair shop, carport（汽車修理廠、車房）

- garage house ph.庫房音樂
- garage sale ph.車庫售物
- truck n.貨車
- breakdown n.損壞

`97`

910.
garbage [`gɑrbɪdʒ] 【gar·bage】 **n.**垃圾、廢話
The sanitation department is in charge of garbage disposal.
環境衛生部門負責處理垃圾。
➤ junk, trash, waste（垃圾）

- garbage can ph.垃圾箱
- garbage collector / man ph.垃圾工
- garbage truck ph.垃圾車
- sanitation n.公共衛生

`105`

911.
garment [`gɑrmənt] 【gar·ment】 **n.**服裝、衣著
I have a client in the garment business on Seventh Avenue.
我有個客戶在第七大道從事成衣生意。
➤ frock, robe, togs（衣服）

- client n.客戶
- avenue n.大道

`66`

912.
gasp [gæsp] 【gasp】 **n.**喘氣 **v.**喘氣、渴望
The teams were at their last gasp when the whistle blew.
球隊正作最後拼搏時哨聲響了。
➤ choke, pant puff（喘氣）

- whistle n.哨子
- blow v.吹響

`81`

913.
gauge [gedʒ] 【gauge】 **n.**尺寸標準、範圍 **v.**估計
He took the gauge of the new secretary's competence.
他估量了一下新祕書的能力。
➤ assess, estimate, judge（估計、判斷）

- competence n.能力

`75`

914.
gaze [gez] 【gaze】 **V n** 注視、凝視 〔140〕

We strained our eager and gazed forward.

我們興高采烈，極目眺望。

同 **gape, gawk, stare**（凝視、注視）

• strain v.拉緊
• eager a.熱心

915.
gear [gɪr] 【gear】 **n** 齒輪、工具 **V** 以齒輪連動、使適應 〔81〕

My whole morning's work has been put out of gear by that mishap.

我一個上午的工作全讓這件倒楣的事給打亂了。

• gear toward ph.為某事或某特定對象而設計發展
• mishap n.災難

916.
general hospital **ph** 綜合醫院 〔58〕

This is a general hospital with various departments.

這是家有各科門診的綜合醫院。

• various a.多樣化的

G

917.
generalize [ˋdʒɛnərəˏlaɪz] 【gen·er·al·ize】 **V** 推斷、概括 〔81〕

It is critical to generalize about people.

以偏概全地談論他人是危險的。

同 **diversify, universalize**（推廣）
反 **specialize**（專攻）

• 字首：general普通的 字尾：ize使成為
• critical a.吹毛求疵的

918.
generate [ˋdʒɛnəˏret] 【gen·er·ate】 **V** 產生、造成、生育 〔114〕

The new business we'll generate should far exceed what's lost.

我們新招攬的生意會遠遠超過丟失的那部分。

同 **cause, produce, originate**（產生、引起）

• generator n.發電機
• 字根：gener產生 字尾：ate進行一項行動
• exceed v.超過

919.
generous [ˋdʒɛnərəs] 【gen·er·ous】 **a** 慷慨的、寬厚的、大量的 〔105〕

The repayment provisions are generous.

償還貸款的條款訂得很寬鬆。

同 **bighearted, ample, plentiful**（慷慨的、大量的）

• 字首：gener產生 字尾：ous充滿…的
• repayment n.付還
• provision n.條款

920.
genuine [ˋdʒɛnjuɪn] 【gen·u·ine】 **a** 真的、真誠的、純血統的 〔87〕

Most of the genuine monopolies were dissolved.

大部分真正的壟斷公司被解散了。

同 **authentic, legitimate, sincere**（真的）
反 **dummy, false, sham**（假的、錯的）

• monopoly n.壟斷企業
• dissolve v.解散

921.
get-together [ˋgɛttəˏgɛðə] 【get to·geth·er】 **n** 聚會、聯歡會 〔64〕

I saw him bustling about making preparation for the New Year get-together.

我看見他正在忙碌地為新年聯歡會作準備工作。

• bustling a.奔忙的
• reparation n.準備

922.
glance [glæns]【glance】**v n**一瞥、掠過、閃爍

Have you got time for a glance at this agenda?

你有時間流覽一下這份議程表嗎？

🔵 **glimpse, look, skim**（看）

🔴 **gaze, stare**（凝視、注視）

- glance over ph.簡略閱讀
- agenda n.議程

923.
gloomy [`glumɪ]【gloom·y】**a**陰暗的、憂鬱的

He saw the patrol ahead in a gloomy vista of fatigue and danger and misery.

他感到這一去前途黯淡，等待著他的不是奔波勞累就是艱危磨難。

🔵 **dreary, glum, melancholy**（沮喪的、悲哀的）

🔴 **cheerful, gay, pleasant**（開心的、快樂的）

- 字首：gloom黑暗
  字尾：y充滿…的
- vista n.展望
- misery n.痛苦

924.
glow [glo]【glow】**v n**發光、臉紅、興高采烈

She felt a glow of pride at her daughter's achievements.

她為女兒的成就感到非常驕傲。

🔵 **blush, flame, radiate**（臉紅、燃燒）

- pride n.驕傲
- achievement n.成就

925.
gossip [`gɑsəp]【gos·sip】**n**閒話、愛傳流言蜚語的人 **v**閒聊

As a matter of fact, this was purely newspaper gossip and speculation.

事實上，這純粹是報紙上的八卦和推測。

🔵 **prattle, tattle**（閒談）

- gossip column ph. 報刊漫談欄
- gossip magnet ph. 焦點問題
- speculation n.推測

926.
graduate [`grædʒʊ͵et]【grad·u·ate】**v**畢業 **n**大學畢業生 **a**研究生的

The full university graduate fellowship covers both tuition and stipend.

研究生的全額獎學金包括學費和生活費。

- graduate school n.研究所
- 字根：gradu步驟
  字尾：ate執行某一行動
- fellowship n.獎學金
- stipend n.津貼

927.
grain [gren]【grain】**n**穀粒、細粒、微量

Our observations may contain a grain of truth for you to refer to.

我們的意見也許會有值得你參考的地方。

🔵 **bit, particle, speck**（顆粒）

- grain alcohol ph.酒精
- grain elevator ph.裝有升降機的穀倉
- observation n.意見
- truth n.事實

928.
grant [grænt]【grant】**v n**同意、允許、財產轉讓

He importuned me to grant his request.

他糾纏著要我答應他的請求。

🔵 **bestow, give, permit**（給予、同意）

🔴 **request, refusal**（要求、拒絕）

- grant-in-aid n.資助款
- grant-maintained a.由中央政府直接資助的
- importune v.強求

929.
grateful [`gretfəl]【grate·ful】**a**感謝的、令人愉快的

I should be grateful if you would send me your estimate as soon as possible.

如果你們能儘快地把你們的估價單寄來，我將非常感謝。

🔵 **appreciative, obliged, thankful**（感激的）

🔴 **ungrateful**（忘恩負義的）

- grateful for ph.為…而感謝
- estimate n.估價單

930.
grave [grev] 【grave】 n墓穴 v雕刻 a重大的
The matter is too grave for haste.
這事很嚴重不能草率從事。
⊜ essential, important, vital（重大的）
⊗ puny, trifling, trivial（不重要的）

- grave accent ph.重音符
- grave mound ph.土冢
- haste n.急速

931.
greeting [`gritɪŋ] 【greet‧ing】 n問候、賀詞
As I approached, Reid gave me a nod of greeting.
我走近時，里德向我點頭示意。
⊜ devoir, regard, missive（問候、祝賀）

- greeting card ph.賀卡
- approach v.靠近
- nod n.點頭

932.
grief [grif] 【grief】 n悲痛、不幸、災難
One inch of joy surmounts grief of a span.
點滴歡樂就能克服大量的憂傷。
⊜ anguish, sadness, torture（悲傷、憂傷）

- grieve v.使悲傷
- grief therapy ph.節哀治療
- grief-stricken a.極度悲傷的
- surmount v.克服

933.
grip [grɪp] 【grip】 n v緊握、控制
Paul was formerly one of our best salesmen, but recently he has begun to lose his grip.
保羅是我們以前最好的推銷員，但最近開始失去應付事務的能力。
⊜ clench, hold, seize（抓住、握緊）
⊗ loosen, release（鬆掉、釋放）

- grip-gripped-gripped
- formerly ad.以前
- recently ad.最近

934.
groan [gron] 【groan】 n呻吟、抱怨 v呻吟、發吱嘎聲
The shelves groan with books.
書架堆滿書撐不住了。
⊜ howl, moan, wail（呻吟）

- shelf n.架子

935.
grope [grop] 【grope】 v n觸摸、探索
You'd better grope after the explanation by yourself.
你最好自己去尋找解釋。
⊜ fumble, poke around（摸索）

- grope after ph.探索
- grope for ph.觸摸
- explanation n.解釋

936.
gross [gros] 【gross】 n總額、總量 a總共的、嚴重的
He made a gross mistake but refused to admit it.
他犯了嚴重的錯誤卻不肯承認。
⊜ entire, total, whole（總的、全部的）
⊗ small, tiny（小的、少量的）

- gross domestic product ph.國內生產總值
- gross income ph.總收入
- gross margin ph.毛利
- gross national product ph.國民生產總額
- gross out ph.惹人討厭

937.
ground crew ph地勤人員
The ground crew is to make ready the airplane for take-off.
地勤人員將為飛機的起飛作準備。

- airplane n.飛機
- take-off n.起飛

155

938.
guarantee [ˌgærənˋti] 【guar·an·tee】 **v n** 保證、擔保
Goods are sold with refund guarantee.
售出商品品質不符保證退款。
同 pledge, swear, warrant（保證）

• refund **n.** 退款 **194**

939.
gym [dʒɪm] 【gym】 **n** 體育館、體操
Graduation was held in the gym because of rain.
由於天氣下雨，畢業典禮是在體育館舉行的。

• gym shoe **ph.** 運動鞋 **81**
• hold **v.** 舉行

MEMO

abbr 縮寫詞
a 形容詞
ad 副詞
aux 助動詞
conj 連接詞
n 名詞
num 數字
ph 片語
prep 介系詞
v 動詞
（美）美式用語
（英）英式用語
（法）法式用語

全書單字取材於：
①10本坊間新多益考試暢銷書籍
②50篇英文新聞、商業文章
③2005~2012年ETS TOEIC歷屆考古題
→ 總計約50,000個單字，以電腦統計出題率高達80%
　 的實用單字1,800個

高頻率單字

> | H 家族 habitat~hypothesis

高 分 錦 囊

940.
habitat [`hæbə͵tæt】【hab·i·tat】 n (動植物)棲息地

Many species are in peril of extinction because of our destruction of their natural habitat.

由於我們破壞了自然環境，許多物種現在正面臨滅絕的危險。

⊕ **milieu, zone** (周圍環境、地區)

- 字根：habit居住
- peril n.危險
- extinction n.滅絕
- destruction n.破壞

`81`

941.
hacker [`hækə】【hack·er】 n 熱衷於使用電腦的人、駭客

Our website is temporarily down due to hacker attack, and will resume later.

本公司網站因遭駭客入侵破壞，將在短期內恢復運作。

- 此字為音譯外來詞
- website n.網站
- temporarily ad.暫時地

`54`

942.
haggle [`hægl】【hag·gle】 v n 討價還價、為利益爭論

Don't haggle lower than 70% list price. It cuts too deep into our margins.

別砍價砍到標價的70%以下，那樣我們的利潤損失太多了。

- list price ph.定價
- margin n.利潤

`104`

943.
handicap [`hændɪ͵kæp】【hand·i·cap】 v n 障礙、不利(條件)

My dual nationality was, in fact, a handicap.

事實上，我的雙重國籍對我是一個不利因素。

⊕ **burden, disadvantage, hindrance** (障礙、不利條件)

⊘ **advantage** (優勢)

- dual a.雙重的
- nationality n.國籍
- in fact ph.事實上

`88`

944.
hands-on a 親自動手的、實用的

The company went to great lengths to give us hands-on experience.

公司竭盡全力讓我們從經驗中學習。

`74`

945.
harmony [`hɑrmənɪ】【har·mo·ny】 n 協調、和睦

Good design has the feeling of a unified whole, in which all parts are in balance and harmony.

優秀的設計讓人感覺是一個整體，以及各部分平衡協調。

⊕ **accordance, concordance, peach** (調和、融洽)

⊘ **discord, disharmony** (不一致)

- in harmony with ph.與…協調一致
- design n.設計
- unify v.使成一體

`101`

946.
headline [`hɛd͵laɪn】【head·line】 n 標題、頭版頭條新聞 v 加標題

He had brightened at having his name in headline again.

他因自己的名字再次出現在頭條上而喜形於色。

⊕ **banner, title** (大字標題)

- 字首：head頭(可引申為重要的)
  字尾：line線
- brighten v.使明亮

`188`

947.
headquarters [`hɛd`kwɔrtɚz] 【 head·quar·ters 】 **n** 總部、司令部

The international corporation's headquarters is in Washington.
這家跨國公司的總部設在華盛頓。
同 **base, central station, main office**（總部）

948.
heap [hip] 【 heap 】 **n** 一堆、許多 **v** 堆積、裝滿

- a heap of ph.一堆

We have heaps of work to do.
我們有許多工作要做。

949.
heave [hiv] 【 heave 】 **v** **n** 舉起、投擲、嘔吐

- heave-hove-hove
- heave-on n.拒絕
- habit n.習慣

It's a very bad habit to heave things around.
把東西到處亂扔是很不好的習慣。
同 **haul, lift, raise**（舉起）

950.
heritage [`hɛrətɪdʒ] 【 her·i·tage 】 **n** 遺產、繼承物

- punctuate v.強調
- academic a.學術的

I have not punctuated every fact or example with its academic heritage.
我對每個事實和例證並不是學術式地強調其出自何處。
同 **birthright, heredity**（繼承、遺傳）

951.
hesitate [`hɛzə͵tet] 【 hes·i·tate 】 **v** 猶豫、躊躇、不願意

- 字根：hes黏著
  字尾：it走動
  字尾：ate行動
- recommend v.推薦

I will not hesitate to recommend this brand.
我會毫不猶豫向您推薦這個品牌。
同 **falter, pause, vaciliate**（停頓、躊躇）
反 **dare, decide, determine**（膽敢、決定）

952.
hideous [`hɪdɪəs] 【 hid·e·ous 】 **a** 醜惡的、駭人聽聞的、令人厭惡的

- 字首：hide隱藏
  字尾：ous充滿…的
- pestilence n.瘟疫
- fatal a.致命的

No pestilence had ever been so fatal, or so hideous.
以往的瘟疫從沒像這次那麼恐怖、駭人聽聞的。
同 **horrid, ghastly, ugly**（可怕的、令人討厭的）
反 **beautiful**（漂亮的）

953.
highlight [`haɪ͵laɪt] 【 high·light 】 **n** 強光、重要部分 **v** 照亮、強調

- 字首：high高
  字尾：light亮
- orientation n.說明會
- seminar n.研討會

One highlight was giving a two-day cross-cultural orientation seminar to a group of French professionals planning to work in Asia.
其中一個重頭戲是，一次為期兩天的對一群計劃在亞洲工作的法國人舉辦的跨文化定位研討會。
同 **accentuate, italicize, illuminate**（強調、照亮）

考来考去都考這些NEW TOEIC新多益單字

954.
hilarious [hɪˈlɛrɪəs] 【hi·lar·i·ous】 **a** 極可笑的、熱鬧的

They may seat you between a hilarious raconteur and a moneybags who awards you a huge contract.

坐在你兩邊的人可能是一位滔滔不絕的健談者和一位給你大筆合約的富翁。

同► joyful, gleeful, merry（歡樂的、愉快的）

• raconteur n.健談者
• moneybags n.闊佬
• award v.給予

955.
holding [ˈholdɪŋ] 【hold·ing】 **n** 保持、（常複數）持有股份

The company's net worth, including all stocks, bonds and holdings, exceeds 5 billion.

這家公司的淨值包含股票、債券、地產等，超過50億美元。

同► ownership, possession, property（所有權）

• holding company ph. 控股公司
• holding operation ph. 維持現狀的做法
• holding pattern ph. 停滯狀態
• exceed v.超過

956.
homogeneous [ˌhoməˈdʒinɪəs] 【ho·mo·ge·ne·ous】 **a** 同種的、同質的

Thorough stirring is essential in order to obtain a homogeneous product.

為了獲得質地均勻的製成品，最主要的是必須充分攪拌。

• stir v.攪拌
• essential a.基本的
• obtain v.達到

957.
hors d'oeuvre **n** 開胃小菜

That's the buffalo wings I plan to serve as a hors d'oeuvre.

那是我打算用來做開胃菜的美式辣雞翅。

• buffalo n.水牛
• wing n.翅膀
• serve v.供應

958.
hospitality [ˌhɑspɪˈtælətɪ] 【hos·pi·tal·i·ty】 **n** 好客、殷勤招待

I want to first thank you for a superlative dinner and magnificent hospitality.

我首先要感謝你舉行的極為豐盛的晚宴和盛情的款待。

• 字首：hospit賓客
字尾：ity性質
• superlative a.最好的
• magnificent a.豪華的

959.
hostage [ˈhɑstɪdʒ] 【hos·tage】 **n** 人質、抵押品

Events soon proved that he had given no hostage to Wall Street by accepting its lavish contributions.

事實很快證明，他並沒有給華爾街抵押品來換取其慷慨捐助。

• prove v.證明
• lavish a.慷慨的
• contribution n.貢獻

960.
hostile [ˈhɑstɪl] 【hos·tile】 **a** 敵人的、不友善的

In recent years the public has generally been hostile to manufacturing industry.

最近幾年，社會輿論普遍對製造業有怨言。

同► antagonistic, belligerent, unfavorable（懷有敵意的、不友善的）
反► amiable, favorable, friendly（友善的、和藹可親的）

• hostile merge ph.惡意併吞
• hostile takeover ph.惡意接收
• manufacturing industry ph.製造業

961.
household [ˈhaʊsˌhold] 【house·hold】 **n** 家庭 **a** 家庭的、普通的

The firm markets various kinds of household appliances.

這家公司銷售各種家用器具。

• household appliance ph.家電產品
• household member ph.住戶成員

160

962.
humble [ˈhʌmbḷ]【hum·ble】 a謙遜的、低下的 v使地位降低
We must do good rather than evil, on however humble a scale.
勿因善小而不為，勿因惡小而為之。
◉ **meek, modest, unpretentious**（謙遜的、簡陋的）
反 **arrogant, grand, insolent**（自大的、傲慢的）

• humble pie ph.屈辱
• 字根：hum地面
  字尾：ble有…性質的
• evil n.邪惡

963.
hyperlink [ˈhaɪpɚˌlɪŋk]【hy·per·link】 n超連結
When a set of source HTML files contains a hyperlink to an image, one or more other images in the document may disappear.
當一組HTML檔包含有一個圖片的動態連結時，在文檔內的圖片可能不會顯示。

• 字首：hyper在…之上
  字尾：link連結
• contain v.包含

964.
hypothesis [haɪˈpɑθəsɪs]【hy·poth·e·sis】 n假設、前提
All these facts have proved the accuracy of hypothesis.
所有這些事實證明了假設的正確性。

• 字首：hypo在…之下
  字尾：thesis論點
• accuracy n.正確

H

MEMO

MEMO

abbr 縮寫詞
a 形容詞
ad 副詞
aux 助動詞
conj 連接詞
n 名詞
num 數字
ph 片語
prep 介系詞
v 動詞
（美）美式用語
（英）英式用語
（法）法式用語

全書單字取材於：

①10本坊間新多益考試暢銷書籍

②50篇英文新聞、商業文章

③2005~2012年ETS TOEIC歷屆考古題

→ 總計約50,000個單字，以電腦統計出題率高達80%
　的實用單字1,800個

高頻率單字

> | 家族 **ideal~itinerary** 01-07

965.
ideal [aɪ`dɪəl]【i·de·al】**a**理想的、不切實際的 **n**理想、典範
There is in reality a gap between the ideal and the actural.
理想和現實之間事實上始終存在著距離。
⑯ **faultless, model, perfect**（理想的、完美的）
⑰ **actual, real**（真實的）

• ideal humidity ph.理想溼度
• ideal temperature ph. 理想溫度
• gap n.差距

215

966.
identical [aɪ`dɛntɪkl]【i·den·ti·cal】**a**同一的、完全相同的
At Golden State Power we're accused of the same thing for identical reasons.
在金州公司我們也為了同樣的原因受到同樣的責備。
⑯ **alike, duplicate, same**（完全相同的）
⑰ **different**（不同的）

• identical twin ph.同卵雙生
• accuse of ph.控告

194

967.
identify [aɪ`dɛntəˌfaɪ]【i·den·ti·fy】**v**確認、使參與
Because market research can help identify an opportunity, it is often the necessary starting point for a design initiative.
市場研究有助於確定市場機會，常常是設計活動不可少的起點。
⑯ **distingusih, recognize**（確認）

• identify oneself with ph.參與
• opportunity n.機會
• initiative n.倡議

188

968.
identity [aɪ`dɛntətɪ]【i·den·ti·ty】**n**身分、相同、特性
The cheque will be cashed on proof of identity.
這張支票憑身分證兌現。

• identity card ph.身分證
• identity crisis ph.青春期個性轉變期
• cheque n.支票

169

969.
ignore [ɪg`nor]【ig·nore】**v**不理睬、忽視、駁回
If you have already sent us your payment, please ignore this letter.
如已經把款匯出，可將此信作廢。
⑯ **disregard, neglect, overlook**（不理會、忽視）
⑰ **acknowledge, notice, watch**（承認、告知）

• ignorance n.無知

212

970.
illegal [ɪ`lɪgl]【il·le·gal】**a**不合法的、非法的 **n**非法移民
Illegal non-payment of tax is "tax evasion."
不合法的稅是「逃稅」。
⑯ **criminal, illegitimate, unlawful**（非法的、犯罪的）
⑰ **legal**（合法的）

• 字首：il無、不
• illegal immigration ph. 非法移民
• illegal transshipment ph.非法轉運

188

971.
illiterate [ɪ`lɪtərɪt]【il·lit·er·ate】**a**文盲的、未受教育的 **n**文盲
To develop special tutorials to assist the illiterate sector of society.
建立特殊教育來幫助社會上不識字的人們。
⑯ **ignorant, uncultured, uneducated**（文盲的、無教育的）
⑰ **literate**（能讀寫的）

• 字首：il無、不
  字根：liter字母
  字尾：ate有⋯性質的
• tutorial a.個別指導的
• sector n.部分

107

972.
illuminate [ɪˋluməˌnet] 【il·lu·mi·nate】 Ⅴ照亮、闡明、興奮
Experiment results illuminate that the model is quite reasonable.
實驗證明，提出的模型頗為合理。
同 brighten, spotlight, illustrate（照亮、闡明）
反 darken, shade（變黑、使陰暗）

- 字首：il加強語氣
  字根：lumin光
  字尾：ate進行一項行動
- experiment n.實驗
- reasonable a.合理的

143

973.
illusion [ɪˋljuʒən] 【il·lu·sion】 Ⅱ幻覺、錯誤的觀念
Along with the increase of age, people do not like the illusion.
隨著年齡的增長，人們就不那麼喜歡幻想了。
同 deception, delusion, trick（幻覺、假象）
反 dusillusion, reality（醒悟、現實）

- 字首：il無、不
  字根：lus遊戲
  字尾：ion行為

94

974.
illustrate [ˋɪləstret] 【il·lus·trate】 Ⅴ舉例說明、圖解、闡明
A few statistics will illustrate the general trend.
少數統計資料就能說明這種總趨勢。
同 clarify, demonstrate, portray（說明、圖解）

- statistics n.統計
- trend n.趨勢

108

975.
imitate [ˋɪməˌtet] 【im·i·tate】 Ⅴ模仿、仿製
The paper is finished to imitate leather.
這種紙是仿皮加工的。
同 copy, duplicate, mock（模仿、仿製）
反 create, invent（創造、發明）

- imitation n.贗品
- leather n.皮革

112

976.
immerse [ɪˋmɝs] 【im·merse】 Ⅴ使浸沒、使埋首於
The translator has to immerse himself in the world of the poet.
譯者必須完全投入詩人的世界。
同 dunk, inundate, submerge（侵入、沈入）

- translator n.譯者
- poet n.詩人

141

977.
immigrant [ˋɪməgrənt] 【im·mi·grant】 Ⅱ移民、僑民 ａ移入的
Immigrant workers were classed as resident aliens.
移民來的工人已歸入外僑類。
反 emigrant（移居他國的）

- 字首：im在…之內
  字根：migr遷移
  字尾：ant…狀態的
- resident n.居民
- alien a.外國人的

150

978.
immortal [ɪˋmɔrtḷ] 【im·mor·tal】 ａ不朽的、長久的 Ⅱ不朽人物
Had we yielded, the system would have been immortal.
如果我們當時作了讓步，這個體系就會永遠存在。
同 eternal, everlasting, unfading（永世的、不朽的）
反 mortal（臨死的）

- 字首：im無、不
  字根：mort會死的
  字尾：al屬於…的
- yield v.投降
- system n.系統

117

979.

immune [ɪ`mjun] 【im‧mune】 **a**免疫的、免疫的 **n**免疫者
Small industries, too, including service industries, have not been immune.
一些較小的行業包括服務行業在內也不例外。
⇨ exempt, resistant（免疫的、免除的）
⇦ susceptible（易受影響的）

- immune system ph. 免疫系統
- service n.服務

980.

impact [`ɪmpækt] 【im‧pact】 **n**衝擊、衝撞力、影響 **v**壓緊、衝擊
These by-products have a greater direct impact on our lives.
這些副產品與我們生活關係更直接。
⇨ bump, collision, shock（碰撞、衝擊）

- impact printer ph. 撞擊式印表機
- impact printing ph. 撞擊印刷
- by-product n.副產品
- direct a.直接的

981.

impartial [ɪm`parʃəl] 【im‧par‧tial】 **a**不偏不倚的、公正的
An impartial judge can settle our argument.
公正的仲裁人能解決我們的爭端。
⇨ dispassionate, fair, neutral（公平的、公正的）
⇦ partial（部分的）

- 字首：im無、不
  字根：part部分
  字尾：ial與…有關的
- judge n.裁判
- settle v.解決

982.

impassive [ɪm`pæsɪv] 【im‧pas‧sive】 **a**無感情的、無感覺的
Sam's face was impassive revealing, as had been the case all morning.
山姆沒有任何表情，整個上午他都是這副模樣。
⇨ apathetic, phlegmatic, stolid（無感情的）
⇦ eager（熱情的）

- 字首：im無、不
  字根：pass遭受
  字尾：ive有…傾向的
- reveal v.顯露出

983.

impatient [ɪm`peʃənt] 【im‧pa‧tient】 **a**無耐心的、盼切的
Philip was impatient to know the news.
菲利浦急於想知道這個消息。
⇨ anxious, fidgety, nervous（忍不住的、焦慮不安的）
⇦ patient（有耐心的）

- impatience n.無耐心
- 字首：im無、不
  字根：pat忍受
  字尾：ent…狀態的

984.

impel [ɪm`pɛl] 【im‧pel】 **v**驅動、激勵
Financial pressures impel the firm to cut back on spending.
財政壓力迫使公司減少開支。
⇨ compel, force, propel（強迫、迫使）
⇦ restrain（抑制）

- 字首：im加強語氣
  字尾：pel推動
- financial a.財政的
- spending n.花費

985.

imperial [ɪm`pɪrɪəl] 【im‧pe‧ri‧al】 **a**帝國的、威嚴的 **n**皇帝鬚
The second reason was altogether more expansive and imperial.
第二個理由整個說來比較廣泛，也比較宏大。
⇨ majestic, regal, supreme（威嚴的）

- expansive a.廣泛的

986.
imperil [ɪmˋpɛrɪl] 【im·per·il】 **V** 使陷於危險

Oil spills devastate the natural environment, endanger public health, imperil drinking water and disrupt the economy.

石油洩漏破壞自然環境，危害公眾健康，污染飲用水且擾亂經濟。

- spill v.溢出
- devastate v.破壞
- endanger v.危及
- disrupt v.使分裂

987.
impetus [ˋɪmpətəs] 【im·pe·tus】 **n** 推動、促進、衝力

The approaching deadline gave impetus to the negotiation.

即將到來的最後期限推動了談判。

🔄 **monentum, stimulus, push**（動力、衝力）

- 字首：im向內
  字根：pet尋找
  字尾：us行動
- deadline n.最後期限
- negotiation n.談判

988.
implement [ˋɪmpləmənt] 【im·ple·ment】 **n** 工具、裝備、手段 **V** 實施

He is the most useful implement to us everywhere.

我們到任何地方都少不了他這麼個有用之人。

🔄 **appliance, device, tool**（工具、用具）

- implement shed ph.農具房

989.
implicit [ɪmˋplɪsɪt] 【im·plic·it】 **a** 不言明、固有的、絕對的

It is implicit in our agreement that she will be a partner.

我們的協議中含有她將成為合夥人的意思。

🔄 **explicit**（詳盡的）

- implicit sign ph.電腦隱式符號
- implication n.暗示
- 字首：im向內
  字根：plic摺疊
- agreement n.協議

990.
implore [ɪmˋplor] 【im·plore】 **V** 懇求、乞求

Please implore someone else's help in a crisis.

危險時請向別人求助。

🔄 **beg, entreat, plead**（懇求、乞求）

- crisis n.危機

991.
imply [ɪmˋplaɪ] 【im·ply】 **V** 暗示、意味

The creation of an employee suggestion system does not imply an administrative monster.

建立職工建議制度不意味行政機構的膨脹。

🔄 **infer, hint, suggest**（暗示）

- 字首：im向內
  字根：ply摺疊
- administrative a.行政的
- monster n.巨大的東西

992.
import [ɪmˋport] 【im·port】 **V** **n** 進口、意味著

Please advise us immediately after you have obtained the necessary import license.

你公司得到所需進口許可證後，請立即通知我們。

🔄 **admit, introduce, receive**（引進）
🔄 **export**（出口）

- import duty ph.進口稅
- import license ph.進口許可證
- import licensing ph.進口許可
- import surcharge ph.進口附加稅
- 字首：im向內
  字尾：port港口

993.
impose [ɪmˋpoz] 【im·pose】 **V** 徵稅、把…強加於、欺騙

The host country may impose foreign exchange control.

東道國可能強行實施外匯管制。

🔄 **charge, force, place**（施加、強加）
🔄 **deprive, free**（免去、自由）

- imposition n.徵收
- 字首：im向內
  字根：pose放置
- host n.東道主
- exchange n.匯兌

994.
impression [ɪmˋprɛʃən]【im·pres·sion】**n**印象、模糊觀念、影響

Frank made a good impression so the manager gave him the job.
法蘭克給經理留下了好印象，因此經理給了他這個工作。

- 字首：im向內
- 字根：press擠壓
- 字尾：ion性質

178

995.
impulsive [ɪmˋpʌlsɪv]【im·pul·sive】**a**衝動的、有推動力的

I don't much care for impulsive people like him.
我不太喜歡像他這樣浮躁的人。
同► impetuous, headlong（衝動的、猛然的）

- 字首：im向內
- 字根：puls推
- 字尾：ive有…傾向的

143

996.
impute [ɪmˋpjut]【im·pute】**v**歸咎於、歸罪於

Don't impute to me that you failed.
不要把你失敗的責任推到我身上。
同► arrogate, ascribe, attribute（歸咎於）

- imputation n.歸罪
- 字首：im向內
- 字根：pute估計
- fail v.失敗

157

997.
inaugurate [ɪnˋɔgjəˌret]【in·au·gu·rate】**v**使正式就任、開始

Open-window envelopes, showing receivers' names and addresses, may inaugurate repeated printout.
使用開窗式信封來顯示收信人的位址和姓名是重複列印的悲劇的開始。
同► begin, instate, launch（使開始、就職）

- envelope n.信封
- receiver n.收件人
- address n.地址
- printout n.印出來的資料

94

998.
incentive [ɪnˋsɛntɪv]【in·cen·tive】**n**鼓勵、動機 **a**刺激的

Higher and more stable prices would provide an incentive for commercial collection.
高昂而穩定的價格對營利本業的回收是一種鼓勵。
同► inducement, motive, stimulus（刺激）

- stable a.穩定的
- commercial a.商業的

81

999.
incident [ˋɪnsədnt]【in·cen·dent】**n**事件、插曲 **a**附帶的

The incident did not affect me any more deeply than that.
這件事對我的影響不過如此。
同► event, happening, occurrence（事件）

- incident room ph.暴力室
- affect v.影響
- deeply ad.深深地

121

1000.
incline [ɪnˋklaɪn]【in·cline】**v**傾向於、傾斜 **n**傾斜、斜面

I strongly incline to the view of our going into cooperation with them.
我很傾向於與他們進行合作的意見。
同► dispose, predispose, tend（有…傾向）
反► disincline（使不願）

- incline to ph.易於…
- 字首：in向內
- 字根：cline傾斜
- cooperation n.合作

140

1001.
inclusive [ɪnˋklusɪv]【in·clu·sive】**a**包含的、包括的

This price is inclusive of 5% commission.
本價格包括5%的佣金在內。
反► exclusive（排外的）

- 字首：in向內
- 字根：clus關閉
- 字尾：ive有…傾向
- commission n.佣金

115

1002.
income [`ɪnˌkʌm] 【 in·come 】 n 收入、收益、所得

His economic income this year approximates to 8,000 dollars.
他今年的收入將近8,000美元。
 earnings, payment, wages（收益、收入）

- income policy ph.收入政策
- income statement ph.損益表
- income support ph.收入補助
- income tax ph.所得稅
- approximate v.接近

250

1003.
incorporate [ɪn`kɔrpəˌret] 【 in·cor·po·rate 】 v 包含、使併入、組成公司

We had to incorporate the company for tax reasons.
鑒於稅務原因，我們得組成公司。
 combine, merge, unite（聯合、連結）
 extract（用力取出）

- 字首：in向內
  字根：corpor團體
  字尾：ate進行一項行動

151

1004.
increase [ɪn`kris] 【 in·crease 】 vn 增加、增大

Along with the increase of tax rates comes an increase in benefits.
隨著稅率的提高，福利也在增加。
 augment, expand, multiply（增大、增加）
 decrease, diminish, reduce（減少、減小）

- 字首：in向內
  字根：crease成長
- rate n.比率

170

1005.
incredible [ɪn`krɛdəbl] 【 in·cred·i·ble 】 a 難以置信的、不可信的

There is an incredible opportunity for developers.
這是開發人員的一次極好機會。
 absurd, doubtful, ridiculous（難以置信的）
 credible（相信的）

- 字首：in無、不
  字根：cred相信
  字尾：ible可…的
- developer n.開發者

104

1006.
incur [ɪn`kɝ] 【 in·cur 】 v 招致、惹起、遭受

An enterprise has to incur certain costs and expenses in order to stay in business.
一個企業為了維持營業就不得不承擔一定的費用和開支。
 catch, contract（招致、引來）

- 字首：in進入
  字根：cur跑
- enterprise n.企業
- cost n.費用
- expense n.開支

113

1007.
incursion [ɪn`kɝʃən] 【 in·cur·sion 】 n 侵略、入侵、進入

Save for this annual incursion, they left literature alone.
除了這一年一度的例外，他們與文學無緣。
 invasion, offense（侵略、進攻）

- 字首：in進入
  字根：cur跑
  字尾：sion行為
- literature n.文學

120

1008.
indemnity [ɪn`dɛmnɪti] 【 in·dem·ni·ty 】 n 賠償金、保障、赦免

To prevent overpaying for policyholders' losses, the insurance industry has established a rule of indemnity.
為防止對投保人所受損失的超額賠付，保險公司已建立了一套賠償規則。
 amends, compensation（賠償、補償）

- overpay v.多付款
- policyholder n.投保人

51

1009.
independence [ˌɪndɪˋpɛndəns] 【in·de·pend·ence 】
n獨立、自主
I prize my independence too much to go and work for them.
我決不願意喪失自己的獨立性去為他們效勞。
同 **freedom, liberty**（自由）
反 **dependence**（依賴）

- Independence Day ph. 美國獨立紀念日
- 字首：in無、不 字尾：dependence依賴
- prize v.重視

1010.
indifferent [ɪnˋdɪfərənt] 【in·dif·fer·ent 】a不關心的、中立的、不重要的
I was concentrating so hard that I was indifferent to the noise outside.
我思緒高度集中，不在乎外面的喧嚷聲。
同 **detached, disinterested, neutral**（冷淡的、中立的）
反 **concerned, interesteed**（關心的、有興趣的）

- concentrate v.專心
- noise n.吵鬧

1011.
indignity [ɪnˋdɪgnətɪ] 【in·dig·ni·ty 】n輕蔑、侮辱
I suffer the indignity of having to apologize in front of all those people.
我蒙受了要在那麼多人面前道歉的屈辱。
同 **affront, insult, offense**（侮辱、傷害）
反 **dignity**（尊嚴）

- 字首：in無、不 字尾：dignity尊嚴
- apologize v.道歉

1012.
indispensable [ˌɪndɪsˋpɛnsəbl] 【in·dis·pen·sa·ble 】
a必需的、不可或缺的
These executives, expert in every phase of corporation, became the indispensable cogs in the industrial machine.
這些高層管理人員精通公司的各項業務，成為整個工業機器中不可缺少的齒輪。
同 **essential, necessary, vital**（不可或缺的、必要的）
反 **dispensable**（非必要的）

- 字首：in無、不 字根：dispense分配 字尾：able能…的
- cog n.鈍齒

1013.
individual [ˌɪndəˋvɪdʒuəl] 【in·di·vid·u·al 】a個人的、獨特的 n個人
Do you think individual investors can really beat the pros?
你認為個人投資者真的能勝過專業人員嗎？
同 **personal, single**（單個的、個體的）
反 **entire, general, whole**（整體的、全部的）

- individual medley ph. 個人混合泳
- individual retirement account ph. 個人退休金帳戶
- investor n.投資者
- pro=professional n.專家

1014.
indubitable [ɪnˋdjubɪtəbl] 【in·du·bi·ta·ble 】a無疑的、明白的
It is indubitable that good region advantage and investment environment are playing important roles.
毋庸置疑，良好的區位優勢和良好投資環境是吸引外資流入的重要因素。

- region n.地區
- advantage n.優勢
- investment n.投資

1015.

induce [ɪn`djus]【in·duce】**Ⅴ**引誘、導致

The price is not attractive enough to induce business.

價格不足以引起興趣，達成交易。

同 **elicit, evoke, influence**（影響、引出）

反 **deduce**（推論）

- 字首：in向內
  字根：duce引導
- **attractive** a.吸引人的

1016.

induct [ɪn`dʌkt]【in·duct】**Ⅴ**正式就任、徵招入伍、引導

He tried to induct the youngsters into the use of their own language.

他設法引導那年輕人使用他們自己的語言。

同 **enroll, initiate, introduce**（引入、就任）

- 字首：in向內
  字根：duct引導
- **youngster** n.年輕人

1017.

indulge [ɪn`dʌldʒ]【in·dulge】**Ⅴ**沉迷於、使高興、縱容

There is no need to indulge in such heroics.

根本沒有必要這樣肆意誇張。

同 **gratify, please, satisfy**（使高興、使滿意）

- **heroics** n.豪壯行為

1018.

industrial [ɪn`dʌstrɪəl]【in·dus·tri·al】**a**工業的、勤勞的 **n**工業股票

We are experiencing an incredible transformation from the age of industrial, mechanical artifacts to an age of digital, information objects.

從工業的機械製品時代到數位的資訊物件時代，我們正經歷著一場令人難以置信的轉變。

- **industrial action** ph.罷工
- **industrial art** ph.工藝課
- **industrial dispute** ph. 勞資糾紛
- **industrial estate** ph. 工業區

1019.

inevitable [ɪn`ɛvətəbl]【in·ev·i·ta·ble】**a**不可避免的、必然的

Condition on arrival unsatisfactory inspect damage further but buyer claim inevitable.

到貨情況不能令人滿意正在進一步檢查受損情況，但買方索賠是不可避免。

同 **destined, fated, ineluctable**（不可避免的、必然的）

反 **avoidable**（可避免的）

- **condition** n.情況
- **unsatisfactory** a. 令人不滿的
- **inspect** v.審查
- **damage** n.損害

1020.

infect [ɪn`fɛkt]【in·fect】**Ⅴ**傳染、汙染、腐蝕

I didn't pay any attention to it because I never infect.

我對這事毫不注意，因為我從來未受感染。

同 **corrupt, disease, pollute**（傳染、腐蝕）

反 **disinfect**（將…消毒）

- 字首：in向內
  字根：fect製作
- **pay attention to** ph.專心

1021.

infer [ɪn`fɝ]【in·fer】**Ⅴ**推斷、暗示

I infer from your statement that you are not willing to agree.

我從你的聲明中推斷你不打算同意。

同 **conclude, deduce, suppose**（推理、推斷）

- 字首：in向內
  字根：fer帶來
- **agree** v.同意

I

1022.
inferior [ɪnˋfɪrɪə] 【in·fe·ri·or】 **a**低等的、較差的 **n**屬下、次品

He tried to foist some inferior goods on me.

他企圖把一些劣質貨強售給我。

同 lower, subordinate, worse（低等的、較差的）

反 superior（較高的）

- inferior to ph.比⋯差
- foist v.把⋯強加於
- 112

1023.
infinite [ˋɪnfənɪt] 【in·fi·nite】 **a**無限的、極大的

If the payments are made over an infinite period of time the annuity is called a perpetuity.

假如支付期是無限的，稱為永久年金。

同 boundless, eternal, perpetual（無限的、無窮的）

反 finite, limited（有限的、限制的）

- infinite loop ph.無限循環
- 字首：in無、不
  字根：fin限制
  字尾：ite有⋯性質的
- annuity n.年金
- perpetuity n.永存
- 181

1024.
inflame [ɪnˋflem] 【in·flame】 **v**燃燒、憤怒、加劇

Insults are only served to inflame the feud.

侮辱只是加劇長期不和的作用。

同 anger, irritate, stir（使興奮、激起情緒）

- 字首：in向內
  字尾：flame火焰
- insult n.侮辱
- feud n.仇恨
- 94

1025.
inflation [ɪnˋfleʃən] 【in·fla·tion】 **n**通貨膨脹、自大

Are wages keeping pace with inflation?

工資的提高能否與通貨膨脹同步？

反 deflation（通貨緊縮）

- 字首：in向內
  字尾：flat吹氣
  字尾：ion狀態
- inflation-proof a.保證不受通貨膨脹影響的
- 179

1026.
inform [ɪnˋfɔrm] 【in·form】 **v**通知、告發

I'm very pleased to inform you that your application has been accepted.

我非常高興地通知您，您的申請已被接受。

同 impart, notify, snitch（通知、告密）

反 conceal, misinform（隱蔽、誤傳）

- information n.消息
- application n.申請
- 204

1027.
infuse [ɪnˋfjuz] 【in·fuse】 **v**灌輸、使充滿

We feel sure that Auchinleck will infuse a new energy and precision into the defense of the Nile Valley.

我們確信，奧金萊克將給尼羅河流域的防務帶來新的活力和謹嚴的作風。

同 animate, infect, saturate（灌入、浸入）

- 字首：in進入
  字根：fuse流、瀉
- precision n.精確
- defense n.防禦
- 116

1028.
ingenious [ɪnˋdʒinjəs] 【in·gen·ious】 **a**足智多謀的、精巧的

It took a lot of imagination to come up with such an ingenious plan.

設計出如此巧妙的方案需有極大的想像力。

同 glorious（光榮的）

- imagination n.想像力
- come up with ph.想出
- 79

1029.

inglorious [ɪnˋglorɪəs]【in‧glo‧ri‧ous】 **a**不名譽的、可恥的、不出名的

He will never forget that inglorious fleeting when he was in the army.

他永遠也不會忘記他當兵時的一次不名譽的逃亡。

反 **glorious**（光榮的）

- 字首：in無、不
- 字根：glory光榮
- 字尾：ious充滿…的
- **army** n.軍隊

1030.

ingredient [ɪnˋgridɪənt]【in‧gre‧di‧ent】 **n**組成部分、因素

On the other hand, there is some bodily ingredient in the labour most purely mental, when it generates any external result.

另一方面，即使是最純粹的腦力勞動，在產生任何外在成果時也有某種體力成分。

同 **component, element, factor**（組成部分、要素）

- **bodily** ad.整體的
- **labour** n.勞力
- **external** a.外部的

1031.

inhabitant [ɪnˋhæbətənt]【in‧hab‧i‧tant】 **n**居民、棲居的動物

Every inhabitant of this planet must contemplate that it may no longer be habitable.

世界上每個人都必須思考到地球上可能不再適合人住的那一天。

同 **citizen, resident**（居民）

- 字首：in進入
- 字根：habit居住
- 字尾：ant執行某行動的人
- **planet** n.行星
- **contemplate** v.仔細考慮

1032.

inherent [ɪnˋhɪrənt]【in‧her‧ent】 **a**固有的、與生俱來的

It imposes on those who practice it specific obligations inherent in it's very nature.

從事這一工作的人承擔著由該工作性質產生的特殊義務。

同 **existing, internal, natural**（固有的、天生的）
反 **acquired**（養成的）

- 字首：in向內
- 字根：her黏著
- 字尾：ent…狀態的
- **specific** a.特殊的
- **obligation** n.責任

1033.

inherit [ɪnˋhɛrɪt]【in‧her‧it】 **v**繼承、遺傳

This government has inherited many problems from the previous one.

上任政府遺留給本屆政府很多問題。

同 **receive**（收到）

- 字首：in向內
- 字根：her黏著
- 字尾：it走動
- **previous** a.先前的

1034.

initial [ɪˋnɪʃəl]【in‧i‧tial】 **a**開始的、最初的

The experiments have given initial results eventually.

那些試驗總算初見成效了。

同 **beginning, introductory, primary**（起始的、最初的）
反 **final**（最後的）

- 字首：in向內
- 字根：it走動
- 字尾：ial與…有關的
- **eventually** ad.最後

1035.

initiative [ɪˋnɪʃətɪv]【in‧i‧tia‧tive】 **n**主動行動、首創精神

Both central and local initiative should be brought into play.

發揮中央和地方兩個積極性。

同 **aggressiveness, hustle, verve**（主動精神）

- **central** a.中央的
- **local** a.地方的

173

1036.
injunction [ɪn`dʒʌŋkʃən] 【 in‧junc‧tion 】 **n**命令、強制令

The government has sought an injunction to prevent the paper from publishing the story.

政府已申請禁制令，禁止該報發表此事。

同 mandate, prohibition（命令、禁止）

- 字首：in無、不
- 字根：junct連接
- 字尾：ion性質
- seek v.請求
- 96

1037.
injustice [ɪn`dʒʌstɪs] 【 in‧jus‧tice 】 **n**不公正、非正義

There have also been ugliness and injustice in corporate yielding of power.

大公司在行使權力上也有過醜陋的事和非正義的行動。

同 inequity, unfairness, unjustness（不公平）
反 justice（公平）

- 字首：in無、不
- 字根：justice公平
- ugliness n.難看
- 81

1038.
in light of **ph**根據、從…觀點

Different ways of investment and cooperation were followed in light of the actual conditions of different countries.

根據不同國家實際的情況，分別採取不同的投資合作方式。

同 considering（就…而論）

- 121

1039.
innovation [ɪnə`veʃən] 【in‧no‧va‧tion】 **n**革新、創新

Technical innovation is instrumental in improving the qualities of products.

技術革新有助於提高產品的品質。

同 novelty（新穎）

- 字首：in向內
- 字根：nov新
- 字尾：ation性質
- instrumental a.有幫助的
- 144

1040.
input [`ɪn‚pʊt] 【 in‧put 】 **n**輸入、投入

To perform these manipulations, we also require input mechanisms that give us the flexibility to do so.

同時為了完成這些操作，我們也需要靈活的輸入機制。

- 來自片語put in ph.加進
- manipulation n.操作
- mechanism n.機械裝置
- flexibility n.彈性
- 168

1041.
inquire [ɪn`kwaɪr] 【 in‧quire 】 **v**詢問、調查

They determined to inquire thoroughly into the matter.

他們決定徹底調查這件事。

同 ask, investigate, question（詢問、訊問）
反 answer, reply, respond（回答）

- inquire after ph.問候
- inquire for ph.求見
- inquire into ph.調查
- 字首：in進入
- 字根：quire尋找
- 94

1042.
insane [ɪn`sen] 【 in‧sane 】 **a**精神錯亂的、瘋狂的

She was seized with insane jealousy.

她被一種瘋狂的妒忌所支配著。

同 crazy, foolish, mad（瘋狂的、笨的）
反 sane（頭腦清楚的）

- 字首：in無、不
- 字根：sane頭腦清楚的
- seize v.抓住
- jealousy n.妒忌
- 65

1043.
inscribe [ɪn`skraɪb] 【 in·scribe 】 **v** 題寫、題贈
This book I inscribe to my old comrades in arms.
謹將本書獻給我的老戰友們。
⊜ **engrave, imprint, stamp**（書寫、銘刻）

* 字首：in向內
  字根：scribe寫
* comrades in arms ph.戰友

1044.
insert [ɪn`sɝt] 【 in·sert 】 **v n** 插入、插話、刊登廣告
Insert personal opinions into an objective statement
在客觀的陳述中插入個人的意見

* 字首：in進入
  字根：sert參加
* objective a.客觀的

1045.
insight [`ɪn,saɪt] 【 in·sight 】 **n** 洞察力、深刻的理解
An investigation of the relationship between inventories, shipments and sales may provide additional insight.
調查庫存表、裝運量和銷售量之間的關係可以提供新的洞察力。
⊜ **acumen, intuition, wisdom**（洞察力、智慧）

* 字首：in向內
  字尾：sight眼光
* additional a.額外的

1046.
insist [ɪn`sɪst] 【 in·sist 】 **v** 堅持、堅決主張、強調
A good administrative personnel should understand that how to insist the principle.
一個好的行政人員應該懂得要怎樣堅持原則。
⊜ **demand, press, urge**（堅持、要求）

* insist on ph.督促
* 字首：in向內
  字根：sist立
* personnel n.員工
* principle n.原則

1047.
inspect [ɪn`spɛkt] 【 in·spect 】 **v** 檢查、檢閱
The Director will leave tomorrow for a tour of overseas branches, to inspect them.
董事長明天動身去視察海外分支公司。
⊜ **contemplate, examine, observe**（檢查、思考）

* 字首：in向內
  字根：spect看
* overseas a.海外的
* branch n.分公司

1048.
inspire [ɪn`spaɪr] 【 in·spire 】 **v** 鼓舞、引起、激起
If you want to inspire your customers, you must first inspire your employees.
要吸引更多的客戶，你就必須首先吸引公司的員工。
⊜ **encourage, influence, prompt**（激勵、引起）
⊜ **deject, languish**（使沮喪、苦惱）

* 字首：in向內
  字尾：spire呼吸
* customer n.顧客

1049.
install [ɪn`stɔl] 【 in·stall 】 **v** 安裝、設置、使就職
When a firm decides to install a computer, the cost of the hardware may only be half the total cost.
當一個工廠決定裝配一台電腦時，硬體成本只占總成本的一半。
⊜ **inaugurate, instate, fix**（安置、固定）

* hardware n.電腦硬體
* half n.一半
* total a.總計的

1050.
instance [`ɪnstəns] 【 in·stance 】 **n** 例子、情況、建議
I did it at the instance of one of my colleagues.
我是經我一位同事的提議才做了這件事。
⊜ **case, example, occasion**（例子、事件）

* for instance ph.例如
* colleague n.同事

1051.
instant [ˈɪnstənt] 【in·stant】 a立即的、速食的 n一剎那
At the critical instant, a change of plan flashed on her mind.
在這關鍵時刻，她的心中突然產生了一個全新的計劃。
📖 **immediate, quick, urgent**（立即的、緊急的）

- instant book ph.速成書
- instant message ph.即時傳訊軟體
- instant noodles ph.速食麵
- instant replay ph.錄影鏡頭的即時重播

1052.
instantaneous [ˌɪnstənˈtenɪəs] 【in·stan·ta·ne·ous】
a 瞬間的、猝然的
Before the invention and diffusion of writing, translation was instantaneous and oral.
在文字還沒有發明和廣泛傳播以前，翻譯是隨時隨地在口頭上進行的。

- 字首：instant立即的
  字尾：aneous有…性質的
- diffusion n.擴散

1053.
instinct [ˈɪnstɪŋkt] 【in·stinct】 n本能、直覺 a充滿著的
We get no help from our instinct or intuition. We can only rely on the empirical.
我們不能從本能和直覺中獲得任何幫助，只能依靠經驗。

- intuition n.直覺
- rely on ph.依賴
- empirical a.經驗上的

1054.
institute [ˈɪnstətjut] 【in·sti·tute】 n學會、學院、協會 v創立、開始
He thought of trying for a position in a research institute.
他想盡一切辦法在一個研究機構找了一份工作。
📖 **create, launch, organize**（開始、建立）

- institution n.制度
- 字首：in向內
  字根：stitute設立
- research n.研究

1055.
intercept [ˌɪntəˈsɛpt] 【in·ter·cep】 v n攔截、截取
This move had not been unforeseen, but our plans to intercept it were foiled by the quickness of its withdrawal.
我們事先並不是沒有料到這種行動，但是因為它迅速撤退使我們要想攔截它的計劃落空。
📖 **arrest, interrupt**（打斷、攔截）

- 字首：inter在…之間
  字根：cept拿取
- unforeseen a.為預見到的
- foil v.挫敗
- withdrawal n.撤回

1056.
intervene [ˌɪntəˈvin] 【in·ter·vene】 v干涉、介入、打擾
Extraneous factors can intervene and cause the shelving of advertising campaigns.
廣告活動會因外部因素影響而推遲進行。
📖 **disrupt, interrupt, intrude**（介入、干涉）

- 字首：inter在…之內
  字根：vene來
- extraneous a.外來的
- campaign n.活動

1057.
introduce [ˌɪntrəˈdjus] 【in·tro·duce】 v介紹、引進
We must introduce some systems into our office routine.
我們須在我們日常公務中引進一些制度。
📖 **inaugurate, launch**（引出、開始）

- 字首：intro向內
  字根：duce引導
- routine n.慣例

1058.
introspect [ˌɪntrəˈspɛkt] 【in·tro·spect】 v內省、反省
Before correcting others, introspect and make a mistake by oneself first.
要糾正別人之前，先反省自己有沒有犯錯。

- 字首：intro向內
  字根：spect看
- correct v.糾正
- mistake n.錯誤

1059.
introvert [ˈɪntrəˌvɜt] 【in·tro·vert】 **n** 內向的人 **v** 使內向

And some looked at personality: are you an extrovert or an introvert?

還有一些涉及個性：你的性格內向還是外向？

反 extrovert（個性外向的人）

- 字首：intro向內
  字根：vert轉
- personality n.個性

1060.
instruct [ɪnˈstrʌkt] 【in·struct】 **v** 指示、教授、通知

The old workers instruct the young workers not only in words, but by deeds.

老工人對青年工人不僅言傳而且身教。

同 educate, dicate, inform（教授、通知）

- instruct in ph.教授
- 字首：in向內
  字根：struct建立
- deed n.行為

1061.
instrument [ˈɪnstrəmənt] 【in·stru·ment】 **n** 工具、儀器、手段、樂器

I am a mere instrument, not an agent.

我純粹被利用而不是主動。

同 device, implement, tool（儀器、器具）

- instrument board ph.儀表板
- instrument flying ph.儀器飛行法
- instrument panel ph.儀表板
- mere ad.僅僅

1062.
insulate [ˈɪnsəˌlet] 【in·su·late】 **v** 隔離、使絕緣

Variable levies can insulate farmers and consumers from world markets.

差價進口稅可以把農民和消費者與世界市場隔離開來。

同 isolate, separate（使孤立、使分離）

- 字首：insul島
  字尾：ate進行一項行動
- variable a.多變的
- levy n.徵稅

1063.
insurance [ɪnˈʃʊrəns] 【in·sur·ance】 **n** 保險、保險業、賠償金

They keep back $20 pounds a month from my salary for National Insurance.

他們從我的薪金中每月扣下20磅付國民保險費。

同 assurance, indemnity, warrant（安全保障、保險）

- insurance adjuster ph.保險理賠員
- insurance broker ph.保險代理人
- insurance policy ph.保險證書

1064.
integral [ˈɪntəgrəl] 【in·te·gral】 **a** 不可或缺的、完整的、組成的 **n** 整體

The annexes are an integral part of this agreement.

各附件為本協定的組成部分。

同 constituent（組成的）

- integrity n.正直
- integral calculus ph.積分學
- annex n.附加

1065.
intellectual [ˌɪntlˈɛktʃʊəl] 【in·tel·lec·tu·al】 **n** 知識份子 **a** 智力的、聰明的

They had no desire nor capacity for any of intellectual pursuit.

他們沒有心思也沒有能力從事需要用腦子的工作。

同 brainy, intelligent, talented（天才的、有學問的）
反 ignorant（無知的）

- intellectual capital ph.知識資本
- intellectual property ph.智慧財產
- capacity n.能力
- pursuit n.事務

1066.
intense [ɪnˈtɛns] 【in·tense】 **a** 強烈的、緊張的、熱情的

Rivalry among business firms grew more intense.

公司間的競爭趨於激烈。

同 drastic, forceful, severe（激烈的、強烈的）
反 faint, feeble（虛弱的）

- 字首：in向內
  字根：tense緊張
- intense pulsed light ph.脈衝光
- rivalry n.競爭

1067.
intent [ɪnˈtɛnt]【in·tent】**n.** 目的、含義 **a.** 熱切的、專心致志的

At least three of these companies have voiced officially their intent to do so.

至少有三個公司已正式表示打算這樣做。

- intent on ph. 熱衷於
- intention n. 意圖
- officially ad. 正式地

1068.
interaction [ˌɪntəˈrækʃən]【in·ter·ac·tion】**n.** 互相影響、互動

Architectural planning for transactional kiosks should occur at the same time as the interaction and industrial design planning.

在進行交互和工業設計計劃時，我們應該同時進行建築學上的規劃。

- 字首：inter在…之間
  字尾：action行動
- architectural a. 建築學的
- kiosk n. 涼亭
- occur v. 發生

1069.
intercom [ˈɪntəˌkɑm]【in·ter·com】**n.** 對講機

Would you page Mr.William over the intercom and tell him to meet me at the front desk?

麻煩你用對講機叫威廉先生到櫃台跟我會面好嗎？

- page v. 廣播叫人
- front desk ph. 櫃台

1070.
intercourse [ˈɪntəˌkors]【in·ter·course】**n.** 交往、交流

English is more widely used in international intercourse than any other languages today.

現今英語在國際交往中比其他任何語言用得都廣。

- 字首：inter在…之間
  字尾：course過程
- international a. 國際的

communication, dealings（交流）

1071.
interfere [ˌɪntəˈfɪr]【in·ter·fere】**v.** 妨礙、衝突、干涉

She never allows her private affairs to interfere with production.

她從不為個人事情耽誤產量。

- interfere with ph. 妨害
- 字首：inter在…之間
  字根：fer帶來
- allow v. 允許
- private a. 私人的

arbitrate, encroach, meddle（介入、妨礙）

1072.
integrate [ˈɪntəˌgret]【in·te·grate】**v.** 使結合、使完整

Why don't we combine the two teams and let them integrate the best aspects of them?

為什麼我們不整合這兩個團隊，使他們將各自的優點合而為一呢？

- aspect n. 方面

amass, combine, merge（使成一體）

1073.
internal [ɪnˈtɜnl]【in·ter·nal】**a.** 內部的、內在的 **n.** 本質

We have no right to interfere in the internal affairs of other countries.

我們無權干涉別國內政。

inner, inside, interior（內部的）
external（外在的）

- internal auditing ph. 內部審計
- internal combustion engines ph. 內燃機
- internal medicine ph. 內科
- internal secretion ph. 內分泌

1074.
international [ˌɪntəˈnæʃənl]【in·ter·na·tion·al】**a.** 國際性的

The company is an international trader in grain.

這家公司是國際糧食貿易公司。

cosmopolitan, global, universal（國際的）
national（全國的）

- International Date Line ph. 國際換日線
- International Film Festival ph. 國際電影節
- International Labor Organization ph. 國際勞工組織

1075.

Internet [ˈɪntɚˈnɛt] [in·ter·net] **n**網際網路

Enormous quantities of information are available on the Internet, but its sheer quantity and heterogeneity almost guarantee that no regular system could ever be imposed on it.

互聯網上有大量的資訊，但是因為其數量龐大結構迥異，一般的系統根本無法管理它。

- internet access **n.**上網
- internet addiction disorder **ph.**網路成癮症
- sheer **a.**全然的
- heterogeneity **n.**異質性

1076.

interpret [ɪnˈtɝprɪt] [in·ter·pret] **v**解釋、說明、翻譯

Don't interpret it without real comprehension when you study a foreign language.

學習外國語切莫望文生義。

⊕ analyze, clarify, translate（解釋、分析）

- comprehension **n.**理解

1077.

interrupt [ˌɪntəˈrʌpt] [in·ter·rupt] **v**打斷說話、中斷、阻礙

We now interrupt our normal transmissions to bring you a special news flash.

我們現在要中斷正常節目，插播一則特別新聞。

⊕ hinder, interfere, intrude（打斷、中止）
⊖ aid, help（幫忙）

- 字首：inter在…之間 字根：rupt破
- normal **a.**正常的
- transmission **n.**節目
- flash **n.**新聞快報

1078.

intersection [ˌɪntɚˈsɛkʃən] [in·ter·sec·tion] **n**交叉、十字路口

The traffic banked up at the intersection.

車輛在交叉路口聚積起來。

⊕ crossing（交叉）

- 字首：inter在…之間 字根：sect切、割 字尾：ion性質
- bank **v.**堆積

1079.

intimate [ˈɪntəmɪt] [in·ti·mate] **a**親密的、熟悉的 **v**暗示、通知

He participated the intimate regulation of the task with all the strength.

他全力投入了自己所規定的任務。

⊕ close, familiar, innermost（親密的、內心的）

- participate **v.**參與
- regulation **n.**規定
- strength **n.**力量

1080.

intrude [ɪnˈtrud] [in·trude] **v**侵入、打擾、把…強加在

I don't want to intrude my opinion upon you.

我不想把我的意見強加於你。

⊕ discommode, intervene, obtrude（入侵、打斷）
⊖ extrude（逐出）

- 字首：in向內 字根：trude推
- opinion **n.**意見

1081.

inventor [ɪnˈvɛntɚ] [in·ven·tor] **n**發明家、創作者

The inventor shall have the right to be mentioned as such in the patent.

發明人有權要求在專利證書上記載自己是發明人。

⊕ creator, initiator, maker（發明人、創建者）

- 字首：in進入 字根：vent來 字尾：or從事…的人
- mention **v.**提名表揚
- patent **n.**專利

1082.
inventory [ˋɪnvənˏtorɪ] 【 in·ven·to·ry 】 **n.** 存貨清單、詳細目錄
I regret not completing the inventory on time.
我很遺憾沒有按時填好庫存單。
同 **collection, list, stock**（存貨、名冊）

• inventory turnover **ph.** 存貨周轉
• regret **v.** 懊悔
• complete **v.** 使完整
• on time **ph.** 準時

1083.
invest [ɪnˋvɛst] 【 in·vest 】 **v.** 投資、耗費、覆蓋
This account is designed for people with $10,000 or more to invest.
這種帳戶是為投資額在一萬元以上的人設立的。
同 **stake, venture**（投資、冒險）
反 **divest**（剝除）

• account **n.** 帳戶

1084.
investigate [ɪnˋvɛstəˏget] 【 in·ves·ti·gate 】 **v.** 調查、研究
To begin with, the ICC was empowered, upon complaint, to investigate and lower rates.
首先，州際商業委員會被授權在有人申訴時進行調查並降低價格。
同 **examine, inspect, probe**（調查、考察）

• investigator **n.** 調查員
• empower **v.** 授權
• complaint **n.** 抗議

1085.
invincible [ɪnˋvɪnsəb!] 【 in·vin·ci·ble 】 **a.** 無敵的、無法征服的
This football team was once reputed to be invincible.
這支足球隊曾被譽為無敵的勁旅。
同 **impregnable, invulnerable, unbeatable**（無敵的）

• football **n.** 足球
• repute **n.** 名譽

1086.
invisible [ɪnˋvɪzəb!] 【 in·vis·i·ble 】 **a.** 看不見的、無形的
Insurance is one of Britain's most profitable invisible exports.
保險業是英國獲益最大的無形出口之一。
同 **imdiscenible, imperceivable**（看不見的）
反 **visible**（看得見的）

• invisible earings **ph.** 無形收入
• invisible hand **ph.** 看不見的手
• invisible ink **ph.** 隱形墨水
• invisible trade **ph.** 無形貿易
• 字首：in無、不
• 字根：vis看

1087.
invoice [ˋɪnvɔɪs] 【 in·voice 】 **n.** 發票、發貨單
A signed invoice presumes receipt of the shipment.
經過簽字的發票表示貨物已經收到。

• presume **v.** 假設
• receipt **n.** 收據

1088.
invoke [ɪnˋvok] 【 in·voke 】 **v.** 請求、懇求、喚起
I'm pleased to say we've never had occasion to invoke this particular clause.
我很高興地說，我們從來沒有機會使用這一特殊條款。
同 **beseech, pray**（祈禱、懇求）

• 字首：in向內
• 字根：voke呼叫
• occasion **n.** 理由

1089.
involve [ɪnˋvɑlv] 【 in·volve 】 **v.** 使捲入、需要、使專注
Part of the design approach must therefore involve harmonizing these perspectives with those of users and customers.
因此，設計工作的一部分就是對各個用戶和顧客的看法進行協調。
同 **concern, implicate, tangle**（包含、使捲入）

• 字首：in向內
• 字尾：volve滾轉
• harmonize **v.** 協調
• perspective **n.** 看法

1090.
irrational [ɪˋræʃənl̩] 【 ir·ra·tion·al 】 **a** 無理性的、不合理的

The irrational structure and weak competitiveness of industries is a protruding problem adversely affecting the sustained development of the national economy.

產業結構不合理、競爭力不強，是影響經濟持續增長的突出問題。

反 **rational** (理性的)

- 字首：ir無、不
- 字根：ration理性
- 字尾：al屬於⋯的
- **weak a.**虛弱的
- **adversely ad.**不利地

84

1091.
irrefutable [ɪˋrɛfjutəbl̩] 【 ir·ref·u·ta·ble 】 **a** 不能反駁的、不可否認的

Only truth that is tested by practice is irrefutable.

只有經過實踐檢驗的真理才是無法反駁的。

- 字首：ir無、不
- 字根：refute拒絕
- 字尾：able能⋯的
- **test v.**測試

88

1092.
irregular [ɪˋrɛgjələ] 【 ir·reg·u·lar 】 **a** 不規則的、不整齊的、不合法的

The contour of the Atlantic coast of America is very irregular.

美國沿大西洋的海岸線甚為曲折。

同 **abnormal, erratic, rough** (不規則的、不平的)
反 **regular** (規則的)

- 字首：ir無、不
- 字根：regular規則的
- **contour n.**輪廓
- **Atlantic a.**大西洋的

79

1093.
irresistible [ˌɪrɪˋzɪstəbl̩] 【 ir·re·sis·ti·ble 】 **a** 不可抵抗的、富有誘惑力的

This claim was not perhaps irresistible.

這種主張並不是駁不倒的。

同 **compelling** (不可抗拒的)
反 **resistant** (抵抗的)

- 字首：ir無、不
- 字根：resist抵抗
- 字尾：ible可⋯的
- **claim n.**主張

65

1094.
irrevocable [ɪˋrɛvəkəbl̩] 【 ir·rev·o·ca·ble 】 **a** 不能改變的、不可撤回的

In general, payment will be made by Irrevocable Letter of Credit negotiable against presentation of shipping documents.

關於付款方式，我們一般採用不可撤銷的使用憑證和運單議付。

反 **revocable** (可撤回的)

- 字首：ir無、不
- 字根：re再、又
- 字根：voc喊叫
- 字尾：able能⋯的
- **negotiable a.**可協商的

81

1095.
irritate [ˋɪrəˌtet] 【 ir·ri·tate 】 **v** 使惱怒、使過敏，刺激

As the minutes ticked away, she became more and more irritated.

隨著時間一分一秒地過去，她變得更加不耐煩。

同 **annoy, infuriate, madden** (使惱怒、激怒)
反 **appease, calm** (平息、冷靜)

- **tick v.**發滴答聲

105

1096.
irruption [ɪˋrʌpʃən] 【 ir·rup·tion 】 **n** 衝進、闖入

The whole body made a disorderly irruption into Mr. Bounderby's dining-room.

這一大堆人莽莽撞撞地擁進了龐得貝先生的餐廳。

同 **invasion** (入侵)

- 字首：ir進入
- 字根：rupt破
- 字尾：ion性質
- **disorderly ad.**雜亂地

114

I

1097.
isolate [ˈaɪsḷˌet] 【i·so·late】 **V** 使隔離、使孤立、使絕緣

In trying to isolate us, they only succeed in isolating themselves.
他們想孤立我們，結果卻只孤立了他們自己。

同 quarantine, seclude, segregate（使孤立、分離）

• succeed v.成功

1098.
issue [ˈɪʃju] 【is·sue】 **V** 發行、配給 **n** 爭論

Attention, please. These tickets are available on the day of issue only.
請注意，這種車票僅在發售當天有效。

• available a.可得的

1069.
itemize [ˈaɪtəmˌaɪz] 【i·tem·ize】 **V** 分條列述、詳細列舉

This benefit is available only to taxpayers who itemize.
只有扣除稅額的納稅人才能獲得該項津貼。

同 list, summarize, total（列述記載、合計）

• 字首：item項目
  字尾：ize使成為
• taxpayer n.納稅人

1100.
itinerary [aɪˈtɪnəˌrɛrɪ] 【i·tin·er·ar·y】 **n** 旅程、旅行計劃 **a** 旅行的

This itinerary leaves us plenty of leeway.
這個旅行計劃給我們留有很多自由活動的餘地。

• plenty a.許多的
• leeway n.餘地

MEMO

J/K

abbr 縮寫詞
a 形容詞
ad 副詞
aux 助動詞
conj 連接詞
n 名詞
num 數字
ph 片語
prep 介系詞
v 動詞
（美）美式用語
（英）英式用語
（法）法式用語

全書單字取材於：

①10本坊間新多益考試暢銷書籍

②50篇英文新聞、商業文章

③2005~2012年ETS TOEIC歷屆考古題

➜ 總計約50,000個單字，以電腦統計出題率高達80%
的實用單字1,800個

高頻率單字

 **J 家族 jaywalk~justify**

高 分 錦 囊

1101.
jaywalk [`dʒeˌwɔk] 【jay·walk】 **v** 不守交通規則橫穿馬路

Pedestrians have to travel farther to cross the street legally unless they want to jaywalk.

行人需要走遠一點從斑馬線上橫過馬路，除非他們想要亂穿馬路。

54
● pedestrian n.行人
● unless conj.除非

1102.
jealous [`dʒɛləs] 【jeal·ous】 **a** 妒忌的、小心守護的

I couldn't help feeling jealous when she was promoted over my head.

她獲升後職位比我高，我壓抑不住忌妒的心情。

（同）**covetous, envious**（嫉妒的、貪婪的）
（反）**generous, tolerant**（慷慨的、寬容的）

88
● jealous of ph.妒忌

1103.
jeopardy [`dʒɛpədɪ] 【jeop·ard·y】 **n** 危險、風險、危難

It is precisely at this juncture that the boss finds himself in double jeopardy.

剛好在這個關鍵時刻，上司發現自己處於進退兩難的境地。

（反）**safety**（安全）

67
● precisely ad.精準地
● juncture n.連結
● double a.雙重的

1104.
jet lag **ph** 時差

Sleep phase disturbances caused by jet lag or shift work can be characterized by early awakening or by awakening later in the day.

時差或輪班引起睡眠相混亂，其特徵是早醒或白天晚醒。

67
● phase n.階段
● disturbance n.打擾
● shift v.轉移

1105.
jot down **ph** 匆匆記下、草草記下

Let me jot down your telephone number so that I can call you later.

讓我記下你的號碼，以後好打電話給你。

88
● jot v.草草記下

1106.
jury [`dʒʊrɪ] 【ju·ry】 **n** 陪審團、評判委員會 **a** 應急的

The jury found for the plaintiff.

陪審團作出了有利於原告的裁決。

68
● jury box ph.陪審員席
● jury-packing n.賄賂陪審員
● jury-rigged a.臨時或應急配備的
● plaintiff n.原告

1107.
justify [`dʒʌstəˌfaɪ] 【jus·ti·fy】 **v** 證明、辯解

Users make commensurate effort if the rewards justify it.

如果回報值得，用戶們願意付出相稱的努力。

（同）**authorize, legitimate, warrant**（使合法、證明）
（反）**condemn**（責備）

104
● justification n.藉口
● 字首：just公平
  字尾：ify使成為
● commensurate a.相稱的
● effort n.努力

高頻率單字

K 家族 **keen~know-how**

keen ~ know-how

高 分 錦 囊

1108.

keen [kin]【keen】 a.熱心的、渴望的、敏銳的
Competition for the nomination was very keen.
爭取提名的競爭非常激烈。
同 **exact, quick, smart**（激烈的、敏銳的）
反 **blunt, dull, obtuse**（鈍的、不鋒利的）

65
• keen to ph.熱心
• keen-edged a.銳利的
• keen-eyed a.眼光銳利的
• keen-witted a.機智敏銳的
• nomination n.提名

1109.

kitchenware [`kɪtʃɪn.wɛr]【kitch·en·ware】 n.廚房用具
Our factory specializes in producing series stainless steel kitchenware products.
本廠專業生產不銹鋼廚具系列產品。

51
• specialize v.專攻
• stainless steel ph.
  不鏽鋼

1110.

know-how n.實際知識、技術
I don't have much know-how about engines.
發動機方面的技術知識我所知甚少。

78
• engine n.發動機

K

MEMO

185

MEMO

abbr 縮寫詞
a 形容詞
ad 副詞
aux 助動詞
conj 連接詞
n 名詞
num 數字
ph 片語
prep 介系詞
v 動詞
（美）美式用語
（英）英式用語
（法）法式用語

全書單字取材於：
①10本坊間新多益考試暢銷書籍
②50篇英文新聞、商業文章
③2005~2012年ETS TOEIC歷屆考古題
→ 總計約50,000個單字，以電腦統計出題率高達80%
　的實用單字1,800個

高頻率單字

> | L 家族 label~luxury

高 分 錦 囊

1111.
label [`lebḷ] 【la·bel】 n 標籤、標記 v 貼標籤於
The most important safty rule is: Read the label.
最重要的安全條例是看清標籤。
📖 **tag**（標籤）

213

1112.
laboratory [`læbrəˌtorɪ] 【lab·o·ra·to·ry】 n 實驗室、研究室
A laboratory must be kept in good order.
實驗室裡必須保持井然有序。
📖 **atelier, lab, studio**（實驗室、研究室）

54
● 字首：labor勞動
字尾：atory領域

1113.
lading [`ledɪŋ] 【lad·ing】 n 裝載、汲取、貨物
The bills of lading are turned over to the shipper, who will surrender the letter of indemnity to the bank.
將提單轉交給承運人，承運人再將保證函交給銀行。

104
● bill of lading ph.提貨單
● surrender v.交出

1114.
landlord [`lændˌlɔrd] 【land·lord】 n 房東、主人、地主
They were persuaded to sign a waiver of claims against the landlord.
經勸說後，他們簽署了放棄向房東索賠的權利。
📖 **lessor, master, proprietor**（房東）
📖 **tenant**（房客）

81
● 字首：land土地
字尾：lord統治者
● persuade v.說服
● waiver n.棄權證書

1115.
lane [len] 【lane】 n 小路、巷、車道
Cycling in the fast traffic lane is really dangerous.
在快車道上騎腳踏車真的很危險。
📖 **avenue, path, road**（路、通道）

155
● cycle v.騎腳踏車
● fast a.快速的
● dangerous a.危險的

1116.
laptop [`læptɑp] 【lap·top】 n 筆記型電腦
I have a laptop. Do I have to declare it at the customs?
我有個手提電腦，需要在海關申報嗎？

61
● declare v.申報
● custom n.海關

1117.
latest [`letɪst] 【lat·est】 a 最新的、最近的、最遲的
These shoes are the latest fashion.
這些鞋子是最新的流行樣式。
📖 **up-to-date**（最新的）

124
● latest fashion ph.最新流行

1118.

launch [lɔntʃ] 【launch】 **V** **N** 發射、開始

Likewise, clicking on the e-mail address in the address book could launch the mail application.

相同地，當按一下這個人的電子郵寄地址時就可以自動地調用電子郵件程式。

🔵 **introduce, start**（開始）

- launch into ph.開始、投入
- launch out ph.出航、開始
- launch pad ph.發射臺
- launch vehicle ph. 運載工具
- launch window ph.最佳發射時機

1119.

laundry [ˋlɔndrɪ] 【laun·dry】 **N** 洗衣店、洗好的衣服

Please check through the laundry and then put it away.

請把洗衣店送來的衣服檢查一下，然後拿去放好。

🔵 **laundromat, launderette**（洗衣店）

- laundry basket ph.洗衣籃
- laundry list ph.冗長的細目清單

1120.

lavish [ˋlævɪʃ] 【lav·ish】 **a** 非常慷慨的、浪費的、豐富的 **V** 揮霍

It was a wealthy company and everything done on a lavish scale.

這是一家有錢的公司，做什麼事都挺有派頭。

🔵 **abundant, ample, extravagant**（豐富的、慷慨的）
🔴 **thrifty**（節儉的）

- wealthy a.富裕的
- scale n.等級

1121.

lawn [lɔn] 【lawn】 **N** 草坪、草地

I spent all day weeding the lawn.

我花了一整天時間除草。

🔵 **grass, meadow, sward**（草地、草坪）

- lawn bowling ph. 草地保齡球
- lawn chair ph.草坪躺椅
- lawn mower ph.割草機
- lawn party ph.露天招待會
- weed v.除草

L

1122.

lay off **V** 解雇、停止

Has Miss Alison decided whether to retrain or lay off?

愛麗森女士決定哪些員工是要重新培訓和哪些要解雇了嗎？

🔵 **fire**（解雇）
🔴 **hire**（雇用）

- retrain v.再訓練

1123.

layout [ˋleˏaut] 【lay·out】 **N** 安排、版面設計

Changing your perspective can often uncover previously undetected issues in layout and composition.

在改變角度看看，這樣就可以發現一些佈局上和構成上的問題。

🔵 **formation**（結構）

- perspective n.觀點
- previously ad.以前
- undetected a.未發現的
- composition n.構成

1124.

leading edge **N** 前沿（指科學技術發展的最先進、最先端方面）

We devote ourselves to providing leading edge technologies, and best value solutions of the highest quality to all our customers.

我們致力為客戶提供最先進的技術與最高品質及最有價值的服務和產品。

- edge n.邊緣
- devote v.致力於
- solution n.解決

1125.

leaflet [ˋliflɪt] 【leaf·let】 **N** 傳單、單張印刷品 **V** 散發傳單

This leaflet contains your operating instructions.

這份傳單印有你應知道的操作說明。

🔵 **brochure, handbill, pamphlet**（傳單、活頁）

- contain v.包含
- operate v.操作
- instruction n.操作指南

1126.

league [lig] 【 league 】 n.聯盟、同盟、種類 v.結盟、聯合

He just isn't in your league.

他和你根本不是同類型的人。

🔄 **alliance, association, federation**（同盟、聯盟）

- League of Nations ph. 國際聯盟
- league table ph.聯賽成績紀錄及名次表

1127.

lease [lis] 【 lease 】 n.租約、租貸 v.出租

The lease stated that tenants should maintain the property in good condition.

租約規定承租人必須保持房產完好無損。

🔄 **charter, hire, rent**（出租）

- tenant n.房客
- maintain v.維持
- property n.所有物

1128.

ledger [ˋlɛdʒɚ] 【 ledg·er 】 n.總帳

Rule out that entry in the ledger, and the transaction was cancelled.

那項交易已取消了，請從總帳裡劃去那筆帳目。

- ledger line ph.音譜的上加線或下加線
- rule out ph.排除
- transaction n.交易
- cancel v.取消

1129.

leftover [ˋlɛ f tovɚ] 【 left·o·ver 】 n.殘餘物、剩飯剩菜

They pieced out a meal from leftovers.

他們用剩下的飯菜將就成一頓飯。

🔄 **surplus**（剩餘物）

- piece out ph.使完整
- meal n.一餐

1130.

legal [ˋligḷ] 【 le·gal 】 a.法律的、法定的、合法的

A corporation is separate legal entity chartered by the state.

股份有限公司是州政特許的獨立法律主體。

🔄 **lawful, legitimate**（法律上的、合法的）
🔄 **illegal**（不合法的）

- legal age ph.法定年齡
- legal aid ph.法律援助
- legal holiday ph.法定假日
- legal proceedings ph.法定程序
- legal profession ph.司法界
- 字根：leg法律

1131.

legible [ˋlɛdʒəbḷ] 【 leg·i·ble 】 a.（字跡）清楚的、易辨認的

Records shall remain legible, readily identifiable and retrievable.

品質記錄應保持清晰，易於識別和檢索。

🔄 **clear, readable, obvious**（易讀的、明瞭的）

- 字根：leg讀字尾：ible易…的
- identifiable a.可辨識的
- retrievable a.可恢復的

1132.

legitimate [lɪˋdʒɪtəmɪt] 【 le·git·i·mate 】 a.合法的、正統的、合理的

The legitimate rights and interests of women have been effectively protected.

婦女合法權益得到有效保護。

🔄 **authorized, justified, valid**（合法的、正當的）
🔄 **illegitimate**（非法的）

- interest n.利益
- effectively ad.有效地
- protect v.保護

1133.

leisure [ˋliʒɚ] 【 lei·sure 】 n.閒暇、悠閒、安逸 a.空閒的、業餘的

All this extra work I'm doing is breaking into my leisure time.

我目前做的這些額外工作用去了我的閒暇時間。

🔄 **comfort, rest, spare time**（空暇時間）
🔄 **business, labour, work**（工作、勞動）

- leisure centre ph.康樂中心
- leisure economy ph.休閒經濟
- leisure suit ph.男士輕便套裝
- leisure wear ph.居家服
- extra a.額外的

1134.
letter of credit ph.信用狀
The bank's responsibility is to verify that the explorer's documents conform to the letter of credit.
銀行的責任在於查核出口商的單據必須與信用證的一致。

- responsibility n.責任
- verify v.核對
- conform v.符合

1135.
liability [ˌlaɪəˈbɪlətɪ] [li‧a‧bil‧i‧ty] n.責任、傾向、負債
He has on excess of assets over liability.
他的資產大於其他負債。
- accountabilty, obligation（責任）
- asset（資產）

- excess n.超過

1136.
liable [ˈlaɪəbl] [li‧a‧ble] a.易於…的、有…傾向的、義務的
The shipping company will be liable for damage.
運輸公司將對損壞負責。
- apt, likely, probable（可能的、易…的）

- liable to ph.易於
- damage n.損害

1137.
liberal [ˈlɪbərəl] [lib‧er‧al] a.自由的、慷慨的、大量的 n.自由主義者
At least he paid them a very liberal premium above the average brick-layer's pay.
至少他付給他們的工資遠比一般砌磚工人的工資高。
- generous, substantial, tolerant（開朗的、足夠的）
- compulsory（強迫的）

- liberal art ph.文科
- liberal studies ph.人文科學
- 字根：liber自由
  字尾：al屬於…的
- premium n.津貼

1138.
life vest ph.救生衣
There's a life vest under your seat for water emergencies.
您的座位下有一件救生衣，在發生水上緊急情況時可以使用。

- vest n.背心
- emergency n.緊急情況

1139.
likelihood [ˈlaɪklɪˌhʊd] [like‧li‧hood] n.可能、可能性
In all likelihood the institutions that emerge over the next 20 years will serve agriculture well.
在爾後的20年裡出現的機構，多半都會好好地做農業服務。

- emerge v.出現
- agriculture n.農業

1140.
liquor [ˈlɪkə] [liq‧uor] n.含酒精飲料、烈酒
He carries his liquor like a gentleman.
他酒量很大，沒有絲毫醉意。
- alcohol（含酒精飲料）

- liquor store ph.小酒店
- gentleman n.紳士

1141.
literary [ˈlɪtəˌrɛrɪ] [lit‧er‧ar‧y] a.文學的、精通文學的、文言的
His writings are very plain, entirely devoid of any literary ornament.
他的作品非常樸素，完全沒有任何的文學雕琢。
- erudite（博學的）
- colloquial（口語的）

- literary criticism ph.文藝批評
- literary film ph.文藝片
- 字根：liter文字
  字尾：ary與…有關的

1142.
loan shark **ph.**放高利貸者

A loan shark's customers were closemouthed.
借高利貸的人都守口如瓶。

- loan n.貸款
- shark n.鯊魚
- closemouthed a.口緊的

1143.
lodge [lɑdʒ] 【 lodge 】 **n.**守衛室、旅舍 **v.**投宿、停留

Where we were to lodge was the problem.
我們要在哪裡住宿是個問題。

同 **dwell, inhabit, reside**（居住、投宿）

- ledge a complaint against ph.控告

1144.
logical [ˈlɑdʒɪkḷ] 【 log·i·cal 】 **a.**邏輯學的、合理的、必然的

Persistent research will uncover a logical justification.
持續的研究將會揭示出邏輯上的正確性。

同 **rational, reasonal, sensible**（邏輯的、合理的）
反 **illogical**（不合邏輯的）

- logical map ph.邏輯映像
- logical positivism ph.邏輯的實證主義
- persistent a.持續的
- justification n.證明為正常

1145.
long-range **a.** 遠程的、長期的

Long-range goals are normally set by a company.
一般都由公司制定長遠的目標。

- goal n.目標
- normally ad.通常

1146.
loyal [ˈlɔɪəl] 【 loy·al 】 **a.**忠誠的、忠心的

Joe managed to remain loyal to both his bosses, Rogers and the President, and served both well.
喬對他的兩位上司羅傑斯和董事長都很忠心，對他們兩人服務也很周到。

反 **isolate, separate**（使孤立、使分離）

- loyalty n.忠誠
- manage v.設法
- remain v.維持

1147.
luggage [ˈlʌgɪdʒ] 【 lug·gage 】 **n.**行李

Can I store my luggage here after checkout?
退房後我能把行李寄存在這兒嗎？

同 **baggage, valise**（行李、手提旅行袋）

- luggage compartment ph.行李置放箱
- luggage rack ph.行李架
- luggage van ph.行李車
- store v.存放

1148.
luxury [ˈlʌkʃərɪ] 【 lux·u·ry 】 **n.**奢侈、享受

Experienced specialty chefs also receive good salaries in luxury restaurants.
在豪華餐廳中，經驗豐富的專門廚師的薪資也頗豐厚。

同 **lavishness, luxuriousness, profuseness**（奢侈、奢華）
反 **economy, penury**（節約、貧窮）

- luxury goods ph.奢侈品
- chef n.主廚
- receive v.接收

abbr 縮寫詞
a 形容詞
ad 副詞
aux 助動詞
conj 連接詞
n 名詞
num 數字
ph 片語
prep 介系詞
v 動詞
（美）美式用語
（英）英式用語
（法）法式用語

全書單字取材於：
①10本坊間新多益考試暢銷書籍
②50篇英文新聞、商業文章
③2005~2012年ETS TOEIC歷屆考古題
→ 總計約50,000個單字，以電腦統計出題率高達80%
　的實用單字1,800個

高頻率單字

M家族 macroscale~mutual

1149.
macroscale [`mækrə͵skel] [ma·cro·scale] **n**大規模、宏觀
On a macroscale it can be considered to consist of two surfaces.
從大規模的角度看來，它能被考慮為含有兩個表面。
同 **milieu, zone**（周圍環境、地區）

> • surface n.表面
> **64**

1150.
mad [mæd] [mad] **a**發瘋的、愚蠢的、惱火的
Everybody that was not invited was as mad as a wet hen.
沒有受到邀請的人每個都很生氣。
同 **crazy, irrated, lunatic**（發狂的、瘋狂的）
反 **calm, sane, peaceful**（神智正常的、和平的）

> • mad cow disease ph.
> 狂牛症
> • mad money ph.
> 自備的零錢
> • as mad as a wet hen
> ph.腦羞成怒
> **101**

1151.
magnet [`mægnɪt] [mag·net] **n**磁鐵、有吸引力的人或物
The West Lake in Hangchow is a magnet for visitors.
杭州西湖使遊客流連忘返。

> • magnet school ph.課程
> 特別設計以吸引學生的公立
> 學校
> • magnetic a.有吸引力的
> **98**

1152.
magnificent [mæg`nɪfəsənt] [mag·nif·i·cent] **a**壯麗
的、豪華的
They were accorded a magnificent reception in France.
他們在法國受到了盛大的歡迎。
同 **grand, majestic, splendid**（壯麗的、堂皇的）
反 **humble, modest**（謙遜的）

> • 字首：magni大
> 字尾：fic引起…的
> 字尾：ent…狀態的
> • accord v.給予
> • reception n.接待
> **125**

1153.
maintain [men`ten] [main·tain] **v**維持、保養、堅持
They agreed to maintain production and refrain from severe
wage reductions.
他們同意維持生產，禁止大量削減工資。
同 **possess, retain, sustain**（保持、維持）
反 **abandon, forsake**（遺棄、拋棄）

> • maintenance n.維護
> • 字首：main主要的
> 字尾：tain持有
> • refrain v.抑制
> • severe a.劇烈的
> **181**

1154.
majority [mə`dʒɔrətɪ] [ma·jor·i·ty] **n**多數
A majority of working women remain in full charge of their home.
大多數職業婦女的家庭仍然完全由她們照管。
同 **bulk, mass, plurality**（多數、大部分）
反 **minority**（少數）

> • majority and plurality
> ph.過半數和相對多數
> • majority leader ph.多數黨
> 領袖
> • Majority Shareholder
> ph.主要股東
> • majority verdict ph.多數
> 裁決
> **211**

1155.
malfunction [mæl`fʌŋʃən] [mal·func·tion] **n**故障
IMPORTANT: Inspection and service should also be performed
anytime a malfunction is observed or suspected.
重要：出現任何故障或懷疑有故障時，均應進行檢視和維修。

> • 字首：mal壞
> 字尾：function功能
> • inspection n.檢察
> • suspect v.察覺
> **71**

1156.

management [ˋmænɪdʒmənt] 【 man·age·ment 】

n 管理、經營手段

Incapable management ruined the company.

無能的經營管理斷送了公司。

- management buyout ph.經理部購股以控制自己公司
- management by exception ph.異常管理

126

1157.

mandatory [ˋmændəˌtorɪ] 【 man·da·to·ry 】 **a** 命令的、義務的

Social welfare insurance, particularly endowment, unemployment and medical insurance, must be made mandatory in urban areas.

城鎮地區要強制推行以養老、失業、醫療為重點的社會保險。

- 字根：mand命令 字尾：atory與…有關的
- welfare n.福利
- endowment n.捐贈
- medical a.醫療的

64

1158.

manipulate [məˋnɪpjəˌlet] 【 ma·nip·u·late 】 **v** 巧妙處理、操作

Improperly implemented, dials can be extremely difficult to manipulate.

如果設計不當，刻度盤將會非常難於操作。

同 handle, manage, operate（處理、操作）

- improperly ad.不適當地
- implement n.器具
- dial n.刻度盤
- extremely ad.非常

143

1159.

manual [ˋmænjʊəl] 【 man·u·al 】 **a** 手的、用手操作的 **n** 手冊、簡介

The use of robots will someday supersede manual labor.

機器人的使用有一天會取代人力。

同 directory, handbook, guidebook（說明書、手冊）

- manual alphabet ph. 手語字母
- manual labor ph.手工
- manual recount ph. 人工計票
- 字根：manu手

119

1160.

manufacture [ˌmænjəˋfæktʃə] 【 man·u·fac·ture 】 **v** **n** 製造

The engineer needs to carefully study the manufacture's data sheets.

技術員需要認真研究產品說明書。

同 build, construct, make（製造、創造）

- 字根：manu手 字根：fact製作 字尾：ure狀態
- sheet n.印刷品

124

M

1161.

marathon [ˋmærəˌθɑn] 【 mar·a·thon 】 **n** 馬拉松賽跑、耐力比賽

People lined the streets to watch marathon.

人們夾道觀看馬拉松賽跑。

同 race, relay（賽跑）

- 此單字字首大寫為希臘地名，馬拉松。

56

1162.

margin [ˋmɑrdʒɪn] 【 mar·gin 】 **n** 邊緣、極限、利潤

After-tax profit margin is the ratio of net income to net sales.

稅後利潤率指淨收入與淨銷售之比。

同 border, edge, rim（邊緣）

- margin fee system ph.收小費制
- margin of error ph.誤差幅度
- margin requirement ph.委託保證金
- ratio n.比率

88

1163.

mask [mæsk] 【 mask 】 **n** 假面具、掩飾 **v** 戴面具、掩飾

Such feelings tend to remain submerged beneath a mask of social politeness.

在社交禮貌的掩飾之下，這樣的情感往往不會顯露出來。

同 camouflage, cover, disguise（掩飾、偽裝）

反 unmask（揭露）

- submerge v.淹沒
- beneath prep.在…之下
- politeness n.禮貌

79

1164.
mass [mæs] 【mass】 **n**團、大部分、大眾 **a**大眾的
A good deal of adult education is accomplished by the mass media.
成人教育的相當一部分是由大眾傳播媒介完成的。
同 **amount, bulk, volume**（大量）
反 **bit**（一點）

- mass medium ph.大眾傳播工具
- mass noun ph.不可數名詞
- education n.教育
- accomplish v.完成
- mass media ph.大眾傳播媒體

【189】

1165.
massage [mə`sɑʒ] 【mas·sage】 **v** **n**按摩、推拿
The massage made the hurt go away.
按摩使疼痛消失了。
同 **knead, rub**（按摩、摩擦）

- massage palor ph.按摩院

【58】

1166.
mattress [`mætrɪs] 【mat·tress】 **n**床墊
The mattress was hard and unyielding.
這床墊很硬，沒有彈性。

- hard a.堅硬的
- unyielding a.不易彎曲的

【52】

1167.
mature [mə`tjur] 【ma·ture】 **a**成熟的、慎重的 **v**使成熟
I'll let you have an answer after mature consideration.
我慎重考慮後再給你答覆。
同 **adult, mellow, ripe**（成熟的、準備好的）
反 **immature**（不成熟的）

- mature student ph.成年人、大學生
- mature transcript ph.成熟轉錄物
- consideration n.考慮

【112】

1168.
maximum [`mæksəməm] 【max·i·mum】 **n**最大量、最大限度 **a**最高的
Our goal is to achieve the maximum of efficiency.
我們的目標是取得最高的效率。
同 **highest, largest, uppermost**（頂點的）
反 **minimum**（最小的）

- achieve v.達成
- efficiency n.效率

【132】

1169.
medium [`midɪəm] 【me·di·um】 **n**媒體、中間、手段 **a**中間的
Commercial television is an effective medium for advertising.
商業電視是有效的廣告宣傳工具。
同 **average, mean, mediocre**（中等的、適中的）
反 **extreme**（末端的）

- media為其複數，亦可表示媒體
- medium of exchange ph.交易媒介
- medium-dry a.不太甜的
- medium-range a.中程的
- medium-sized a.普通型的

【211】

1170.
melt [mɛlt] 【melt】 **v** **n**溶化、溶解、消失
Support for the manager melted into nothingness.
對經理的支持化為烏有。
同 **dissolve, liquefy, soften**（融化、溶解）
反 **freeze, solidify**（結冰、凝固）

- melt away ph.融化、消失
- melt down ph.熔化

【84】

1171.
memo [ˋmɛmo]【mem·o】 n 備忘錄 v 把…記入備忘錄

Everyone's curiosity was piqued upon circulation of a memo announcing the senior vice-president's resignation.

由於一項宣佈資深副總裁要離開的備忘錄在公司內流傳，激起每個人的好奇心。

- 原為memorandum
- curiosity n.好奇心
- pique v.激起
- resignation n.辭職

219

1172.
mental [ˋmɛnt!]【men·tal】 a 精神的、智力的、內心的 n 精神病患者

People's expectations about a product and the way it works are highly informed by their mental model.

人們對於產品的期望和對於產品工作方式的想像大部分來自於他們的心理模型。

- cerebral, intellecrual, psychological（精神的、腦力的）
- bodily, material, physical（身體的、物質的）

- mental age ph.智力年齡
- mental arithmetic ph.心算
- mental deficiency ph.智能不足
- mental deterioration ph.智能退化
- mental home ph.精神病院
- mental retardation ph.智力遲鈍

83

1173.
menu [ˋmɛnju]【men·u】 n 菜單、功能選擇單

You click on the menu, and it drops down.

按一下選單，它就向下展開。

133

1174.
merely [ˋmɪrlɪ]【mere·ly】 n 僅僅、不過

This principle merely states that people will willingly work harder for something that is more valuable to get.

這個原則只不過是說，人們願意為更有價值的事物努力工作。

- barely, purely, simply（僅僅）

- principle n.原則
- willingly ad.願意地
- valuable a.有價值的

214

1175.
merge [mɝdʒ]【merge】 v 合併、融合

The directors have decided to merge the two small firms together.

董事們已決定把這兩家小商店合併起來。

- blend, combine, mingle（混合、合併）

- merger n.合併
- merge together ph.混合起來

105

1176.
merit [ˋmɛrɪt]【mer·it】 n 價值、優點、功績 v 應得

Promotion goes by merit.

晉升以功績為依據。

- excellence, value, worth（價值、優點）
- defect, demerit, fault（缺點、過失）

- merit pay ph.功績制薪酬
- merit system ph.實績制人材制度

94

1177.
messy [ˋmɛsɪ]【mess·y】 a 混亂的、骯髒的

Give me a few seconds with messy here.

給我幾秒鐘來整頓這裡的混亂，好嗎？

- neat（整齊的）

79

1178.
metal detector ph 金屬探測器

Sorry, but you have to go through the metal detector again.

對不起，您必須再過一次金屬探測器。

- metal n.金屬
- detector n.探測器

63

M

1179.
metropolis [mə`trɑplɪs]【me·trop·o·lis】**n**大都市、中心

The metropolis is a confusion of old and new.

大都市是新與舊的大雜燴。

同**capital, downtown, megalopolis**（大城市、主要都市）

- 字首：metro母親
  字根：polis城市
- confusion n.混亂

165

1180.
mild [maɪld]【mild】**a**溫和的、不濃烈的、輕微的

Most experts forecast a mild decline in housing starts.

大多數專家預計住房建築的開工率將有所下降。

同**lenient, moderate, temperate**（溫和的、親切的）
反**harsh, strict, wild**（粗糙的、嚴格的、猛烈的）

- mild-mannered
  a.溫文爾雅的
- forecast v.預測
- decline n.下降

83

1181.
military [`mɪlə͵tɛrɪ]【mil·i·tar·y】**n**軍隊 **a**軍事的、陸軍的

He seems more like a military officer than a business executive.

他似乎比較像一個軍官，而不像一個商業行政主管。

同**army, troop**（軍隊）
反**naval**（海軍的）

- Military Academy ph.軍事
  學院
- military drill ph.軍事練習
- military law ph.軍法
- military police ph.憲兵
- military service ph.兵役

77

1182.
mingle [`mɪŋgl]【min·gle】**v**使混合、相混

It is characteristic of city life that all sorts of people meet and mingle together who never fully comprehend one another.

城市生活的一個極大特徵就是各種各樣的人互相見面又互相混雜在一起，但卻從未互相充分瞭解。

同**associate, blend, mix**（使混合、使結合）

- mingle-mangle n.混合
- fully ad.完全地
- comprehend v.理解

124

1183.
minimum [`mɪnəməm]【min·i·mum】**a**最小的、最低的
n最小值

The engineer contractor will set up the minimum specifications.

工程師訂合約者要規定最低的技術要求。

同**least, lowest, smallest**（最小的）
反**maximum**（最大的）

- 字首：mini小
- minimum lending rate
  ph.最低利率
- minimum security prison
  ph.不設防監獄
- minimum wage ph.
  最低工資
- contractor n.立契約者
- set up ph.創立

131

1184.
minority [maɪ`nɔrətɪ]【mi·nor·i·ty】**n**少數、少數民族、未成年

We're in the minority; more people are against us than with us.

贊成我們的佔少數，我們成了少數派。

同**contingent, faction, handful**（少數派、少數）
反**majority**（多數）

- minority government
  ph.少數黨政府
- minority leader ph.
  少數黨領袖
- against prep.反對

105

1185.
miscellaneous [͵mɪsɪ`lenjəs]【mis·cel·la·ne·ous】**a**混雜
的、多才多藝的

Does the entertainment of visitors fall under the heading of miscellaneous expenditure?

來訪者的娛樂費用是列在雜項開銷下嗎？

同**conglomerate, jumbled, scrambled**（繁雜的）

- entertainment n.娛樂
- expenditure n.消費

74

1186.

mission [`mɪʃən] 【 mis·sion 】 **n**任務、使節團、傳教 **v**派遣

We have overcome every objection and completed the mission on time.

我們排除了各種障礙並按時完成了任務。

🔄 **errand, stint, task**（使命、任務）

- mission control ph.太空航行地面指揮中心
- mission statement ph.宗旨
- mission critical system ph.緊急任務系統
- 字根：miss送
- 字尾：ion行為、狀態
（188）

1187.

mistake [mɪ`stek] 【 mis·take 】 **n**錯誤 **v**弄錯、誤解

He charged off the mistake to inexperience.

他把錯誤歸咎於缺乏經驗。

🔄 **blunder, error, fault**（錯誤、疏忽）

- charge v.指責
- inexperience n.無經驗
（210）

1188.

mobile [`mobɪl] 【 mo·bile 】 **a**移動的、多變的 **n**汽車

A mobile clinic visits this village every week.

巡迴醫療隊每週來這個村子一次。

🔄 **changeable, fluid, movable**（可動的、善變的）
🔙 **immobile**（不能動的）

- Mobile Belt of Earth Crust ph.地殼活動帶
- mobile communication ph.行動通訊
- mobile phone ph.行動電話
- 字根：mob動
  字尾：ile易…的
- clinic n.會診
（94）

1189.

mode [mod] 【 mode 】 **n**方法、形式、文體

I hope to come back to the mode of payment.

我希望回過頭來討論付款方式。

🔄 **form, method, style**（方式、風格）
（187）

1190.

modem 【 mo·dem 】 **abbr**數據機

For example, transferring a 10 megabyte file over a 56 Kbps modem takes about 24 minutes.

例如，通過56Kbps數據機傳一份10百萬位元組的檔案需要24分鐘。

- modulator-demodulator ph.數據機的縮寫
- megabyte n.電腦百萬位元
（68）

1191.

moderate [`mɑdərɪt] 【 mod·er·ate 】 **a**適度的、普通的、溫和的 **v**使緩和

Judging by the chairman's instructions, the "moderate line" was still in effect.

照董事長的指示看來，仍然要採用「溫和路線」。

🔄 **fair, gentle, medium**（溫和的、平靜的）
🔙 **excessive, extreme, immoderate**（過度的、極端的）

- chairman n.董事長
- instruction n.指示
（121）

1192.

modest [`mɑdɪst] 【 mod·est 】 **a**謙虛的、端莊的、適度的

There has been a modest decrease in house price this year.

房價今年略有下降。

🔄 **bashful, humble, unpretentious**（謙虛的）
🔙 **arrogant, immodest, pretentious**（傲慢的、做作的）

- decrease n.減少
- price n.價錢
（94）

M

1193.

modify [ˋmɑdəˌfaɪ] 【mod·i·fy】 **v** 更改、緩和、修飾

The union has been forced to modify its position.

工會被迫稍稍改變立場。

（同）**alter, diversify, vary**（更改、改變）

（反）**fix**（固定）

- union n.工會
- force v.強迫

1194.

monitor [ˋmɑnətə] 【mon·i·tor】 **n** 監督器、班長 **v** 監控、監測

A business must monitor changes and needs in society in order to behave in a social responsible way.

企業必須密切關注社會的變化和需求，以便更好地承擔社會責任。

- 字根：mon警告
  字尾：it走動
  字尾：or從事…的人
- behave v.表現
- responsible a.有責任的

1195.

monocracy [moˋnɑkrəsɪ] 【mo·noc·ra·cy】 **n** 獨裁統治

The idea of state "ruled by law" is in association with a constitutional state but it is in opposition of such states not ruled by law as monocracy, autocratic state, as well as state ruled by police.

法治國家與人治國家、專制國家、員警國家等非法治國家相對立與憲政國家相聯繫。

（同）**dictatorship, tyranny**（專制、獨裁者的職位）

- 字首：mono單一
- association n.聯合
- constitutional a.憲法的
- autocratic a.獨裁的

1196.

monopoly [məˋnɑpḷɪ] 【mo·nop·o·ly】 **n** 獨佔、壟斷、專賣權

The factory has a monopoly of medical equipment in the country.

這家工廠在該國獨占醫療設備市場。

（同）**control, corner, possession**（控制、支配）

- 字首：mono單一
  字尾：poly多
- medical a.醫療的
- equipment n.設備

1197.

moral [ˋmɔrəl] 【mor·al】 **a** 道德的、教訓的 **n** 道德、品行

His behavior transgressed the moral rules of the social conduct.

他的行為違背了社會行為的道德準則。

（同）**ethical, righteous, virtuous**（正確的、倫理的）

（反）**immoral**（不道德的）

- 字根：mor習慣
  字尾：al屬於…的
- behavior n.行為
- transgress v.違背
- conduct n.品行

1198.

moreover [morˋovə] 【more·o·ver】 **ad** 並且、此外

Moreover, domestic prices were usually at least as variable as export prices and in some cases more so.

此外，國內價格通常至少與出口價格同樣易變，在某些情況下變化更多。

（同）**besides, furthermore**（此外）

- domestic a.國內的
- at least ph.至少
- variable a.多變的

1199.

motel [moˋtɛl] 【mo·tel】 **n** 汽車旅館

The motel business went to pot when the new highway was built.

這條新公路建成後，汽車旅館的生意冷變得冷清。

- 為motor與hotel二詞的縮合

1200.
mortgage [ˋmɔrgɪdʒ] 【mort‧gage】 **v** **n** 抵押

The mortgage is a drain on our financial resources.

償還抵押借款是我們財務上的一大負擔。

🔷 **guaranty, pledge**（抵押）

- mortgage loan ph.抵押貸款
- mortgage-backed securities ph. 抵押擔保證券
- drain n.負擔
- financial a.財政的

1201.
motive [ˋmotɪv] 【mo‧tive】 **n** 動機、目的 **a** 推動的

His motive for working so hard is that he needs money.

他這麼賣力工作的目的在於他需要錢。

🔷 **cause, motivation, reason**（動機、理由）

- motivate v.作為…的動機
- 字根：mot動
  字尾：ive小事物

1202.
mountaineering [ˌmauntəˋnɪrɪŋ] 【moun‧tain‧eer‧ing】
n 登山運動、登山

Mountaineering is attractive especially to young people because it is accompanied with hardship and adventure.

登山很吸引人，特別是對年輕人來說，因為它伴隨著艱難險阻。

- mountaineering bag ph.登山包
- attractive a.吸引的
- hardship n.艱難
- adventure n.冒險

1203.
multicultural [ˌmʌltɪˋkʌltʃərəl] 【mul‧ti‧cul‧tur‧al】
a 多種文化的、融合多種文化的

Since Australia is a multicultural and unique society, it is probably hard for overseas students to fit in with it.

由於澳大利亞是一個有著多元文化的獨特社會，所以對海外學生來說或許較難適應。

- 字首：multi多
  字根：culture文化
  字尾：al屬於…的
- unique a.獨特的
- fit in with ph.適合

1204.
multilingual [ˋmʌltɪˋlɪŋgwəl] 【mul‧ti‧lin‧gual】 **a** 使用多種語言的

Translation Service Center provides the service of multilingual translation of technical and non-technical literature.

翻譯服務中心提供科技及其他方面的各種文字翻譯服務。

- 字首：multi多
  字根：lingua語言
  字尾：al與…有關的
- technical a.科技的

1205.
multiple [ˋmʌltəpl̩] 【mul‧ti‧lin‧gual】 **n** 倍數 **a** 多樣的、由許多部分

We use the hall for multiple purposes.

這個大廳對我們有多種用途。

- multiple alleles ph. 等位基因
- multiple birth ph.多胎生產
- multiple choice ph.多項選擇的
- multiple store ph.連鎖商店

1206.
multiply [ˋmʌltəplaɪ] 【mul‧ti‧ply】 **v** 相乘、增加、繁殖 **a** 多層的

Buy lots of raffle tickets and multiply your chances of success.

多買彩票增加你中獎的機會。

🔷 **increase, gain, procreate**（增加）
🔻 **divide**（除數）

- 字首：multi多
  字根：ply折疊
- raffle n.獎券銷售
- chance n.機會

1207.
multitude [ˋmʌltətˌjud] 【mul‧ti‧tude】 **n** 許多、大量、民眾

Advanced figures are emerging in multitude in this era of ours.

在我們這個時代的卓越人物正大量地湧現出來。

🔷 **crowd, group, mass**（大群、集合）

- figure n.人物
- era n.時代

M

1208.
munch [mʌntʃ]【munch】 **v** 津津有味地嚼
Cows munch mostly grasses and hay, yet they grow strong and hefty.
牛吃的是草，但卻長得身高體壯。
chew（嚼）

- hay n.乾草
- hefty a.肌肉發達的

(181)

1209.
multimedia [mʌltɪˋmidɪə]【mul·ti·me·di·a】 **n** 多媒體
a 多媒體的
Stadiums are multimedia marketing platforms.
體育場成了利用多種媒體為進行市場行銷提供機會的場所。

- multimedia database ph.多媒體數據庫
- multimedia technology ph.多媒體技術
- 字首：multi多
  字尾：media媒體
- stadium n.體育場

(50)

1210.
muscle [ˋmʌsl̩]【mus·cle】 **n** 肌肉、體力 **v** 使勁擠出
He concentrates on the bone and muscle of his tale.
他集中全力構思故事的結構和內容。

- muscle spasm ph.肌肉痙攣
- muscle-bound a.肌肉僵硬的
- concentrate on ph.全神貫注的
- tale n.故事

(61)

1211.
mutual [ˋmjutʃʊəl]【mu·tu·al】 **a** 相互的、共有的
I believe the measure would redound to our mutual benefit and reputation.
我相信這項措施將有助於我們共同的利益和名譽。
common, joint, reciprocal（相互的、共同的）

- mutual fund ph.共同資金
- mutual insurance ph.互助保險
- mutual reality ph.共同現實
- redound to ph.提高
- reputation n.名譽

(126)

MEMO

abbr 縮寫詞
a 形容詞
ad 副詞
aux 助動詞
conj 連接詞
n 名詞
num 數字
ph 片語
prep 介系詞
v 動詞
（美）美式用語
（英）英式用語
（法）法式用語

全書單字取材於：
①10本坊間新多益考試暢銷書籍
②50篇英文新聞、商業文章
③2005~2012年ETS TOEIC歷屆考古題
→ 總計約50,000個單字，以電腦統計出題率高達80%
 的實用單字1,800個

高頻率單字

N 家族 napkin~nutrition 01-09

高 分 錦 囊

1212.
napkin [ˋnæpkɪn] 【nap·kin】 n 餐巾、小毛巾

He put a napkin by my plate.

他把一條餐巾放在我盤子旁邊。

🔁 **linen, serviette, towel**（餐巾紙）

• napkin ring ph.
套餐巾的小環
• plate n.盤子

1213.
nasty [ˋnæstɪ] 【nas·ty】 a 令人作嘔的、脾氣不好的、不愉快的
n 討厭的人

They cut their own throats by being nasty to the boss.

他們對上司不禮貌是自討苦吃。

🔁 **disgusting, nauseating, unpleasant**（不愉快的、噁心的）

• nasty-nice a.笑裡藏刀的
• throat n.喉嚨

1214.
navigation [ˌnævəˋgeʃən] 【na·vig·nation】 n 航行、導航、水上運輸

The council also affirmed the requirement to guarantee free navigation through international waterways.

安理會還會確認需要保證國際水道的航行自由。

• 字根：nav船
字尾：ig駕駛
字尾：ation性質
• affirm v.確認

1215.
negative [ˋnɛgətɪv] 【neg·a·tive】 n 否定、拒絕 a 否定的、消極的

She could not be negative or perfunctory about anything.

她對任何事情都不抱消極或敷衍的態度。

🔄 **affirmative, positive**（確定的、積極的）

• negative campaigning
ph.攻擊型的選戰
• negative declaration
ph.否定聲明書
• negative equity ph.負資產抵押

1216.
neglect [nɪgˋlɛkt] 【ne·glect】 n 忽視、疏忽 v 忽略、疏漏

He tried to remedy this neglect during his own administration.

他努力在他的任期內彌補這個缺陷。

🔁 **disregard, ignore, omit**（忽視、忽略）
🔄 **endeavor, exert, respect**（努力、盡力）

• 字根：neg否定
字根：lect選擇
• remedy n.補救
• administration n.管理

1217.
negligible [ˋnɛglɪdʒəbḷ] 【neg·li·gi·ble】 a 可以忽略的、微不足道的

Their losses were negligible.

他們的損失微不足道。

🔁 **insignificant, scanty**（不重要的、不足的）

• 字根：neg否定
字根：lig選擇
字尾：ible可…的

1218.
negotiate [nɪˋgoʃɪet] 【ne·go·ti·ate】 v 談判、商議

We've decided to negotiate with the employers about our wage claims.

我們已經決定和雇主談判關於我們的工資要求。

🔁 **arbitrate, intervene, mediate**（談判、交涉）

• negotiation n.談判
• employer n.雇主
• wage n.薪資

1219.
neighborhood [`neibɚhud]【neigh·bor·hood】**n** 鄰近地區、整個街坊、接近

We will plan to rehabilitate the run-down neighborhood.

我們計劃重建這個破落的街區。

同 district, location, zone（區域、地區）

- rehabilitate v.重建
- run-down a.破敗的

1220.
neon sign **ph** 霓虹燈招牌

The neon signs are lit up.

霓虹燈招牌亮了。

1221.
network [`nɛt͵wɝk]【net·work】**n** 網眼織物、網狀系統、廣播網

Banks develop a network of correspondent banks abroad with which they maintain accounts.

銀行在國外建立代理行網並在這些銀行開立帳戶。

同 fretwork, mesh, web（網狀物）

- network architecture ph.通訊網路的設計與結構
- network banking ph.網路銀行業
- Network Information Center ph.網路資訊中心
- correspondent a.符合的

1222.
neutral [`njutrəl]【neu·tral】**a** 中立的、模糊的 **n** 中立者

He continued to keep a neutral attitude towards both sides.

他對雙方繼續保持中立的態度。

同 detached, impartial, unprejudiced（中立的、公平的）

- neutral country ph.中立國
- neutral spirits ph.中性酒精
- attitude n.態度

1223.
newscast [`njuz͵kæst]【news·cast】**n** 新聞廣播

An anchor coordinates a newscast in which several correspondents give reports.

新聞節目主播在新聞節目中綜合整理若干記者的報導。

- anchor n.新聞節目主播
- coordinate v.調節
- correspondent n.特派員

1224.
nominal [`nɑmənl]【nom·i·nal】**a** 名義上的、微不足道的

She is only the nominal chairman, and the real work is done by somebody else.

她只是名義上的主席，實際工作是別人執行的。

反 real, practical, veritable（實際的、名副其實的）

- nominal group ph.名詞組
- nominal wages ph.名義工資
- 字根：nomin名字
  字尾：al屬於…的

1225.
nominate [`nɑmə͵net]【nom·i·nate】**v** 提名、任命、命名

If I were a sole owner, I could nominate you this moment.

假如我是獨資老闆，我現在就可任命你。

同 assign, designate, name（任命、提名）

- 字首：nomin名字
  字尾：ate進行一項行動
- sole a.單獨的

1226.
nonetheless [͵nʌnðə`lɛs]【none·the·less】**ad** 但是、仍然

Nonetheless, very few managers look forward to dealing with "messy" declining performance situations.

不管怎麼說，很少有經理希望去處理工作每況愈下的「混亂」局面。

- look forward to ph.期待
- deal with ph.處理
- messy a.混亂的

1227.
nosy [`nozɪ]【nos·y】**a** 好管閒事的

That old lady is very nosy, so no one likes to talk to her.

那個老婦人是個包打聽，因此沒有人喜歡跟她說話。

同 curious（好奇的）

- nosy parker ph.好管閒事的人

1228.
notable [`notəbḷ] 【 no·ta·ble 】 **a**顯著的、著名的 **n**名人
The policy of staying in close, keeping at work and waiting for the breaks had its most notable success in Guinea.
堅持到底，不斷工作和等待時機的政策，在幾內亞獲得最顯著的成功。
⑩ **famous, noteworthy, prominent**（顯著的、著名的）

• notation n.標誌
• 字根：not標記
  字尾：able可…的

1229.
noteworthy [`not͵wɝðɪ] 【 note·wor·thy 】 **a**值得注意的、顯著的
A young surgeon took the noteworthy operation and became noted ever since.
年輕的外科醫生做了這個引人注目的手術並從此出名。

• surgeon n.外科醫生
• operation n.手術

1230.
notify [`notə͵faɪ] 【 no·ti·fy 】 **v**通知、報告、公佈
Please notify them of the change of the office's address.
請把辦公地址的更改通知他們。
⑩ **inform, report, tell**（通知、報告）

• 字根：not標記
  字尾：ify使成為

1231.
notion [`noʃən] 【 no·tion 】 **n**概念、想法、意圖
She has no notion of the difficulty of this problem.
她不瞭解這個問題的難處。
⑩ **idea, opinion, thought**（想法、主意）

1232.
nourish [`nɝɪʃ] 【 nour·ish 】 **v**養育、支持、懷抱
I could find nothing to nourish my suspicion.
我找不到任何懷疑的根據。
⑩ **feed, nature, nurse**（養育、培育）

• suspicion n.懷疑

1233.
novice [`novɪs] 【 nov·ice 】 **n**新手、初學者
These savvy speakers have some tips for novice speakers.
這些演講老手有一些祕訣可供新手參考。
⑩ **beginner, freshman, newcomer**（初學者、新進者）

• savvy n.理解能力
• tip n.提示

1234.
nuisance [`njusṇs] 【 nui·sance 】 **n**討厭之人或事物、麻煩事
People who park on the pavement are a public nuisance.
把汽車停在人行道上的人很討厭。
⑩ **annoyance, bother, irritation**（討厭的人或事）

• nuisance tax ph.小額消費品稅
• pavement n.人行道

1235.
numerous [`njumərəs] 【 nu·mer·ous 】 **a**許多的、為數眾多的
The examples are too numerous to mention individually.
例子不勝枚舉。
⑩ **abundant, many, multitudinous**（許多的、很多的）
⑫ **unmask**（揭露）

• 字根：num數字
  字尾：er小事物
  字尾：ous充滿…的
• individually ad.逐個地

1236.
nutrition [nju`trɪʃən] 【 nu·tri·tion 】 **n**營養、滋養物、食物
Variety is not a guarantee of good nutrition.
品種多並不能確保營養好。
⑩ **food, nourishment**（食物、營養）

• variety n.多樣化
• guarantee n.保證

abbr 縮寫詞
a 形容詞
ad 副詞
aux 助動詞
conj 連接詞
n 名詞
num 數字
ph 片語
prep 介系詞
v 動詞
（美）美式用語
（英）英式用語
（法）法式用語

全書單字取材於：
①10本坊間新多益考試暢銷書籍
②50篇英文新聞、商業文章
③2005~2012年ETS TOEIC歷屆考古題
→ 總計約50,000個單字，以電腦統計出題率高達80%
  的實用單字1,800個

高頻率單字

O 家族 obedient~owe

高分錦囊

1237.
obedient [ə`bidjənt] [o·be·di·ent] **a** 服從的、恭順的

No one should fawn on his superiors or be obedient and "loyal" to them in an unprincipled way.

下級也不應當對上級阿諛奉承或無原則地服從「盡忠」。

同 acquiescent, duteous, loyal（順從的、服從的）
反 disobedient（違抗的）

- fawn v.奉承
- unprincipled a.無原則的

165

1238.
object [`abdʒɪkt] [ob·ject] **V** 反對 **n** 物體、目的、受詞

Some people work with the sole object of earning fame.

有些人工作以求得名聲為唯一的目標。

同 complain, disagree, protest（反對、不服）
反 agree, consent, support（同意、支持）

- object code ph.電腦語言
- object glass ph.街物透鏡
- object lesson ph.實物教學
- object to ph.對…反對
- fame n.名聲

213

1239.
obligation [ɑblə`geʃən] [ob·li·ga·tion] **n** 義務、恩惠、合約

You're under no obligation to pay for goods which you did not order.

沒有訂購貨物就無需付款。

同 commission, duty, responsibility（責任、義務）

198

1240.
oblivious [ə`blɪvɪəs] [o·bliv·i·ous] **a** 健忘的、不注意的

He was quite oblivious to the danger he was in.

他完全忘記了自己處於危險中。

同 forgetful, preoccupied, unconscious（忘掉的、忽略的）

- danger n.危險

121

1241.
obsolete [`absə,lit] [ob·so·lete] **a** 廢棄的、過時的 **V** 淘汰

Today's competition renders obsolete huge chunks of what we know.

今天的競爭使得我們的大部分知識變得陳舊了。

同 antiquated, extinct, outmoded（陳舊的、過時的）
反 new（新的）

- render v.使成為
- chunk n.相當的部分

57

1242.
obstacle [`abstək!] [ob·sta·cle] **n** 障礙物、妨礙

What may be a stimulus at one time may become an obstacle later.

在某個時期的刺激之後也可能變成障礙。

同 barrier, block, deterrent（障礙、阻礙）
反 help（幫忙）

- obstacle course ph.障礙超越訓練場
- obstacle race ph.障礙賽跑
- stimulus n.刺激

81

1243.
obtain [əb`ten] [ob·tain] **V** 獲得、達到

Having increased our manufacturing facilities, we are advertising to obtain more users.

為了增加製作便利，我們刊登廣告以爭取更多的用戶。

同 acquire, gain, receive（獲得、得到）
反 forgo, relinquish, surrender（放棄、交出）

- 字首：ob朝向
- 字根：tain握、持
- facility n.便利

143

1244. `165`

obvious [ˈabvɪəs] 【 ob·vi·ous 】 **a**明顯的、平淡無奇的

Indeed, there are many obvious advantages to a five-day week.

的確，實行五天工作制有許多明顯的優點。

⑩ apparent, clear, explicit（明顯的）

⑫ obscure（黑暗的）

• indeed ad.確實
• advantage n.優點

1245. `143`

occasion [əˈkeʒən] 【 oc·ca·sion 】 **n**場合、時機、理由
　　　　　　　　　　　　　　　　v惹起、引起

He wished to make the most of the occasion, maintaining the suspense.

他想充分利用這場合，以保持這緊張的局面。

⑩ condition, motivation, rationale（時機、動機）

• wish v.希望
• suspense n.懸疑

1246. `98`

occlude [əˈklud] 【 oc·clude 】 **v**堵塞，阻擋、牙齒咬合

This method can occlude the invalid user and greatly improve the security of the DBMS software.

此種方法可封閉非法用戶的許可權，大大提高資料庫管理軟體的安全性。

• 字首：oc朝向
　字根：clude關閉
• invalid a.無效的
• security n.安全

1247. `143`

occupation [ˌakjəˈpeʃən] 【 oc·cu·pa·tion 】 **n**職業、消遣、佔領

Coal mining has always been a dangerous occupation.

採煤向來是一種危險職業。

⑩ affair, business, employment（工作、生意）

• coal n.煤
• mine v.開採

1248. `112`

occupy [ˈakjəˌpaɪ] 【 oc·cu·py 】 **v**佔領、佔用、使從事

Today women are striving to occupy positions previously closed to them.

現今婦女正在努力爭取以往不對她們開放的職位。

⑩ capture, dominate, seize（征服、統治）

• strive v.努力
• previously ad.以前

O

1249. `164`

occur [əˈkɝ] 【 oc·cur 】 **v**發生、出現、被想起

The time when a solar eclipse will occur can be calculated.

日蝕發生的時間可以被推算出來。

⑩ happen, transpire（發生）

• occur to ph.在…心裡出現
• 字首：oc朝向
　字根：cur跑
• eclipse n.蝕

1250. `184`

offense [əˈfɛns] 【 of·fense 】 **n**犯罪、冒犯、攻擊

His words gave great offense to everybody present.

他的發言冒犯了在場的所有人。

⑩ dereliction, infraction, violation（侵犯、過失）

⑫ defense（防禦）

• offensive a.冒犯的

1251. `221`

offer [ˈɔfɚ] 【 of·fer 】 **v**提供、試圖、出價、貢獻

The job offers prospects of promotion.

這份工作有晉升的機會。

⑩ attempt, propose, submit（提交、建議）

⑫ accept, give, receive（接受、得到）

• offer for sale ph.公開發售
• offer for subscription ph.公開認購
• 字首：of朝向
　字根：fer帶來

1252.
offset [ˈɔfˌsɛt] 【off·set】 **V** **n** 補償、抵消

He put up his prices to offset the increased cost of materials.

他提高了售價以補償材料成本的增加。

- offset printing ph. 膠版印刷
- 字首：off相反
  字尾：set設置

1253.
omit [oˈmɪt] 【o·mit】 **V** 遺漏、省略、忘記

He did not omit to avail himself of the opportunity, cautiously and briefly.

他不但謹慎且迅速的，並沒有錯過這個機會。

同 bar, exclude, neglect（忽略、排斥）
反 keep（保持）

- cautiously ad.謹慎地
- briefly ad.短暫地

1254.
on and off **ph** 斷斷續續地

He has been working here, on and off, for two years.

他在這裡斷斷續續工作了兩年。

同 apt, likely, probable（可能的、易…的）

1255.
opaque [oˈpek] 【o·paque】 **a** 不透明的、難理解的

During these tests she was able to read a newspaper through an opaque screen.

在這些測試中，她能夠隔著一塊不透明的擋板閱讀報紙。

同 murky, obtuse, vague（晦暗的、朦朧的）
反 transparent（透明的）

- 字首：op相反
  字首：aque水
- screen n.遮擋物

1256.
operate [ˈɑpəˌret] 【op·er·ate】 **V** 操作、運轉、經營

This facility is very effective because it is so simple to operate.

因為易於操作，所以這項設施非常有效。

同 conduct, handle, manage（經營、管理）

- 字根：oper工作
  字尾：ate進行一項行動
- effective a.有效的

1257.
operator [ˈɑpəˌretə] 【op·er·a·tor】 **n** 操作者、接線生

If you know the extension of the party you wish to reach, dial it now or wait on the line for operator assistance.

如果你知道這個黨的分機號碼請直撥，或稍後由總機為您服務。

- 字首：operate操作
  字尾：or從事…的人
- extension n.電話分機
- dial v.撥號
- assistance n.幫助

1258.
opponent [əˈponənt] 【op·po·nent】 **n** 對手、反對者 **a** 對抗的

He closed in with his opponent.

他向自己的對手妥協了。

同 adversary, combatant, foe（競爭者、敵人）
反 ally, association, confederate（聯盟、結合）

- 字首：op相反
  字根：pon放置
  字尾：ent執行某行動的人

1259.
opposite [ˈɑpəzɪt] 【op·po·site】 **a** 相對的、對面的、相反的

The other places were all filled with the exception of the one opposite him.

其餘的地方都已坐滿，只有他對面的一個位置還空著。

同 antagonistic, contrary, contrastive（相反的、對立的）
反 identical, same（相同的）

- opposite number ph.職務、地位對等或相當者
- opposite sex ph.異性
- 字首：op相反
  字根：pose放置
  字尾：ite有…性質的

1260.

oppress [əˋprɛs] 【 op·press 】 **V**壓迫、壓抑、使沉重

Somehow, the room oppressed him.

這房間不知為何使他有壓迫感。

🔒 **harass, saddle, tyrannize**（壓抑、壓迫）

🔒 **relieve**（釋放）

• 字首：op朝向
• 字根：press壓

1261.

optical [ˋɑptɪkl̩] 【 op·ti·cal 】 **a**眼睛的、視力的、光學的

The area that is visible through an optical instrument.

通過光學儀器可以看到的範圍。

🔒 **seeing, visual**（視覺的）

• optical art ph.視覺藝術
• optical fiber ph.光纖
• optical illusion ph.視錯覺
• 字首：opt視覺
• 字尾：ical與…有關的

1262.

optimistic [ˏɑptəˋmɪstɪk] 【 op·ti·mis·tic 】 **a**樂觀的

My estimate of the situation is not so optimistic.

我對形勢的估計不那麼樂觀。

🔒 **pessimistic**（悲觀的）

1263.

optimum [ˋɑptəməm] 【 op·ti·mum 】 **n**最適宜條件 **a**最理想的

Unfortunately, figuring out the optimum time to place orders is never easy.

很不幸，抓準下訂單的最佳時機是不容易的。

• unfortunately ad.不幸地
• figure out ph.算出

1264.

option [ˋɑpʃən] 【 op·tion 】 **n**選擇、選修科目

He ruled out the impractical option.

他拒絕考慮不切實際的選擇。

🔒 **alternative, equivalent, surrogate**（供選擇的事物）

• 字根：opt選擇
• 字尾：ion狀態
• rule out ph.排除
• impractical a.不切實際的

1265.

order [ˋɔrdɚ] 【 or·der 】 **n**訂單、順序、命令 **V**訂購

The publisher was inundated with orders.

出版社接到雪片般飛來的訂單。

🔒 **arrangement, formation, mode**（安排、佈置）

🔒 **disorder**（混亂）

• order about ph.不斷差遣
• order arms ph.持槍立正的姿勢
• order book ph.定貨簿
• order paper ph.議事日程表
• 字根：ord次序
• 字尾：er小事物

1266.

organ donor **ph**器官捐贈者

They were given islet cells from the pancreas of a dead organ donor.

他們被移植了死亡的器官捐獻者的胰臟細胞。

• organ n.器官
• donor n.捐贈者
• pancreas n.胰腺

1267.

origin [ˋɔrədʒɪn] 【 or·i·gin 】 **n**起源、出身

He is a researcher of working class origin.

他是工人出身的研究員。

🔒 **derivation, source, parentage**（出身、根源）

• originate v.來自
• working class ph.工人階級

211

1268.
ornament [ˋɔrnəmənt] 【 or‧na‧ment 】 n裝飾品、修飾
v裝飾、美化

He is an ornament to his profession.
他為專業添增光彩。
同► adornment, decoration, garnish（裝飾、裝飾品）

1269.
outage [ˋautɪdʒ] 【 out‧age 】 n運行中斷、中斷供應

A freak storm was to blame for the power outage.
停電的起因是一場特大怪異的暴風雪。
同► bar, exclude, neglect（忽略、排斥）
反► keep（保持）

* freak a.怪異的
* blame v.把…歸咎於

1270.
outbid [ˏautˋbɪd] 【 out‧bid 】 v在開價上戰勝

We offer 100,000 pounds for the warehouse, but another company outbid us.
我們出價100, 000英磅購買這個倉庫，但另一家公司出價高於我們。

* 字首：out出
  字尾：bid出價
* warehouse n.倉庫

1271.
outbreak [ˋautˏbrek] 【 out‧break 】 n爆發、暴動

A piece of incredible folly on the part of the company precipitated an outbreak.
公司做出一件難以置信的蠢事，因而促成了這次暴動。
同► eruption, rebellion, revolt（暴動、爆發）

* 字首：out出
  字尾：break破裂
* incredible a.難以置信的
* folly n.蠢事
* precipitate v.促使

1272.
outgoing [ˋautˏgoɪŋ] 【 out‧go‧ing 】 a外出的、直率的

Would you describe yourself as outgoing or more reserved?
你認為你是個外向的人還是內向的人？

* describe v.描述
* reserved a.含蓄的

1273.
outflow [ˋautˏflo] 【 out‧flow 】 n流出（物） v流出

Capital inflow shall be recorded as a credit item, while capital outflow shall be recorded as a debit item in the capital account.
當資本流入被記為資本項目中的貸方時，資本流出則記為借方。

* inflow n.流入物
* debit n.借方

1274.
outlet [ˋautˏlɛt] 【 out‧flow 】 n出口、發洩途徑、銷路

There is a huge sales outlet for pocket caculators.
袖珍計算機有極大的市場。
同► exit, loophole, postern（出口）

* pocket a.袖珍的

1275.
outline [ˋautˏlaɪn] 【 out‧line 】 n大綱、輪廓、概要 v概述

It is necessary to outline the premises upon which they should be based.
必須明確這些項目是基於什麼前提。
同► contour, profile, skeleton（外形、輪廓）

* 字首：out外
  字尾：line線條
* premise n.前提

1276.

outpatient [ˋaʊtˏpeʃənt] 【 out‧pa‧tient 】 **n**門診病人

I'd like to know whether basic health insurance coverage should include benefits for outpatient, hospital, surgery and medical expenses.

我想知道基本健康保險所列的項目是否應包括醫院門診、住院、手術及藥品等費用的賠償。

反 impatient（住院病人）

- health insurance **ph.**健康保險
- coverage **n.**保險項目
- expense **n.**費用

1277.

output [ˋaʊtˏpʊt] 【 out‧put 】 **V** **n**出產、產量

Factory managers understate their potential output.

工廠的管理人員少報他們的潛在產量。

同 proceed, production, yield（出產、產量）

- 源自於片語put out
- understate **v.**保守地說
- potential **a.**潛在的

1278.

outset [ˋaʊtˏsɛt] 【 out‧set 】 **n**最初、開始

At the outset of her career she was full of optimism but not now.

她事業一開始十分樂觀，但現在已今非昔比了。

同 beginning, commencement, opening（最初、開始）

- career **n.**職業
- be full of **ph.**充滿
- optimism **n.**樂觀

1279.

outside [aʊtˋsaɪd] 【 out‧side 】 **n**外面、外觀 **a**外面的 **ad**在外面

Excise is the extra work that satisfies either the needs of our tools or those of outside agents as we try to achieve our objectives.

附加工作是在我們努力實現目標的同時，滿足工具或者某些外部因素需要的其他工作。

同 edge, exterior, surface（外部、外面）
反 inside（內部）

- outside broadcast **ph.**實況播播
- outside lane **ph.**外車道
- outside-the-box **a.**創造性

O

1280.

outskirts [ˋaʊtˏskɝts] 【 out‧skirts 】 **n**（複數）郊外、郊區

In some large cities, people from outskirts prefer commuting to the city than driving by themselves.

在大城市裡，住在郊區的人們喜歡搭乘公車進城上班而不願自己開車。

同 borders, suburbs（郊區）

- commute **v.**通勤

1281.

overcoat [ˋovɚˏkot] 【 o‧ver‧coat 】 **n**外套、大衣

It is so warm today that I can dispense with an overcoat.

今天天氣很暖和，我可以不用穿大衣。

同 coat, greatcoat（大衣、長大衣）

- dispense with **ph.**省掉

1282.

overcome [ˏovɚˋkʌm] 【 o‧ver‧come 】 **V**戰勝、克服、壓倒

In order to succeed here you will need to overcome your prejudices.

你需要消除偏見才能在這裡獲得成功。

同 conquer, defeat, surmount（擊敗）
反 submit, surrender, yield（服從、投降）

- 源自於片語come over
- prejudice **n.**偏見

1283.
overcrowd [͵ovəˋkraud]【o·ver·crowd】**v** 過度擁擠
It was the height of the rush hour. An overcrowded bus ploughed its way through the busy streets.
上下班的尖峰時刻，一輛擁擠不堪的公車緩慢地駛過大街鬧市。

• rush hour ph.尖峰時刻
• plough v.開路

1284.
overdraft [ˋovə͵dræft]【o·ver·due】**n** 透支、透支數額
We honored the check as the overdraft was only 5 dollars.
我們支付這張支票的透支額只有5元。

• overdraft facility ph. 透支法
• 字首：over超過 字尾：draft匯票
• honor v.支付

1285.
overdue [ˋovəˋdju]【o·ver·due】**a** 過期的、未付的、遲到的
Now they are overdue and I shall have to pay a penalty.
現在它們過期了，我不得不付罰款。
📖 **belated, tardy**（誤期的、遲延的）

• 字首：over超過 字尾：due期限
• penalty n.罰款

1286.
overhaul [ovəˋhɔl]【o·ver·haul】**v** **n** 徹底檢修、詳細檢查
I'm going to the doctor for my annual overhaul, i.e. physical examination.
我要到醫生那裡作年度身體檢查。
📖 **fix, mend, repair**（修理）

• annual a.年度的
• physical a.身體的
• examination n.檢查

1287.
overhead [ˋovəˋhɛd]【o·ver·head】**a** 管理的 **n** 經常費用、天花板
The large overhead reduced the company's profits.
大筆的管理費用減少了公司的利潤。

1288.
overlap [ovəˋlæp]【o·ver·lap】**v** **n** 部分重疊
Obviously, the two sets of policies overlap and can complement each other.
顯然，兩套政策有互相重複的地方也可以互補。
📖 **overlay, overspread**（與…交搭、疊蓋住）

• overlap-overlapped-overlapped
• complement v.補充

1289.
overlook [ovəˋluk]【o·ver·look】**v** 俯瞰、寬恕、忽視
I will overlook your late arrival because it is the first time.
我可以寬恕你的遲到，因為這是第一次。

• arrival n.抵達

1290.
overseas [ˋovəˋsiz]【o·ver·seas】**ad** 在海外 **a** 在海外的
Our overseas commerce has increased a great deal.
我們的海外貿易已大大增加。
📖 **abroad**（在海外）

• commerce n.貿易

1291.
overthrow [ˌovəˋθro] 【 o·ver·throw 】 **v.n.** 翻、打倒
The overthrow of his plans left him much discouraged.
他的計劃失敗使得他很氣餒。
🔄 **defeat, overturn, subvert**（使失敗、挫敗）

- overthrow-overthrew-overthrown

186

1292.
overtime [ˋovəˌtaɪm] 【 o·ver·time 】 **n.** 加班、延長時間 **a.** 超時的
Although the work is always urgent, overtime payment is unusual.
雖然工作經常刻不容緩，但加班費則很優厚。

- urgent **a.** 緊急的
- unusual **a.** 獨特的

94

1293.
overturn [ˌovəˋtɝn] 【 o·ver·turn 】 **v.n.** 翻轉、顛覆、廢除
I have convictions that his testimony could overturn situation.
我很有信心他的證言可能會讓形勢逆轉。

- conviction **n.** 說服力
- testimony **n.** 證詞
- situation **n.** 形勢

87

1294.
overwork [ˋovəˋwɝk] 【 o·ver·work 】 **v.n.** 過度勞累
The great mental strain and overwork shattered his mind.
過度的精神負擔和勞累使他心靈受損。

- mental **a.** 精神的
- strain **n.** 負擔
- shatter **v.** 筋疲力盡

126

1295.
overwhelm [ˌovəˋhwɛlm] 【 o·ver·whelm 】 **v.** 壓倒、覆蓋
If I cannot overwhelm with my quality, I will overwhelm with my quantity.
如果我不能以品質壓倒，我就一定要以數量取勝。
🔄 **crush, vanquish**（擊敗）

- 字首：over超過
- 字尾：whelm壓倒

67

1296.
owe [o] 【 owe 】 **v.** 欠債、歸功於、應給予
How much do I owe you?
我要付你多少錢？
🔄 **pay**（付費）

- owe to **ph.** 應把…歸功於

176

O

MEMO

MEMO

abbr 縮寫詞
a 形容詞
ad 副詞
aux 助動詞
conj 連接詞
n 名詞
num 數字
ph 片語
prep 介系詞
v 動詞
（美）美式用語
（英）英式用語
（法）法式用語

全書單字取材於：

①10本坊間新多益考試暢銷書籍

②50篇英文新聞、商業文章

③2005~2012年ETS TOEIC歷屆考古題

→ 總計約50,000個單字，以電腦統計出題率高達80%
　的實用單字1,800個

高頻率單字

>|P 家族 package~pushcart (MP3) 01-10

1297.
package [`pækɪdʒ] 【pack·age】 **n** 包裹、包裝箱 **v** 包裝
The bulk of your pay package is shares, not the basic monthly salary.
你的待遇主要是股票，而不是以底薪為主。
同 **bundle, pack, parcel**（包裹、綑）

`128`
- package deal **ph.**整批交易
- package holiday **ph.**承包旅遊
- package store **ph.**酒店
- package tour **ph.**包辦旅行

1298.
packing [`pækɪŋ】 【pack·ing】 **n** 包裝、填料
We agree to use cartons for outer packing.
我們同意用紙箱做外包裝。

`179`
- packing case **ph.**裝運貨物的箱子
- carton **n.**紙板箱

1299.
palatable [`pælətəbḷ] 【pal·at·a·ble】 **a** 美味的、使人愉快的
The truth is not always very palatable.
事實真相並非盡如人意。
同 **delicious, tasty**（美味的）

`75`

1300.
panic [`pænɪk] 【pan·ic】 **v n** 恐慌、驚恐
In spite of the panic, she remained serene and in control.
儘管人心惶惶，但她卻泰然自若。
同 **fear, scare, terror**（恐慌、驚慌）

`145`
- panic buying **ph.**瘋狂搶購
- panic grass **ph.**黍
- panic purchase **ph.**搶購風
- panic-striken **a.**受恐慌的
- serene **a.**穩重的

1301.
paradox [`pærəˌdɑks] 【par·a·dox】 **n** 自相矛盾的議論
Rising benevolence and falling profits seem a paradox at the best of times.
捐款增加而利潤下降，這在經濟狀況最好的年代也似乎是一種矛盾現象。
同 **antilogy, contradiction, oxymoron**（矛盾）

`166`
- paradox of thrift **ph.**節儉的矛盾
- benevolence **n.**善意

1302.
parch [pɑrtʃ] 【parch】 **v** 烘、烤、使乾枯
Parched corn was a staple of the Indian diet.
烤玉米是印度人的主要食物。
同 **roast**（烤）

`51`
- staple **n.**主食
- diet **n.**食物

1303.
pardon [`pɑrdṇ] 【par·don】 **v n** 原諒、寬恕
Please pardon my presumption in writing to you.
請原諒我很冒昧地寫信給你。
同 **absolve, excuse, forgive**（原諒、饒恕）
反 **punish**（處罰）

`106`
- presumption **n.**冒昧

144

1304.
part-time [`part`taɪm] 【part-time】 **a** 部分時間的、兼職的
I have a part-time job now, so I work in the evenings.
我目前有份兼職工作，所以都在夜晚上班。
反 full-time（全部時間的）

107

1305.
partial [`parʃəl] 【par·tial】 **a** 部分的、偏袒的
His partial attitude called forth a lot of criticism.
他的偏袒態度招致了不少批評。
同 fractional, fragmentary, limited（部分的、局部的）
反 total（全部的）

- partial to ph.偏袒
- partial towards ph.特別喜歡
- 字根：part部分
  字尾：ial與…有關的

165

1306.
participate [par`tɪsə,pet] 【par·tic·i·pate】 **v** 參與、分享、分擔
We cherish the opportunity to participate in the decision-making process.
我們很重視參加決策過程的機會。
同 affair, business, employment（工作、生意）

- participant n.參與者
- participate in ph.參加
- cherish v.珍惜
- process n.過程

143

1307.
partition [par`tɪʃən] 【par·ti·tion】 **n** 分開、分隔物 **v** 分隔
To prefer one at the expense of the other would bring on civil war and worse disunity than that would result from peaceful partition.
如果偏愛一方而犧牲另一方，將會引起內訌和分裂，和平劃分造成的不統一更糟。
同 division, separation（分開、分割）

- partition off ph.分隔成
- disunity n.不團結
- peaceful a.和平的

105

1308.
passion [`pæʃən] 【pas·sion】 **n** 熱情、情欲、忿怒
Nothing could rekindle her extinct passion.
她熱情已逝，無法回心轉意。
同 enthusiasm, fervor, rage（熱情、忿怒）
反 coolness, indifference（冷淡、漠視）

- passion fruit ph.百香果
- passion killer ph.熱情殺手
- passion play ph.耶穌受難復活劇
- Passion Sunday ph.苦難主日
- rekindle v.使再振作

P

141

1309.
passive [`pæsɪv] 【pas·sive】 **a** 消極的、被動的
He had a passive expression on his face.
他臉上有一種漠然的表情。
同 docile, inactive, quiescent（不主動的、沉默的）
反 active（主動的）

- passive microwave system ph.被動式微波系統
- passive resistance ph.消極抵抗
- passive smoking ph.吸二手煙
- passive voice ph.被動式

91

1310.
pastime [`pæs,taɪm] 【pas·time】 **n** 娛樂、消遣
Playing tennis, for some it is a career and a pastime for others.
打網球對有些人來說是一項職業，對其他人來說卻是種消遣。
同 amusement, recreation（娛樂）

- tennis n.網球

81

1311.
pass up 【ph.】 拒絕、放棄
You can't afford to pass up too many openings like that.
你不可以像這樣放棄太多的就業機會。

- afford v.足夠去做
- opening n.職位空缺

1312.
passenger [`pæsn̩dʒɚ]【pas‧sen‧ger】n.乘客、旅客

This aircraft company deals with freight only; it has no passenger service.

這家航空公司只辦理貨運業務，沒有客運服務。

📖 **boatman, commuter, rider**（乘客、旅客）

- passenger pigeon ph. 候鴿
- passenger seat ph.乘客座
- aircraft n.飛機
- freight n.貨運

145

1313.
passport [`pæs,port]【pass‧port】n.護照、通行證、手段

After disembarkation, we went through passport control.

我們下飛機接受護照檢查。

- passport control ph. 護照檢察處
- disembarkation n.登陸

65

1314.
pastry [`pestrɪ]【pas‧try】n.麵團、酥皮點心

The pastry is light and crisp.

這點心鬆脆可口。

- pastrycook n.作西點麵包的人
- crisp a.酥的

54

1315.
patent [`pætn̩t]【pat‧ent】n.專利、特權 v.取得…的專利

If the fees are not paid, then the patent is said to have lapsed.

如果不付專利費，這項專利就宣告失效。

📖 **copyright, franchise, trademark**（專利、商標）

- patent leather ph.漆皮
- patent log ph.拖曳式計程儀
- patent medicine ph.成藥
- patent office ph.專利局
- lapse v.失效

165

1316.
patron [`petrən]【pa‧tron】n.贊助者、主顧客

Steven did not think it was fit to question his patron any further at that time.

史帝芬覺得那時不便向他的老闆追問這件事。

📖 **client, customer, frequenter**（顧客、常客）

- patron saint ph.最初的領導人

121

1317.
payment [`pemənt]【pay‧ment】n.支付、付款、報償

Payment by installments is one of the terms of payment that has been accepted.

分期付款是常被接受的一種付款方式。

📖 **defrayal, expenditure, payout**（支付）

- payment by remittance ph.匯付
- payment card ph.付款卡
- installment n.分期付款

184

1318.
peak [pik]【peak】n.山頂、最高點 a.最高的 v.達到高峰

A business cycle can be measured from peak to peak or from trough to trough.

一個商業週期可以用從高峰到高峰或者從谷底到谷底來測定。

📖 **apex, crest, hilltop**（尖端）

🔄 **foot**（底部）

- peak experience ph.顛峰經驗
- peak gust ph.最大陣風
- peak hour ph.顛峰時刻的
- peak time ph.高峰時間

165

1319.
pedestrian [pə`dɛstrɪən]【pe‧des‧tri‧an】n.行人 a.徒步的、行人的

Pedestrian's vehicle on the street is a lot in the rush hour.

高峰時刻，街上的行人車輛很多。

📖 **hiker, walker**（步行者）

🔄 **equestrian**（騎馬者）

- pedestrian crossing ph.人行橫道
- pedestrian precinct ph.機動車禁駛區
- 字根：ped足
- 字尾：ian…的人

127

220

1320.
penalty [`pɛnḷtɪ] 【 pen·al·ty 】 **n**處罰、罰款、罰球、苦難
It is part of the contract that there is a penalty for late delivery.
合約中有延遲交貨的懲罰規定。
辨 **deprivation, fine, forfeit**（罰金、苦難）
反 **remuneration, reward**（獎金、酬勞）

- penalty area ph.罰球區
- penalty clause ph.罰款條例
- penalty kick ph.罰球
- penalty point ph.違章記錄
- penalty shoot-out ph.平局決勝賽

1321.
74
pending [`pɛndɪŋ] 【 pend·ing 】 **a**懸而未決的
All pending orders will be executed this month.
所有未完成的訂單將於本月內執行。
辨 **waiting**（等候的）

- 字根：pend懸掛
- execute v.執行

1322.
57
peninsula [pə`nɪnsələ] 【 pen·in·su·la 】 **n**半島
Dalian is in the south of the Liaodong Peninsula.
大連位於遼東半島南部。
辨 **cape, chersonese, promontory**（半島、河灣）

- peninsular n.半島居民

1323.
87
pension [`pɛnʃən] 【 pen·sion 】 **n**養老金、津貼
After a certain period of employment, the employee qualifies for a pension.
職員在工作一定時間後，就有資格領取養老金。
辨 **stipend, subsidy**（津貼）

- pension book ph.養老金單據簿
- pension fund ph.養老基金
- pension plan ph.養老金制
- pension sb. off ph.發給某人養老金使其退休

1324.
84
pensive [`pɛnsɪv] 【 pen·sive 】 **a**沉思的、悲傷的
Things did not come to their height with him, and I observed he became pensive and melancholy.
情況並沒有發展到嚴重的程度，我卻看他變得苦心焦思、愁悶萬狀。
辨 **contemplative, deliberating, thoughtful**（沉思的、哀愁的）

- 字根：pens懸掛
  字尾：ive有…性質的
- melancholy n.憂鬱

P

1325.
123
perceive [pə`siv] 【 per·ceive 】 **v**察覺、意識到
I plainly perceive some objections remain.
我清楚地察覺到還有一些反對意見。
辨 **detect, feel, observe**（察覺、感知）

- 字首：per穿越
  字根：ceive拿取
- plainly ad.清楚地
- objection n.異議

1326.
125
perception [pə`sɛpʃən] 【 per·cep·tion 】 **n**查覺、洞察力
Contrary to public perception, we were under no pressure with respect to it.
同大家的看法相反，我們在這方面並沒有受到壓力。
辨 **comprehension, percipience, recognition**（理解力、知覺）

- 字首：per穿越
  字根：cept拿取
  字尾：ion性質
- contrary a.相反的
- pressure n.壓力

1327.
241
perfect [`pɝfɪkt] 【 per·fect 】 **a**完美的、精通的、十足的
The job was perfect; there was not a single rejection.
這件工作做得非常好，沒有發生退貨情形。
辨 **absolute, excellent, flawless**（完美的、理想的）

- perfect game ph.完全比賽
- perfect participle ph.【文】過去分詞
- perfect pitch ph.完全音感
- rejection n.拒絕

221

1328.

perform [pɚˋfɔrm]【per·form】 ⅴ執行（任務）、表演

A conscientious person has a larger perspective on what it means to perform a task.

一個盡責的人會從長遠的角度來觀看所執行任務的意義。

圓 **accomplish, execute, transact**（履行、完成）
反 **neglect**（疏忽）

• performance n.表演
• conscientious a.認真的
• perspective n.觀點

1329.

perfume [ˋpɚf jum]【per·fume】 ⓝ芳香、香水 ⅴ充滿香氣

By degrees, the night became impregnated with the perfume of the flowers.

夜色裡漸漸地充滿了馥鬱的花香。

圓 **aroma, incense, scent**（香味、香氣）
反 **stink**（惡臭）

• impregnate v.使充滿

1330.

periodical [ˌpɪrɪˋɑdɪk!]【pe·ri·od·i·cal】 ⓝ期刊 ⓐ週期的、間歇的

I expect periodical reports from you.

我希望你定期向我彙報。

圓 **gazette, journal, magazine**（定期刊物、雜誌）

1331.

permanent [ˋpɚmənənt]【per·ma·nent】 ⓐ永久的、固定的 ⓝ燙髮

I'm not a permanent employee; but I'm working here on a fixed-term contract.

我並不是永久雇員，而是根據定期合約在此工作的。

圓 **constant, durable, enduring**（永久的）
反 **impermanent, momentary, temporary**（暫時的）

• permanent press ph.乾後不皺的
• permanent secretary ph.常務次官
• permanent tooth ph.恆齒
• permanent wave ph.燙髮

1332.

permeate [ˋpɚmɪͺet]【per·me·ate】 ⅴ滲入、瀰漫

If there is a security breach in a small area, it can permeate the entire system.

如果在小範圍內有安全性的漏洞，它將擴散到整個系統。

圓 **penetrate, saturate, soak**（滲入）

• security n.安全
• breach n.裂痕

1333.

permissible [pɚˋmɪsəb!]【per·mis·si·ble】 ⓐ可允許的

Unless a credit stipulates that the quantity of the goods specified must not be exceeded or reduced, a tolerance of 5% more or 5% less will be permissible, always provided that the amount of the drawings does not exceed the amount of the credit.

除非信用證規定貨物的指定數量不得有增減外，在所支付的款項不超過信用證金額的條件下，貨物數量准許有 5 %的增減幅度。

• 字首：per穿過
字根：miss送
字尾：ible可…的
• exceed v.超過
• tolerance n.寬容
• drawing n.提款

183

1334.
permit [pɚˋmɪt]【 per·mit 】**V**允許、容許 **N**許可證

An enlightened government should permit the free expression of political opinion.

一個開明的政府應當允許自由發表政見。

同▶ allow, consent, grant（允許、容許）
反▶ forbid, prohibit（禁止）

- permit of ph.容許
- permit-permitted-permitted
- 字首：per穿過
  字根：mit送
- enlightened a.開朗的

76

1335.
perpetual [pɚˋpɛtʃʊəl]【 per·pet·u·al 】**a**永久的、終身的

It doesn't cater to the beginner or to the expert, but rather devotes the bulk of its efforts to satisfying the perpetual intermediate.

它既不迎合新手也不迎合專家，而是把大部分工作放在滿足永久的中間用戶上。

同▶ continuous, eternal, infinite（永久的、持續的）
反▶ momentary, temporary, transient（短暫的、暫時的）

- perpetual calendar ph. 萬年曆
- perpetual motion ph. 永恆運動
- cater to ph.迎合
- intermediate n.中間事物

74

1336.
perplexed [pɚˋplɛkst]【 per·plexed 】**a**困惑的、複雜的

He is sorely perplexed to account for the situation.

那種情況使他感到很為難。

- 字首：per穿過
  字根：plex折疊

121

1337.
persist [pɚˋsɪst]【 per·sist 】**V**堅持、持續

We must persist in taking the road of self reliance.

我們必須堅持自力更生的道路。

同▶ continue, endure, last（持續、耐久）
反▶ refrain（克制）

- persist in ph.堅持
- 字首：per穿過
  字根：sist站立
- reliance n.依賴

188

1338.
personnel [ˌpɝsnˋɛl]【 per·son·nel 】**N**總稱員工、人事部門

All the managerial personnel at the factory are hired on contract.

工廠所有管理人員都是約聘的。

同▶ employees, staff, workers（全體職員）

- 此單字表複數
- personnel carrier ph. 人員運輸車
- personnel management ph.人員管理

P

125

1339.
perspective [pɚˋspɛktɪv]【 per·spec·tive 】**N**看法、遠景、透視圖

They had no idea how to evaluate from a financial perspective what management was doing.

這些人根本不知道如何從財務角度來評價當前的管理工作。

同▶ prospect, standpoint, viewpoint（遠景、觀點）

- 字首：per穿過
  字根：spect看
  字尾：ive性質
- evaluate v.評價
- financial a.財政的

157

1340.
persuade [pɚˋsweɪd]【 per·suade 】**V**說服、勸服

He had to spell out the plan in detail to persuade the investors.

為了說服投資人，他不得不把整個計劃細細說明清楚。

同▶ convert, convince, induce（說服、勸服）
反▶ dissuade（勸阻）

- 字首：per穿越
  字根：suade力勸
- detail n.詳情

1341.

pertain [pɚˋten]【per·tain】Ⅴ從屬、相關、適合

The file contained all documents that pertain to the new project.

這份檔案包括所有關於新工程的文件。

🔁 **belong, concern, refer**（附屬、有關係）

116
- pertain to **ph.**有關
- 字首：per穿過
  字根：tain握持

1342.

pervade [pɚˋved]【per·vade】Ⅴ彌漫於、遍及於

Science and technology have come to pervade every aspect of our lives.

科學和技術已經滲透到我們生活的每一個方面。

🔁 **fill, penetrate, permeate**（充滿）

147
- 字首：per穿越
  字根：vade走動

1343.

pervert [pɚˋvɝt]【per·vert】Ⅴ使變壞、曲解、誤用

To pervert the course of justice is to prevent justice being done.

誤用司法過程就是阻止司法的實施。

🔁 **exploit, misuse, prostitute**（誤用、濫用）

93
- 字首：per橫過
  字尾：vert轉
- justice **n.**司法
- prevent **v.**防止

1344.

petition [pəˋtɪʃən]【pe·ti·tion】ⁿ請願、申請 Ⅴ請願

When a person or corporation decides that debt has become too burdensome, a petition of bankruptcy is filed.

如果某人或某公司負債累累無力償付時，可申請宣告破產。

🔁 **appeal, demand, request**（請求）

135
- 字根：pet尋找
  字尾：it走動
  字尾：ion行為
- burdensome **a.**累贅的
- bankruptcy **n.**破產

1345.

petroleum [pəˋtroliəm]【pe·tro·le·um】ⁿ石油

Kerosene is a by-product of petroleum refining.

煤油是提煉石油的副產品。

🔁 **petrol**（汽油）

75
- petroleum jelly **ph.**凡士林
- 字首：petro含油的
- refine **v.**提煉

1346.

pharmaceutical [ˌfɑrməˋsjutɪkl̩]【phar·ma·ceu·ti·cal】
ⓐ製藥的

Reports about side effects of drugs, including adverse effects, came to pharmaceutical companies from several sources.

製藥公司通過好幾個管道得到有關藥物副作用，包括有害副作用的報告。

63
- pharmaceutical Co. Ltd **ph.**製藥有限公司
- 字首：pharmac藥
- adverse **a.**有害的

1347.

phase [fez]【phase】ⁿ階段、方面 Ⅴ分階段實行

The first phase of the project was completed two months ahead of schedule.

第一期工程提前兩個月完工。

🔁 **aspect, stage, state**（時期、方面）

117
- phase in **ph.**逐步引入
- phase out **ph.**逐步淘汰
- phase-in **n.**逐漸採用
- phase-out **n.**分階段撤銷

1348.

phenomenon [fə`nɑmə͵nɑn] 【phe·nom·e·non】 n現象、奇蹟

- phenomena為其複數
- common a.普遍的
- recession n.衰退

Bankruptcy is a common phenomenon in an economic recession.

在經濟衰退時，破產是常見的現象。

⑩ **incident, episode, marvel**（事件、奇蹟）

1349.

pickpocket [`pɪk͵pɑkɪt] 【pick·pock·et】 n扒手

- 字首：pick採
  字尾：pocket口袋
- run away ph.逃跑
- pursue v.追捕

The pickpocket ran away and hotly pursued by the police.

那扒手倉皇而逃，員警緊追不捨。

⑩ **ganef, picker**（扒手）

1350.

pilot [`paɪlət] 【pi·lot】 n駕駛員 a試驗性的 v引導

- pilot balloon ph.測風氣球
- pilot lamp ph.領航燈
- Pilot Officer ph.空軍少將
- pilot whale ph.巨頭鯨

The first part was the pilot program.

第一部分是試驗性計劃。

⑩ **conductor, engineer, operator**（駕駛員、領航者）

1351.

plateau [plæ`to] 【pla·teau】 n高原、穩定水準

- inflation n.快速膨脹

After a period of rapid inflation, prices have now reached a plateau.

急遽通貨膨脹之後物價現已趨於平穩。

⑩ **interim, lull, respite**（平穩時期）

1352.

platform [`plæt͵fɔrm] 【plat·form】 n平臺、月臺、講臺

- platform ph.電腦遊戲
- platform scale ph.臺秤
- platform shoe ph.厚底鞋
- concert n.一致
- interaction n.互相影響

Decisions about technical platform are best made in concert with interaction design efforts.

選擇技術平臺時，一定要與交互設計工作一致。

⑩ **balcony, rostrum, stage**（臺、講臺）

1353.

platitude [`plætə͵tjud] 【plat·i·tude】 n發生、出現、被想起

He seems to have no original idea, and his speech is full of platitude.

他似乎沒有什麼獨到的見解，他的講話充滿了陳腔濫調。

1354.

plausible [`plɔzəbḷ] 【plau·si·ble】 a貌似真實的、花言巧語的

Of these three possibilities, the last one seems the most plausible.

在這三個可能性中，最後一個是最可取的。

⑩ **believable, logical, reasonable**（似合理的）
⑱ **actual, genuine**（真實的）

1355.

playwright [`ple͵raɪt] 【play·wright】 n劇作家

- foremost a.最前的

Bernard Show was the foremost playwright of his time.

蕭伯納是他那個時代最重要的戲劇作家。

P

1356.

plenty [`plɛntɪ] 【 plen·ty 】 **n**豐富、充足 **a**足夠的

Plenty of Web sites still exist out there, in the form of personal sites, corporate marketing and support sites, and information-centric intranets.

現在存在大量的網站，有各種形式的個人網站、公司的銷售、支援網站以及提供大量資訊的企業內部網站。

同▶ mass, quantity, volume（大量）

反▶ famine, want（饑荒、不足）

• plenty of ph.很多
• plenty of other fish in the sea ph.天涯何處無芳草
• intranet n.內部網路
• intranet n.內部網路

1357.

plumbing [`plʌmɪŋ] 【 plumb·ing 】 **n**鉛管業、配管工程

We employed a local man to do the plumbing.

我們雇了一個當地人做管道裝修工作。

• plumb n.鉛錘

1358.

playground [`ple͵graʊnd] 【 play·ground 】 **n**運動場、遊戲場

Parents heartily endorsed the plan for a school playground.

家長們熱心支持學校修建運動場的計劃。

同▶ field, park（操場、運動場）

• 字首：play玩樂
  字尾：ground場地
• endorse v.贊成

1359.

pointer [`pɔɪntɚ] 【 point·er 】 **n**指針、暗示

You can move the pointer to select commands from the pull-down menu.

你可以移動指標從下拉式功能表中選擇命令。

• 此單字大寫為大熊星座中的兩顆指極星

1360.

polish [`pɑlɪʃ] 【 po·lish 】 **v**擦亮、使優美

The teacher asked students to polish all windows in the classroom.

老師要求學生擦亮教室裡的所有玻璃。

同▶ burnish, glaze, shine（使發光）

反▶ tarnish（使失去光澤）

• 此單字大寫表示波蘭語
• polish off ph.趕快做完
• polish remover ph.去光水
• polish up ph.潤色

1361.

ponder [`pɑndɚ] 【 pon·der 】 **v**仔細考慮、回想

These are minor problems over which you needn't ponder too long.

這都是些次要的問題，你不必考慮太久。

同▶ consider, deliberate, meditate（仔細思考）

• ponder over ph.考慮
• minor a.次要的

1362.

porch [portʃ] 【 porch 】 **n**門廊、走廊

I sat on the porch a long time waiting for my emotions to ebb.

我在門廊裡坐了好久，等我的情緒穩定下來。

同▶ gallery, portico, veranda（門廊、走廊）

• ebb v.退潮

1363.

portable [`portəbl̩] 【 port·a·ble 】 **a**便於攜帶的、輕便的

What I look at is the sacrifice of so much portable property.

我的意思是，好大一筆動產就這樣付之東流了。

同▶ conveyable, transferable（便於攜帶的）

• sacrifice n.犧牲
• property n.財產

1364.

portage [`portɪdʒ] 【 por·tage 】 **n** 搬運、運費 **v** 轉到陸上運輸

Due to the attack of hurricane, the marine transit company portaged their orders immediately.

因為颶風來襲，船運公司將立即將所有訂單轉由陸上運輸。

- attack n.攻擊
- hurricane n.颶風
- marine a.海的
- transit n.運輸

1365.

porter [`portɚ] 【 por·ter 】 **n** 搬運工人、雜務工、門房

He once worked as a porter in a commercial bank.

他曾在一家商業銀行當雜務工。

⑮ carrier, carter, redcap（搬運工人、雜務工）

- 字首：port港口
  字尾：er從事…的人
- commercial a.商業的

1366.

portion [`porʃən] 【 por·tion 】 **n** 部分 **v** 分配

He left the major portion of his money to the foundation.

他將大部分錢捐給了這個基金會。

⑮ division, part, section（部分）

- portion out ph.分配
- foundation n.基金會

1367.

portfolio [port`folˌo] 【 port·fo·li·o 】 **n** 文件夾、公事包

My stockbroker manages my portfolio for me.

我的證券經紀人替我管理投資組合。

- 字首：port拿、帶
  字根：folio葉
- portfolio career ph.組合型自由職業

1368.

position [pə`zɪʃən] 【 po·si·tion 】 **n** 位置、職位、立場

He cannot abide to stay in one position for long.

他無法忍受長久待在同一職位。

⑮ duty, post, spot（職位、位置）

- position paper ph.立場聲明書
- 字根：pos放置
  字尾：it走動
  字尾：ion狀態
- abide v.忍受

1369.

positive [`pɑzətɪv] 【 pos·i·tive 】 **a** 積極的、確實的、絕對的

You'll have to make a positive decision, not just let things slide.

你必須作出積極的決定，而不是順其自然。

⑯ negative（消極的）

- positive discrimination ph.正面歧視
- positive vetting ph.個人情況全面調查

P

1370.

possession [pə`zɛʃən] 【 pos·ses·sion 】 **n** 擁有、財產

A good job was a prized possession.

一個好的職業是一種珍貴的財富。

⑮ domain, occupancy, ownership（持有、佔據）

1371.

postage [`postɪdʒ] 【 post·age 】 **n** 郵資、郵費

Can you refund the cost of postage in a case like this?

若發生這種情況你能退還郵資嗎？

- postage meter ph.郵資機
- postage stamp ph.郵票
- 字首：post郵政
  字尾：age費用

1372.

postal [`postl̩] 【 post·al 】 **a** 郵政的、郵遞的

The companies were greatly inconvenienced by the postal delays.

郵件延誤給這些公司造成極大不便。

- postal card ph.郵政明信片
- postal code ph.郵政編號
- postal order ph.郵政匯票
- postal service ph.郵政業務

1373.

postgraduate [post`grædʒuɪt] 【 post·grad·u·ate 】 a 大學畢業後的、研究生的 n 研究生

After college, Mary hopes to do postgraduate work in law faculty.

大學畢業後，瑪麗想在法學院從事研究工作。

- 字首：post在…之後
- 字尾：graduate大學畢業生
- faculty n.系院

`74`

1374.

postpone [post`pon] 【 post·pone 】 v 延遲、延期

Arise in price will make people postpone expenditure.

價格的上漲會使人們延遲支出。

🔄 delay, suspend, put off（延期、延緩）

🔄 advance（向前推進）

- 字首：post在…之後
- 字尾：pone放置

`198`

1375.

postscript [`post.skrɪpt] 【 post·script 】 n 附錄、附筆

She mentioned in a postscript to her letter that the parcel had arrived.

她在信末備註說已收到包裹。

- 可以P.S.縮寫表示
- 字首：post在…之後
- 字尾：script寫

`61`

1376.

potential [pə`tɛnʃəl] 【 po·ten·tial 】 a 潛在的、可能的 n 潛能

The factory manager understated their potential output.

工廠的管理人員低估他們的潛在產量。

🔄 conceivable, likely, possible（可能的）

- potential energy ph.位能
- output n.產量

`81`

1377.

precaution [prɪ`kɔʃən] 【 pre·cau·tion 】 n 預防措施、謹慎

There wake the local government to the need for safety precaution.

這些使當地政府認知到必須採取安全預防措施。

- 字首：pre事先
- 字尾：caution小心

`96`

1378.

precede [pri`sid] 【 pre·cede 】 v 優於、領先

He dissatisfied that my promotion was preceded.

他不滿我比他早升職。

🔄 forerun, head, lead（領先）

🔄 follow（跟隨）

- 字首：pre在…之前
- 字根：cede走動

`157`

1379.

precedent [`prɛsədənt] 【 prec·e·dent 】 n 先例 a 在前的

If he is allowed to do this, it will be a precedent for others.

如果允許他這麼做，就會為別人開先例。

- 字首：pre在…之前
- 字根：ced走動
- 字尾：ent進行一項行動的人

`104`

1380.

precious [`prɛʃəs] 【 pre·cious 】 a 珍貴的 n 寶貝

Time is so precious that you must make full use of it.

時間很寶貴，你必須充分利用它。

🔄 expensive, valuable（貴重的、珍貴的）

🔄 cheap, inexpensive（便宜的）

- precious metal ph. 貴重金屬
- precious stone ph.寶石
- make use of ph.利用

`127`

1381.
precise [prɪ`saɪs] 【 pre·cious 】 **a** 精確的、清楚的、嚴格的

These raw numbers, precise as they are, do little to help make sense of the facts.

這些原始資料儘管很精確，但對於釐清這些事實一點幫助也沒有。

🔊 **accurate, exact**（準確的、確切的）

- 字首：pre事先
  字根：ciset切割
- raw a.原始的

`89`

1382.
preclude [prɪ`klud] 【 pre·clude 】 **v** 排除、阻礙

My present finances preclude the possibility of buying a car.

按我目前的財務狀況我是不可能買車的。

🔊 **bar, deter, exclude**（妨礙、阻止）

- 字首：pre在…之前
  字根：clude關閉
- finance n.資金

`108`

1383.
predict [prɪ`dɪkt] 【 pre·dict 】 **v** 預言、預報

It is very difficult at this juncture to predict the company's future.

此時很難預料公司的前景。

🔊 **divine, prophesy, foresee**（預言、預料）

- 字首：pre在…之前
  字根：dict說
- juncture n.時刻

`169`

1384.
preempt [prɪ`ɛmpt] 【 pre·empt 】 **v** 以先買權獲得、先佔有

Discussion of the water shortage will preempt the other topics on this week's agenda.

在這星期的日程表上關於用水短缺的討論將優先於其它議題。

- shortage n.短缺
- agenda n.議程

`84`

1385.
preface [`prɛfɪs] 【 pref·ace 】 **n** 前言、序幕

Our defeat might be the preface to our successor's victory.

我們的失敗可能是我們後繼者獲勝的開端。

🔊 **introduction, foreword, preamble**（序言、緒言）

- defeat n.失敗
- victory n.勝利

`126`

1386.
prefer [prɪ`fɝ] 【 pre·fer 】 **v** 寧可、更喜歡、提出控告

If the cost is very heavy, potential hedgers will prefer not to hedge.

如果成本太高，潛在的套利交易者就寧可不進行套利交易。

🔊 **fancy, pick**（選擇、愛好）

- 字首：pre事先
  字根：fer拿
- hedge n.避免

`184`

P

1387.
prejudice [`prɛdʒədɪs] 【 prej·u·dice 】 **n** 偏見、歧視

His judgment was warped by his prejudice.

他的判斷因偏見而變得不公正。

🔊 **jaundice, preconception**（偏見、成見）

- warp v.使有偏見

`93`

1388.
preliminary [prɪ`lɪmə‚nɛrɪ] 【 pre·lim·i·nar·y 】 **a** 預備的、初步的

They refused to negotiate unless three preliminary requirements were met.

如果三項先決條件得不到滿足，他們就拒絕談判。

🔊 **initiatory, preclusive, preparatory**（預備的、開始的）

- preliminary group match ph.小組預賽
- preliminary hearing ph.初步聽證
- 字首：pre事先
  字根：limin光
  字尾：ary與…有關的

`125`

1389.

premiere [prɪˋmjɛr] 【pre·miere】 **v**首次公演 **n**女主角

We rehearsed frenziedly the last few days before the premiere.

公演前的那幾天我們如火如荼地進行訓練。

- rehearse v.排練
- frenziedly ad.極其激動地

1390.

premise [ˋprɛmɪs] 【prem·ise】 **n**前提、假設 **v**預先提出

Advice to investors was based on the premise that interest rates would continue to fall.

給予投資者的建議是以利率將繼續下降這一點為前提的。

1391.

premium [ˋprimɪəm] 【pre·mi·um】 **n**獎品、津貼

Such hours attract a pay premium.

這種工時需給付加班津貼。

- Premium Bond ph.以獎金代息儲蓄債券

1392.

prepay [priˋpe] 【pre·pay】 **v**預付

Normally, the seller is obligated to prepay the ocean freight.

在一般的情況下，賣方有責任預付海運費。

- 字首：pre事先
- 字尾：pay付費

1393.

prerequisite [͵priˋrɛkwəzɪt] 【pre·req·ui·site】 **a**不可或缺的 **n**必要條件

Honesty is the prerequisite condition to apply for the work.

申請這份工作的先決條件是誠實。

- 字首：pre在…之前
- 字首：re加強語氣
- 字根：quis尋找
- 字尾：ite有…性質的

1394.

prescient [ˋprɛʃɪənt] 【pre·sci·ent】 **a**有先見的、預知的

The General Manager, Mr. Chen's summitry has gained him much respect in business field.

陳總經理有先見之明的最高層級外交為他在商場上贏了不少敬意。

- 字首：pre在…之前
- 字根：sci知
- 字尾：ent…狀態的
- summitry n.外交手法

1395.

prescribe [prɪˋskraɪb] 【pre·scribe】 **v**囑咐、開藥方、指定

He likes to prescribe to others how they should act.

他喜歡指示別人應該怎麼做。

↔ assign, direct, order（指定）

- prescription n.處方

1396.

preservative [prɪˋzɝvətɪv] 【pre·ser·va·tive】 **n**防腐劑 **a**保存的

Salt is a common food preservative.

鹽是一種常用的食物防腐劑。

- 字首：preserv保存
- 字尾：ative與…有關的

1397.

pressure [ˋprɛʃɚ] 【pres·sure】 **n**壓、壓力、困難

Ordinarily, tightening supplies and increased demand would cause upward pressure on prices.

通常供應緊張和需求增長會迫使價格上升。

↔ burden, force（壓力）

- pressure point ph.施壓點
- 字根：press壓
- 字尾：ure行為
- tighten v.變緊
- upward a.升高的

1398.

pretend [prɪ`tɛnd] 【 pre·tend 】 **V**假裝、自稱

She pretended to be friendly with me when we first met.

當我們第一次見面時，她假裝對我友善。

act, feign, make believe（假裝）

- pretend to ph.妄求
- 字首：pre事先
  字根：tend伸展

1399.

pretext [`pritɛkst] 【 pre·text 】 **n**藉口、託辭

It cannot fire women or unilaterally annul their labor contracts on the pretext of marriage, pregnancy, maternity leave or baby nursing.

不得以結婚、懷孕、產假、哺乳等為由辭退女職工或單方面解除勞動合約。

excuse, pretence（藉口）

- 字首：pre事先
  字尾：text編織
- unilaterally ad.單方面地
- pregnancy n.懷孕
- maternity n.母愛

1400.

prevail [prɪ`vel] 【 pre·vail 】 **V**優勝、流行、普遍

This view did not prevail in all parts of the executive branch.

這一觀點並不是在政府的所有部門都佔優勢。

dominate, govern, preponderate（獲勝、控制）

- prevail on / upon / with ph.說服
- 字首：pre在…之前
  字根：vail強力

1401.

prevent [prɪ`vɛnt] 【 pre·vent 】 **V**防礙、阻止

Most discarded material is mutilated or destroyed to prevent unauthorized resale elsewhere.

大部分登出的資料應加以毀損以防止未經批准的轉售他處。

block, inhibit, prohibit（阻止、妨礙）
allow, permit（允許）

- prevent from ph.阻止
- 字首：pre事先
  字根：vent來
- discard v.拋棄
- mutilate v.毀壞

1402.

preview [`pri͵vju] 【 pre·view 】 **n**預習、預告 **V**預看

I showed the sales director a preview of the proposal to whet his appetite for the main advertising campaign.

我給銷售經理預先看所提的建議以增加他對廣告宣傳活動的興趣。

- 字首：pre事先
  字尾：view觀看
- appetite n.愛好
- campaign n.活動

P

1403.

previous [`priviəs] 【 pre·vi·ous 】 **a**以前的、過急的

Typically, when a selection is made, any previous selection is unmade.

一般來說，當做出抉擇後以前的任何選擇都作廢了。

earlier, former, prior（以前的、先的）

- previous to ph.在…之前
- unmade a.尚未做好的

1404.

primary [`praɪ͵mɛrɪ] 【 pri·mar·y 】 **a**最初的、首要的

Shape is the primary way we recognize what an object is.

形狀是我們辨識物體的最主要方式。

chief, main, paramount（首要的、主要的）
secondary（次要的）

- primary accent ph.主重音
- primary education ph. 初等教育
- primary election ph.初選
- 字根：prim最初
  字尾：ary與…有關的

1405.

primitive [`prɪmətɪv`] 【prim·i·tive】 **a** 原始的、簡單的 **n** 原始人

Arrangements were very primitive in the House of Commons in those days.

那時候下院的工作條件很差。

同 ancient, original, native（原始的、遠古的）

● 字根：prim 最初
字尾：it 走動
字尾：tive 有…性質的
● House of Commons ph.【英】下議院

1406.

principal [`prɪnsəpḷ`] 【prin·ci·pal】 **a** 主要的、首要的 **n** 校長、資本

The low salary is her principal reason for leaving the job.

工資太低是她辭去工作的最重要的原因。

同 dominant, important, prominent（主要的、最重要的）

● principal boy ph. 啞劇男主角
● principal parts ph. 動詞的主要變化形式

1407.

principle [`prɪnsəpḷ`] 【prin·ci·ple】 **n** 原則、主義

We implement the principle of assuming responsibility for mistakes.

我們貫徹對錯誤承擔責任的原則。

同 belief, dogma, doctrine（原理、信條）

反 exception（例外）

● implement v. 履行
● assuming a. 傲慢的

1408.

printed matter **n** 印刷品

Please check all the letters with printed matter on them as we can get a better rate for them at the post office.

請把註明印刷品的信件找出來，因為我們可以在郵局以比較低的郵資寄送。

● post office ph. 郵局

1409.

priority [praɪ`ɔrətɪ`] 【pri·or·i·ty】 **n** 優先、優先考慮的事

Financial controls were given to priority.

他們把財務管理當成頭等大事。

同 anteriority, precedence, seniority（較早、優先）

● priority seat ph. 博愛座

1410.

private [`praɪvɪt`] 【pri·vate】 **a** 個人的、祕密的

It is the principle I contend for, not individual or private benefit.

我奮鬥爭取的是原則而不是個人的私利。

同 individual, personal, privy（個人的、祕密的）

反 official, public（官方的、公開的）

● private company ph. 私人公司
● private detective ph. 私家偵探
● private education ph. 私立學校
● 字根：priv 個人
字尾：ate 有…性質的

1411.

privilege [`prɪvḷɪdʒ`] 【priv·i·lege】 **n** 特權、恩典 **v** 給予…特權

I esteem it a privilege to address such a distinguished audience.

我認為能向各位貴賓演講十分榮幸。

同 freedom, license（特權）

● 字根：priv 個人
字尾：lege 法律
● distinguished a. 卓越的

1412.

probable [`prɑbəbl] 【prob·a·ble】 **a**很可能發生的

- 字根：prob證實
- 字尾：able能…的
- **alternative** n.二擇一
- **propound** v.提議

This latter alternative, which was first propounded by Pallas, seems by far the most probable.

巴拉斯最初提出的較後面的選擇似乎是最可能是。

🔄 **apt, likely, presumable**（可能的）

🔄 **improbable**（不可能的）

1413.

procedure [prə`sidʒɚ] 【pro·ce·dure】 **n**程式、手續

- 字首：pro之前
  字根：ced走動
  字尾：ure性質
- **run back over** ph.重溫

I'll run back over the procedure again.

我要把整個過程再重溫一遍。

🔄 **means, process, way**（程序、步驟）

1414.

proceed [prə`sid] 【pro·ceed】 **v**繼續進行、進展

- **proceed from** ph.從…發出
- **proceed to** ph.繼續下去
- 字首：pro向前
  字根：cede走動

Let's proceed to the next.

讓我們進入下一個議程。

🔄 **advance, progress**（繼續進行）

🔄 **recede**（撤退）

1415.

proceeds [`prosidz] 【pro·ceeds】 **n**收益、實收款項

- **loan** n.貸款

All purchases shall be financed with the proceeds of loan.

全部貨款用貸款支付。

🔄 **earnings, income, receipts**（收益、收入）

1416.

process [`prɑsɛs] 【proc·ess】 **n**過程、步驟 **v**加工、處理

- **process printing** ph.彩色印刷術
- 字首：pro向前
  字根：cess走動
- **short-circuit** v.縮短

This is a necessary part of the process and shouldn't be short-circuited.

這是這個過程的必要部分，不應該縮短。

🔄 **course, operation, step**（步驟、程序）

P

1417.

proclaim [prə`klem] 【pro·claim】 **v**宣告、聲明、顯示

- 字首：pro向前
  字根：claim喊叫
- **notify** v.通知
- **decree** n.法令

We ask that carriers to send all the departments to notify them of the decrees that you proclaim here.

我們要求派人到所有部門去傳達你們在這裡公佈的各項指令。

🔄 **announce, declare, herald**（宣告、聲明）

1418.

procure [pro`kjur] 【pro·cure】 **v**努力取得、導致、達成

- 字首：pro向前
- 字尾：cure跑

One of my friends asked me to procure a position in the bank for him.

我的一個朋友要求我幫他在銀行中謀得一個職位。

🔄 **acquire, get, obtain**（獲得、取得）

1419.
produce [prə`djus]【pro·duce】 Ⅴ生產、製造 Ⅱ產品

Firms can now produce huge quantities and employ the division of labor to much greater advantage.

現在廠商可以生產大量產品，並更充實地利用勞動分工。

- create, generate, make（製造、創作）
- consume（消耗）

• 字首：pro向前
字根：duce引導
• huge a.大量的

184

1420.
product [`prɑdəkt]【prod·uct】 Ⅱ產品、結果

Your new product has a strong footing in the market.

你們的新產品在市場上很有銷路。

- creation, merchandise, production（產品、生產物）

• 字首：pro向前
字根：duct引導
• footing n.立足點

151

1421.
profess [prə`fɛs]【pro·fess】 Ⅴ公開宣稱、承認

With such censures I cannot profess that I completely agree.

對於這些指責我不能說我完全同意。

- allege, claim, contend（宣稱、主張）
- deny, suppress（否認、廢止）

• 字首：pro向前
字根：fess承認
• censure n.責備

112

1422.
profession [prə`fɛʃən]【pro·fes·sion】 Ⅱ職業、聲明

He is a doctor by profession and a novelist by avocation.

他的職業是醫生，副業是作家。

- career, occupation, vocation（職業）

• novelist n.小說家
• avocation n.副業

108

1423.
proficient [prə`fɪʃənt]【pro·fi·cient】 ᵃ精通的、熟練的 Ⅱ專家

He was feeling the satisfaction of doing a job at which he knew he was proficient.

他心裡止不住感到得意因為他精通於這類工作。

- clever, expert, masterful（靈巧的、熟練的）

• proficient at / in ph.精通
• 字首：pro在…之前
字根：fic製作
字尾：ient…狀態的

84

1424.
profile [`profaɪl]【pro·file】 Ⅱ側面、輪廓、概況 Ⅴ描出…輪廓

The BBC is working on a profile of the British nuclear industry.

英國廣播公司正在報導英國核子工業概況。

• nuclear a.核子的

96

1425.
profit [`prɑfɪt]【prof·it】 Ⅱ利潤、收益 Ⅴ有利於

The company has targeted a profit for the year.

公司已經規定了今年的利潤指標。

- advantage, benefit, gain（收益、得益）
- loss（虧損）

• profit and loss ph.
盈虧帳目
• profit and loss account ph.企業經營情況一覽表
• profit by / from ph.得益於
• profit margin ph.
利潤百分比
• profit-making a.營利的

213

1426.

profuse [prə`fjus]【pro·fuse】**a** 十分慷慨的、極其豐富的

He was so profuse with his money that he is now poor.

他大肆浪費金錢，結果現在變窮。

- abundant, generous, lavish（大方的、很多的）
- scanty, spare（不足的、多餘的）

- 字首：pro向前
- 字尾：fuse流入

1427.

progressive [prə`grɛsɪv]【pro·gres·sive】**a** 先進的、逐漸的

The most direct approach to income redistribution is to levy progressive taxes.

收入再分配的最直接的方法就是推行累進稅。

- ameliorative, improving, progressing（前進的、發展的）
- conservative, regressive（保守的、後退的）

- **Progressive Party ph.** 美國進步黨
- **progressive tax ph.** 累進稅
- **progressive tense ph.** 進行時態
- **redistribution n.** 重新分配

1428.

prohibit [prə`hɪbɪt]【pro·hib·it】**V** 禁止、妨礙

The high cost prohibited the widespread use of the drug.

該藥物昂貴而影響被廣泛應用。

- ban, forbid, restrict（禁止、妨礙）
- admit, allow, permit（允許）

- **prohibit from ph.** 禁止
- **widespread a.** 普遍的
- **drug n.** 藥物

1429.

prolific [prə`lɪfɪk]【pro·lif·ic】**a** 多產的、豐富的

Along with the rapid spread of urbanization has come the prolific growth of huge slums and shantytowns.

在城市化中迅速發展的同時，貧民區的數目也不斷增長。

- fruitful, plentiful, rich（豐富的、多產的）

- **prolific in / of ph.** 盛產
- **urbanization n.** 都市化
- **slum n.** 貧民窟
- **shantytown n.** 貧民窟

1430.

prominent [`prɑmənənt]【prom·i·nent】**a** 突出的、顯著的、重要的

Many prominent enterprises have had serious problems in the area.

許多傑出的公司在這方面仍然存在許多嚴重的問題。

- eminent, famous, outstanding（重要的、出名的）
- common, inconspicuous, obscure（普通的、不重要的）

- **enterprise n.** 企業

P

1431.

promote [prə`mot]【pro·mote】**V** 晉升、促進、創立

If you keep your nose clean, the boss might promote you.

你若是規規矩矩的，老闆就可能提拔你。

- boost, encourage, upgrade（促進）
- degrade, demote（使降級）

- 字首：pro向前
- 字尾：mote動

1432.

prompt [prɑmpt]【prompt】**a** 敏捷的、即期的

For this lot, could you consider prompt shipment?

我們這批貨能不能考慮即期裝運？

- immediate, instant, punctual（敏捷的、準時的）
- dilatory, slow, tardy（慢的、拖延的）

- **lot n.** 一批商品
- **shipment n.** 船運

1433.
proofread [ˋprufˏrid] 【proof·read】 **v** 校對
Live copy is ready to be set in type or already set but not yet proofread.
前稿就是準備好排版或者已經排好版但沒有校對的稿件。

- 字首：proof證明
  字尾：read閱讀

1434.
propel [prəˋpɛl] 【pro·pel】 **v** 推進、驅策
To take responsibility will propel you forward and onward to your greater good.
承擔責任能推動你不斷前進創造更美好的前程。
同 impel, motivate, shove（推進、驅使）

- 字首：pro向前
  字尾：pel推動
- onward ad.向前

1435.
property [ˋprɑpətɪ] 【prop·er·ty】 **n** 財產、資產、所有權
He made his pile during the property boom.
在房地產生意興隆期間他發了大財。
同 belongings, possession（財產、所有物）

- property developer ph. 房地產商
- property manager ph. 道具員
- property tax ph.房地產稅
- pile n.大筆錢財

1436.
proposition [ˏprɑpəˋzɪʃən] 【prop·o·si·tion】 **n** 提議、主張
Any seemingly viable proposition will be tested by market research.
任何表面上可行的建議都要通過市場研究予以檢驗。
同 deal, proposal（提議）

- 字首：pro向前
  字根：pos放置
  字尾：it走動
  字尾：ion行動
- viable a.可實行的

1437.
propriety [prəˋpraɪətɪ] 【pro·pri·e·ty】 **n** 適當、禮貌
I am doubtful about the propriety of grant such a request.
我懷疑答應這項要求是否合適。

- doubtful a.懷疑的
- grant n.同意

1438.
proprietor [prəˋpraɪətɚ] 【pro·pri·e·tor】 **n** 所有人、經營者
On this public domain the government, as proprietor, can lease grazing lands.
作為這塊國有土地的所有者，政府可在該土地上出租牧地。
同 freeholder, possessor, owner（所有人）

- domain n.領域
- lease v.租借
- grazing n.放牧

1439.
prosecute [ˋprɑsɪˏkjut] 【pros·e·cute】 **v** 對…起訴、執行
In view of his age, the police have decided not to prosecute.
考慮到他的年齡，警方決定對他撤銷起訴。
同 execute, pursue, transact（執行）

- in view of ph.考慮到

1440.
prospect [ˋprɑspɛkt] 【pros·pect】 **n** 盼望的事物、前景
She balanced the attractions of a high salary against the prospect of working long hours.
她對高薪和長工時兩者的利弊作了權衡比較。
同 anticipation, expectation, outlook（期望）
反 retrospect（回顧）

- prospect for ph.尋找
- 字首：pro向前
  字根：spect看
- attraction n.吸引

1441.
prospectus [prəˋspɛktəs] 【 pro·spec·tus 】 **n.** 創辦計畫書、說明書

In making a public offer of shares, promoters must publish a prospectus and prepare share subscription application.

發起人向社會公開募集股份時，必須公告招股說明並且製作認股書。

- promoter n.創辦人
- subscription n.認捐
- application n.申請

57

1442.
prosperity [prasˋpɛrətɪ] 【 pros·per·i·ty 】 **n.** 繁榮、成功、興隆

In times of prosperity, money circulates quickly.

在商業繁榮時期，錢流通得快。

- circulate v.循環

94

同 **affluence, fortune, wealth**（繁榮、富裕）
反 **adversity, misfortune**（窘境、不幸）

1443.
protect [prəˋtɛkt] 【 pro·tect 】 **v.** 保護、防護

Happily, there's more than one way to protect software from bad data.

令人高興的是，有很多方法可以保護軟體免受壞資料的侵害。

- protect against / from ph.使免受
- software n.軟體
- data n.資料

183

同 **defend, guard, shield**（保護、防護）
反 **assail, attack, forsake**（攻擊、侵略）

1444.
protest [prəˋtɛst] 【 pro·test 】 **v.n.** 抗議、斷言

Our chief representative's withdrawal was construed as a protest.

我們的首席代表退場被看作是一種抗議的表示。

- protest against ph.反對
- protest rally ph.抗議大會
- protest song ph.抗議之歌
- 字首：pro向前
  字根：test證據

144

同 **dispute, object, squawk**（抗議、反對）
反 **agree, support**（同意、支持）

1445.
protocol [ˋprotəˌkal] 【 pro·to·col 】 **n.** 外交禮儀、草約 **v.** 擬定

Once in a while, emergency justified a break with protocol.

偶爾遇到緊急情況時就得破例。

- protocol stack ph.協定堆
- once in a while ph.有時

124

P

1446.
protract [proˋtrækt] 【 pro·tract 】 **v.** 延長、伸展

Three hours have passed since the discussion began, and I'm afraid they will protract it still longer.

這個討論會已經開了3個小時了，而且恐怕他們還會拖延下去。

- 字首：pro向前
  字根：tract拉

107

反 **curtain, shorten**（減短）

1447.
protrude [proˋtrud] 【 pro·trude 】 **v.** 伸出、突出

He manages to hang on to a piece of rock protrude from the cliff face.

他設法抓住懸崖表面向外伸出的岩石。

- 字首：pro向前
  字根：trude推
- piece n.片
- cliff n.懸崖

94

同 **bulge, project**（推出、突出）

1448.
proverb [`prɑvɝb] 【prov‧erb】 **n**諺言
A proverb is the wisdom of men and the wit of one.
諺語是眾人的智慧也體現個人的機智。
圖► adage, dictum, maxim（俗語、箴言）

- 字首：pro在…之前
  字尾：verb動詞
- wisdom n.智慧
- wit n.機智

1449.
provident [`prɑvədənt] 【prov‧i‧dent】 **a**有先見之明的、節儉的
In his usual provident manner, he had insured himself against this type of loss.
他辦事一貫深謀遠慮，早給自己保了這類的損失險。
反► improvident（無先見之明的）

- Provident Society ph.
  互助會
- 字首：pro向前
  字根：vid看
  字尾：ent…狀態的

1450.
provoke [prə`vok] 【pro‧voke】 **v**激怒、導致
Such tendentious statements are likely to provoke strong opposition.
這種有傾向性的說法可能招致強烈的反對。
圖► infuriate, pique, stir（激怒、激起）
反► appease, calm, soothe（平息、緩和）

- 字首：pro向前
  字尾：voke喊叫
- tendentious a.傾向的

1451.
publicity [pʌb`lɪsətɪ] 【pub‧lic‧i‧ty】 **n**公開、宣傳、名聲
Mr. Smith takes care of marketing and publicity.
史密斯先生負責產品的銷售與推廣。

- publicity agent ph.宣傳員
- take care of ph.負責
- marketing n.行銷

1452.
punctual [`pʌŋktʃuəl] 【punc‧tu‧al】 **a**準時的、精確的
To ensure punctual payments, great care must be taken in checking the credits opened by banks abroad.
為了保證及時交貨必須仔細審核外國銀行的來證。
圖► exact, immediate, precise（準確的、快的）

- 字根：punct刺、點
  字尾：ual與…有關的

1453.
purchase [`pɝtʃəs] 【pur‧chase】 **v n**購買
The indent agent takes a commission on the value of his purchase.
航空公司的職員可以優惠價購買飛機票。
圖► buy, shop（買、購買）
反► sell（賣）

- purchase order ph.請購單
- purchase order tracking ph.採購訂單跟蹤
- purchase price ph.購買價

1454.
purification [ˌpjurəfə`keʃən] 【purification】 **n**洗滌、精鍊
A tremendous amount of work has been done on the purification of the starting material.
人們在提純原始材料方面做了大量的工作。

- 字根：puri純
  字尾：fic製作
  字尾：ation行動
- tremendous a.巨大的

1455.
purport [`pɝport] 【pur‧port】 **n**涵義、目地 **v**意圖
His plans are not what they purport to be.
他的計劃並不如他們所聲稱的那樣。
圖► connotation, meaning（言外之意、意義）

201

1456.
purpose [ˋpɝpəs] 【pur‧pose】 **n.**目的、意圖 **v.**打算

If the main purpose of menus were to execute commands, terseness would be a virtue.

如果功能表的主要目的是執行命令的話，那麼就應該精練一些。

🔁 **aim, goal, intention**（目標、意圖）

- **purpose-built ph.**為特定目的建造的
- **terseness n.**精練
- **virtue n.**優點

54

1457.
pushcart [ˋpʊʃˏkɑrt] 【push‧cart】 **n.**手推車

A pushcart is a handy way to take a young child shopping.

用手推車帶小孩去購物很方便。

- 字首：push推
  字尾：cart車子
- **handy a.**便利的

P

MEMO

MEMO

abbr 縮寫詞
a 形容詞
ad 副詞
aux 助動詞
conj 連接詞
n 名詞
num 數字
ph 片語
prep 介系詞
v 動詞
（美）美式用語
（英）英式用語
（法）法式用語

全書單字取材於：

①10本坊間新多益考試暢銷書籍

②50篇英文新聞、商業文章

③2005~2012年ETS TOEIC歷屆考古題

→ 總計約50,000個單字，以電腦統計出題率高達80%
的實用單字1,800個

高頻率單字

>|Q家族 quantity~quote

高 分 錦 囊

1458.
quantity [`kwɑntətɪ] [quan‧ti‧ty] **n** 量、數量
Don't strive merely for quantity of production.
在生產中不要單純地追求數量。
同 amount, number, sum（量、分量）
反 quality（質）

132
- quantity surveyor ph. 估算師
- strive v.努力

1459.
quarrel [`kwɔrəl] [quar‧rel] **v n** 爭吵、責備
He's trying to keep out of this quarrel.
他不想置身於這場糾紛中間。
同 argument, tiff, wrangle（爭吵、吵架）
反 agreement, concord, harmony（同意、和諧）

74
- quarrel with ph.不同意

1460.
quota [`kwotə] [quo‧ta] **n** 定額、配額
The result was a quota on U.S. imports but the foreign suppliers pocketed windfalls from the price markup.
其結果就是對美國的進口商品實行一種配額，但外國供應商卻因提價攫取了暴利。
同 allotment, ratio, proportion（配額、分擔額）

104
- supplier n.供應者
- windfall n.意外的收穫
- markup n.漲價

1461.
quote [kwot] [quote] **v** 報價、引述 **n** 報價、引號
I can quote you a price lower than anybody else's.
我能向你提出低於任何人的價格。
同 cite, illustrate（引用）

156

MEMO

abbr 縮寫詞
a 形容詞
ad 副詞
aux 助動詞
conj 連接詞
n 名詞
num 數字
ph 片語
prep 介系詞
v 動詞
（美）美式用語
（英）英式用語
（法）法式用語

全書單字取材於：
①10本坊間新多益考試暢銷書籍
②50篇英文新聞、商業文章
③2005~2012年ETS TOEIC歷屆考古題
→ 總計約50,000個單字，以電腦統計出題率高達80%
　的實用單字1,800個

高頻率單字

> R 家族 random~runway

高 分 錦 囊

1462. 113

random [ˋrændəm] 【ran·dom】 a 隨便的、無目的的 n 隨意

This random approach is not as dubious as one might expect.

這種隨意的途徑並不像人們所預期的那樣沒把握。

同 haphazard, irregular, unorganized（偶然的、無規則的）
反 deliberate（謹慎的）

• at random ph.任意地
• random access ph. 隨機存取
• random variable ph. 隨機變數
• dubious a.可疑的

1463. 101

rapid [ˋræpɪd] 【rap·id】 a 迅速的、快速的

Her colleagues were all surprised at her rapid advance in the company.

她的快速升遷令公司同仁均感到驚訝。

同 fast, speedy, swift（快的、迅速的）
反 slow, tardy（慢的、緩慢的）

• rapid transit system ph.都市捷運系統
• rapid-fire a.一連串的

1464. 84

rapture [ˋræptʃɚ] 【rap·ture】 n 狂喜、著迷 v 使著迷

The beauty of the sunset filled everybody with rapture.

美麗的夕陽日使得每個人皆為之出神。

同 delight, enchantment, glee（癡迷、狂喜）

• rapture of the deep ph. 氮麻醉
• 字根：rapt著迷的 字尾：ure行為

1465. 211

rate [ret] 【rate】 v 分級、等級

An income tax is graduated so that people who make more money pay a higher rate of taxes.

所得稅分等累進使賺錢者付較高的稅率。

同 categorize, grade, measure（分等、估價）

• rate of exchange ph. 貨幣兌換率
• rate of return ph.利潤率
• rate tart ph.為賺取最低利率而不斷更換信用卡的人
• rate-cap v.對…實行稅率
• rate-capping n.稅率限制

1466. 81

ravage [ˋrævɪdʒ] 【rav·age】 v n 破壞、劫掠

The floods ravaged 25 percent of Texas and leave over one billion dollars in damage.

洪水蹂躪德州25%的土地，造成超過10億美元的損失。

同 damage, destroy, ruin（破壞、毀壞）
反 preserve, protect（保存、保護）

• flood n.洪水

1467. 74

ravenous [ˋrævɪnəs] 【rav·en·ous】 a 饑餓的、貪婪的

I was working so hard that I forgot to have lunch and now I'm ravenous.

我太努力工作了以至於忘記吃午餐，現在我都快餓暈了。

同 hungry, starved, greedy（飢餓的、貪婪的）

1468.
ravish [ˋrævɪʃ] 【rav·ish】 **V** 使陶醉、狂喜

I know groups of trees that ravish the eye with their perfect picture like effects.

我知道有許多樹由於外表完全像是一幅幅的畫，讓人看得眼花撩亂。

1469.
raw material **ph** 原料

We are faced with a shortage in manpower, not in raw material.

我們面臨的問題是缺乏人力而不是缺乏原料。

- raw a.原始的
- shortage n.短缺
- manpower n.人力

1470.
real estate **ph** 不動產

The company cleaned up in real estate.

這家公司在不動產方面受益頗大。

- real estate agent ph.房地產經紀人
- estate n.地產

1471.
rearrange [͵riəˋrendʒ] 【re·ar·range】 **V** 重新整理

Can you rearrange your schedule and make my order your top priority?

你能否重新安排一下你的排程計劃，讓我的訂貨優先處理？

- 字首：re再、又
  字尾：arrange安排
- schedule n.時間表
- priority n.優先

1472.
reassure [͵riəˋʃʊr] 【re·as·sure】 **V** 使安心、向…再保證

The manager tried to reassure her that she will not lose her job.

經理試圖使她解除不會失去工作的疑慮。

- 字首：re加強語氣
  字尾：assure確認

1473.
rebate [ˋribet] 【re·bate】 **V n** 折扣、退還

Will you give us a premium rebate just as other underwriters do?

你們能不能像其他保險公司一樣在保險費上給予優惠呢？

- premium n.優惠
- underwriter n.保險商

1474.
recipe [ˋrɛsəpɪ] 【rec·i·pe】 **n** 食譜、烹飪法、訣竅

We must keep rigidly the recipe.

我們必須嚴格按照配方行事。

同 formula, direction, instruction（命令、指定）

- rigidly ad.緊緊地

1475.
receipt [rɪˋsit] 【re·ceipt】 **n** 收據、收入 **V** 開收據

The warrants are duplicate warehouse receipt or, better a combined warehouse and trust receipt.

保單是一種雙重含義的倉儲單。更確切地說，是倉儲和信託的聯合收據。

同 stub, voucher（收據）

- 字首：re返、回
  字根：ceip拿
- warrant n.證書
- duplicate a.二倍的
- warehouse n.倉庫

1476.
receptionist [rɪˋsɛpʃənɪst] 【re·cep·tion·ist】 **n** 接待員

Before entering the boardroom, Mr. William told the receptionist to hold all of his calls until after the meeting.

在進入會議室前，威廉先生告訴接待員在會議結束前不接任何電話。

- 字首：reception接待
  字尾：ist從事…的人
- boardroom n.會議室

R

1477.
recess [rɪ`sɛs] 【 re·cess 】 **V n** 休息、隱居
I hope you enjoyed a short recess from hard work.
工作很辛苦，我希望你們在短暫的休息期間過得很愉快。
🔁 **adjourn, pause, rest**（休息）

- 字首：re返、回
- 字根：cess走動

1478.
recession [rɪ`sɛʃən] 【 re·ces·sion 】 **n** 撤退、交還、衰退
In the recession, our firm went through a bad time.
我們公司在經濟衰退時期歷盡艱辛。
🔁 **affluence, fortune, wealth**（繁榮、富裕）
🔄 **adversity, misfortune**（窘境、不幸）

- recession chic ph.衰退時尚
- 字首：re返、回
- 字根：cess走動
- 字尾：ion行動

1479.
reclaim [rɪ`klem] 【 re·claim 】 **V** 取回、回收
You may be entitled to reclaim some of the tax you paid last year.
你或許有權要求退回去年你交付的部分稅金。

- 字首：re返、回
- 字根：claim喊叫
- entitle v.給…權力

1480.
recommendation [ˌrɛkəmɛn`deʃən]
【 rec·om·men·da·tion 】 **n** 推薦、推薦書、勸告
I got the job on the strength of your recommendation.
承蒙您的推薦，我已獲得這份工作。
🔁 **credential, endorsement, reference**（推薦信）

- strength n.效力

1481.
recompense [`rɛkəmˌpɛns] 【 rec·om·pense 】 **V n** 回報、報酬
His work met people's approbation and then received the great recompense.
他的辛苦贏得了人們的認可，最終也得到了充分的報償。
🔁 **compensate, pay, reward**（報酬）

- 字首：re返、回
- 字首：com一起
- 字根：pense付款
- approbation n.許可

1482.
reconcile [`rɛkənsaɪl] 【 rec·on·cile 】 **V** 調和、調解
I can't reconcile these figures with the statement you prepared.
我無法使這些數字與你的財務報表相符。
🔁 **harmonize, mend, settle**（使和解、改善）
🔄 **argue**（爭執）

- figure v.認為
- prepare v.準備

1483.
record [`rɛkəd] 【 re·cord 】 **V n** 記錄
In order to accomplish this, we must formally record these expectations.
為了達到這個目標，我們必須正式記錄這些期望。
🔁 **chronicle, inscribe, write**（記錄、寫下）

- record changer ph.自動換片裝置
- record library ph.唱片儲藏室
- record-breaker n.破記錄者
- record-holder n.保持最高記錄者

1484.
recourse [rɪ`kors] 【 re·course 】 **n** 依賴、求助
He tackled the knotty problem without recourse to any help.
他不依靠任何人的幫助而獨立處理這難題。

- 字首：re返、回
- 字根：course跑
- tackle v.處理
- knotty a.難解決的

1485.
recreation [ˌrɛkrɪˋeʃən] 【rec·re·a·tion】 n娛樂、消遣、休養

They have no recreation or recess in their work.

他們並沒有休息或停工時間。

🔄 **amusement, entertainment, relaxation**（娛樂）

- recreation ground ph. 遊樂場
- recreation room ph.家中之娛樂室
- recess n.休息

1486.
recruit [rɪˋkrut] 【re·cruit】 v徵募、聘用 n新手

Business and government recruit first-degree graduates.

企業和政府部門都錄用剛讀完大學本科系的畢業生。

🔄 **enlist, enroll, muster**（徵募）

- 字首：re加強語氣
  字根：cru成長
  字尾：it走動

1487.
rectify [ˋrɛktəˌfaɪ] 【rec·ti·fy】 v改正、矯正

We should rectify the undesirable tendencies in time.

我們應該及時糾正不良傾向。

🔄 **adjust, correct, remedy**（矯正、調節）

- 字根：rect正直
  字尾：ify使成為
- tendency n.傾向

1488.
referee [ˌrɛfəˋri] 【ref·e·ree】 n裁判員、仲裁者

You have to abide by the referee's decision.

你必須遵從裁判員的決定。

🔄 **arbitrator, judge, mediator**（裁判、仲裁）

- 字首：refer指
  字尾：ee動作承受者
- abide v.忍受

1489.
reflect [rɪˋflɛkt] 【re·flect】 v回想、反射

The look and behavior of a product should reflect how it is used, rather than the personal taste of its designers.

產品的外觀和行為應該反應產品將如何被使用，而不是設計者的個人喜好。

🔄 **consider, ponder, mirror**（思考、反映）

- reflect on ph.仔細考慮
- 字首：re返、回
  字根：flect彎曲
- taste n.愛好

1490.
reform [rɪˋfɔrm] 【re·form】 v改革、改造

Our election victory has given us a mandate to reform the economy.

我們在選舉獲勝，這就使我們有權進行經濟改革。

🔄 **convert, improve, revise**（改正、轉變）

- reform school ph.少年感化院
- 字首：re再、又
  字根：form形狀
- mandate n.指令

R

1491.
refreshment [rɪˋfrɛʃmənt] 【re·fresh·ment】 n茶點(常用複數)

The spectators dropped off to get refreshment.

觀眾紛紛離座去吃點心。

- spectator n.觀眾

1492.
refund [rɪˋfʌnd] 【re·fund】 vn退還、償還

You may exchange the shirt but not return it for a refund.

你可調換這件襯衫但不能退貨。

🔄 **pay back, reimburse**（償還）

- 字首：re返、回
  字尾：fund資金

1493.
regard [rɪˋgɑrd]【re·gard】 n 問候、致意、認為
Please pass on my regards to your parents.
請代我向你的父母問好。
🔄 **consider, judge, think of**（認為）

• regard as ph.把…視為

1494.
register [ˋrɛdʒɪstə]【reg·is·ter】 v n 登記、註冊
Attendance figures normally include only the people who actually register for the convention.
出席人數一般只包括實際登記參加會議的人。
🔄 **enroll, enter, log**（登記）

• register office ph. 戶籍登記處
• attendance n.出席

1495.
rehearsal [rɪˋhɝsl]【re·hears·al】 n 預演、排練
They need another rehearsal to link the production into shape.
他們還需要再排練，演出才會像樣。
🔄 **drill, exercise, practice**（訓練、練習）

• shape n.情況

1496.
reimburse [ˏriɪmˋbɝs]【re·im·burse】 v 償還、補償
We will reimburse the customer for any loss or damage.
我們願賠償顧客受到的一切損失和損害。

1497.
reinforce [ˏriɪnˋfors]【re·in·force】 v 加強、鞏固
to further reinforce enterprise management and improve the entire quality of enterprises
進一步加強企業管理以提高企業整體素質
🔄 **brace, fortify, intensify**（增加、增強）

• 字首：rein控制 字尾：force武力
• entire a.整個的

1498.
reinstate [ˏriɪnˋstet]【re·in·state】 v 使恢復、使復職
His supporters failed in their attempt to reinstate the President in the White House.
他的支持者試圖使總統重新入主白宮的努力失敗了。

• 字首：re再、又 字尾：instate擔任
• supporter n.支持者
• attempt n.企圖

1499.
reiterate [riˋɪtəˏret]【re·it·er·ate】 v 重做、反覆做
Let me reiterate that we have absolutely no plan to increase taxation.
讓我再一次重申我們絕對沒有增稅的計劃。
🔄 **recount, repeat**（重述）

• absolutely ad.絕對
• taxation n.徵稅

1500.
relaxation [ˏrilæksˋeʃən]【re·lax·a·tion】 n 放鬆、緩和、休息
Hard work is essential, but there's also a time for rest and relaxation.
勤奮工作當然是必要的，但是每人也必須有時間休息和娛樂。
🔄 **easing, moderation, palliation**（放鬆、減緩）

• essential a.必須的

1501.
relevant [`rɛləvənt] 【 rel·e·vant 】 **a** 有關的、有意義的

Be responsible for coordinating with relevant departments to ensure the effective running of QMS.

負責與相關部門做好協調工作，以確保品質管理系統運行的有效性。

同 **apropos, fitting, suitable**（合適的）
反 **inappropriate, irrelevant**（不適當的、不相關的）

• coordinate v.協調

1502.
relocate [ri`loket] 【 re·lo·cate 】 **v** 重新安置

The company is relocatting its headquarters in the Midlands.

公司將把總部遷往英格蘭中部。

• 字首：re再、又
  字根：loc地點
  字尾：ate進行一項行動
• headquarters n.總部

1503.
remind [rɪ`maɪnd] 【 re·mind 】 **v** 提醒、使想起

Please remind me again nearer to the time of the interview.

到快面試時請再提醒我一下。

同 **prompt, suggest to**（提醒、提示）

• remind of ph.使回想起
• 字首：re再、又
  字尾：mind注意
• interview n.面試

1504.
remote [rɪ`mot] 【 re·mote 】 **a** 遙遠的、冷淡的

The connection between the two events is remote.

這兩件事之間沒有什麼聯繫。

同 **distant, far, secluded**（遙遠的）
反 **close, near**（近的）

• remote access ph.遠程存取
• remote control ph.遙控
• Remote host ph.遠端主機
• remote-controlled a.遙控的

1505.
remuneration [rɪ͵mjunə`reʃən] 【 re·mu·ner·a·tion 】
n 報酬、酬勞、賠償金

Our remuneration increased with the turnover.

我們的報酬隨營業額的增加而調高。

反 **penalty**（罰款）

• turnover n.營業額

1506.
renovate [`rɛnə͵vet] 【 ren·o·vate 】 **v** 更新、修理、恢復

If we renovate the existing enterprises and produce 20 million more tons of steel, we shall be able to curtail the import of steel products.

如果在現有企業的基礎上加以改造增加兩千萬噸，就可少進口鋼材。

同 **recondition, redo, remake**（修理、重做）

• 字首：re再、又
  字根：nov新
  字尾：ate進行一項行動
• ton n.公噸
• steel n.鋼
• curtail v.縮減

R

1507.
repel [rɪ`pɛl] 【 re·pel 】 **v** 擊退、拒絕

A masculine man is never discouraged, as pressure can never repel him.

有男子氣概的男人從不氣餒，因為他從不屈服於壓力。

同 **offend, revolt, rebuff**（擊退、拒絕）
反 **attract**（吸引）

• 字首：re返、回
  字尾：pel驅趕
• masculine a.男子氣概的
• pressure n.壓力

1508.
replacement [rɪ`plesmənt]【re·place·ment】**n**代替、歸還
We need a replacement for the secretary who left.
我們需要一個人代替已離職的祕書。

- 字首：re返、回
- 字根：place放置
- 字尾：ment性質

`81`

1509.
replenish [rɪ`plɛnɪʃ]【re·plen·ish】**v**把…裝滿、補充
We have to import an extra 4 million tons of wheat to replenish our reserves.
我們不得不額外進口四百萬噸小麥以補充我們的儲備。
🔁 **furnish, provide, supply**（提供、供給）
🔄 **exhaust**（耗盡）

- 字首：re再、又
- 字根：plen充足
- 字尾：ish使成為
- wheat n.麥

`94`

1510.
replete [rɪ`plit]【re·plete】**a**充滿的、詳盡的、飽食的
His house is replete with domestic appliances, like air-conditioner, washing machine, refrigerator, dish washer, etc.
他的房子家庭電器一應俱全，有冷氣、洗衣機、冰箱、洗碗機等應有盡有。
🔁 **abundant, wealthy**（充足的、富裕的）

- 字首：re再、又
- 字根：plete充足
- domestic a.家庭的
- appliance n.設備
- refrigerator n.冰箱

`73`

1511.
replicate [`rɛplɪˏket]【rep·li·cate】**v**摺疊、複製 **n**複製品
On principle, to replicate any human technologically is against the basic dignity of the uniqueness of each human being.
原則上，以技術複製人違反了每一個人獨特性的尊嚴。

- 字首：re再、又
- 字根：plic折疊
- 字尾：ate進行一項行動
- dignity n.尊嚴

`97`

1512.
reply [rɪ`plaɪ]【re·ply】**v** **n**回答、反響
We request the favour of a reply at your earliest convenience.
請方便時儘早給予答覆。
🔁 **answer, respond, retort**（回答）
🔄 **ask, inquire, question**（詢問）

- reply for ph.代表…作答
- reply-paid a.回函郵資已付的
- reply man ph.收回人
- 字首：re再、又
- 字根：ply折疊
- convenience n.便利

`151`

1513.
repose [rɪ`poz]【re·pose】**v** **n**休息、躺、信賴
Her manner expressed the repose and confidence which came from a large experience.
她的舉止倒是表現了沉靜和信心，這是來自豐富的閱歷。
🔁 **lounge, recline, sleep**（休息、睡眠）

- repose in ph.把…寄託於
- 字首：re向後
- 字根：pose放置
- confidence n.信心

`64`

1514.
reprove [rɪ`pruv]【re·prove】**v**責備、指責
I have to reprove you for repeating the same mistakes over and over again.
你屢屢重犯同樣的錯誤，我不得不嚴厲地批評你。
🔁 **blame, rebuke, scold**（責備、責罵）

- 字首：re再、又
- 字根：prove證明
- over and over again ph. 再三

`95`

1515.
repulsive [rɪ`pʌlsɪv]【re·pul·sive】**a**排斥的、使人反感的
It is hard to forget repulsive things.
不堪入目的景象往往難以忘懷。
🔁 **disgusting, ghastly, terrible**（可怕的、厭惡的）
🔄 **attractive, pleasant**（吸引的、喜悅的）

- 字首：re向後
- 字根：pulse推
- 字尾：ive有…性質的

`121`

1516.
reputation [ˌrɛpjəˈteʃən] 【 rep·u·ta·tion 】 **n** 名聲、信譽

I believe the measure would redound to our mutual benefit and reputation.

我相信這項措施將有助於我們共同的利益和名譽。

同 **celebrity, dignity, honor**（名譽、光榮）

- reputation risk ph.信譽風險
- measure n.措施
- redound v.有助於
- mutual a.相互的

1517.
request [rɪˈkwɛst] 【 re·quest 】 **v n** 要求、懇請

I won't request you any more since you cannot keep your promise.

既然你無法遵守諾言，那我不會再請求你了。

同 **beg, coax, implore**（懇求、請求）
反 **grant**（同意）

- request stop ph.招呼站
- 字首：re再、又
  字根：quest詢問
- promise n.諾言

1518.
requisite [ˈrɛkwəzɪt] 【 req·ui·site 】 **a** 需要的 **n** 必需品

They are accompanied by the requisite shipping documents in order.

正確無誤的裝船單據是必須隨附的。

同 **necessity**（必需品）

- 字首：re再、又
  字根：quis尋找
  字尾：ite有…性質的

1519.
resent [rɪˈzɛnt] 【 re·sent 】 **v** 憤慨、怨恨

Some directors might resent not having been informed in advance.

某些董事可能因為沒有事先接到通知而生氣。

同 **bristle, growl, scowl**（憤怒、發怒）
反 **submit**（服從）

- 字首：re相反
  字根：sent感覺
- in advance ph.事先

1520.
reservation [ˌrɛzəˈveʃən] 【 res·er·va·tion 】 **n** 保留、預約

I support this measure without reservation, completely, wholeheartedly.

我毫無保留地支持這一措施。

同 **booking, engagement, retaining**（預訂）

- completely ad.完整地
- wholeheartedly ad.全心全意地

R

1521.
residence [ˈrɛzədəns] 【 res·i·dence 】 **n** 居住、住所

I learned Spanish during my residence in Mexico.

我住在墨西哥時學會了西班牙語。

同 **abode, dwelling, lodging**（住所）

- 字首：re回
  字根：sid坐
  字尾：ence性質

1522.
resign [rɪˈzaɪn] 【 re·sign 】 **v** 辭職、放棄

There's no suggestion that she should resign, that would be completely unthinkable.

沒有任何跡象顯示她要辭職。

同 **abandon, relinquish, vacate**（放棄、屈服）
反 **achieve**（達成）

- resign oneself to ph.順從
- 字首：re相反
  字根：sign標記
- unthinkable a.不可思議的

1523.
resist [rɪ`zɪst] 【re·sist】 **V**反抗、抵抗 **n**防腐劑

General Motors presented Henry Ford with an opportunity he couldn't resist.

通用汽車公司給亨利福特提供了一個無法拒絕的好機會。

同 counteract, oppose, withstand（反抗）
反 obey, submit（遵從、服從）

- 字首：re相反
  字根：sist站立
- opportunity n.機會

1524.
resolve [rɪ`zɑlv] 【re·solve】 **V n**解決、決定

Resolve to perform what you ought to; perform without fail what you resolve.

該做的一定要做且一定要做好。

同 decide, determine, settle（決定）

- 字首：re加強語氣
  字尾：solve釋放
- ought v.應該

1525.
resolute [`rɛzə,lut] 【res·o·lute】 **a**堅決的、不屈不饒的

There was nothing to be done; he remained resolute.

他始終堅定不移，毫無商量的餘地。

同 bold, firm, willful（堅定的、果斷的）
反 irresolute（優柔寡斷的）

- 字首：re相反
  字尾：solute釋放

1526.
response [rɪ`spɑns] 【re·sponse】 **n**回答、回覆

Our appeal for help met with a meager response.

我們求助的呼籲反應冷淡。

同 answer, replication, respondence（回答）

- 字首：re再、又
  字根：sponse許諾
- appeal n.請求
- meager a.粗劣的

1527.
restate [rɪ`stet] 【re·state】 **V**再聲明、重新敘述

Before the formal contract is drawn up we'd like to restate the main points of the agreement.

在正式簽約之前我們想先重申一下協議的重點。

- 字首：re再、又
- 字尾：state站立
- draw up ph.制訂

1528.
restriction [rɪ`strɪkʃən] 【re·stric·tion】 **n**限制、約束

Australia announces restriction on ships near the Great Barrier Reef.

澳洲宣佈將限制船隻駛近大堡礁附近。

同 limit（限制）

- 字首：re加強語氣
  字根：strict約束
  字尾：ion性質
- reef n.暗礁

1529.
resume [rɪ`zjum] 【re·sume】 **n**簡歷、摘要

It would be helpful if you were to bring both your resume and your college transcript to the job interview.

如果你可以在工作面試時把履歷表和大學成績單帶來的話會很有幫助。

- helpful a.有助益的
- college n.大學
- transcript n.成績單

1530.

retailer [ˈriteləʳ] 【re·tail·er】 Ⓥ零售商、詳述者

The retailer will be primarily interested in locating at the market centre where he is accessible to the maximum possible number of shoppers and is likely to do the greatest amount of business.

零售商主要想選擇在市場中心的位置上，在那裡他能最大限度地接近顧客，生意可以做得最大。

- 字首：re再、又
  字根：tail切
  字尾：er從事…的人
- primarily ad.主要地
- accessible a.可接近的

1531.

retire [rɪˈtaɪr] 【re·tire】 Ⓥ退休、撤回

Many companies in this country grant their old employees annuities after they retire.

這個國家的許多公司在老年雇員退休後發給他們養老年金。

🔄 abdicate, relinquish, withdraw（退休、撤回）

- grant v.同意
- annuity n.年金

1532.

retort [rɪˈtɔrt] 【re·tort】 Ⓥ Ⓝ反駁、報復

The retort raised a cheer in support of the speaker.

發言人的反擊搏得一片支持的歡呼聲。

- retort pouch ph.密封條封口保鮮袋
- 字首：re返、回
  字根：tort扭曲
- speaker n.發言人

1533.

retract [rɪˈtrækt] 【re·tract】 Ⓥ縮回、收回

She had committed herself so fully to the policeman that she could not well retract.

她已經對警察局裡的人全部招認，現在無法翻供。

🔄 cancel, repeal, revoke（撤回、撤銷）

- 字首：re返、回
  字根：tract拉
- commit v.承認

1534.

retreat [rɪˈtrit] 【re·treat】 Ⓥ後退、撤退

After a week's work I like to retreat to the country to relax.

工作一週之後我喜歡躲到鄉下放鬆一下。

🔄 reverse, retire, withdraw（倒退、撤退）

1535.

retribution [ˌrɛtrɪˈbjuʃən] 【ret·ri·bu·tion】 Ⓝ報應、報答

Justice will not sleep long. The retribution will ripen sooner or later.

正義不會長久湮沒，心存善念果報必然早晚現前。

- 字首：re返、回
  字根：tribut分配
  字尾：ion性質

R

1536.

retrieval [rɪˈtrivl] 【re·triev·al】 Ⓝ取回、恢復、補償

Dr. Li is a specialist in information retrieval.

李博士是位資訊檢索專家。

- 此單字大寫表示檔案復原

1537.

retrogress [ˌrɛtrəˈgrɛs] 【ret·ro·gress】 Ⓥ倒退、退化

Practice has shown that the relations between these two countries will go ahead steadily once this political foundation is maintained; otherwise the relations will be undermined, become stagnant or even retrogress.

實驗已經證明嚴守和維護這個政治基礎，這兩國關係就能前進並持續穩定發展；背離和違反這個政治基礎兩國關係就會受損、停滯甚至倒退。

- 字首：retro向後
  字尾：gress行走
- steadily ad.穩固地
- undermine v.逐漸受損

1538.
retrospect [`rɛtrə,spɛkt] 【 ret·ro·spect 】 **v** **n** 回顧、追溯
In retrospect the elaborate preparations seemed de trop.
回顧繁雜的準備工作似乎是多餘的。
反 **prospect**（預期）

- 字首：retro向後
- 字根：spect看
- elaborate a.複雜的
- de trop ph.【法】太多的

1539.
revenue [`rɛvə,nju] 【 rev·e·nue 】 **n** 收益、稅收
They are of two main classes, protective duties and revenue duties.
關稅主要分兩種：保護稅和所得稅。
同 **income, profits, receipts**（收入、收益）
反 **expenditure**（消費）

- revenue cutter ph.緝私船
- revenue stamp ph.
  印花稅票
- revenue stream ph.
  收益流
- protective a.保護的

1540.
reverse [rɪ`vɝs] 【 re·verse 】 **v** **n** 顛倒、相反 **a** 相反的
Children's shoes are not cheap quite the reverse.
兒童的鞋並不便宜反而更貴。
反 **obverse, recto**（表面、正面）

- reverse charge call ph.
  受話方付費電話
- reverse discrimination
  ph.反向歧視
- reverse mortgage ph.
  倒貸
- 字首：re相反

1541.
revert [rɪ`vɝt] 【 re·vert 】 **v** 恢復原狀、重提
I was soon to revert to these matters.
我不久還要重新談到這些事情。
同 **regress, reverse, return**（歸屬、回到）

- revert to ph.回復到
- 字首：re返、回
  字根：vert轉

1542.
revise [rɪ`vaɪz] 【 re·vise 】 **v** **n** 修正、校訂
They accepted the plan with the reservation that they might revise it later.
他們以日後可以修改為條件接受了那項計劃。
同 **alter, correct, rewrite**（改正、糾正）

- 字首：re再、又
  字根：vise看
- reservation n.保留

1543.
revoke [rɪ`vok] 【 re·voke 】 **v** 取消、撤回
A testator may revoke or alter a will he previously made.
遺囑人可以撤銷或變更自己所立的遺囑。
同 **cancel, repeal, withdraw**（撤回、取消）
反 **decide**（決定）

- 字首：re返、回
  字根：voke喊叫
- testator n.立遺囑人
- will n.遺囑

1544.
revolve [rɪ`vɑlv] 【 re·volve 】 **v** 旋轉、反覆思考
Their troubles revolve around money management.
他們的麻煩圍繞在金錢的管理。
同 **circle, turn**（旋轉）

- revolve around ph.以…為
  中心
- 字首：re再、又
  字根：volve轉

1545.
ridiculous [rɪ`dɪkjələs] 【 ri·dic·u·lous 】 **a** 可笑的、荒謬的
Their ridiculous demands torpedoed the negotiations.
他們荒謬的要求破壞了談判。
同 **bizarre, ludicrous, preposterous**（可笑的、荒謬的）

- 字首：rid笑
  字尾：ulous充滿…的
- torpedo v.破壞
- negotiation n.談判

1546.
rigor [ˋrɪgə] 【 rig·or 】 n.嚴格、苛嚴待遇、精確

It was necessary that this should be done in one single day, on account of the extreme urgency and rigor of events.

由於局勢嚴峻時間極端緊迫，這項工作必須在一天之內完成。

- rigor mortis ph.死後僵硬
- urgency n.緊急

1547.
risk [rɪsk] 【 risk 】 n.危險 v.使遭受危險、冒…的危險

Fire-fighters risk life and limb every day in their work.

消防隊員的工作每天都是出生入死的。

- **hazard, imperil, venture**（冒險）
- **safety**（安全）

- risk analysis ph.風險分析
- RAMP= risk analysis and management of projects ph.項目的風險分析和管理
- RMB=risk management budget ph.風險管理預算
- risk-proof a.防範風險的
- risk-taking n.冒險行為

1548.
rival [ˋraɪvl̩] 【 ri·val 】 n.競爭者 v.競爭

He is taken over by his new and successful rival.

他的買賣被新成功的競爭者兼併。

- **compete with, match, vie with**（與…競爭）
- **ally**（結盟）

- take over ph.接管
- successful a.成功的

1549.
round-trip a.來回的、環遊的

Do you want to buy a single fare or a round-trip ticket?

你想買單程票還是往返票？

- RTT=Round-Trip Time ph.一個資料在網路上延遲的時間
- fare n.票價

1550.
route [rut] 【 route 】 n.路線、路程

The route was designed to relieve traffic congestion.

這條路是為緩解交通擁擠而開闢的。

- **itinerary, path**（路線、路程）

- route march ph.訓練行軍
- relieve v.緩和
- congestion n.擁塞

1551.
run into v.撞到、偶遇

We'll run into that time and again.

這個問題我們還會不時地碰到。

- time and again ph.屢次

1552.
runner-up n.第二名、亞軍

She beat out Miss Colombia and Miss Peru who came in as the runner-up and third place holder.

她擊敗了分獲亞軍和季軍的哥倫比亞小姐和秘魯小姐。

1553.
rural [ˋrʊrəl] 【 ru·ral 】 a.農村的、田園的、農業的

George was sending him out into the rural districts to drum up trade.

喬治贊成派他到鄉下招攬生意。

- **bucolic, provincial, rustic**（農村的、田園的）
- **urban**（城市的）

- rural area ph.鄉村
- district n.地區
- drum v.召集

R

1554.
runway [ˋrʌnˌwe]【run·way】**n** 飛機跑道、坡道的

The runway of this airport is undergoing expansion to accommodate large planes.

這個機場的跑道正在擴建以適應大型飛機起落。

同► path, road, track（跑道、車道）

- 字首：run跑
  字尾：way道路
- undergo v.經歷
- expansion n.擴展
- accommodate v.能容納

MEMO

abbr 縮寫詞
a 形容詞
ad 副詞
aux 助動詞
conj 連接詞
n 名詞
num 數字
ph 片語
prep 介系詞
v 動詞
（美）美式用語
（英）英式用語
（法）法式用語

全書單字取材於：
①10本坊間新多益考試暢銷書籍
②50篇英文新聞、商業文章
③2005~2012年ETS TOEIC歷屆考古題
→ 總計約50,000個單字，以電腦統計出題率高達80%
的實用單字1,800個

高頻率單字

➤ | S 家族 sacrifice~synthesis  01-12

高 分 錦 囊

1555.
sacrifice [ˋsækrəˌfaɪs] 【 sac·ri·fice 】 **V**犧牲 **n**犧牲品、祭禮
It's the company's policy to sacrifice short-term profits for the sake of long-term growth.
為長期發展而犧牲短期利潤是公司的方針。
➡ forego, forfeit, waive（喪失、放棄）

> • sacrifice fly ph.犧牲高分球長打
> • 字根：sacri神聖 字尾：fice製作
> • short-term a.短期的
> • long-term a.長期的

`73`

1556.
salary [ˋsælərɪ] 【 sal·a·ry 】 **n**薪資 **V**給…薪水
Smith's monthly salary is paid into the bank by the cashier.
史密斯的每月工資由出納員存入銀行。
➡ pay, wages（薪資、薪水）

> • cashier n.出納員

`214`

1557.
salute [səˋlut] 【 sa·lute 】 **V**向…致敬、讚揚
I also salute the vice president and his supports for waging a spirited campaign.
我同時也要感謝副總統先生，感謝他的支持。
➡ greet, hail（歡迎、致敬）

> • 此單字可為義大利人乾杯用語
> • wage v.進行

`78`

1558.
sample [ˋsæmpl̩] 【 sam·ple 】 **n**樣品、實例
Free samples are offered by this factory.
本廠提供免費樣品。
➡ example（例子）

`145`

1559.
satellite [ˋsætl̩ˌaɪt] 【 sat·el·lite 】 **n**衛星、人造衛星
They receive television pictures by satellite.
他們通過人造衛星接收電視圖像。

> • satellite dish ph.碟型衛星信號接受器
> • satellite television ph.衛星電視

`81`

1560.
scandal [ˋskændl̩] 【 scan·dal 】 **n**醜聞、誹謗
He suffered a loss of prestige when the scandal was publicized.
這件醜事公開後他便威信掃地。
➡ disgrace, humiliation, shame（醜聞、丟臉）
反 praise（稱讚）

> • scandal sheet ph.渲染醜聞的報刊
> • prestige n.聲望

`128`

1561.
scanner [ˋskænɚ] 【 scan·ner 】 **n**掃描機
The antenna enables the chip to send the identification information to a scanner.
天線可使晶片把確認資訊發送到掃描器上。

> • 字首：scan掃描 字尾：ner小事物
> • antenna n.天線
> • chip n.晶片

`73`

1562.

scenario [sɪˋnɛrɪˏo] 【sce·nar·i·o】 **n** 情節、事態

That grim scenario is now unfolding.

這種嚴酷的事態目前正在漸漸揭露。

- grim a.嚴厲的
- unfold v.顯露

1563.

schedule [ˋskɛdʒʊl] 【sched·ule】 **n** 時間表、日程安排表 **v** 安排

All these activities gave him a full schedule, but somehow he managed.

這些活動使他一天忙到晚，但他還是撐下來了。

- schedule management ph.進度管理
- somehow ad.不知怎麼的

1564.

scheme [skim] 【scheme】 **v n** 計劃、策劃

The land developer hoped the mayor would play ball on the scheme.

土地開發資商希望市長在那項方案上能夠合作。

- play ball ph.合作

connive, intrigue, plan (計劃、密謀)

1565.

screen [skrin] 【screen】 **n** 隔板、螢幕 **v** 遮蔽

Maximized windows fill the entire screen, covering up whatever is beneath them.

最大的視窗充滿了整個螢幕，覆蓋了底下的內容。

- screen door ph.紗門
- screen out ph.遮擋
- screen test ph.試鏡
- beneath prep.在⋯之下

cover, shelter, veil (掩蔽)

1566.

scriptwriter [ˋskrɪptˏraɪtə] 【script·writ·er】 **n** 編劇、作家

The film was a largely successful adaptation of the stage play, though sometimes one felt that the scriptwriter had taken rather too many liberties with the original text.

這部電影大體上來說是對原舞臺劇的成功改編，儘管有時讓人覺得電影編劇者對原著的處理過於隨意。

- 字首：script手稿
  字尾：writer撰稿人
- original a.原始的

1567.

search engine **n** 搜尋引擎

The website, Sina, with news, a search engine and auctions, offers a broader business.

新浪以其新聞、搜尋引擎和拍賣功能強大帶來廣闊商機。

- search v.搜尋
- engine n.引擎
- search engines ph.一些較受歡迎的搜尋工具
- auction n.拍賣

1568.

seasoning [ˋsizṇɪŋ] 【sea·son·ing】 **n** 調味料

Chinese seasoning made by grinding star anise and fennel and pepper and cloves and cinnamon.

中國調味品由磨碎的星形大茴香、茴香、胡椒粉、丁香和肉桂製成。

- grind v.磨碎
- anise n.大茴香
- fennel n.茴香
- clove n.丁香
- cinnamon n.肉桂

1569.

seat belt **n** 安全帶

You must buckle your seat belt in a plane before it takes off.

在飛機起飛之前你一定要扣緊安全帶。

- belt n.帶狀物
- buckle v.扣住
- take off ph.起飛

1570.
secret [`sikrɪt] 【se·cret】 **a** 祕密的 **n** 祕密

Actual secret rendezvous need not be settled till later.

實際祕密會晤地點待以後再定。

同 mysterious, private (隱蔽的)
反 public, obvious, open (公開的、明顯的)

> **164**
> • secret agent ph.特務
> • secret ballot ph.
>   無記名投票
> • secret police ph.祕密警察
> • Secret Service ph.
>   特務工作
> • rendezvous n.會面地點

1571.
secretary [`sɛkrəˌtɛrɪ] 【sec·re·tar·y】 **n** 祕書

The manager was mad at his secretary because she failed to remind him of an important appointment.

經理對他的祕書很不悅，因為她未提醒他去參加一個重要的會議。

同 assistant, bookkeeper, helper (助手、記帳人)

> **131**
> • secretary bird ph.鷺鷹
> • secretary general ph.
>   祕書長
> • Secretary of State
>   ph.【美】國務卿【英】國務
>   大臣
> • appointment n.約會

1572.
segment [`sɛgmənt] 【seg·ment】 **v** **n** 部分、切片

Our approach was to segment the diplomacy into a series of steps.

我們的做法是把外交工作分成一系列的步驟來進行。

同 division, part, section (部分)

> **84**
> • segment sequence ph.
>   程式段序列
> • segment terminator
>   ph.程式段落終止者
> • diplomacy n.外交

1573.
segregate [`sɛgrɪˌget] 【seg·re·gate】 **v** 隔離、分離

A power firm, for example, might segregate its industrial customers from its residential customers.

一個電力廠可把它的顧客區分成工業顧客和居民顧客。

反 aggregate (聚集)

> **131**
> • 字首：se分開
> • industrial a.工業的
> • residential a.居住的

1574.
select [sə`lɛkt] 【se·lect】 **v** **n** 選擇、挑選

I can select anyone I desire to fill vacant positions.

我可以選我喜歡的人去填補空缺。

同 choose, pick (挑選、選擇)

> **146**
> • select committee ph.為某
>   一特案組成的特別委員會
> • 字首：se分開
>   字根：lect選擇
> • vacant a.空的

1575.
self-explanatory **a** 不解自明的、明顯的

To be quite fair, the phrase is by no means self-explanatory.

公平地說，這個說法並不明瞭。

> **104**
> • select committee ph.為某
>   一特案組成的特別委員會
> • 字首：se分開
>   字根：lect選擇
> • vacant a.空的

1576.
semiconductor [ˌsɛmɪkən`dʌktə] 【sem·i·con·duc·tor】
n 半導體

A further refinement in semiconductor technology is the integrated circuit.

在半導體科技中，積體電路是一次革新。

> **91**
> • 字首：semi一半
>   字尾：conductor導體
> • refinement n.精細的改進
> • integrated circuit ph.積體
>   電路

1577.
semimonthly [ˌsɛmɪ`mʌnθlɪ] 【sem·i·month·ly】 **n** 半月刊
a 半個月一次的

The publishing house launched the semimonthly in 1938, and edited from the first 18 issues.

出版社於1938年創辦了半月刊，並編輯了前18期。

> **47**
> • 字首：semi一半
>   字尾：monthly月刊
> • launch v.開辦
> • issue n.期號

1578.
seminar [ˈsɛmə‚nɑr] 【 sem·i·nar 】 n 專題研討會
188
The economy and trade seminar among these nations is about to be held in Singapore.

這些國家的經貿研討會即將在新加坡舉行。

 conference, discussion, workshop（會議、專題研討會）

• be about to ph.即將

1579
sentiment [ˈsɛntəmənt] 【 sen·ti·ment 】 n 感情、情緒、觀點
67
Her passion for money excluded every other sentiment.

她對金錢的熱愛已經把其他的感情都排擠掉了。

• 字根：senti感覺
字尾：ment狀態
• exclude v.排斥

1580.
server [ˈsɝvɚ] 【 serv·er 】 n 伺服器
86
If the application is having trouble creating a connection to a server, don't put up a dialog box to report it.

如果應用程式無法連接伺服器，不要用對話方塊來報告。

• Server Appliance（精簡型伺服器）
• connection n.聯結
• dialog box ph.對話框

1581.
settlement [ˈsɛtḷmənt] 【 set·tle·ment 】 n 解決、結算、殖民地
141
The trade contract stipulates for the settlement of balances in US dollar.

貿易合約規定餘額以美金結算。

• 字首：settle解決
字尾：ment狀態
• stipulate v.規定

1582.
severe [səˈvɪr] 【 se·vere 】 a 嚴重的、純潔的
145
Commerce is paralyzed in consequence of a severe earthquake.

由於嚴重的地震所以商業全面停頓了。

 harsh, rough, strict（嚴厲的、苛刻的）
 indulgent, lenient, mild（寬大的、溫和的）

• SARS=severe acute respiratory syndrome ph.嚴重急性呼吸道症候群
• paralyze v.全面停頓
• consequence n.後果
• earthquake n.地震

1583.
shareholder [ˈʃɛr‚holdɚ] 【 share·hold·er 】 n 股東
104
The right granting to shareholders the first opportunity to buy a new issue of stock; provides protection against dilution of the shareholder's ownership interest.

為防止分散股益，發行新股時股東有優先購買的權利。

• 字首：share股票
字尾：holder n.持有者
• dilution n.稀釋

S

1584.
shift [ʃɪft] 【 shift 】 v n 轉移、輪班
164
Peter is on the day shift and I am on the night shift.

彼得上白天班，我上夜班。

 alter, substitute, vary（替換、變動）

• shift for oneself ph.自謀生計
• shift gear ph.改變方法
• shift the goalposts ph.改變目標

1585.
shipment [ˈʃɪpmənt] 【 ship·ment 】 n 裝運、裝載的貨物
78
We'll send the shipment details by fax shortly.

我們會立即將出貨明細傳真出去。

• 字首：ship船
字尾：ment狀態
• shortly ad.立刻

261

1586.
shopping mall ph.大型購物中心
* mall n.大規模購物中心
You can have a larger choice in the shopping mall.
在購物中心的選擇較多。

1587.
shortcut [ˈʃɔrtˌkʌt] 【short‧cut】 n.近路、捷徑
* 字首：short短的
* 字尾：cut切
* fame n.名望
* fortune n.財產
My father was always looking for a shortcut to fame and fortune.
我父親總是在找成名發財的捷徑。

1588.
shorthand [ˈʃɔrtˌhænd] 【short‧hand】 n.速記、簡略方式表達
* shorthand typist ph.速記員
A secretary must learn shorthand and typing.
祕書一定要學會速記和打字。
📖 stenography, tachygraphy（速記法）

1589.
shut down ph.停工
Many U.S. industries operate overtime during part of the year, then shut down for several months to save operating expenses.
許多美國工業在一年中一段時期超時間工作，然後就關門幾個月以節省開工的開支。

1590.
side effect ph.副作用
* absorption n.吸收
* toxic a.有毒的
* pollution n.汙染
The pysical absorption does not have toxic side effect or secondary pollution.
物理吸收無任何有毒的副作用和二次污染。

1591.
sightseeing [ˈsaɪtˌsiɪŋ] 【sight‧see‧ing】 n.觀光、遊覽
* pack v.擠滿
She managed to pack a lot of sightseeing into the short time she had in London.
她在倫敦逗留的短短時間中，緊湊地安排了一連串的觀光活動。

1592.
signature [ˈsɪɡnətʃɚ] 【sig‧na‧ture】 n.簽名、特徵
* signature file ph.簽名檔
* signature tune ph.信號曲
* imperative a.必要的
* identification card ph.身分證
It's imperative that your signature appear on your identification card.
身份證上必須有你的親筆簽名。
📖 autograph, endorsement, subscription（簽名、簽署）

1593.
significance [sɪɡˈnɪfəkəns] 【sig‧nif‧i‧cance】 n.重要、意義
* 字根：sign標記
* indicate v.指出
* assess v.評估
Because of the public health significance, much work is indicated to assess these results.
鑑於公共健康的重要性，需要做出更多的工作以評估這些結果。
📖 connotation, importance, gist（重要性、要點）
📖 insignificance（不重要）

1594.
silverware [`sɪlvɚ͵wɛr] [sil·ver·ware] **n**銀器、鍍銀餐具
Place the silverware on the table for dinner.
請將餐具擺放在桌子上吃晚飯。

- 字首：silver銀
- 字尾：ware器皿

1595.
simulate [`sɪmjə͵let] [sim·u·late] **v**假裝、模仿
Door mounted push-button to simulate float switch operation.
在門上安裝按鈕，模仿浮動開關操作。

- 字根：simul相類似
  字尾：ate進行一項行動
- push-button a.按鈕操作的
- float n.浮動

1596.
simultaneous [͵saɪm]`tenɪəs] [si·mul·ta·ne·ous]
a同時發生的
The conference hall is provided with facilities for simultaneous interpretation in five languages.
這個會議大廳配有五種語言的同步口譯設備。
Ⓢ **coincident, contemporary, parallel**（同時發生的）

- simultaneous interpreter ph.同步翻譯員
- 字根：simult相類似
  字尾：aneous有…性質的
- conference n.會議

1597.
slogan [`slogən] [slo·gan] **n**口號、標語
The slogan was a pun on the name of the product
那廣告用語與其產品名稱一語雙關。
Ⓢ **motto**（口號）

- pun n.雙關語

1598.
snack [snæk] [snack] **n**小吃、點心 **v**吃點心
I prefer to snack when I'm travelling rather than have a full meal.
我旅行時喜歡吃小吃而不吃正餐。
Ⓢ **morsel, nosh**（小吃）

- snack bar ph.簡速餐廳
- rather than ph.而不是…

1599.
soccer [`sakɚ] [soc·cer] **n**足球
Next to bullfight and soccer, lotteries are Spain's biggest sport.
發行彩票在西班牙是僅次於鬥牛和足球的最大娛樂活動。
Ⓢ **football**（【美】足球）

- bullfight n.鬥牛
- lottery n.彩券

1600.
solar [`solɚ] [so·lar] **a**太陽的、日光的
The exploitation of solar energy is gradually moving into high gear.
太陽能的開發漸漸進入高速發展。
Ⓐ **lunar**（月亮的）

- solar battery ph.太陽能電池
- solar battery charger ph.太陽能充電器
- solar eclipse ph.日蝕
- solar system ph.太陽系
- exploitation n.開發

1601.
solicit [sə`lɪsɪt] [so·lic·it] **v**請求、懇求、徵求
We solicit a continuance of your order.
我們懇切希望貴公司能繼續訂購。
Ⓢ **appeal, beg, request**（請求）

- solicitation n.懇切地要求
- solicitor n.懇求者
- continuance n.繼續

S

1602.
special [`spɛʃəl]【spe·cial】a特別的、專門的
A special chapter of the General Agreement deals with trade and development.
總協定中專門有一章節談論貿易和發展方面的問題。
🔄 **extraordinary, particular, unsual**（特別的、專門的）
🔄 **common, general, ordinary**（普通的、一般的）

- special agent ph.特務
- Special Branch ph. 政治保安處
- special delivery ph. 限時專送
- special education ph. 特殊教育
- special effect ph.特殊效果

1603.
specialty [`spɛʃəltɪ]【spe·cial·ty】n特質、專長
Her specialty is biochemistry.
她的專業是生物化學。
🔄 **feature, mannerism, peculiarity**（特質、特徵）

- biochemistry n.生物化學

1604.
specific [spɪ`sɪfɪk]【spe·cif·ic】a具體的、特殊的
Until now, the medical industry still cannot figure out any treatment to cure such specific disease.
目前為止，醫學界還沒找到可以醫治這特殊疾病的療法。
🔄 **definite, particular, precise**（明確的、特殊的）
🔄 **general**（廣泛的）

- specific gravity ph.比重
- figure out ph.理解
- treatment n.治療法
- cure v.治療

1605.
specimen [`spɛsəmən]【spec·i·men】n樣本、標本
Job applicants have to submit a specimen of handwriting.
求職者必須遞交自己的手寫樣本。
🔄 **example, sample, type**（樣品、典型）

- applicant n.申請人
- submit v.提交
- handwriting n.手稿

1606.
spectator [spɛk`tetə]【spec·ta·tor】n觀眾、目擊者
He remained a mere spectator of the great happenings of his time.
對於他所處的那個時期的大事件，他只是一個旁觀者而已。
🔄 **bystander, witness, viewer**（旁觀者、觀眾）

- spectator sport ph.吸引大量觀眾的體育運動
- 字根：spect看 字尾：ator動作執行者
- happening n.事件

1607.
specification [ˌspɛsəfə`keʃən]【spec·i·fi·ca·tion】
n把…裝滿、補充
Can you give me a price list with specification?
你能給我一份有規格說明的價目單嗎？

- price n.價錢
- list n.清單

1608.
speculate [`spɛkjəˌlet]【spec·u·late】v思索、投機、推斷
One can either hedge or speculate in the spot market for foreign exchange.
人們可以在即期外匯市場上進行套期保值或投機。
🔄 **conjecture, guess, reflect**（思索、沉思）

- 字根：spec看 字尾：ate進行一項行動
- hedge v.兩面下注以防損失
- spot market ph.現貨市場

1609.
spice [spaɪs]【spice】**n**香料、調味品
Ginger, salt, pepper, sugar and vinegar are common spices.
薑、鹽、胡椒粉、糖和醋都是常見的調味品。
同 flavor, seasoning（調味料）

- ginger n.薑
- pepper n.胡椒粉
- vinegar n.醋

1610.
spreadsheet [ˋsprɛd.ʃit]【spread·sheet】**n**空白表格程式
In the spreadsheet, a single-click will select exactly one whole cell.
在空白表格程式中，按一下就是選擇整個儲存格。

- click n.喀嚓聲
- exactly ad.完整地

1611.
stadium [ˋstedɪəm]【sta·di·um】**n**體育場、競技場
The crowds drifted away from the stadium.
人群慢慢從體育場散去。
同 arena, bowl, hippodrome（競技場、運動場）

- stadium concert（=gig） ph.在露天體育場舉行的大型搖滾音樂會
- drift v.漸漸趨向

1612.
staff [stæf]【staff】**n**全體職員**v**給…配備職員
He spoke on behalf of all the members of the faculty and staff.
他代表全體教職員工發言。
同 committee, crew, personnel（成員）

- staff nurse ph.醫院護士
- staff officer ph.參謀
- staff room ph.教ardingroom教師室
- staff sergeant ph. 參謀軍士
- on behalf of ph.代表

1613.
stapler [ˋsteplə]【sta·pler】**n**釘書機
The stapler gets jammed every time I want to use it.
每次我要用這釘書機都會卡住。

- staple n.訂書針
- jammed a.卡住的

1614.
startle [ˋstɑrt!]【star·tle】**v n**使驚嚇、驚奇
I hope my sudden attendance didn't startle you.
但願我的突然出現沒有嚇著你。
同 fright, shock（驚嚇）

- sudden a.突然的
- attendance n.出席

1615.
starve [stɑrv]【starve】**v**餓死、挨餓、渴求
Such a system might dictate that some people starve from lack of income.
這種制度使某些人缺乏收入以致餓死。
同 crave, hunger（挨餓、渴求）
反 satiate（使飽足）

- starve for ph.渴望
- lack n.缺乏
- income n.收入

1616.
statement [ˋstetmənt]【state·ment】**n**聲明、陳述
All the department reports should be integrated into one annual statement.
各部門的報告應結合在一起成為一份年度報告。
同 announcement, declaration, report（陳述、宣言）

- Statement of income ph.損益表
- 字根：state站立 字尾：ment性質

S

1617
state-of-the-art a最先進的、最高級的

The Olympic Games in any country will also enjoy state-of-the-art technology systems.

各個國家舉辦的奧運會享有一流的技術系統。

- **Olympic Games ph.**奧林匹克運動會
- **technology n.**科技

74

1618.
static [ˋstætɪk] 【stat·ic】 a靜態的、固定的 n靜電

Don't take a static view of things.

不要用固定的眼光看問題。

- **dormant, sluggish, still**（靜止的、少動的）
- **dynamic**（動態的）

- **static electricity ph.**靜電
- 字根：**stat**站立
  字尾：**ic**有…性質的

64

1619.
stationery [ˋsteʃənˏɛrɪ] 【sta·tion·er·y】 n文具、信紙

Miller travels in office stationery.

米勒到各地去推銷辦公用品。

71

1620.
stock [stɑk] 【stock】 n儲存、證券、股票

The London Stock Exchange is in turmoil today.

今天倫敦股票交易市場一片混亂。

- **stock car ph.**普通車改裝成賽車
- **stock certificate ph.**股票
- **stock control ph.**庫存核算
- **stock in trade ph.**存貨
- **turmoil n.**騷亂

124

1621.
stockbroker [ˋstɑkˏbrokə] 【stock·bro·ker】 n證券或股票經紀人

His stockbroker announced his portfolio as being valueless.

他的證券經紀人宣稱他的有價證券毫無價值。

- **stockbroker belt ph.**城市遠郊
- 字首：**stock**股票
  字尾：**broker**經紀人

118

1622.
stopover [ˋstɑpˏovə] 【stop·o·ver】 n中途停留

You will have a two-hour stopover in Tokyo before continuing to Melbourne.

你們要在東京停留兩小時，再繼續飛往墨爾本。

71

1623.
storage [ˋstorɪdʒ] 【stor·age】 n儲藏、倉庫

Surplus wheat is put in storage and shipped abroad.

剩餘的小麥被儲存起來運到海外。

- **cache, space, stowage**（儲藏所、堆積處）

- **storage battery ph.**蓄電池
- **storage heater ph.**電蓄熱器
- **storage snapshot ph.**資料快照軟體
- 字根：**stor**儲存
  字尾：**age**地方

104

1624.
stretch [strɛtʃ] 【stretch】 vn伸展、拉直

Can we stretch the rules to allow them to join in our club?

我們能放寬規定允許他們加入我們的俱樂部嗎？

- **elongate, expand, spread**（伸展、展開）
- **shrink**（收縮）

- **stretch a point ph.**做出讓步
- **stretch limo ph.**家常的豪華小汽車
- **stretch mark ph.**妊娠紋
- **stretch out ph.**延長
- **stretch-out ph.**增加勞動強度的工業管理制度

148

1625.

strike [straɪk] 【 strike 】 **V n** 打擊、罷工

Communication with other countries was difficult during the telephone and postal strike.

郵電工人罷工期間與各國的通訊很困難。

⬤ bat, hit, smack（打、敲擊）

- strike a false note **ph.** 說或做得不恰當
- strike a match **ph.** 點火柴
- strike all of a heap **ph.** 使大吃一驚
- strike an attitude **ph.** 裝腔作勢
- strike down **ph.** 擊倒

1626.

stroke [strok] 【 stroke 】 **n** 中風、突然發作

The stroke left him paralyzed on one side of his body.

他因患中風而致半身不遂。

⬤ attack, convulsion, seizure（病的突然發作）

- stroke down **ph.** 安撫

1627.

stroll [strol] 【 stroll 】 **V n** 散步、閒逛

A few passengers would have a stroll on the afterdeck before the evening meal.

幾位乘客將在晚飯前到後甲板上散步。

⬤ amble, saunter, stride（散步）

- afterdeck **n.** 後甲板

1628.

stunt [stʌnt] 【 stunt 】 **n** 特技、噱頭 **V** 表演絕技

A stunt man needs to have a good guardian angel.

當特技替身演員需要有個守護天使來保佑。

⬤ exploit, feat, performance（技藝、表演）

- stun man **ph.** 拍攝危險鏡頭時作電影演員替身的雜技演員
- stun woman **ph.** 女特技替身演員
- guardian angel **ph.** 守護天使

1629.

subconscious [sʌbˋkɑnʃəs] 【 sub·con·scious 】 **a** 潛意識的

Making your subconscious work for you is only the first for many steps.

使潛意識發揮作用只是邁向成功的第一步而已。

- 字首：sub在…之下
- 字尾：conscious意識到的

1630.

submerge [səbˋmɝdʒ] 【 sub·merge 】 **V** 淹沒、覆蓋

We were not prepared to submerge our doubts about some of the existing trends and procedures.

我們不準備掩蓋我們對目前某些傾向和程序的懷疑。

⬤ dunk, immerse, inundate（沉浸、浸泡）

⬤ emerge（浮現）

- 字首：sub在…之下
- 字根：merg沉、浸
- existing **a.** 現存的
- procedure **n.** 程序

S

1631.

submissive [səbˋmɪsɪv] 【 sub·mis·sive 】 **a** 服從的、柔順的

Their early training programs led them to be obedient and submissive.

他們早先受過的教育已把他們訓練得俯首貼耳、唯命是從。

- training **a.** 訓練的
- obedient **a.** 服從的

1632.

submit [səbˋmɪt] 【 sub·mit 】 **V** 使屈服、提出

Please submit your application form in quadruplicate.

請交申請表，一式四份。

⬤ comply, obey, surrender（使屈服）

⬤ resist（抗拒）

- submit oneself to **ph.** 歸順於
- submit to **ph.** 屈服於
- quadruplicate **n.** 一式四份

1633.
subnormal [sʌb`nɔrml̩] 【sub·nor·mal】 **a** 普通以下的、低能的
Much of the area of the country has received subnormal precipitation since the end of January.
一月底以來,這個國家的多數地區雨水都比以往少。

- 字首:sub在…之下
- 字根:norm標準
- 字尾:al屬於…的
- precipitation n.猛然落下

143

1634.
subordinate [sə`bɔrdn̩ɪt] 【sub·or·din·ate】 **a** 次要的、附屬的
n 屬下
He contented himself with a subordinate job.
他對自己不起眼的工作感到滿足。
同 **dependent, inferior, secondary**(下級的、從屬的)
反 **dominant, leading**(支配的、統治的)

- subordinate clause ph. 附屬子句
- 字首:sub在…之下
- 字根:ordin次序
- 字尾:ate有…性質的

104

1635.
subscribe [səb`skraɪb] 【sub·scribe】 **v** 捐款、訂購
The magazine is trying to get more readers to subscribe.
該雜誌正大力發展新訂戶。
同 **contribute, support**(捐助)

- subscribe for ph.預訂
- subscribe to ph.同意
- 字首:sub在…之下
- 字根:scrib寫

138

1636.
subside [səb`saɪd] 【sub·side】 **v** 消退、平息
At the San Francisco sales meeting after waiting for applause to subside, Celia continued her address.
在舊金山的推銷會議上,西莉亞等掌聲平靜後繼續發言。
同 **decrease, diminish, lessen**(減少)

- applause n.鼓掌歡迎
- 字首:sub在…之下
- 字根:sid坐

91

1637.
subsidiary [səb`sɪdɪˌɛrɪ] 【sub·sid·i·ar·y】 **a** 輔助的、次要的
n 子公司、輔助物
The investor has substantial control over the foreign subsidiary enterprise.
投資者對於國外子公司具有實際的控制權。

- subsidiary company ph.附屬公司
- substantial a.實在的

84

1638.
subsist [səb`sɪst] 【sub·sist】 **v** 維持生活、存在
I was very sorry to tell him that the little money I had would not subsist.
我很抱歉地告訴他,我的那一點存款不夠維持我們的生活。
同 **exist, live, survive**(存在)

- 字首:sub在…之下
- 字根:sist站立

114

1639.
substandard [sʌb`stændəd] 【sub·stan·dard】 **a** 不夠標準的、不合規格的
No permission shall be granted for the export of export commodities found to be substandard in a random inspection.
出口商品經抽查檢驗不合格的,不准出口。

- permission n.允許
- commodity n.商品
- random a.隨意的
- inspection n.檢查

104

1640.
substantially [səb`stænʃəlɪ] 【sub·stan·tial·ly】 **ad** 實質上、相當多地
Our concern and theirs substantially overlap.
我們的利害關係和他們的大致相合。

- concern n.關係
- overlap v.重疊

110

1641.
substitute [`sʌbstətˌjut] 【sub·sti·tute】 **n**代理人或物 **v**代替

If you cannot attend the conference in person, please find someone to substitute you.

你如果不能親自出席會議，請找人代替你。

- substitute for ph.代替
- substitute teacher ph. 代課老師
- 字首：sub在…之下 字根：stitute設立
- in person ph.親自

108

1642.
subtract [səb`trækt] 【sub·tract】 **v**減去、去掉

From this amount you need to subtract something to cover fixed overheads.

從這個總額中你需要扣除一些來支付固定的經費開支。

- **⑩** deduct, remove, withdraw（減去、扣除）
- **⑫** add, increase（增加）

- 字首：sub向下 字根：tract拉
- overhead n.經常費用

97

1643.
suburb [`sʌbɝb] 【sub·urb】 **n**近郊、郊區、邊緣

He lives in the suburb and works in the central business district.

他住在郊區而在商業中心上班。

- **⑩** outskirts, suburbia, vicinage（郊區、鄰近地區）

- 此單字多用於複數形式
- suburban a.郊區的
- district n.地區

141

1644.
subway [`sʌbˌwe] 【sub·way】 **n**【美】地下鐵、【英】地下通道

You'll find a map in each subway car showing where all the stops are.

在每一班地下鐵裡，你都能看到列著各站站名的地圖。

- **⑩** metro, tube, tunnel（地鐵）

- 字首：sub在…之下
- 字尾：way道路

231

1645.
succeed [sək`sid] 【suc·ceed】 **v**成功、繼任

In order to succeed here you will need to overcome your prejudices.

你要消除偏見才能從這裡獲得成功。

- **⑩** achieve, prosper, thrive（成功、興旺）
- **⑫** fail, precede（失敗、領先）

- succeed in ph.成功
- 字首：suc向下 字根：ceed行走
- overcome v.克服

183

1646.
suffer [`sʌfɚ] 【suf·fer】 **v**遭受、經歷

If only we don't have to suffer too great a decline.

只要我們不遭受太大的跌價就好了。

- **⑩** bear, endure, stand（遭受、忍受）

- suffer from ph.受…之苦
- suffer through ph.挨過
- 字首：suf在…之下
- 字根：fer帶來

147

S

1647.
sufficient [sə`fɪʃənt] 【suf·fi·cient】 **a**充分的、足夠的 **n**足量

Her fortune is already more than sufficient to attract those unscrupulous adventurers.

她的財產已經多得足以引起那些貪得無厭的冒險者的覬覦。

- **⑩** adequate, ample, enough（足夠的）
- **⑫** deficient, inadequate, insufficient（不足的）

- 字首：suf在…之下 字根：fic製作 字尾：ient…狀態的
- unscrupulous a.無恥的
- adventurer n.冒險者

175

1648.
suffuse [sə`fjuz] 【suf·fuse】 **v**遍佈、充滿

They want to move everyone with their behaviors and suffuse the world with love.

他們表示要用自己的行為去感染世界上的每一個人，讓愛心充滿全世界。

- 字首：suf在…之下
- 字根：fuse流、瀉

1649.
suite [swit] 【 suite 】 **n**套房、系列

The secretary booked a luxurious suite for the CEO on his business trip to Russia.

執行長到俄羅斯出差時，祕書幫他訂了一間豪華套房。

- book v.登記
- luxurious a.豪華的

1650.
superficial [ˌsupəˋfɪʃəl] 【 su·per·fi·cial 】 **a**表面的、膚淺的

The pressures of his job drive the manager to be superficial in his actions.

管理職務的壓力迫使他採取表面性的行動。

⊜ **cursory, surface, shallow**（表面的、膚淺的）
⊗ **essential, radical**（實質的、基本的）

- 字首：super在…之上
  字根：fic製作
  字尾：ial與…有關的

1651.
superfluous [suˋpɝfluəs] 【 su·per·flu·ous 】 **a**過剩的、不必要的

The introductory style seemed a little superfluous.

這種客套未免有點多餘。

- 字首：super過度
  字根：flu流、瀉
  字尾：ous充滿…的
- introductory a.介紹的

1652.
supervise [ˋsupəˌvaɪz] 【 su·per·vise 】 **v**監督、管理

She supervises six subordinates in the account department.

她在財務部門管6個部屬。

⊜ **administer, govern, regulate**（監督）

- supervisor n.管理人
- 字首：super在…之上
  字根：vise看

1653.
supplant [səˋplænt] 【 sup·plant 】 **v**取代、排擠

TV and computers shouldn't supplant time with others and cyber chats don't develop social skills.

電視和電腦不應取代與他人共度的時光，而且上網聊天並不能提高社交技巧。

⊜ **displace, replace, supersede**（取代）

- cyber n.電腦異度
- chat n.聊天
- skill n.技巧

1654.
supplement [ˋsʌpləmənt] 【 sup·ple·ment 】 **vn**補充、補給

She got a part-time job to supplement the family income.

她找了一個兼職工作以補充家庭收入。

⊜ **augment, fortify, reinforce**（補充、增加）

- 字首：sup向下
  字根：ple折疊
  字尾：ment行為

1655.
supplicant [ˋsʌplɪkənt] 【 sup·pli·cant 】 **n**懇求者

During the depression, the job supplicants submit at least hundreds of resumes to get a job.

在景氣大蕭條時期，求職者至少要投遞上百封履歷才能找到工作。

- depression n.不景氣
- hundreds of ph.數以百計
- resume n.履歷表

1656.
supply [səˋplaɪ] 【 sup·ply 】 **vn**供給、補充

Either we will find a supply, or we will make the goods.

我們將尋求供貨或自己製造。

⊜ **afford, endow, obilge**（供給、供應）
⊗ **demand**（要求）

- supply and demand ph.供求
- supply department ph. 採購部
- supply line ph.生產線
- supply teacher ph. 代課老師

1657.
support [sə`port]【sup·port】**Ⅴ**支持、保持、忍受
I support this measure without reservation, i.e. completely, wholeheartedly.
我毫無保留地支持這項措施。
同- maintain, prop, uphold（支持、維持）
反- betray, oppose（背叛、反對）

- **support group** ph.搖滾音樂會的配角樂團
- **support level** ph.支撐水準
- **support stocking** ph.彈性襪
- **support the weak and retrain the powerful** ph.扶弱抑強
- 此單字當忍受解釋時,多與 can, cannot連用
▸ 181

1658.
suppose [sə`poz]【sup·pose】**Ⅴ**猜想、推測
I don't suppose there'll ever be a remedy for that.
我想那件事不會有任何補救辦法。
同- assume, consider, think（認為）
反- prove（證實）

- 字首:**sup**在…之下
  字根:**pose**放置
- **remedy** n.補救辦法
▸ 165

1659.
suppress [sə`prɛs]【sup·press】**Ⅴ**鎮壓、抑制
He was trying to suppress the hope he was feeling.
當內心的盼望蠢蠢欲動,他就拼命克制。
同- arrest, bridle, subdue（抑制、壓制）

- 字首:**sup**向下
  字根:**press**壓
▸ 104

1660.
surcharge [`sɝ.tʃɑrdʒ]【sur·charge】**n**超載、額外費 **Ⅴ**罰款
We demand a surcharge of four cents per gram for the overweight.
我們另外要收每克4分錢的超重費用。

- 字首:**sur**超過
  字尾:**charge**索費
- **cent** n.分
- **gram** n.克
- **overweight** n.超重
▸ 113

1661.
surface [`sɝfɪs]【sur·face】**n**表面、外表
Beneath her self-confident surface, she's quite unsure of herself.
她看上去信心十足,實際上很缺乏信心。
同- face, exterior, outside（表面、外面）
反- interior（內部）

- 字首:**sur**在…之上
  字尾:**face**表面
- **beneath** prep.在…之下
- **self-confident** a.自信的
▸ 54

1662.
surfing [`sɝfɪŋ]【surfing】**n**衝浪遊戲
He goes surfing every summer vacation.
每個暑假他都會去衝浪。

- **surfing the web** ph.網路衝浪
▸ 73

1663.
surgery [`sɝdʒərɪ]【sur·ger·y】**n**外科、手術室
He will have his rotating internship in medicine, surgery, obstetrics, and pediatrics.
他將在內科、外科、產科及小兒科輪流實習。
反- medicine（內科）

- **rotate** v.輪流
- **internship** n.實習醫生的地位
- **obstetrics** n.產科醫學
- **pediatrics** n.小兒科
▸ 131

1664.
surpass [sə`pæs]【sur·pass】**Ⅴ**優於、勝過
In order to catch up with and surpass the advanced world levels we'll have to accelerate our speed.
要趕上且超越世界水準,我們還得快馬加鞭。
同- exceed, excel（勝過）

- 字首:**sur**超過
  字尾:**pass**通過
- **catch up with** ph.趕上
- **accelerate** v.增速

S

271

1665.
surplus [ˋsɝpləs] [sur·plus] **n** 剩餘、盈餘 **a** 過過剩的、剩餘的
A surplus of exports over imports will boost employment.
出口大於進口的順差自然將提供就業。
同 extra, leftover, superfluous（過剩的、多餘的）
反 deficit（不足額）

- surplus value ph.剩餘價值
- 字首：sur超過
  字尾：plus外加額
- boost v.提高
187

1666.
surprise [səˋpraɪz] [sur·prise] **v** 吃驚、感到意外
The customer neither expressed suprise at the price nor attempted.
客戶對於這個價格既沒有表示驚訝也沒想接受。
同 administer, govern, regulate（監督）

- attempt v.企圖
- accept v.接受
144

1667.
surrender [səˋrɛndə] [sur·ren·der] **v** 投降、自首、聽任
The bills of lading are turned over to the shipper, who will surrender the letter of indemnity to the bank.
銀行將提單轉交給承運人，承運人再將保證函交給銀行。
同 abdicate, relinquish, submit（投降、放棄）

- surrender value ph.被保險人中途解約時的退休金
- indemnity n.賠償
94

1668.
surround [səˋraʊnd] [sur·round] **v** 包圍、圍住
Listen to the sounds of the summer that surround us.
仔細傾聽環繞我們的夏夜聲息。
同 encircle, enclose, encompass（圍住、圍繞）

- 字首：sur向下
  字尾：round圓圈
165

1669.
surrounding [səˋraʊndɪŋ] [sur·round·ing] **n** 環境 **a** 周圍的
The alms are from the surrounding countries, so they have been travelling for days.
救濟品來自鄰近的地區，在路途上要行駛數日。
同 ambient, circumfluent, circumvolutory（圍繞的）

- alms n.救濟品
131

1670.
survival [səˋvaɪvl] [sur·viv·al] **n** 倖存、殘存物
This industry depends for its survival on government subsidies.
這個行業靠政府津貼而得以維持。

- survival kit ph.救生背包
- survival of the fittest ph.適者生存
- 字首：sur在…之下
- 字根：viv生命
113

1671.
suspect [səˋspɛkt] [sus·pect] **v** 懷疑、猜想 **n** 嫌疑犯
I suspect that he is more or less involved in the affair.
我猜他和這件事多少有點牽連。

- 字首：su在…之下
  字根：spect看
- more or less ph.多少有些
- affair n.事件
143

1672.
suspend [səˋspɛnd] [sus·pend] **v** 懸掛、暫緩
Let us suspend judgment until we know all the facts.
讓我們在瞭解全部事實之前暫時不要作出判斷。
同 hang, sling, postpone（懸掛、延緩）

- suspended animation ph.假死
- suspended load ph.懸浮載
- suspended sentence ph.緩刑
181

1673.
suspense [sə`spɛns] [sus·pense] **n**擔心、懸而不決

He wished to make the most of the occasion, maintaining the suspense.

他想充分利用這場合保持緊張的局面。

🔄 **anxiety, concern, fear**（擔心、害怕）

136
- keep sb. in suspense ph.使擔心
- 字首：sus在…之下
  字根：pense懸掛
- occasion n.情況

1674.
sustain [sə`sten] [sus·tain] **v**支持、承受、忍受

It is well known that displaced workers sustain prolonged income losses while trying to find new jobs.

眾所周知，被解雇的工人在試圖找到新的職業的同時他們的收入會遭受長時期的損失。

🔄 **bear, endure, tolerate**（支持、忍受）

157
- 字首：sus向下
  字根：tain握、持
- displace v.免職
- prolong v.延長

1675.
switch [swɪtʃ] [switch] **n**開關、變更 **v**轉換、打開或關掉

Be sure to switch off the light when you leave the office.

你離開辦公室時務必把燈關掉。

🔄 **shift, swap, turn**（交換）

181
- switch off ph.關閉
- switch on開啟
- switch card ph.一種銀行發的信用卡
- switch-hitter n.在左右打擊位置都能擊球的打擊手

1676.
symbol [`sɪmbl̩] [sym·bol] **n**符號、象徵

If it does meet those standards, it can then use the name and advertising symbol, the logo, as it is called, for the group

如果（某方）符合標準，驗收合格方可使用此名稱和廣告標誌，即所謂商標。

177
- standard n.標準
- logo=logotype n.商標

1677.
symmetry [`sɪmɪtrɪ] [sym·me·try] **n**對稱、勻稱

What they did ask for was that we demand in negotiations the perfect symmetry.

他們要求的則是，在談判中要取得完全的對等。

104
- 字首：sym相同
  字根：metry測量
- perfect a.完整無缺的

1678.
sympathy [`sɪmpəθɪ] [sym·pa·thy] **n**同情、憐憫

A bond of sympathy developed between members of the group.

該團體的成員間產生了志同道合的凝聚力。

🔄 **compassion, mercy, sensitivity**（同情、憐憫）

🔄 **antipathy**（厭惡）

125
- sympathy strike ph.同情罷工
- 字首：sym相同
  字根：pathy感情
- bond n.聯結

S

1679.
symphony [`sɪmfənɪ] [sym·pho·ny] **n**交響樂

Beethoven's Ninth Symphony is a glorious piece of music.

貝多芬的第九交響曲是壯麗的音樂篇章。

57
- 字首：sym相同
  字根：phon音調
  字尾：y有…性質的
- glorious a.優美的

1680.
symposium [sɪm`pozɪəm] [sym·po·si·um] **n**討論會、宴會

The specialists and scholars present at the symposium come from all corners of the country.

出席研討會的專家學者們來自全國各地。

132
- 字首：sym相同
  字根：pos放置
  字尾：ium地方
- scholar n.學者

1681.

synchronous [ˋsɪŋkrənəs] 【syn·chro·nous】 **a** 同時發生的、同步的

In a synchronous counter all stages are triggered by a common clock.
在同步計算器中，所有觸發器均由同一個時鐘觸發。

• synchronous communication ph. 同步通訊
• Synchronous Connection ph. 同步連絡
• 字首：syn相同
• 字根：chron時間

`121`

1682.

synopsis [sɪˋnɑpsɪs] 【syn·op·sis】 **n** 概要、對照表

A new synopsis on the Aspirin Triad, authored by an international expert in this area, is posted on the WAO Web site this month.
本月在WAO的網站上我們上傳了一份由國際知名專家講述的關於阿司匹林三聯征的最新簡介。

`105`

1683.

synthesis [ˋsɪnθəsɪs] 【syn·the·sis】 **n** 綜合體、合成

Her novels are an odd synthesis of English reserve and Welsh emotionalism.
她的小說把英格蘭人的拘謹和威爾士人的情感外露很獨特地結合在一起。

同► combination, fusion, unification（結合、聯合）
反► analysis（分析）

• syntheses為其複數型
• 字首：syn相同
字根：thesis放置
• novel n.小說
• emotionalism n.多愁善感

`124`

MEMO

abbr 縮寫詞
a 形容詞
ad 副詞
aux 助動詞
conj 連接詞
n 名詞
num 數字
ph 片語
prep 介系詞
v 動詞
（美）美式用語
（英）英式用語
（法）法式用語

全書單字取材於：
①10本坊間新多益考試暢銷書籍
②50篇英文新聞、商業文章
③2005~2012年ETS TOEIC歷屆考古題
→ 總計約50,000個單字，以電腦統計出題率高達80%
　的實用單字1,800個

高頻率單字

> | T 家族 take off~turnover (MP3) 01-13

高 分 錦 囊

1684.
take off **ph** 起飛、移去
Come aboard quickly, the plane will take off in a minute.
快登機，飛機馬上就要起飛了。

`145`

1685.
tactic [ˈtæktɪk] 【 tac·tic 】 **n** 戰術、策略
Different circumstances call for different tactics.
不同的情勢需要不同的策略。

`73`
- 此單字多用於複數
- call for ph.需要

1686.
tardy [ˈtɑrdɪ] 【 tar·dy 】 **a** 遲到的、緩漫的
Too swift arrives as tardy as too slow.
欲速則不達。
同 delayed, late, overdue（延遲的）
反 prompt, quick（快的、敏捷的）

`103`
- arrive v.到達
- slow a.慢的

1687.
tariff [ˈtærɪf] 【 tar·iff 】 **n** 關稅、價目表 **v** 課以關稅
Removing an existing tariff would clearly displace workers in import-competing industries.
免除某種現有關稅顯然會使與進口競爭的工業中的工人失業。
同 duty, levy, tax（稅、稅款）

`124`
- tariff escalation ph.關稅級距
- import v.進口
- compete v.競爭

1688.
taxicab [ˈtæksɪˌkæb] 【 tax·i·cab 】 **n** 計程車
Each taxicab is fitted with a meter ticking off the fare due.
每輛計程車都有一個算出應付車費的計程表。

`71`
- 字首：taxi計程車
  字尾：cab計程車
- tick off ph.用記號標出

1689.
telephone [ˈtɛləˌfon] 【 tel·e·phone 】 **n** 電話 **v** 打電話
I'll be in the office all day, in case you telephone.
我今天將整日在辦公室，你若有事可以打電話過來。

`96`
- 字首：tele遠
  字尾：phone聲音
- telephone book ph.電話簿
- telephone booth ph.電話亭

1690.
television [ˈtɛləˌvɪʒən] 【 tel·e·vi·sion 】 **n** 電視、電視業
Television advertisers can exploit a captive audience.
電視廣告商能吸引觀眾。

`88`
- television license ph.【英】電視機許可證
- 字首：tele遠
- 字根：vis看
  字尾：ion事物

1691.
temporary [ˈtɛmpəˌrɛrɪ] 【 tem·po·rar·y 】 **a** 臨時的
n 臨時工、臨時雇員
They feel that you'd better announce a temporary suspension, anyhow.
總之，他們覺得你還是宣佈暫時停業較好。
同 momentary, passing, transient（暫時的）
反 eternal, lasting, permanent（持續的、永久的）

`157`
- 字首：tempor時間
  字尾：ary與…有關的
- suspension n.中止
- anyhow ad.無論如何

1692.

temper [ˈtɛmpɚ] [tem·per] **n**脾氣、情緒

Be patient. Don't lose your temper over matters.

忍著點，別為了一點小事發火。

同 character, mood（性情）

- be out of temper with sb. ph.對某人生氣
- get / go / fly / into a temper ph.發脾氣
- keep / control one's temper ph.不發火

1693.

temptation [tɛmpˈteʃən] [temp·ta·tion] **n**引誘、誘惑物

He had resisted temptations to immorality with strength of purpose that was creditable to him.

他曾經抵制了不道德行為的種種誘惑，而那種意志力是可以給他增光的。

- 字根：tempt企圖
  字尾：ation行為
- immorality n.不道德
- creditable a.可信的

1694.

tenant [ˈtɛnənt] [ten·ant] **n**房客、住戶 **v**租借

A clause in the agreement provides that the tenant shall bear the cost of all repairs to the building.

合約中有一條規定，房客將負擔修理房屋的一切費用。

同 dweller, inhabitant, resident（居民）

反 landlord n.屋主

- tenant farmer ph.佃農
- clause n.契約
- repair n.修復

1695.

tendency [ˈtɛndənsɪ] [ten·den·cy] **n**傾向、趨勢

There was an upward tendency in oil shares yesterday.

石油股票昨天有上漲的趨勢。

同 bent, disposition, proclivity（傾向）

- 字根：tend傾向
  字尾：ency性質
- upward a.升高的
- share n.費用

1696.

terminology [ˌtɝməˈnɑlədʒɪ] [ter·mi·nol·o·gy] **n**術語、專門用語

Loose terminology must be avoided.

應避免使用意義含糊的術語。

1697.

terminate [ˈtɝməˌnet] [ter·mi·nate] **v**結束、終止、解雇

It is said that the General Motors is going to terminate your contract.

據說通用汽車公司要解除和你訂的契約。

同 conclude, finish, stop（結束、終止）

反 lengthen（延長）

- 字根：termin結束
  字尾：ate進行一項行動

1698.

term [tɝm] [term] **n**條款、期限

After you decide to buy that car, you don't really care who finances it as long as the terms are competitive.

在決定購買汽車之後只要物有所值你不會在意為其籌錢。

同 duration, period, time（期間）

- term insurance ph.定期人壽保險
- term paper ph.學期研究報告
- competitive a.競爭的

1699.

territory [ˈtɛrəˌtorɪ] [ter·ri·to·ry] **n**領土、領域

No small territory to cover in a two-hour question period!

要在2小時之內回答這些問題可不簡單！

同 area, district, domain（領土、地區）

- 字根：ter土地
  字尾：it走動
  字尾：ory領域

T

1700.

theater [ˋθɪətɚ]【thea·ter】 **n** 戲院、戲劇（界）

The acoustics of this theater are admirable.

這個劇院的音響效果很好。

同 **hall, playhouse, stadium**（劇場）

- theater of the absurd
  ph.荒謬劇場
- theater-in-the-round
  ph.舞台起碼有兩面被席次包
  圍的現場
- acoustics n.音響效果

1701.

theme [θim]【theme】 **n** 主題、話題、題目

The main theme of this discussion was press censorship.

此討論的主題是新聞審查制度。

同 **subject, topic**（主題）

- theme park ph.主題樂園
- theme party ph.化裝舞會
- theme pub ph.以奇想主題
  佈置的酒吧
- theme restaurant ph.以奇
  想主題佈置的餐廳

1702.

ticket office **ph** 售票處

The ticket office is at the rear of the station concourse.

售票處在車站大廳的後部。

- concourse v.集合

1703.

thrift [θrɪft]【thrift】 **n** 節儉、繁茂

By practising thrift we can cut out a great deal of unnecessary expenditure.

通過節約我們可以省去大量不必要的開支。

同 **conservation, frugality, saving**（節省、儉省）
反 **waste**（浪費）

1704.

thrive [θraɪv]【thrive】 **v** 繁榮、興旺、茁壯成長

In addition, a stable financial and regulatory environment is needed if futures markets are to thrive.

此外，必須要有穩定的金融和規定制度的環境期貨市場才能興旺。

- in addition ph.另外
- stable a.穩定的
- regulatory a.管理的

1705.

time-out **n** 暫停、休息時間

A coach should call a time-out when his team loses three consecutive points.

當他的隊連失三分時就應叫暫停。

- coach n.教練
- consecutive a.連續不斷的

1706.

timetable [ˋtaɪmˌtebl̩]【time·ta·ble】 **n** 時間表、時刻表

The timetable is subject to change without notice.

本時刻表隨時可能改變不另行通知。

同 **list, program, schedule**（時刻表、時間表）

- 字首：time時間
  字尾：table圖表
- subject a.須經…的

1707.

tournament [ˋtɝnəmənt]【tour·na·ment】 **n** 錦標賽、比賽

Last tournament is open to amateur as well as professionals.

上次錦標賽不僅職業運動員可以參加，而且業餘運動員也可以參加。

同 **contest, game, tourney**（比賽）

- amateur n.業餘從事者
- as well as ph.不但…而且…
- professional n.職業選手

1708.

track record **ph** 過去的記錄、徑賽成績

The job needs someone with a good track record in investment.

這個工作需要的是一個良好投資記錄的人。

- track n.行蹤

121

1709.
trademark [ˋtredˏmɑrk] 【trade‧mark】 **n**商標、標記
v註冊商標

Goods bearing famous trademarks sell well.
標有名牌商標的產品暢銷。
⊕ brand, label, tag（商標、標記）

- 字首：trade貿易
字尾：mark標記

94

1710.
tradition [trəˋdɪʃən] 【tra‧di‧tion】 **n**傳統、慣例

It is a tradition that the young look after the old in my family.
在我家族裡，年輕的照顧年長的是一個傳統。
⊕ custom, folklore, usage（習俗、慣例）

- look after ph.照料

74

1711.
tranquility [trænˋkwɪlətɪ] 【tran‧quil‧li‧ty】 **n**平靜、寧靜、平穩

It needed all Monica's steady mildness to bear these attacks with tolerable tranquility.
幸虧莫妮卡從容不迫、柔和鎮定，好不容易才忍受了這些讒言誹語。

- steady a.平穩的
- mildness n.溫和
- tolerable v.忍受

117

1712.
transaction [trænˋzækʃən] 【trans‧ac‧tion】 **n**交易、辦理

In view of our longstanding business relationship, we can conclude the transaction at a discount.
鑒於你我雙方的長期貿易關係，我們可以以優惠的價格做成這筆交易。

- 字首：trans穿越
字尾：action行動
- longstanding a.長年的
- conclude v.決定
- discount n.折扣

143

1713.
transcend [trænˋsɛnd] 【tran‧scend】 **v**超越、優於

We must admit that they transcend, in relative importance, all the subsequent works.
可能我們必須承認，從相對重要性而言，他們的成就超過了後人的一切事業。

- 字首：trans穿過
字尾：scend攀爬
- relative a.相對的
- subsequent a.隨後的

194

1714.
transfer [trænsˋfɝ] 【trans‧fer】 **v n**調動、改變

He has been transferred to another department.
他已經被調往另一個部門。

- transfer syntax ph.資料形態敘述
- 字首：trans轉變
字根：fer帶來

187

1715.
transit [ˋtrænsɪt] 【tran‧sit】 **v n**運輸、通過

Bus and rapid transit fares are certain to rise following welfare settlements.
在福利問題解決之後，公共汽車和高速交通的費用肯定上漲。

- transit camp ph.臨時難民營
- transit lounge ph.轉機候機室
- transit visa ph.過境簽證
- 字首：trans橫過
字尾：it走動

T

191

1716.
transmission [trænsˋmɪʃən] 【trans‧mis‧sion】 **n**傳輸、傳送

The package was delayed in transmission.
這包裹在傳送中被耽誤了。
⊕ displacement, move, transfer（運輸、遷移）

- Transmission Control Protocol ph.電腦傳輸控制協定
- transmission electron microscope ph.透射式電子顯微鏡
- 字首：trans橫越

279

考來考去都考這些NEW TOEIC新多益單字

1717.
transparent [træns`pɛrənt] 【trans·par·ent】 **a**透明的、一目瞭然的

It was transparent that his pride was hurt.
顯然地，他的自尊心受到了傷害。

opaque（不透明的）

- 字首：transpar橫過
  字尾：ent…狀態的
- pride n.自尊心

`173`

1718.
transplant [træns`plænt] 【trans·plant】 **V**移植、移居

Adults are not flexible; they do not transplant comfortably to a new place.
成年人適應性不強，他們移居異地會感到不舒服。

graft, shift, transfer（移居、轉移）

- transplant operation ph.器官移植手術
- 字首：trans橫過
  字尾：plant種植
- flexible a.有彈性的
- comfortably ad.舒服地

`164`

1719.
transport [træns`port] 【trans·port】 **V**運輸 **n**運輸、交通工具

New York Transport runs extra trains during the rush-hour.
紐約運輸公司在交通高峰時間，增開加班列車。

conveyance, freightage, hauling（運輸）

- transport café ph. 【英】路邊小餐館
- Transport Layer ph.傳輸層
- transport ship ph.運輸船
- 字首：trans橫過
  字尾：port港口

`213`

1720.
trauma [`trɔmə] 【trau·ma】 **n**外傷、感情方面的創傷

It's the deepest trauma of his existence.
這在他的生命中是最慘重的一次打擊。

- existence n.生存

`57`

1721.
treaty [`tritɪ] 【trea·ty】 **n**條約、協議

A new clause was annexed to the treaty.
條約上附加了一項新條款。

agreement, concordat, contract（協定、契約）

- Treaty of Versailles ph.凡爾賽條約
- treaty port ph.根據條約開放之通商口岸

`181`

1722.
tremendous [trɪ`mɛndəs] 【tre·men·dous】 **a**巨大的、極度的、極好的

Last month saw a tremendous boost in profits.
上個月的利潤激增。

enormous, giant, immense（巨大的、極大的）

- boost n.提高
- profit n.利潤

`104`

1723.
trendy [`trɛndɪ] 【trend·y】 **a**時髦的、流行的 **n**追求時髦的人

People in big cities are easy to catch trendy information from different countries.
在大城市裡的人較容易得到來自各國家的流行資訊。

- 字根：trend趨勢
  字尾：y有…傾向的
- information n.資訊

`124`

1724.
triangle [`traɪˌæŋgḷ] 【tri·an·gle】 **n**三角形

The Changjiang River's "golden triangle" becomes a new investing hotspot.
長江金三角成為新的投資熱點。

- triangle trade ph.三角貿易
- 字首：tri三
  字尾：angle角度
- hotspot n.電腦熱度

`84`

280

1725.
triple [`trɪpl̩] 【 tri·ple 】 **a**三倍的

I received triple pay for my extra work.

我因超額工作得到三倍的報酬。

同 **ternate, treble, trinal**（三倍的）

- triple jump ph.三級跳遠
- triple measure ph.音樂三拍子
- triple play ph.棒球三殺
- 字首：tri三
  字根：ple折疊

`125`

1726.
triumph [`traɪəmf] 【 tri·umph 】 **v n**勝利、成功

I gloried in my triumph.

我因獲勝而洋洋得意。

同 **conquest, success, victory**（勝利、成功）

反 **defeat**（失敗）

- glory v.自豪

`114`

1727.
trophy [`trofɪ] 【 tro·phy 】 **n**戰利品、獎品

The defending champion Tony succeeded in retaining the trophy.

上屆冠軍東尼衛冕成功。

同 **award, laurels, prize**（戰利品、獎品）

- champion n.冠軍
- retain v.保留

`91`

1728.
troubleshooting [`trʌbl̩ˏʃutɪŋ] 【 trou·ble·shoot·ing 】

n疑難排解

Mike is an expert at troubleshooting.

麥可是位排解爭端的高手。

- 字首：trouble麻煩
  字尾：shooting發射

`86`

1729.
typist [`taɪpɪst] 【 typ·ist 】 **n**打字員

Don't forget to remind the typist to delete the last two sentences.

不要忘了提醒打字員把最後兩句話刪掉。

- 字首：type打字
  字尾：ist從事…的人
- delete v.刪除

`73`

1730.
turn down **v n**轉小、拒絕

Jessie, turn down the record player, please. I'm trying to read.

婕西，請把錄音機關小聲點。我想看書。

- turn down the thumb ph.表示反對

`164`

1731.
turnover [`tɜˏnˏovə] 【 turn·o·ver 】 **n**翻轉、營業額、人員替換率

That company has a fast turnover because of the poor wages.

那家公司因為薪水很少，所以員工流動得很快。

- 源自片語turn over
- turnover for the insured activity ph.
  受保證活動成交額
- turnover volume ph.
  營業額

`141`

T

MEMO

abbr 縮寫詞
a 形容詞
ad 副詞
aux 助動詞
conj 連接詞
n 名詞
num 數字
ph 片語
prep 介系詞
v 動詞
（美）美式用語
（英）英式用語
（法）法式用語

全書單字取材於：
①10本坊間新多益考試暢銷書籍
②50篇英文新聞、商業文章
③2005~2012年ETS TOEIC歷屆考古題
→ 總計約50,000個單字，以電腦統計出題率高達80%
　的實用單字1,800個

高頻率單字

U 家族 ultimately~utility

高 分 錦 囊

1732.
ultimately [ˋʌltəmɪtlɪ]【ul·ti·mate·ly】 **ad**最後、終極地
Ultimately all the starting material is converted into finished goods.
最後全部原料都轉變為成品。

• 字首：ult最後的
• convert v.轉變

1733.
umpire [ˋʌmpaɪr]【um·pire】 **v n**裁判、仲裁
The umpire's decision is usually final.
裁判員的裁決通常是不可改變的。
arbitrator, judge, mediator（仲裁人、裁判）

• arrive v.到達
• slow a.慢的

1734.
unanimous [juˋnænəməslɪ]【u·nan·i·mous】 **a**一致同意的、無意義的
The vote that followed, establishing the doctrine as official enterprise policy, was unanimous.
接下來進行的表決一致同意把這一原則正式奉為企業的方針。
agreed, concurrent, solid（一致同意的、無異議的）

• 字首：un單一
　字根 anim精神
　字尾：ous與…有關的
• doctrine n.政策
• official a.官方的

1735.
uncivilized [ʌnˋsɪvḷaɪzd]【un·civ·i·lized】 **a**野蠻的、未開化的
She can knock you down, which is uncivilized.
她可以迫使你屈服，但這太野蠻。
barbarous, bestial, savage（野蠻的）
civilized（文明的）

• 字首：un無、不
• knock down ph.擊倒

1736.
uncover [ʌnˋkʌvɚ]【un·cov·er】 **v**揭開、發現
Next year we need to concentrate on examining the modern corporate system established in listed companies to uncover problems and solve them.
明年要重點檢查上市公司建立現代企業制度的情況，找出存在問題認真加以解決。
disclose, expose, reveal（暴露）
cover（覆蓋）

• 字首：un無、不
　字尾：cover覆蓋
• concentrate v.專心
• corporate a.公司的
• establish v.建立

1737.
underdeveloped [ˋʌndɚdɪˋvɛləpt]【un·der·de·vel·oped】
a不發達的、發展不完全
The underdeveloped country is active its diplomacy with other countries to solve its financial crisis.
這不發達的國家正積極拓展外交以解決國內的財政危機。

• 字首：under在…之下
• diplomacy n.外交
• crisis n.危機

1738.

underestimate [ˋʌndɚˋɛstəˏmet] 【 un·der·es·ti·mate 】
v **n** 估計不足、低估

Don't underestimate the difficulties of the program.

不要低估了這專案的艱鉅性。

🔄 **contemn, disdain, underrate**（低估、輕視）

🔄 **overestimate**（高估）

- 字首：under在⋯之下
  字尾：estimate v.估計
- difficulty n.困難

151

1739.

underline [ʌndɚˋlaɪn] 【un·der·line 】 **v** 在⋯的下面劃線、強調

The illustration underlines the consequences of bad management.

這個例證突顯了管理不好的後果。

🔄 **highlight, underscore, stress**（劃線在下面）

- 字首：under在⋯之下
  字尾：line線
- illustration n.說明
- consequence n.結果

174

1740.

underling [ˋʌndɚlɪŋ] 【 un·der·ling 】 **n** 下屬、部下

He seemed to be a leader, not an underling, now.

他現在像是個領導者而不是個下屬了。

94

1741.

undermine [ʌndɚˋmaɪn] 【un·der·mine 】 **v** 暗中破壞

We are trying to undermine his position.

我們在試圖損傷他的地位。

🔄 **destroy, sabotage, weaken**（暗中破壞）

- 字首：under在⋯之下
  字尾：mine破壞

121

1742.

undertake [ʌndɚˋtek] 【 un·der·take 】 **v** 保證、承擔、試圖

I undertake to replace any product not up to the specifications.

產品不合規格我保證退換。

🔄 **agree, contract, promise**（同意、保證）

- 字首：under在⋯之下
  字尾：take拿取
- specification n.規格

131

1743.

undervalue [ʌndɚˋvælju] 【 un·der·val·ue 】 **v** 低估、輕視

Don't undervalue Jason's contribution to the research.

不要低估了傑森在研究工作中的貢獻。

🔄 **overvalue**（對⋯評價過高）

- 字首：under在⋯之下
  字尾：value評價
- contribution n.貢獻

97

1744.

unfortunate [ʌnˋfɔrtʃənɪt] 【un·for·tu·nate】 **a** 不幸的、可惜的 **a** 不幸的人

I hope that this unfortunate circumstance will not deprive me of my position.

我希望這不幸的事件不會導致我被革職。

🔄 **ill-fated, unlucky**（不幸的）

🔄 **fortunate**（幸運的）

- deprive of ph.使喪失

104

1745.

uniform [ˋjunəˏfɔrm] 【 u·ni·form 】 **a** 相同的、一致的 **n** 制服

The staff at this factory wear uniform clothing.

這家工廠的員工穿統一的制服。

🔄 **balanced, even, symmetrical**（相同的、一致的）

🔄 **various**（不同的）

- Uniform Resource Locator ph.電腦一致資源定址器
- 字首：uni單一
  字尾：form形狀
- clothing n.總稱衣著

132

U

1746.
unique [ju`nik] 【u·nique】 adj 獨一無二的、唯一的、稀罕的

The developing nation's economic resurgence was based on a unique set of institutions.

這發展中的國家在經濟復甦上有一套獨特的制度作為基礎。

同 **single, sole, solitary**（唯一的、單獨的）

- unique fauna and flora ph.奇花異草
- resurgence n.復活
- institution n.制度

1747.
unity [`junəti] 【u·ni·ty】 n 團結、單一性、個體

There is a requirement for great unity in the corporation.

這公司有必要加強團結。

同 **highlight, underscore, stress**（劃線在下面）

- requirement n.需要
- corporation n.公司

1748.
unprecedented [ʌn`prɛsə,dɛntɪd] 【un·prec·e·dent·ed】

adj 無前例的、空前的

House prices raised up and up to an unprecedented level.

房價不斷地急劇上升，達到了空前的水準。

同 **exceptional, extraordinary, unduplicated**（無前例的、空前的）
反 **precedented**（有前例可循的）

- 字首：un無、不
  字首：pre事先
  字根：ced前進
  字尾：ent…狀態的

1749.
untoward [ʌn`toəd] 【un·to·ward】 adj 不幸的、倔強的

We'll come if nothing untoward happens.

我們要是沒有特殊情況一定會出席。

1750.
unusual [ʌn`juʒʊəl] 【un·u·su·al】 adj 不平常的、獨特的

The work is always urgent, but overtime payment is unusual.

雖然工作總是刻不容緩，但加班費則很優厚。

同 **odd, queer, rare**（不平常的、稀有的）
反 **usual**（平常的）

- urgent a.緊急的
- overtime n.超時

1751.
upgrade [`ʌp`gred] 【up·grade】 v 升級、提高品質、上坡

Her main errand is to determine how we can best upgrade the services we offer our major clients.

她的主要任務是確定如何最大幅度地提高我們對主要顧客的服務品質。

反 **downgrade**（下坡）

- upgrade fever ph.電腦升級熱
- 字首：up向上
  字根：grade級數
- errand n.任務
- determine v.決定

1752.
uphold [ʌp`hold] 【up·hold】 v 支持、維護、舉起

It is necessary to uphold diversity of the world and respect diversity of civilization.

應該堅持世界多樣化，尊重文明多樣性。

同 **bolster, corroborate, support**（支撐、支持）
反 **subvert**（推翻、破壞）

- 字首：up向上
  字首：hold握持
- diversity n.多樣化
- civilization n.文明

1753.
upset [ʌp`sɛt] 【up·set】 v 打翻 adj 心煩的

That behavior would upset the wage differential.

這樣做會打亂工資級別制度。

同 **capsize, overturn, unsettle**（使倒下、翻倒）

- upset price ph.拍賣的低價
- differential a.差別的

1754.
up-to-date a最新的、現代的

- **statistics n.**統計資料
- **unemployment n.**失業
- **favorable a.**順利的

An up-to-date statistics reports that the unemployment takes a favorable turn in recent months.

一份最新統計報告指出，失業狀況在最近幾個月有漸漸好轉。

⬆ **advanced, contemporary, modern**（現代的、最新的）
⬇ **out-of-date**（舊式的）

1755.
urban [ˋɝbən]【ur·ban】a城市的

- **urban decay ph.**城市衰落
- **urban forest ph.**城市森林
- **urban renewal ph.**都市環境改造
- **urban sprawl ph.**都市擴張
- **urban tribe ph.**都市族群
- **phenomenon n.**現象

It's a common phenomenon that more and more people are migrating to urban areas.

越來越多的人向市區遷移是個普遍現象。

⬆ **civic, metropolitan, municipal**（城市的）
⬇ **rural, rustic**（鄉下的）

1756.
urgent [ˋɝdʒənt]【ur·gent】a緊急的、催促的

- **chore n.**困難的工作
- **complicated n.**複雜的

The chore is very urgent and complicated and colleagues all work together.

這工作非常複雜且緊急，所有員工共同進行。

⬆ **imperative, motivating**（緊急的、急迫的）

1757.
usher [ˋʌʃɚ]【ush·er】n引座員、招待員 v引領

- **usher in ph.**領進、引進

The usher took him to his seat.

招待員引導他找到了座位。

⬆ **conduct, escort, guide**（引領）

1758.
utility [juˋtɪlətɪ]【u·til·i·ty】n公用事業公司、有用之物 a實用的、多種用途的

- **utility person ph.**劇務人員
- **utility pole ph.**電線杆
- **utility room ph.**洗衣間
- **territory n.**領域

The utility was entering a new and cutting-edge territory.

公司進入了一個陌生且尖端的領域。

⬆ **adaptability, helpfulness, usability**（有用、實用）

U

abbr 縮寫詞
a 形容詞
ad 副詞
aux 助動詞
conj 連接詞
n 名詞
num 數字
ph 片語
prep 介系詞
v 動詞
（美）美式用語
（英）英式用語
（法）法式用語

全書單字取材於：
①10本坊間新多益考試暢銷書籍
②50篇英文新聞、商業文章
③2005~2012年ETS TOEIC歷屆考古題
→ 總計約50,000個單字，以電腦統計出題率高達80%
　 的實用單字1,800個

高頻率單字

V 家族 vacant~voyage

 01-14

高 分 錦 囊

1759.
vacant [ˋvekənt] 【va·cant】 **a** 空的、未被佔用的
Vacant positions can be made known through the medium of the web.
職位空缺可借由網站公佈於眾。
同 empty, desolate, unoccupied（空的、未被佔用的）
反 full（滿的）

> **147**
> • vacant lot ph.空地
> • vacant possession ph. 空屋
> • 字根：vac空的 字尾：ant…狀態的
> • medium n.媒介

1760.
vague [veg] 【vague】 **a** 模糊不清的、含糊的
I should not make vague promises.
我不該作含糊不清的承諾。
同 dim, faint, shadowy（模糊不清的）
反 clear, district（清楚的）

> **124**
> • 字根：vag走動

1761.
vain [ven] 【vain】 **a** 徒然的、無益的、自負的
We tried in vain to get into contact with the local branch.
我們試圖與當地分部取得聯絡，但沒有成功。
同 futile, ineffectual, unsuccessful（徒然的、無益的）
反 effective, effectual（有效的）

> **146**
> • in vain ph.徒勞
> • contact n.聯繫

1762.
valid [ˋvælɪd] 【val·id】 **a** 有根據的、有效的
The ticket is valid for two months.
這票兩個月內有效。
同 effective, legal, true（合法的、有效的）
反 fallacious, false, invalid（無效的）

> **181**
> • 字根：val強力 字尾：id引起…狀態的

1763.
variation [͵vɛrɪˋeʃən] 【var·i·a·tion】 **n** 變化、差異
Production quotas, budget constraints, etc. might restrict the variation of the variables.
生產定額、預算限制等等可以限制變數的變化範圍。

> **174**
> • variation margin ph.變動 保證金
> • 字根：vari變 字尾：ation性質
> • constraint n.限制
> • variable n.變量

1764.
vegetarian [͵vɛdʒəˋtɛrɪən] 【veg·e·tar·i·an】 **a** 素食的
n 素食者
I opened a vegetarian restaurant in my hometown.
我在家鄉開了一間素菜餐廳。

> **75**
> • 字根：veget蔬菜 字尾：arian信仰者
> • hometown n.家鄉

1765.
vehicle [ˋviɪkl̩] 【ve·hi·cle】 **n** 交通工具、傳播媒介
Electronic gauges attached to various parts of the vehicle measure impact forces.
電子儀錶裝在汽車不同的部件上測量各種撞擊力。
同 carriage, conveyance（運載工具、車輛）

> **104**
> • vehicle guide system ph.行車導引繫統
> • Vehicle Identification Number ph.車輛識別號碼
> • vehicle requirement planning ph.車輛需求規劃
> • gauge n.測量儀器

1766.

vendor [`vɛndɚ] 【vend·or】 **n**小販、賣主、自動售貨機

When you visit the night market, you'll see a lot of vendors along the street.

當你逛夜市時，你會發現路邊有很多攤販。

⑩ hawker, peddler（小販）

⑫ vendee（買主）

- 亦可拼寫為vender
- **vendor scheduler ph.**
  採購計劃員
- **vendor scheduling ph.**
  採購計劃法

1767.

ventilate [ˈvɛntʃˌet] 【ven·ti·late】 **v**公開討論、使通風

Delegates are asked not to ventilate delegation problems outside this meeting.

要求代表們在這次會議之外勿公開討論本代表團的問題。

⑩ deliberate, discuss（自由討論）

108

- 字根：vent風
  字尾：ate進行一項行動
- **delegate n.**會議代表
- **delegation n.**代表團

1768.

venture [ˈvɛntʃɚ] 【ven·ture】 **v n**冒險、投機

The joint venture is integrated into the parent's management system.

合資企業的管理業務全部納入母公司的管理系統。

⑩ adventure, undertaking（冒險、投機活動）

143

- **venture capital ph.**冒險資本
- **venture capitalist ph.**風險資本家
- 字根：vent來
  字尾：ure行為
- **joint venture ph.**合資

1769.

verdict [ˈvɝdɪkt] 【ver·dict】 **n**裁決

We are in no condition to give a verdict on the matter.

我們沒有資格就這件事作出判決。

⑩ decree, determination, judgement（裁決、裁定）

126

- 字根：ver真實
  字尾：dict說
- **condition n.**條件

1770.

verify [ˈvɛrəˌfaɪ] 【ver·i·fy】 **v**核對、證實

Please verify each item you have pricked down.

請把你已用小記號標出的每一個項目核對一下。

⑩ confirm, testify, validate（證明、證實）

⑫ guess（猜測）

152

- 字根：ver真實
  字尾：ify使成為
- **item n.**項目
- **prick v.**標出

1771.

versatile [ˈvɝsətl] 【ver·sa·tile】 **a**引多才多藝的、多功能的

Only a versatile person can settle such a complex problem.

只有多才多藝的人才能解決這麼複雜的問題。

⑩ competent, talented, skilled（多才多藝的）

98

- 字根：vers轉變
  字尾：ile易於…的
- **complex a.**複雜的

1772.

vertical [ˈvɝtɪkl] 【ver·ti·cal】 **a**垂直的

The southern side of the mountain is almost vertical.

這座山的南側幾乎是垂直的。

⑩ perpendicular, standing, upright（垂直的、豎的）

⑫ horizontal（水平的）

103

- **vertical circle ph.**垂直圈
- **vertical integration ph.**
  垂直整合
- **vertical union ph.**全體工人的工會

V

1773.

via [`vaɪə] 【vi·a】 **prep**經由、通過

My boss flew to New York via Hong Kong.

我老闆經香港飛往紐約。

201

- **via crucis ph.**苦難之路
- **via media ph.**中庸之道

1774.
vigorous [ˋvɪgərəs] 【vig·or·ous】 a 強有力的、精力充沛的
The supervisor of my department makes a vigorous speech.
我部門長官發表了一場強有力的演說。
forceful, mighty, potent (強有力的)

- 字首：vigor活力
  字尾：ous充滿…的
- supervisor n.長官
- speech n.演說

1775.
VIP abbr 重要人物
Aim at VIP high level customers of company offers a specialized service.
針對公司貴賓高端使用者群提供專門服務。

- 即very important person 的縮寫
- service n.服務

1776.
virus [ˋvaɪrəs] 【vi·rus】 n 病毒、毒害
Researchers have isolated the virus.
研究人員已經把這種病毒隔離起來。

- virus protection ph.防毒軟體
- virus signature ph.病毒碼
- virus spam mail ph.病毒垃圾郵件，亦可以v-spam email表示

1777.
vital [ˋvaɪtl] 【vi·tal】 a 必需的、重要的 n 重要器官、要害
Their support is vital for our project.
他們的支援對我們的計畫是不可或缺的。
essential, fundamental, necessary (必需的、不可少的)

- vital capacity ph.肺活量
- vital signs ph.脈搏
- vital statistics ph.生命的統計
- 字根：vit生命
  字尾：al與…有關的

1778.
vivid [ˋvɪvɪd] 【viv·id】 a 逼真的、鮮豔的、活潑的
The anxiety she felt about the future is still vivid in her mind.
那種前途渺茫的焦慮，她至今仍然歷歷在目。
brilliant, glaring, splendid (鮮明的、生動的)
dull (不鮮明的)

- 字根：viv活
  字尾：id…狀態的
- anxiety n.焦慮

1779.
violin [ˌvaɪəˋlɪn] 【vi·o·lin】 n 小提琴、小提琴手
She's the first violin at Vienna Philharmonic
她是維也納愛樂交響樂團的第一小提琴手。

- 字根：vers轉變
  字尾：ile易於…的
- complex a.複雜的

1780.
vocational [voˋkeʃənl] 【vo·ca·tion·al】 a 職業的
The bill provided traineeships in vocational rehabilitation.
公司招聘了一批新手，預算裡要增加培訓費這一項。

- vocational school ph.職業學校
- vocational training ph.職業訓練
- rehabilitation n.更新

1781.
volleyball [ˋvɑlɪˌbɔl] 【vol·ley·bal】 n 排球
Volleyball is growing in popularity in America.
在美國愛打排球的人越來越多了。

- 字首：volley發射
  字尾：ball球
- popularity n.普及

1782.
volume [ˋvɑljəm] 【vol·ume】 n 卷、冊、量、額
Both imports and exports continue to grow in volume.
進出口量繼續增長。
amount, capacity, proportion (容積、量)

1783.
voluntary [`vɑlən͵tɛrɪ] 【vol·un·tar·y】 **a** 自願的、有意的

About half of one's salary had to be earmarked for voluntary subscription.

每人的工資約有一半得留起來付各種各樣的志願捐獻。

🔵 **intentional, premeditated, purposeful**（自願的、自發的）
🔴 **accidental, compulsory, involuntary**（意外的、強制的）

• voluntary liquidation **ph.**無償產權處置
• voluntary muscle **ph.** 隨意肌
• 字根：volunt意志
  字尾：ary有…傾向的
• earmark **v.**標誌
• subscription **n.**捐款

1784.
voucher [`vaʊtʃɚ] 【vouch·er】 **n** 保證書、證書、收據

What's their voucher number?

他們的訂單號碼是多少?

73

1785.
voyage [`vɔɪɪdʒ] 【voy·age】 **v n** 旅行、航行

The voyage from America to France used to take almost two months.

從美國到法國的航行過去差不多要花二個月時間。

🔵 **cruise, navigate, journey**（航海、航行）

MEMO

V

高頻率單字

W 家族 waive~write-up

高 分 錦 囊

1786.

waive [wev]【waive】 **V** 撤回、擱置

We have decided to waive the age-limit for applicants in his case.

針對他的情況，我們決定免除申請人年齡限制。

1787.

warehouse [ˋwɛrˌhaʊs]【ware·house】 **n** 倉庫、【英】批發店

As a high turnover warehouse we operate 12 hours a day, moving inventory in and out.

作為一周轉率很高的倉庫，我們一天工作12小時把庫存貨物搬進搬出。

同 depository, depot, storehouse（倉庫）

- warehouse club ph. 批發店
- warehouse supermarket ph. 倉儲式超市
- 字首：ware器皿 字尾：house房子
- inventory n.存貨

1788.

warranty [ˋwɔrəntɪ]【war·ran·ty】 **n** 保證書、理由

The product comes with three year warranty.

這產品有三年的保固期。

1789.

wealth [wɛlθ]【wealth】 **n** 財富、豐富

Taxation on wealth typically involves personal and corporate taxes.

財產稅一般針對個人和公司的財產。

同 abundance, fortune, prosperity（財富、豐富）
反 poverty（貧窮）

- wealth elasticity of demand ph.財富需求彈性
- wealth gap ph.貧富差距
- taxation n.課稅
- involve v.包含
- personal a.個人的

1790.

wholesale [ˋholˌsel]【whole·sale】 **V n** 批發、批售

They wholesale the T-shirts at $8 each.

他們以每件8美元的價格批發出售這些T恤。

反 retail（零售）

- wholesale price ph. 批發價格
- whole price index ph. 基售物價指數
- 字首：whole全部 字尾：sale銷售

1791.

withdraw [wɪðˋdrɔ]【with·draw】 **V** 提取、撤回、退出

I want to withdraw 300 dollars from my deposit account.

我要從我的定期存款中領取300美元。

同 deduct, extract, recede（取消、撤退）
反 deliver, disperse（傳送、解散）

- deposit account ph.儲蓄存款
- withdrawal n.提款

1792.

withhold [wɪðˋhold]【with·hold】 **V** 阻擋、保留

Visas were withheld from some delegates of the delegation.

代表團的一些成員被拒發簽證。

同 keep, preserve, reserve（保留）

- withhold-withheld-withheld
- visa n.簽證

1793.
workmanship [ˋwɝkmənˌʃɪp] 【 work·man·ship 】

74

n 工藝品、手藝

They've received a lot of complaints of bad workmanship.
很多人向他們投訴產品工藝低劣。

• complaint n.抱怨

1794.
worthwhile [ˋwɝθˋhwaɪl] 【worth·while】 **a** 值得花時間的、有
真實價值的

123

It's worthwhile taking the trouble to explain a job fully to new colleague.
給新同事詳細解釋一下工作要求費點事也是值得的。

• 字首：worth值得
　字尾：while一段時間
• explain v.解釋
• colleague n.同事

1795.
write-up [ˋraɪtˌʌp] 【write-up】 **n** 報導、評論

137

There is a brief write-up and some drawings.
那裡有一份簡單的文字介紹和一些圖樣。

• brief a.簡短的
• drawing n.圖形

MEMO

W

295

MEMO

X/Y

abbr 縮寫詞
a 形容詞
ad 副詞
aux 助動詞
conj 連接詞
n 名詞
num 數字
ph 片語
prep 介系詞
v 動詞
（美）美式用語
（英）英式用語
（法）法式用語

全書單字取材於：
①10本坊間新多益考試暢銷書籍
②50篇英文新聞、商業文章
③2005~2012年ETS TOEIC歷屆考古題
→ 總計約50,000個單字，以電腦統計出題率高達80%
　的實用單字1,800個

高頻率單字

▶ | X/Y 家族 xerox~yield

高 分 錦 囊

1796.
xerox [ˋzɪrɑks] 【xer·ox】 **V** 影印
I cannot take it home, but I can xerox what I need.
我不能帶它回家，但可以影印我需要的內容。

93
- Xerox machine ph.影印機
- Xerox Network System ph.Xerox網路系統

1797.
yield [jild] 【yield】 **V** **N** 產生、結果、服從
They must do everything to rise the per unit yield.
他們要千方百計提高單位面積產量。
同 furnish, provide, produce（產生、供給）

157
- yield average ph.收益優勢
- yield maintenance ph.收益維護
- yield the palm to sb.向某人認輸
- yield to ph.屈服

MEMO

298

試題篇

NEW TOEIC TEST
新多益全真模擬試題

LISTENING TEST

In the Listening Test, you will be asked to demonstrate how well you understand spoken English. The entire Listening Test will last approximately 45 minutes. There are four parts, and directions are given for each part. You must mark your answers on the separate answer sheet. Do not write your answers in the test book.

PART 1

Directions: For each question in this part, you will hear four statements about a picture in your test book. When you hear the statements, you must select the one statement that best describes what you see in the picture. Then find the number of the question on your answer sheet and mark your answer. The statements will not be printed in your test book and will be spoken only one time.

Sample:

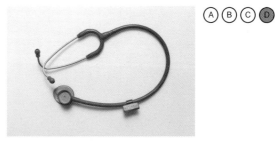

Statement (D), "It's a stethoscope." is the best description of the picture, so you should select answer (D) and mark it on your answer sheet.

1.

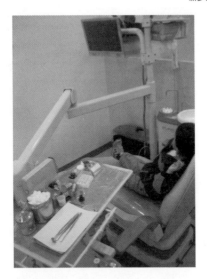

2.

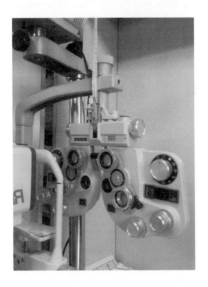

3.

4.

5.

6.

7.

8.

9.

10.

PART 2

Directions: You will hear a question or statement and three responses spoken in English. They will be spoken only one time and will not be printed in your test book. Select the best response to the question or statement and mark the letter (A), (B), or (C) on your answer sheet.

You will hear: Where is the General manager's room?

You will also hear: (A) To meet the new director.

(B) It's the first room on the right.

(C) Yes, at two o'clock.

Ⓐ Ⓑ Ⓒ

The best response to the question "Where is the General manager's room?" is choice (B), "It's the first room on the right," so (B) is the correct answer. You should mark answer (B) on your answer sheet.

---

11. Mark your answer on your answer sheet. Ⓐ Ⓑ Ⓒ

12. Mark your answer on your answer sheet. Ⓐ Ⓑ Ⓒ

13. Mark your answer on your answer sheet. Ⓐ Ⓑ Ⓒ

14. Mark your answer on your answer sheet. Ⓐ Ⓑ Ⓒ

15. Mark your answer on your answer sheet. Ⓐ Ⓑ Ⓒ

16. Mark your answer on your answer sheet. Ⓐ Ⓑ Ⓒ

17. Mark your answer on your answer sheet. Ⓐ Ⓑ Ⓒ

18. Mark your answer on your answer sheet. Ⓐ Ⓑ Ⓒ

19. Mark your answer on your answer sheet. Ⓐ Ⓑ Ⓒ

20. Mark your answer on your answer sheet. (A) (B) (C)

21. Mark your answer on your answer sheet. (A) (B) (C)

22. Mark your answer on your answer sheet. (A) (B) (C)

23. Mark your answer on your answer sheet. (A) (B) (C)

24. Mark your answer on your answer sheet. (A) (B) (C)

25. Mark your answer on your answer sheet. (A) (B) (C)

26. Mark your answer on your answer sheet. (A) (B) (C)

27. Mark your answer on your answer sheet. (A) (B) (C)

28. Mark your answer on your answer sheet. (A) (B) (C)

29. Mark your answer on your answer sheet. (A) (B) (C)

30. Mark your answer on your answer sheet. (A) (B) (C)

31. Mark your answer on your answer sheet. (A) (B) (C)

32. Mark your answer on your answer sheet. (A) (B) (C)

33. Mark your answer on your answer sheet. (A) (B) (C)

34. Mark your answer on your answer sheet. (A) (B) (C)

35. Mark your answer on your answer sheet. (A) (B) (C)

36. Mark your answer on your answer sheet. (A) (B) (C)

37. Mark your answer on your answer sheet. (A) (B) (C)

38. Mark your answer on your answer sheet. (A) (B) (C)

39. Mark your answer on your answer sheet. (A) (B) (C)

40. Mark your answer on your answer sheet. (A) (B) (C)

PART 3

Directions: You will hear some conversations between two people. You will be asked to answer three questions about what the speakers say in each conversation. Select the best response to each question and mark the letter (A), (B), (C), or (D) on your answer sheet. The conversations will be spoken only one time and will not be printed in your test book.

41. What was the fundraiser for?
   A)   A school
   B)   A hospital
   C)   An orphanage
   D)   A corporation

42. What disappointed the man?
   A)   The weakness of the economy
   B)   IntelliCorp just cut 30,000 workers
   C)   The orphanage was forced to close
   D)   They didn't raise as much money as they hoped.

43. What does the woman imply led to the disappointing fundraiser?
   A)   Recent job cuts and the weakness of the economy.
   B)   Chicago is experiencing an economic boom.
   C)   It was poorly organized.
   D)   People didn't care much about orphanages.

44. What will the man and the woman go on Saturday?
   A)   To a movie
   B)   To a jazz concert
   C)   To dinner and a classical music concert
   D)   To a Mexican restaurant

45. What do they decide to do before the concert?

    A)   Get dinner in Little India

    B)   Get dinner in Little Italy

    C)   Get dinner in Chinatown

    D)   Make a traditional Indian dinner

46. What does the woman imply she doesn't like?

    A)   Foreign food

    B)   Indian food

    C)   Mexican food

    D)   Very hot and spicy food

47. What problem does the woman raise?

    A)   Their expenses have gone up.

    B)   Their taxes have gone up.

    C)   Their landlord has sold their building.

    D)   Their landlord is demanding that they move next month.

48. What does the man imply they should do?

    A)   Buy the building

    B)   Sell the building

    C)   Take out a loan

    D)   Raise their prices or find a cheaper location

49. Why does the woman think they should look for a cheaper location?

    A)   They should buy their own building.

    B)   They can't keep raising prices.

    C)   The building needs to be renovated.

    D)   Because the building will be sold soon.

50. What does the man ask the woman to do?

    A)   Lower her prices

    B)   Send him some samples

    C)   Send his order by overnight messenger

    D)   Change the design

51. What reason does the woman give for not having sent out the samples?
A) She didn't receive his order.
B) She already sent them out.
C) She forgot.
D) His company has not paid yet.

52. What does the woman say she'll do?
A) Lower the price
B) Redesign the lamps
C) Talk to her purchasing team
D) Send them out by overnight messenger today

53. What does the woman start by doing?
A) Apologizing
B) Giving a presentation
C) Giving justification for missing work
D) Defending herself against an accusation

54. What is the man's attitude towards her coming late?
A) Angry
B) Suspicious
C) Understanding
D) Indignant

55. How were the sales figures this quarter?
A) Very poor
B) Very good
C) They fell by over 12%
D) Stagnant

56. What can be inferred about the woman?
    A) She just returned to her office.
    B) She has just spoken with Mr. Prescott.
    C) She just placed an order.
    D) She is just leaving for the day.

57. When was the order supposed to arrive?
    A) At the end of last week
    B) Three weeks ago
    C) At the beginning of last month
    D) Two months ago

58. What will the man probably do next?
    A) Re-order the necessary parts
    B) Write a check to pay for the order
    C) Visit his company's warehouse
    D) Inquire about the shipment

59. How many times has the man apparently made the same request before?
    A) None
    B) Once
    C) Two times
    D) Three times

60. What does the man say about his family?
    A) Most of them work in the professions.
    B) He hasn't been able to meet them recently.
    C) He prefers not to talk about the situation.
    D) Most of them have never read his books.

61. What does the woman tell the man?
    A) She has some flexibility about the deadline.
    B) She must confer with her marketing department.
    C) She doesn't have time to review his manuscript.
    D) She may not be able to publish his work.

62. Who is the man?
   A) A flight attendant
   B) A customer service agent
   C) A baggage handler
   D) A ground staff member

63. What is the woman's problem?
   A) The baggage she wants to check is too large.
   B) Her suitcase has been damaged by the airline.
   C) She neglected to put her box through security.
   D) She has too many pieces of luggage.

64. What does the man suggest the woman do?
   A) Pay an additional service charge
   B) Try to book a ticket for a later flight
   C) Shift some items into her carry-on bag
   D) File a claim for reimbursement

65. Who is the woman?
   A) A job applicant
   B) A potential employer
   C) A school principal
   D) A language instructor

66. Why did the man first go to Thailand?
   A) To take a vacation
   B) To work in personnel
   C) To get a teaching job
   D) To visit a friend

67. How did the man get his first job in marketing?

    A) Through a connection with a previous student

    B) By using his university career placement center

    C) By answering a job ad in a business magazine

    D) Through the recommendation of his Marketing professor

68. What had the man asked the woman to do?

    A) Conduct a financial review

    B) Make some travel arrangements

    C) Preparing a marketing report

    D) Contact the phone company

69. What can be inferred about the man?

    A) He is launching a new product.

    B) He is about to take a trip.

    C) He is negotiating a tax payment.

    D) He is about to make some personnel changes.

70. What does the woman recommend to the man?

    A) He should consider some cost-cutting measures.

    B) He should concentrate on increasing earnings.

    C) He ought to return an important telephone call.

    D) He ought to find a new tax accountant.

PART 4

Directions: You will hear some short talks given by a single speaker. You will be asked to answer three questions about what the speaker says in each short talk. Select the best response to each question and mark the letter (A), (B), (C), or (D) on your answer sheet. The talks will be spoken only one time and will not be printed in your test book.

71. What type of merchandise does the store sell?
A) Dining ware and cooking utensils only
B) Furniture for the office
C) Garden accessories
D) Furniture and accessories for bedrooms, bathrooms and kitchens

72. What types of discounts will be offered?
A) Everything in the store will be 20 to 40% off.
B) Select merchandise will be 20 to 40% off.
C) Only bed and bath ware will be 20 to 40% off.
D) Only kitchen appliances will be 20 to 40% off.

73. In addition to discounts, what is the store offering customers?
A) Greater quantities than before
B) Their usual low prices
C) Interest free credit for one year, and free delivery
D) 5% off when they pay with cash

74. What is the main subject of the announcement?
A) The loss of jobs in Florida
B) Various strategies for encouraging business growth
C) Incentives introduced by the legislature to encourage business growth
D) Film and TV production in Florida

75 What do the bills that passed in the Florida legislature on Friday do?
A) Promote corporation between universities and corporations.
B) Allocate funds to promote business
C) Give tax cuts to low income residents
D) Give tax cuts to the tourism industry

76. How will the state entice film production companies to shoot films and TV series in the state?
A) By paying their salaries
B) By providing free use of camera and lighting equipment
C) By providing free health care and insurance
D) Through tax cuts and the free use of state services

77. Who is the intended audience of the announcement?
A) Delta Airlines ground staff
B) A group of people waiting for a flight to arrive
C) A group of people waiting for a flight to depart
D) Passenger on Delta Airlines Flight 433

78. Why has the flight been delayed?
A) Due to a problem with passengers who deboarded at LAX
B) Due to a problem at LA
C) Due to a technical problem with the landing gear
D) Due to bad weather in Japan

79. What does the airline offer to family and friends waiting for the flight?
A) A discount on coffee and donuts at a café nearby
B) Free coffee and donuts
C) A discount on their next flight
D) Free coffee and donuts on their next Delta Airlines flight

80. What is the speaker doing?
A) Describing a product
B) Describing duties
C) Explaining a problem
D) Explaining how to use something

81. Who is most probably listening to the talk?
   A) A new salesperson
   B) A new accountant
   C) A new machine
   D) A new secretary

82. What is the first thing the listener has to do in the morning?
   A) Make a pot of coffee
   B) Check the mailbox
   C) Turn on the copier
   D) Answer the e-mail from clients

83. Where is this announcement most likely being made?
   A) On an airplane
   B) In an airport
   C) On a boat
   D) On a bus

84. What should passengers who remain seated do?
   A) Refrain from smoking
   B) Unbuckle their seatbelts
   C) Watch a movie
   D) Keep their seatbelt fastened

85. What is the government worried about?
   A) Its slow economic growth
   B) Too few mothers of childbearing age
   C) Its increasing population
   D) A low birth rate

86. What does a birthrate of 2.0 per woman of childbearing age mean?
   A) The population will decrease slowly.
   B) The population will increase slowly.
   C) The population will decrease quickly.
   D) The population will increase quickly.

87. What recommendation was given to the government?
- A) Slowly increase taxes on childbearing couples
- B) Increase the financial burden on childbearing couples
- C) Reduce the tax burden on childbearing couples
- D) Decrease the tax burden on children

88. What kind of business is JetSet?
- A) A bookstore
- B) A travel agency
- C) A hotel
- D) A restaurant

89. What does JetSet do for its customers?
- A) Escape from prison
- B) Break their daily routine
- C) Arrange travel packages
- D) Focus on the planet

90. What is the main point of this announcement?
- A) How to preserve natural forests
- B) How to preserve the natural habitats of animals
- C) What to do to make animals tame
- D) What to do when wild animals are around

91. Where is the information about animals available?
- A) At the park entrance office
- B) In guidebooks sold at the visitors' center
- C) At the park rangers' offices and on sign boards
- D) On the radio operated by the park

92. Who is talking?
- A) The chief representative of consumers
- B) The CEO of the company
- C) The chief of market research company
- D) The president of the bank

93. Why was production changed to the new machines?
   A)   They believe the board of directors want them.
   B)   They believe the CEO wants them.
   C)   They believe the chief of market research wants them.
   D)   They believe the consumers want them.

94. What was the meeting about?
   A)   About the reshuffling of directors
   B)   About the performance of the new computer models
   C)   About the change in marketing targets and products
   D)   About the weakening of a rival company

95. Who won the Orange County Business Leader Award?
   A)   A deer
   B)   Max Patterson
   C)   Orange County
   D)   A motivational speaker

96. How long has the award recipient lived in Orange County?
   A)   He was born there
   B)   For fifteen years
   C)   Since 1985
   D)   From the time he was 19 until he turned 85

97. Why did he win the award?
   A)   For his community service
   B)   For building a new library
   C)   For rebuilding the downtown center
   D)   For his ability to play basketball

98. Where was this announcement most likely made?
   A)   On a conference call
   B)   In Toronto
   C)   On an airplane
   D)   In a bathroom

99. Why does he congratulate the Toronto branch?
A) The Toronto branch came in second in a sales contest.
B) It is the Toronto branch's fifth anniversary.
C) Its sales were the highest in the country.
D) Its customer service was ranked number one.

100. What does the speaker imply about how well the Toronto Branch has performed in the past?
A) Its current quarter is a lot better than previous quarter.
B) It has always had good sales numbers.
C) Its sales numbers have steadily declined.
D) It is a new branch.

READING TEST

In the Reading Test, you will read a variety of texts and answer several different types of reading comprehension questions. The entire Reading Test will last 75 minutes. There are three parts, and directions are given for each part. You are encouraged to answer as many questions as possible within the time allowed.

You must mark your answers on the separate answer sheet. Do not write your answers in the test book.

PART 5

Directions: A word or phrase is missing in each of the sentences below. Four answer choices are given below each sentence. Select the best answer to complete the sentence. Then mark the letter (A), (B), (C), or (D) on your answer sheet.

101. Rampant _____ is undermining the economies of several developing countries in Asia.
   A) corruption
   B) integrity
   C) charity
   D) enthusiasm

102. From next year, all final year high school students _____ to pass an English exam before they can enter University.
   A) are being required
   B) will be required
   C) will be requiring
   D) will have been required

103. The National Assembly was considered outdated and unnecessary, so the Legislature voted overwhelmingly to _____ it.
   A) come down on
   B) make up for
   C) stand in for
   D) do away with

104. _____ such strong position throughout the country, the government would have introduced sweeping financial reforms last year.

- A) If there wasn't
- B) Had there not
- C) If there hadn't been
- D) Was there not

105. Although the police search far and wide, the missing child was _____ to be found.

- A) whereabouts
- B) nowhere
- C) elsewhere
- D) nearby

106. "_____ , this looks like a good business offer." The lawyer said. "But, we must study the contract thoroughly before making a final decision."

- A) On the face of it
- B) On the safe side
- C) On the right track
- D) On the spot

107. Despite everything he had said during the meeting, the owner failed to _____ on his promise to improve working conditions in the factory, so the staff went on strike.

- A) pull through
- B) make out
- C) come around
- D) make good

108. The report revealed that the company's financial problem were _____ anyone anticipated.

- A) very worse than
- B) bad more than
- C) worse much more than
- D) much worse than

109. William's English proficiency is already very good because his mother, who is a renowned English professor, has been coaching him _____ he started kindergarten.

A) way beyond
B) since before
C) even during
D) while at

110. Even though AIDS has already claimed millions of lives throughout the world, many people still don't _____ the need to take precautions against the disease.

A) appreciate
B) eventuate
C) obligate
D) confiscate

111. The project was a failure because the manager's instructions were _____ . Consequently, none of the staff knew what was expected of them.

A) tangible
B) explicit
C) ambiguous
D) reliable

112. In the last two hundred years, millions of people have migrated to America _____ a better life.

A) in view of
B) in line with
C) in place of
D) in search of

113. There's no point _____ constantly dwelling on past mistakes. The key is to learn from them and then look into the future.

A) about
B) in
C) at
D) on

114. The opera singer, _____ critics were divided, was given a standing ovation by the audience.

A) who about
B) about whom
C) whose
D) about her

115. _____ stall-holders in the night markets is a good way to save money. It can also be a lot of fun.

A) Attending to
B) Bargaining with
C) Standing by
D) Glancing at

116. The government made the decision to push ahead with _____ of the nuclear power plant.

A) constructing
B) constructed
C) construction
D) constructs

117. Normal business hours are posted in each office or branch and are _____ upon request.

A) furnish
B) furnished
C) furniture
D) furnishing

118. Contributions will benefit STM Reads, a non-profit organization _____ literacy programs.

A) support
B) supported
C) supporting
D) supports

119. Being an entrepreneur is all _____ finding creative ways to show the world your great idea.

A) about
B) for
C) of
D) to

120. The federal government estimates that 90 percent of all the sports _____ that is sold to collectors is fake.

A) memorandum
B) memorial
C) memorabilia
D) memory

121. An important thing to remember when buying stocks is that past performance isn't necessary an _____ of future results.

A) indecision
B) infraction
C) indictment
D) indication

122. Managers who can head off problems before they develop into something serious are two steps _____ of the game.

A) ahead
B) behind
C) about
D) below

123. The recent success of Tim's restaurant has served only to increase his _____ for the future.

A) enthused
B) enthusiasm
C) enthusiastic
D) enthuse

124. During the 1980's, Japan's fast-growing GNP was _____ to be the highest in the world by the year 2000.

A) predict
B) predictor
C) predicted
D) prediction

125. Construction jobs, fueled by the housing boom, have also _____ plentiful in the past year, and the need for skilled workers isn't abating.

A) remained
B) reminded
C) recreated
D) remitted

126. Payment is to be received _____ 10 days of the statement date printed on the bill.

A) about
B) within
C) at
D) from

127. Annual reports are the best tool for the public to _____ the performance of companies.

A) review
B) extract
C) demand
D) expect

128. There were several layovers at the airport last month _____ to bad weather.

A) because
B) owed
C) due
D) since

129. Many companies manufacture their products in other countries _____ cheap labor is easier to find.

A) although
B) so that
C) than
D) because

130. There's always something interesting to do in New York. It's a really _____ city.

A) notorious
B) abstract
C) vibrant
D) terrible

131. _____ government regulations, everyone must submit an annual statement of income to the Department of Taxation.

A) In lieu of
B) In accordance with
C) In reference to
D) In spite of

132. During the blizzard, the hikers were lucky to find a disused barn where they could take _____ from the howling wind and driving snow.

A) refuge
B) peace
C) refugee
D) asylum

133. Although one engine had failed during the flight, the aircraft
_____ safely at the airport.
A) took off
B) turned around
C) shot down
D) touched down

134. You can exchange the goods within seven days, _____
you keep the receipt.
A) unless
B) despite
C) so long as
D) in case

135. The speaker, who _____ physically by a group of anti-
government demonstrators, was escorted from the meeting under a
heavy police guard.
A) having been attacked
B) had been attacked
C) has been attacked
D) is being attacked

136. Julie was really happy when she was admitted to law school. She
felt like she was _____ .
A) walking on air
B) making a hit
C) keeping up appearances
D) off her head

137. When questioned by the judge, the defendant was _____
to explain his behavior on the night of the crime.
A) at a loss
B) at first hand
C) at cross-purposes
D) at face value

138. Ian Thorpe, the Olympic swimming champion, has always kept himself _____ fit.

A) exclusively
B) approximately
C) unanimously
D) superbly

139. A great deal of emphasis is placed on academic success, but it's not always easy for children to _____ their parents' expectations.

A) live up to
B) come up against
C) drop in on
D) feel up to

140. In this company, the staff normally retires at the age of sixty-five. Mr. Wang _____ last year, but he wants to keep working for at least another five years.

A) must have retired
B) could have retired
C) should have retire
D) would have been retire

PART 6

Directions: Read the texts on the following pages. A word or phrase is missing in some of the sentences. Four answer choices are given below each of these sentences. Select the best answer to complete the text. Then mark the letter (A), (B), (C), or (D) on your answer sheet.

Questions 141-144 refer to the following memo.

To: Sandy Parks
From: Michael Evans
Subject: Quarterly Financial Report
Date: April 2

This is to remind you that the initial draft of the quarterly financial report should be _____ by this Friday. Gary in accounting has finished compiling budget

141. A) implemented
B) completed
C) invented
D) constructed

and revenue data, and should have it on your _____ by tomorrow afternoon.

142. A) office
B) account
C) word
D) desk

if there's any other information you need, just let him know.
After I read the initial draft, I'll set up a meeting with you on Monday so we can go over the figures before you write the final draft. Our

auditor will also be there to make sure our accounts are ＿＿ .

143. A) in order
B) in effect
C) on time
D) overdue

I know this is short notice, but you did such a great job on last quarter's report, and I'm sure you'll come ＿＿ for us again.

144. A) over
B) off
C) back
D) through

Questions 145-148 refer to the following article.

The digital age is dawning, and that is good news for Asian companies. Already, a high percentage of the world's new digital products, such as DVD players and digital cameras, are being produced in Asia, not only ＿＿ manufacturing costs are lower there than in

145. A) because
B) that
C) after
D) until

North America and Europe, but also because Asia has become a center for ＿＿ .

146. A) recreation
B) animation
C) innovation
D) cooperation

Japanese companies, of course, have long been admired for their ability to design and manufacture consumer products that incorporate the latest technology while _____ the most-desired functions.

147. A) offered
B) did offer
C) offering
D) would offer

Now other Asian countries like Taiwan and Korea are taking Japan's lead. With the worldwide demand for digital products _____ at a furious pace,

148. A) extending
B) expanding
C) developing
D) growing

the future looks bright for the Asian companies that make them.

Questions 149-152 refer to the following e-mail.

From: frieda@intc.ned.de
To: jerry@intc.ac.de
Date: March 22
Subject: New Pricing Scheme

Jerry,
Thanks for your e-mail last Friday. I think you raised some important issues which we need to consider. At the same time, though, there appear to be some points where you may _____ what we are trying to do with this new pricing structure.

149. A) maintain
B) misdirect
C) match
D) misunderstand

For one thing, you incorrectly assume that there will be a substantial discount offered to all customers, irrespective of the size of the order. There is no such blanket markdown; only those customers ＿＿＿ at least 100 units will be entitled to it.

150. A) purchase
B) purchased
C) have purchased
D) purchasing

＿＿＿ , the proposed discount only applies to Model XG-10, not to versions XG-11 and later, as you indicate in your e-mail.

151. A) Then
B) Furthermore
C) Markedly
D) Because

I hope that ＿＿＿ helps to clear up the questions you raised. As always, I greatly appreciate your input on pricing and I

152. A) the above
B) as follows
C) as previous
D) the subsequent

look forward to having a chance to discuss this and other topics with you in person soon.

Best,
Frieda

PART 7

Directions: In this part you will read a selection of texts, such as magazine and newspaper articles, letters, and advertisements. Each text is followed by several questions. Select the best answer for each question and mark the letter (A), (B), (C), or (D) on your answer sheet.

Question153-155 refer to the following pamphlet.

Do you know that more than 40% of Americans live the last, golden years of their lives in a nursing home? Do you know that more than half of the homes currently offer levels of care that are far, far below the lifestyles previously enjoyed by their clients, and that many are critically understaffed and downright negligent when it comes to therapy, organizing activities, or even properly administering medication?

The Department of Health & Human Services maintains a website, updated once per year that reports on deficiencies found in nationally licensed nursing homes and offers comparative evaluations of cost, quality of life, quality of care, and other factors. This resource is available to you free of charge. Don't let yourself or a loved one land in a death trap.

153. What service is this pamphlet advertising?
A) In home care for seniors
B) A high-quality nursing home
C) Information on nursing homes
D) The importance of family care

154. Which of the following is NOT listed as a problem in American nursing homes?

A) Improper medication

B) Extremely high costs

C) Lack of staff

D) Low quality of life

155. What type of nursing homes is reviewed annually?

A) State-run care facilities

B) Class A1 and A2 homes

C) Hospital-sponsored homes

D) Nationally licensed homes

Question 156 - 157 are based on the following letter

The Sherwood Hotel

Marc Brown, Convention Chair

American Association of Photoengravers

125 45th Street

Watertown, NY 11201

Dear Mr. Brown:

Mr. Patterson, our general manager, passed on your letter requesting information regarding our convention facilities and asked me to respond. I am happy to comply.

As you can see from our brochure, we offer large meeting rooms for plenary sessions and display areas, and an ample number of small "breakout" rooms for workshops and concurrent meetings. Banquet facilities are also available. Our centralized location is convenient to other hotels, fine restaurants, and all the sights of downtown New York, as you can see from the map I've sent. I'm also enclosing a list of special room rates for convention attendees.

I think you will find the Sherwood Hotel the perfect place for your

---

convention. Our experienced and courteous staff really knows what it takes to make a convention run smoothly.

Please let me know if there's any other information or help I can provide.

Sincerely,

Lisa Setten

Lisa Setten, Convention and Banquet Manager

Encl: (3)

---

156. What is the main purpose of this letter?

A) To ask for further information

B) To respond to a request

C) To confirm a reservation

D) To explain the general manager's opinion

157. Which of the following is NOT enclosed?

A) A schedule of events

B) A publicity of brochure

C) A map of downtown Chicago

D) A list of room rates

Question158-160 refer to the following announcement:

25th Annual Children's Book Fair

Seoul, Korea

City Of Seoul Exhibition Center

March 19-23 10 a.m. – 8 p.m. daily

The Korean Book Foundation will open the doors of the 25th children's book fair from Thursday March 19th through Monday March

23rd. More than 300 exhibitors will take part, including the most important book stores and publishing houses devoted to children's literature and education. For the first two days, from 10 to 2, the fair is open exclusively to groups of pupils on official school excursions. After 2 on these days, and from the 21st to the 23rd, it is open to all interested members of the public. There will be workshops on literature, art and computing as well as dancing, music, and puppet shows.

This year, for the first time, Darren the Magnificent will be performing magic on Saturday and Sunday. Meet-the-author sessions and book-signings take place daily.

158. At which of these times may only official school groups attend the fair?
- A) Thursday at 3 p.m
- B) Friday at 11 a.m
- C) Friday at 5 p.m
- D) Saturday at 10 a.m

159. Who may attend the fair from March 21 to March 23?
- A) Only members of the Korean Book Foundation
- B) Only children and their parents
- C) Anyone who wants to
- D) Only publishers and book store owners

160. What is taking place at the book fair for the first time this year?
- A) Magic shows by Darren the Magnificent
- B) Computer workshops
- C) Sessions at which books are signed by the author
- D) Puppet shows

Questions 161-162 are based on the following newspaper article:

Trevor Baylis, inventor of the wind-up radio designed for areas of Africa and other locales where there is not electricity and batteries are expensive, has now developed a wind-up computer. The laptop, powered by a spring that runs a small generator, is just the first of 150 new wind-up products Baylis is perfecting

Next up: a wind-up television and a wind-up indoor lighting system.

161. Which of these wind-up products was first developed by Trevor Baylis?
A) A television
B) An indoor lighting system
C) A radio
D) A laptop computer

162. It can be inferred from the article that Baylis' products could also be marketed in which of these ways?
A) As a high-technology substitute for existing products
B) As a substitute for existing products in case of an electrical emergency
C) As a low-cost substitute for existing products
D) As a substitute for existing products when little or no maintenance is required

Questions 163 -167 are based on the following book review:

The Art of Communicating Globally
by Maxine Paetro and Andrew Gross Hachette Book Group

What's the best time to call Australia if you are in New York? What greeting do you use to begin a business letter to someone in Turkey? How do you find the email address of a company in South Africa? What's the country code you'll need to call someone in Brazil? These and countless other questions are answered in this new guidebook.

It covers the ins and outs of transnational contact by phone, fax, mail and email. There are more than 700 pages of useful tips on how to address business people in 110 countries, how to polish your English for international correspondence, how to design stationery and forms for use in various nations, and how to say hello, thank you, and other important phrases in more than 70 languages. The book also provides information about translation software, postal codes, the meaning of various telephone signals in different countries, and many other topics. Like the popular guidebook Negotiating Your Way Around the Globe that the couple previously collaborated on, this volume should occupy a prominent place on the office bookshelves of all our readers.

163. The magazine in which this review appeared is probably directed at which of these groups?

A) Commercial artists

B) International businesspersons

C) Communication experts

D) World travelers

164. The book that is reviewed probably does NOT answer which of these questions?

A) What does it mean if I telephone an office in Malaysia and hear a series of chimes?

B) What is the country code I need to send a fax to someone in Venezuela?

C) How do I say "hello" if I call someone in Finland?

D) What should I wear to a business luncheon in Egypt?

165. The phrase "ins and outs" in line 5 of the review is closet in meaning to

A) latest developments

B) common difficulties

C) important points

D) helpful suggestions

166. How many pages does the book The Art of Communicating Globally probably have?

A) 70

B) 110

C) 712

D) 1,246

167. What does the review say about the book Negotiating Your Way Around the Globe?

A) It's not as popular as The Art of Communicating Globally.

B) It was written by the same authors who wrote The Art of Communicating Globally.

C) It will not be needed by someone who has the book The Art of Communicating Globally.

D) It is more expensive than The Art of Communicating Globally.

Question168-170 refer to the following contest advertisement.

The SunCool Hot Summer Wheels Contest

Purchase a 16- or 22-oz bottle of any SunCool beverage, and you may spend a cool summer in the seat of a hot new Grand Z car, Apollo motorcycle, or Hi-Trekker mountain bike! Just look under the bottle cap and see if you are an instant winner.

(Rules and Details: Must be over 18 to play. One prize per contestant. Offer valid for US and Canadian residents only. Current employees of SunCool Corporation or members of their immediate families not eligible for prizes. Prizes must be redeemed by midnight, October 31, 2010. Odds of winning: car 1:400,000; motorcycle 1:45,000; bicycle 1:10,000.)

---

168. Based on the information in the ad, which of the following is most likely to be true?

A) This ad was published in a car magazine.

B) Most customers will win a prize.

C) SunCool is sold more than one country.

D) There is one flavor of SunCool.

169. Which of the following statements is clearly NOT true?

A) Suncool prints prize notices on the caps of its beverages.

B) One is more likely to win a car than a motorcycle.

C) No one may be awarded both a car and a motorcycle.

D) SunCool Cola is sold in more than one size bottle.

170. Who among the following cannot win an Appollo Motorcycle in this contest?

A) One who dislikes SunCool products

B) Someone born in November, 1998

C) A former SunCool executive

D) Someone not born in the US or Canada

Questions 171-173 refer to the following promotional information.

Running Start Program:
Giving Kids a Running Start towards Education
Take part in the Price/Bellhouse Corporation Running Start Program

When: Saturday, July 15ᵗʰ @ 9:00 a.m.
Where: State University Athletic Complex

The Running Start Program is designed to supply children in need with a backpack, school supplies, and new clothing in order to prepare them for a successful school year. The money raised from the Price/Bellhouse Corporation's 5-kilometer run benefits the Running Start Program as well as other Combined Charities youth programs and services. Last year, with over 300 runners competing, more than $10,000 was raised – making all the kids served by Combined Charities the real winners.

---

171. What information is NOT contained in the promotion?
   A) The amount of money expected to be raised.
   B) The names of the commercial sponsor.
   C) The objectives of the Running Start Program.
   D) The scheduled distance of the run.

172. What best describes the event advertised?
   A) A state-sponsored inter-school competition
   B) An effort to improve student physical fitness
   C) A fund-raiser to help poor children
   D) A race between employees of two companies

173. When is the event scheduled to be held?
   A) On a fall morning
   B) On a summer morning
   C) On a spring afternoon
   D) On a summer afternoon

Questions 174-176 refer to the following instructions on an application form.

PHOTOS. You must submit 2 identical natural color photographs of yourself taken within 30 days of this application. The photos must have a white background, be unmounted, printed on thin paper, and not have been retouched. They should show a three-quarter frontal profile showing the right side of your face, with your right ear visible and with your head bare (unless you are wearing a headdress as required by a religious order of which you are a member). The photo should be no larger than 5cm x 5cm. With a pencil, print your name, application number, and the date taken on the back of each submitted photograph.

---

174. Which of the following is NOT a requirement for the two photographs?

    A) That they be taken the day before being submitted.

    B) That they show the right side of the applicant's face.

    C) That they be exactly the same.

    D) That the date they were taken be indicated.

175. What is the only requirement for which an exemption is stated in the instructions?

    A) The photos must be no larger than a certain size.

    B) The information on the reverse must be written in pencil.

    C) The head of the applicant must be shown bare.

    D) The background of the photo must be a specific color.

176. What should appear on the back of the photo?

    A) The application number

    B) The size of the photo

    C) The photographer's name

    D) The address

Question177-180 refer to the following product information.

Thank you for purchasing this CompuEd Product.

Our Product Development Philosophy

Since 1988, The CompuEd company has consistently developed and marketed the most innovative and effective children's educational software available. Our award-winning products help develop your child's creative and cognitive abilities, while targeting important areas of school curriculum, such as reading, writing, social studies, and math. Before hitting the market, everyone program from CompuEd is subject to extensive research and with input from teachers, curriculum designers, education researchers, and – importantly – parents and children. Each product is designed not only to be educational, but also highly entertaining. In fact, our company's motto is, "For Learning to Get Done, Learning Must Be Fun."

CompuEd pioneered the use of Adaptive Learning Technology, whereby the software is designed and programmed to become more challenging as the skill level of the user increases. This means that it will be years before your child outgrows his or her CompuEd product!

Finally, CompuEd itself is continually learning from its customers. When we design new products or upgrades of existing products, we do so paying close attention to feedback from our consumers. So, if you have any comments or suggestions – positive or negative – please do not hesitate to pass them on to us.

177. Where this information would most likely be found?

   A) In a magazine advertisement

   B) Included with purchased software

   C) In a review of newly released program

   D) Attached to a letter from customer service

178. Which of the following would probably NOT be found on a CompuEd product's package?

   A) "Learn geography with your favorite cartoon character!"

   B) "Spend hours memorizing historical dates!"

   C) "CompuEd: Over two decades of making learning fun."

   D) "Prepare your child for the upcoming school year."

179. Among the following, who is NOT mentioned as being involved in the product development process?

   A) Software engineers

   B) Parents and their children

   C) Researchers

   D) Education professionals

180. According to the reading, which of the following is true?

A) CompuEd offers upgrades for all its older software.

B) CompuEd has been the most popular educational software since 1988.

C) CompuEd products have won awards in the past.

D) CompuEd's software is only for very young children.

Question181-185 refer to the following faxes.

FAX: URGENT

To:　Samantha Brown, Leila Fashions

From:　Annette Lyons, Head of Ladies Fashions, Anderson Department Store

Re:　Order

Date:　December 15th

Sam,

The clothes and shoes that you sent us in the last delivery have proved to be an amazing success. They are just flying off the racks. Therefore, I would like to place an order for the following items:

An additional 5 dresses in each of the size you delivered before (a total of 50 dresses);

7 skirts in sizes 6 through 12 (even sizes only, a total of 28 skirts);

4 blouses in sizes 6 through 18 (2 pink and 2 black, even sizes only, a total of 28 blouses);

and if you have any of those silver and pearl earrings, send as many as you can. We want to have the clothes ready to go on sale within the next couple of days. Can you get them to us by midday on the 17th?

Let me know as soon as you can,

Thanks,

Annette

FAX

To: Annette Lyons, Anderson Department Store
From: Samantha Brown, Leila Fashions
Re: Order
Date: December 15th

Dear Annette,

I'm sending this fax in reply to the fax you sent early this morning. I've spent the morning telephoning around our suppliers and factories, trying to gather all of the items you have requested. Unfortunately, this being the holiday season, the factory we use on a regular basis is already working at full capacity, trying to complete orders from other clients. I've tried to pull a few strings and get some favors done, but I'm not having a lot of lucks. What I can do is send you everything that we currently have in stock immediately, and try to get the other stuff to you later, if at all. I doubt that we will be able to get the rest of your order made before Christmas, and I imagine that you won't want to be stocking these items once Christmas has passed and you start moving into the bargain sale season.

Let me know what you think.

Regards,

Samatha

181. Why were these two faxes sent?
   A) To discuss an order of clothes
   B) To cancel an order
   C) To discuss Christmas plans
   D) To discuss the bargain sale season

182. Why does Annette want more of the same items?

    A) The shelves look empty.

    B) There is a great demand for them.

    C) She wants to buy some for herself.

    D) She is flying to a meeting.

183. What is the problem at the factories?

    A) They are closed for the holidays.

    B) They are busy fulfilling other orders.

    C) They are going out of business.

    D) There is no problem.

184. What has Samantha been doing all morning?

    A) Christmas Shopping

    B) Telephone manufacturers and suppliers

    C) Making clothes

    D) Making deliveries

185. How likely is it that Samantha will be able to send everything that Annette wants?

    A) There is a very high possibility.

    B) She had already sent the items.

    C) She gives no indication of this.

    D) It is very doubtful.

Question186-190 refer to the following complaint and response.

To: Customer Response (customer.care@hanley.co)

From: zelda33@hotmail.com

Subject: Faulty goods

Date: January 19, 2011

I found this address on the side of the packet of one of your products, so I hope this is the correct address for complaints. If not, would you please forward this to the correct address? I am emailing you because of a problem that I experienced with a Hanley Electronics product. I've been using Hanley products for many years, and it was the first time that I have had any trouble. I recently purchased the Hanley Straight/Wave Hair tongs from the online shopping mall on your website.

I had seen them advertised on TV and in various fashion magazines. The problem is that even after waiting for the recommended 5 minutes, the tongs did not really seem to heat up. I waited a further 5 minutes, but they still didn't get any hotter. I tried using them to straighten my hair, but nothing happened, and it was a waste of time. I would, therefore, like to receive a refund. Could you tell me how I should go about this?

Thank you for your time.

Zelda Barnard

To: zelda33@hotmail.com
From: Alison McCain (amccain@hanley.co)
Subject: Re: Faulty goods
Date: January 20, 2011
Dear Ms. Barnard,

Thank you for your email alerting us to the problem you have had with one of our products. I'm sorry to hear that this has inconvenienced you. This is the first complaint of this kind regarding this particular product, and I can only imagine that a wire has become disconnected. We would be happy to refund your money in full, including postage and packing. To obtain a refund we ask you to send the product (in its original packaging if possible), together with your name, address and order reference number to the following address:

Returns

Hanley Electronics
100 W, Capitol Drive
Seattle, Washington 45002

Again, I apologize for any inconvenience and hope you will continue
to use our products.
Sincerely,
Alison McCain

186. Why did Zelda Barnard send an email?

  A) To place an order

  B) To ask for her money back

  C) To ask for an exchange

  D) To demand an apology

187. Which of the following statements best describes Zelda Barnard?

  A) She is a new customer.

  B) She doesn't often make electronics purchases.

  C) She frequently makes complaints.

  D) She is a loyal customer of Hanley Electronics.

188. How long did Zelda Barnard wait for the tongs to heat up?

  A) 5 minutes

  B) A total of 10 minutes

  C) 15 minutes

  D) Many years

189. How many other complaints has the company received?

  A) None for this particular product

  B) A dozen

  C) Several

  D) Hundreds

190. What information should Zelda Barnard send?

  A) Phone number

  B) Credit card number

  C) Name, address, and reference number

  D) Name and email address

Questions 191-195 refer to the following two pieces of information.

The Stonewall Hotel and Conference Center is found in the historic and enchanting city of Laurel, Virginia, centrally located in the heart of bustling downtown. Enjoy your business trip while you step back in time and visit numerous historic sites in this colonial city. For those important business meetings, the Stonewall Hotel offers the ideal settings for seminars and conferences of all sizes. The Stonewall Hotel has nearly $8,500 square feet of elegant meeting space that can accommodate up to 400 for a banquet or 495 theater-style.

The Stoney Brook Inn in Laurel, Virginia is just right for your intimate engagement. Our beautiful stone lodge beckons you through its doors. The vaulted ceilings and warm earth tones make the perfect setting for a romantic location. From adventurous hiking to exquisite food, you'll find the historic setting a dream getaway as you spend time in the gorgeous mountain areas. Live nightly entertainment and a lovely gift and craft shop will offer you just the right souvenir to remember your time here. We have the right combination to take you to a different level of privacy and comfort. Come for a visit. We're confident you'll find our Southern hospitality and personal service beyond compare.

191. What does the Stoney Brook Inn offer as its setting?

  A) A family setting

  B) A modern setting

  C) A professional setting

  D) A historic setting

192. What does the Stonewall Hotel NOT offer its guests?
- A) An intimate setting
- B) A conference area for business
- C) Historic sites
- D) A central location in the city

193. Where is The Stonewall Hotel located?
- A) On the outskirts of town
- B) In a modern district
- C) In the town center
- D) On a quiet, private lane

194. Which kinds of guests might be most interested in The Stoney Brook Inn?
- A) Large families
- B) Honeymooners
- C) Business conferences
- D) Beach-goers

195. What kind of city is Laurel?
- A) A purely urban environment
- B) A city located on the plains of the Midwest
- C) A city by the Atlantic Ocean
- D) A city that offers both urban and rural settings

Question196-200 refer to the following notice and letter.

October 25

Thank you for joining the Stallions' team of supporters again this year! We have carefully read the comments you sent us and we get the message loud and clear. We promise to do anything we can to provide a family-friendly and safe atmosphere for all who attend Stallions games. In order to accomplish this, there are a few reminders we would like to pass along to you, our most valued supporters.

If you are not able to attend a game yourself, we ask that you exercise discretion in what you do with your tickets. If you give them away or decide to sell them, you are responsible for the actions of the individuals using your tickets. If someone using your tickets acts inappropriately, your tickets to future games or seasons could be revoked. Fans who demonstrate inappropriate or disruptive behavior, including the following, will be subject to ejection and you will risk losing your season tickets:

1. Abusive language or actions
2. Fighting or other dangerous behavior
3. Unruly behavior which prevents other fans from enjoying the game
4. Interfering with the progress of the game in any way, including throwing objects onto the field.
5. Smoking, except in designated areas.

We want everyone to come to the stadium, relax, and enjoy a great day. If one fan's experience is ruined by the actions of others, it's one too many.
We look forward to seeing you this Sunday and at every future home game of the Stallions.

November 5
Dear Mr. McGee:
I regret to inform you that two of the fans who bought your tickets to last Sunday's game were apprehended by stadium security for repeatedly tossing things at the opposing team's players and action was taken against them as outlined in the notice sent to all season ticket holders on October 25.

We understand that you had no expectation that people purchasing your game tickets would act this way. Nonetheless, as clearly stated in the policy letter, your must take responsibility for their actions. We urge you to contact Rickard Wieder at the Stallions office immediately to discuss the situation. He can be reached at 807-1580.

Sincerely,
Thomas L. DuPont
Director of Security

196. What was probably the reason for the notice of October 25?

    A) No more tickets were available for Sunday's game.

    B) The team was facing legal action from some fans.

    C) Some fans had complained to the team in writing.

    D) Too many fans had been selling their tickets.

197. To whom is the notice of October 25 mainly directed?

    A) People attending this Sunday's game

    B) People owning season tickets

    C) People wishing to purchase tickets

    D) People thinking about joining the team

198. Why has the letter of November 5 been written?

    A) Mr. McGee misplaced his tickets.

    B) Mr. McGee's behavior to the game was unruly.

    C) Some fans objected to the new policy.

    D) Some fans threw objects onto the field.

199. What action was taken against the fans Mr. McGee sold his tickets to?

    A) They were asked to leave the stadium.

    B) They were arrested by the police.

    C) They had their season tickets revoked.

    D) They had to remain in their seats.

200. What will Mr. McGee most likely do?

    A) Speak with the fans who bought his tickets

    B) Visit the team's offices in person

    C) Phone a team representative

    D) Contact the agency that sold his tickets

詳解篇

NEW TOEIC TEST
新多益全真模擬試題

聽力測驗：在聽力試題中，將會測試考生掌握口說英語的程度。整個測驗將會進行約45分鐘，共分四個部分，每個部分都有作答說明。考生必須在答案卡上劃記答案，不得在試題冊上書寫答案。

> ## PART 1
> **作答說明：**閱讀底下的數篇文章，其中有些句子缺少一個單字或片語。從四個選項中選出最適合的填入空格內，以完成該篇文章，然後塗黑答案紙上(A)、(B)、(C)或(D)中的一個選項。

破題解析

1. A) These photographs are now on display.
　　B) A patient is waiting to sit in the dentist's chair.
　　C) The faxmachine is ready for use in the office.
　　D) This assembly line uses only the latest machinery.

中譯
　　A) 這些照片目前正在展示中。
　　B) 一位病患正等著坐上牙科診療椅。
　　C) 這部傳真機在辦公室裡待機供人使用。
　　D) 這條裝配線只使用最新的機械。

關鍵字彙

- photograph (n.) 照片
- be on display = be on exhibition 展示中
  例 Her paintings are on display at the gallery. 她的畫作正在美術館展出。
- assemble (v.) 集合；裝配、安裝
- assembly line = production line 裝配線、生產線
  例 The bookcase can easily be assembled with a screwdriver.
  這書櫃用一把螺絲起子就可以很容易地安裝起來。
- machinery (n.)（不可數）（泛指）機器、機械
  machine (n.) 機器、機械
- copy (v.) 抄寫、複製

2. A) According to the thermometer, the man has a fever.
　　B) The nurse is giving the baby an injection.
　　C) My grandfather is having his blood pressure checked.
　　D) An eye examination takes a long time.

中譯
A) 溫度計顯示這名男子發燒了。
B) 護士正在為嬰兒打針。
C) 我祖父正在接受血壓檢測。
D) 檢查眼睛要花很多時間。

關鍵字彙

- blood pressure (n.) 血壓
  例 check sb.'s blood pressure 量某人血壓
    take sb.'s temperature 量某人體溫
    feel sb.'s pulse 量某人脈搏
- nurse (n.) 護士
- injection (n.) 注射
  give sb. an injection 幫某人打針
  例 The morphine was administered by injection. 那嗎啡是注射進去的。
- examination (n.) 檢驗、檢查
  例 a physical examination 體檢
- thermometer (n.) 溫度計

3.
A) He's writing an article.
B) He's delivering the newspaper.
C) He's at a newsstand.
D) He's reading the newspaper.
中譯
A) 他在寫一篇文章。
B) 他在送報紙。
C) 他在一家書報攤。
D) 他在閱讀報紙。

關鍵字彙

- article (n.) 文章
- deliver (v.) 遞送、傳送
  例 We deliver your order to your door! 我們送貨到府！
- newspaper (n.) 報紙
- newsstand (n.) 書報攤
  同 news vendor, news agency（英式用法）

4. A) He's giving directions.
   B) He's writing a ticket.
   C) He's directing traffic.
   D) He's conducting an orchestra.

   中譯
   A) 他正在指引方向。
   B) 他在開罰單。
   C) 他在指揮交通。
   D) 他在指揮交響樂團。

關鍵字彙

- conduct (v.) 指揮（管絃樂隊、合唱團、樂曲等）
- conductor (n.) （管絃樂隊、合唱團的）指揮
- orchestra (n.) （通常為大型的）管絃樂隊
  例 He conducts the National Symphony Orchestra. 他指揮國家交響樂團。
- write (v.) 填寫文件、表格
  例 I don't have any cash. I'll have to write you a check.
  我沒有現金。得開張支票給你。
  In a day, a doctor may write 30 prescriptions for patients.
  一位醫生一天可能要幫病人開出30張處方。
- ticket (n.) 〔口〕（交通違規）通知單、罰單
  例 get a parking/speeding ticket 接到違規停車／超速罰單

5. A) This is a business district downtown.
   B) These are residential homes in the suburbs.
   C) This is an amusement park in the countryside.
   D) This is a retirement community in a rural area.

   中譯
   A) 這是是中心的一處商業區。
   B) 這是郊區的住家。
   C) 這是鄉村地區的一間遊樂園。
   D) 這是鄉村地區的一處退休社區。

關鍵字彙

- district (n.) 區域，行政區
  例 mountainous district 山區；outlying district 偏遠地區
- residential (adj.) 住宅的
  resident (n.) 居民

- suburb (n.) (the ~s) 郊區
- amusement (n.) 娛樂，消遣
  amusement park 遊樂園
  例 The hotel offers its guests a wide variety of amusements.
  這家旅館為住客提供了各種各樣的娛樂活動。
- retirement (n.) 退休
  例 reach retirement age 達到退休年齡
  retire (v.) 退休
  例 retire early （未達退休年齡）提前退休
- rural (adj.) 鄉村的
  同 country, rustic, pastoral, bucolic, countryside
  反 urban

6. A) People are leaving their briefcases on the platform.
   B) The door of the train is closed.
   C) People are boarding the airplane.
   D) The train has already departed from the station.

   中譯
   A) 人們把他們的公事包留在月台上。
   B) 列車的車門是關閉的。
   C) 人們正在上登機。
   D) 列車已從車站離站。

關鍵字彙

- board (v.) 上（船、火車、飛機、公車）等交通工具
  例 Flight BA193 for Paris is now boarding.
  搭乘往巴黎的BA193班機的旅客現在正在登機。
- door (n.) 門
- depart (v.) 走開、離開
  例 We departed for New York at 10 am. 我們上午十點出發去紐約。
- briefcase (n.) 公事包
- platform (n.) 月台
  例 Which platform does the Sydney train leave from?
  開往雪梨的火車在哪個月台發車？

7. A) They're looking at the wine display.
   B) They're drinking in a pub.
   C) They're visiting a vineyard.
   D) They're sampling some wine.

A) 他們在看陳列的酒類商品。
B) 他們在酒吧喝酒。
C) 他們在參觀葡萄園。
D) 他們在品嚐一些酒。

關鍵字彙

- sample (v.) 試用、抽樣檢查
  例 sample the delights of Chinese food 品嚐中國美食
- vineyard (n.)（尤指為釀酒而種植的）葡萄園
  vine (n.) 葡萄藤
- display (n.) 陳列的貨物
  例 The displays in Harrods are one of the sights in London.
  哈洛德百貨公司的陳列品是倫敦的一景。

8. A) They are dancing in a ballroom.
B) They are shaking hands.
C) They are standing in line.
D) They are playing sports on the field.

A) 他們在舞廳裡跳舞。
B) 他們在握手。
C) 他們在排隊。
D) 他們在球場上運動。

關鍵字彙

- ballroom (n.) 跳舞廳
  例 ballroom dancing 交際舞
- sport (n.) 運動、體育競技活動
- field (n.) 作某用途的場地
  例 a baseball field 棒球場

9. A) Driving through the countryside is relaxing.
B) No more cars can be parked in the parking lot.
C) There are a lot of new cars on display.
D) There're many cars on the overpasses.

A) 開車徜徉鄉間感覺很輕鬆。

B) 停車場無法再停更多車了。

C) 有許多新車正在展示中。

D) 高架橋上有許多車輛。

關鍵字彙

- overpass (n.) 天橋；高架道
  - 相 underpass〔美〕地下通道；下穿交叉道
- be on display 展示中
- parking lot (n.) 停車場

10. A) The girl is waiting for the elevator.

B) She is waiting for someone to answer the door.

C) The toilet is out of order.

D) Someone is already inside the telephone booth.

中譯

A) 這個女孩正在等電梯。

B) 她正在等人應門。

C) 馬桶壞掉了。

D) 有人已在電話亭裡面。

關鍵字彙

- toilet (n.)（有沖洗式馬桶的）廁所；沖洗式馬桶
  be out of order 故障、損壞
- elevator (n.)〔美〕電梯
  - 同 lift（英式用法）
  - 相 escalator 自動扶梯
  - 例 elevator music〔口〕商店或公共場所播放的乏味音樂
- booth (n.) 亭子；小隔間
  - 例 polling booth 投票間

> **Part 2**
> **作答說明：**你會聽到以英語播放的問句或敘述句，以及3個答句選項。問句或敘述句
> 以及答句均只播放一次，也不會印在試題冊上，請選出最適合問句或敘述句的答案，
> 並在答案卡上劃記。現在請聽參考範例。

破題解析

11. Why didn't Mr. Peters bring the situation to the attention of his manager?
  A) Yes, he was promoted last week.
  B) No, I didn't know who the manager was.
  C) He thought he could handle it himself.

關鍵字彙

- bring sth. to the attention of sb. 讓某人注意到某事

  例 We are grateful that you have brought the matter to our attention. If you wish, we would be happy to take issue with the shipping company on your behalf.
  本公司感激貴公司知會本公司這事宜，如果你們願意，我們樂意代表來向船公司爭論這問題。

  ★ "bring" 其它的片語：
  ■ bring sb. or sth. up 提及某個話題或人物
  I want to bring this matter up for a vote.
  我希望提出這件事，讓大家表決一下。
  ■ bring sb. to justice 繩之以法
  The police officer swore she would not rest until she had brought the killer to justice.
  那位警官發誓除非將兇手繩之以法，否則她不會罷休。
  ■ bring the house down 贏得最大的掌聲；博得滿堂彩
  This is a great joke. The last time I told it, it brought the house down.
  這笑話很棒，我上次講的時候就博得滿堂彩。

12. Is this shirt already marked down?
  A) Yes, that's the sale price on the tag.
  B) The flea market is open every Sunday morning.
  C) Yes, I think it fits you perfectly.

關鍵字彙

- mark down 減價

  In order to increase their market share, the company has decided to mark down

a wide range of goods to boost sales.
為了提升市場占有率,公司決定將多數產品降價來刺激買氣。
- tag (n.) 標籤
- flea market 跳蚤市場
- fit (v.) 合身
  These shoes don't fit me.
  這雙鞋不合我的腳。

13. Why does Ms. Otto want to see the invoice?
  A) Yes, you should speak louder.
  B) There's a problem with the shipment.
  C) Yes, I will find it for you.

關鍵字彙

- invoice (n.) 發票
  I used to get invoices through the mail but now I get it via email.
  以前發票是用郵寄寄給我,現在則用電子郵件傳送。
- shipment (n.) 貨運
  Shipment of the merchandise was held up because of the railroad strike.
  由於鐵路罷工,這批貨品的裝運被耽擱了。

14. Should we move the end table to the right or over by the lamp?
  A) Yes, your apartment looks great.
  B) I think it looks good where it is.
  C) No, the lamps didn't need to be moved.

關鍵字彙

- end table 茶几

15. Isn't that the same problem we talked about last time?
  A) Yes, but things have changed since then.
  B) No, the meeting is called off.
  C) No, it was a different person.

關鍵字彙

- call off 取消
  I insist on calling off this wedding.
  我堅持要取消這場婚禮。
  [同] cancel
- then (n.) 那時候

16. Would you mind saving a seat for me?
    A) No, I don't mind at all.
    B) I don't have a savings account.
    C) Yes, the seats are taken.

關鍵字彙

- savings account 儲蓄存款帳戶

17. Why don't you let me drive for a while so you can take a break?
    A) Because I need you there.
    B) I can handle it.
    C) I've had a driver's license for a long time.

關鍵字彙

- driver's license 駕照
- handle (v.) 處理
  handle a problem 處理問題
  = deal with a problem
  = cope with a problem
  例 There doesn't seem to be anybody who can handle the problem.
  似乎沒有人能處理這問題。

18. You've worked here longer than Ms. Schmidt, haven't you?
    A) No, it's very close to the office.
    B) No, we were hired at the same time.
    C) No, you don't have to wait much longer.

關鍵字彙

- hire (v.) 雇用
  例 The companies hired several new employees last month.
  這家公司上個月雇用了好幾名新員工。
  同 employ
  反 fire, dismiss

19. The orientation for the new hires begins at ten o'clock, doesn't it?
    A) No, he left at eleven.
    B) I don't know who just got hired.
    C) I thought it was at nine.

關鍵字彙

- orientation (n.) 新生訓練
  - 例 Your orientation will begin at 10 o'clock next Monday. Don't be late.
    你的新生訓練下星期一上午十點開始，不要遲到。
  - 相 orient (v.) 使…適應
    disorient (v.) 使…困惑
- new hire 新進員工
  - 相 rookie (n.) 新手；新人

20. Should I turn off these lights before I go?
   A) No, you should turn right at the next stoplight.
   B) No, only the ones in your office.
   C) Yes, the lights need to be fixed.

關鍵字彙

- stoplight (n.) 紅綠燈；停止行進燈號

21. Do you like this new sweater, or do you prefer the old one?
   A) I have trouble with the cold weather.
   B) The old one is much more comfortable.
   C) Yes, I'm feeling much better, thanks.

關鍵字彙

- sweater (n.) 毛衣
- prefer (v.) 偏好
  prefer A to B 喜歡A甚於B
  prefer V-ing to V-ing 喜歡從事前者甚於後者
  prefer to V rather than V 比較喜歡…，而不願…
  = prefer to V instead of V-ing
  - 例 Mary prefers chocolate to strawberry ice cream.
    瑪莉喜歡巧克力甚於草莓冰淇淋。
  - 例 I prefer hiking to skiing in the mountains.
    = I prefer to hike rather than ski in the mountains.
    = I prefer to hike instead of skiing in the mountains.
    我喜歡在山中健行而不喜歡滑雪。

22. When should I hand in this report?
   A) By the end of next week.
   B) At window number five.
   C) Yes, you need to report to the manager.

關鍵字彙

- hand in 交出；呈交
  同 submit

23. What's the most popular sightseeing spot in this country?
A) The sightseeing bus starts at 9:00.
B) You can go by train.
C) The National Palace Museum.

關鍵字彙

- sightseeing spot 觀光景點
- National Palace Museum 台灣的故宮博物院

24. How many factories are we visiting on this tour?
A) Just one, I think.
B) That's one of the attractions of the city.
C) The tour costs about $2,000.

關鍵字彙

- attractions (n.) 吸引物；吸引力
  She felt an immediate attraction to him.
  她對他一見鍾情。
  相 attract (v.) 吸引
  attractive (adj.) 動人的；吸引人的

25. When did the burglary take place?
A) In the new conference room.
B) At the end of next month.
C) I heard it was late last night.

關鍵字彙

- burglary (n.) 竊盜
  例 The burglary took place when Frank was out playing golf.
  法蘭克外出打高爾夫球時發生了竊案。
- take place 發生
  例 The meeting took place in the president's office.
  會議在董事長辦公室舉行。

同 happen, occur

26. Why is there such a rush to buy this stock?
  A) The rush won't stop.
  B) Because stocking up on supplies is a waste of time.
  C) That's a good question.

關鍵字彙

- stock (n.) 股票；商品的存貨
  例 If you have a long term perspective, the stock market's a good place to put your money.
  如果你眼光放遠一點，股市是不錯的投資環境。
- stock up on sth. 囤積某物
  例 As soon as they heard about possible food shortages, they began to stock up.
  他們一聽到食物可能短缺，就立刻囤積起來。
- a waste of time 浪費時間
  例 In my opinion, playing online games all day is a waste of time.
  以我看來，整天玩線上遊戲很浪費時間。
  ■ 相關片語：waste one's breath 白費口舌
  例 Don't waste your breath on that rascal; he's a hopeless case.
  別再對那無賴多費唇舌了，他已無可救藥。

27. Is there an optician around here?
  A) I think there's one in the shopping mall.
  B) Her glasses have round frames.
  C) They handle optical products.

關鍵字彙

- optician (n.) 眼鏡商；配鏡師
- optical (adj.) 視覺的；視力的
  例 optical products 光學製品
  例 optical fiber 光學纖維
- frame (n.) 框架
  The frame is prettier than the picture.
  畫框比畫作更美。
- handle (v.) 經營；經銷
  例 He asked me to handle the business for him.
  他請我替他經營生意。

28. Would you like me to write down the directions?
    A) I'll get to you directly.
    B) Yes, I'll appreciate that.
    C) Yes, would you tell me again?

關鍵字彙

● appreciate (n.) 感謝；感激
    例 Your help was greatly appreciated.
    非常感謝您的幫助。
    反 depreciate

29. When was the merger first suggested?
    A) Do you remember the visit by those New York lawyers?
    B) It was suggested once before.
    C) There's always a first time.

關鍵字彙

● merger (n.) 合併
    例 The merger will make us the largest convenience store in the nation.
    這次的合併將使我們成為國內最大規模的連鎖便利商店。

30. Is our budget for a new computer cut as well, boss?
    A) The new system has the best cost performance.
    B) Yes, it's the best computer, I know.
    C) I hate to tell you, Sarah, but yes.

關鍵字彙

● budget (n.) 預算
    on a tight budget 缺錢；拮据
    例 A family on a tight budget can't afford meat every day.
    經濟拮据的家庭無法每天都享用得到肉食。
● performance (n.) 表現；效益
    performance review 工作績效考核
    例 My sales figures were disappointing last quarter so I am not looking forward to my upcoming performance review.
    我上一季的銷售數字令我失望，所以我並不期待即將來到的工作績效考核。

31. How often do you access the Net?

    A) Not more than twice a day.

    B) The net has a hole in it.

    C) I once had contact with it.

關鍵字彙

● access (v.) 進入；使用

    例 This password will allow you to access the secret website. Don't share the password with anyone.

    這密碼可以讓你進入祕密網站。千萬不要與任何人共用這密碼。

    同 get into

32. Who is supposed to handle the case anyway?

    A) The case isn't closed yet.

    B) Yes, I suppose so.

    C) Mr. Newton was named for this one.

關鍵字彙

● case (n.) 案件；案例（常用於法律案件或病例）

    例 Lawyers handle several cases every day.

    律師們每天都要處理好幾件案子。

● name (v.) 提名；任命

    例 Miss Lopez has been named as the new CEO.

    羅培茲小姐已被提名為新的總執行長。

    同 nominate, appoint

33. How much do they charge you for this service?

    A) They can't charge that.

    B) You should have paid much less.

    C) Fifteen percent off the regular rate.

關鍵字彙

● charge 索價

    例 As long as you've paid in advance, we won't charge you for delivery.

    只要你預先付款，我們就不收你運費。

● regular (adj.) 一般的

    例 My regular routine gets me to the office at about 8:30 in the morning.

    我一般日常的習慣是早上大約八點半到辦公室。

● rate (n.) 價格；費用

    advertising rate 廣告費

    insurance rate 保險費

34. Is it permissible to bring a dog into this store?
    A) Yes, you must have a permit to have a pet.
    B) No, I cannot take the puppy with me to work.
    C) No, animals are not allowed in this shop.

關鍵字彙

- permissible (adj.) 容許的
  例 Delay is not permissible, even for a single day.
  不得延誤，即使一天都不可以。
- permit (n.) 許可證；通行證
  例 You cannot enter a military base without a permit.
  你沒有通行證就不能進入軍事基地。
- allow (v.) 允許；准許
  例 Photography is not allowed in this theater.
  這家戲院裡不准攝影。

35. Would you give me the recipe for this dish?
    A) Oh, I'm glad you like it.
    B) I'm afraid I can't give you this dish.
    C) I'm sure you know why.

關鍵字彙

- recipe (n.) 食譜
  例 I'd like to have your recipe for the cheese cake.
  我想跟你要乳酪蛋糕的食譜。
- dish (n.) 菜餚
  例 Fried eggs are my favorite dish.
  煎蛋是我最喜歡的菜餚。

36. Have you consulted a doctor about your high blood pressure yet?
    A) The consultant fee is going up quickly.
    B) Yes, Mr. Page still has high blood pressure.
    C) Oh, honey, it's not that serious.

關鍵字彙

- consult (v.) 找(醫生)看病；請教
  例 "We'll have to consult the surgeon before we decide what to do with your test results," said the doctor.

「在決定如何處理你的檢驗結果前，我們必須先徵詢外科醫生的意見」醫生說。

- consultant (n.) 顧問
- high blood pressure 高血壓
  同 hypertension

37. How about eating out tonight?
  A) You always eat too much Italian food.
  B) Tonight was a little busy.
  C) That's a nice idea.

關鍵字彙

- eat out 外出用餐
  例 Eating in is cheaper than eating out.
  在家吃飯比上館子用餐便宜。

38. Why did Mr. Wang visit the factory?
  A) He wanted to talk directly to the quality control room.
  B) He would visit the factory often.
  C) The factory workers want to invite them.

關鍵字彙

- quality control (簡稱QC)品質控管
  相 quality assurance (商品及服務的)品質保證
  quality audit 品質審查

39. Who else wants a copy of the report?
  A) Don't copy my style.
  B) A report on illegal copies was featured in the paper.
  C) Both Helen and myself, if you don't mind.

關鍵字彙

- illegal (adj.) 違法的
  例 illegal immigrant 非法移民
  同 unlawful, illicit
  反 legal, legitimate, lawful

40. Have you heard the rumor, Tommy?
  A) Yes, I really like that part about the room.
  B) No, please tell me.

C) That's hardly the case with her.

關鍵字彙

- rumor (n.) 謠言
  - 同 gossip, tale, hearsay, buzz, anecdote
  - 反 fact, truth
- hardly (adv.) 幾乎不；簡直不（用以表示不太可能發生的事）
  - 例 You can hardly expect me to lend you money again.
    你別指望我再借給你錢。
  - ■ 相關片語: hardly have time to breathe 忙到幾乎連喘氣的時間都沒有
  - 例 This was such a busy day. I hardly had time to breathe.
    今天好忙，我幾乎沒時間喘口氣。

MEMO

Part 3

作答說明：你會聽到兩個人之間產生的一些會話，聽完每段會話後，皆須回答有關說話內容的3個問題。請就問題敘述句選出最適切的答案後，在答案卡上劃記(A)、(B)、(C)或(D)。會話內容都不會印在試題冊上，而且只會播放一次。

破題解析

41-43

W: Hi Tom, how much money did you raise at the fundraiser for the orphanage last night?

M: Only $5,000. We were really hoping to make over $20,000, so it's a real disappointment.

W: The economy is very weak right now. Bank of Chicago and IntelliCorp just cut 30,000 workers, and a lot of them must have been based here in Chicago at their headquarters. Everyone's nervous about the economy.

M: Yes, I know. We'll just have to hope things improve next year.

41. What was the fundraiser for?
A) A school
B) A hospital
C) An orphanage
D) A corporation

42. What disappointed the man?
A) The weakness of the economy.
B) IntelliCorp just cut 30,000 workers.
C) The orphanage was forced to close.
D) They didn't raise as much money as they hoped.

43. What does the woman think led to the disappointing fundraiser?
A) Recent job cuts and the weakness of the economy.
B) Chicago is experiencing an economic boom.
C) It was poorly organized.
D) People didn't care much about orphanages.

關鍵字彙

- fundraiser (n.) 募款人；募款活動
- orphanage (n.) 孤兒院
  相 orphan (n.) 孤兒
- base (v.) 以…為基地
- boom (n.) 景氣繁榮
  例 Many people were driven by greed when they bought homes during the housing boom.
  許多人因貪心驅使，在房市旺的時候購屋。

44-46

W: Sasha, are we still on for the classical concert this Saturday?

W: Yes, definitely. It begins at 7:30 p.m., right? Do you want to meet at the concert hall, or do you want to meet for dinner first...?

M: Let's get dinner in Little India... That is, if you don't mind...I've been really craving spicy food lately.

W: Sure, I like Indian food... So long as we don't go somewhere where all the food is super hot and spicy. I definitely don't want to go to that Mexican restaurant we went to last time.

---

44. What will the man and the woman go on Saturday?
- A) To a movie
- B) To a jazz concert
- C) To dinner and a classical music concert
- D) To a Mexican restaurant

45. What do they decide to do before the concert?
- A) Get dinner in Little India
- B) Get dinner in Little Italy
- C) Get dinner in Chinatown
- D) Make a traditional Indian dinner

46. What does the woman imply she doesn't like?
- A) Foreign food
- B) Indian food
- C) Mexican food
- D) Very hot and spicy food

關鍵字彙

- crave (v.) 渴望得到;迫切需要
  例 That little kitten craves affection.
  那隻小貓渴望有人愛。

47-49

W: As I was saying, our rent has increased by 20% this month and utilities have gone up by almost 30% in the last year. There's no way we can make a profit with an overhead like this.

M: Yes, I've been thinking the same thing. We've got to do something – either increase our prices or move to a cheaper location.

W: I think we should look for a cheaper location. We can't go on raising our prices forever.

---

47. What problem does the woman raise?
  A) Their expenses have gone up.
  B) Their taxes have gone up.
  C) Their landlord has sold their building.
  D) Their landlord is demanding that they move next month.

48. What does the man imply they should do?
  A) Buy the building
  B) Sell the building
  C) Take out a loan
  D) Raise their prices or find a cheaper location

49. Why does the woman think they should look for a cheaper location?
  A) They should buy their own building.
  B) They can't keep raising prices.
  C) The building needs to be renovated.
  D) Because the building will be sold soon.

關鍵字彙

- overhead (n.) 經常費用
  例 reduce expenditure on overhead
  減少經常費用的開支。
- renovate (v.) 修復;刷新
  例 They renovated the house to make more room.

373

他們重新翻修房子，讓空間更大。

同 refurbish, restore, revamp, give a face-lift

50-52

W: Could you send me those samples you spoke about at our meeting last week?

W: Sure, I'd be happy to. I'm sorry, I have been so busy. I just forgot to send them out.

M: That's O.K. We are getting ready to order now and I really think we'd like to order some of your lamps, but we definitely need to show them to everyone on our purchasing team before we can make a decision.

W: I'll send them out by overnight messenger today. You should receive them tomorrow morning.

---

50. What does the man ask the woman to do?
A) Lower her prices
B) Send him some samples
C) Send his order by overnight messenger
D) Change the design

51. What reason does the woman give for not having sent out the samples?
A) She didn't receive his order.
B) She already sent them out.
C) She forgot.
D) His company has not paid yet.

52. What does the woman say she'll do?
A) Lower the price
B) Redesign the lamps
C) Talk to her purchasing team
D) Send them out by overnight messenger today

關鍵字彙

● sample (n.) 樣品
● overnight messenger 快遞

53-55

W: I apologize for coming to the meeting late today. My babysitter called me at the last minute to let me know she was sick, so my husband and I had to take the kids to his sister's house. She was the only person who could look after the kids.

M: That's O.K. I know that experience well. My wife and I have four kids. Today's meeting wasn't really important, and we cut it short after you called in to say you'd be late. We can have a longer meeting next week.

W: Thanks so much. By the way, how are this quarter's sales figures?

M: Excellent! Sales rose by over 12% last month.

53. What does the woman start by doing?
A) Apologizing
B) Giving a presentation
C) Giving justification for missing work
D) Defending herself against an accusation

54. What is the man's attitude towards her coming late?
A) Angry
B) Suspicious
C) Understanding
D) Indignant

55. How were the sales figures this quarter?
A) Very poor
B) Very good
C) They fell by over 12%
D) Stagnant

關鍵字彙

- justification (n.) 正當理由

  相 justify (v.) 為…辯護

  例 The accused justified his killing a burglar by saying he had done it in self-defense.
  被告為自己辯護說他殺死竊賊完全是出於自衛。

- accusation (n.) 指控

  例 She brought an accusation of theft against the man.
  她指控這名男子犯有竊盜罪。

- indignant (adj.) 憤怒的
  例 Mark became indignant when the policeman accused him of stealing the gun.
  當警察控告馬克竊取槍枝時,他變得很憤怒。
- stagnant (adj.) 停滯的;不景氣的
  例 The stagnant economy shows few signs of an immediate recovery.
  蕭條的經濟顯然不會在短時間內復甦。

Questions 56-58 refer to the following conversation.

W: Nick, did you get a phone call from Prescott Machines while I was out this morning? I've been waiting to hear from them for three days.

M: No, Ms. Stacy. Nothing at all. Is this about the order we placed with them at the beginning of last month?

W: It sure is. The parts were supposed to have been delivered last Friday, but I haven't heard anything from them at all about what's going on. Could you check on it for me before you leave? I'd really appreciate it.

---

56. What can be inferred about the woman?
   A) She just returned to her office.
   B) She has just spoken with Mr. Prescott.
   C) She just placed an order.
   D) She is just leaving for the day.

57. When was the order supposed to arrive?
   A) At the end of last week
   B) Three weeks ago
   C) At the beginning of last month
   D) Two months ago

58. What will the man probably do next?
   A) Re-order the necessary parts
   B) Write a check to pay for the order
   C) Visit his company's warehouse
   D) Inquire about the shipment

關鍵字彙

- place an order 下訂單
  例 They have placed an order with us for three new aircraft.

他們向我們訂購了三架新飛機。

(aircraft 為單複數同型的名詞，所以不加s)

● parts (n.) (常用複數)零件

　auto parts 汽車零件

　例 lose one of the part of the lawn mower

　　遺失割草機上的一個零件

● reorder (v.) 追加訂貨

　相 back-order (v.) 延後出貨

● inquire (v.) 打聽；查詢

　例 Peter wrote to inquire into the possibility of joining our company.

　　彼得來信詢問加入我們公司的可能性。

Questions 59-61 refer to the following conversation.

W: Susan, I hate to ask you this again, but I need some more time to finish up the first draft of my manuscript.

W: But Jack, we've granted you two extensions already. What seems to be the problem?

M: There's a lot of stuff going on in my family right now. Every day I'm dealing with lawyers, accountants, insurance companies – I really don't want to go into it in detail.

W: OK. Listen, I'll give you until the end of this month. But after that there's a good chance we won't be able to accept your submission. If we don't get your book on the market before the end of the year, we'll miss the publication window we've set out.

---

59. How many times has the man apparently made the same request before?

　A) None

　B) Once

　C) Two times

　D) Three times

60. What does the man say about his family?

　A) Most of them work in the professions.

　B) He hasn't been able to meet them recently.

　C) He prefers not to talk about the situation.

　D) Most of them have never read his books.

61. What does the woman tell the man?
A) She has some flexibility about the deadline.
B) She must confer with her marketing department.
C) She doesn't have time to review his manuscript.
D) She may not be able to publish his work.

關鍵字彙

- draft (n.) 草稿；草案
- manuscript (n.) 手稿；原稿(尚未印刷成書者)
- grant (v.) 同意給予
  The minister granted journalists an interview.
  部長答應接受記者訪問。
  反 deny
- extension (n.) 延期；延長
  He's got an extension to finish writing his thesis.
  他獲准延期交論文。
- submission (n.) 提交；呈遞
  the submission of an appeal 上訴書的呈遞
  相 submit (v.) 提交；呈遞
- on the market 出售；上市
  例 put a house on the market 出售房子
  例 These computers are not yet on the market.
  　　這些電腦還沒上市。
- publication window 出版品的櫥窗陳設
- set out 擺放；陳列
  Before the operation, the surgeon set out his instruments.
  手術前，外科醫生擺出他的器具。
- confer (v.) 討論；協商

Questions 62-64 refer to the following conversation.

W: I'm sorry, Ma'am, but we won't be able to check in that box. It exceeds the maximum permissible dimensions by more than 10 centimeters on each side.

W: But what can I do? I need everything I've packed inside. Can't you make an exception? What if I pay an extra fee?

M: I'm afraid that's not possible. Today's flight is completely sold out and space is at a premium. The only thing I could suggest is that you repack using a smaller box. Maybe you could put some of the things that don't fit in the box into your carry-on luggage.

62. Who is the man?
A) A flight attendant
B) A customer service agent
C) A baggage handler
D) A ground staff member

63. What is the woman's problem?
A) The baggage she wants to check is too large.
B) Her suitcase has been damaged by the airline.
C) She neglected to put her box through security.
D) She has too many pieces of luggage.

64. What does the man suggest the woman do?
A) Pay an additional service charge
B) Try to book a ticket for a later flight
C) Shift some items into her carry-on bag
D) File a claim for reimbursement

關鍵字彙

- exceed (v.) 超過
  The number admitted must not exceed 200.
  容納的數目不得超過200。
- permissible (adj.) 容許的
  Delay is not permissible, even for a single day.
  不得延誤，即使一天也不能。
- dimensions (n.) 大小；體積
- at a premium 因稀少而難得或寶貴
  Space is at a premium in this building.
  在這個建築物裡空間很稀少。
- carry-on luggage 手提行李
  同 hand luggage
- shift (v.) 移動
  例 She was uncomfortable and kept shifting in her chair.
  她覺得不自在，坐在椅子上一直動來動去。
- file a claim 申請索賠
- reimbursement (n.) (費用的)償還；報銷
  相 reimburse (v.) (費用的)償還；報銷
  All expenses will be reimbursed to you.
  一切費用都能給你報銷。

Questions 65-67 refer to the following conversation.

W: It says here on your application that you have overseas experience. Could you tell me a little about that?

M: Right after I graduated from university, I taught English to businesspeople in Thailand for three years. That led to my first business job. One of my former students was the personnel director for a multi-national firm.

W: So, basically everything you learned about marketing you learned on the job?

M: Well, not everything. My major in university was business. The English teaching thing was just a way to gain some life experience. My plan all along was to eventually find a job in sales or marketing.

65. Who is the woman?
A) A job applicant
B) A potential employer
C) A school principal
D) A language instructor

66. Why did the man first go to Thailand?
A) To take a vacation
B) To work in personnel
C) To get a teaching job
D) To visit a friend

67. How did the man get his first job in marketing?
A) Through a connection with a previous student
B) By using his university career placement center
C) By answering a job ad in a business magazine
D) Through the recommendation of his marketing professor

關鍵字彙

● potential (adj.) 有潛力的；可能的
  例 She hasn't realized her full potential as tennis player; she can perform even better in the future.
  她不知道自己具有成為網球好手的潛能；以後她可以有更好的表現。

● connection (n.) (常作複數)生意上的關係；熟人
  例 I heard about it through one of my business connections.
  我透過一個生意上的熟人聽說了這件事。

● career placement 職業介紹

Questions 68-70 refer to the following conversation.

W: I just finished the cost-cutting report you asked me to do, Mr. Harrison. Should I send it to you by e-mail?

M: Actually, could you please print out a copy and put it in my inbox? I'll read it on the plane this evening. Anything you want to let me know about right off the bat?

W: Your suspicions were certainly on target. Our profit margin is way down this quarter. But it's not because of the revenue side of things – it's just that our costs are really up. We had a one-time tax payment that couldn't be helped, but the main problem is with our communications providers. Our phone and Internet costs are much higher than they need to be.

68. What had the man asked the woman to do?
A) Conduct a financial review
B) Make some travel arrangements
C) Preparing a marketing report
D) Contact the phone company

69. What can be inferred about the man?
A) He is launching a new product.
B) He is about to take a trip.
C) He is negotiating a tax payment.
D) He is about to make some personnel changes.

70. What does the woman recommend to the man?
A) He should consider some cost-cutting measures.
B) He should concentrate on increasing earnings.
C) He ought to return an important telephone call.
D) He ought to find a new tax accountant.

關鍵字彙

● right off the bat (美式口語) 馬上
    同 right off
● suspicion (n.) 懷疑
    例 After a crime, suspicion naturally falls on the person who has a motive for it.
        一件犯罪案件發生後，有作案動機的人自然受到懷疑。
    同 doubt, misgiving, skepticism
    反 trust

- on target 達到目標
  - 例 Production so far this year is on/off target.
    今年到目前為止生產已達到／未達到目標。
- profit margin 利潤率
  - 相 margin (n.) 成本與售價間的差額
  - 相 a business operating on tight margins 蠅頭小利的生意
- way (adv.) 很遠
  - 例 The price is way above what we can afford.
    價格高得我們實在付不起。
- launch (v.) 發動(活動)
  - 例 The company is launching a new model next month.
    下個月公司將推出新型號產品。

MEMO

Part 4
作答說明：你將會聽到由一個人說的一些簡短談話。在每段簡短談話後，需回答有關說話內容的三道問題。請就每道問題選出最適切的答案，在答案卡上劃記(A)、(B)、(C)或(D)。每次談話只會播放一次，內容不會印在試題冊上。

Questions 71-73 refer to the following advertisement.

Hi, I'm Joan Irwin from Beds, Baths and Kitchens International, located in the Huntington Mall at the corner of Deltona Road and Sanford Road in Kenmore, and I want to let you know about our huge spring clearance sale! We're slashing prices on bed and bath ware, furniture and kitchen furnishings and appliances. In fact, for the month of March, all our merchandise will be discounted from 20 to 40% off our usual low prices. We're also offering interest free credit for one year to all customers, and free delivery to all customers on all our furniture. So tell your family and friends to come on down to Beds, Baths and Kitchens International for the deal of a lifetime! But don't delay! Our sale ends on March 31st, and quantities are limited!!!

71. What type of merchandise does the store sell?
A) Dining ware and cooking utensils only
B) Furniture for the office
C) Garden accessories
D) Furniture and accessories for bedrooms, bathrooms and kitchens

72. What types of discounts will be offered?
A) Everything in the store will be 20 to 40% off.
B) Select merchandise will be 20 to 40% off.
C) Only bed and bath ware will be 20 to 40% off.
D) Only kitchen appliances will be 20 to 40% off.

73. In addition to discounts, what is the store offering customers?
A) Greater quantities than before
B) Their usual low prices
C) Interest free credit for one year, and free delivery
D) 5% off when they pay with cash

關鍵字彙

- clearance (n.) 清倉大拍賣
- slash (v.) 大幅度削減
  例 The government has decided to slash taxes.
  政府決定大幅度減稅。
- utensil (n.) 器具
  例 kitchen/cooking utensils 廚房用具
- furnishings (n.) (常用複數)家具；室內陳設
- appliance (n.) 用具；設備
  例 The kitchen is equipped with modern appliances.
  廚房安裝了各種現代化的設備。
- accessory (n.) 配件
  例 The magazine offers advice on choosing clothes, shoes and accessories.
  這本雜誌提供選擇衣服、鞋子及配件的建議。

Questions 74-76 refer to the following announcement.

As a result of the loss of jobs in the state due to downsizing in the tourism industry, Florida officials have decided to create special incentives for business to expand or develop new offices or projects in the state. The special fund, which was approved by both houses of the Florida Legislature at a vote on Friday, will set aside $50 million in economic incentives, including tax cuts, and the sale or rental of state land for new businesses at an exceptionally low price. A second bill, specifically aimed at enticing film production companies to shoot films and TV series in the state, was also passed. It offers over $20 million in tax cuts and free use of state land and offices, and free assistance from state transportation and police services during film and TV shoots.

---

74. What is the main subject of the announcement?
A) The loss of jobs in Florida
B) Various strategies for encouraging business growth
C) Incentives introduced by the legislature to encourage business growth
D) Film and TV production in Florida

75. What do the bills that passed in the Florida legislature on Friday do?
A) Promote corporation between universities and corporations
B) Allocate funds to promote business
C) Give tax cuts to low income residents
D) Give tax cuts to the tourism industry

76. How will the state entice film production companies to shoot films and TV series in the state?
A) By paying their salaries
B) By providing free use of camera and lighting equipment
C) By providing free health care and insurance
D) Through tax cuts and the free use of state services

關鍵字彙

- incentive (n.) 刺激；鼓勵；獎勵
    - 例 What incentives does your company offer its employees?
      貴公司給與員工甚麼樣的獎勵?
    - 同 motivation, encouragement
    - 反 punishment
- legislature (n.) 立法機關
    - 相 legislation (n.) 立法
    - 例 The major function of the congress is to introduce legislation.
      國會的主要功能是制訂法律。
- set aside 留出；撥出
    - 例 We plan to set aside some money for our son's education.
      我們打算存一些錢，作為兒子的教育基金。
- bill (n.) 議案；法案
    - 例 The House of Commons has not yet passed the bill.
      下議院尚未通過該議案。
- entice (v.) 誘使；慫恿
    - 相 enticing (adj.) 引誘的；迷人的
    - 例 Sally's invitation seemed too enticing to refuse.
      莎莉的邀請太誘人，叫人難以拒絕。
- shoot (v.) 拍攝
    - 動詞三態為shoot, shot, shot
    - 例 That movie studio shot a movie in my hometown last year.
      那家製片廠去年在我的老家拍了一部電影。
- House (n.) 議院
    - 例 She is speaker of the House of Representatives.
      她是眾議院的議長。
- allocate (v.) 分配；分派
    - 例 They will allocate funds for housing.
      他們將分配資金作為購屋用。
- series (n.) 連續；系列
    - a series of... 一連串…；一系列…
    - 例 There have been a series of burglaries on the east side of town.
      城裡的東區發生了一系列竊盜案件。

Questions 77-79 refer to the following message.

This is a message for family and friends waiting for passengers on Delta Airlines Flight 433 which originated in Tokyo and stopped off at LAX on its way to Las Vegas. Due to a technical problem with the landing gear, the flight may be delayed in Los Angeles for another hour or so, while technicians work on the problem. We expect the plane to be landing here in Las Vegas at around 3:20 p.m. today. We apologize for any inconvenience this unexpected delay may have caused you. Free coffee and donuts will be provided by ground staff in the arrivals area near Gate 33, where passengers will be deboarding. Thank you again for your patience, and we hope you'll fly Delta Airlines sometime soon.

77. Who is the intended audience of the announcement?
A) Delta Airlines ground staff
B) A group of people waiting for a flight to arrive
C) A group of people waiting for a flight to depart
D) Passenger on Delta Airlines Flight 433

78. Why has the flight been delayed?
A) Due to a problem with passengers who deboarded at LAX
B) Due to a problem at LAX
C) Due to a technical problem with the landing gear
D) Due to bad weather in Japan

79. What does the airline offer to family and friends waiting for the flight?
A) A discount on coffee and donuts at a café nearby
B) Free coffee and donuts
C) A discount on their next flight
D) Free coffee and donuts on their next Delta Airlines flight

關鍵字彙 |

- originate (v.) 發源；來自
  例 No one is quite sure of where that strange custom originated.
  沒有人知道那奇特的風俗習慣究竟起源於哪裡。
- landing gear 起降落裝置
- ground staff 地勤人員
- deboard (v.) 下飛機
- LAX 洛杉磯國際機場

> **Questions 80-82 refer to the following passage.**
> Ok, follow me around, and I'll show you where everything is. Here is the copy machine. It's an old machine and needs some time to warm up, so you've got to switch it on before 8:50, and that's your first responsibility every morning. After you get that done, you have to make a pot of coffee, and here is the coffeemaker. Remember, the coffee should be ready before the others come in. OK...now...here is the mailbox – you should sort the mail and put it on everyone's desk. We get a lot of mail, so you'll have to do this a couple of times a day.

80. What is the speaker doing?
- A) Describing a product
- B) Describing duties
- C) Explaining a problem
- D) Explaining how to use something

81. Who is most probably listening to the talk?
- A) A new salesperson
- B) A new accountant
- C) A new machine
- D) A new secretary

82. What is the first thing the listener has to do in the morning?
- A) Make a pot of coffee
- B) Check the mailbox
- C) Turn on the copier
- D) Answer the e-mail from clients

關鍵字彙

- duty (n.) 責任；職責
  同 responsibility, obligation, job, task

> **Questions 83 and 84 refer to the following announcement.**
> Ladies and gentlemen, this is your captain speaking. We have reached our cruising altitude of 30,000 feet and I'm going to go ahead, and turn off the fasten seatbelt sign. You can feel free to move about the cabin, but I'm going to ask that you keep your seatbelts fastened while you're in your seats. You never know when we might hit some turbulence. Thank you and enjoy the flight.

83. Where is this announcement most likely being made?
   A) On an airplane
   B) In an airport
   C) On a boat
   D) On a bus

84. What should passengers who remain seated do?
   A) Refrain from smoking
   B) Unbuckle their seatbelts
   C) Watch a movie
   D) Keep their seatbelts fastened

關鍵字彙

- cruise (n.) 巡航；巡遊
- altitude (n.) 海拔；高度
- cruising altitude 飛行高度
  相 cruise control 定速裝置
- cabin (n.) 機艙；船的客艙
  例 cabin crew 航班空服人員
- turbulence (n.) 亂流
  例 We experienced some slight turbulence flying over the Atlantic.
     我們飛越大西洋時，遇到了一點亂流。
  相 turbulent (adj.) 動盪的；混亂的
- refrain (v.) 克制
  refrain from V-ing/sth. 克制不要做某事
  例 You should refrain from eating candy before dinner or you'll kill your appetite.

你應克制自己不要在晚餐前吃糖果，否則你會沒有胃口。

● unbuckle (v.) 解開(皮帶或釦子等)
反 buckle (v.)

Questions 85-87 refer to the following news story.

Only a decade ago, the government was worried about overpopulation. Now, it's worried that mothers are not having enough children. With the fertility rate at 1.2 children per woman of childbearing age – one of the lowest in the world – the government has begun to realize the problems of a suddenly shrinking population.

Key to returning the birthrate to a more stable birthrate of 2.0 children per woman of childbearing age, one which allows for a very gradual decline in the population, is giving families economic incentives to have more children. A recent poll revealed that only eight percent of mothers who have at least one child want more children. The reason? Financial difficulties in raising children, they said. According to population specialists, the government must offer better tax breaks for couples of childbearing age.

---

85. What is the government worried about?
A) Its slow economic growth
B) Too few mothers of childbearing age
C) Its increasing population
D) A low birth rate

86. What does a birthrate of 2.0 per woman of childbearing age mean?
A) The population will decrease slowly.
B) The population will increase slowly.
C) The population will decrease quickly.
D) The population will increase quickly.

87. What recommendation was given to the government?

A) Slowly increase taxes on childbearing couples

B) Increase the financial burden on childbearing couples

C) Reduce the tax burden on childbearing couples

D) Decrease the tax burden on children

關鍵字彙

- fertility (n.) 繁殖力

  例 fertility rate 生育率

  例 fertility drug 受孕藥

  相 fertile (adj.) 能生育的

- childbearing (n.) 分娩

  例 She's past childbearing age.

  她已過生育年齡。

- allow for 考慮到

  例 It will take you half an hour to get to the station, allowing for traffic delays.

  把交通延誤的情況算進去，你要花半小時才能到車站。

- gradual (adj.) 逐漸的

  同 slow, moderate

  反 sudden, swift, abrupt

- decline (v.) 衰退；下降

  例 Unemployment declined to 2 percent last month.

  上個月失業率降到百分之2。

- incentive (n.) 獎勵；刺激

  例 Paul has a strong incentive to learn English.

  保羅有強烈的動機學英文。

  同 motive

- poll (n.) 民意調查；投票

  例 We're going to conduct a public opinion poll.

  我們將進行一項民意調查。

- tax break 減稅

Questions 88 and 89 refer to the following advertisement.

Are you working hard and feeling tired? Are you bored with the routine of your life? Why not visit JetSet and plan the perfect escape from your stressful reality? We offer packages of two-day to two-week tours of some of the most exotic and exciting destinations on the planet! JetSet takes care of your paperwork, from your passport to your hotel and restaurant accommodations, so you can focus on what you need most: fun and relaxation! With five offices in the Greater Los Angeles area, we're in easy to reach or call our hotline at 1-800- JetSet. Need a break? Who doesn't? Come to JetSet for the best break of them all!

88. What kind of business is JetSet?
   A) A bookstore
   B) A travel agency
   C) A hotel
   D) A restaurant

89. What does JetSet do for its customers?
   A) Escape from prison
   B) Break their daily routine
   C) Arrange travel packages
   D) Focus on the planet

關鍵字彙

● routine (n.) 例行公事；慣例
   例 In our daily routine, we are likely to get bored from time to time.
   在日常生活中，我們常會感到無聊。
● exotic (adj.) 具有異國風味的
   例 I was attracted to the exotic scenery on that island.
   那個島上充滿異國風味的景色很吸引我。
● destination (n.) 目的地
   例 Although we will be laying over in Houston, our final destination is Nashville, Tennesse.
   雖然我們將在休士頓中途停留，但我們目的地是田納西州的那須維爾。

- accommodation (n.) (常用複數)住宿
  - 例 These are your accommodations for the duration of your stay, I hope you like them.
    這些是您停留期間的住宿安排，希望您會喜歡。
- Greater (adj.) 包括市區和郊區的
  - 例 Greater London 大倫敦區 (包括倫敦市及其郊區)

Questions 90 and 91 refer to the following announcement.

Welcome aboard the Yosemite National Park tour bus. You are now in one of the best maintained and best preserved natural forest areas in North America. The population of wildlife is quite large here, and we will encounter a variety of both tame and dangerous animals. The animals behave as they would in any natural habitat, so please take heed of all sign boards informing you as to their whereabouts and activity patterns. But there are three basic rules we ask you to observe in all cases: one, do not feed the animals; two, do not approach them; three, do not scare them. For more details, please visit the park ranger offices throughout the park. We thank you for your cooperation and wish you a happy ride.

---

90. What is the main point of this announcement?
   A) How to preserve natural forests
   B) How to preserve the natural habitats of animals
   C) What to do to make animals tame
   D) What to do when wild animals are around

91. Where is the information about animals available?
   A) At the park entrance office
   B) In guidebooks sold at the visitors' center
   C) At the park rangers' offices and on sign boards
   D) On the radio operated by the park

關鍵字彙

- preserve (v.) 維護；保存

例 The most popular way to preserve fruit is to cook it with sugar and then seal it in a jar.
保存水果最常見的方式是和糖一起煮，然後封入罐子中。

● encounter (v.) 遇到；面臨
例 Every time he encounters a problem, he asks the teacher for advice.
他每次遇到問題，總是徵詢老師的意見。

● tame (v.) 使…馴服或服從
例 It takes skills and a lot of energy to tame a wild lion.
馴服野生獅子需要技巧和充沛的精力。
同 domesticate, break

● habitat (n.) (動物的)棲息地；(植物的)產地

● take heed of... 留意或聽從…
例 Take heed of your doctor's advice.
聽醫生的話吧。

● whereabouts (n.) 行蹤；下落(恆用複數)
例 The police are trying to find the whereabouts of the fugitive.
警方正設法找尋那名逃犯的行蹤。

● observe (v.) 遵守；奉行
例 observe the speed limit
遵守速限

● approach (v.) 接近
例 We approached the dying animal with caution.
我們小心翼翼地接近這隻垂死的動物。

Questions 92 to 94 refer to the following speech.

To conclude this meeting, let me restate my policy for next year. Because we are approaching a rapid shift in the market from a preference for high-end, high-performance computers to low-priced, limited capacity computers, we have shifted our production accordingly. We have the backing of the entire board of directors. They realize and we realize that consumers are becoming smart, all consumers, not just the lower-end machine users. Let us provide them with what they want, not what we want to sell them. That is our theme for the next year. It cost us more than 50 million dollars to develop the new machines and shift the production, but the investment will come back to us as profits, twofold, at least. We are moving faster than any other company. We'll finally catch up with IBM. Let's go get them!

92. Who is talking?
 A) The chief representative of consumers
 B) The CEO of the company
 C) The chief of a market research company
 D) The president of the bank

93. Why was production changed to the new machines?
 A) They believe the board of directors wants them.
 B) They believe the CEO wants them.
 C) They believe the chief of market research wants them.
 D) They believe the consumers want them.

94. What was the meeting about?
 A) About the reshuffling of directors
 B) About the performance of the new computer models
 C) About the change in marketing targets and products
 D) About the weakening of a rival company

關鍵字彙

- shift (v.) 改變；轉移

  例 Don't try to shift the responsibility onto others!
  別想把責任推給別人！

- preference (n.) 偏愛

  have a preference for.... 對…有偏好

  例 Many of my friends enjoy singing, but I have a preference for dancing.
  我許多朋友喜歡唱歌，但我偏好跳舞。

- high-end (adj.) 昂貴的；高檔的

  反 low-end

- capacity (n.) 能力

  beyond one's capacity 超過某人的能力

  例 At the moment this book is beyond my son's capacity.
  目前我兒子還沒有辦法讀這本書。

- board of directors 董事會

- twofold (adj.) 兩倍的

- reshuffle (v.) 調整；改組

  同 reorganize, rearrange, restructure

- rival (n.) 競爭對手

  例 business rivals 商業對手
  例 rivals in love 情敵

- catch up with... 趕上…

  例 Try as we could, we could not catch up with the leaders.
  不管我們怎麼努力，還是無法趕上領先的人。

Questions 95 to 97 refer to the following speech.

Every year we give the Orange County Business Leader Award to the person who has made the greatest positive impact on our community. This year it is with great pleasure that I present this award to Max Patterson. Max has been a leader in this community and a dear friend since he moved here in 1985. However last year he really outdid himself. He renovated our downtown center, adding 15 stores and a basketball court. His renovation alone added twenty five jobs for our city. Now, would you join me in congratulating Max?

95. Who won the Orange County Business Leader Award?
   A) A deer
   B) Max Patterson
   C) Orange County
   D) A motivational speaker

96 How long has the award recipient lived in Orange County?
   A) He was born there
   B) For fifteen years
   C) Since 1985
   D) From the time he was 19 until he turned 85

97. Why did he win the award?
   A) For his community service
   B) For building a new library
   C) For rebuilding the downtown center
   D) For his ability to play basketball

關鍵字彙

- outdo (v.) 超過；勝過
- renovate (v.) 修復或整修(尤指舊建築物)
   同 refurbish, restore, revamp, remodel
- motivational (adj.) 激勵人心的
   相 motivate (v.) 刺激；給予動機
- recipient (n.) 接受者
   例 She's one of the recipients of prizes.
   她是獲獎者之一。

Questions 98 to 100 refer to the following speech.

Hi, this is the National Sales Director, Jack Robins. Before we go through the numbers for the whole country, I'd like to congratulate the Toronto branch on another terrific quarter. Their sales were once again off the charts, more than doubling their quota. They finished the year number one in sales for the fifth year in a row.

98. Where was this announcement most likely made?
   A) On a conference call
   B) In Toronto
   C) On an airplane
   D) In a bathroom

99. Why does he congratulate the Toronto branch?
   A) The Toronto branch came in second in a sales contest
   B) It is the Toronto branch's fifth anniversary
   C) Its sales were the highest in the country
   D) Its customer service was ranked number one

100. What does the speaker imply about how well the Toronto branch has performed in the past?
   A) Its current quarter is a lot better than previous quarter.
   B) It has always had good sales numbers.
   C) Its sales numbers have steadily declined.
   D) It is a new branch.

關鍵字彙

- conference call 電話會議
- quarter (n.) 區域
  例 Living conditions in poor quarters were horrible. 城裡窮人居住區的生活條件惡劣
- off the charts 出乎意料地好
  例 His new car was off the charts! 他的新車出乎意料地拉風！
- quota (n.) 配額
  例 The sales department fell short of their sales quota by about fifteen percent.
  業務部未達成他們的業績，大約少百分之十五。
- in a row 連續
  Poor Hedy was sick for 5 days in a row last week.
  可憐的海蒂上禮拜病了連續五天。
  同 consecutively, successively
- current (adj.) 目前的
  例 current affairs 現今的議題

Part 5

作答說明： 以下的每個句子都是不完整的句子，句子底下都標上了4個答案選項。請從中挑選出1個最適當的字彙或片語來完成句子，然後在答案卡上劃記(A)、(B)、(C)、(D)。

破題解析

101. Rampant _____ is undermining the economies of several developing countries in Asia.

A) corruption

B) integrity

C) charity

D) enthusiasm

因為句意以及關鍵字economies，故選A。

關鍵字彙

- rampant (adj.) 猖獗的；蔓延的

  例 Cholera was rampant among the slum dwellers.

  霍亂在貧民區的居民間蔓延開來。

- corruption (n.) 貪汙

  例 There's corruption in almost every government.

  幾乎大多數的政府都貪汙。

  相 corrupt (adj.)

- integrity (n.) 正直

  例 The integrity of a person is much more important than his wealth.

  一個人的正直比他的財富重要得多。

- charity (n.) 慈善

  例 The old man left all his property to charity.

  老人把所有財產捐給慈善團體。

- enthusiasm (n.) 熱忱

  例 Joe was a basketball fan and he showed little enthusiasm in any other sports.

  喬是個籃球迷，他對其它運動就不怎麼熱衷。

譯文

貪汙猖獗的問題正侵蝕著好幾個亞洲發展中國家的經濟。

102. From next year, all final year high school students _____ to pass an English exam before they can enter university.

A) are being required

B) will be required

C) will be requiring

D) will have been required

根據句意，主要子句要用未來式，而且主詞all final year high school students 是被要求要通過測驗，所以應是未來被動語態，故選B。

關鍵字彙

● require (v.) 要求；需要

例 They were required to study three years of English.

他們必須修三年英文。

譯文

自明年起，所有高三學生在進入大學之前，都被要求要通過一項英文測驗。

103. The National Assembly was considered outdated and unnecessary, so the Legislature voted overwhelmingly to _____ it.

A) come down on

B) make up for

C) stand in for

D) do away with

根據句意和關鍵字outdated以及unnecessary，故選D。

關鍵字彙

● come down on 斥責

例 His boss came down on him very harshly.

他的老闆非常嚴厲地斥責他。

● make up for 補償

例 There is no way she can make up for her reckless behavior.

她沒有辦法彌補她不顧後果的行為。

● stand in for 代替

例 I'm very busy. Do you mind standing in for me?

我很忙。你可以代替我嗎？

- do away with 廢除；擺脫

  例 The mayor endeavored to do away with all the red tape.
  市長致力於廢除官僚的行政作風。

譯文

國民大會被視為過時而且無必要存在，因此立法院壓倒性地表決將它廢除。

104. _____ such strong opposition throughout the country, the government would have introduced sweeping financial reforms last year.

A) If there wasn't

B) Had there not

C) If there hadn't been

D) Was there not

本句描述的是與過去事實相反的情況，因此if子句要用had + p.p.，結果子句用 would have + p.p.。以If there hadn't been (若不是有)最恰當，故選C。

關鍵字彙

- introduce (v.) 帶領；傳入；介紹

  例 He was introduced to a whole new concept.
  他被介紹了一個全新的觀念。

- reform (n.) 改革;改造

  例 Ten years of imprisonment has completely reformed him.
  十年的牢獄生涯已徹底改造了他。

譯文

若不是有全國各地的反對聲浪，政府去年就會進行財經改革。

105. Although the police search far and wide, the missing child was _____ to be found.

A) whereabouts

B) nowhere

C) elsewhere

D) nearby

根據句意和關鍵字search和missing，故選B。

關鍵字彙

● nowhere (adv.) 到處都沒有…；到處都不…

例 The necklace was nowhere to be found.
那項鍊到處都找不到。

譯文

警方雖然遍地搜尋，走失的小孩還是無法尋獲。

106. _____, this looks like a good business offer." The lawyer said.
" But, we must study the contract thoroughly before making a final decision."

A) On the face of it
B) On the safe side
C) On the right track
D) On the spot

根據句意和關鍵字looks like...，故選A。

關鍵字彙

● on the face of it 表面上看來
● on the safe side 為保險起見
● on the right track 正確

例 Tim is on the right track and will solve the mystery soon.
提姆的推理正確，他很快就能解出謎題。

● on the spot 當場

譯文

「表面上看來這是一筆好交易。」律師說：「可是在做最後決定之前，我們必須再仔細研究一下契約內容。」

107. Despite everything he had said during the meeting, the owner failed to
_____ on his promise to improve working conditions in the factory, so the staff went on strike.

A) pull through
B) make out
C) come around
D) make good

根據句意和關鍵字failed和promise，故選D。

關鍵字彙 |

- pull through 渡過難關
  - 例 The doctor pulled the patient through his illness.
    醫生幫助這病患渡過病痛。
- make out 瞭解
  - 例 No one could make out what she was talking about.
    沒有人聽得懂她在說甚麼。
- come around 甦醒；恢復知覺
  - 例 Doctor! Doctor! The patient is coming around now.
    醫生！醫生！病人現在甦醒了。
- make good 實現；成功
  - 例 He is a hard worker, and I am sure that he will make good in that job.
    他很勤勞，我深信他一定能勝任那份工作。

譯文 |

儘管在會議中說得天花亂墜，老闆還是沒能實現他的承諾去改善工廠的工作環境，員工因而罷工。

108. The report revealed that the company's financial problem were
_____ anyone anticipated.

    A) very worse than

    B) bad more than

    C) worse much more than

    D) much worse than

關鍵字彙 |

- reveal (v.) 揭發；透露
  - 例 The guilty party is often not revealed until the end of the program.
    通常要到節目最後才知道犯罪的是哪一方。
  - 同 disclose, divulge, publicize
  - 反 conceal, hide
- anticipate (v.) 預期
  - 相 anticipation (n.)

譯文 |

報告批露出這家公司的財務問題遠比任何人預期的還要更嚴重。

109. William's English proficiency is already very good because his mother, who is a renowned English professor, has been coaching him _____ he started kindergarten.

A) way beyond
B) since before
C) even during
D) while at

空格處連接兩個子句，需要的是連接詞，四選項中只有since是附屬連接詞，後接before he started kindergarten為表達時間的子句，故選B。

關鍵字彙

- proficiency (n.) 精通
  例 Her proficiency in foreign languages is quite impressive.
  她精通外語的能力令人印象深刻。
- renowned (adj.) 著名的
  例 renowned for her acting 以她的演技著稱

譯文

威廉的英文能力很強，因為他母親身為著名的英文教授，從他上幼稚園前就開始教他英文了。

110. Even though AIDS has already claimed millions of lives throughout the world, many people still don't _____ the need to take precautions against the disease.

A) appreciate
B) eventuate
C) obligate
D) confiscate

根據句意和關鍵字still don't以及the need，故選A。

關鍵字彙

- precaution (n.) 警戒；預防措施
  例 Government agencies concerned had taken all necessary and possible precautions against an imminent and likely far-reaching financial storm.
  相關的政府機構在之前即已針對一場近迫眉睫且可能影響深遠的金融風暴做了一切必要且可能的預防措施。

同 safeguard, safety measure, prevention, heedfulness

- claim (v.) 奪取(生命)
  claim a life 奪走一條人命
  例 The typhoon claimed seven lives in that small coastal town.
  這颱風造成那濱海小鎮有七人死亡。

- appreciate (v.) 重視；體會；察覺
  例 I am afraid you have not appreciated the urgency of the matter.
  恐怕你還沒有意識到這件事的緊迫性。

- eventuate (v.) 結果；最終導致
  例 A rapid rise in prices soon eventuated in mass unemployment.
  價格的快速上漲很快就導致了大量的失業。

- obligate (v.) 使…負責任
  相 obligation (n.) 責任；義務

- confiscate (v.) 充公；沒收
  例 The drugs he was trying to smuggle into the country were confiscated by customs.
  他原本試圖要走私入境的毒品被海關沒收了。
  同 take, seize, appropriate, commandeer

譯文

雖然愛滋病已奪走無數人的生命，許多人仍然不重視採取預防措施的必要性。

111. The project was a failure because the manager's instructions were _____. Consequently, none of the staff knew what was expected of them.

A) tangible
B) explicit
C) ambiguous
D) reliable

根據句意和關鍵句 none of the staff knew what was expected of them，故選C。

關鍵字彙

- tangible (adj.) 確實的
  例 The judge had to let the accused free because the prosecutor couldn't come up with any tangible proof of his crime.
  法官必須釋放被告，因為檢察官提不出他犯罪的確實證據。

up with any tangible proof of his crime.

法官必須釋放被告，因為檢察官提不出他犯罪的確實證據。

- explicit (adj.) 明確的

  例 The more explicit the directions, the less room for error.

  方向越明確，犯錯的空間就越小。

  同 exact, obvious

  反 implicit, vague

- ambiguous (adj.) 模糊的；不明確的

  例 When asked if he had broken the vase, Paul gave an ambiguous reply.

  當問到他是否打破花瓶，保羅給了令人摸不著頭緒的答覆。

  同 unclear, uncertain, vague

  反 clear

- reliable (adj.) 可靠的

  同 trustworthy, dependable

  反 unreliable

譯文

這項計畫失敗了，因為經理模糊不清的指示，因此員工都不知道他們該做些甚麼。

112. In the last two hundred years, millions of people have migrated to America _____ a better life.

A) in view of

B) in line with

C) in place of

D) in search of

根據句意和關鍵字migrated以及a better life，故選D。

關鍵字彙

- in view of 鑑於

  例 In view of her eloquence, Jessica could be a great speaker.

  從潔西卡的口才來看，她說不定會成為一個很棒的演說家。

- in line with 一致

  例 The company's profits were in line with what was expected.

  公司的獲利情況與原本預期的一樣。

- in place of 代替

- in search of 尋求
    例 The explorers went to South America in search of gold and jewels.
    探險家們到南美洲尋找黃金和珠寶。

譯文│

過去兩百年來，數百萬的民眾移居美國去尋求更美好的生活。

113. There's no point _____ constantly dwelling on past mistakes. The key is to learn from them and then look into the future.
    A) about
    B) in
    C) at
    D) on
    名詞point後應接介系詞in，故選B。

關鍵字彙│

- dwell on... 老是想著…
    例 Do not dwell too long on past mistakes; look to the future.
    不要老想著過去所犯的錯，展望未來吧。

譯文│

經常沉浸於過去犯的錯誤是沒有意義的，重點是要從中學到教訓，然後展望未來。

114. The opera singer, _____ critics were divided, was given a standing ovation by the audience.
    A) who about
    B) about whom
    C) whose
    D) about her
    這裡需要的是關係代名詞，而且要表達出「對於此人」的意思，因此about whom最正確，介系詞about後面需用受格，故選B。

關鍵字彙│

- critic (n.) 評論家；吹毛求疵的人
    例 Despite the critics' positive review of the movie, the people who have gone to

see it don't really like it.

儘管影評人的評價是正面的，但是去看過那部電影的觀眾們並不是那麼喜歡這片。

- divided (adj.) 分歧的
  相 divide (v.) 分割；分開
  division (n.) 分配；歧見
- standing ovation 起立喝采

譯文

這位歌劇家，儘管評論家們對於此人意見分歧，仍得到觀眾的起立喝采。

115. _____ stall-holders in the night markets is a good way to save money. It can also be a lot of fun.

A) Attending to

B) Bargaining with

C) Standing by

D) Glancing at

根據句意以及關鍵字save money，故選B。

關鍵字彙

- attend to 照顧
  例 Our hostess attended to our every need.
  我們的女主人顧及我們的各種需求。
- bargain with 討價還價
  例 If we bargain with them, they might reduce the price.
  如果我們跟他們討價還價，他們可能會降價。
- stand by 支持
  例 I will stand by you whenever you are in trouble.
  你有困難時我一定會支持你。
- glance at 瞄一眼
  例 I glanced at the menu, but I didn't see anything I wanted.
  我看了一下菜單，但看不到任何我想要的東西。

譯文

和夜市的小販討價還價是省錢的好方法，也很有趣。

116. The government made the decision to push ahead with _____ of the nuclear power plant.

A) constructing

B) constructed

C) construction

D) constructs

從句子結構和空格位置可看出with後面和of前面需接名詞或名詞片語。四個選項中，只有construction是名詞，故選C。

關鍵字彙

● push ahead with... 推動…

例 The country is pushing ahead with economic development.

這個國家正推動經濟發展。

● nuclear power plant 核能電廠

譯文

政府決定推動興建核能電廠。

117. Normal business hours are posted in each office or branch and are _____ upon request.

A) furnish

B) furnished

C) furniture

D) furnishing

句中 "are posted in the office" 為被動語態，因此是同樣主詞business hours，對稱句也用被動語態，故選B。

關鍵字彙

● upon request 回應要求

例 Catalogs are available upon request.

備有目錄以供索取。

● furnish (v.) 提供；供應

例 a furnished flat (英)連同家具一同出租的公寓

同 supply, provide, equip

● furnishing (n.) 裝備

譯文

一般的營業時間表張貼在每一間辦公室或分公司，並且一旦有人索取就會提供。

118. Contributions will benefit STM Reads, a non-profit organization
_____ literacy programs.

A) support
B) supported
C) supporting
D) supports

主要子句 Contributions will benefit STM Reads中已有主要動詞 "benefit" ，
所以後面空格位置應填入修飾主詞的形容詞。選項A和D是動詞，不符合。選項B
的supported是過去分詞，也可視為形容詞，但是還原成which is supported的
關係子句時可看出，過去分詞的時態並不符合題意。只有選項C的supporting是
現在分詞，可當形容詞，還原句是which is supporting才符合題意，故選C。

關鍵字彙

- non-profit organization非營利機構(簡稱NPO)
- contribution (n.) 捐助
  相 contribute (v.)

譯文

外界的捐獻將有助於STM Reads，它是個支援識字計畫的非營利機構。

119. Being an entrepreneur is all _____ finding creative ways to show
the world your great idea.

A) about
B) for
C) of
D) to

根據句意以及關鍵字all和名詞子句finding creative ways to....，故選A。

關鍵字彙

- entrepreneur (n.) 企業家；事業創辦者
  相 enterprise (n.) 企業
  enterprising (adj.) 有事業心的；有膽量的

譯文

當一個企業家，就是找出有創意的好方法，把你的好點子呈現給全世界。

120. The federal government estimates that 90 percent of all the sports
_____ that is sold to collectors is fake.
A) memorandum
B) memorial
C) memorabilia
D) memory

根據句意以及關鍵字sports和collectors，故選C。

關鍵字彙

- fake (adj.) 假的；偽造的
  同 false, counterfeit, phony, bogus, sham
  反 real, genuine
- memorandum (n.) 備忘錄(簡稱memo)
- memorial (n.) 紀念館；紀念碑
- memorabilia (n.) 紀念品

譯文

聯邦政府估計，賣給收藏者的運動紀念品，有九成都是假的。

121. An important thing to remember when buying stocks is that past
performance isn't necessary an _____ of future results.
A) indecision
B) infraction
C) indictment
D) indication

根據句意以及關鍵字past performance和future results，故選D。

關鍵字彙

- indecision (n.) 優柔寡斷；遲疑不決
- infraction (n.) 違背；違法
  例 a minor infraction of the rules 輕微犯規
- indictment (n.) 告發；起訴

例 bring in an indictment against sb. 控告某人

● indication (n.) 表示；跡象

例 There are indications that the situation may be improving.

有跡象顯示情勢可能好轉。

相 indicate (v.)

譯文

買股票的時候，要記得一件重要的事，就是過去的市場表現未必可當成未來結果的參考。

122. Managers who can head off problems before they develop into something serious are two steps _____ of the game.

A) ahead

B) behind

C) about

D) below

根據句意以及子句head off problems before.....和two steps_____ of the game，故選A。

關鍵字彙

● head off 阻止；避免

例 The nuclear plant is going to explode! It is impossible to head off a disaster.

核能電廠就要爆炸了！災難無可避免。

同 block, intercept, cut off

譯文

能阻止問題擴大成嚴重事態的經理，總是領先別人兩步。

123. The recent success of Tim's restaurant has served only to increase his _____ for the future.

A) enthused

B) enthusiasm

C) enthusiastic

D) enthuse

所有格his後面應接名詞，故選B。

關鍵字彙

● enthusiasm (n.) 熱情

　　同 eagerness, keenness, fervor, passion, zeal

　　反 apathy

譯文

提姆的餐廳近來經營得很成功，更增加他對未來的熱情。

124. During the 1980's, Japan's fast-growing GNP was ＿＿＿＿＿ to be the highest in the world by the year 2000.

A) predict

B) predictor

C) predicted

D) prediction

從句子結構中可看出空格應填入動詞的過去分詞，配合前面的was成為被動語態，故選C。

關鍵字彙

● GNP = gross national product 國民生產總額

● prediction (n.) 預測

　　例 Have you heard the weather prediction for tomorrow?

　　　你有聽到明天的氣象預報嗎？

　　同 forecast, prophecy

譯文

在1980年代，日本快速增長的國民生產總額，當時曾預言將在2000年成為世界第一高。

125. Construction jobs, fueled by the housing boom, have also ＿＿＿＿＿ plentiful in the past year, and the need for skilled workers isn't abating.

A) remained

B) reminded

C) recreated

D) remitted

根據句意以及關鍵字fueled by, plentiful和isn't abating，故選A。

關鍵字彙

- fuel (v.) 激起；刺激
  例 His rude remarks fueled her anger.
    他粗魯的言詞使她怒上加怒。
- boom (n.) 繁榮時期
  例 baby boom (第二次世界大戰後的)嬰兒潮
  例 The oil market is enjoying a boom.
    現階段的石油市場欣欣向榮。
- abate (v.) 減少；減輕
  例 People are campaigning to abate the noise in our cities.
    大家正在進行一場減低我們城市中噪音的活動。
  同 reduce, lessen, alleviate
  反 increase, augment, strengthen
- remit (v.) 赦免；寬恕(常用於被動語態)
  例 The taxes have been remitted.
    稅款已免除。

譯文

建築業的工作量，因為房地產興起，在過去一年也仍然居高不下，對技術性工人的需求也沒有減少。

126. Payment is to be received ＿＿＿＿＿＿＿ 10 days of the statement date printed on the bill.
   A) about
   B) within
   C) at
   D) from
   本題主要是考介系詞的用法，由句意判斷，句中提到支付的款項應在某個期限內收到，因此只有選項B的within最符合題意，表示要在10天內收到，故選B。

關鍵字彙

- statement (n.) (銀行等的)報告或結算單；聲明
  例 My bank sends me monthly statements.
    銀行按月把結算單寄給我。

譯文

應支付的款項應在帳單上印製的日期十天內收到。

127. Annual reports are the best tool for the public to _____ the performance of companies.

   A) review

   B) extract

   C) demand

   D) expect

根據句意以及關鍵字the best tool和performance，故選A。

關鍵字彙

- review (v.) 再檢查；重新探討；檢視

   例 The government is reviewing the situation.

     政府正重新研究形勢。

- extract (v.) 採掘；設法得到(情報等)

   例 The police finally extracted the information after hours of questioning.

     警方在數小時的盤問後，終於套出情報。

譯文

年度報告是讓大眾檢視公司表現的最佳工具。

128. There were several layovers at the airport last month _____ to bad weather.

   A) because

   B) owed

   C) due

   D) since

根據句意以及關鍵字layovers和bad weather，空格前後的兩件事應互有因果關係。加上空格後面接介系詞to，所以不能選because，故選C。

關鍵字彙

- layover (n.) 臨時滯留；中途停留

   同 stopover

- due to 因為；由於

   例 Maggie's failure is due to her laziness.

     瑪姬的失敗是因為她懶惰。

譯文｜

機場上個月因氣候不佳而有幾起班機誤點的狀況。

129. Many companies manufacture their products in other countries
_____ cheap labor is easier to find.
A) although
B) so that
C) than
D) because

根據句意以及子句manufacture their products in other countries和關鍵字
cheap labor，空格前後的兩件事應互有因果關係，故選D。

關鍵字彙｜

● labor (n.) 勞力；勞動
例 My dad didn't have much education, which is why he makes a living doing manual labor.
我老爸沒受過什麼教育，這就是為什麼他要靠雙手勞動來謀生的原因。

譯文｜

許多公司都在別的國家製造它們的產品，因為較容易找到廉價的勞工。

130. There's always something interesting to do in New York. It's a really
_____ city.
A) notorious
B) abstract
C) vibrant
D) terrible

根據句意以及關鍵字interesting，故選C。

關鍵字彙｜

● notorious (adj.) 聲名狼藉的
同 infamous, disreputable, ill-famed
● abstract (adj.) 抽象的
例 My art teacher says she doesn't like abstract art.
我的美術老師說她不喜歡抽象藝術。
同 conceptual, intangible

反 concrete

● vibrant (adj.) 有活力的

例 The vibrant atmosphere of Wall Street at noon is offset by its relative stillness at midnight.

華爾街中午時分的活躍氣氛被午夜時相對的寂靜給抵消。

同 lively, vivacious, pulsating, alive

反 listless

譯文

在紐約永遠都有有趣的事可做，它真是一個有活力的城市。

131. _____ government regulations, everyone must submit an annual statement of income to the Department of Taxation.

A) In lieu of

B) In accordance with

C) In reference to

D) In spite of

根據句意以及關鍵字regulations和must submit.....，故選B。

關鍵字彙

● in lieu of 代替

例 accept a check in lieu of cash 接受支票來代替現金

● in accordance with 依照

例 act in accordance with custom/ the law 依照慣例／法律

● in reference to 關於

例 I'm writing in reference to your job application.

敬啟者，此封信乃有關您應徵工作一事。

● in spite of 儘管(後接名詞或名詞子句)

例 In spite of all Jennifer's efforts she failed.

儘管珍妮佛已盡全力，但還是失敗了。

譯文

依照政府的規定，每個人都應繳交年收入申報表給稅捐處。

132. During the blizzard, the hikers were lucky to find a disused barn where they could take _____ from the howling wind and driving snow.

A) refuge
B) peace
C) refugee
D) asylum

根據句意以及關鍵字blizzard和子句take_____ from the howling wind and driving snow，故選A。

關鍵字彙

- disused (adj.) 不再使用的；廢棄的
  反 in use
- driving (adj.) 強勁的
- refuge (n.) 保護；避難處
  例 seek refuge from the storm 躲避暴風雨
- refugee (n.) 難民
- asylum (n.) (尤指政治上的)庇護

譯文

在暴風雪中，登山客們很幸運地能找到一處廢棄的穀倉，在那躲過狂風暴雪。

133. Although one engine had failed during the flight, the aircraft_____ safely at the airport.
A) took off
B) turned around
C) shot down
D) touched down

根據句意以及子句the aircraft _____ safely at the airport，故選D。

關鍵字彙

- take off 起飛
- turn around 轉回來
- shoot down 射下
- touch down 著陸
  例 The plane touched down, and then there was a loud bang.
  飛機著陸，接著就發出巨大的聲響。

譯文│

雖然飛行途中一具引擎失靈，飛機還是在機場安全著陸。

134. You can exchange the goods within seven days, _____ you keep the receipt.
A) unless
B) despite
C) so long as
D) in case

根據句意以及關鍵字exchange the goods和keep the receipt，故選C。

關鍵字彙│

- receipt (n.) 收據
- so/as long as 只要

  例 I will pay you extra money as long as you promise to finish the job tomorrow.
  只要你答應我明天完工，我就會付你加倍的錢。

譯文│

只要保留收據，在七天內都可換貨。

135. The speaker, who_____ physically by a group of anti-government demonstrators, was escorted from the meeting under a heavy police guard.
A) having been attacked
B) had been attacked
C) has been attacked
D) is being attacked

因修飾speaker的形容詞子句有by，所以一定是被動語態，而且形容詞子句比主要子句更早發生（先遭到攻擊才離開），所以時態應為過去完成式，故選B。

關鍵字彙│

- physically (adv.) 身體上

  例 After her vacation, she was in fine condition both physically and mentally.
  她度完假後，身心狀況都很好。

- demonstrator (n.) 示威運動者

  相 demonstration (n.) 示威遊行

  相關片語: stage a demonstration 發動示威

  例 The women staged a demonstration in protest of sexual discrimination.

  這些婦女發動示威來抗議性別歧視。

- escort (v.) 護送

  例 I'm going to escort her home.

  我準備要送她回家。

譯文

遭到反政府示威群眾攻擊的演講者，在警方重重戒護下離開了演講會場。

136. Julie was really happy when she was admitted to law school. She felt like she was _____.

A) walking on air

B) making a hit

C) keeping up appearances

D) off her head

根據句意以及關鍵字really happy，故選A。

關鍵字彙

- admit (v.) 使…入會／入學（常用被動語態）

  例 This year, ten students were admitted into the music program.

  今年有十位學生獲准選修音樂課程。

  相 admittance (n.) 許可進入

  admission (n.) 入學許可

- walk on air 如置雲端；洋洋得意

- make a hit 造成轟動

- keep up appearances 裝面子

  例 There's no point in keeping up appearances when everyone knows we're nearly bankrupt.

  人家都知道我們快破產了，何必還打腫臉充胖子呢？

- off one's head 發瘋

譯文

茱莉獲准入學法學院感到非常高興，感覺如走在雲端之上。

137. When questioned by the judge, the defendant was _____ to explain his behavior on the night of the crime.

  A) at a loss

  B) at first hand

  C) at cross-purposes

  D) at face value

根據句意以及關鍵字explain his behavior，故選A。

關鍵字彙

● defendant 被告

  例 The judge ordered the defendant to stand up and raise his right hand.

    法官要求被告起立並舉起右手。

● at a loss 不知如何

  例 He was at a loss for words. 他不知該說什麼。

● at cross-purposes 雞同鴨講；相互誤解

  例 The two students found themselves at cross purposes with the professor.

    兩位學生發覺自己與教授之間有誤會。

● at face value 字面意義；表面價值

  例 Tina took his stories at face value and did not know he was joking.

    蒂娜對他的故事信以為真，卻不知他是在開玩笑。

譯文

被告被法官質問時，不知如何解釋他在犯罪當晚的行為。

138. Ian Thorpe, the Olympic swimming champion, has always kept himself _____ fit.

  A) exclusively

  B) approximately

  C) unanimously

  D) superbly

根據句意以及子句has always kept himself _____ fit，故選D。

關鍵字彙

● exclusively (adv.) 專有地

● approximately (adv.) 大概地

- unanimously (adv.) 全體一致地
- superbly (adv.) 絕佳地

譯文

奧運游泳冠軍伊恩索普一直以來都讓自己保持絕佳的健康狀態。

139. A great deal of emphasis is placed on academic success, but it's not always easy for children to_____ their parents' expectations.

A) live up to

B) come up against

C) drop in on

D) feel up to

根據句意以及關鍵字expectations，故選A。

關鍵字彙

- emphasis (n.) 強調
  lay emphasis on... 強調…
  例 Our boss lays great emphasis on punctuality.
  我們老闆很重視守時。
- live up to 達到標準
  例 However hard he tried, he failed to live up to his parents' expectations.
  不管他多努力，還是無法達到他父母的期望。
- come up against 遇到問題
  例 We expect to come up against a lot of opposition to the scheme.
  我們預期這項方案會遇到很多人反對。
- drop in (on sb.) 順便拜訪(某人)
  例 After disappearing for ten years, he just dropped in last night.
  他在失蹤十年後，昨夜突然來訪。
- feel up to 突然想做；覺得可以對付
  例 Kevin didn't feel up to the task. 凱文覺得擔當不了這項工作。

譯文

孩子在學業上的成就雖然很受重視，但要達到父母的期望並不容易。

140. In this company, the staff normally retires at the age of sixty-five. Mr. Wang _____last year, but he wants to keep working for at least another five years.

A) must have retired
B) could have retired
C) should have retire
D) would have been retire

空格處應填「助動詞+have+ p.p.」的句型。must have p.p.指過去一定做過…; could have p.p. 指原本可以…; should have p.p. 指原本應該做…，但選項C沒有retire的過去分詞retired; would have p.p.指原本將要做…。根據以上分析，故選B。

關鍵字彙

● staff (n.) 職員
例 We have a small staff in our office.
我們辦公室的職員並不多。

譯文

在這家公司，一般員工在65歲退休。王先生去年原本可以退休，但他想至少再繼續工作個五年。

Part 6

作答說明：閱讀底下的數篇文章，其中有些句子缺少一個單字或片語。從四個選項中選出最適合的填入空格內，以完成該篇文章，然後塗黑答案紙上(A)、(B)、(C)或(D)中的一個選項。

141. " the quarterly financial report should be _____ by this Friday " 中的financial report 為無生命物品，所以空格的動詞時態應為被動語態。而選項B最符合題意故為正解。

A) implemented (v.) 生效；實施

B) completed (v.) 完成；結束

C) invented (v.) 發明

D) constructed (v.) 建造

142. " and should have it on your _____ by tomorrow afternoon. " 中的介系詞為on，所以選項D的desk最符合句意故為正解。

A) office (n.) 辦公室

B) account (n.) 帳戶

C) word ((n.) 言語

D) desk (n.) 辦公桌；書桌

143. "Our auditor will also be there to make sure our accounts are _____. " 中的 " make sure our accounts are _____. " 為附屬子句，而選項A最符合題意故為正解。

A) in order 依照順序

B) in effect (指規則、法律等)有效，(而本文指的是帳戶而非法律)

C) on time 準時

D) overdue 逾期

144. " I'm sure you'll come _____ for us again. " 中的come _____ 應為動詞片語，而選項D的come through最符合題意故為正解。

A) come over 順道來訪

B) come off 脫落

C) come back 恢復

D) come through 經歷（困難）

關鍵字彙

- implement (v.) 生效；實施
  例 They planned on implementing a new economic program to relieve the current economic stress.
  他們計畫要執行一項新的經濟方案，來減輕目前的經濟壓力。

- initial (adj.) 最初的
  例 Construction of this building is still in the initial stage.
  這棟大樓的建造還只在初步階段。

- in order 按照順序
  例 Make sure the legal documents are signed and in order.
  確認這些法律文件都有簽名並且照順序排列。

- in effect（指規則、法律等）有效
  例 Some ancient laws are still in effect.
  有些古時的法律仍然有效。

- come through 經歷（困難）
  例 To get here, we have come through great difficulty.
  我們經歷了很大的困難才到達這裡。

145. 上句的後半部為 " not only...but also... " 的句型，而由該句所連結的應為對等的子句， " but also " 之後緊接著 " because " ，因次空格應填入 " because " 最符合題意故正解為選項 A。
  A) because (conj.) 因為
  B) that (conj.)（用以引導子句）
  C) after (conj.) 在…之後的時間
  D) until (conj.) 直到…為止

146. " Asia has become a center for _____. " 的空格之前為介系詞 " for " ， " for " 之後應接名詞，而四個選項中最符合句意為選項C。
  A) recreation (n.) 休閒
  B) animation (n.) 生氣；活力
  C) innovation (n.) 改革；創新
  D) cooperation (n.) 合作

147. " that incorporate the latest technology while _____ the most-desired functions. " 中空格前的 " while " 所引導的為表時間的從屬子句(" while they offer the most-desired function ")，由於空格內僅能填入一個字，因此該子句簡

化為分詞片語，也就是省略主詞，並改主動語態為現在分詞 ("while offering the most-desired function")，因此選項C為正解。

A) offered
B) did offer
C) offering
D) would offer

148. " With the worldwide demand for digital products＿＿at a furious pace, "
中空格所引導的關係子句 ("which＿＿at a furious pace ")簡化成的分詞片語(" which ＿＿ing at a furious pace ")， " which " 所代替的是先行詞 " digital products "，而產品需求量與速度之間的關係若以動詞表示，則以選項D最為恰當。

A) extending (v.) 延長
B) expanding (v.) 擴張
C) developing (v.) 發展
D) growing (v.) 成長

關鍵字彙

● innovation (n.) 發明

　相 innovate (v.) 發明；革新

　例 An electronics company needs to keep on innovating new products in order to survive.

　　一家電子公司必須不斷地開發新產品，才能繼續經營下去。

● incorporate (v.) 合併；包含

　例 Please remember to incorporate the latest data in your weekly report.

　　請記得在你的每週報告裡納入最新的資料。

　同 include

　反 exclude

● extend (v.) 延伸；擴大

　例 I'd like to extend my stay another two days.

　　我想在這多待兩天。

● expand (v.) 擴張；膨脹

　例 The company expanded their business by now catering to overseas customers as well.

　　這家公司現在已擴展業務，也迎合海外顧客的需求。

　相 expansion (n.) 擴張；膨脹

149. " there appear to be some points where you may ____ what we are trying to do with this new pricing structure. " 中may後面的空格應填入原形動詞，而選項C最符合題意故為正解。
A) maintain (v.) 保持
B) misdirect (v.) 誤用；濫用
C) match (v.) 相配
D) misunderstand (v.) 誤會

150. " only those customers ____ at least 100 units will be entitled to it. " 中有主詞those customers，有動詞will be entitled，所以空格內應填現在分詞，因為 ____ at least 100 units為修飾those customers的附屬子句。故選項D為正解
A) purchase 原形動詞
B) purchased 簡單過去式
C) have purchased 現在完成式
D) purchasing 現在分詞

151. " ____, the proposed discount only applies to Model XG-10 " 中的空格應填入副詞來修飾整句，選項B最符合題意故為正解。
A) Then (adv.) 然後
B) Furthermore (adv.) 此外；而且
C) Markedly (adv.) 清楚地；顯著地
D) Because (conj.) 因為

152. " I hope that ____ helps to clear up the questions you raised. " 中that的後面空格應填入名詞，選項A最符合題意故為正解。
A) the above 前文
B) as follows（用於列舉事項）
C) as previous 應為 as previously stated...
D) the subsequent 後來的事件

關鍵字彙

- scheme (n.) 計畫；方案
  例 Bruce's scheme for raising money is practicable.
  布魯斯籌款的計畫是可行的。
- substantial (adj.) 豐富的
  例 She left him a substantial sum of money.

她留給他一大筆錢。

同 considerable, large, sizable

- irrespective (adj.) 不顧一切的；與⋯無關的

  例 We will get the work done, irrespective of cost.

  不管花多少成本，我們也要把這項工作做好。

- blanket (adj.) 全體的

  例 The boss promised a blanket wage increase.

  老闆答應全面提高工資。

- mark down (v.) 減價

  例 In order to increase their market share, the company has decided to mark down a wide range of goods to boost sales.

  為了提升市場佔有率，公司決定將大多數產品降價以刺激買氣。

- entitle (v.) 使⋯有資格

  例 Every citizen over twenty years of age is entitled to vote.

  年滿二十歲的公民就有選舉權。

  同 authorize, allow, empower

  反 deprive

- version (n.) 版本

  例 You're still using the beta-testing software? You need to upgrade to the latest version before you can continue your project.

  你還在使用試用版軟體嗎？在繼續進行你的案子前，需要把軟體升級至最新的版本。

  同 edition

- previous (adj.) 先前的

  例 It takes a mature person to admit previous mistakes.

  成熟的人才能夠承認之前所犯的錯誤。

  同 prior, earlier, former

  反 later, following, subsequent

Part 7
作答說明：本部份的測驗是篩選報章雜誌的文章、信件和廣告等讀物命題。請在讀完每篇文章後，根據短文所陳述或蘊含的內容回答文後的幾道問題。請就每個問題，從(A)、(B)、(C)、(D)之中，選出一個最適當的答案，請在答案卡上劃記。

破題解析

153. What service is this pamphlet advertising?
A) In home care for seniors
B) A high-quality nursing home
C) Information on nursing homes
D) The importance of family care
由本文大意和關鍵句The Department of Health & Human Services....factors 可以判斷出本文應出自政府機關印製的宣傳小冊子，選項C為正解。

154. Which of the following is NOT listed as a problem in American nursing homes?
A) Improper medication
B) Extremely high costs
C) Lack of staff
D) Low quality of life
根據關鍵句many are critically understaffed...medication中有提到服藥照顧不周、人手不足和生活品質低落，但沒提到收費高昂，因此選項B為正解。

155. What type of nursing homes is reviewed annually?
A) State-run care facilities
B) Class A1 and A2 homes
C) Hospital-sponsored homes
D) Nationally licensed homes
從關鍵句The Department of Health & Human services maintains a website, updated once per year that reports on deficiencies found in nationally licensed nursing homes得知衛生署每年有更新有國家執照的安養中心的缺失報導，因此選項D為正解。

關鍵字彙

● understaffed (adj.) 人手不足

回 undermanned

反 overstaffed, overmanned

- downright (adv.) 完全地；徹底地

  例 a downright lie 徹頭徹尾的謊言

- negligent (adj.) 疏忽的；粗心大意的

  例 She was negligent in her work.

  她對工作粗心大意。

  回 neglectful, careless, slipshod

  反 careful, attentive

- administer (v.) 給某人服藥

  例 The morphine was administered by injection.

  那嗎啡是注射進去的。

- medication (n.) 藥物

  例 What is the best medication for this condition?

  這種病況用什麼藥最好？

- deficiency (n.) 缺點

  回 fault, defect, flaw, shortcoming

  反 perfection, flawlessness

- sponsor (v.) 主辦；贊助

  例 This concert was sponsored by Microsoft.

  這場演唱會是微軟公司贊助的。

156. What is the main purpose of this letter?

   A) To ask for further information

   B) To respond to a request

   C) To confirm a reservation

   D) To explain the general manager's opinion

開頭就清楚地交代，...passed on your letter requesting...and asked me to respond. 可見本信的目的是回覆要求，因此選項B為正解。

157. Which of the following is NOT enclosed?

   A) A schedule of events

   B) A publicity of brochure

   C) A map of downtown Chicago

   D) A list of room rates

根據第二段的關鍵句得知作者隨信附上了三樣東西：

1) As you can see from our brochure,...
2) ...as you can see from the map I've sent
3) I'm also enclosing a list of special room rates...
可見沒有附上的東西是 A) schedule of events。

關鍵字彙

● regarding (prep.) 關於

例 Your question regarding bonuses will have to wait until the next meeting.
= Your question with regard to bonuses will have to wait until the next meeting.
你所提出有關紅利的問題必須等到下次會議才能做決定。

● facilities (n.) 設備

例 The facilities in that building are of the highest quality.
那棟建築物的設備品質最好。

● comply (v.) 遵守
comply with... 遵守

例 A good citizen always complies with the law.
好國民始終都守法。

同 abide by, conform to, obey

● plenary session 全體大會

● ample (adj.) 充裕的；足夠的

同 abundant, plentiful

反 insufficient, inadequate

● enclose (v.) 附上

例 I enclosed a photo in my letter to my girlfriend.
我在給女友的信中附上我的照片。

158. At which of these times may only official school groups attend the fair?

A) Thursday at 3 p.m.
B) Friday at 11 a.m.
C) Friday at 5 p.m.
D) Saturday at 10 a.m.

關鍵句For the first two days, from 10 to 2, the fair is open...pupils on official school excursions. 又依據先前提到的開幕時間為Thursday March 19th，可見開放學童參觀時間為星期四和星期五10:00 a.m.~ 2:00 p.m.因此選項B為正解。

159. Who may attend the fair from March 21 to March 23?

A) Only members of the Korean Book Foundation

B) Only children and their parents

C) Anyone who wants to

D) Only publishers and book store owners

關鍵句...and from the 21st to the 23rd, it is open to all interested members of the public. 可見這三天是開放給一般大眾，因此選項C為正解。

160. What is taking place at the book fair for the first time this year?

A) Magic shows by Darren the Magnificent

B) Computer workshops

C) Sessions at which books are signed by the author

D) Puppet shows

關鍵句This year, for the first time, Darren the Magnificent will be performing magic...可見魔術表演為今年的創舉，因此選項A為正解。

關鍵字彙

- exhibition (n.) 展覽會
  例 They went to an exhibition of Chinese paintings at the museum.
  他們去博物館參觀中國畫展。
- devote (v.) 奉獻
  例 With five children, how could my mother devote a lot of time to each one?
  擁有五個孩子，我母親是如何對每一位都貢獻大量時間呢？
  同 apply, dedicate, give
  反 relinquish, withdraw, withhold
- exclusive (adj.) 獨有的；專用的
  例 The interview is exclusive to this magazine.
  本雜誌獲得獨家訪問權。

161. Which of these wind-up products was first developed by Trevor Baylis?

A) A television

B) An indoor lighting system

C) A radio

D) A laptop computer

關鍵句...inventor of the wind-up radio..., has now developed a wind-up computer 接著又表示他正在研發a wind-up television and a wind-up lighting system 可以推測他最早的發明是收音機，因此選項C為正解。

162. It can be inferred from the article that Baylis' products could also be marketed in which of these ways?

A) As a high-technology substitute for existing products

B) As a substitute for existing products in case of an electrical emergency

C) As a low-cost substitute for existing products

D) As a substitute for existing products when little or no maintenance is required

關鍵句...where there is not electricity and batteries are expensive...可見他設計的產品不需要電力，適用於停電時的代替品，因此選項B為正解。

關鍵字彙

- wind-up 上發條的
- generator (n.) 發電機
- locale (n.)（法語）現場；場所
- perfect (v.) 使…完美

  例 He went to France to perfect his French.

  他去法國是為了讓法語更精進。
- substitute (n.) 替代品；代替者

  例 I'm not good enough to be a regular player, but I'm substitute.

  我當固定球員還不夠資格，但我是替代者。

  同 replacement, surrogate, stand-in
- existing (adj.) 現存的

  例 We have to find ways of making the existing system work better.

  我們必須得找出能使現行系統實施得更好的辦法。
- maintenance (n.) 維持；維修

  例 This is a delicate machine, maintenance and repairs are costly.

  這是台需要小心處理的機械，例行保養和修理都很花錢。

163. The magazine in which this review appeared is probably directed at which of these groups?

A) Commercial artists

B) International businesspersons

C) Communication experts

D) World travelers

關鍵句It covers the ins and outs of transnational contact by phone, fax, mail, and email. 可見本書主要討論國際之間溝通方面的細節，因此研判適合做國際生意的商人，因此選項B為正解。

164. The book that is reviewed probably does NOT answer which of these questions?

A) What does it mean if I telephone an office in Malaysia and hear a series of chimes?

B) What is the country code I need to send a fax to someone in Venezuela?

C) How do I say "hello" if I call someone in Finland?

D) What should I wear to a business luncheon in Egypt?

關鍵句It covers the ins and outs of transnational contact by phone, fax, mail, and email. 可見是著重商業書信和電話溝通，因此像午餐場合的穿著就沒包括，因此選項D為正解。

165. The phrase "ins and outs" in line 5 of the review is closet in meaning to

A) latest developments

B) common difficulties

C) important points

D) helpful suggestions

關鍵句These and countless other questions are answered in this new guidebook. 由此研判本書鉅細靡遺地處理許多問題，最符合ins and outs意思的選項為重點呈現，因此選項C為正解。

166. How many pages does the book The Art of Communicating Globally probably have?

A) 70

B) 110

C) 712

D) 1,246

關鍵句 There are more than 700 pages of useful tips ...可見本書有700多頁，由此推測最接近的頁數是選項C。

167. What does the review say about the book Negotiating Your Way Around the Globe?

A) It's not as popular as The Art of Communicating Globally.

B) It was written by the same authors who wrote The Art of Communicating Globally.

C) It will not be needed by someone who has the book The Art of Communicating Globally.

D) It is more expensive than The Art of Communicating Globally.

關鍵字彙 │

- ins and outs 詳細情形；裡裡外外

    例 She knows the ins and outs of effective marketing.

    她摸清楚了有效用的行銷技巧。

- polish (v.) 提升或修飾（技巧、名譽等）

    例 I polished up my Korean before visiting the country.

    我到韓國玩之前先練好我的韓文。

- collaborate (v.) 合作

    例 The two students have collaborated in preparing the term paper.

    這兩位學生一起合作準備學期研究報告。

    同 cooperate

- prominent (adj.) 顯眼的

    例 The error in the statistics was too prominent to be ignored.

    數據裡的錯誤實在太明顯，不能被忽略。

    同 noticeable, obvious, conspicuous

168. Based on the information in the ad, which of the following is most likely true?

    A) This ad was published in a car magazine.

    B) Most customers will win a prize.

    C) SunCool is sold more than one country.

    D) There is one flavor of SunCool.

關鍵句Offer valid for US and Canadian residents only可知這飲料有在這兩個國家以上的地方銷售，選項C為正解。

169. Which of the following statements is clearly NOT true?

    A) Suncool prints prize notices on the caps of its beverages.

    B) One is more likely to win a car than a motorcycle.

    C) No one may be awarded both a car and a motorcycle.

    D) SunCool Cola is sold in more than one size bottle.

關鍵句Odds of winning: car 1:400,000; motorcycle 1:450,000 可知中汽車比摩托車的比例低，因此選項B為正解。

170. Who among the following cannot win an Appollo Motorcycle in this contest?

A) One who dislikes SunCool products

B) Someone born in November, 1998

C) A former SunCool executive

D) Someone not born in the US or Canada

關鍵句Must be over 18 to play，領獎日期為2010年，所以出生於1998年的人還未滿十八歲。所以選項B為正解。

關鍵字彙

- beverage (n.) 飲料

  例 In America, anyone who is 21 years old can buy alcoholic beverages.

  在美國，任何人滿21歲就可買酒類飲料。

- valid (adj.) 有效的

  例 The free lunch coupon is valid for only one person.

  這張免費午餐優待券只限一人使用。

- eligible (adj.) 有資格的；合格的

  例 Being a student, she was eligible for free medical care.

  由於是學生，她有資格享受免費的醫療服務。

  同 entitled

- resident (n.) 居民

  例 All of the residents of this area are against the construction of a nuclear plant.

  這地區所有居民一致反對興建核電廠。

171. What information is NOT contained in the promotion?

A) The amount of money expected to be raised.

B) The names of the commercial sponsor.

C) The objectives of the Running Start Program.

D) The scheduled distance of the run.

關鍵句Last year...more than $10,000 was raised為去年募款金額，今年預期的金額沒提到，選項A為正解。

172. What best describes the event advertised?

A) A state-sponsored inter-school competition

B) An effort to improve student physical fitness

C) A fund-raiser to help poor children

D) A race between employees of two companies

關鍵句The Running Start Program is designed to supply children in need with....可知此活動為幫助需要的學童，選項C為正解。

173. When is the event scheduled to be held?

A) On a fall morning

B) On a summer morning

C) On a spring afternoon

D) On a summer afternoon

由關鍵句 When: Saturday, July 15@ 9:00 a.m.可得知選項B為正解。

關鍵字彙

● fund (v.) 基金

raise funds for... 為⋯籌募基金

例 They are raising funds for those orphans.

他們正為那些孤兒籌募基金。

● benefit (v.) 受惠

例 Working here will benefit you in a number of ways. For one thing, you'll gain work experience.

在這工作將會使您在許多方面受惠，例如可以獲得工作經驗。

174. Which of the following is NOT a requirement for the two photographs?

A) That they be taken the day before being submitted.

B) That they show the right side of the applicant's face.

C) That they be exactly the same.

D) That the date they were taken be indicated.

關鍵句 You must submit...taken within 30 days of this application是申請期30天內而非前一天照相，所以選項A為正解。

175. What is the only requirement for which an exemption is stated in the instructions?

A) The photos must be no larger than a certain size.

B) The information on the reverse must be written in pencil.

C) The head of the applicant must be shown bare.

D) The background of the photo must be a specific color.

關鍵句 (unless you are wearing a headdress...) 可得知頭上不能帶任何物品這規定是有例外，如因宗教因素就可免除，選項C為正解。

176. What should appear on the back of the photo?

    A) The application number

    B) The size of the photo

    C) The photographer's name

    D) The address

關鍵句print your name...on the back of each submitted photograph可知申請
序號要寫在相片背後,選項A為正解。

關鍵字彙

- submit (v.) 交付;呈遞

  例 Submit your outline to the professor before writing your research paper.
    將你的綱要呈遞給教授看,然後再寫研究報告。

- identical (adj.) 完全相同的
  be identical to... 與…完全相同

  例 Her reply is identical to mine.
    她的答覆與我完全相同。

- exemption (n.) 免除

  相 exempt (adj.) 免除於…

  例 He was exempt from gym class due to his broken leg.
    他因為斷了腿所以不用上體育課。

177. Where would this information most likely be found?

    A) In a magazine advertisement

    B) Included with purchased software

    C) In a review of newly released program

    D) Attached to a letter from customer service

關鍵句Thank you for purchasing this CompuEd Product可知這資訊應是在購
買的產品內可看到,選項B為正解。

178. Which of the following would probably NOT be found on a CompuEd
product's package?

    A) "Learn geography with your favorite cartoon character!"

    B) "Spend hours memorizing historical dates!"

    C) "CompuEd: Over two decades of making learning fun."

    D) "Prepare your child for the upcoming school year."

關鍵句 our company's motto is, "For Learning to Get Done, Learning Must
Be Fun!"可知CompuEd的宗旨是在樂趣中學習,所以死記歷史不可能是他們標
榜的,選項B為正解。

179. Among the following, who is NOT mentioned as being involved in the product development process?

   A) Software engineers

   B) Parents and their children

   C) Researchers

   D) Education professionals

關鍵句with input from teachers...parents and children可知只有軟體工程師沒有參予產品內容發展，因此選項A為正解。

180. According to the reading, which of the following is true?

   A) CompuEd offers upgrades for all its older software.

   B) CompuEd has been the most popular educational software since 1988.

   C) CompuEd products have won awards in the past.

   D) CompuEd's software is only for very young children.

關鍵句 Our award-winning products....可知CompuEd產品在過去有得過獎，選項C為正解。

關鍵字彙

- adapt (v.) 使適應

   例 When living in another country you have to adapt to the local customs.

     住在另一個國家時，你必須適應當地的風俗習慣。

   同 conform, suit, modify, adjust, fit

- release (v.) 釋放；透露（消息）

   例 The authorities have just released the names of those who were killed in the plane crash.

     有關當局剛剛發佈一份飛機失事罹難者的名單。

- review (n.) 評論

   例 I wasn't going to read the review of my play, but I did and now I wish I hadn't.

     我原本並不打算看有關我表演的評論，但還是看了，現在我希望當初不要看。

   同 appraisal, commentary, critique, judgment, opinion

- memorize (v.) 記憶；背誦

   相 memory (n.) 記憶

     memorial (adj.) 紀念的

181. Why were these two faxes sent?

    A) To discuss an order of clothes

    B) To cancel an order

    C) To discuss Christmas plans

    D) To discuss the bargain sale season

這兩份傳真信的主題都是成衣訂單Re: Order，因此選項A為正解。

182. Why does Annette want more of the same items?

    A) The shelves look empty.

    B) There is a great demand for them.

    C) She wants to buy some for herself.

    D) She is flying to a meeting.

第一封信關鍵句The clothes.....amazing success. They are just flying off the racks. 可得知因非常暢銷所以下訂更多數量，選項B為正解。

183. What is the problem at the factories?

    A) They are closed for the holidays.

    B) They are busy fulfilling other orders.

    C) They are going out of business.

    D) There is no problem.

第二封信關鍵句the factory we use on a regular basis is already working at full capacity, trying to complete orders from other clients可知工廠也忙著處理其他訂單，選項B為正解。

184. What has Samantha been doing all morning?

    A) Christmas Shopping

    B) Telephone manufacturers and suppliers

    C) Making clothes

    D) Making deliveries

第二封信關鍵句I've spent the morning telephoning around our suppliers and factories可知選項B為正解。

185. How likely is it that Samantha will be able to send everything that Annette wants?

    A) There is a very high possibility.

    B) She had already sent the items.

    C) She gives no indication of this.

    D) It is very doubtful.

第二封信關鍵句I doubt that we will be able to get the rest of your order made before Christmas可知Samantha自己也不能確定能否把訂單的商品湊齊，因此選項D為正解。

關鍵字彙

- fly off the racks 非常暢銷（形容商品放在架上，馬上跟飛走了似地銷售一空）

  其他形容暢銷的片語：

  a) in great demand

  b) have a ready market

  c) sell like hotcakes

  d) do a roaring trade in sth.

  e) a brisk sale

- place an order 下訂單

- full capacity 全能生產

  例 When all of our machines are all working and our plant is running at full capacity, it really is a wonder to behold.

  當我們所有機器全都在運作，廠房在全能生產的狀況運轉，那幅景象真是美妙。

  相 half capacity

- pull a few strings 動用關係

  例 I didn't have any experience, so my dad pulled a few strings to get me the job.

  我並沒有任何經驗，所以我父親動用關係幫我取得這份工作。

- fulfill (v.) 達成

  例 The courier failed to fulfill the shipping needs of his clients.

  快遞員未能達成客戶的送件需求。

  同 complete, satisfy

- indication (n.) 指示

  相 indicate (v.) 指出；顯示

  indicative (adj.) 指示的

- doubtful (adj.) 可疑的

  be doubtful of... 懷疑…

  例 I am doubtful of his ability to handle the problem.

  我懷疑他處理這問題的能力。

186. Why did Zelda Barnard send an email?

A) To place an order

B) To ask for her money back

C) To ask for an exchange

D) To demand an apology

第一封信關鍵句I would, therefore, like to receive a refund可知她要求退款，選項B為正解。

187. Which of the following statements best describes Zelda Barnard?

A) She is a new customer.

B) She doesn't often make electronics purchases.

C) She frequently makes complaints.

D) She is a loyal customer of Hanley Electronics.

第一封信關鍵句I have been using Hanley products for many years可知Zelda用該品牌已多年，因此選項D為正解。

188. How long did Zelda Barnard wait for the tongs to heat up?

A) 5 minutes

B) A total of 10 minutes

C) 15 minutes

D) Many years

第一封信關鍵句The problem is....a further 5 minutes可知她總共等了十分鐘，選項B為正解。

189. How many other complaints has the company received?

A) None for this particular product

B) A dozen

C) Several

D) Hundreds

第二封信關鍵句This is the first complaint of this kind regarding this particular product可知這公司是收到第一次收到關於此項產品的客訴，選項A為正解。

190. What information should Zelda Barnard send?

A) Phone number

B) Credit card number

C) Name, address, and reference number

D) Name and email address

第二封信關鍵句To obtain a refund.....address:可知申請退款必須附上姓名、地址和參考序號,因此選項C為正解。

關鍵字彙

● refund (n.) 退款

例 Kevin took the DVD player back to the shop and asked for a refund.
凱文把DVD放映機帶回店裡並要求退款。

● disconnect (v.) 使分離

例 She disconnected the electric fan by pulling out the plug.
她把插頭拔出使電風扇斷電。

反 connect

● apology (n.) 道歉

例 The President made a formal apology on the radio this morning.
今早總統在廣播節目中正式表示道歉。

相 apologize (v.) 道歉

191. What does the Stoney Brook Inn offer as its setting?

A) A family setting

B) A modern setting

C) A professional setting

D) A historic setting

第二篇文章關鍵句you'll find the historic setting a dream getaway...可知the Stoney Brook Inn具有歷史文化的環境,選項D為正解。

192. What does the Stonewall Hotel NOT offer its guests?

A) An intimate setting

B) A conference area for business

C) Historic sites

D) A central location in the city

從第一篇文章全文可知the Stonewall Hotel位於市中心、也位於歷史悠久的環境、也可在此舉辦會議,但並不適合想要隱密和私密環境的旅客,因此選項A為正解。

193. Where is The Stonewall Hotel located?

A) On the outskirts of town

B) In a modern district

C) In the town center

D) On a quiet, private lane

第一篇文章關鍵句centrally located in the heart of bustling downtown，可知選項C為正解。

194. Which kinds of guests might be most interested in The Stoney Brook Inn?

A) Large families

B) Honeymooners

C) Business conferences

D) Beach-goers

第二篇文章關鍵句The Stoney Brook Inn.....is just right for your intimate engagement可知度蜜月者最適合，選項B為正解。

195. What kind of city is Laurel?

A) A purely urban environment

B) A city located on the plains of the Midwest

C) A city by the Atlantic Ocean

D) A city that offers both urban and rural settings

由這兩篇文章的全文可得知Laurel是一個同時具有城市和鄉村風貌的地方，選項D為正解。

關鍵字彙

- bustling (adj.) 活躍的；奔忙的
  例 The city center was bustling with life.
  市中心充滿了生活的繁忙景象。
- intimate (adj.) 親密的
  例 We're not exactly on intimate terms, but we see each other fairly often.
  我們雖算不上關係密切，但還算常見面。
  同 private, personal
- hospitality (n.) 慇勤待客
  例 Thank you for your kind hospitality.
  謝謝您的盛情款待。
- beyond compare 無與倫比
  例 She is lovely beyond compare.
  她真是無與倫比的可愛。

● outskirts (n.) 市郊

　　例 They live on the outskirts of Paris.

　　　他們住在巴黎市郊。

196. What was probably the reason for the notice of October 25?

　　A) No more tickets were available for Sunday's game.

　　B) The team was facing legal action from some fans.

　　C) Some fans had complained to the team in writing.

　　D) Too many fans had been selling their tickets.

　　第一封信關鍵句We have carefully read the comments you sent us...可知有

　　球迷寫信投訴，安全部門才會發出此通知，選項C為正解。

197. To whom is the notice of October 25 mainly directed?

　　A) People attending this Sunday's game

　　B) People owning season tickets

　　C) People wishing to purchase tickets

　　D) People thinking about joining the team

　　第一封信的第2段和第3段是敘述如果把季票給別人，就可能會承擔風險，因此該

　　通知的主要訴求對象是季票的擁有者，選項B為正解。

198. Why has the letter of November 5 been written?

　　A) Mr. McGee misplaced his tickets.

　　B) Mr. McGee's behavior to the game was unruly.

　　C) Some fans objected to the new policy.

　　D) Some fans threw objects onto the field.

　　第二封信關鍵句I regret to.....tossing things at the opposing team's players，

　　因此選項D為正解。

199. What action was taken against the fans Mr. McGee sold his tickets to?

　　A) They were asked to leave the stadium.

　　B) They were arrested by the police.

　　C) They had their season tickets revoked.

　　D) They had to remain in their seats.

　　由第二封信關鍵句action was taken against them as outlined in the notice

　　sent to all season ticket holders on October 25，以及第一封信關鍵句Fans

　　who demonstrate.....will be subject to ejection可得知不守規矩的球迷必須被

　　驅逐出場外，因此選項A為正解。

200. What will Mr. McGee most likely do?

A) Speak with the fans who bought his tickets

B) Visit the team's offices in person

C) Phone a team representative

D) Contact the agency that sold his tickets

第二封信關鍵句We urge you to contact.....situation可見Mr.McGee被要求去聯絡球隊的代表人,選項C為正解。

關鍵字彙

- exercise (v.) 運用

  例 exercise judgment/power 運用判斷力／權力

  例 exercise one's rights as a citizen 行使公民權

- revoke (v.) 撤銷;廢除

  例 His driving license was revoked after the crash.

  他撞車後駕駛執照吊銷了。

  同 cancel, annul, rescind, withdraw

- subject to... 遭受到…

  例 Trains are subject to delays after the heavy snowfalls.

  一下大雪火車就往往會誤點。

- ejection (n.) 驅逐

  相 eject (v.) 驅逐

  例 The noisy youths were ejected from the cinema.

  吵鬧的那群年輕人都已被驅逐在電影院外。

- object (v.) 反對;抗議

  例 She wanted to cut down the hedge, but her neighbor objected.

  她想把樹籬剪低些,可是鄰居反對。

  同 protest, disapprove of, complain

  反 approve, agree, assent

- apprehend (v.) 逮捕;拘押

  例 The thief was apprehended by the police in the act of stealing a car.

  竊賊在偷汽車時當場被警察逮捕。

  同 catch, arrest, seize, capture

- misplace (v.) 放錯地方

  例 I've misplaced my glasses ＿＿they're not in my bag.

  我把眼鏡放錯地方了 ＿＿沒在我的包包裡。

NEW TOEIC TEST
新多益全真模擬試題
Answer Sheet

LISTENING TEST (PART 1~4)

NO.	ANSWER	NO.	ANSWER	NO.	ANSWER	NO.	ANSWER	NO.	ANSWER
	A B C D		A B C D		A B C D		A B C D		A B C D
1	a b c d	21	a b c d	41	a b c d	61	a b c d	81	a b c d
2	a b c d	22	a b c d	42	a b c d	62	a b c d	82	a b c d
3	a b c d	23	a b c d	43	a b c d	63	a b c d	83	a b c d
4	a b c d	24	a b c d	44	a b c d	64	a b c d	84	a b c d
5	a b c d	25	a b c d	45	a b c d	65	a b c d	85	a b c d
6	a b c d	26	a b c d	46	a b c d	66	a b c d	86	a b c d
7	a b c d	27	a b c d	47	a b c d	67	a b c d	87	a b c d
8	a b c d	28	a b c d	48	a b c d	68	a b c d	88	a b c d
9	a b c d	29	a b c d	49	a b c d	69	a b c d	89	a b c d
10	a b c d	30	a b c d	50	a b c d	70	a b c d	90	a b c d
11	a b c d	31	a b c d	51	a b c d	71	a b c d	91	a b c d
12	a b c d	32	a b c d	52	a b c d	72	a b c d	92	a b c d
13	a b c d	33	a b c d	53	a b c d	73	a b c d	93	a b c d
14	a b c d	34	a b c d	54	a b c d	74	a b c d	94	a b c d
15	a b c d	35	a b c d	55	a b c d	75	a b c d	95	a b c d
16	a b c d	36	a b c d	56	a b c d	76	a b c d	96	a b c d
17	a b c d	37	a b c d	57	a b c d	77	a b c d	97	a b c d
18	a b c d	38	a b c d	58	a b c d	78	a b c d	98	a b c d
19	a b c d	39	a b c d	59	a b c d	79	a b c d	99	a b c d
20	a b c d	40	a b c d	60	a b c d	80	a b c d	100	a b c d

NEW TOEIC TEST
新多益全真模擬試題
Answer Sheet

READING TEST (PART 5~7)

NO.	ANSWER A B C D	NO.	ANSWER A B C D	NO.	ANSWER A B C D	NO.	ANSWER A B C D	NO.	ANSWER A B C D
101	a b c d	121	a b c d	141	a b c d	161	a b c d	181	a b c d
102	a b c d	122	a b c d	142	a b c d	162	a b c d	182	a b c d
103	a b c d	123	a b c d	143	a b c d	163	a b c d	183	a b c d
104	a b c d	124	a b c d	144	a b c d	164	a b c d	184	a b c d
105	a b c d	125	a b c d	145	a b c d	165	a b c d	185	a b c d
106	a b c d	126	a b c d	146	a b c d	166	a b c d	186	a b c d
107	a b c d	127	a b c d	147	a b c d	167	a b c d	187	a b c d
108	a b c d	128	a b c d	48	a b c d	168	a b c d	188	a b c d
109	a b c d	129	a b c d	149	a b c d	169	a b c d	189	a b c d
110	a b c d	130	a b c d	150	a b c d	170	a b c d	190	a b c d
111	a b c d	131	a b c d	151	a b c d	171	a b c d	191	a b c d
112	a b c d	132	a b c d	152	a b c d	172	a b c d	192	a b c d
113	a b c d	133	a b c d	153	a b c d	173	a b c d	193	a b c d
114	a b c d	134	a b c d	154	a b c d	174	a b c d	194	a b c d
115	a b c d	135	a b c d	155	a b c d	175	a b c d	195	a b c d
116	a b c d	136	a b c d	156	a b c d	176	a b c d	196	a b c d
117	a b c d	137	a b c d	157	a b c d	177	a b c d	197	a b c d
118	a b c d	138	a b c d	158	a b c d	178	a b c d	198	a b c d
119	a b c d	139	a b c d	159	a b c d	179	a b c d	199	a b c d
120	a b c d	140	a b c d	160	a b c d	180	a b c d	200	a b c d

www.17buy.com.tw

現在就加入▶

 I'm 我識出版集團 I'm Publishing Group **專屬網站**

 17Buy 一起買 購物網站

facebook

現在就加入**我識出版集團**的粉絲團！每天都有最新的學習資訊，不定期並有**17buy一起買購物網站**的優惠活動喔！

www.facebook.com/ImPublishing

17buy 一起買

現在就加入**17buy一起買購物網站**會員！只要是會員購物就能享有**最特別的優惠**！你買、我買、一起買，買愈多愈便宜！

www.17buy.com.tw

I'm 我識出版集團 I'm Publishing Group | 17Buy 一起買 購物網站 | 會員登入 | 加入會員 | 會員專區 | 客服中心 | 購物車 0 件 0 元 ▶ 結帳 |

首頁　書籍館

銷售排行榜 | 特價書區 | 語言學習 | 檢定考試 | 財經企管 | 心理勵志 | 生活藝術 | 親子共享 | 人文科普 | 文學小說 | 下載專區

熱門搜尋 | 高國華、圖解英文的原理、第一次投資就賺錢、讓女人買單、躺著背單字

特價書

定價 129 元
7折特惠價90元
放入購物車

熱門關鍵字 Hot Words

▶ 2014年站長推薦!!
▶ 2014年秋季暢銷首選!
▶ 女人，妳這是什麼態度？
▶ 就算再被，也可以躺著背單字
▶ 一個人也可以去旅行!
▶ 新多益滿分要向誰學？
▶ 連聖星都是這樣學日文
▶ 用Facebook也可以學英文
▶ 第一次絕不能花錯
▶ 窮女人最快樂
▶ 女人要夠壯
▶ 當父母的第一課

特別企劃 Special Program

獨創 圖像・單字・句型　用「圖像」記住「單字」用「單字」套用「句型」

懶人御用首選自學書。

結合圖像式記憶法＋串聯式記憶法圖像式記憶法！

只要1小時，日文功力馬上倍增！　單字、萬用句型全收錄MP3

站長推薦 Hots Picks

看見10年後的自己

你看見你未來嗎？10年後的你，會是個什麼樣的你？你滿意現在嗎？現在的自己，是你滿意的自己嗎？時間未去匆匆！對於未來，你茫然嗎？小學作文寫「我的志願」很容易，若此時再接到同樣的題目，你，答得出來嗎？小時候我們急著……

more .....

▶ 不會韓文也能玩樂韓國
▶ 現在你做什麼，決定未來你會變成什麼！
▶ 只要學會風景照原理，什麼照片都能拍!
▶ 會說話的女人最迷人
▶ 向老闆偷時間!

今日秒殺

商用英語書信大全

全球化商用英語書信大……

今日最熱門

我的第一本日文行事曆
全世界都在用的英語旅遊會話8,000
看圖學會日本語文法 — 30天學會「東京日本語專門學校」文法精華
只享一個人：愛自己最快樂，原來獨處是種難得的幸福!
給未來的33個禮物
...more

搶鮮新書 | 編輯推薦 | 讀者最喊讚

| 語言學習 | 檢定考試 | 財經企管 | 心理勵志 |

TOP 本週新進榜

我用這幾句英文在全世界交朋友

我用這幾句英文在全世界交朋友

我識出版集團

我識客服：(02) 2345-7222　http://www.17buy.com.tw
我識傳真：(02) 2345-5758

〔全國各大書店熱烈搶購中！大量訂購，另有折扣〕

國家圖書館出版品預行編目（CIP）資料

考來考去都考這些新多益單字（隨身
版）／蔣志榆・楊可馨 著. -- 初版. --
臺北市：我識，2013. 01
面；　公分
ISBN 978-986-6163-78-4（平裝附光碟
片）
1. 多益測驗 2. 詞彙

805.1895　　　　　　101025879

Examination KING

考來考去
都考這些新多益單字
（隨身版）
NEW TOEIC

書名 / 考來考去都考這些新多益單字（隨身版）
作者 / 蔣志榆・楊可馨
發行人 / 蔣敬祖
編輯顧問 / 常祈天
主編 / 戴媺凌
執行編輯 / 謝昀蓁・曾羽辰
視覺指導 / 黃馨儀
內文排版 / 果實文化設計
法律顧問 / 北辰著作權事務所蕭雄淋律師
印製 / 金漾印刷事業有限公司
初版 / 2013年01月
二版二十二刷 / 2016年08月
出版單位 / 我識出版集團－我識出版社有限公司
電話 / (02) 2345-7222
傳真 / (02) 2345-5758
地址 / 台北市忠孝東路五段372巷27弄78之1號1樓
郵政劃撥 / 19793190
戶名 / 我識出版社
網址 / www.17buy.com.tw
E-mail / iam.group@17buy.com.tw
facebook網址 / www.facebook.com/ImPublishing
定價 / 新台幣 349 元 / 港幣 116 元（附光碟）

總經銷 / 我識出版社有限公司業務部
地址 / 新北市汐止區新台五路一段114號12樓
電話 / (02) 2696-1357　傳真 / (02) 2696-1359

地區經銷 / 易可數位行銷股份有限公司
地址 / 新北市新店區寶橋路235巷6弄3號5樓

港澳總經銷 / 和平圖書有限公司
地址 / 香港柴灣嘉業街12號百樂門大廈17樓
電話 / (852) 2804-6687　傳真 / (852) 2804-6409

版權所有・翻印必究

2011 不求人文化

2009 懶鬼子英日語

I'm 我識出版集團
I'm Publishing Group
www.17buy.com.tw

2006 意識文化

2005 易富文化

2004 我識地球村

2001 我識出版社

2011 不求人文化

2009 懶鬼子英日語

I'm 我識出版集團
I'm Publishing Group
www.17buy.com.tw

2006 意識文化

2005 易富文化

2004 我識地球村

2001 我識出版社

2011 不求人文化

2009 懶鬼子英日語

I'm 我識出版集團
I'm Publishing Group
www.17buy.com.tw

2006 意識文化

2005 易富文化

2004 我識地球村

2001 我識出版社

2011 不求人文化

2009 懶鬼子英日語

I'm 我識出版集團
I'm Publishing Group
www.17buy.com.tw

2006 意識文化

2005 易富文化

2004 我識地球村

2001 我識出版社